THE TROJAN PEACE:

FIRST LIGHT

JILL BARTELT

ALYMENE PRESS

Kewanee, Illinois

Publisher's Cataloging-in-Publication data

Names: Bartelt, Jill, author.
Title: The Trojan peace : first light / Jill Bartelt.
Description: Kewanee, IL: Calymene Press, 2016.
Identifiers: ISBN 978-0-9982932-0-2 | LCCN 2016920185
Subjects: LCSH Troy (Extinct city)--Fiction. | Greece--History--To 146 B.C.--Fiction. | Mythology (Greek)--Fiction. | Andromache (Legendary character)--Fiction. | Hector (Legendary character)--Fiction. | BISAC FICTION / Historical.
Classification: LCC PS3602.A83858 T76 2016 | DDC 813.6--dc23

For Marc and Luke

Contents

PART ONE:

The Trojan Woman

High summer

Chapter 1

“That’s her? Good. She can tell us what happened.”

“What for? I already *told* you what happened!”

“And why should I believe *you?*”

“Because I told you the truth, you ponderous old ass!”

The young woman moaned. The angry voices were still arguing about her — coming into the room hadn’t stopped them, after all. She should have stayed where she was! But she couldn’t leave now. Her whole body hurt. Moaning again, she slumped sideways on the bench.

Meanwhile, the voices raged on.

“Listen, boy —”

“No, *you* listen!”

“I will — but to *her*, not to you!”

“Not if I —”

A third voice interrupted the other two: “Silence! She will speak. It was her choice to come in here, and she’ll be heard.”

The young woman felt everyone’s attention shift to her.

“Tell us what happened,” prompted the third voice.

She shuddered. This voice was the worst one of all! It cut through her like ice crystals, sharp and white.

“Well, then?”

Dumbly, the young woman stared at the floor.

“Speak, girl!” cried the first voice, hot and blustery. After another brief silence, it asked, “Why won’t she answer?”

“Because — she can’t understand braying,” said the second voice, gravelly and deep.

The white voice ignored its two comrades and focused instead on the young woman. "Tell us," it demanded.

She shrank back further.

"Go on, now!" pressed the blustery voice, impatient.

"Why don't you just whip her?" taunted the gravelly voice. "Is it because you're too old and fat?"

"I'll whip *you*, if you don't —"

"Oh, I'd like to see that!"

"I mean it!"

"So do I!"

"A whip — a *ship*," interrupted the young woman, to silence the chorus of angry voices. "Coming for us."

The sea was dazzling under the midday sun. The very waves seemed to catch fire. For two straight weeks, the heat had been ferocious, leading some of the villagers to mutter about sorcery. Even the young woman, who was weary of their superstitions, had to admit a certain strangeness to the world. In the shimmering air, nothing looked like what it really was.

The young woman sat down in the shade of a platana tree and dipped her bare feet into the creek. The water was surprisingly cold. In the space of a moment or two, she could no longer feel her toes.

She didn't move them, didn't make even the slightest effort to bring feeling back to them. Numb...her feet matched her insides. She hadn't felt anything for days. What was there left to feel? Auntie was gone. Auntie, who had taken care of her since the death of her parents. Auntie, who had brought her here to Lyrnassa all those years ago. Auntie, the last member of her family — the last person on earth who loved her!

There had been no time for a bedside farewell, no chance for a last imparting of wisdom. The young woman had simply awoken to find herself alone in the world.

The death hadn't come as a surprise. Auntie had been old and sick; she'd worked herself into the ground making a life for them in Lyrnassa. Still, the inevitability of the loss made it no easier to bear — especially since all of Auntie's efforts would now come to nothing. Alone, the young woman wouldn't be welcome there. The villagers thought she was cursed. They'd tolerated her for Auntie's sake because Auntie's skills were useful to them, but now, they would jump at the chance to get rid of her.

They certainly weren't inviting her to stay.

Someone had left her a few tidbits of food, none of which she'd touched. She had no appetite. But other than that small gesture, no one had come near her since Auntie's death. No one had mourned with her. No one had helped her with the burial. Alone, she'd hauled the dead weight of Auntie's body to the sea. Alone, she'd floundered over to the place where the currents pulled out hard. No one had been there with her as Auntie slipped beneath the waves and disappeared...

The villagers probably wished that the young woman would disappear.

If only she could! She had no one left, here, nothing to hold her back, nothing good to look forward to. She wouldn't mind disappearing, if there was a way that didn't hurt.

She looked around at the platana trees. How lucky they were, never moving, never feeling, growing forever in loveliness in the grove beside the creek. If only she could take root and become one of them, or be suspended in time beneath them! If only —

She was jolted from her thoughts. Down by the shore, one of the village boys was hollering what sounded like, 'A ship! A ship!'

The young woman frowned. A ship? Despite the blistering heat, a chill ran through her. The fog she'd been in since Auntie's death thinned. Could it be true? Was there a ship? No, surely the boy was wrong! But how could she know unless she went down to see? She moved on toward the beach, the other villagers close behind her.

At first, no one else could see it — their vision wasn't sharp enough to pierce the gleaming air. Then they looked again, and that time they saw something. A seabird, someone said; a ripple, said another. By the time that no one could deny it was a ship, the thing was almost upon them.

"How far away was the ship when you spotted it?"

Again, the young woman flinched at the white, abrasive voice. "Don't know," she mumbled.

"Would you say it was ten ship's lengths away, or twenty, or forty?" interjected a new voice, an older man.

"Don't know," she repeated.

"Try to think!" the blustery voice commanded.

The gravelly voice growled, "What do *you* think — that she had a goddamn measuring stick?"

There was a groan of dismay, and then the blustery voice again began to yell at the gravelly one.

The young woman shrank back from it all. Her thoughts were alarmingly muddy. Blood was oozing from her feet, where the bands of cloth had peeled away. They must have caught on a rough spot on the floor...

A sudden silence caused her to look up once more. Everyone was staring at her.

The white voice repeated its question: "I said, was the ship coming fast or slow?"

"Fast."

"She knows it was coming fast, but can't tell us how far away it was?" asked someone else. "Is she deliberately trying to mislead us?"

"Oh, *come* now!" snapped yet another voice. A woman. <u>*The mother*</u>, thought the young woman. "Don't be ridiculous! She's not an enemy agent, she's *ill!* She shouldn't even be in here!"

"She *chose* to come in here," the white voice repeated. "She *chose* to tell us her version of the events, and we *will* listen to her!" Turning back to the young woman, it asked, "What did you do, after the ship was spotted?"

"Ran," she whispered.

The villagers stood there, transfixed. Ships never came to their village to trade — they always went down the shore to Thebe. And this ship didn't look lost, as though it had stumbled into their harbor by chance. It was coming straight toward them.

<u>*No*</u>*! thought the young woman, with a shimmering of terror. It was an old, familiar feeling, the fluttering in her stomach that quickened to a buzz — the cloud of sharp, hot wings that swelled until they filled her whole belly and boiled up into her throat.* <u>*Please, no!*</u>

Many years had passed since the young woman had seen a ship of raiders, but she recognized it at once and knew what it meant. Raiders! Raiders, streaming in from the sea to steal — burn — capture — kill. They were covered in armor and bristling with weaponry. Beneath their helmets, their eyes were blank. Their teeth were bared.

The young woman had never seen a raider up close, but she'd heard stories of what they looked like, and she'd seen what they left behind. Burnt wreckage, bitter ash. A pool of blood. Flesh as pale as oyster shells...

"<u>*Run! Run!*</u>*" her mother had always told her when they came, and she'd obeyed. From afar, she'd seen the flash of metal spears and armor.*

No, the young woman had never seen a raider up close — and she didn't want to now! She wouldn't have minded disappearing, but the thought of pain scared her. She had to get to the hills! She had to get to safety, and fast! She had to <u>run</u>*!*

Around her, though, the Lyrnassans were packed together in an unmoving horde. They seemed stunned.

'Let me through,' cried the young woman, shoving her way into the crowd. 'I need to get through!' The villagers ignored her. Their eyes were fixed on the ship. They didn't move for her, but she was small and could squeeze in among them. Not much further, *she told herself.* Not much further, and I can —

'A spear!' someone shrieked. 'I see a spear!'

The other villagers began to shout:

'A spear?'

'Oh, no! Oh, gods!'

'Who is it?'

'Raiders!'

'Raiders?'

Raiders. The word burned a hole in the young woman's gut. It was even more powerful, more terrifying, now that someone had spoken it aloud. Raiders! Raiders were coming! She had to run*! Oh, gods, but she was stuck in the middle of the crowd! Why weren't the other people moving?*

Then, suddenly, they were. They were moving, shouting.

'Get the axes!'

'Where's my baby? Where's Dares?'

'Help!'

'Oh, gods!'

'Help!'

'HELP!'

The villagers surged around the young woman without seeing her. They knocked her forward, then to the side, hitting her in the eyes and throat.

'Stop!' she cried, covering her face with her hands. 'Stop! Stop!' In terror, she unwittingly slipped out of Truvan — the villagers' language — and into her native tongue, Lukkan.

The others never noticed. They were intent on fleeing the shore. 'Help!' they cried. 'Axes! Dares! Oh, gods! Help! HELP!'

They crashed into the young woman, their heels battering her shins, their arms blocking her escape. When an elbow caught her square in the chest, she fell to her knees, then her side, and was lost in a sea of legs. She couldn't stand up — couldn't breathe! A foot was crushing her. As she curled to protect herself, more feet came pounding down on her, one after the next, grinding her face into the sand. And then there was nothing to breathe, nothing but sand. She was suffocating, struggling, fighting for breath — just as her parents had —

<u>Mom…Dad</u>! *She wanted to cry out to them for help, but she couldn't make a sound — and they were dead — and she was going to die just as they had, gasping for breath — choking on the earth — crushed — facedown on the earth —*

All at once, the feet stopped pounding her, and there was air. Air! She could breathe again. She could breathe!

For a moment, the young woman lay on the ground, trembling — coughing. She coughed out the sand that had been choking her and took deep gulps of air. Oh, gods! Oh, gods…She was bruised, but safe.

Safe?

The young woman hurriedly sat up.

Safe??

Peeking out at the sea, she saw it: the ship. A ship full of raiders, coming to chase her — to stab her — to drain her blood —

<u>Fool</u>! *she screamed to herself.* <u>You're not safe! Run!</u> <u>*Run*</u>!

Forgetting about her bruises, she ran as hard as she could toward the hills. Hills meant safety. Long ago, in the Lukka lands, when raiders had come to her village, the young woman and her mother had always run up the mountainside. The raiders had never followed them. Her mother had told her why…

"<u>They know we know the mountains better than they do. Always run *up* when they come, my girl. Leave everything behind and run.</u>"

"<u>Everything? Even Dad? Even Auntie?</u>"

"<u>They'll be fine, hiding in the cave, but we can't *all* fit in there. You and I are safer in the mountains…</u>"

With her mother, the young woman had always been safe, but this time she was hurt and alone. Her head was spinning. How long had it been since she'd eaten? She wasn't sure if she could make it…

"<u>Run, my little girl! Run!</u>" *The young woman could almost hear her mom crying out to her, and she did as she was told — she ran for the cliffs above Lyrnassa. Up there, up high, she could find a place to hide.*

The going was easy at first, on the grassy stretches near the valley floor. Thistles and prickle plants scratched her, but she fled onward.

Halfway up the hill, though, she began to hear — or imagine, she wasn't sure which — sounds from down below. There was a steady thudding — a crackling — screams, sickeningly muted. Screams! The ship must have landed, then, and the Lyrnassans hadn't known what to do. They hadn't known to run upward! They'd fled to their houses, instead. What were the raiders doing to them? Straining her ears, the young woman thought she heard cries of 'Help!' *Should she turn back? Should she try to help them?*

In her mind's eye she saw a form, pale and still, facedown on the ground...

Faster, dammit, faster! *she told herself.* Faster, or that will be you! *But her lungs and legs were already burning, and the surface of the path had changed. In her haste to flee Lyrnassa, she hadn't thought about the roughness of the rocky upper slope. Her feet were tough, but not that tough. She'd never come this way without shoes, before. The sharp stones were shredding her bare feet.*

I can't go back for shoes, now! *she thought frantically. Neither could she try to find an easier path up the hill. To go any way but onward would mean running into the raiders, and raiders would do far worse things to her. They would drain her blood and leave her facedown in the grass. They would —*

'Run! Run! They're coming!" *Once again, the young woman heard her mother's voice. She stumbled onward, her feet now bleeding badly. They hurt — they* hurt! *She opened her mouth to scream —*

'No, don't, my girl! The raiders will hear you!" *Whimpering softly, she sat down for a moment to catch her breath. In the silence, she heard more chilling sounds down in Lyrnassa.* Thock, thock, thock! *A rock against a skull...*

The sounds conjured images of things her parents had told her about — or were they things she'd seen? Blank eyes. Bared fangs. Gory spears. Charred wood. Smoke. Splinters of bone. Torn flesh, like meat, raw and bloody. The man! The man, facedown and waxy-pale, drained of blood —

Run! *The young woman gritted her teeth and started running again, but each step drove stones into the raw soles of her feet. The pain of it made her keel over and vomit, and that was when she knew.*

I'm not going to make it, *she thought.* I'm going to die. *But then, once more, she heard her mother's voice:*

'Go, dammit! They're coming! They're right behind you! Go!"

The young woman saw herself stumbling, sliding down the hill. The raiders would catch her — seize her — tear her skin, drain her blood —

'Go, I said! RUN!"

The young woman obeyed. The first steps were the worst — she could feel each jagged stone as it thrust up into her flesh — but after a few more steps, the pain dimmed. She hobbled up to the crest of the hill. Just off the

path, there was an outcropping. She crawled around behind it and vomited
again.

"You ran?" asked the white voice.

The young woman nodded, shivering slightly. She burrowed deeper into the folds of her borrowed cloak.

"Where did you run?"

"Up."

"To the top of the hill?"

Again, the young woman nodded.

"And then what?"

Her feet were throbbing. She started to cry.

"I said, and then what?"

"Rested…"

"How long were you there?"

As her eyes glazed over, she slipped once more into Lukkan. "Don't know," she whispered. "Long…" She began to drift away, away from the protests of the white voice and the others, who couldn't understand what she was saying.

She lay behind the outcropping for what felt like hours. The rock had a sheer face with no ledges to shelter under. The sun was beating down on her. She wanted to find a new place to hide, but her feet hurt too much. When she looked down at them, she saw two lumps of raw, shredded meat. Pulpy — red — glistening —

Her stomach heaved, and she covered her face. Hastily, she tore strips of cloth from her dress to wrap around her feet so that she wouldn't have to see them. Walking wasn't an option.

A breeze from the sea brought the scent of smoke toward her. Peering out, she saw black ribbons rising into the sky above Lyrnassa. She thought of her old house, the tiny place she'd once shared with Auntie. A one-room shack made of wood.

The ribbons thickened into ropes.

"How long were you there?" the white voice insisted.

"Don't know," said the young woman, in Truvan this time.

"Did you see anything while you were up there?"

"Burning," murmured the young woman, twisting the cloak in her hands. Lyrnassa had burned, and she'd been helpless to stop it. In sorrow, she looked up and was surprised to see a comforting face, a man with a grey beard and dark, gentle eyes. He was dressed as a priest. "They can't fight," she said to him. She was crying again. "They can't fight."

"Who can't fight?" asked the blustery voice. "The villagers?"

"Of course, the villagers, you ass!" snapped the gravelly voice. "That's why —"

"Silence!" the white voice interrupted. "Let her speak. Now, did you see anything else?"

The young woman shuddered.

"Did you see anything else?"

"Raiders…"

The young woman lay still, straining her ears for the sound of raiders coming up the hillside. She heard it in the pounding of blood in her ears and in the torrent of wind over the hills. She heard it in the rustling grass and in the dim roar of the sea. She heard hoof beats thundering toward her from the other side of the very hill she was on.

She froze. That sound, the last one, didn't fade as the others had. It grew louder. She peeked out in time to see six people on horseback. They were armed. She choked back a scream. More raiders, from the land this time! Raiders from the land, raiders from the sea. Lyrnassa was surrounded!

The young woman cowered behind her rock as the raiders charged down toward the village. They hadn't seen her. She was safe. All she had to do was wait until they passed by again, thundering back to wherever they'd come from. All she had to do was wait.

The sun was still beating down on her. Her skin had turned fiery red and hurt when anything brushed against it. <u>Shade</u>, *she thought longingly. In that moment, her need for shade outweighed her fear of being seen. She stood and tried to take a step, but her feet wouldn't hold her. The pain was too great.* <u>Try again</u>! *But what if she collapsed on the way? The raiders would find her when they came back up…*

She saw herself, facedown and waxy-pale.

She saw her whole body, red and glistening, like her feet.

She heard the crack of splintering bone.

She began to cry so hard that she almost vomited again. No, she couldn't bear it! She couldn't let them find her! But neither could she stay where she was, in the sun…

The young woman looked out across the path and saw a tall rock close to the cliff's edge. The other side of it was shaded. <u>I'll just *have* to make it over there</u>! *And if she tripped and fell off the cliff, so be it! She would dis-*

appear after all — she would find her parents again — she would find Auntie...

"Riders?" asked the white voice, mistaking the word she'd said. "How many?"

The young woman didn't correct him. Riders or raiders, it made no difference in this case. "Six," she said.

"No more?"

She shook her head.

"Did you see what happened in Lyrnassa, after they came?"

"No — no —" She felt herself slipping away again. Her whole body was trembling. "Too far."

"Did you *hear* anything?"

She shook her head. "Sleeping..."

As the young woman turned toward the cliff, her world began to spin. Her skin was on fire, burned by the blazing midday sun. The ground felt like a thousand broken shells. After only a few steps, she crumpled. Blood was trickling from her feet.

She moaned. She would have to get to the tall rock on her knees. Little by little, she dragged herself onward, stopping twice to throw up. After the second time, too exhausted to go on, she lay down and closed her eyes...

When she came to — she had no idea how much later — a monster was hovering over her.

And not just any monster! It was the monster from her childhood nightmares, the monster her parents had always warned her about. A brutal monster, covered in gore. Blood ran tracks through soot on its skin and armor. Blood. Lyrnassan blood — her neighbors' blood! The hulking brute loomed over her, its eyes fixed on her throat. No, not eyes! Less than eyes! Two black hollows where there should have been eyes! It was everything she'd always dreaded but far, far worse in the flesh. Oh, gods, it was so close to her! It was breathing her very air. She could smell the monster's vile stench — acrid smoke, sweat, putrescence, the heavy smell of blood. The thing's mouth gaped open, ready to sink its teeth into her — to drink her blood — and then to leave her, pale and still, facedown upon the earth —

No!

She screamed and punched the thing on its black, ravenous mouth. The helmet scraped her sunburned hand, but she hardly felt it. Her attacker swore and backed away.

'Alive,' it said. The voice was hoarse and rough. Gravelly.

The young woman moaned and curled into a ball, terrified at what the monster might do to her now that she'd attacked it. It was between her and the cliff. There was no escape. The thing was a giant — a bloodthirsty giant, and it was going to —

She screamed.

'It's all right,' said a different voice. A female voice. 'Ssssh.' To the gruesome giant, she asked, 'What do we do?'

'Take her to Thebe,' rasped the monster.

Thebe? *thought the young woman.* <u>These raiders came here from</u> Thebe? <u>But why? We never did anything to</u> Thebe! *And why did the monster want her taken there? To keep her as his slave? That didn't mean he wouldn't kill her. When raiders tired of their captives, they cut them open and let the ground soak up their blood...*

'I'll deal with the rest.' The monster mounted a horse, a pale gold creature streaked in black and drizzled in gore from its hideous master's hands. The two of them sped away.

Meanwhile, the giant's comrade spoke again. 'Let's get you onto my horse,' she said.

The young woman lay where she was, in a ball on the ground. She wasn't going anywhere with any of the raiders — male, female, or otherwise!

'Come on. You can't stay here.'

The young woman screamed as a hand grasped her bruised, sunburned flesh. She started shuddering and couldn't stop. 'No,' she whispered feebly.

'You're cold. Here.'

A cloak was wrapped around her shoulders.

'No! No!' shrieked the young woman, recoiling.

A moment later, two arms were around her, lifting her up off the ground. At that point, she succumbed. She had no more strength to fight. She was heaved up onto the horse, where she landed on her stomach, across the animal's back. As her tender skin scraped against the coarse riding blanket, she screamed. The horse spooked at the sound, and the young woman reflexively pulled out handfuls of its hair, trying not to slide off.

Two strong hands calmed the horse and held the young woman steady. "I'm not taking you to Thebe. We're going straight to the city."

To which city, exactly? And why? Was this raider woman planning to sell her? To ransom her? What would she do when she found out that her captive wasn't worth anything? That no one wanted her? The young woman shuddered. She wouldn't go! No, she would not *go!*

But she couldn't get off the horse — the other woman was holding her there.

'I'll help you sit up.'

The young woman was pulled into a sitting position, and one of her legs was moved to the other side of the horse. An arm looped around her waist — a strong, sweaty arm, smelling of blood and smoke. She tried to squirm away from it but there was nowhere to squirm. She was pinned.

At a signal, the horse galloped off to the northwest, bumping the young woman up and down, turning her tailbone into a misery of bruises.

"So, you were sleeping when the — er, riders — found you?"

The young woman shivered at the memory of what she'd seen upon awakening. "Two — two of them."

"Two," repeated the white voice.

"What about the other four?" a different voice asked. "She said there were six, at first."

"They're still down in Lyrnassa, guarding the prisoners!" the gravelly voice answered. "I told you, I left them —"

"As if we can believe *you*!" the blustery voice interrupted.

The white voice ignored their fighting and addressed the young woman: "Did the two riders who found you say anything about what happened in Lyrnassa?"

She closed her eyes and saw the ropes of smoke in the sky. No one had had to tell her what had happened, there. "Gone," she whispered.

"That's it?"

She nodded.

"And then you were brought here?"

She nodded again.

Night had long since fallen. The young woman knew she must have fainted again. They'd passed from hilly country to the banks of a river, and from there to a broad plain. In the starlight, she saw city walls appear and then grow larger until they dominated the plain.

It took much longer than the young woman would have guessed to reach the city walls. Once they did, her captor hollered something up to the gatekeepers. The gates opened, and the two women clattered up a series of dark streets.

<u>*Where's she taking me?*</u> *wondered the young woman, although it hardly mattered.*

At last, they stopped at a door. 'This is the place.'

The young woman was suddenly alone on the horse. A moment later, she felt herself being tugged off of it. When her bloodied feet hit the ground, she cried out and crumpled against her captor, who helped her limp up several steps to the door.

After one knock, the door opened to reveal a shadow. It looked at them, only to disappear without speaking.

<u>A ghost</u>, thought the young woman. <u>Maybe I'm dead</u>. A moment later, she wished she was: the next phantasm to appear was the monster from the cliff, still blood-spattered and reeking of smoke. The giant. The Raider. It was no longer wearing a helmet, but in the dark, its eyes were as cavernous as ever. A violent tremor overtook the young woman. Why, of all places, had she been brought here?

The thing's hollow eyes bored into the women in a stream of palpable ire. 'I told you to take her to Thebe,' said a voice that was still rough but quieter and somehow more terrible than before.

The young woman shrank; her captor did not. 'She's hurt — and your mother is here.'

'They're all *here!' snarled the monster.*

Wherever 'here' was. Not Lyrnassa — not Thebe — somewhere deep in the land of shadows.

The monster wheeled and disappeared, leaving the door open.

The young woman was dragged into the house by her captor. They stopped in a sort of entry hall with warm tan walls and a floor of impeccable cleanliness. The young woman felt a vague sense of shame for contaminating the place with her blood.

'Wait here,' said her captor, helping her to a bench. 'He'll be back with his mother. I have to get my horse to the stable.' Without another word, she hurried away, leaving the young woman to curl once more into a ball.

From the interior of the house, she heard an approaching clamor. <u>The Raider and its mother</u>, she thought. Too afraid to look directly at the living nightmares, she peeked out at them from between her knees.

'Yes, yes,' the mother was saying. 'I'll see to it.' Looking down at the young woman, she cried, 'Oh, gods! What's she done to her feet?'

'I don't know.'

'You didn't mention…Oh, no, she can't come to the meeting like that!'

'Of course not!' rasped the gravelly voice.

The mother shook her head, as if trying to make the scene before her right itself. 'I can't imagine what you were thinking, dragging her here!'

The Raider didn't answer but radiated silent fury.

The mother turned her attention to the young woman. 'Are you awake? Can you hear me?'

'Go away,' the young woman mumbled. 'Go away.'

'Babblery! She's out of her mind!' the mother shrieked at her son, adding, 'You see? You see!'

Voices began to drift in from a nearby room.

'You have to get back,' said the Raider's mother.

The monster stormed off toward the other voices.

'Control yourself!' the mother howled at her son. 'Name of all the gods, don't provoke them! Don't make things any worse for yourself than they already are!'

I'm in hell, *thought the young woman.* I must be in hell. Everything hurts, and everyone is yelling. *She didn't realize that she was whimpering until the Raider's mother touched her arm. A sun blister popped, and she screamed. The mother backed away and offered her water, which was cold and brought her somewhat back to her senses.*

'I'll be right back,' said the mother.

In her absence, the young woman gulped down more of the water, and then more, until she threw up again.

'A Lyrnassan? She must come in here,' proclaimed a muted voice. It was coming from the direction the Raider had taken.

More and more voices joined in the cacophony.

'She's the only witness.'

'Except the prisoners — '

'Prisoners!'

'Can we believe what they say?'

'They're not even here, yet.'

'If there are any!'

'What do you mean, "if?"'

'I think it's clear!'

'I tell you, the prisoners don't matter either way! We need to hear her.'

'She might be able to sort things out for us.'

'No,' growled the gravelly voice.

'No, what?'

'No, she's not coming in here.'

He didn't want the young woman there...*he'd wanted her in Thebe. He'd meant to give her to a comrade, a raider just as monstrous as he was, a brute who would tear her to pieces...*

'What are you afraid of, boy?' demanded a blustery voice. 'What are you trying to hide?'

'Afraid, my ass! I'm not afraid of you!'

'You should be! I'm warning you!'

'What my son failed to mention,' the mother interrupted, *'is that this Lyrnassan girl is ill. She's in no condition to talk to anyone tonight.'*

'Convenient,' said the blustery voice.

'Excuse me?'

'Convenient that the only witness is ill. Who are you protecting — her, or your reckless son?'

'I don't need protection from you, you ass!' the gravelly voice broke in. *'I'm warning you!'*

'Again? You just did that. Didn't you mean it?'

'I mean to have you shackled to the oars of a slave ship!'

'You're speaking out of turn,' said a new, soft voice.

The blustery voice ignored it. *'A few trips around the sea will put your impudent little tongue in its place, and then — '*

'YOU'RE SPEAKING OUT OF TURN!' boomed the new voice, suddenly terrible.

The young woman shuddered from fear or fever — she couldn't tell which, anymore. Her ears ached from all the yelling. She was tired of it and wanted it to stop. Stumbling over to the doorway, she paused just inside and looked into the other room. It was swirling. The whole house was now a monstrous eddy, but at least the voices had stopped.

She couldn't stand, anymore. She needed —

Her knees buckled and she fell, landing on a bench. As soon as she was sitting, the voices began to argue again, and then to question her. She was far too weary to get up, to escape them. All she could do was answer their questions in the hope that they would let her go...

"Do you have anything to add?" asked the white voice.

The young woman wearily shook her head and slumped in her seat, exhausted. From that point on, everything sounded wavery, as though from a dream. She heard nothing but a muddle of more loud voices — and then there was a sudden, brilliant pain as she collapsed and cracked her head against the floor.

Chapter 2

The young woman spent most of the next week in bed, alternately sleeping and crying. Every time she stirred, she put pressure on some part of her that was bruised, blistered, or torn. Her whole body hurt. She'd never slept on such sheets — on such a mattress — on such a sumptuous excess of linens and velvety cushions — and yet for the pain she was feeling, she might as well have been lying on the rocky trail above Lyrnassa.

Even in those few moments when she managed to settle her body on the mattress, her mind tossed on in an agony of memories and nightmares…

Fire — smoke — screams — the eerie sound of faraway hacking — a thick wall of mud devouring the village — a heap of waxy-white corpses suffocating her — invaders overtaking her on the cliff path and pounding her beneath their feet — the hollow-eyed Raider, gleaming as if on fire — looming over her and soaking her in gore — grinding her bones — slashing her skin until it was a mass of red, glistening meat — lapping up her blood — cutting her — ripping her — tearing her —

Every time she awoke, she was screaming. Nothing brought her comfort until a large, blackish dog mysteriously joined her on the bed. The animal had pointed ears, a curly tail, a greying muzzle, and a belly long since gone to flab.

Vaguely, the young woman remembered someone hissing, "Shoo, Mukadiah, you silly old dog! Shoo, I say! How did you get in here, anyway? Off, Muka! Off! You're drooling. Get!" The intruder pulled the scruff of Muka's neck, trying to remove her, but the young woman held fast and wouldn't let go.

"No!" she cried, over and over, until the intruder sighed and left. Weeping, the young woman tightened her arms around Muka's ribcage. That warm, furry body, the heart beating against her hand — everything about the dog was so *alive*! Muka licked her fingers placidly and allowed herself to be squeezed.

After a while, they both fell asleep…

Lyrnassa was burning. A dozen fiery ships had sailed into the harbor. She was there, on the beach, watching everything burn. The other villagers were with her, standing close to the flames but not burning. They were frozen instead. She wanted to get away — she had to get away! — but all around her, their arms and legs pinned her in place. They were trapping her! She was stuck! She —Suddenly, she was away from them, high on a cliff. Safe. A hulking shadow swept past her. The Raider was joining the invaders from the sea, and all of them were closing in on the villagers. The villagers. Oh, gods, she'd left them! She'd left them! She could have saved one or two, at least — if only she'd thought to drag a few with her! They didn't know to run uphill. She'd doomed them. She could hear their muffled screams as the Raider found them. They were left, cold and pallid, on the sand. The last thing they saw was the blackness of the Raider's hollow eyes…

"It's my fault," moaned the young woman, over and over. So what if they'd never liked her? They were just simple villagers. They didn't deserve to be slaughtered. She'd *left* them! "It's my fault!"

A cool hand brushed the hair off her forehead, and a voice murmured soft, comforting sounds.

Mom! thought the young woman, sobbing in relief. It had all been a nightmare. She was ten, and she'd had a bad fall in the mountains above her home, but now her mom was there, taking care of her. "Mom! You're here!" But where was her dad? He had to be close by — he seldom left the house. And where was Auntie? She reached out, flailing her arms. "Auntie? Dad? Dad!"

"Hush, dear. It's all right. It's all right."

A Truvan speaker. Not her mom, after all, but someone from the northern coast. From the region near Lyrnassa…

The young woman turned her head, blinking at the unfamiliar face beside her — and then, with a shudder, remembering.

Not *her* mother — the *Raider's* mother! The Raider's mother was there, touching her! Too weak to flee, she shrieked and curled herself as best she could around Muka. The dog, content to serve as a shield, nuzzled her chin.

The Raider's mother sighed and left the room, but hours later, she returned to bathe and wrap the young woman's feet. Again and again the young woman fell asleep, only to awaken to this same scene. For whatever reason, she was being cared for.

The Raider's mother made many dozens of rounds without speaking to the young woman. One day, though, when the latter was once again weeping into Muka's flank, the Raider's mother gave her a stern shake of the shoulders. "My dear," she said, "this isn't doing you any good!"

Her forceful tone made the young woman gasp.

"You need to *stop*," the mother insisted.

Not daring to disobey, the young woman wiped the tears from her eyes. She sniffled and buried her hands deeper in Muka's fur but managed not to cry.

The Raider's mother smiled at her, pleased. "That's better. Now, what's your name, dear?"

"Andromache," whispered the young woman, pronouncing her name in the Truvan way, with four syllables.

"That's a pretty name."

Andromache didn't answer.

"Do you know where you are?"

Andromache shook her head.

"You're in a city called Troy."

Eyes wide, Andromache gaped.

"You've heard of it, then."

Andromache nodded. She'd heard of Troy. Everyone in Lyrnassa had heard of it! Troy was the biggest city around. The villagers had loved to babble about the riches, there — the towering palaces faced in gold and the herds of winged horses.

Andromache had never believed those tales. Her father, who had once lived in Troy, had painted her a very different picture. His Troy was a wealthy city full of merchants and ships from all over the world. It had bustling streets, high walls, and taverns where neighbors gathered. He'd never mentioned Trojan raiders, but then *he* wouldn't have associated with them! Andromache's family had loved to hear his stories about Troy; among themselves, however, they'd always called the city by its Lukkan name, <u>Taruisha</u>…

Tears sprang to her eyes. *<u>Don't think about that</u>,* she warned herself.

The Raider's mother touched Andromache's hand. "Do you remember what happened?" she murmured.

Ropes of smoke — a ship — the villagers crushing her — sand choking her — her feet torn to pieces — a monster hovering over her — a horse — angry voices —

A few tears spilled over and rolled down Andromache's cheeks. She wiped them away. "Most of it," she whispered.

The woman nodded gravely. "After all that, I don't wonder that you needed to retreat from the world for a while! But of course, you've also been ill. Fever, sunburn, all those bruises…"

Bruises. Andromache winced at what the word meant…

Fists in her throat — knees in her back — her stomach pounded by a thousand feet — her lungs choking, filling with sand —

"I thought by now you'd want some clean clothes." The Raider's mother held out a dress that was plain but well-made, like the one the woman herself was wearing. "My daughter's," she said. "It's probably too big, but it'll work well enough for now. I'll put a few more in the clothing chest."

"Thank you, uh, my lady," said Andromache. *My lady.* In saying the words, Andromache was acknowledging her fate. She'd been brought here by raiders, after all, and this woman — kindly though she seemed — now owned her. Andromache was now her slave, or at least her servant, and servants called their mistresses '*My lady.*' But the sense of deference went deeper. The woman had an obvious air of dignity, even nobility, about her. Andromache felt suddenly ashamed of her night dress, grungy from a week of wear. What had happened to her own dress, the one she'd worn in from Lyrnassa? Thrown away, she supposed.

"You're welcome, dear, but I must introduce myself. My name is Hecuba."

"Hecuba," whispered Andromache. An informal mistress, then — or perhaps a nurse employed by the real lady of the house. Whoever she was, Andromache was grateful to call her something besides '*the Raider's mother.*' She didn't want to think about anything in relation to *him.*

Hecuba patted her hand again, frowning as she did so. "Most of the skin has peeled off your arms, but it looks worse than it is, I can assure you."

"Oh," said Andromache. She studied her arms and found that she looked like a cicada, freshly molted, tender and soft. Wisps of dead skin still clung to her, and the bruises were an ugly greenish color, but nothing hurt as much as it had.

"May I see your feet?"

Meekly, Andromache extended them. She felt a gentle brushing as the woman's fingers moved over her skin. It shocked her that the woman — Hecuba — could stand to touch her, bloody as she'd been. The Lyrnassans had seen blood as an abomination…

"You certainly did a number on yourself," clucked Hecuba.

Andromache shuddered. She thought of the raw meat she'd seen on the ends of her legs. It made her sick.

"If I'd known the full extent of your injuries, I never would have allowed you to stay in that council meeting, no matter *what* Ucalegon said or *how* Laoganus brayed!" The woman gave Andromache's feet a look of fury before adding, "I have to say, though, they're healing well. Between the salt bath and the salve, they've stayed clean. Scabs are forming and I think you can walk any time, as long as we wrap your feet to pad them. Shoes will have to wait."

Andromache didn't care if her feet were healing. She didn't *want* to walk ever again, to run ever again — to leave the bed, ever again. She'd never had a bed before, and certainly not one like *this.* Plush and silken, it was like something out of a dream, and the dog who went with it seemed to like her.

"Shoes will have to wait," Hecuba repeated with a firm nod. "And I'm afraid it will be some time before you can leave for Thebe."

Andromache shot Hecuba a look of mute horror. Thebe? '*Take her to Thebe!*' The Raider's gravelly voice rang in her ear. Had Hecuba merely tended to her so that she could be shipped there after all, a prize for one of the Raider's monstrous comrades? Andromache clutched Muka's ruff and fought back tears. Muka turned to lick her hand.

"Dear? Don't you want to go there?"

Andromache still couldn't speak but managed to shake her head. No, she didn't want to go to Thebe! Whatever the Raider's plans for her had been, she wanted no part in them!

"Don't you have family in Thebe?" asked Hecuba, frowning. "It was our understanding that most Lyrnassans do."

Andromache shook her head once again. Family? Hecuba planned to return her to her family? Was *that* why the Raider had wanted her taken to Thebe? Oh, surely not! His mother had probably thwarted some darker plot and was hoping to sell Andromache back to her family for a ransom. She would be disappointed to find out that Andromache was alone in the world...

"You can't go back to Lyrnassa, dear," Hecuba said gently. "It's been burned. And surely your family —"

"I didn't have any," whispered Andromache. "I was alone."

"Oh!" Hecuba looked startled. "Well, if — if you didn't have family in Lyrnassa, nor in Thebe, then where..." She let her voice trail off, hinting for Andromache to fill in a location.

Where? There was Auntie, under the waves. There were her parents, under the earth. Andromache began to cry — not a dribble, this time, but a heavy stream of tears. "Nowhere," she whimpered. "My f-family is — all — g-g-gone!"

"Oh — oh, my!" Hecuba cleared her throat. "Then is there someone else you might be reunited with? Friends, perhaps?"

Friends? *What* friends? Andromache didn't have any friends! The Lyrnassans had never liked her, and anyway, they were all dead. The raiders had killed them. The village had been burned. It was gone. Everyone and everything were gone, and she was alone. There was no one who wanted her, no one to claim her as their own. *No one!*

Sobbing, Andromache seized two fistfuls of her hair. She didn't care anymore that Hecuba had told her to stop crying! She didn't care if crying was doing her no good! What did that matter? She had nothing — *was* nothing! "<u>Nothing</u>!" she shrieked. "<u>I have nothing and no one and *nobody* wants me</u>!"

"Sssssh, dear," Hecuba murmured soothingly, taking Andromache's fists in her hands and holding them still. "We'll say no more about it. Ssssh..."

Andromache was so tired — so tired of crying, so generally drained — that little by little, she stopped struggling and let herself be calmed.

There was an awkward silence, finally broken by Hecuba: "What language was that, dear?"

"Wh-what?" asked Andromache, frowning.

"All along, we've been speaking Truvan, but a moment ago you said something in another language."

"I did?" asked Andromache, surprised. She was at home in both Truvan and Lukkan, but usually she noticed herself shifting from one to the other.

"Yes, you did — and not just then. You did it at the meeting, and also several times when I was in here, changing your bandages. At first I thought it was gibberish, but once your voice cleared a little, I could tell it was another language. Where are you from — before Lyrnassa, I mean?"

"Hurapi," said Andromache, thinking of her homeland, far to the southeast. "The closest big city is Awarna."

"You're from the Lukka lands!" Hecuba concluded triumphantly. "You were speaking Lukkan!"

Andromache nodded.

"I thought it was something like that. How on earth did you come to live all the way up here?"

"It's a long story." And Andromache didn't want to tell it. She didn't want to risk more tears by talking about the death of her parents, the tragedy that had driven her and Auntie away from the Lukka lands…

"I imagine it is." Hecuba gave her a thoughtful look and began muttering to herself, so softly that Andromache caught only snippets: "Lukkan…new one…useful?…too late…" Finally, Hecuba nodded. Looking once more at Andromache, she said in a decided tone, "As I told you before, dear, you were very sick when you came here. My husband and I always planned to care for you as our guest until you were well enough to rejoin your family. However, since —" She coughed. "Well, I have a different proposition for you."

Andromache gave her a wary look. The word 'guest' made her feel better. Trojans were fiercely protective of guests; her father had always said so. She'd never heard of raiders taking guests into their family but supposed there was no rule against it.

And Hecuba — who was, so it seemed, the lady of the house after all — had been kind to her. Still, Andromache was alone. Vulnerable. What would she do — who would help her — if she didn't like Hecuba's *'proposition?'*

Hecuba went on: "There's a job that I'd like you to do for as long as you care to stay with us."

"A job?" Andromache frowned. What exactly would she be asked to do? Gather crops? Fetch water? Scrub floors? Spin and weave? She knew how to weave, although not as well as Auntie. Whatever the job was, though, what could she say? She was an exile with no prospects and no family to her name. Meanwhile, Hecuba was offering her a place to stay — a lavish bed all her own. Hauling water and scrubbing floors might not be so bad if, at the end of the day, she could sink into the delicious comfort of this bed.

"It's nothing onerous, I assure you," said Hecuba. "I was thinking that you might speak some Lukkan."

Speak Lukkan? Her native tongue? The language she'd spoken with Auntie? With her parents and all their friends, so many years ago? The language she'd thought she would never speak again, once Auntie died? That was the so-called *'job'* she was supposed to do? For the first time in weeks, Andromache felt her world start to brighten. "Lukkan?" she asked, to make sure she'd heard right.

Hecuba nodded. "With my son. I'd like you to teach it to him."

The shadows swept back in around Andromache. Her voice quavered as she asked, "Y-your — s-son?"

"Yes."

"The *Raider?*" Andromache murmured in dread.

"Rider?" asked Hecuba, mistaking the word just as the man in the meeting had. "Yes, I suppose that's how you'd know him."

Andromache choked back a scream as she saw him once more, looming over her, his eyes hollow and black — his face streaked with smoke — his armor drenched in blood — his skin laced with the scents of burning and death —

"His name is Hector," said Hecuba, seeming not to notice Andromache's fright. "Think about it. When you feel up to it, you can talk to him and decide."

Decide? There was no decision to be made! She never wanted to see that gore-spattered monster again, let alone teach him Lukkan! "No!" croaked Andromache.

"But why not, dear?" asked Hecuba, looking confused. "I thought you might enjoy speaking your native language."

"I can't! I don't —"

"You don't know how to teach?" offered Hecuba.

That wasn't at all what Andromache meant! She shook her head.

Hecuba took the gesture as an answer of '*no*' to her own question. "I'm sure you'll manage," the woman said reassuringly. "If you grew up in the Lukka lands, speaking Lukkan, then someone must have taught you to speak Truvan. Whoever it was did a fine job. You're perfectly fluent, and your accent is slight. You can teach my son Lukkan however that person taught *you* Truvan."

Andromache began to panic. "Teach him to say *what?*" she whispered. What use would that walking horror have for the kinds of things she knew? Once she'd taught him the words for *stab*, *slice*, *kill*, and *blood*, how would they pass the hours? It chilled her to picture those cavernous eyes staring at her; she shuddered to think of that gravelly voice asking _How do you do?_

Hecuba sighed. "For now, anything would be fine. We can always talk about specifics later, if things go well." Sighing again, she added, "I'll be frank with you. He hasn't always been the easiest of pupils."

Not the easiest of pupils? Andromache moaned in desperation. What did *that* mean? Had he run his teachers to the hilt when he tired of his studies?

Whatever he'd done to them, he would surely do worse things to *her*. He was already angry with her for being there, instead of in Thebe. He might tear her open — drain her blood — leave her on the ground, her flesh waxy-pale, her throat red and raw —

For the third time, Hecuba sighed. "This might be his last chance. So, whatever you can manage will be fine, dear. You might start with phrases of politeness and refinement. As you no doubt noticed, he could use a bit more of both."

Until that moment, consumed as she was by dread, Andromache hadn't paused to wonder *why* Hecuba wanted lessons for her raider son. So, it was to help him learn to be polite? Hecuba thought a few language lessons would be enough to fix him? What a laugh! She might as well try to quench fire with oil!

Andromache gulped and looked miserable.

So did Hecuba. "He's a good boy," she said softly. "Just a little headstrong."

A little headstrong? A good boy? Andromache barely stifled a snort. Here, if she needed it, was proof that even the foulest monster had a mother to love it!

"Please consider talking to him," Hecuba beseeched. "Just see what he says."

Doubt bubbled up, deep in Andromache's stomach. Hecuba had taken her in and cared for her, rubbing salves into her sunburned skin and piecing her feet back together. It made no sense for the woman to go through all of that, only to send her to her doom. She was Hecuba's guest, her sacred responsibility as a Trojan. And surely even the Raider, gruesome though he might be, wasn't going to attack Andromache under his parents' roof — *was* he?

(*Even if he did,*) wondered a snide little voice from a dark, hidden region of her mind. (*Who would care?*)

Who *would* care? Andromache closed her eyes. She was tired. Why fight? What was the point? It was easier just to let things happen...to close up like an oyster shell and let the waves crash over her.

"So," said Hecuba. "You'll talk to him?"

Andromache was tired of talking. She just wanted Hecuba to go away.

"Excellent!" Hecuba beamed, taking Andromache's silence for a '*yes.*' "I'll speak to him, to see how soon he can meet with you." She bustled out, leaving Andromache to burrow wretchedly down between Muka and the mound of pillows.

Chapter 3

*S*he was lying on the sand, facedown under a pile of bodies — Lyrnassans, stiff and pale, all of their blood gone. They were crushing her.
They were squeezing her slowly into the earth. The air was turning
black. No matter how hard she tried, she couldn't wriggle out from under
them. Suddenly, they were gone, and she was running. Her feet were whole
and the earth was smooth and level. She was running! But then the ground
turned steep, and she started sliding backward. Slipping. Rolling. She
crashed to a halt at the bottom of the hill and instantly, the Raider was
looming over her. His armor was gleaming red — slick, sticky red. He held
a rock in his hands — <u>No</u>! — he was going to bash in her skull —
<u>Please, no</u>! — then she heard the sickening thock! of rock on bone —

Thock, thock, thock.

"Andromache?"

Andromache stifled a scream. It was only Hecuba, knocking
at her door.

"I'm coming in, dear."

As the door swung open, Andromache fought to catch her
breath.

"But you're not ready!" Hecuba clucked in disapproval.
"You're still in your night dress! I told you I'd stop by in the late
afternoon, didn't I?"

Andromache gave the faintest of nods. Oh — Hecuba had
told her, all right! That very morning, after bathing Andromache's feet and changing the bandages, the woman had passed
along a dreadful piece of news: *My son said he could meet you this afternoon. I'll come back then, to take you to him.*

Why couldn't *that* have been a dream?

34

"Put this on, dear." Hecuba was holding out a dress, the one she'd brought the day before. "I'll be waiting for you in the hall."

What would happen if Andromache stayed in the room? Would Hecuba march back in and drag her through the door, regardless of what she was wearing? Terrified that the woman might do just that, Andromache slipped out of her night dress and pulled on the gown that had belonged to Hecuba's daughter.

It sagged over her torso and fell well past her toes.

A giantess's dress! she thought, shuddering. *Of course!* It made sense. Hecuba's daughter would be none other than the Raider's sister. Andromache was about to tear off the hateful gown when Hecuba called out to her from the hallway:

"Andromache? Do you need help with something?"

I need you to help me stay away from the Raider, thought Andromache. *Not lead me to him!*

"Dear?"

(*What difference does it make?*) sneered the snide little Voice from the night before. (*If he bashes in your skull, who's going to care?*)

"Andromache?" The door swung open, revealing Hecuba's worried face.

Hecuba *would care if my skull got bashed in,* Andromache told the Voice. *I'm her guest. Guests are sacred, here.* Hoping she was right, she brushed her knotted hair behind her ears, tugged up her gown's sagging shoulders, and clutched a wad of the hemline in her hand. She stepped through the doorway, leaving her sanctuary behind.

Hecuba gave her a kindly smile. "We don't have far to go, just down the hall to the library."

Hall? Library? Andromache didn't know what a library was, but if this house was big enough to have hallways, it might have anything else. A library might be a sort of storage room. Or a dungeon. Maybe Hecuba was going to lock her in a dungeon with the Raider...

Grasping her arm firmly, Hecuba pulled her along. The two women plodded down the hallway, followed by gentle old Muka. Andromache was grateful for their slow pace. Her feet may well have been healing, but they still ached and throbbed beneath the bandages. *How much farther?* she wondered, moaning aloud.

"You're doing well," soothed Hecuba. When they reached a door about halfway down the hall, she announced, "Here it is!"

Andromache gulped.

"Go on in, dear," said Hecuba, holding the door open for her.

In terror, Andromache asked, "Aren't — aren't *you* coming with me?"

"Oh, no. I have to run over to the neighbor's house." Hecuba sighed. "She's been hounding me for an unguent, and honestly, if I had toes as scaly as hers, I'd be doing the same. I really can't put her off any longer."

Andromache gave a pleading look. She didn't want Hecuba to leave! She didn't want to face the Raider alone!

"I shouldn't be too long," said Hecuba.

This woman took care of you, Andromache reminded herself. *She wouldn't just leave you to be slaughtered*...

"I'll come by in an hour or so to help you back to your room."

An hour? A whole hour? Newly terrified, Andromache balked.

"Off you go, then." Hecuba gave her a firm but gentle push. "And you — Muka — come here!"

With a doleful look, Muka skulked after Hecuba, leaving Andromache to enter the library alone. She limped in, ready to limp back out at the least sign of danger, but instead, what she saw inside the room filled her with wonder. Delight.

The library wasn't a dungeon, or a storage space, or a meeting hall. *It was a room full of texts!* There were thin panels of wood and clay tablets, as well as scrolls made of leather, linen, and an off-white material that Andromache didn't recognize. There were broken bits of pottery and rock with writing on them. Her dad's four beloved leather scrolls — the collection he'd guarded so jealously — would have disappeared among the riches before her. He must never have been to a library, or he would surely have taught her the word. *He would've loved it, here!* she thought. *It's just beautiful.* There was even a quiet place to sit and read — a table near the window on the far wall.

Andromache turned this way and that, drifting along, gaping at the texts around her. *They're in* Truvan! she realized, awe-struck. Long ago, before the death of her parents, she'd studied Truvan writing with her dad. Now, she couldn't quite dredge up the knowledge she would have needed to read the library's texts, but she recognized their script as Truvan. The symbols had a sacred power. They took her back through time…

She watched her dad's movements, knowing she would have to copy them exactly. He was pulling a stick across the dirt floor of their cottage, leaving a trail of shapes behind him: 'Just like this, Little Cricket,' he said…

Andromache shook her head, dizzy with the strength of her vision. She hadn't seen her dad's face so clearly in years! If a simple glance at the texts could do *that*, what would *touching* one of them do? She had to find out.

With a single, trembling finger she reached out for a clay tablet. Before she could touch it, though, her eye was drawn over to a shelf with three linen scrolls. Scrolls! Her dad's texts had been scrolls — it seemed fitting to choose one of those, rather than a tablet. Each of the three scrolls had a wooden label, the inscriptions of which looked identical. *They must go together*, she thought. She'd just taken hold of the first one when she heard her name:

"Andromache?"

She froze, dropping the scroll. She shouldn't have touched it! She had no right to touch it! She was going to be beaten, or whipped! She was —

"It's all right."

Andromache shivered. She knew that voice, deep and gravelly! But no, that wasn't right — it wasn't gravelly now, just a little husky. Not *quite* the same voice she'd heard from that gory, sooty —

She gasped. Soot? Smoke! All the smoke at Lyrnassa — had it scratched the Raider's throat? Was *that* what had made him sound so horrifying? The possibility gave her just enough courage to turn around.

There were feet on the floor behind her — sandaled feet, fastidiously clean. Big, it was true…but maybe not *giant*. Ankles. Nice, average ankles. Comforting ankles. Unarmored shins. Calves, brown and trim. A tunic laundered to the point of softness. Normal clothes — no dirt, and no gore.

Reassured, Andromache let her eyes move upward to the man's chest.

He was standing perfectly still, as though afraid she might spook. "It's all right," he repeated. "It's not going to hurt you." Cautiously, he walked over to where she was, picked up the fallen scroll, and coughed in disgust. "I take that back — I didn't know which one you had. The biography of Sarcho is definitely painful."

He's read *it?* wondered Andromache. *He's read the biography of Sarcho, whoever that is?* Surely the monster from the cliff wouldn't spend his free time reading texts, would he? Perhaps she'd mistaken the voice altogether. She raised her eyes a little further.

The man was giving Sarcho's biography a stern look, as though remembering a nasty prank it had once pulled on him.

This can't *be the Raider!* thought Andromache as she stared. The person in front of her was ordinary; if he'd had a full beard instead of stubble, he could have passed for a Lyrnassan fisherman. He was tall, but no giant, and while he looked strong enough, he wasn't hulking. The dreaded hollows in his face were nothing more than dark eyes, shadowed by fatigue. And what *was* that in the corner of his mouth? A sprig of mint, of all things? Andromache was unprepared for mint.

The man looked up from the scroll he was holding and tried once more to engage her in conversation. "My mom said you asked to see me."

"No — no — not exactly," stammered Andromache, finding a sliver of voice. "It was — it was, um — it was *her* idea."

The man tilted his head, revealing a faintly swollen lip. *But it* must *be him*, Andromache thought in bemusement. *I remember punching the Raider.*

"My mom's idea?" The man frowned and set the scroll on the reading table. "What did she say?"

"She wants — she wants me to — to teach you — Lukkan," said Andromache. "The language. My language."

It was the man's turn to fall silent. For an eternity he stood there, nibbling on the mint and drumming his fingers against the Sarcho scroll. At last, he shook his head. "Teach me Lukkan," he muttered.

His voice held a note that sent Andromache cowering back against the shelf. There, she awaited the full force of his anger — his fist cracking against her skull, or his hands crushing her throat.

Nothing. No sounds, no movements from his corner.

When curiosity overwhelmed her fear, she raised her eyes again. The man's expression was sorrowful. He had removed the mint from his mouth and wound it around his index finger in a delicate floral ring.

Andromache didn't know what to say. Nothing about this meeting had gone as she'd expected, and in any case her feet were hurting too much for her to think. Wincing, she sat down on a stool beside the table.

The man noticed her look of pain. "How are you?" he asked, sitting down across from her.

How was she? Andromache thought of Lyrnassa, of *that day*. She thought of being trampled, of stumbling over broken rocks. She thought of poor, lost Auntie and the parents she would never see again. Tears rolled down her cheeks. A sense of emptiness overwhelmed her.

The man cleared his throat once or twice before exchanging his question for an easier one: "How are your feet?"

Picturing the horrible lumps of raw meat at the ends of her legs, Andromache shuddered. "Better, I guess," she murmured. "They're getting scabs." The shoulder of her dress fell down, and she brushed it back into place. "Your — your mom has me soak them in some kind of salt bath." Too late, she realized that he probably hadn't wanted all the gruesome details — just a simple, *'They're fine.'*

The man looked more somber than disgusted, though. He sucked on his swollen lip for a moment and murmured, "I'm sorry...about your feet." His gaze flickered over the greenish bruises on her arms and the last shreds of peeling, sunburned skin.

Andromache lowered her eyes, mumbling automatically, "What can you do? Life is a bag of goat shit."

It was a phrase her parents had used all the time. It was good for any occasion, from small disappointments — *You lost your favorite pebble, Ahndromahk? Oh, well. What can you do? Life is a bag of goat shit'* — to major misfortunes — *'Yes, raiders came and took our animals. What can we do? Life is a bag of goat shit. We have to get on with it.'* Her dad had always used the phrase whenever someone showed pity for his legs...

The Raider was eyeing her with interest. "What did you say?" he asked.

Andromache hesitated. Her phrase was neither polite nor refined. Surely, the Raider's mother wouldn't want him to learn it. On the other hand, she didn't want to disappoint him. He might get angry. "Life is a bag of goat shit," she translated.

The man stopped short, his eyes wide, but he wasn't silent for long. Laughing, he added onto her phrase: "A bag of goat shit that smacks you in the face."

Andromache's own eyes widened. She'd never heard such a laugh — black, bitter, rippled with grime and rot. This man had obviously seen his share of goat shit. He *understood* — yet somehow he'd found a way to *laugh* at it! Momentarily forgetting her fear, she whispered, "That smacks you in the face *repeatedly*."

The man nodded.

"It's a saying people use, where I'm from," she said. "We have a lot of goats down there."

"In the Lukka lands?" he asked.

Andromache gave the barest of nods. Exhaustion had suddenly overcome her. What was she doing there, talking about goats with the Raider? He had no interest in learning Lukkan — he hadn't wanted her to come to Troy in the first place. Meanwhile, mint or no, she didn't want to be in the library with *him*. All she wanted was to sleep. She covered her face with both hands and mumbled, "This is absurd."

"What's absurd?"

"Sitting here. You don't want Lukkan lessons, and I..."

The man shifted. His hands were fidgeting over the scroll, the biography of Sarcho. "I never said I don't want them."

"Oh." Andromache frowned. She supposed that he hadn't., but —

"But?" he prompted.

"But you sounded so —" She paused, searching for the right word to describe his tone of voice — '*menacing*' or '*dangerous*' might offend the unremarkable person in front of her. He might vanish, only to leave the monster in his place.

"Annoyed?" he suggested, smiling ruefully.

Close enough. Andromache nodded.

"Because of my mom."

"Oh." He was annoyed at his *mom*?

"Just because *she* comes from the east and can speak seventy-seven languages, it humiliates her that I can't." The man rolled his eyes. "She drives me up the wall."

"Oh," said Andromache, flinching as pain shot through her feet again. She'd made the mistake of moving them too quickly. "So you *do* want lessons?"

The man's busy hands froze. "It would take up a lot of time," he said. "I need to think about it."

"Oh," Andromache said again. She wasn't sure how to feel about his response. On the one hand, she didn't *want* to meet with the Raider every day. On the other hand, what right did he have to reject *her*? What right did *he* — a horrible, bloodthirsty brute — have to refuse Lukkan lessons, if she could bring herself to offer them?

The man stood. "Do you need help getting back to your room?" he asked politely.

Andromache imagined leaning against him — against the Raider — and shuddered. Even now that he was clean, she didn't like the idea one bit. "No, thank you. Your mother — er, *mom* — is coming to get me."

He gave a single nod. "All right, then," he said. "See you."

"See you," whispered Andromache.

See you…an unthinkable end to a surreal conversation. Perhaps she was feverish again. Perhaps it had all been a dream. Her brain hurt. Her feet hurt. She wanted to lie down.

Dropping her head to the table, she came face to face with the Sarcho scroll. She considered the text. It couldn't be as bad as the Raider said, could it? What did *he* know about texts? He probably couldn't even read — he was just pretending. All *he* knew about were spears, and smoke, and blood!

Andromache unrolled the scroll and stared at the writing, but to no avail. Other than the word '*Sarcho*' itself, which she could decipher now that the Raider had said it, the lines on the scroll were all gobbledygook. Too many years had passed since she'd last read a text of any kind. She tried to think back to what her dad had told her…

'*That shape says* 'rrr.''
'*Why, Dad?*'
'*Well — I don't know, Cricket. It just does.*'

'But why doesn't that shape say "rrr?"'
'I don't know.'
'I think that one should say "rrr..."'
'You can't pick, like that.' He laughed. *'Just try to memorize them.'*

But it was no use. Andromache had forgotten. Once more, her eyes brimmed with tears. She set Sarcho's biography back down on the table; there was no point in trying to read it. Not only had she lost her dad, she'd lost everything he'd ever tried to teach her! What had once been symbols with meaning now looked like worms.

(*What gives you the right to compare that text to worms?*) asked the snide little Voice.

And Andromache knew it was right — *she* was the worm! Low, ignorant, worthless, useless. Her weak worm's mind was too full of dust to draw meaning from the symbols. If she had any respect for the library, for the hundreds of precious texts within it, she should slither on back to her room. She was an intruder! She had no right to be there!

The Sarcho scroll sat before her, beatific in its pallor. It was the most perfect object she'd ever seen — smooth, unsullied, replete with its own intrinsic worth. Here was the true wealth of Troy, a treasure that neither the Lyrnassan villagers nor her father had ever imagined.

How had she ever dared touch it, intruder that she was? *How had she ever dared touch it?* She, who had sunk so low that a raider could despise and snub her — that a village could stampede over her without even realizing it! She, who was nothing! Her family might have loved her, once, but they were gone, and who would ever love her now?

"Andromache?" called a voice.

Andromache jumped.

"I'm here to take you back to your room, dear."

"Oh," sighed Andromache. Weariness overcame her feelings of despair. "Thank you, my lady." The title slipped out, an involuntary nod of respect to someone grand enough to own a library.

"Please, no more of that! You must call me Hecuba."

Andromache choked the word out: "Hecuba."

Hecuba took her arm. As soon as they'd made it back to the bedroom, Andromache collapsed onto her bed and snuggled down among the pillows. Muka, who was already there, greeted her with kisses and a chorus of happy grunts.

Tucking a blanket around both of them, Hecuba asked, "So, how did it go?"

"Fine," whispered Andromache. The Raider hadn't bashed in her skull or torn out her throat. Far from it, he'd been polite to her — more polite than Hecuba had given him credit for. Perhaps the mere threat of Lukkan lessons had been enough to civilize him.

"My son's going to learn Lukkan, then?"

"He — he said he needs to think about it," Andromache murmured sleepily.

"Think about it?" Hecuba's voice sounded pinched. "I see. Well, in any case, now that you're walking, you'll want to know your way around. This house is your house, for as long as you stay here. I mean that, dear. My daughter, Cassandra, will give you a tour. She's eager to spend time with you."

Andromache's eyes popped open. Tour? Each of her previous dwellings had had a single room. She'd realized this place was much, much bigger, what with its halls and libraries — but still! What kind of house needed a *tour*? And how, with her sorry feet, would she manage to keep up with a giantess?

"Andromache, dear?"

"Huh?"

"I said, would you like her to come this evening or tomorrow morning?"

Andromache closed her eyes — she didn't want *her* to come at all! She wanted to sleep…and sleep…and sleep…

"Tomorrow," Hecuba decided. She smoothed Andromache's hair. "Tonight, get some rest."

As she drifted off, Andromache thought about the other hands that had soothed her: her mom's, her dad's, her aunt's. Those memories led her back to the mountain winds that had blown through her hair when she was a child — back to the droplets of water that had plopped onto her head from the branches of the Lyrnassan platana trees — back to those trees' star-shaped leaves and downy seeds.

She fell asleep to a string of beautiful thoughts, yet when she dreamed, it was of the ship, glittering. Of Lyrnassa, burning. Of the Raider, chasing her. Pushing her face into the sand. Blotting her out.

Chapter 4

ndromache stretched, then squirmed. Her sleeping rug felt wrong — too comfortable. Far too soft. Had Auntie laid another rug beneath it without telling her? She sank into its luxury, not wanting to get up. The birds outside were singing, though...soon, the sun would be hot. She had to get up to water the vegetable garden.

She frowned. Birds *were* singing, but not very many — not as many as she was used to, anyway. She couldn't even hear the rowdy squawking of the shore birds. Had something happened to them? For that matter, had something happened to the *sea?* She couldn't hear it, either.

Was something wrong with her ears?

Andromache sat up in panic. The moment she opened her eyes, she saw the strange environs of her room in the Trojan house — or was it a palace? — and remembered everything. She remembered Auntie's death, her own flight from Lyrnassa, and her injured feet. She remembered the Raider and his mother. She remembered *that day.*

Lyrnassa was gone, now. Her vegetables there would wither, if the marauders from the ship hadn't trampled them to pulp. Either way, she would never go back to tend them. Her Auntie had long since been carried out to sea, and she, Andromache, was alone in the world.

She began to whimper — soft, sad little sounds that awoke the dog lying at her feet. Muka! She'd forgotten about Muka. Twisting around in bed, she stroked the dog's thick fur.

Muka licked her arm.

"You like me, don't you?" whispered Andromache.

The dog waved her plumy black tail.

Scritch, scritch, scritch.

Startled, Andromache clutched the blanket in her fist. What *was* that sound? It seemed to be coming from the door.

Scritch, scritch, scritch.

Was someone knocking? "H-hello?" she said warily.

The door opened and in flew a girl, weighed down by a tray of food.

Andromache gasped. The girl, she realized, was none other than the ghost she'd seen her first night in the city — the one who had briefly appeared at the front door of the house. Andromache was utterly lost for words, and so, it seemed, was her visitor.

Muka made her way over to the girl and licked her toes. "Hi, Muka," the girl murmured. Then, having broken the silence, she turned to Andromache and whispered, "I'm Cassandra. I have breakfast for you." She thrust the tray forward.

Andromache took a piece of bread, more to be polite than because she wanted it. "Thank you," she said.

Cassandra gave her an earnest smile. The girl was tall, but no giantess — she just wore her dresses very long and flowing. "You're Andromache," she said. "I've heard all about you."

"I've heard about you, too," said Andromache, brushing a strand of hair out of her eyes. "You're Hecuba's daughter."

The girl nodded. "Mom said you wanted me to — to show you around. Around the house, I mean. But —" Her expression turned wary, as though she feared Andromache might crumple to the floor at any moment.

What's she looking at? wondered Andromache. *The bruises? My feet? Or is something else wrong with me?*

Tentatively, Cassandra went on: "But is — are — I mean, can you walk?"

Andromache nodded. "A *little*." She stressed the last word. Even with thick bandages on her feet, she didn't want to go too far, and if this house was as palatial as everyone let on —

"We — we don't have to go *everywhere*." Cassandra still seemed flustered, afraid to say the wrong thing.

Andromache now felt guilty for making the girl uncomfortable. "It's fine," she said. "I'm fine."

"Maybe just the upstairs."

Stairs? thought Andromache as they made their way slowly down the hall. *A house with separate rooms, a library* — in her mind, she gave the Truvan word a Lukkan pronunciation — *hallways — and now stairs?*

"It's a short staircase," Cassandra assured her.

Stupefied and sore, Andromache climbed without speaking. Cassandra was more than happy to fill the silence.

"The third floor — that's where we're going — isn't *really* a third floor. It's actually on top of part of the banquet hall, so it's a second floor, but since it's over the *tall* end of the banquet hall, and you have to take two flights of stairs to get to it, we call it the third floor. Does that make sense?"

It didn't…not in the least. Andromache knew nothing about how floors were counted. All she cared about was making it to the end of whatever staircase they were on.

Once they'd reached the top, Cassandra led her down the hall.

"Anyway, you can see how small these rooms are, up here, compared to the ones on the real second floor. That's why none of us use them. Most of them aren't even set up as bedrooms, anymore. People used to use them, though, back when my grandparents — Dad's parents — lived here, but they're long gone, of course. My cousins spent a lot of time here, too, until they all got married. Now, they have better things to do. Well, *they* think it's better, anyway — me, I'd much rather study than take care of babies — not that babies aren't nice! But they're not easy, you know? In the old days, some of my brothers' tutors lived with us, too, but *my* tutors all live in their own houses and only come here for lessons. Not very many people stay, anymore. It's not like when we were growing up and the house was always full…I think my parents are disappointed that they just had the three of us."

Andromache nodded along, too overwhelmed by the girl's volume of chatter to think about what she was saying. Only the last few words sank in. "Three?"

"Yes."

"It's not just you and the —" Andromache barely stopped herself from saying '*the Raider.*'

"Just me and Hector?" asked Cassandra. "Oh, no, I have two brothers." She sighed lightly. "The other one's away, right now. His room is down a floor. Near the library."

Andromache could tell that Cassandra was hedging — hiding something about the other brother — but she didn't ask what it was. She was probably better off not knowing, and anyway, her feet had begun to ache. "I think I need to rest for a while," she whispered, turning back toward the stairs.

"Oh — oh — of course. I have lessons to go to, anyway." The girl furrowed her eyebrows in a pretty frown. "Have I kept you too long? Are you all right?"

"I'm fine," Andromache assured her. "Just tired."

"Then let's get you back to your room." Slowly, Cassandra led the way down the stairs to the second floor, stopping at the door Andromache now recognized as hers.

"Is there anything you need?" asked the girl. "Anything I can get you?" Plainly, she was bursting to be helpful.

Andromache thought hard until she came up with something. "Could — could I please borrow a sash?" she asked, lifting the hemline of her dress above her ankles. "So I can tie the dress up a little?"

Cassandra brightened. "Of course! I'll bring you one after my lessons." As she turned to leave, she cried, "Oh, honey — this was so much *fun*!"

Once the girl had darted off, Andromache crept into her room and lay down on the bed. She sank immediately into a dream...

Villagers were lining the beach, reaching their waxy-pale arms toward her, moaning for help. She climbed a tall tree to get away from them, but soon she could go no further. The branch gave a crack! and sagged under her. She knew what was waiting at the bottom, when she fell. She could see the ragged claws reaching for her, the hollow eyes burning, the teeth gnashing...

Andromache awoke in a sweat, her heart racing, her mind blurry. *Where am I? And where is* he? Frightened, she looked around, but she saw only safe things. There was the end of the bed — there was Muka — there was the door —

The door! She held her breath. She could hear someone on the other side, in the hallway. *He* was there — he was coming —

"...think it's...good idea."

Andromache exhaled. It was only Hecuba.

A muffled voice — Cassandra? — mumbled something in reply. Whoever it was was standing further down the hall, where Andromache couldn't hear the responses.

"Yes, yes...days...busy...Lukkan, on top of the rest. Don't you think I know that?" said Hecuba, her voice rising.

Mumble, mumble.

"Listen to me! If we don't give the poor girl something to do, I'm afraid she'll cry herself to oblivion!"

Could someone really cry herself to oblivion? Surely not, or Andromache would already be there!

Something to do. Poor girl. Cry herself to oblivion. Oblivion. Andromache repeated the words over and over in her mind. *Oblivion.* She'd felt it yesterday in the library, in front of the Sarcho scroll, and now she knew that everyone could see it. She was nothing — empty — so pathetic that she had no reason not to fade away. Hecuba, moved by the Trojan impulse to protect guests — and no doubt fearing disgrace if her guest faded to oblivion — had thought up a task to keep Andromache occupied. Lukkan lessons. Lukkan lessons with a *monster.*

Andromache shuddered. *The Raider!*

She'd seen him in her nightmares, with his fangs and his cavernous eyes — she'd seen him ever since she was a little girl. Her mom had frightened her with tales of massacres and burnings. She'd warned Andromache to run whenever raiders came near their home...

'You run when they come here, Ahndromahk! Run up the mountainside, as fast as you can. Don't let them near you! Their eyes are black hollows, and they have fangs for teeth. They're monsters! They kill men, Ahndromahk — they'll kill your dad if they find him. And do you know what they'll do if they catch you? They'll take you away! And then, if they decide they don't want you, they'll tear you open and drink your blood!'

The lurid details were meant to scare Andromache into running away from raiders; the slower she was to obey her mother, the more gruesome the stories became. Andromache hadn't really believed them until one day, just after a raid on Hurapi, when her childhood friend Haliosh had come to find her. She must have been seven or eight at the time...

'Look at this!' said Haliosh, pulling her toward the edge of their village. 'I almost tripped over it.' When he pushed aside the tall grass, Andromache saw a body — a man, facedown on the earth, his skin waxy-pale.

Haliosh, who was two years older than Andromache, always liked to show off how much he knew. 'His blood's gone,' he said. 'That's why he's white.'

Andromache screamed — and screamed — and screamed. She didn't know how long she screamed before her mom found her and carried her home, but even then she couldn't stop screaming. Only when her dad played her favorite lullaby did she finally calm down. For days afterward, Andromache wasn't allowed out of her parents' sight. Even once she had permission to wander, Haliosh avoided her for a while. He'd been spanked for showing her the corpse.

Andromache never knew for sure who the man was. Although she had several guesses, she never found out which was right. She preferred not knowing. The bloodless body had terrified her. It had brought all of her mom's ghastly tales to life. From then on, Andromache had believed every word about the raiders' blank eyes, their gnashing teeth, their spears, and their jagged claws. In her childhood nightmares, she'd often been hunted by them — bloodthirsty, hulking, hollow-eyed brutes with gore-spattered armor. Monsters who would drain her blood and leave her facedown in the grass. She was never fast enough to escape them.

Those fears had gone dormant during her tranquil years in Lyrnassa, but they'd never truly vanished. They'd lain where she'd buried them, deep in her mind. They'd festered there quietly, only to resurge with the attack on Lyrnassa and the sight of the Raider, looming over her.

The incarnation of her oldest fears. A monster — a *real* one, in flesh and blood. The very image of the raiders who'd chased her through her nightmares — who'd destroyed so many homes in Hurapi — who'd drained a man's blood and left him lying facedown on the earth —

Andromache's cheeks went white. *Never!* she thought. She would *never* have any kind of lesson with *him!* She would rather sob down to nothingness than face *him* every day! Tears flooded to her eyes. _Good,_ she thought bitterly. _Every time I cry, I'm that much closer to oblivion._

There was a final mumble from the other person in the hallway, and then the sound of feet retreating. Andromache's door creaked open.

"Hello, dear?" whispered Hecuba. "Are you awake?"

Andromache sniffled.

"Good. I didn't want to disturb you if you weren't." Hecuba came to sit on the bed. "How are you feeling?"

"Fine." It was an obvious lie — tears were still streaming down her cheeks.

Hecuba looked at her and sighed. "My daughter showed you around?"

Andromache nodded.

"Good," said Hecuba. Clearing her throat, she added, "I spoke with my son —"

Andromache began to tremble. Hecuba's son — the Raider — *he'd* been the other person out there in the hallway! He knew where she was hiding! He might come back at any time! Fear tore through her — she opened her mouth to scream —

"— and he's decided to take Lukkan lessons," said Hecuba. "He asked if you would be free to meet the same time as yesterday."

Andromache snorted back her scream. Was that a *joke?* What else did he think she might be doing, dancing through the city square? Weeding her trampled vegetable garden? For the first time since waking, she thought of the man from the library, laughing his black laugh. He was faint, a mere shadow compared to the Raider — but then, the grotesque monster from her nightmares never would have asked if she was free that afternoon. Was she free that afternoon!

"I'll tell him you are, if that's all right..." Hecuba let her words trail off.

If that's all right? Andromache froze. Of course it wasn't all right! If she went to the library, she would have to see the Raider — and who knew what he might do?

While Andromache sat unmoving, unspeaking, Hecuba began laying out plans. "I think you can find the library on your own," she said. "So I won't stop by for you. But I suppose you might want an afternoon nap…" Hecuba thought for a moment. "Well, that's no problem, either. I'll tell my son that if you're not in the library, he should just come down the hall and knock on your door to wake you up."

That did it. "I — I'll be there on time," Andromache said hoarsely. She would do whatever she had to, to keep the Raider from knocking on her door!

"Splendid," said Hecuba. "I'll leave you, then — you and silly old Muka."

Muka…Andromache hugged the dog gratefully. When she went to the library, later, at least she would have a friend with her.

ॐ

WHEN THE SLANT of the sun was right, Andromache left her room to meet Hecuba's son for their first official lesson.

To her dismay, she was forced to go alone. She'd fallen asleep, and sometime during her nap, Muka had disappeared. *I won't go without her!* Andromache had vowed, but the thought of the Raider pounding on her door changed her mind. Grimly, she hobbled down the hall to the library.

She slipped inside. No one was there. On the table near the window, Sarcho's biography was still sitting where she'd left it.

The Raider hated that text, she remembered, although he hadn't explained why. Had Sarcho been a lover of flowers, trees, or something else peaceful that raiders naturally despised? As she unrolled the scroll, though, she saw nothing but a knot of indecipherable scrawls. *You're nothing!* they seemed to remind her. *You can't read. Even if the Raider is wrong about Sarcho, you can't prove it. You might as well cry yourself to oblivion*…

Out in the hallway, footsteps sounded.

Oh, shit! It was too late for Andromache to scurry back to her room, and in any case, her feet were in no shape for scurrying. Instead, she dropped the Sarcho scroll and sat down on the same stool as yesterday, hoping the Raider would do likewise.

Pitiable as it was, the table would serve as a barrier between them.

A moment later, he walked in, looking quite as benign — and be-minted — as he had the day before. In response to her look of confusion, he offered a tentative smile.

As he was sitting down, Andromache noticed a streak of brown on the front of his tunic. She began to tremble. _Brown!_ _Dried blood — clots of gore — spurting blood —_

"I'm sorry," said the Raider, almost in a whisper. His cheeks were flushed, and his smile had died. "There wasn't time to change on my way in from the stables."

A crimson stain spread on Andromache's own cheeks. The stables! The streak of brown was dirt, or manure at worst, not that she could smell any manure on him. For all her hideous thoughts, he'd only been taking care of his horses — and to make matters worse, he looked apologetic rather than affronted.

"Of course, it had to be my best tunic," the Raider said wryly. "Lahff EESS a bahkOFF gotSHEET."

On some level, Andromache was impressed. She'd only said the phrase once, after all, and in passing. Even so, this stranger's voice tore at her. It was like hearing an echo of her lost family, but twisted. Distorted. "It's all wrong!" she cried.

"I'm sorry," said the Raider, with a rueful smile. "My ear isn't very good. My brother's the family musician, not me."

Andromache flushed again. Despite who this man was, she felt mortified at having insulted him — now _twice_. "Oh, gods," she moaned, crumpling in on herself, clutching the table until her knuckles went white.

"Do you want me to get Mom?" the Raider asked worriedly.

"No, I — I —" Andromache let go of the table to pinch her thigh, instead. Just then, she despised herself even more than she feared _him_.

(_He has better manners than you do_,) the snide Voice sneered.

That did it! Maybe Andromache didn't want to tutor him, but she should at least try to explain herself! "You — actually, you _do_ have a good ear," she murmured. "I just meant, uh —" How to describe what she'd heard? "Well, it's just that you —" What _was_ it, exactly? "You —" She thought about what he'd said: '_Lahff EESS a bahkOFF_ — ' Oh! She had it! "When you said that, you stressed things differently than my — than Lukkan speakers do."

"Stressed things differently?"

He looked interested — or at least pitying — so Andromache went on. "Different words, different parts of words, different parts of the phrase. Here. Uh, here, listen."

With that, she began to babble about the first things that came to her mind — observations about the library that surely made no sense to the Raider, but he sat in perfect stillness and seemed to be listening.

When she stopped, he asked, "Like this? LAHFF eess a bahkov GOT sheet."

"Oh!" gasped Andromache. "That's much closer."

He looked pleased. "Can you say more?"

She nodded. She spoke of the breezes coming in through the window; of the scrolls and tablets lining the shelves; of the fine grain of wood on the reading table.

"Hmmm…" The Raider frowned in concentration.

"Could you understand anything?"

"Was I supposed to?"

"Well, I…sometimes it just happens." Andromache bit her lip. Hecuba had told her to teach the same way her Truvan teacher had taught — and all her dad had ever done was speak to her. The more he'd spoken, the more she'd understood, until finally, Truvan was as clear to her as Lukkan. His was the only way of teaching that she knew.

The Raider hesitated. "I think there was something about reading."

"Reading, yes!" she exclaimed. "You *did* understand!"

"It sounds almost the same."

The same. "Oh, gods, Ahndromahk!" she moaned, feeling stupid for her burst of enthusiasm. "Never mind. It *is* the same. None of the Lukkan people in my area could read. They didn't even have a word for reading, so my dad borrowed the Truvan word and changed the pronunciation."

"Hreeting," said the Raider.

Andromache nodded, but her face was turned downward.

The Raider sighed and ran his fingers over the dust-covered table. He then coughed, either to break the silence or because he'd inhaled some of the dust. "I was wondering…"

Andromache looked up.

"Just now, you said '*Oh gods, Ahndromahk.*'" He pronounced the last word very precisely.

Andromache's mouth went dry. "I did?" she whispered.

"Mm-hmm. What does that mean?"

"It's my name, in Lukkan," she murmured, knotting her fingers together under the table. "Ahndromahk."

"Ahndromahk," the Raider said again, trying to make his sounds match hers.

The room began to swim. "I have to go," she whispered, stumbling away before he could offer to help her. *Ahndromahk!* she heard as she hobbled away. She wasn't sure if he'd called out to her or if she was only hearing an echo in her mind.

Ahndromahk. . .

She'd buried Auntie thinking that she would never again be called by that name.

⅋

"SSSH — GO BACK TO SLEEP."

Andromache groaned. In the flickering lamp light, she could see Hecuba sitting at the foot of her bed.

"I just came in to check your feet," the woman whispered.

"Oh."

"Not that it's easy to get to them. There's something here." Hecuba held up a wad of cloth.

"My sash," mumbled Andromache, feeling a strange stab of warmth. The girl had remembered! "I asked your — Cassandra — for a sash."

"Oh, that's right." Hecuba nodded. "She did mention that. But between the sash, and this creature at your feet — this silly black creature!"

Muka thumped her tail against the bed.

"I like her," whispered Andromache.

"I know." Hecuba smiled. "They're getting better and better — your feet, I mean."

"Thank you for taking care of them." Andromache was all the more grateful to Hecuba since she couldn't bear to look at them herself. All she saw was meat, raw meat...

Hecuba nodded. "You're most welcome, of course." She gave the tops of Andromache's feet a gentle squeeze and asked, "How did the lesson go?"

Andromache stiffened, thinking back to her ignominious flight from the library.

"Did something happen?" Hecuba was frowning.

"No — it — it went well." That wasn't a total lie. Some parts of the lesson *had* gone well.

"I'm delighted to hear it. Tell me more, dear."

Andromache hesitated. What could she say? Nothing about the substance of the first lesson. It would *not* please Hecuba to learn that her son could now swear in another language. True, the woman had said to teach him '*anything,*' but profanities stretched even *that* broad limit — and they were certainly not '*phrases of politeness and refinement...*'

"Your — your son — has a good ear," Andromache offered cautiously.

Hecuba looked content. "Let me know *immediately* if he's anything but well-mannered and kind."

Andromache's eyes widened, standing out against her suddenly ashen skin.

"What's gotten into you?" asked Hecuba. "You've gone toadbelly white!"

"You think — he might — he might — *hurt* me?"

"Goodness no, girl!" Hecuba bristled. "He's not a fiend, for pity's sake."

"Oh — I'm sorry! I'm sorry! I'm sorry!" Andromache blubbered, although part of her was rebelling. She wasn't the crazy one, to think he might hurt her! No matter how he looked in the house, she'd seen his other self, the violent brute all covered in blood!

"It's all right," said Hecuba, softening. "I can only imagine what you'd think of us, after your first night here. All I meant is that, in the past, he was not always quick to do the tasks his language teachers asked of him."

"Oh," said Andromache, relieved. "Oh, no, he — he was — uh, studious — and — and — nice."

56

Hecuba nodded approvingly. "That's good to hear. Well, you must be tired. I'll let you sleep."

He was nice, thought Andromache, when she was alone. Patient and nice. So patient, and so nice, that when she'd insulted him — repeatedly — he'd apologized to *her*. If he was *really* the monster of her nightmares, shouldn't he have slain her, or pummeled her, or at least gotten angry? Instead, the man in the library had been *nice*. He seemed like someone who would want to save a girl from weeping herself to oblivion. Who, out of pity — or at least to placate his mother — would agree to unwanted Lukkan lessons.

Then again, if he was so nice, why had he chosen the life of a raider — a life that sometimes left him covered in blood? Because he'd obviously had some choice in the matter. Andromache could understand how someone with no family, no wealth, and no advantages might turn to raiding out of sheer desperation; the son of *this* house, though, must have had other options. He knew how to read — he had his own library! Why would someone with all of *that* go out marauding?

(*Unless*…)

It was the snide little Voice from before.

(*Unless you have it backward, and they have such a big house, and all those texts, because of his marauding*.)

Andromache's heart sank. Of course the Voice was right. She felt stupid for not seeing it before. The Raider's family had no doubt amassed its wealth over generations of raiding and looting. Even those who didn't do the raiding, like Cassandra, lived off of it.

(*So do you, now,*) taunted the Voice. (*Just think of where it all comes from…your bed…your food…your clothes*…)

Andromache fought back a wave of nausea. Everything she had, here, everything she used — brought in by the spoils of raiding! Why hadn't she thought of that before? She couldn't eat any of it! Wear any of it! Everything she had was tainted!

(*What are you going to do then, run around naked? Sleep on the floor? Starve?*)

Andromache had spent her whole life sleeping on the floor and could do it again if she had to, although now that she knew what beds were like, she hated to give hers up. *I have bruises all over*, she told herself. *I need somewhere soft to sleep*. Going naked was an even sillier idea. What could she hope to prove by doing *that*? Hecuba would just think she'd lost her wits and order her to get more sleep. As for starving herself in protest, the amount of food she ate couldn't have much impact on the family's finances, anyway.

(*So, you're just going to wear the tainted clothes, eat the tainted food, and sleep in the tainted bed?*) the Voice demanded.

What choice did she have? *Maybe giving food and clothes to me helps them make up for everything they've stolen*, Andromache answered weakly.

(*Stolen from your fellow villagers, you mean.*)

Andromache frowned. Fellow villagers. Lyrnassans. Lyrnassa. The village had been even poorer than the place where she was born, Hurapi. Beyond a few animals, there wasn't much to steal. Certainly nothing that someone from a house like Hecuba's would want. So what had the Raider been doing there?

(*Maybe he didn't know what a dump the place really was,*) the Voice suggested.

But Trojans had passed through Lyrnassa before, Andromache remembered. They'd seen how little the villagers had. She couldn't imagine them returning home, spinning wild tales about Lyrnassa's golden palaces and herds of winged horses.

For that matter, everyone around seemed to know that Lyrnassa wasn't worth raiding. In all Andromache's years there, no one had bothered them — not until the sea invaders came, presumably from far away.

She frowned again. The sea invaders — were *they* what the Raider had been after? Had his true goal been to steal weapons and glittering armor from those other raiders? The idea made a twisted sort of sense. The Raider and his comrades had been drawn to the smoke over Lyrnassa like flies to a rotting carcass.

(*What does it matter, why he came? When you saw him, he was covered in blood.*)

But if I'm right, it was the sea invaders' blood, Andromache argued. *Not the villagers'. And the sea invaders deserved it*. So what if an even more violent Raider had killed them? It served them right for attacking a peaceful village.

(*He probably just killed whoever was down there, so he could get his loot. Why would he spare the villagers?*) the Voice argued. (*And anyway, blood is blood.*)

Blood is blood...

Closing her eyes, Andromache saw the Raider charging down the trail, spear in hand, greedy for plunder, ready to mow down anyone in his path — but she also saw her student, drawing on the dust-covered table. She heard him say, *'Hreeting. Got sheet. Ahndromahk.'*

She couldn't imagine *him* covered in anyone's blood and didn't want to believe it. Her brain started spinning in her skull. *They're not the same person*, she thought wildly. *Maybe it was a ghost, that thing I saw at Lyrnassa.*

(*A ghost with a fat lip,*) mused the little Voice.

Maybe my student just tripped, and fell, and bumped his lip. Maybe he tripped over the Sarcho *scroll, and that's why he hates it.*

(*And maybe you're still ten, living in the mountains with your parents,*) sneered the Voice.

Andromache hugged Muka tightly to stop the tears from rolling down her cheeks.

⅌

THE FULL MOON was bathing the room in light when Andromache awoke, shuddering. Terrified. The nightmare hovered at the edges of her mind, not quite allowing itself to be seized.

It's nothing, she told herself. *You're safe. You're here. Muka is here.* She petted the snoring creature so hard that Muka awoke. "I'm sorry," whispered Andromache, as Muka sneezed in befuddlement. "Oh, sssssh, I'm sorry!" She stroked the dog's soft fur, hoping to fall back to sleep, but all she could see were burning houses — legs, churning above her, crushing her to the ground — ribbons of smoke. She turned onto her right side — then her left — then back again to the right — so many times that a disgusted Muka hopped down to the floor.

Think of something else, Andromache told herself. *Now!* Nothing from her recent past, which was gruesome; nothing from her distant past, either, because if she thought about her family or her old home she would start to cry. But what else did she have?

All she'd done in the past week was talk to the Raider, and — *No! Not that. Don't think about that! Something peaceful!*

The library. Niches lined with beautifully crafted shelves, cinnamon against the creamy white of the walls. A low table. A window that was more like a door, with a porch jutting out over the courtyard. A peaceful place to sit and read. Not too high — someone who fell off of it probably wouldn't die. Now, if someone were *thrown* off, on the other hand, she might not make it. Her last sight would be the empty eyes of her murderer, staring down —

Stop that! Flip. Flop. Flop, flop, flip. Twist. It was no use. No matter which way Andromache lay, her feet ached and her bottom hurt. She opened her eyes and stopped trying to think.

The polished wood of the bed gleamed like water in the moonlight. She imagined it coming to life, flowing across her chamber floor and down the hall in a silver sheen. Given enough time, reeds would spring up, a home for birds. Great clouds of long-legged storks, dancing through the water, shedding feathers onto the surface until it was white, like moonlight or a fine linen sheet...

Chapter 5

Andromache awoke to a timid knocking.

Scritch, scritch, scritch.

"Are you awake?" Cassandra whispered through the door. "Do you want some breakfast? Do you want to finish the tour before my tutors come?"

Andromache didn't know what to make of Cassandra. She felt both assaulted by and attracted to the girl's joie de vivre. The rosy aura surrounding her was almost palpable, while Andromache was veiled instead by a noxious black miasma. She'd been like Cassandra, once, joyous and beloved. She didn't want Cassandra to become like her. She hated to dirty the girl by spending too much time with her.

"Here…" Cassandra's voice was louder, no longer muffled by the door. She was standing inside of it, holding out a piece of fruit as if to a frightened, feral dog.

Andromache took the fruit, an apricot.

"It's from our tree," said Cassandra. "Want to see it?"

Fresh air, Andromache thought longingly. She nodded.

"Now, which staircase should we take?" Cassandra murmured to herself.

The house had *more than one* staircase?

"Hmmm…we took the back one, yesterday, because it's closer to this room, so let's take the front one, for variety. We can swing by the kitchen on our way to the courtyard, too. You'll probably want to know where the food is, now that you're up and walking. Not that I mind bringing food up to you," Cassandra said hastily. "I'm happy to! But you might want to see for yourself what there is. I mean, I don't know your tastes, and —"

"Good idea," said Andromache, before the girl could upset herself further.

Cassandra smiled. "Let's go!"

Andromache hesitated.

"Is something wrong?"

"No, I just need to — to put on the — your —" Andromache picked the sash up off the bed.

"Oh, of course! Let me help you, honey." Cassandra looped the sash around Andromache's waist so that it pulled the hem of her dress above her feet. She admired her work, nodding. "Yes — oh, that looks nice on you! When I saw it at the market, I just had to get it for you. I *thought* it might work with your coloring!"

In the daylight, Andromache could see that the sash was a bilious shade of yellow. She devoutly hoped that it *didn't* go with her coloring, but she didn't want to hurt the girl's feelings by saying so — Cassandra had chosen it specifically for *her*. How long had it been since anyone had given her a present? She couldn't remember. And besides, the sash would at least keep her from tripping.

"Are you coming, Mukadiah?" asked Cassandra.

The dog wagged her tail but didn't move.

"Poor old thing," murmured the girl. "All you do is sleep, these days. We'll leave you here, then."

The two young women set out, passing the library and several other doors. Andromache's feet were already throbbing by the time they reached the stairs, and then they had to descend. The staircase, too, was long.

At the bottom, Andromache stopped to catch her breath and realized that she was in a vaguely familiar place. It was the room where the council — or so Hecuba had called it — had been meeting when they'd questioned her. The room where she'd fainted and hit her head. For a moment, she stared, marveling at the dimensions of the space. She was sure that Lyrnassa could have fit inside it twice over.

Once again, she was astonished by the family's wealth — sickened, too, by where it came from. Raiders! She knew all about raiders. They'd been the one blemish on her childhood in Hurapi, her old Lukkan village. It had sat on the flanks of the mountains where they stretched to meet the sea, and raiders had found it a convenient prize. How many times had the Hurapian animals been stolen? The houses burned? How many times had Auntie and Andromache's dad struggled out to the secret cave in the slope behind their house? How many times had Andromache run up the mountainside with her mother? How many Hurapians had suffered an even worse fate?

Enough that her parents had considered '*raider*' a dirty word. '*Raiders take it!*' her dad had muttered, if one of his tools slipped while he was making a lute. Her mom had said the same thing when her thread snarled. What would they say to their daughter, now that she was living among a family of raiders — profiting from generations of thievery and crimes?

Andromache could almost hear them: *Don't you remember what it was like for us? For our neighbors? Everything you're eating — everything you're wearing — was stolen from someone else. How can you live with that?'*

Tears sprang to her eyes at her family's imagined rebuke, but they were as much tears of anger as of shame. *It's not my fault,* she cried out to her parents. *I didn't ask to come here. I tried not to come, but that woman dragged me onto her horse! There was no one there to help me. In case you haven't noticed, Auntie died and left me all alone.* You *left me all alone!* The tears rolled down her cheeks; hurriedly, she wiped them away. *And I'm with a family of raiders, now. What can I do about it, Mom and Dad? Life is a bag of goat shit!*

Cassandra slipped her hand into Andromache's and pulled her gently into the room. "This is the banquet hall," she said. "You can get to it from either stairway." She motioned to the other side of the room, where the back staircase was located. "Mostly we just use the front one, though." Her eyes twinkled. "For climbing, anyway…"

Cassandra's tone had turned rather devious, but Andromache didn't ask why. She was too busy looking around. The ceiling was supported by rows of pillars, so beautifully spaced that they didn't clutter the room. As Cassandra had mentioned the day before, one side of the hall had a higher ceiling than the rest. *Yesterday, we were walking above that part,* thought Andromache, trying to orient herself. *The false third floor is up there.*

Looking around the banquet hall, Andromache saw that its generally U-shaped outline was broken by numerous alcoves, which she imagined would lend the room either an inviting or a menacing air, depending on the function being held there.

"It's big, isn't it?" asked Cassandra.

Andromache nodded. "What do you use it for?"

"Oh, sometimes we have parties in here, if it's chilly outside. But my parents use it for other things, too, like meetings — you know, like the night you — oh!" Cassandra broke off, flustered. "I'm so sorry! Mom told me I shouldn't mention —"

"It's all right," Andromache said softly.

Cassandra squeezed her hand, and Andromache felt a glimmer of warmth like the one from the night before, when she'd discovered the sash at her feet. She also felt ashamed of the harsh way she'd been judging Cassandra's family. Whatever else they did in their lives, they'd shown *her* nothing but kindness — bringing her food, smoothing her hair, offering her presents and comforting her. They'd given her a much nicer welcome than the villagers had, the day she'd arrived in Lyrnassa...

Andromache shivered and told herself not to think about *that*. There were lots of things, now, that she couldn't afford to think about.

"Are you cold? There must be a draft coming in from the entry hall. It's over there," said Cassandra, pointing at a doorway to her right. "That's the portal, if you need to go out anywhere in the city!"

Out in the city? For *what*? Andromache might now be living among raiders, but at least their behavior in the house was civilized. Who knew what Trojan raiders were like outside, in the streets? She wasn't going to risk finding out!

Besides, no matter how well they behaved, there were too many of them. Too many Trojans, raiders or otherwise. Her dad had told her that Troy was a big city, thick with people. Choked with people. Teeming with people who would crush her beneath their feet without ever knowing — or caring — that they'd killed her. For the others, even Cassandra, leaving the house might be safe. They were tall. They were Trojans. Andromache was small and vulnerable and easily overlooked. She didn't belong in Troy, no more than she'd belonged in Lyrnassa. She could get smashed out of existence without anyone noticing.

Andromache looked at the fading bruises on her arms and shuddered. The house was spacious. No one crowded her, there. She was in no danger of being trampled. Why would she ever want to leave? She'd seen what the world had to offer and wanted no part in it! Whatever horrors were lurking out there in the city, she would stay far away from them. She knew better than to leave the safety of a house with thick walls.

"You're still shivering! Let's get you out of that draft. Mom says it's very important that you don't catch a chill, after the fever you had! The courtyard should be fine. It's nice and sunny, out there, and the walls keep the wind down. Oh, my lands, though!" Cassandra exclaimed. "If you ever go up on the city ramparts, watch out! But — hmm, that's right. I was going to show you the kitchen...how on earth did I get started on winds and walls?" She gave a warbling little laugh.

"I — uh, don't know," mumbled Andromache. The girl's exuberance left her flustered.

"Well, the kitchen is that way." Cassandra indicated a doorway on the far side of the hall, beyond the back stairs. "Let's go in."

As they passed into the kitchen, Andromache saw that it was really one end of the banquet hall — a large, lower-ceilinged alcove made into its own room by a screen of wood paneling. The kitchen was jam-packed. There was a hearth, of course, as well as a large table, surrounded by stools. The far corners of the room held an array of smaller tables as well as shelves on which dishware and food were stored. On one wall, though, a bank of tall windows opened onto the courtyard and gave the kitchen some sense of spaciousness.

"There's always a lot to eat." Cassandra motioned to the main table, which was practically caving in under the mass of food atop it. Andromache gaped at the stunning plates of breads, cheeses, tarts, and stews, but her eyes grew widest at the sight of the fruit. There were all kinds of figs, cherries, and apricots, as well as fruits she didn't recognize. Lyrnassa hadn't had much fruit, just one lone wild fig tree and some sour berries that grew along the creek.

"Help yourself to anything you want, any time," Cassandra went on. "We all pitch in with tidying, so it's probably best if you..." She looked hesitantly at Andromache, who nodded. She'd always cleaned up after herself and hadn't expected to do things any differently here, at least once she was up and about.

"On a side note, about cleaning, when your clothes get dirty, you can throw them in with ours — we take them down to a launderer. Well, all of us except my brother, but he's really fussy about how his clothes get washed. Anyway, back to the kitchen. I'm sorry in advance, because I'm doing most of the cooking right now." Cassandra sighed. "Just until Paris — that's my other brother, the middle one — gets back. He's really the best — and the least busy. That's who usually ends up cooking, the person with the least to do. I have lessons all morning and part of the afternoon, but I'm still less busy than Hector. Or my parents. Between going to meetings — did you know my mom's an ambassador? — well she is, and between that and tending to sick people, she's hardly ever here. And then my dad has a whole slew of other duties, of course."

Andromache was used to busy people. Her whole life, she'd lived among fisher folk, shepherds, weavers, and craftsmen: villagers, always working hard. She herself had labored over gardens and herds of animals, and she could cook simple foods. *Once I can spend more than an hour out of bed without collapsing, I'll help out in the kitchen*, she decided. She was sure to be even less busy than the mysterious Paris, unless he spent his days in a trance.

"You see, as early as it is and everyone's already come and gone," remarked Cassandra. "They've got so much to do!"

From the kitchen windows, Andromache could see hints of lushness out on the courtyard. The girl noticed where she was looking and said, "Let me show you around the garden."

Andromache's feet were throbbing, but she ignored them. The lure of the courtyard was stronger, for the moment, than her pain.

"There's a proper doorway out there from the banquet hall, but if we're in here, we usually just use the windows. It's the quickest way out to the bath chamber or the gardens. I know — you must think we're lazy, not to go to the next room, but the windows are big enough to walk through, so why not use them?"

Andromache nodded. The windows *were* large, and anyway, she had too little experience with rooms to judge what was lazy and what wasn't. She followed Cassandra through the window and out to the greenery beyond.

"So, this is the courtyard!" chirped Cassandra when they were outside. "When the weather's nice, we eat out here, or meet friends, or host weddings, or have parties. The best parties are when Hector comes back from — well, from *engagements*." She pronounced the word delicately. "Mom and Dad have all their friends over, and we drink wine and dance all night, when he comes back. Except this last time, I mean — that was different." The girl looked contrite. To cover her discomfort, she prattled on. "For parties they put lamps everywhere, and garland — it looks so beautiful!"

"It's beautiful now," Andromache said sincerely. She shuffled over to one of the trees and pressed her palms flat against it. It seemed like years had passed since she'd felt the roughness of bark beneath her hands.

"The apricot tree," said Cassandra. "We also have a few little pear trees — Dad planted them when the quince died, just to try something new — and there's the huge old fig tree, and the apples."

In amongst the trees, someone had set raised boxes full of other, smaller plants. There was an abundance of vegetables and herbs including — Andromache couldn't help but notice — a large bed of mint. Beautiful, smooth paving stones made paths around these boxes and led out to a table even larger than the one in the kitchen. For outdoor parties, she supposed; the people of Lyrnassa and Thebe combined could have fit around it.

Even so, the table was not the most impressive object out there.

"A *fountain?*" Andromache asked in shock, when Cassandra guided her to one side of the courtyard. "A private fountain?" Even in the tales she'd heard about royal palaces, people seldom had private fountains.

"An upflowing spring," Cassandra amended.

Andromache looked again at the spring, bubbling up and out to form a small pool with a wall around it. At the lowest end of the pool, a stone-lined channel took the outflow through the courtyard, toward the nearest wall.

"One of Dad's ancestors had the house and courtyard built around it. We're really lucky to have the spring. It gives us all the water we need, and the extra goes out under the wall, down to the city cisterns."

"It's incredible," murmured Andromache.

"Thank you," said Cassandra. In a hushed voice, her eyes wide and solemn, the girl added, "Did you know that for a while, before I was born, it went dry? It's true — you can even ask my parents."

"I'm sorry," said Andromache. It sounded inadequate, but she didn't know the right words to say to someone whose spring had failed.

"Well, it's in the past," Cassandra said crisply. "People like to get married here, now. The ritual requires flowing water, of course, and it's not as though you can find *that* just anywhere in the city."

Andromache hadn't actually known about the requirement. She didn't know anyone — including her own parents — who had been ritually married.

"Oh! Speaking of water, there's something else I have to show you!" Cassandra led her back toward the kitchen and pointed at a room jutting out onto the courtyard. "There's nothing wrong with sponge baths, but if you want to soak for a while, there's a basin in that room. That's our bath chamber."

"Wait — did you say *bath chamber?*"

The girl nodded. "Of course! I told you before that we had one."

"I — I must have been distracted," said Andromache. But even so, how had she *not* noticed the mention of a bath chamber? How could she have taken *that* in stride?

"That's understandable," soothed Cassandra. "You've been sick, remember?"

Before Andromache could answer, the girl had moved on.

"See those tiles slanting off the roof? Dad designed it that way to make rain run into the cistern below. We have other rain barrels, of course — what if the spring were to fail again? — but this one is especially for the bath. You can't tell from here, because of the cover — the cover helps stop it from drying out during the summer months — see, it's my brother's job to fill it with spring water if it *does* dry out, and he doesn't want to be doing that all the time, so Dad made a cover. Anyway, what I was saying is that the wall is cut out around the cistern, so part of it is actually *inside* the bath chamber. Dad's a genius to have thought of that, I tell you! Anyway, there's a hearth in the room, and a kettle, so you can heat water to add to the cold. When you're done, just bail out the bath water and pour it on a shrub." The girl gave a trilling laugh. "And now I'm hearing everything I've said to you, and it sounds like a huge pain — not relaxing, the way a bath *should* be! Well, I'm sure everyone would understand if you left the water in the bath chamber, at least. There's no reason *you* should be carrying it around! But even so, if all that seems like too much, the public baths aren't far from here."

Andromache stared at the door. All her life, she'd bathed in pools, streams, or the sea. She now had a choice between public or private *baths*? She wouldn't, of course, be using the public ones, since that would mean leaving the house — but *still*!

"If you use the bath chamber here, just be careful," warned Cassandra. "Make sure it's empty before you go in, and lock the door behind you, or else it could be embarrassing." She cleared her throat. "With the boys here, and all…"

Andromache imagined the Raider or his brother catching her naked and flushed a furious shade of purple. She would be careful, all right!

"I'll tell you right now, it can be hard to get in there, sometimes," sighed Cassandra. "The people in this house take a *lot* of baths — not that I'm saying it's bad to care about one's hygiene, but honestly! Some days, I swear, it's a wonder the shrubs don't mold over, with all the water getting poured out on them!"

The family's concern about hygiene didn't surprise Andromache. Along with clothes, she'd been allotted a small brush for cleaning her teeth. Her own family had always made do with the shredded end of a twig — which must have worked well enough, considering she still had her teeth, unlike some of the villagers she'd known. Still, the little brush was gentler.

"And on the topic of frequently used rooms…" Cassandra coughed delicately. "When you have any — *ahem* — necessity basins to dump, take them there." She pointed to yet another doorway. "Mom and Dad insist on calling it the '*moldering pit*,' but we kids just call it '*the Chute*.'"

Andromache nodded. She was grateful to Cassandra for having pointed out the room, which was useful, if not as charming as the rest of the courtyard.

"Let's walk around a little more," the girl suggested.

Across the courtyard from the kitchen and banquet hall, in a quiet, overgrown corner, Andromache noticed a small building with a lean-to attached. "What's that?" she asked, pointing at the lean-to. She hoped it wasn't a dungeon.

"That's the shed where my brother — Hector, I mean, not Paris — keeps all his gear. His gear for trainings and *engagements*. Here, we can look in, he won't care." Cassandra dragged Andromache over to the building and ran inside, but Andromache took only a cautious peek from the doorway.

Underneath the sloping rafters, she saw trunks and neatly organized shelves. It was too dark in the windowless shed for her to see exactly what kind of gear was stored there, but even if she could have, she would have been too distracted to notice.

There, on a rack in front of everything else, stood the Raider's — her *student's* — armor.

She sucked in her breath and backed hurriedly away, tripping over a garden box and yelping as she landed on her backside.

"Are you all right?" called Cassandra from inside the shed.

Andromache fought the urge to curl up into a ball. That armor! The night before, she'd tried to convince herself that her student and the Raider weren't the same person. A few more lessons and she might have believed it. But now that she'd seen the armor...

"What happened, honey?"

"Tripped," grunted Andromache, pointing at the garden box.

"I can't imagine!" Cassandra made a moue of disapproval. "You probably never saw it in all the overgrowth. Dad really needs to get out here! This part of the courtyard is a disaster. I'm so sorry!"

"It's all right." Andromache brushed off her hands and, with Cassandra's help, pulled herself upright.

"Well, thank the stars for that!" said the girl. She then gestured to the small building adjoining the shed. "Anyway, this is Hector's room, if you ever need to find him. He used to live in the main house, with us, but he was always coming and going at weird hours, and it used to wake everyone up when he dragged his stuff up and down the stairs. My parents finally told him to move out here or find something else to do with his life."

"I don't want to go in there," said Andromache, still shuddering at the thought of the armor. She was glad that the room's windows had curtains — that she couldn't see in. "I'm tired. Can you take me back upstairs, please?"

"Of course! I really should get to my lessons, anyway. If I'm late, my tutor will make me pay — drill after drill after drill, and you can bet we'll never get to the good stuff."

Andromache was too exhausted to ask what '*the good stuff*' was. Mutely, she followed Cassandra back up the stairs to her room, where she collapsed on the bed with Muka.

"Will you be all right?" asked Cassandra.

Andromache nodded. Her eyelids were already drooping.

"I'll see you later, then."

ℰℂ

SHE WAS RUNNING up the hill. Behind her she heard terrifying noises — crackling, hacking, screaming. She had to go faster — faster! She was almost to the top when a phantom swept down at her, its glowing bronze armor floating as if on the wind. The horrible greaves, slick with reddish ooze, kicked out at her. The helmet, empty and black, bent toward her. Crack, crack, crack. *Armor crashing onto bone…*

Andromache gasped herself awake.

Crack, crack, crack. The sound went on, even as her dream faded to a dim sense of horror. Muka leapt off the bed and gave a sharp bark.

Crack, crack, crack. It was coming from the door — a commanding knock, unlike Cassandra's timid scratching. Who — or *what* — wanted to enter? An image of the blood-soaked Raider passed through Andromache's mind. *Don't be stupid*, she told herself. *It was just a dream.*

"C-come in," she croaked.

The knocking continued; the visitor hadn't heard her. Andromache sighed and slid out of bed. As soon as her feet hit the floor, she tripped over the end of her sash and fell down. Muka, delighted, ran over and began licking her forehead. "Stop!" she pleaded.

Just then, the door creaked open to reveal a tall and stunning woman, aglitter in tones of copper, bronze, and silver. "Are you all right?" she asked, extending a hand. She was of the type who passed through life without ever looking ridiculous.

"Yes. Fine." Andromache felt her cheeks redden. She refused the hand and stayed on the floor as though she'd meant to sit there all along. She neither asked the woman what she wanted, nor asked her to come in, nor even looked at her.

"You don't remember me."

Then, the woman's voice registered: Andromache's captor. "Oh!" she cried. "You're the one who brought me here — from Lyrnassa."

The woman nodded.

"You look different," said Andromache, although the instant she did, it seemed a foolish thing to say, like telling the rain it felt damp. Of *course* the woman looked different, now that she wasn't coated in gore!

The woman nodded again. "I'm Penthesilea," she said, moving into the room.

Andromache hesitated. She hadn't invited this Penthesilea in — didn't want a raider in her private sanctuary! — but she was afraid of insulting the woman by asking her to leave. "I'm Andromache," she said reluctantly.

Penthesilea crossed the room with a graceful, athletic step. She sat down on a trunk, arms folded in her lap. Once she was settled, Muka went over to sniff her and received a perfunctory pat.

Thump, thump, thump, went the dog's tail against the chest. Andromache wondered how long the other woman would sit there without speaking. Why had she come?

Thump, thump, thump. Thump, thump. Thwack.

Penthesilea finally cleared her throat and said, "I wanted to see how you were doing."

"Oh," said Andromache, surprised. "Fine. Better."

"Hecuba's the best healer I know, anywhere. She's the reason I brought you here instead of to Thebe."

"Oh!" Andromache said again. She remembered the disagreement between Penthesilea and the Raider. Had it really been about which *healer* to take her to? What a strange thing for raiders to fight about! But then, many things were strange about the raiders she'd landed among.

"I know Troy was a lot farther away, but Thebe's full of sorcerers."

Andromache couldn't tell if the words were defensive or apologetic. Either way, they were laced with scorn for Thebe's second-rate healers. "Hecuba's been wonderful," she agreed.

"Is she keeping you here awhile?"

Andromache nodded.

"And once you're well, you're going to Thebe."

"No. I'm — I'm — staying *here*."

"In Troy?"

"Here. In the house. I speak Lukkan, so I'm giving Lukkan lessons to the —" *Watch it!* Andromache warned herself. She'd almost slipped again and said '*the Raider.*'

"To Cassandra," suggested Penthesilea.

Andromache shook her head. "To — to —" She gulped. She hadn't had to say the name yet and almost choked on it: "To Hector."

Penthesilea gave her a catlike look that might have hidden deep thoughts or utter blackness. "Hector."

Andromache thought of the armor lurking out there, across the courtyard, and shivered.

"Are you cold?" asked Penthesilea.

"No," said Andromache, but the question reminded her of something. "I don't know where your cloak is."

"My cloak?"

"The one you lent me, that day. It must be in the house somewhere, but I don't —"

"It's all right."

"If I'd known you were coming, I could've asked —" To Andromache's embarrassment, tears were flooding down her cheeks.

"I'll get it another time."

"Thank you, though," Andromache half-whispered. "F-for the cloak, and — for —" She swallowed hard, remembering the long and miserable ride they'd both endured so that she could be taken to a healer.

Penthesilea raised an eyebrow.

"For everything," Andromache finished lamely.

"It's nothing," said the other woman. She stood to leave, adding in a low voice, "Listen. This part of the city can be hard on outsiders. If you don't like it, let me know. I can give you a place to stay. It's small, but I'm not there much, anyway."

The offer caught Andromache off guard. She didn't know about the different parts of Troy, much less which one she was in or why it would be hard on outsiders. "Oh — uh, thanks," she stammered.

Penthesilea nodded once and swept out of the room.

Relieved to be alone again with Muka, Andromache sighed. She felt utterly spent and wanted a nap, but she could tell by the sunlight coming through her window that it was almost time for her to go to the library. It was almost time to face the Raider...

The dream she'd been having when Penthesilea arrived came back in sickening flashes: *metal, slick and bloodied — hacking — cracking —*

(*Face him? You don't* have *to face him,*) the little Voice reminded her. (*If you went to live at* Penthesilea's *house, you'd never have to see him again.*)

Live at Penthesilea's house? Andromache froze. That option seemed no better! What if it wasn't safe for her to live there? Here, at least the house had thick walls to protect her from the outside world. Penthesilea had said that her place was small. Small might mean flimsy, easily destroyed. And then there was the horror of getting to it in the first place — clawing her way through the streets of Troy — the hideous, crowded streets, teeming with people — people who might hit her, knock her down —

(*Then you want to stay with the Raider and see him every day?*) the Voice concluded with relish.

Andromache gritted her teeth. No, she didn't want to do that, no matter how he seemed in the library! She knew what he could turn into. She knew what he looked like after he'd been raiding. And she knew that it was all real, because she'd just seen his armor. *I don't* want *to see him!*

(*But you're choosing to,*) the Voice argued.

No, I'm not! My life just turned out this way! The fact was that she'd wound up in the Raider's house, and she'd wound up tutoring him in Lukkan. It wasn't a situation she would have chosen, but so far, she had no good reason to fight against it. She had no good reason to consider Penthesilea's offer. She didn't *want* choices, now — especially not when all of them were bad!

(*Well, then you'd better get down to the library,*) said the Voice in its sneering little way.

Andromache scowled, but the Voice was right. If she was choosing not to choose — to accept the reality she'd landed in — then it was time for her to go.

(*If you're late, he might come knocking at your door…*)

Andromache swallowed a sudden welling of fear. She certainly didn't want *that.* "Come on, Muka," she said aloud. At least she wouldn't have to go alone.

₮)

JUST LIKE THE PREVIOUS two days, the library was empty when Andromache arrived. She settled in with Muka at her feet, looked around, and frowned. Something about the table was different. Not Sarcho's biography — the scroll was still where she'd left it. No, the change was in the table itself. It almost seemed — but that was impossible! — no, no, sure enough, it was a different color. Brighter. The dust was gone.

Andromache thought of the drawings the Raider had made, the day before. Had he come back to erase them? Had Cassandra done so, inadvertently, during her lessons that morning? Had Hecuba been cleaning? Andromache half stood up, leaning over the table, to see if anything was left.

Squiggles along the edge. One angle, acute. An oval — no, parts of two ovals, half-effaced. Fingerprints?

"Hello?"

The Raider had arrived.

Andromache gasped and thudded back into her seat, mercifully not landing on that morning's fresh bruise. "How are you?" she cried. It sounded like a challenge, as though she'd meant to throw the words '*the hell*' into the middle of the phrase. *Just as well,* she thought. If she sounded bold, she might *feel* bold as well. She might be able to forget about what was in that shed.

The Raider had stopped short at the edge of the table and was blinking in confusion. Andromache noticed that his hair was even darker than it had been the previous day. It looked damp.

She also smelled a hint of green — a clean-scented bath oil. His hands were red and raw from scrubbing; his tunic was freshly laundered.

She flushed, remembering the first few moments of their lesson the day before, and how embarrassed he'd been by the dirt on his clothes. "<u>How are you</u>?" she repeated, more slowly and less aggressively.

"Um…" The Raider laughed and sat down. "Fine?"

Her eyes widened: even if he hadn't spoken Lukkan, he'd understood. Well, that was something. "<u>You can say, '*I am all right*</u>.'" She pronounced the last words very precisely.

"<u>Ah-ee…ham…all…rahght</u>," her student repeated. "<u>Ah-ee ham all rahght</u>, Ahn — Ahn —"

"<u>Ahndromahk</u>," she whispered. She supposed he might as well call her that; she was teaching him Lukkan, after all.

"<u>Ahndromahk</u>," he said. He then surprised her by asking, "<u>How…ham…um…um</u>." He pointed at her. "<u>Yeuh</u>?"

Ashamed at how rude she'd been about his accent the day before, she didn't correct it. "<u>I'm all right. Just a little tired</u>." It was too much, she could tell, so she yawned to show what she meant. "<u>Tired</u>."

"Oh." He nodded, yawning in turn. After a brief pause, he pointed to her feet. "<u>How ham…uh…</u>"

"<u>How are my feet? They hurt. A lot</u>. Cassandra <u>took me all over the house, today</u>."

Again, most of it had gone over his head, but he heard his sister's name and kept trying. "<u>How ham — how *hahre*</u>? — uh, Cassandra?"

Glancing down at the bilious yellow sash, Andromache said, "<u>She's very sweet. I like her</u>."

"What?"

"<u>I — like — her</u>," repeated Andromache, with a fake, exaggerated smile.

The Raider laughed. "You think she's crazy?"

Andromache's lips twitched, just at the corners. "Not crazy — nice. I *<u>like</u>* her." She placed both hands on her chest, over her heart. "<u>Like</u>."

The Raider's face brightened, and he grew serious. "<u>Ah-ee</u> — no, *yeuh*? — <u>lahke heh</u>."

"Yes," said Andromache. Conversing with the Raider was slow, painstaking work, but he'd already come further than her aunt had gone in Truvan. She decided to press on. "What do *you* like?" she asked.

The Raider frowned, and Andromache regretted her question. It had seemed like a natural follow-up, but he didn't have the words to answer it — and, now that she thought about it, she probably wouldn't want to know what he liked, anyway. She hastily decided to give him a few harmless ideas. "I like *trees*," she said, pointing out the window at the courtyard trees. "And I like *Muka*." She pointed to the dog at her feet.

"Mukadiah!" roared the Raider.

The sleeping creature was startled awake. Andromache, too frightened to scream, could only stare out of moon-wide eyes. It was happening! The man before her was changing from someone mild and inoffensive to the gravelly-voiced monster of her nightmares. Now that he'd seen Muka, he would start yelling, the way he had at the council meeting. He would spring up and strike the dog — perhaps because she wasn't allowed in the library, or perhaps just *because*. Andromache had doomed Muka by bringing her here.

But the Raider didn't move, and as Andromache watched in disbelief, Muka went over to him and laid her head on his knee. He scratched the dog's ears; her expression was blissful. Far from yelling at her, he murmured little endearments that sounded like, "Good girl. Good girl."

Andromache gulped down the scream she hadn't been able to muster.

The Raider looked up at her. Smiling, he said, "Ah-ee lahke Muka."

He *liked* Muka? Apparently so. What was more, the creature liked *him*. She'd gone right over to him, in spite of his roaring. Although, in retrospect, Andromache supposed he might not have been roaring at all, but only exclaiming in surprise. She felt stupid and somehow small.

"Ah-ee lahke Muka," he repeated.

Andromache cleared her throat. It was time to move along. "Muka is a *dog*," she murmured. "Do you like *dogs*?" This time, she wasn't just asking him a '*harmless*' question. She was honestly curious.

"Um — um — um — um —" The Raider concentrated. "<u>Yes!</u>"

Muka licked his hands as if to congratulate him for finding the word.

"Ssh, stop that," he protested, shoving lightly at her shoulder. When the dog continued to lick, he turned to Andromache with a pained look and modified his answer: "<u>Ah-ee lahke dok — *sometimes*.</u>"

"<u>Sometimes</u>," she agreed. "<u>What about horses? Do you like dogs or *horses* more</u>?"

He frowned. "<u>Hohsemoh?</u>"

There was almost a lightening at the corners of Andromache's mouth. "Uh, no — *horse*. <u>A horse is a big animal, with four legs</u>…" She stopped, seeing that she'd lost him. There were too many words he didn't know. How could she make him understand '*horse*?' She didn't want to just say '*horse*.' Her dad had usually refused to translate words when he was teaching her Truvan. *'I want us to stay in Truvan, Cricket,'* he'd said. *'It's too hard to go back and forth. You'll confuse yourself.'*

Her dad had been very good at finding a path around the unknown word, a different way of explaining it that she could understand. But now, her own student knew so little Lukkan that she saw no other way. Unless —

Impetuously, Andromache repeated the word '*horse*' and gave a piercing neigh.

The Raider burst into laughter. "Whoa, there!" he cried, tugging an imaginary set of reins.

He was mocking her! A *raider* was mocking her, and what was worse, she deserved it! She'd made herself ridiculous. Blood rushed to her cheeks, and tears began welling in her eyes. It was more humiliation than she could bear, for him to see her cry after hearing her neigh! A combination of pain, anger, and injustice boiled up inside her. "You understood!" she shouted, glaring at him through her tears — willing them not to fall. "You understood, didn't you?"

The Raider sobered. "You're right," he said, tacitly agreeing to move past the incident. "<u>Ah-ee — lahke — hohse.</u>"

But his diplomacy had come too late. From that moment on, nothing went right. Andromache's eyes stayed watery while her lips went dry. The shoulder of her dress kept falling down, and every time she pushed it back into place, dead skin flaked off her arms.

When, on top of it all, Mukadiah began to snore, Andromache called an end to their farce of a lesson and slunk back to her room. She flopped down onto the bed, wishing it would swallow her. She deserved to be swallowed. She'd made a laughingstock of herself. Brought shame upon all her relatives.

Thinking of them, of the comfort they would offer her despite their shame, she finally wept the tears she'd held back in front of the Raider.

'Don't worry about it, Little Cricket,' her dad would say. *'Not everyone is meant to teach.'*

'Dad's right,' her mom would add. She would then stroke Andromache's hair and say, *'It might take a while — and goodness knows it did for* him *— but I'm sure you'll find your place in life.'*

'Go to a wool shop,' Auntie would suggest. *'Nothing too embarrassing can happen in a wool shop.'*

Andromache doubted *that*. No matter where she was, she was sure to find a way of disgracing herself. Besides, she didn't *want* to work in a wool shop, or anywhere else. She didn't *want* to have to start all over again. She was alone, and tired, and hurting. If she couldn't succeed at teaching Lukkan, then she might as well cry herself to oblivion. Or be swallowed by the bed.

₭⇒

SHE WAS WALKING up in the hills. It was a beautiful, clear day, but suddenly, she couldn't see the path before her. Something dark was looming there. Something dark that smelled of smoke and —

Scritch, scritch.
Andromache gasped herself awake.
Scritch, scritch.
Probably Cassandra, she thought. Sitting up, she saw Muka on the floor, eyes closed, ears straight up like a bat's. Her tongue protruded in the front, where there were no teeth to hold it back.

While the dog lay sleeping, saliva had slowly evaporated from the tongue, stiffening it to leather.

"Andromache! Are you awake?" Cassandra whispered through the door.

"Mmmrph…"

Muka stirred and licked her lips, smacking moisture back into the tip of her tongue.

"Are you hungry? Mom sent me up with your dinner."

Andromache looked out the window. It was late. The evening-blue sky was speckled with the first few stars. "Come in," she said wearily.

The door swung open, and Cassandra danced in, holding a heaping tray of food. "Hi, honey! How are you?"

"Pretty tired," said Andromache, hoping the girl would see that she didn't want to talk.

Her hint was lost on Cassandra. "Oh, lessons are hard work, aren't they?" sighed the girl. She set the tray down on the clothing chest and curled up on the bed. "I mean, they're tiring enough for me, the pupil, with all that memorizing and synthesis and — gentle stars!" She clapped both hands to her cheeks. *"There's just so much to know!* I can't imagine what it's like for you poor teachers, trying to stay one step ahead."

Thinking back to the '*neigh*,' Andromache cringed. "It's not easy."

"Did you teach, before you came to the — oh!"

"What's wrong?"

"I'm sorry!"

"For what?"

"Mom and Dad said not to bother you — not to ask you too many questions or make you think too much about *before* — but I — oh!"

"It's all right," Andromache said soothingly. "You didn't do anything wrong. And no, I've never taught before."

Cassandra's eyes widened. "Never? You've had to start from *nothing?*"

Andromache nodded. "I don't know what I'm doing," she whispered. "And I don't think it's going very well."

The girl wrapped an arm around her. "Oh, I'm sure you're doing fine!"

How long had it been since anyone besides Auntie had hugged her? Andromache couldn't remember. The villagers of Lyrnassa certainly hadn't. They'd tolerated her for the sake of Auntie's skill with weaving — and because she was Auntie's interpreter — but they'd never warmed to her, even after all the years she'd lived there. Most of them had seen her arrival as a bad omen and had, on the whole, avoided her. Meanwhile, Cassandra, who had known her only a few days, was hugging her. Befriending her. Andromache couldn't imagine what this sunny creature would want with her, but she was grateful. Tentatively, she rested her cheek on the girl's shoulder.

Cassandra squeezed her. "Oh, poor honey! I hope you get good sleep, tonight."

"I'll need it," said Andromache.

"Especially after today, with Penthesilea here, and all," the girl added, with poorly feigned nonchalance.

Andromache's spirits flagged again. So *that* was all Cassandra cared about — gossip. She didn't really want to be friends. And yet, Andromache was so pathetic — so starved for physical contact — that she didn't break the girl's embrace.

Cassandra went on: "When I saw her at the door, I figured she was coming to see my brother."

"Oh, the R —" Andromache caught herself in time. "I mean, H-H-Hector?" The name was no easier to say the second time.

Cassandra nodded, then frowned. "But then she asked for *you*, not him. I just thought it was funny, since she and Hector are sweethearts and all. Did you know that?"

Andromache hadn't, and she found the idea odd. The one time she'd seen them together, they hadn't acted much like sweethearts. She tried to imagine the tender conversations they might have while lying in each other's arms:

'So, how many people did you bludgeon today, dearest?'
'Only two — it was an off day.'
'Tomorrow will be better.'
'Let's hope so.'

On the other hand, what sweetheart could the Raider possibly have, if not the formidable Penthesilea? What other woman would want him? As for the strong and beautiful Penthesilea, it was obvious why a man might choose *her* for a sweetheart.

"It's true," confirmed Cassandra. "My uncle sent her back here with Hector about a year ago, and they've been sweethearts ever since. Except I feel like I don't even know her. She hardly ever comes to the house."

"Oh," said Andromache. She supposed that Penthesilea wouldn't have much time to chat with her lover's family, in between all her raiding parties.

"Do you think that's normal for sweethearts — not to go to each other's houses, I mean?"

Normal — like sweethearts, it wasn't a word Andromache would have used either for Cassandra's brother or for Penthesilea. Holding hands, lingering beside a bank of flowers — those weren't activities she could imagine them enjoying together. But, then again, women didn't always chose lovers based on enjoyment. Some sought status, or even simple protection...

A twinge of pain ran through her. "I don't know," she said.

"So, honey — what did she want?" asked a keenly interested Cassandra.

"Nothing much. To see if I was all right," said Andromache. She thought of Penthesilea's offer of housing but said nothing about it to Cassandra. Instead, without knowing why, she told the girl a small fib. "Plus, I borrowed a cloak from her, before, and she wanted it back. But I didn't know where it was."

"A cloak? I'll ask Mom about that."

"Thanks."

"I should probably let you sleep." Cassandra gave Andromache a quick squeeze and stood to leave. "Good night."

"Good night."

The squeeze, unlike Cassandra's earlier hug, seemed free from ulterior motives. Andromache wondered if the girl might yet become her friend. She wanted a friend; other than her Auntie, she hadn't had one in years.

Suddenly, she was glad that she hadn't mentioned Penthesilea's offer. Cassandra's family might evict her if they knew that someone else was willing to take her. And while Penthesilea didn't give her nightmares, the way the Raider did, she also wasn't friendly like Cassandra. Andromache looked down at the floor. *Or like Muka,* she thought.

Penthesilea also wasn't home, much, and she'd said her house was small. If Andromache went to live with her, she would be trading a grand house with room to breathe for a cramped little shack — thick, solid walls for thin ones — this delightful bed for a sleeping rug — Muka and Cassandra for emptiness. Both houses came from the spoils of raiding, but Penthesilea's was a lot less comfortable.

On top of it all, Andromache now knew that she couldn't escape the Raider by living with Penthesilea. Not if the two of them were lovers. He would inevitably go there to visit her, perhaps wearing his armor...

Andromache clenched the sheet tightly in her hand. No! If she was going to have to see him, one way or the other, better that it be in the library. The library seemed to have a civilizing effect on him.

So far, their meetings hadn't been as bad as she'd expected. She'd embarrassed herself during that day's lesson, but her fate could have been a lot worse. She'd gotten mad at the Raider — yelled at him as though he were a normal person — and he hadn't lopped off her head, or thrown her against the wall, or even shouted back at her. Far from it, he'd retreated.

And Muka licked his hands, she thought, stroking the dog's fur. Muka hadn't startled when he cried out her name, either. She trusted him. They liked each other.

'*Ah-ee lahke dok*...'

Even if *he* was the one saying those words, and even if his accent was strange, Andromache liked hearing Lukkan again. She liked speaking it. It was a connection, however slight, to her long-lost family. And while part of her worried that her family would have despised her for teaching their language to a raider, another part of her hoped that they would have understood the small comfort it gave her in a world where she was alone.

Andromache sighed. If she would be going to go back to the library tomorrow, she didn't want to make a fool of herself again. What had Cassandra said, about tutors staying a step ahead of their students? It *would* be hard, Andromache knew, but one step wouldn't be impossible. She would just need to plan a little — decide on a few words to use and figure out simple ways of explaining them, much as her dad would have done.

Andromache groaned suddenly as she remembered another old trick of her dad's. Once, when she hadn't understood his explanation for the word '*bird*,' he'd simply taken a stick and drawn a bird on their dirt floor. He'd drawn so many pictures for her! If only she'd remembered, she might have saved herself the humiliation of the '*neigh*.' If only she'd been a good listener — a good student — a good daughter —

Tears ran down her cheeks. They started with a trickle, but a deluge was imminent.

Stop that, she told herself. *Just do better tomorrow.*

Chapter 6

'R*un, dammit, run!' She heard the words and obeyed them. Up, up, higher, higher. 'Run, Ahndromahk! He's right behind you!' She could hear the clinking of his armor.* Clink, clink. *She could smell blood — fetid sweat — and another, more pungent odor. It made her think of guts, sliced open, spilling out.* Clink! CLINK! *He was* THERE! *She had to get away! Her lungs were splitting open. But with a final burst of speed, she —'Aaaaaaaaaaaaaah!' She never even saw the edge of the cliff, but before the Raider could catch her, she was falling…*

Andromache awoke to find herself sprawled on the floor of her room. Panting, she told herself, *It was only a dream. Just a dream. You're safe. You're in your room…*

At that moment, though, the room itself felt menacing. The walls were closing in. They seemed determined to crush her, to make up for the fact that she'd escaped death in her dream. Andromache wished vehemently that Cassandra would stop by to take her on a tour, or that Hecuba would come to check on her. Anything! But she heard no knock, no scritching of fingernails on her door.

Breathe, Ahndromahk. Calm down.

Little by little, her pulse and breathing slowed. She was left feeling calm but stifled. Stale. She wished she could jump into the sea, then stand stark naked and dripping on the beach while the wind swirled all around her.

Oh, the wind! How she missed the breezes of Lyrnassa! At dusk, they'd come in from the sea or the hills, breathing freshness into even the hottest summer days. Troy, with all its walls and buildings, was sweltering by comparison — her corner of it was, anyway. However much the wind might have roared above the ramparts, what reached her room was only a sigh.

Why don't you take a bath? she asked herself, thinking of the room Cassandra had shown her, the little room near the kitchen. *She said you could...and her mom said the house was your house.* Even if Hecuba hadn't really meant those words, Andromache thought she would be able to sneak in a soak.

"Muka," she murmured.

The dog looked up at her.

"Want to go downstairs?"

Muka waved her plumy tail but didn't move.

"All right." Andromache sighed. She was nervous about taking the stairs on her own. Her feet hurt less than they had the day before, but her legs still felt ungainly.

She chose the back stairway, the one closer to her room. She put her right foot on the first stair, then carefully moved the left one beside it. In this slow way, concentrating on her movements, she made it to the main floor without stumbling.

Seeing the banquet hall for the third time, she realized that it couldn't have held *all* of Lyrnassa inside it, but its size still impressed her. The whole house impressed her. Everything she needed was there — water, shelter, food, clothes. Out on the courtyard, there were even trees and flowers. The place was like a whole village, but with walls.

If Lyrnassa had had walls, all the breezes would have been broken — but if Lyrnassa had had walls, the sea invaders might have left it alone.

I'll take the walls, thought Andromache. Years of tranquil village life had dulled her awareness to danger. After the raid on Lyrnassa, though, her senses were razor-sharp once more. She was keenly alert to all the threats looming around her, and walls meant more to her than wind.

Still doddering, she passed through the kitchen and out onto the courtyard. She stopped to rest by a raised garden box and saw that the plants within looked leggy and dry. As Cassandra had said, they weren't being taken care of. *Maybe when I'm feeling better...*

Andromache opened the bath chamber door and went inside. Remembering Cassandra's warning, she locked the door firmly behind her. The room wasn't large, although the ceiling was high. Slits on the wall admitted enough light to see by. Set into the floor was a large basin, and near it, the wall jutted into the room.

The cistern, she realized. *That's the end that's inside the bath chamber. Cassandra's dad really is clever.* Andromache had not yet seen the man and wondered if he was gone so much because he was a genius, an inventor, an engineer needed for all manner of city projects. *And how do a healer and a builder feel, having a raider for a son?* Andromache wondered. She supposed they didn't care what he did, so long as it allowed them to practice their arts. He could kill, burn, and back girls off the edge of cliffs...

Hurriedly, Andromache glanced around the bath chamber. There was a jar on the floor, beside the cistern. She grabbed it and began filling the basin with water. When there was enough for a bath, she removed her clothes and bandages, squinting so as not to see the bottoms of her feet. They were feeling a little better each day, but what if they still *looked* raw? Her bruises hadn't even fully faded, yet...

As she stepped into the bath, she gasped. The chilly water took her breath away. It felt horrible — and, at the same time, delicious. Her injured feet first throbbed, then relaxed. Once the rest of her body had acclimated, she lay back and soaked, letting her hands float up to the surface.

Andromache had never known water so soft, or so still. No current. No ripples. It almost didn't seem real, until she started shivering. Then, too cold to soak anymore, she scrubbed her skin red. The last few bits of dry, sunburned skin peeled off and floated in the water. Horrified, she tried to skim them out but couldn't catch all of them. She would have to start bailing the water. It was high time to get out of there anyway, and —

Oh, no!

She'd brought nothing to dry off with. She looked around, but the room had only a small kettle and a box full of tiny jars — no blankets, no linens, no spare clothes. Nothing absorbent. She had no choice but to sit, dripping, on the edge of the basin, her knees drawn to her chest.

The dry summer air quickly warmed her. As she stood to retrieve her dress, her eyes fell once more on the box of jars. Curious, she opened one and sniffed the liquid inside. *Olive blossoms*, she thought. *These must be bath oils.* She stared at the jars of oil, wondering whether or not to try one. She'd never used bath oil, before.

Well, why not?

One by one, Andromache opened the jars, smelling roses, cedar, herbs, and other smells she didn't recognize — some light, others rich. She chose a soft, breezy scent. *A yellow flower smell*, she thought, as she rubbed it into her skin.

Once finished with the oils, she dressed and re-bandaged her feet. Feeling energized, she bailed her bath water into a set of large jars — the ones that would later be emptied onto a shrub, she assumed. Out on the courtyard, she didn't stop to rest but went straight back to the kitchen.

The table was covered in food, as it had been the day before. Andromache thought of the dinner that Cassandra had brought her — the meal that had largely gone uneaten — and her stomach growled. She was overwhelmed at first by all the choices before her, but finally she settled on bread, a handful of almonds, and an apricot.

While nibbling her snack, she noticed that several plates were still sitting out from the family's breakfast. Someone had washed them without putting them back on the shelf. *'We all help out with cooking and cleaning,'* Cassandra had said, and this was a chance for Andromache to do her share.

One by one, she put the plates away, and when that task was done, she began brushing crumbs from the tabletop into her palm. She'd cleared almost half the table when she heard a strident set of footsteps marching from the main door toward the kitchen.

Andromache yelped, hid the handful of crumbs behind her back, and froze, her widened eyes fixed on the doorway. Why, oh, why, had she taken that bath? Why had she come to the kitchen? Why hadn't she stayed in her bedroom, where she was safe?

It was Hecuba who entered. "Hello, dear," she said. "I'm surprised to see you down here." Noticing Andromache's face, she frowned. "Are you all right? What on earth do you have behind your back?"

Miserably, Andromache extended her hand, opening it for inspection.

The other woman grew somber. "My dear, I don't know what life was like in your village —"

Andromache blinked back tears. She'd obviously done something wrong.

"— but you certainly don't have to eat *that* here! Please take whatever you like. I won't have our guest eating *crumbs*!" Hecuba sniffed.

Surprised, Andromache wiped her eyes and looked up. "I wasn't *eating* them."

"You weren't?"

She shook her head. "I was cleaning."

Again, Hecuba frowned. "Who put you up to *that*?"

Andromache didn't answer.

"My daughter?"

Guiltily, Andromache mumbled, "She told me to pitch in."

"Oh, when I get my hands on her!" The woman's eyes narrowed ominously. "Pitch in, indeed! We did *not* take you in to be our servant, no matter what *some* might think!"

"I don't mind pitching in."

Hecuba softened. "That's very kind of you, dear — and I didn't mean to sound ungrateful for your contributions. But you've been through a lot, recently. You need rest. It's enough to ask that you keep up with lessons."

Lessons. Andromache groaned. She hadn't even begun to prepare for them, as she'd been planning to do the night before. Her mind had been consumed by thoughts of the Raider, chasing her off a cliff...

"Are they going all right?" Hecuba asked in concern.

"I guess," said Andromache. "It's just —" She broke off as two images warred within her mind. The Raider, spattered with gore. Her student, laughing at her neigh. They were so different, yet both abominable.

"Is there anything I can do to help?" asked Hecuba.

Not with the Raider. Andromache shuddered internally. *But maybe with the student.* She thought of her dad, drawing on the floor of her childhood home. The library didn't have a dirt floor, of course, but Hecuba might be able to provide something else. Timidly, Andromache said, "Well, I need — I mean, it would — it would be helpful if I — if I had something to write with —"

"To *write* with?" Hecuba asked sharply. "You can *write*?"

"Well, yes — but I mean, it's more to draw with — for pictures — to explain — to explain words, and —"

"You can write! Can you *read*, as well?"

Andromache hesitated. She was too ashamed to admit that she'd lost the secret of reading. "It's been a long time since I really had the chance."

Hecuba was gaping at her. "I didn't think Lukkan people read *or* wrote Truvan."

"My dad was Trojan," Andromache explained. "He moved to the Lukka lands a long time ago."

"My goodness! Did his family move with him?"

Andromache shook her head.

Hecuba's look was pinched and uncomfortable. "When — when you said all your family was — er —" She cleared her throat. "Gone, did you mean the Trojan side as well?"

Andromache nodded. "Dad's family died a long time ago," she murmured. "That was why he left."

(*So, why aren't you telling her the truth?*) asked the snide little Voice.

That is *the truth!* Andromache protested. *He left because his mother died.* At least, that was part of the reason.

(*And what about the rest of his family?*) taunted the Voice. (*What about his father?*)

That man wasn't family! Andromache shot back. *He threw my dad out. He disinherited him.* Whatever ties there might once have been were broken.

(*Then why not tell* Hecuba *about him?*) the Voice persisted. (*Are you afraid she won't keep you as her guest anymore? That she'll send you off to be with your grandfather?*)

Andromache shuddered. She didn't want to leave Hecuba's house, not to move to Penthesilea's place and certainly not to seek out her grandfather.

(*He wouldn't want you, anyway.*)

It was true. Andromache's grandfather wouldn't welcome her. He wouldn't even acknowledge her. And just then, she wasn't strong enough to face the inevitable rejection. Maybe in time...

(*Maybe in time.*) The Voice sneered. (*Until then, don't you feel guilty about lying to* Hecuba, *after all she's done for you?*)

"I'm sorry, dear," said Hecuba, pulling Andromache out of her thoughts.

"Thank you," she murmured.

"So…" Hecuba cleared her throat again. "So, in any case, your father was the one who taught you to read?"

Andromache nodded. She thought about the scrolls on which she'd learned to read — all leather, all focused on the making of lutes.

"I see." Hecuba looked at her with more curiosity than before, but she didn't press for information. "Well, dear, I hope you'll take advantage of our library."

"It's all right to look at the texts?"

"Goodness, yes! What use are they if no one reads them? Back in my country, Santiya, tablets are rare enough and scrolls, rarer still. Even *I* seldom got to see them. You can imagine my delight when I came here to find that Priam's house had its own library." Hecuba smiled. "Of course, it meant learning a different system of writing, but no matter. It's been worth it."

Andromache shifted back and forth on her feet, which had begun to ache again.

"You look tired, dear," said Hecuba. "Why don't you go upstairs and sleep awhile? I'll come up later, to check your feet — and I'll leave your writing materials in the library."

"Thank you," murmured Andromache.

"Of course, dear, of course. Oh, and you should take a snack with you." Hecuba's eyes swept meaningfully from one end of the table to the other. "I'd be happy to throw together a few odds and ends."

'A few odds and ends!' Was that what Cassandra had been lugging up to her the past few days? Leery of Hecuba's *'few odds and ends,'* Andromache snagged a small handful of figs. "This is all I want," she said. "Thank you."

"Very well," said Hecuba, giving the figs a suspicious look. "Have a good sleep, then."

ANDROMACHE WENT TO the library before she was due there for lessons. She wanted to see what Hecuba had left for her. On the table, she found a reed pen, soot ink, and a basket full of broken bits of pottery. The Sarcho scroll was back in its place on the shelf; Hecuba must have moved it to make room for all the writing materials.

Nervously, Andromache sat toying with the reed pen. She wasn't sure how to use it, and she still hadn't made any plans for the lesson. She felt tired and rested her head, hoping a moment of sleep would clear her mind…

The Raider was advancing toward her, his hand gripping a spear, his armor streaked with blackened blood, his hollow eyes fixed on her throat. She took a step backward to flee him, then another step — and then, as she tried to take another, she realized to her horror that her feet were stuck to the ground…

"Hay-lo?"

Andromache gasped. Her eyelids fluttered open.

"Yeuh — am — tahed?" The Raider was grinning.

Tied?! thought Andromache. Her heightened sense of danger sounded the alarm. Why would the Raider ask if she was *tied?* Did he plan on lashing her to the table? Trembling, she looked over to see if he had rope in his hands.

The Raider smiled mildly at her, yawned, and snored.

"Tired!" exclaimed Andromache, her voice shrill with relief. "Yes, I'm tired! Are you tired?"

He shrugged, frowning as though undecided.

"A little?" Andromache held her thumb and forefinger just a miniscule distance apart from each other. The shoulder of her dress fell down. Irritated, she brushed it back up.

"A leetle." The Raider paused, then added, "A leetle tahed. Ah-ee — uh — am — Ah-ee am hohse." He stared at her, awaiting a response.

Andromache stared back. *I am horse?* Was he poking fun at her about the day before? She didn't think so. His face was far too earnest for mockery. *I am horse…*

"You were *with* a horse?" she guessed. "You went riding?"

"Rahting?"

Taking the reed pen and a potsherd, Andromache sketched a stick horse with a stick man astride it.

The Raider laughed.

He was mocking her — *again*! Why, now? Was she using the pen wrong? Well, how was she to know? It was a new tool for her! Before, she'd always written with a stick, in the dirt. She almost shrank in dismay — almost cried — but before she could, the Raider seized the pen from her.

"Ah-ee *rahting*!" he agreed, completing the man's face: squiggly lines of hair standing out from his head, three ludicrous O's of surprise for the eyes and mouth.

"Riding fast?" Andromache guessed.

"Fahst?"

She whooshed her hand along the tabletop. "Fast." Next, she made it dawdle. "Slow."

The Raider nodded. "Oh — yes — Ah-ee rahting fahst." Tilting his head, he considered the drawing. "I look scared," he said. "Like I'm running away from something. Hmmm…" He took the pen once more.

Andromache blanched. Scared? What could *possibly* scare the Raider? What horror, what fright — oh, gods! She didn't want to know! She *couldn't* —

"Here." He turned the drawing around for her inspection. Behind the horse, he'd sketched three scrolls. There were marks on one of the objects; by squinting, she could just make out the word '*Sarcho.*' He'd drawn himself fleeing the biography!

Andromache wasn't quite sure how to feel. On the one hand, what right did he have to hate those fine and perfect scrolls? What right did he have to mock them? He was a raider — a monster — a living nightmare! His picture was unfair. On the other hand, she felt lucky. He might have drawn something much, much worse…

"It's the complete set," said the Raider, touching each scroll. "One — two — three."

Andromache blinked. Softly, almost involuntarily, she said, "Three."

"Free," he repeated, holding up three fingers.

Just then, Andromache saw how chapped his hands were — even worse than the previous afternoon. Did he always scrub so hard, or was it because of the way she'd reacted to that brown stain on his tunic? Guiltily, she looked away.

Her student coughed as though preparing to say something momentous. "<u>Ah-ee *lahke* rahting</u>," he announced, pulling out a word he'd learned the day before: '<u>*like*</u>.'

Andromache nodded in approval and let her gaze fall back to the sketch. The rider looked absurd — nothing could be farther from the terrifying Raider of her nightmares. Raider. Rider. The words were easily confused. Both Hecuba and the white-voiced man from the council meeting had mistaken the first word for the second — because of her Lukkan accent, she supposed. What if Andromache, too, switched the words in her own mind?

Perhaps in time she would forget about her student's Raider self. He never appeared that way inside the house, and as long as she never left...

"<u>Ah-ee lahke rahting *fast*</u>," added her student.

<u>The Rider</u>, Andromache told herself. It was worth a try.

Chapter 7

Andromache remembered a time when she'd awoken each morning wondering what new joy the day would bring. Would her mom take her out to find the first spring wildflowers? Would they look for birds' nests or watch clouds skim over the mountaintops? Would her dad play a new song for her? Would he *compose* a new song for her? She looked everywhere for beauty and enchantment and never failed to find them.

Everything had changed with her parents' death. There was still love in her life — she and Auntie had each other — but their existence had been about survival, not a search for beauty. Every decision they made hinged on how it would help them carry on. They'd never meant to land in Lyrnassa, but by then they hadn't had much choice. They'd both been so weak...

Stumbling down to Lyrnassa — her dress stiff with blood —

Don't think about that! Andromache warned herself. Regardless of what had brought them to Lyrnassa, life there had been the routine of hard work all day and dark sleep all night. Practical Auntie hadn't cared much about birds' nests or clouds. Weaving cloth to wear and trade had taken up most of her time. Weaving, always weaving, to earn — then keep — their place in Lyrnassa.

While Auntie was busy weaving, Andromache had cooked, hauled water from the stream, or tended the goats or her vegetable garden. She'd bathed in the sea and gone running in the hills. Beauty had sometimes stumbled across her path, but she hadn't gone out looking for it. She'd told herself she had no time, but in truth she'd lost the will.

In Troy, her life had grown even smaller. The people were kind, there was no denying that — much kinder than the Lyrnassan villagers. Hecuba checked on her at least once a day and often sent Cassandra up with trays of food; Andromache was to have no need, excuse, or occasion for subsisting on crumbs! But other than those visits, Andromache had few routines to follow. Still drained from her recent ordeals, she spent hours at a time in bed, cuddling with Muka. If not for Lukkan lessons, she might never have left at all.

But every afternoon, when the sun's rays were slanting at just the right angle, she dragged herself down the hall to the library. It was expected of her, in this new reality.

So far, Andromache thought that the lessons had gone well enough. Even though she still hadn't planned any of them out, with the help of Hecuba's writing materials, she'd managed to stay one step ahead of the Rider. It wasn't easy, although not for the reasons Hecuba had warned her about. The Rider never balked at what she asked him to do and never refused to cooperate, but he was a fast learner and sometimes changed directions unexpectedly.

As his vocabulary grew, Andromache tried to explain new words in Lukkan before resorting to drawings. Her student did likewise. When he didn't know the word for *robe*, he called it a '*person bag*.' The *stable* became the '*horse house*' and the *kitchen*, the '*food house*.' He tossed out the phrases without caring how silly they might sound.

Andromache couldn't help but admire his nimble mind.

More importantly, though, phrases like '*horse house*' took the edge off her nightmares. She hadn't stopped having them — not by a long shot! Every night, the Raider chased her, cornered her, and menaced her. She awoke terrified and short of breath, certain that the being across the courtyard — the Raider with his blood-slicked bronze armor — would find and slaughter her. But then, once she was in the library, her student's greeting — '*Haylo*' — and his quirky little phrases reined in her galloping fears. No Raider would be caught saying '*horse house*' — let alone how her student pronounced it, '*hohse house*.'

Andromache would never have chosen to teach Lukkan to a raider, and she certainly never would have chosen to live in his house, but at least the one made the other bearable.

ॐ

THE RAIDER WASN'T the only being to haunt Andromache's nightmares. The Lyrnassan villagers also stumbled about, moaning with fear, pinning her down. Pawing at her. Suffocating her. When they weren't crushing her outright, they were blocking her escape and dumbly driving her toward the Raider, who was waiting to finish her off. Always, they walked about as demighosts, pale, stiff, and drained of blood.

(*Why do you hate them so much?*) asked the Voice. (*They aren't raiders — they're innocent.*)

Innocent? cried Andromache. *They hurt me!*

The Voice scoffed. (*They didn't mean to.*)

They almost killed me! They would have smashed me to a pulp and never noticed!

(*They were scared.*)

Well, I'd probably notice that I was stepping on someone, even if I was scared! Andromache retorted.

The Voice seemed to give a nasty grin. (*Oh, now, really?*) it said. (*Would you really think about anyone else, if you were scared?*)

Andromache began to tremble. *It's my fault*, she remembered moaning, during her first few fevered days in Troy. She hadn't warned the Lyrnassans to run uphill — hadn't tried to pull anyone up with her — hadn't answered their cries for help. She'd —

(*You deserted them,*) the Voice sneered with relish.

No, Andromache protested weakly. *I didn't desert anyone. They didn't want to be with me. They didn't even like me! They didn't help me bury Auntie.*

(*You knew what the raiders would do and you didn't even warn them,*) the Voice persisted.

Andromache sagged. The Voice was right. Who was *she* to condemn the villagers? She'd deserted her own neighbors, left them at the mercy of raiders. What did it matter if they liked her or not? They hadn't deserved to be slaughtered. Now, here she was, safe and smug behind the walls of Troy, condemning the

Lyrnassans who hadn't made it. Judging them! She was offensive. Revolting. Foul.

Andromache's thoughts festered on, growing so black that she almost wished for the relief a nightmare would bring. But sleep didn't come. Her body was growing stronger, and she had new energy to dwell on the things that upset her.

When her parents died, Auntie had been there to help pull her through. Not unlike Hecuba, Auntie had believed that staying busy was the key to survival. She'd taught Andromache to garden and had made her help with other chores. Even in those rare moments when the two of them were sitting idle, though, Auntie had been a consoling presence. She, too, had loved Andromache's parents.

In Troy, no one understood what Andromache was feeling. No one had known her parents or Auntie. No one knew the terror of being chased by raiders, of being trampled. No one knew the shame of leaving neighbors to be slaughtered. Andromache had no one to grieve with — and far too much time to fret.

Do something! she thought desperately. *Think of something nice.* She pictured the library with its cinnamon shelves, but that image wasn't as strong as the one of herself, deserting the Lyrnassan villagers.

Don't just think about it, then — go there. Hecuba *said you could look at the texts.*

Andromache took her lamp and crept down the hall to the library. Her first thought was to take Sarcho's biography off the shelf. She owed it to the text — she'd betrayed it by allowing the Rider to mock it with his drawing. Coward that she was, she'd stood up neither for her neighbors, nor for Sarcho.

At least I can make up for Sarcho, she told herself. If she read his biography, she could prove the Rider wrong about how terrible it was. She could redeem herself.

But as soon as her fingers brushed against the scroll, she thought of her first day in the library. She saw herself, cringing against the shelves — pathetic — unable to read. Unworthy of the scroll, the most perfect item in the library — unworthy of the library, the most wondrous room in Troy — unworthy of Troy, the grandest city in the north. So low, she could be trampled to death without anyone noticing...

Hastily, Andromache drew back from the Sarcho scrolls. She would never manage to start reading again, if all her confidence was stripped away before she even looked at a text!

Maybe, she told herself, *maybe he hates the biography of Sarcho because it's too hard for him. What if it's the hardest text in the library? No wonder I couldn't read it.* And no wonder the text looked so perfect — few had ever dared attempt it. She might have better luck with a different text. *A clay tablet*, she decided. *So it feels different*.

Grabbing one at random, she sat down at the table and tried to read. A phrase leapt out at her:

...trunks noringdee...

Andromache frowned. It made no sense at all, but at least it made *sounds*. It wasn't just a squiggly mess. Somewhere, deep in her brain, she must still have the secrets of reading. She strained and thought. She spun the symbols around in her mind until, at last, they had a different shape, one that made sense — *drinks morning dew.*

...drinks morning d —

Andromache snapped her head up before her chin could hit her chest. Yawning, she shuffled back to her room, where she lay down and fell immediately to sleep.

෮

FROM THEN ON, reading became a part of Andromache's bedtime ritual. It had been so long since the reading lessons with her dad that even short poems or scraps of history took hours to decipher. Most of the texts had words she'd never seen or heard before, but she didn't mind. What really mattered was the effort. Struggling through difficult passages exhausted her and distracted her from her black thoughts.

There were only two groups of texts that she avoided. One shelf was full of clay tablets written in a language she didn't think was Truvan. The writing looked similar, but there were far too many symbols — more than her dad had taught her, more than there were in the library's other texts. Just looking at the tablets gave her a headache.

The other texts she shunned were the Sarcho scrolls. Once or twice, she'd reached for one, only to be sent back to her very first time in the library. She relived it all — the perfection of the Sarcho scrolls set against her own ignorance, inadequacy, and fear. She was regaining her ability to read, but the biography of Sarcho still intimidated her, so she decided to leave it on the shelf.

The library had plenty of other texts for her to read. She could always find something to fit her mood. On nights when she felt especially agitated, she dug through Trojan law codes. Their dense language soothed her as nothing else could:

> *In the event of ellipsoid dumpage of materials unfit for hurran conception, known hereafter as 'washte' or 'trush,' amends to the amount of thrace the wyant of disheartened trush shall be enworded to the city council, for use in butterfication porgents.*

Andromache was deeply grateful for the law codes. For a time, while she was reading them, her fear and self-hatred were chased away by *'trush'* and *'butterfication.'*

Chapter 8

Outside Andromache's window stood one of the court-yard's apple trees. It was a mature tree, full of fruit, ripening to golden-yellow except where the sun's rays had tinted them with rose.

The tree entranced her. Every morning while she ate breakfast, and then again in the afternoon when she was resting before her lesson, she gazed out at it. Wind made the leaves first overlap each other, then stand apart, changing their color from shadowy black to gem green. Birds flitted through the branches, squawking or pecking at the fruits.

Andromache dearly wished that she could have an apple. The plump fruits on the branch nearest her window looked close enough to touch, but they were just beyond her reach. She knew that if she went downstairs, she could easily pick one. She could sit in the shade of the tree and nibble at the fruit or just hold it in her hand, running her fingers over the silken peel.

After three weeks in the house, though, she still made only occasional trips downstairs, when she needed a bath or something to eat.

Three weeks in the house. Three weeks without the sea, or the stream, or the village platana grove. Three weeks without the villagers she'd so cravenly deserted. She thought of them, bloodless and pale, lying facedown on the sand — and shuddered. Even if they'd never embraced her, they were still her neighbors. They hadn't deserved to be left at the mercy of raiders...

Stop, Ahndromahk — think about something else.

Three weeks in Troy. Auntie had wanted to bring her there, to her dad's homeland, but they'd stopped in Lyrnassa and never completed the move. In the week or so before she died, Auntie had been especially regretful. Her face downcast, she'd gone on and on about the cosmopolitan life Andromache might have lived, the genteel company she might have kept.

Andromache stared out the window at the quaking leaves of the apple tree. _Well_, she thought, _here I am_. She wondered what Auntie would have thought about her living situation — about her hosts. A healer. A builder. A daughter. A student. A raider.

A _raider_! How quickly Andromache had come to accept living in the same house as a raider! Eating food and wearing clothes bought with the spoils of raiding! What a fragile thing her morality had turned out to be, compared to the comforts of filling her stomach and sleeping in a sumptuous bed!

It's not like I have much choice, she reminded herself. She could live with the Raider and his family, or she could live with Penthesilea. Both houses were paid for by raiding.

(_You're getting better_,) taunted the snide little Voice. (_You could go out into the city and find somewhere else to live if you really wanted to — if you were really worried about what Auntie would think_.)

Andromache dug the heels of her hands into her eyes. Her head hurt. She couldn't imagine _what_ Auntie would have thought of it all and was just glad the poor woman had been spared the horrors of _that day_ in Lyrnassa...

Scritch, scritch, scritch.

At the sound, Muka shook herself out of a nap. Andromache kissed the dog's head and wiped her eyes against the fur. Cassandra might leave if she found Andromache in tears, and just then, Andromache wanted a guest. Especially Cassandra — the girl's chatter would be a welcome distraction.

Scritch, scratch, scritch.

Andromache cleared her throat. "Come in."

Cassandra threw open the door. "Hi, honey!" she sang, sweeping into the room. "How are you? I'm done with lessons for the day!"

"How were they?" asked Andromache, feeling the surge of nervousness she felt before her own lessons.

"Delightful!" trilled Cassandra. "I love them! Every day it's something new — history, poetry, astronomy, music, languages, numbers, plants —"

"Languages?" Andromache interrupted.

"Oh, yes! Surely, you can't imagine that Mom would let *me* slip by without them, when the boys were such a disappointment to her! I'm taking two — Luwian and Hittite. Those are the ones Mom knows. She's lucky, though — she comes from the east and grew up speaking them both. It's like breathing, for her. In my case, it's more like trying to breathe while at the bottom of a huge vat of olive oil." Cassandra giggled. "Standing on my head."

"Are your friends learning them, too?" asked Andromache.

The girl's giggle died, and she looked pained. "They're learning *southern* languages, like Ugaritic," she murmured. "I have to learn *eastern* ones. It's so unfair! I'm left out of *everything*, when they start talking. I can't wait to start on *those* languages, too, and Mom says I'll get to, but not yet. She wants me to perfect the eastern ones first. She says that no matter how many alliances we make to the south, we'll still have to deal with the east, too, so the council will *always* need members who speak those languages. If I'm the only one who can, I'll just be that much more influential." Cassandra gave a sigh of resignation. "I suppose she's right. And at least she's not making me learn the *Mudder* language."

"Mudder?" asked Andromache.

Cassandra blushed a fiery red. "Oh! Oh, dear! Please don't tell Mom I said that! It just slipped out!"

"All right, all right. I won't. But what does it mean?"

Her color fading to pink, Cassandra explained: "Well, it's what we sometimes call the Achaeans."

"Who?"

"They're people from the west, from across the sea. They make a lot of pottery. Pretty things, you know, jars and vases. Trojans say that the only thing the Achaeans can do well is make clay pots. That's where '*Mudders*' comes from. It's not a very nice name, I know, and that's why Mom doesn't want *me* saying it, but then again, the Achaeans aren't very nice people. For the past few years, all up and down the coast, they've been —"

Cassandra looked up, her eyes wide and her lips pressed tightly together. Andromache guessed that the girl had once again said too much — and that the ship bearing down on Lyrnassa had been full of Achaeans. Mudders.

"Well — so, it — it could be worse," stammered Cassandra. "But learning eastern languages is so old-fashioned, don't you think?"

Andromache frowned, thinking of the ship — of the Mudders — and how appropriate the name was. A mudslide of horror, crashing down on Lyrnassa…

Seeing her frown, Cassandra's face went pale. "Oh, honey!"
she cried. "Oh, I'm so sorry! Please, please, don't be mad at me!
No, wait — never mind. You have every right to be mad!"

Mad?

Dewy-eyed, Cassandra gripped her hand. "I didn't mean to
sound that way — I just wasn't thinking — I do that, sometimes,
talk without thinking, I mean — Mom says I really need to work
on it, and —"

"Sound *what* way?" Andromache interrupted.

"Like I thought *you* were old-fashioned, for speaking an
eastern language," the girl whispered miserably.

"Oh, I didn't think *that*," said Andromache. And she hadn't
— until now. "Lukkan is from the *south*east, anyway."

Cassandra brightened. "That's true! And it's beautiful, the
snippets I've heard — not that I listen at the door, or anything,
when you and my brother are working! But sometimes I can't
help but hear a word or two, and —"

The girl looked so close to spinning out of control that Andromache broke in with soothing words: "It's all right."

Cassandra gave her a watery smile. "It really *is* beautiful."

"Thanks."

"Oh, honey, would — no, hush! — that's rude to ask —"

"Ask what?"

"Would you — would you —"

"Say something in Lukkan?" guessed Andromache.

"Yes!"

"If *you* say something in Luwian."

"It's a deal." The girl thought for a moment, and then said,
"~~Ayam soo glatt yooer heer~~."

Touched, Andromache responded, "I'm so glad to be here,
too."

"So pretty!" sighed Cassandra. "What did you say?"

"You didn't understand?" asked Andromache, surprised.

The girl blinked. "You understood *me*?"

Andromache nodded. "You said you're glad I'm here, and I
said I'm glad to be here."

"You really *did* understand!"

"Mm-hmm." Cassandra's words had sounded strange, and Andromache couldn't have produced them, but Lukkan and Luwian were similar enough for her to get the gist. She wondered why Hecuba had only recognized Lukkan and not understood it. Perhaps it was too rustic for her, or perhaps she'd been away from the east for too long.

"Say something else in Lukkan — let's see if I get it this time," Cassandra pleaded.

Andromache mentally pawed through her favorite sayings, discarding the ones with profanities — just in case. "The future is stable like a rotten roof," she said slowly.

Cassandra shook her head. "I'm sorry."

"It's all right. You've got enough languages in your head as it is."

"Not *just* languages! If I want to be on the council one day, I have to know *everything*. It's expected of council members. Some days I feel like my brain's about to split open with of all that poetry, astronomy, and the rest jammed in, but what can you do? We have to know it."

"What does the council do?" asked Andromache. *Besides yell at each other*, she thought to herself. *And make rulings on* 'trush.'

"Oh, lots of things! They decide how much to tax ships that pass through our waterways or stay in our harbors. They make treaties with other countries and oversee day-to-day regulations — who can build where, who can sell what, and how much it needs to be taxed. Then there are relations with the city temple to sort out, and grievances people bring against each other. You name it!"

"That sounds — complex." It sounded like a headache, and Andromache couldn't imagine why Cassandra would want to take part in it.

"Oh, it *is*! There's so much I have to do to get ready for it! Lucky for me, there's time. Dad won't want to retire for quite a while. It's his spot I'd take over, *if* I get approved by the other council members, of course. Everyone thought it would be Hector, because he's the oldest, but he went another direction. If you ask me, he just couldn't be bothered with the final project. Before being accepted as a council member, you have to serve as an attendant — you know, tracking down texts for the council members, that sort of thing. And then you also have to write a treatise on something important — that's broad, isn't it? Something important? Mom wants me to write mine on healing herbs, but I don't know… I'd probably have to study sick people, then, too, and I *really* don't like vomit!" Cassandra shuddered. "I don't know how Mom can stand it! But anyway, I was thinking about something more interesting, like optimizing tax rates on the tin trade."

Andromache was stunned. She never would have expected honey-sweet Cassandra to be interested in tin taxes. It showed how little she knew about the family — besides the *direction* Cassandra's brother had chosen, anyway.

As if sharing Andromache's thoughts, Cassandra returned to talk of her brother. "But anyway, I don't think Hector wanted to write a treatise of any kind. Too much sitting still!" The girl smiled fondly. "I suppose he's not the only one to feel that way. Did you know, there are places where people don't read? Not even the council members! Can you imagine? I find it hard to believe, but that's what Mom and Dad told me, and they're too busy to make things up."

Andromache nodded. She knew about such places. She'd grown up in one.

"Say," said the girl, abruptly changing topics. "Do you like your room?"

"What?"

"Do you like your room?" Cassandra repeated patiently.

It was a strange question. As far as Andromache knew, rooms weren't to be liked or disliked, just lived in. Neither her parents nor her Auntie had ever asked her if she liked her room — or rather, her corner of their home's one and only room. If she hadn't, nothing much could have been done about it. "I don't know," she answered. "Why?"

"Oh, Mom thought it would be good for you to change — to move somewhere with a better view. If nothing else, she thought it might be nice for you to break up your routine a little. There are those spare rooms upstairs, remember? If the one you like doesn't have a bed, we can always move one in."

Suddenly recalling Penthesilea's athletic grace, Andromache nodded. If she were forced to walk from the top floor to the library — not to mention to the kitchen — and back every day, maybe she would get back into shape herself. More importantly, the exertions would allow her to burn off energy she might otherwise spend obsessing about Lyrnassa, Auntie, the villagers and the Raider.

"Do you want to see them again? I could show you now," offered Cassandra. "You have time, don't you?"

"A little, I guess."

"Oh, good! Let's go!"

Once again, Andromache followed Cassandra up the back stairs to the third floor. "I'll take this one," she said, gesturing to the room at the top of the staircase.

"But you haven't even looked inside!" Cassandra argued.

Andromache sighed and opened the door. The bed — the most important thing — looked just as comfortable as her current one. As she crossed the floor and looked out the window, she realized that she couldn't see much of the apple tree — just the top. She could, however, see all the way out to the sea. "I like it," she said.

"It's even smaller than I remembered," Cassandra protested.

"It has a nice view."

"Hmmm," said the girl. "That's true. Well, if you want, I can bring up your things while you're having lessons with my brother. It's about time for that, isn't it?"

Andromache nodded vaguely. She was looking out the window, at the sea.

Chapter 9

*S*he awoke to the slow creak of her door opening. In the gap, she saw a
shadow. A huge, hulking shadow. He was coming into her room —
her new room, far from other family members, where no one could hear
her cry out. He stood in the doorway, blocking her exit, staring at her from
hollows so black —

Andromache screamed. She was crying and shaking all over.
She couldn't stay here. Not here! It wasn't safe. *He* might come
— he might even now be lurking in the shadows of the hallway.
She crept to the door and peered out, half expecting a bronze-
covered arm to strike her from the dark —

Nothing.

Go now — hurry, before it's too late! Grabbing her lamp, Andromache limped as quickly as she could down the stairs to her
old room. Muka was there, looking bemused. She wagged her tail
as if to say, '*Where have you been?*' Andromache snuggled down beside her and wrapped her arm around the dog, but cuddling with
Muka wasn't enough to calm her. Her heart was still racing from
the horror of her dream.

I'll go read, she decided.

The library was an eerie silver from the faint light of the
stars, and Andromache's lamp cast weird shadows on the walls.
She tried to ignore them as she crept back and forth among the
shelves, searching for something to read. A treatise on madness?
The memoirs of a battle surgeon? Shuddering, she passed both
of those texts by. A third one, a law code, looked promising until
she made out three key words: *thieves*, *vilest*, and *criminals*. She
thought of her dad and hastily stopped reading.

Finally, she settled on a history of Troy. It seemed like a safe subject.

> *The city has an anobobolous govnernmant quilt favenable to the common fork, blanched as it is along numinous members, not concantated in a swindle man. Unlike nabby states, no real family has regented here for tow handed years. Unstaid, a wise council admonishes city fairs.*

<u>*What?*</u> Andromache frowned and rubbed her forehead. The text made no sense — none at all. It was like looking into fog, or a dark hole. A terrible dark hole, one of two set beside each other. A third dark hole, larger, beneath them and between. Blood, slick and red, streaming from —

She gasped and snapped her eyes back to the text. This time, she would focus.

> *The city has an anomalous government quite favorable to the common folk, branched as it is among numerous members, not concentrated in a single man. Unlike nearby states, no royal family has reigned here for two hundred years. Instead, a wise council administers city affairs.*

Andromache sat there, reeling. She understood — and not just the gist, but *every word!* Each one glowed like an ember in the dark of her mind. No text's meaning had ever been clearer — sharper. Not even her dad's texts, which she'd studied dozens of times. How she wished Cassandra were there to hear her recite it all back and prove once and for all that she could *read* — she wasn't like everyone else from those places where *people couldn't read!*

Warm with triumph, Andromache thought about what she'd read. Troy's council — the one Cassandra wanted to join, the one that had been meeting in Hecuba's banquet hall her first night in the city — was unique. Most places had councils. Even Lyrnassa had had a council. True, its members had all been hurled off a cliff into burning ships while she, Andromache, ran away and hid in the old hollow tree, but —

Andromache stopped. Where had *that* thought come from? She shook her head. *The text, Ahndromahk*, she told herself. *That's what you're supposed to be thinking about.*

Most places had councils. What set Troy apart from other large settlements was that it had no royal family — no king, no queen, no princes. The council had to work together to make rules. No one person had all the power, which was better for the common Trojans. Of course, this arrangement didn't protect common Trojans from the raiders in their midst, raiders wearing fishermen's cloaks with the hoods drawn low to cover their gnashing teeth —

Desperately, Andromache turned back to the text and read on.

> *If a council member dies, falls ill, or for any other reason vacates his seat, the remaining council members choose a replacement. While there is no official rule of succession, in practice a family member is usually chosen, provided there is one sufficiently knowledgeable in the required areas of study: civic history, the medical arts, foreign languages, military history and tactics, fine arts, poetry, trade history, engineering, astronomy, the numerical arts…*

One who knows everything, Andromache summarized. *Everything!* She looked down at the text and saw that its words had turned back to squiggles. Their meaning was now fuzzed over, like bread blurred by mold. All she could remember was that council members had to know everything.

Council members.

Cassandra would have to know everything — numbers, astronomy. Languages. *She* would need this knowledge in order to set taxes and mark the seasons and make treaties with other countries. *She* would…

Her brother, on the other hand — the Rider — the *Raider* — didn't need to know *anything*. He'd taken *another direction. He* didn't tax, he plundered — in any season and in any country. *He* chased treaty-makers up hillsides and shredded their treaties and swallowed them.

And yet *he* was the one here in the library with Andromache every day. He was here even now, hovering — suffocating — hot.

Why?

Andromache dropped the text. Her ears were flaming. Her head felt thick. Before her, she saw the monster's malevolent, empty eyes. The blood dripping from his armor — the streaks of smoke and gore — and then she knew the truth with perfect clarity.

He didn't pity her and didn't care if she cried herself to oblivion. He wasn't taking Lukkan to save her or to placate his mother — he was doing it so he could talk to the raiders from her homeland! He wanted to bring them into his swarming, pillaging horde. He wanted minions. Minions for his mayhem. Raiders flooding from the sea to the mountains, leaving behind them a trail of bloodless corpses. Mudders and riders and winter-black ships —

'*And you're helping him!*' the voices of her family cried out.

'*How can you help* him, *when you deserted our neighbors?*' Auntie accused.

'*Don't you remember what raiders like him did to our village?*' her dad broke in.

'*Didn't I tell you to run from raiders, Ahndromahk?*' asked her mom. '*Why aren't you running?*'

"My feet," Andromache pleaded aloud.

'*Figure something out,*' they all answered. '*Don't help* him!'

Andromache clutched the table until her fingers went white. *I won't*, she thought to her family. *I won't help him!* She would run straight out of the house and throw herself on the mercy of the first passers-by. She would get them to hide her in a basket and carry her out of Troy. Up the coast — north, this time. Away from the city. Far, far from the Raider!

Andromache rose to her feet, ready to run, but sank immediately back to the table. She laid her head down. It was heavy, so heavy. It hurt. Someone was squeezing it and there was nothing she could do but weep…

꿍

"HONEY?" SAID A SOFT, GIRLISH VOICE.

Andromache groaned. Where was she? And why was the place spinning?

"What are you doing in the library, honey? Don't you like your new room?"

"Ah — ah — smary."

"What's that? Oh, I see! You came down to read a little, before breakfast. I used to do that, before my tutors started coming so early. What do you have, there?" Cassandra peeked at the text that had fallen from Andromache's hands. Her eyes grew wide in delight. "Oooh! That's a good one! I should read it again. It's been — oh — maybe five years, now? Six? Well, who knows, anymore. I couldn't have been more than nine or ten, and I'm sure I didn't understand it properly, but you see, it's not the only authoritative text on that subject and — honey?" She paused, frowning. "Are you all right? You look a little flushed."

"Fern...slap," mumbled Andromache. She buried her face in her hands.

"Oh, honey! You're shivering! Hang on, I'll get Mom."

"No — no —"

But the girl was already standing out on the balcony. "MO-OOOOOOOM!" she shrieked.

Andromache's head split open. Cassandra's shrieking was more than she could bear. She stood and wobbled away as fast as her scabby feet would allow. Her mouth tasted like she'd been sucking on copper. She needed to lie down.

Instead of going up to her new room, she crept down the hall to her old one. It was closer, safer. She collapsed on the bed, shivering and afraid to sleep. As soon as she did, *he* would come for her.

The door crashed open. She screamed.

"Sssh, dear — it's all right. I'm here, now. My daughter said you needed me." Hecuba touched a hand to Andromache's cheek and forehead. "Goodness! You're burning up." She bent to pick something up off the floor. "Drink this."

A cup of water was pressed to Andromache's lips. Obediently, she swallowed twice.

"More, dear — a little more."

Three more sips.

"Good. Good," Hecuba tucked a blanket loosely around her. "Now, rest. Sleep. If you can't sleep, I'll bring you something to help."

"Lukka," whimpered Andromache. She had to get up — she *had* to. She had to get out of here before the Raider took over her homeland and —

"I think *not*," ordered Hecuba. "No lessons for you, today. You're not leaving this bed until the fever's broken. I'll let my son know you're ill. You just sleep, and keep drinking water. I'll come up to check on you in a while." She smoothed the hair from Andromache's forehead.

Hecuba's hand felt good — cool. Like the smooth, curved shell Andromache had once found on the beach.

Chapter 10

Andromache awoke periodically, first to sunlight, then to darkness, then to sunlight again. Sometimes Hecuba was in the room with her, feeling her forehead and offering her water or a plate of fruit slices. Other times, she saw evidence that the woman had been there — an extra blanket, a cup of juice, Muka. Andromache drank the juice greedily, cuddled the dog close to her, and fell back to sleep.

Late on what she supposed was the second night, her fever broke. She had a dream that she was running through a field full of hot water springs. They were spraying her, dousing her. When she awoke, her sheets and night dress were soaked through with sweat. She changed into a clean dress that Hecuba must have left for her, wrapped up in the extra blanket, and lay back down feeling weak but more herself than she had in days. She slept peacefully until late the next morning.

When Hecuba stopped in to check on her, she brought a tray of honey cakes and fruit. "A late breakfast," she said. "Or early lunch."

"Thank you," Andromache said shyly.

"You're looking better," the other woman approved. "I can almost see a spark in your eye again. Is the fever gone?"

Andromache nodded.

"Well, let's check, anyway." Hecuba touched her forehead. "Good. You'll need to rest for another day or so, though — and for goodness' sake, eat something!"

She shoved the tray at Andromache, who had no choice but to take it.

"That's what you need: rest, food, and drink. Now, I have to run out for a bit. My ridiculous neighbor, Alybe, will be crying for her salve." Hecuba lowered her voice to a mutter. "She has a nasty case of the pimples and blames them for her inability to find a second husband. The first one died a year or so ago, and Alybe has been hot to have another ever since. I wish her luck! The first one married her when she was sixteen, fresh out of Sestos village. He'd never spoken to her and had no way of knowing that she sounded just like a baying wolf. Can you imagine it, all day long, the hairs on the back of your neck standing up? I tell you, it's a lesson to all those who would marry someone they've never met!" Hecuba gave a slight frisson. "In any case, the city is wise to her, now. Salve or no salve, the best company *she'll* ever be able to rustle up is her late husband's fish bone collection."

Fish bone collection? It was almost as strange an image as some that had come to Andromache during her delirium, but she was given no chance to ask about it. Hecuba was already backing out the door.

"I'll drop back in to check on you, but I need to stop at the herb market, first. Priam's joints are acting up again, although I'll thank you not to tell him I said so."

Andromache shook her head. The request would be easy to honor. She didn't even know a Priam.

"All right, dear. Remember — eat and sleep."

Andromache obeyed, first nibbling at half of a honey cake and then dozing away the afternoon.

ℰↃ

ANDROMACHE AWOKE to the sound of rustling apple leaves, when sunlight was slanting at a low angle into her room. Hecuba wasn't there but had come and gone at least once: the half-eaten honey cake had been replaced by two whole ones.

Andromache considered them but instead took an apricot and squeezed it. She pressed the fruit's flesh to the point where it was about to split, then released it. Her fingers left a dent but no gash.

She felt very awake.

Awake and bored. She'd been sleeping for days and needed a break from her bed. With few options open to her, she decided to go to the library. Maybe she would be able to find something pleasant to read — a tale from the mountain country, or a poem about flower-covered meadows.

Dawdling down the hallway, she felt a little weak but solid. It was good to be out of her room. As she passed by the doors, she looked at each with interest, as though she'd never seen them before. The colors were all slightly different. They'd been made from the same type of wood, she thought, but different trees.

The library door was larger than the others — not taller, but wider. Heavy. She put her shoulder into it and pushed; her face was turned toward the floor as she entered the room.

"Hay-lo?" said a deep voice. "Ahndromahk?"

She gasped.

The Rider was sitting at the table, looking up, clearly as surprised to see her as she was to see him. His forearms lay flat against the table, forming a parapet around the text he was reading. A stray lock of hair fell over his forehead. "How ahre yeuh?"

Andromache bit her lip. How was she? Confused. She didn't know who she was looking at. Not the Raider who'd hunted her through her fevered dreams. Not someone who would revel in setting fire to villages, or attacking girls in the night, or forming bands of marauders all the way to the Lukka lands. At least, he didn't look like that. He looked kind and ordinary — once more, like someone who would take Lukkan lessons out of pity.

Had it all been a dream, before, in Lyrnassa? If not, then how much had been real? Or was *this* the dream, now?

"Ahndromahk?" The Rider's forehead wrinkled in concern.

"I — I — don't know," she stammered. "I don't know how I am."

He nodded as though he understood.

Dizzy — she was definitely dizzy. Stumbling over the bandages on her feet, she made for her place at the table and collapsed onto the stool. The forgotten apricot fell out of her hand, rolled across the table, and stopped against the Rider's — her student's — arm.

He picked up the golden fruit and held it cupped in his hand, turning it so that it caught the late afternoon sunlight. "Yeuh lahke…" He waited for her to fill in the word.

"Apricots," she whispered. She couldn't help but notice that his hands weren't as raw as usual, after the three-day break from lessons. They were clean — he was clean — but not painfully so.

"*Ay*-bricoats," he repeated. "Yeuh lahke?"

Andromache nodded. She cleared her throat. "Yes, I like them. I like all fruits."

Her student wrinkled his brow again. "Fruits…" he said. "Hmm." He took the ink and a potsherd. With his left hand, he drew a bowl filled with a crude pear, an apple and a quince; he then switched the pen to his right hand to sketch in a bunch of grapes, a fig, and a pomegranate. "Fruits?" he asked when the drawing was finished.

Gawking, Andromache asked, "How do you do that?"

"What?" He looked confused. He hadn't understood the question.

"You use both hands."

"Boff?"

"First the left, then the right," she said slowly, imitating the way he'd switched hands. "You use both. How?"

Her student stared at his hands as though he'd never seen them before. "How? Ah-ee know — uh — Ah-ee know *not*. They've always been that way," he added in Truvan.

Still stupefied, Andromache shook her head and murmured, "I wish *I* could switch hands like that."

"But *you* can switch languages," her student said graciously. "You can go straight from Lukkan to Truvan."

He was right — once again, she'd switched between them without realizing it. "From Lukkana to Táruvan," she agreed.

"Tah-roo-vahn," he repeated, laughing at the word.

Andromache almost smiled. "What about you?" she asked, returning to their original topic. "Do *you* like apricots?"

"Yes. And —" Her student pointed to the bunch of grapes.

"Grapes."

"Grapes."

"This one is an apple."

"Mm-mm. Ah-ee lahke. And zees one —"

"A fig."

"Mmm." He smiled. "So good. Baht zees one, no."

"The pomegranate? Why not? You don't like the taste?"

He thought for a moment. "Eet taste *not*."

"It has no taste. No flavor."

"No," he agreed. "Eet *hass* no tasty."

With that, they exhausted the topic of fruit.

"Do you read a lot?" asked Andromache, gesturing to the text on the table, then to the ones on the shelves.

"Oh — um — Yes. A lot, Ah-ee read."

"Here, in the — er, text house? The library?"

The Rider held up his thumb and forefinger, close together. "A leetle. Baht mohre — ah — the sleep house?"

"Your bedroom?" Andromache pointed out the window, across the courtyard, toward the secluded little building.

Her student nodded. "Eet hass mohre airs. Eet hass two — uh —" He pointed to the window.

"Windows," she supplied. "Two windows?"

He nodded again, then added, "Ah-ee lahke airs."

"So do I," said Andromache. He was lucky, she reflected, to have a bedroom with two windows. Her own bedroom wasn't quite that airy. Comfortable, though…it was definitely comfortable…so comfortable…

The thought made her yawn.

"Yeuh ahre tahed?" asked the Rider, his face once more concerned.

"A little." She glanced guiltily at the doorway. She wasn't sure that she was supposed to be up, out of bed. Hecuba might scold her. "Don't tell your mom I was here."

"I won't," promised the Rider.

Andromache stood but didn't leave. "Your hands look better," she whispered, in a rush of post-febrile bluntness.

As he had earlier, the Rider stared perplexedly at his hands. "Uh…thanks," he said.

"See you tomorrow."

"See yeuh."

She left the library, trudging toward her old room. As she reached the doorway, Muka's head poked out to greet her. Andromache hesitated for a moment but didn't go inside.

"Come on, girl," she said. The dog plodded out to her, and together they climbed to the top floor.

Curled up with Muka on her new bed, Andromache planned the next day's lesson. *Maybe we can talk about the sea*, she thought as she drifted off. *Or rivers, or the hills. And I can't forget to teach him the word for* 'wind.'

Late summer

Chapter 11

*H*e was almost there. If she ran, she could get to the tree in time *and climb up, away from him — but no, her feet were stuck! They'd been chained to the rocks. No, the rocks had melted around her feet and she was now sinking deep into mud. No one was there to pull her out. They'd all run away. They were all far from her, safe in a distant walled city. She kept sinking — sinking — she couldn't breathe — but then she hit the bottom and passed through and she, too, was behind walls. A shack. Her shack from Lyrnassa, but thinner than she'd remembered. The walls weren't safe, and she knew what was waiting on the other side. He would throw the door open, and she would see him, towering, backlit by fire, glistening red.* Thwack, thwack, thwack! *He was pounding on the door — he was trying to break it down —*

Thwack, thwack, thwack!

"Honey!" called Cassandra's voice.

Andromache shuddered awake, her heart pounding.

"Can I come in?"

"Su — sure," stammered Andromache, still half asleep and terrified. *It was just a dream*, she told herself. *Just a dream*. But her heart kept racing.

"Hi, honey!" sang Cassandra, swinging open the door. As she skipped into the room, she bent to fondle Muka's ears. The dog, who had also been napping, sneezed and wagged her tail.

"Good girl! Pretty dog!" Cassandra took Muka's front feet in her hands and moved them gently in a running motion. "Time for *you* to wake up, too!" Turning to Andromache, she asked, "How are you doing?"

Just a dream, Andromache reminded herself. Her breathing was almost back to normal. "I'm all right," she said to Cassandra. "A little tired."

"Well, then you'll have to wake up! Paris is here!" Cassandra laughed for joy and clapped her hands.

"Paris?"

"My other brother! He's back! I can't wait for you to meet him. We're having dinner down on the courtyard."

"What...now?" Andromache's heart began to pound again.

"Yes, now, sleepyhead!"

"With — with — uh, who's going to be there?"

"Everyone! My parents — my brothers — you. Oh, you have no idea how good this is! Another girl, after all these years! It's always been me against a troop of brothers. Well, only two really, but they're a lot to take when they get going! Finally!" Eyes gleaming with satisfaction at having found an ally, Cassandra set about braiding Andromache's hair.

Brothers, Andromache thought in horror. *Brothers*. She was supposed to have dinner with the Rider and whatever his brother was? No way!

"There! Your hair's done," said Cassandra. "Are you ready to go down?"

Andromache cleared her throat. "Actually, no, I —"

"You look ready to me. Are your bandages all right?"

"Yes, but —"

"Here, stand up, then. I'll fix your sash." Cassandra gently pulled Andromache to her feet and readjusted the bilious yellow cloth.

Andromache was trapped, cornered. There was no escaping Cassandra. The most she could do was pull her dress up over the sash a little so she wouldn't trip.

"You look beautiful!" sang the girl.

Andromache looked like a mushroom — and knew it.

"Let's go, or the boys will eat everything in sight!" Cassandra skipped back out of the room, followed by Andromache and Muka.

When they reached the main floor, Andromache whispered, "Where was your brother? The one who was gone, I mean." Had he been out on a raiding mission, charged with bringing back riches for the family? Was *that* why they were having a feast?

"Oh," said Cassandra. "He was staying with my uncle, in Santiya, to the east. Both my brothers have spent some time there." Her tone was evasive, and Andromache didn't dare probe the matter further. The brother had obviously been off doing something too terrible for Cassandra to talk about!

When they emerged onto the courtyard, Andromache was shocked to see not a younger version of the Rider, as she'd expected, but instead the gentle-eyed priest from the council meeting. "Is — is there going to be a ceremony?" she whispered to Cassandra, glancing at the priest.

"Oh, no. That's Dad!" The girl laughed. "Haven't you met him?"

"Uh, not really." Even though Andromache had been there over a month, she'd never met the man of the house. He was very busy, Cassandra had said — not that Andromache had tried to seek him out.

"Dad," sang Cassandra, running over to her father. Andromache followed more slowly. "Dad! She hasn't met you, yet!"

The priest hugged and kissed Cassandra and beamed at Andromache. "My name is Priam," he said, his voice mild and low. "And you're the Andromache my daughter keeps chattering on about."

Andromache nodded; Cassandra laughed.

"It's good to see you up and about, my dear," said Priam.

"Thank you," murmured Andromache.

Cassandra took her arm and whispered to her, "Sit by me, honey — the boys can sit over *there*." She waved dismissively at the other side of the table, which was heaped with many platters of food. Andromache was glad. She felt safer with a mound of vegetables between her and Cassandra's brothers.

Maybe dinner out here won't be all bad, Andromache decided. It was a beautiful evening. The courtyard was glowing in the soft, golden light, and a gentle breeze was carrying in the scent of late summer plants. Birds were twittering streams of song as they fluttered through the branches of Andromache's favorite apple tree.

Suddenly, the birds' twitters turned to squawks. Their serenade was interrupted by a burst of shouting from the kitchen:

"Hey! Stop that!"

"No!"

"It's mine!"

"Knock it off!"

Squawk! Squaaaaaaawk! The birds fled to safer, more distant perches.

"Just carry them out, will you?" Basket in hand, Hecuba marched out onto the courtyard. "You can save your squabbling for after dinner, I think!"

"Sorry, Mom."

"Sorry."

Hecuba's two sons were a step behind her, laboring under trays and enormous clay jars. Cassandra squealed and flitted over to them, embracing first the newcomer, then the Rider. The sight of Cassandra flinging her arms so blithely around *him* gave Andromache an instinctive rush of fear. She had to cover her mouth to avoid crying out a warning.

"Good evening, Andromache dear," said Hecuba. Nodding at the newcomer, who was now standing in between his siblings, she said, "Andromache, this is Paris, our younger son. And Paris, this is Andromache, the woman I told you about — your brother's Lukkan tutor."

Andromache caught her breath as Paris approached the table. She'd never seen anyone with such an elegant face. Still, she could tell that he was part of the Rider's family. Beautiful and polished, Paris looked like the finished work for which his brother was a study, rough and angular. They were of similar height and had the same dark hair, although Paris didn't let his fall in his face. Nothing blocked the view of his startling grey eyes...

While Andromache stared, Paris was taking stock of her, too. "What's wrong with your dress?" he asked snidely. "And your *feet?*" There was a hiss and he bobbled as though jabbed in the side.

Andromache fought back tears. What was wrong with her feet? What was wrong with her *feet?* Oh, even if that hateful little jerk had three weeks, she couldn't begin to tell him everything that was wrong! Hateful little jerk, slick and smug, with his family and his colossal house! What right did he have to taunt *her?* There was *no way* she was going to let him see her cry!

"They're stilts," she snapped. "Your sister's dresses are too long for me." To her surprise, she heard laughter from the others — at Paris's expense, not hers. She'd scored a point against him.

"Indeed," sniffed Hecuba, her critical eye examining Andromache's sash and the fabric bulging over it. "It's time we got you some clothing of your own."

"Paris is loads of fun, but he can be a real pest sometimes," whispered Cassandra as they took their seats. "Mom thought you might be happier not living down the hall from him." She squeezed Andromache's hand.

Thankful for her new bedroom on the uppermost floor, Andromache squeezed back.

Before the meal, silence fell and the priest drew a deep breath to ready himself for an oration — a prayer, Andromache supposed, although she couldn't be sure, since her family had never been devout. All she knew about religion was that priests wore their robes longer than other men did.

The priest shut his eyes, affixing an expression of beatific serenity. "The brightest evening star has drawn closer to the moon than is its habit, a joyous sign not only for the reunion of our family — Paris returned home from the east — but also for the arrival of our guest. In Troy, we have always seen guests as a blessing, and so it is in this spirit that we greet Andromache, who faced such adversity before coming to enrich our lives. She is to be, for as long as it pleases the stars to keep her with us, a member of our household. And so, together, we sit down to this meal…"

The florid expressions touched but also greatly embarrassed Andromache. She peered sidelong at the others to see how they were reacting. Cassandra and her mother wore expressions identical to that of the priest; horrid Paris, while he too had closed his eyes, was smirking as though titillated. Beside him, though, the Rider was staring into space. He caught the slight movement of Andromache's face and turned toward her. Their eyes met.

She fixed her gaze back on the table, sure that she shouldn't have been looking around. Was the Rider going to report her to his father? Nothing interrupted Priam's prayer, though, and several moments later she peeked up again. Again, the Rider caught her eye. This time, he smiled at her, nodded his head once in his father's direction, rolled his eyes, and pretended to fall asleep.

Andromache coughed and looked at her plate.

Priam went on and on about the beauty of the countryside, the health of the city, the renewal that would come with the autumn rains, and myriad other topics. Andromache felt herself drifting off, and beautiful though his words were, she wasn't sorry when they stopped flowing.

"We can eat now," whispered Cassandra, picking up a bowl and passing it to Andromache.

As Andromache accepted the bowl, she was relieved to see only chick pea stew inside. If she could fill her plate quickly with enough stew and vegetables, the family members might not notice her refusal to take meat...

She needn't have worried. The family was far too focused on chattering to care about anything else. Back when Andromache was living with her parents, they'd often had the neighbors over for dinner. The meals had been lively, merry — at the time, she might even have said rowdy. They were nothing, however, compared to the cacophony of dining with Cassandra and her family.

That night, Paris was the center of everyone's attention. Even as the others were eating, they peppered him with questions. Questions about his trip to Santiya, questions about his stay there, questions about what he'd eaten, whom he'd seen, and how he'd passed his time. Sometimes, whoever asked a given question didn't even wait to hear the answer before firing off another. A single family member often managed to sustain two or three conversations at once, talking to each other while waiting for a turn with Paris.

"What news is there from my brother? Is he well?" Hecuba asked Paris, at a moment when all the side conversations had converged in a single main stream.

"As well as ever — and to make sure that *you* are, he sent along a flask of your favorite honeywine."

"Oh! How lovely!" Hecuba's cheeks flushed with pleasure.

"He told me lots of stories about all the times you drank it when you were young —"

"Thank you, Paris — that's quite enough!" snapped his mother.

Cassandra giggled, and her brothers laughed.

"Was the river high?" wondered Priam in the midst of all the jollity.

"No, but I'd bet my life's fortune the ferryman was!" Paris snickered.

The Rider snorted.

"Boys, for shame!"

"Well, my dear, he may be right," Priam said with gravity. "The countries in between the coast and Santiya do have some interesting religious practices."

"Oh, Dad," sighed the Rider, under his breath. "'*Religious practices?*'"

His father didn't seem to have heard him, and neither did his mother. "Not that *I'm* aware of!" Hecuba huffed. "Upon my word, Priam, there was nothing of the sort going on so long as *I* lived there! I shudder to think of what might have happened if this — this *altered* ferryman — had upset the boat with *my son* on it!" Her face roiled like a storm over the sea.

"No doubt you'd have melted away, honey tart that you are," whispered the Rider, elbowing his brother in the side. Paris shoved him back.

"What were they studying?" Cassandra warbled. "Did you hear any concerts? Which new dances did you learn? Did they have a feast for you? Did they give you any gifts? Is everyone just *brilliant?*"

Paris gave his sister an affectionate smile. "Not as brilliant as you, Songbird."

Cassandra smiled back, her eyes shining.

"What's the first thing you want to do, now that you're back in Troy?" asked Priam.

"He wants to come to archery practice tomorrow morning," answered the Rider, smiling sweetly even as Paris scowled.

Their mother gave an approving nod. "Yes, his life wouldn't suffer from a bit of discipline."

"I would've thought you'd be too busy, with your new duties and all," Paris griped.

Smirking, his brother replied, "I'll never be too busy for you, Honey Tart."

New duties? Still in the shadow of her nightmare, Andromache couldn't help but wonder, *More pillaging? More villages to burn?*

More doors to crash through? She shot the Rider a look of terror and suspicion, but he didn't see it. He was too busy laughing at a joke his father had made — he looked no scarier than the neighbors who'd come over long ago to drink her parents' wine.

Who are you? she wondered. *I don't understand.* The Rider — her student — seemed more separate than ever from the monster of her nightmares. He was laughing again, now at his brother. He'd rolled his eyes during the prayer. Just that afternoon, in the library, he'd drawn a picture of the river Scamander and called it a '*leetle theen sea.*' No Raider — no monster — would think up '*little thin sea,*' would he?

Don't try to understand, she told herself. *Just go along with it. Be glad he only shows* this *self in the house. Stay on guard, but don't obsess. And don't run out of the house and leap into a basket unless he's actually attacking you…*

It seemed like sound advice.

As the night wore on, the family ate, drank, chatted, and bickered. They asked so many questions about Santiya and Troy, and had so many side conversations, that Andromache didn't try to follow any of it. Instead, she stroked Muka's fur and breathed in the night air.

Eventually, the family's commotion faded to silence. *Time for bed,* Andromache thought with relief, but it wasn't to be.

"So, now can you play us something you learned there?" begged Cassandra.

"Sure, Songbird," said Paris, fetching a lute from the kitchen and shocking Andromache with the music he was able to draw from it. She hadn't heard such playing since she was a child, when her dad was testing the lutes he'd made…

He was holding the newest one on his lap, adjusting the pegs. Twang! He plucked each string and let it resonate with his voice. Twing, twang! 'Ready, Little Cricket! Now, what should we sing?'

Andromache laughed. "The Cricket Song!"'

'Again?' asked her dad, pretending to groan. 'How about "The Twisting Pine?"'

'Again?' she asked, groaning back…

The groan was their joke. Her dad had always loved playing '*The Cricket Song*' for her, and she'd loved all of his music. Everyone had loved his music! He had a spark — some special, native talent that no amount of practicing could emulate. The same was clearly true for Paris. In fact, his playing sounded hauntingly similar to her dad's. She thought she knew why...

'Why does your lute sound different, Daddy?'
'Different from what?'
'From all the other lutes...the ones the neighbors play. And even if they play your lute, it doesn't sound the same.'
'Because I'm better at it, Little Cricket.'
'Daddy!'
He laughed. *'Because I'm playing in a Taruishan mode.'*
'Mode?'
'A certain family of notes...'

The Trojan family of notes: it felt like forever since she'd heard a lute played like this! Closing her eyes, Andromache forgot the horrible little jerk who'd ridiculed her bandages. She let Paris's music take her over grassy yellow hillsides, far off in deep valleys, and under the pine-tipped starry skies of her youth.

And to think, she'd taken her student's comment about the *'family musician'* as a figure of speech!

When the music finally ended, the family members began hauling the remnants of the dinner back to the kitchen. Paris sidled over to Andromache and said, "So — you're my brother's Lukkan tutor..."

She nodded, feeling more kindly toward him than she had earlier.

"In that case, it's nice to spend time with you." He flashed a smile so radiant that it warmed her, until he added, "It's nice to spend time with you *now*, I mean, since you won't be here much longer. None of my brother's past language tutors lasted more than a few months. I don't see why *you'd* succeed where all the professionals failed."

Chapter 12

*F**ail*. Even the next morning, the word was still gnawing at. Andromache. Was Paris right? Would she fail? She hadn't really considered the idea until now. Once the Rider had agreed to take lessons — and, rather than slaughtering, her had politely done anything she asked — she'd taken the lessons for granted. They were a given, a part of her new routine, a part of what her life had become.

But it was true, she wasn't a professional. She didn't know how to teach. Her second lesson was proof of *that* fact! *'Whoa, there!'* the Rider's voice echoed in her mind. Her only comfort was that Paris hadn't been around to hear her neighing.

Now that she thought about it, that first day Hecuba *had* said *'if things go well.'* What did that mean? What were the expectations? Was the Rider meeting them? Andromache didn't know. He could say more words every day, but perhaps that wasn't enough. As for Hecuba's other goal, that her son learn *'phrases of politeness and refinement,'* Andromache didn't think much progress had been made. He didn't seem any more or less polite than he'd ever been.

Fail.

Why did that awful Paris have to come home, anyway? Why couldn't he have just stayed in the east?

(*Why do you care about failing?*) asked the snide little Voice. (*I didn't think you wanted lessons with the Rider anyway.*)

No one likes to fail! Andromache snapped. Maybe she hadn't wanted lessons at first, but they were a fact of her life now, and she didn't want them to end in disaster. She had so little to be proud of, lately, even without adding failure into the mix.

Besides, what would happen to her if she failed? Would she waste away to oblivion after all?

Andromache flopped back and forth on the bed. The linens were irritating her. It was mid-morning, and she was hungry, but she didn't dare leave the room to find food. Now that Paris was back, he might be in the kitchen, cooking. If she ran into him, he would taunt her again — *fail, fail, fail.* How she hated him!

In the corner of her room sat a tray with two shriveled figs and a stale crust of bread: the remains of an earlier breakfast. Paltry as it was, it would have to suffice until the heat of the day, when many Trojans napped. Andromache was sure that Paris was a napper — he had a lazy air about him.

As she began nibbling at one of the figs, someone rapped on her door. A firm sound, unlike Cassandra's scritching.

"Andromache, dear?"

"Come in," said Andromache, trying to speak around the half-chewed fruit.

Hecuba swept into the room. "It's a beautiful morning," she announced.

Andromache nodded.

"I'm glad to see you're up. I have to run to several houses, later today, but if we hurry, we'll be able to go to the dressmaker's beforehand."

Andromache froze. Her breathing grew ragged. Go to the dressmaker's? Leave the *house*? She was *never* leaving the house! Her idea of running away to be shipped off in a basket had been nothing but feverish nonsense. She couldn't leave the house! She couldn't walk the streets of Troy, with their thousands upon thousands of people — thousands of feet that would crush her without even realizing it —

"So, dear, are you ready?" asked Hecuba.

The flood of people crashed into her, their heels battering her shins, their arms blocking her escape. She fell to her knees, then her side, and was lost in a sea of legs. She couldn't stand up — couldn't breathe! A foot was crushing her. As she curled to protect herself, more feet came pounding down on her, one after another, grinding her face into the sand —

"No!" cried Andromache.

Hecuba frowned. "It's about time you had some clothes that fit you properly."

Andromache shook her head, clenching her fists until her fingers went white. She didn't care about clothes! She would much rather look like a mushroom than go out! And she didn't see how it would hurt Hecuba if she stayed in the house forever, wearing whatever old clothes she could find.

"It's not far, dear."

"I don't want to go," whispered Andromache.

"Why on earth not? What do you think is going to happen to you?" asked Hecuba, either astonished or disgusted. "Do you think they'll poke pins into you? Sew your hands together?"

What was going to happen? The memories came faster — faster —

Heels battering her — feet crushing her — her face ground into the earth — she couldn't breathe — she couldn't breathe —

"Honestly, my girl, I —"

"I DON'T WANT TO GET TRAMPLED AGAIN!" Andromache screamed.

Hecuba stared open-mouthed at Andromache's arms, now all but free of yellowing bruises, but Andromache took no notice. She'd begun to shake, and tears were streaming down her cheeks.

Raiders landing on the beaches near Hurapi — a waxy-pale corpse at her feet — a pile of rocks on her house — Auntie, heavy in her arms —

Nothing could stop the memories. They were all raining down on her, even those that she'd pushed back during her years in Lyrnassa, while she and Auntie were scraping together a life.

The screaming — oh gods, the screaming! — Crack — crack — crack — the screaming! — crack — crack —

Everything was toppling down on her.

She was stumbling down the hill toward Lyrnassa — her dress was soaked in blood —

"NO!" Andromache cried out, before she could see any more. She grabbed two fistfuls of her hair.

"Sssssh," Hecuba said softly, covering Andromache's hands with her own. "Sssh, poor child. I'm sorry. You must have had quite a shock."

A shock? Which one did Hecuba mean? Her parents' death? Her Auntie's death and burial? Andromache's own near-death and burial on the beach? Or perhaps her flight up the hill? Her mutilated feet? The Raider looming over her? Or was it one of the other ones?

"A *terrible* shock," Hecuba amended. "I can't begin to know how terrible."

No, she couldn't! Nobody here understood how it felt to lose their family members one by one! Nobody here knew the terror of breathing in sand, of being crushed by dozens of feet! Nobody here had been face-to-face with death — looked into its cavernous eyes —

Hecuba gently loosened Andromache's hands from her hair. "But I'm sure it's not the sort of thing you can just forget."

Did she mean that she thought Andromache wasn't trying hard enough? Would Hecuba have been able to forget? Didn't she realize that Andromache would have given *anything* to erase it all from her mind?

"You can stay in the house as long as you like," Hecuba said soothingly.

Andromache sniffled.

"You can't heal on anyone else's schedule," Hecuba went on. "I'm sorry — I never should have forced the issue. You alone will know when the time is right to leave and explore the city."

Explore the city? For *what?* There was nothing for her, out there! "I don't *want* to go!" cried Andromache, her cheeks slick with tears. "Not *ever!*"

Hecuba stroked her hair. "All right. Ssssh... You don't have to go anywhere, dear," she murmured. "Calm yourself — just breathe."

Andromache tried to shut out her memories and focus on her breathing. Little by little, she felt it slow. Once her tears had stopped, Hecuba patted her shoulder and said, "There, there. That's it. I'll just take your measurements and send them down to the shop with Cassandra."

"Thank you," Andromache managed to whisper.

There was an awkward pause. "How are your feet doing?" asked Hecuba.

Andromache shrugged. Her feet weren't hurting, but she still couldn't bring herself to look at them.

"Well, let's have a peek." Hecuba unwrapped Andromache's bandages. "You know, I think you should try walking without the bandages. Your injuries look well enough healed to stand it — so to speak — and now they need to be toughened up."

"All right," said Andromache.

"Try it now."

Obediently, Andromache stood up beside her bed. The floor felt strange beneath her bare feet, but not uncomfortable. "It's fine," she said.

"Oh, my dear! That's wonderful!" Hecuba beamed.

Andromache didn't answer. What use were healthy feet to her? The last thing she wanted was to go running or exploring outside of the house, where she might have another '*shock*.' She'd had her fill of '*shocks!*'

Besides, if Paris was right, soon she wouldn't even need her feet for afternoon visits to the library.

℘

AS THE RIDER walked in for his lesson, he didn't say '*Hay-lo*,' as usual. Instead, he smiled at Andromache's bare feet and asked, "No more stilts?"

Andromache teared up. The run-in with Hecuba had left her fragile.

"I'm sorry," said the Rider, looking abashed. When Andromache didn't answer, he added, "About my brother. He sucks."

"He *what?*" Andromache had an image of Paris, slurping away at a big jar of wine. What did *that* have to do with anything?

"It means, he's awful," explained the Rider. "Truvan slang."

"Oh."

"He thinks the heavens spin around him." The Rider rolled his eyes. "It's all Dad's fault."

Andromache frowned. "The priest? What did he do?"

The Rider looked uncomfortable.

Suddenly anxious, Andromache recoiled. What could Priam have done that was bad enough to shock his raider son?

"It's a long story," said the Rider. "And it's lesson time."

Andromache blinked, unsure of the connection. "So?"

"I could try to say it in Lukkan…"

"But?"

"But you'd probably be annoyed."

"Oh," she said, relieved. So *that* had been the reason for his unease! "That's fine — just say it in Truvan."

The Rider nodded. "The first thing you have to know is that Mom lost some babies in between me and Paris."

This blunt beginning made Andromache's stomach clench, but the Rider didn't seem to notice her sudden pallor. He went on: "Then one night, when she was pregnant with Paris, Dad went out on the courtyard to think about the baby…and he got zapped."

Got zapped? Was that another bit of Truvan slang? "What do you mean?" asked Andromache.

"He says light fell upon him from the sky," said the Rider. "He took it as a sign from the gods that the baby would be all right, and the next day he joined the priesthood."

"Oh." Andromache furrowed her brow. "So you *don't* think it was a sign from the gods?"

The Rider gave her a pitying look, as if to say he'd hoped better of her.

"Well, *I* don't know about those things!" she said defensively. "*My* dad wasn't a priest."

"There's nothing to know," said the Rider, shrugging. "Either Dad had had a little too much wine to drink, or else he saw a falling star. Maybe more than one — some nights, you can see dozens."

"I know *that!*" hissed Andromache, her cheeks flaming with indignation. She wasn't some ignorant bumpkin!

"Then you know that there are far too many for them to be signs," said the Rider. "You could ask anything you wanted, and a star would fall: '*Will the grape harvest be good? Will I be married by next year? Will I step in dog crap on the way to the market?*'"

Andromache coughed.

"Are you all right?"

"Yes — yes," she sputtered. "Fine." The words '*Dog crap*' had just caught her off guard. In fact, the whole conversation was catching her off guard! When her coughing fit ended, she asked, "What do you think they are, then?"

"What?"

"Falling stars."

"They're metal."

"Metal?" she repeated, shrinking back from the edge of the table, distancing herself from the Rider. Metal — of *course* he would think that, obsessed as he was with armor, swords, and spears! His whole life was metal; small wonder he would think the stars were, too.

He nodded. "Metal."

"How do you know?"

"I've seen one."

Shocked, Andromache leaned in once more toward the table. "You *have*?"

"There's one in Dad's temple," said the Rider, brushing a stray lock of hair from his forehead. "What did *you* think stars were?"

"I don't know," said Andromache. "I just thought they were pretty."

"Pretty," he repeated. "Pretty…"

Andromache nodded.

"Well, whatever they are, Dad saw their light as a sign." The Rider raised an eyebrow. "And then there was what happened with the spring."

"The spring?"

"In our courtyard. It was dry for a long time."

"Cassandra told me that."

The Rider nodded. "It's true — I remember it. But then, just after Paris was born, the earth moved and the spring started flowing again."

"The earth moved?" asked Andromache. "How much?"

"A lot. Everything in the house was shaking…all the plates, and jars, and things."

"Giants dancing," Andromache mused aloud, thinking of a story her mom had told her when she was four or five, and they'd felt a tremor while out walking in the mountains.

The Rider gave her another pitying look. "I've traveled to a lot of places, Ahndromahk, and not one of them had a giant."

"I *know* that!" she bristled, yanking up the shoulder of her dress. "I don't really think there are giants! I know it's just something people say for fun."

"If you know there aren't giants, then why *do* you think the earth moves?" challenged the Rider.

Andromache froze. In her mind's eye, she saw a fallen pile of boulders where a cottage used to be. "Rocks," she said softly. "When a lot of rocks fall all at once, off a high cliff. That makes the earth move."

The Rider nodded solemnly.

Grateful that he'd accepted her explanation, Andromache picked up an earlier thread of their conversation. "So, between the star signs — or whatever — and the spring —"

"— my parents declared Paris a miracle," said the Rider, finishing her thought. "Which means that all his life, he's been spoiled rotten, getting whatever he wants. That's why he's such a brat." Muttering, he added, "I doubt even Uncle could do much with him."

"That's why he was in San —"

"Santiya," said the Rider.

"Santiya," Andromache repeated. She'd never heard of the country but knew from Cassandra's stories that it lay to the east. "He was there to be straightened out?"

"Kind of," said the Rider, in the tone of an exasperated elder sibling. "He got in trouble over a girl."

"Oh!" cried Andromache, color flooding to her cheeks. She could see now why Cassandra had been so evasive about her brother!

"No — not *that*," said the Rider, his own dark cheeks flushed. "The problem was, she told everyone my stupid brother asked to marry her, and he denied it. Her parents believed him — or, more likely, they said they did because they didn't *want* him for a son-in-law. But since people around here have nothing better to do than talk, and since she's a niece of one of the council members, my parents sent Paris to Uncle's for a while to let things simmer down. You know — far from the eyes, far from the heart."

"Out of sight, out of mind," Andromache agreed. It was, she thought, the ideal place for Paris to be.

ಹಿ

"HOW ARE YOUR FEET?" Hecuba was visiting again. "How did they hold up on your first day without bandages?"

"Fine," said Andromache.

"You seem like you're feeling better. Did you find the sour cherries Paris brought back from the market?"

"Yes," said Andromache. "They're good."

"I thought you might like them!" Hecuba crowed. "I've noticed you eat a lot of fruit — although, dear, you can't live on it. You need something more substantial." She turned a critical eye to Andromache's physique and to the gown that was once again slipping off her shoulder. "I should have told the dressmaker to put a rush on that order," she muttered.

Andromache didn't mind. Ill-fitting or not, Cassandra's old dresses were the nicest clothes she'd had in a long time.

"Speaking of orders, do you need any more potsherds, pens, or ink for your lessons?"

"I think I have enough for a while," said Andromache. "Thank you, though."

"Of course. Anything you need, just let me know." A smile spread on Hecuba's face. "It seems like things are going well. The other morning, when I came into the kitchen, my son was muttering Lukkan over the fruit bowl."

Andromache brightened. If her student was practicing outside of lessons, maybe she wouldn't fail after all. On the other hand, if Hecuba thought fruits were insubstantial food, she might not approve of them as a lesson topic, either. Clearing her throat, Andromache asked, "Is there — I mean, we talked about maybe — if things were going well — you might have specific things for me to teach him?"

After pondering the question for a moment, Hecuba said, "No, dear, as long as he's progressing, I leave his program up to your judgment. My only goal is that he keep learning Lukkan." Pensively, she murmured, "A mountain language…"

Andromache nodded. "Mountains, pine trees, and the sea — that's the Lukka lands."

"I've heard it's beautiful, there."

Beautiful... Deep emotions stirred within Andromache as she thought of the wind-tossed pines. She nodded again, not trusting herself to speak.

Hecuba didn't pry. She seemed wary of creating another scene like the one they'd had earlier, over the dressmaker. "Well, dear, I should head downstairs. You wouldn't believe all the babies arriving this week!" She shook her head. "I need to snag rest whenever I can."

The mention of babies reminded Andromache of those that Hecuba had lost — babies she and her husband had desperately wanted. And yet, there she was, dashing around the city, delivering other people's children into the world. Feeling a strong surge of sympathy and admiration for Hecuba, Andromache touched her hand. "Thank you for coming to talk to me," she said softly. "All these times, I mean."

Hecuba smiled and patted her shoulder. "It's my pleasure."

Chapter 13

*S**he was running, running from the beach. The raiders were almost on shore, and if they caught her, they would tear her throat. Her blood would soak into the sand. But she was running fast — faster than she ever had — and she knew she could escape them. She passed by the shacks and cottages of Lyrnassa. She was almost onto the hill path when she heard it:***

'Help!'

But was it real? Or was she imagining it?

'Please, help!'

The voice sounded like —

'It's me, Eriopis! Myrine and I are trapped!'

Behind her, Andromache could hear the clatter of spears. Sweat poured down her body. She almost fainted. Woozy with fear, she ran on, up into the hills. There was a man sitting on the path up ahead. He stared at her without speaking.

'Phaenops!' she gasped. Old Phaenops. As she passed by him, he reached out a hand to her, and she saw that his feet were gone. She screamed.

His mouth formed a word: Help. *But the clattering spears were closer than ever, and she ran on. She ran on, hearing all the voices behind her — the whimpering and moaning of Eriopis, Myrine, even Phaenops, now. The roaring of the raiders as they charged.*

Then all of the other sounds were drowned out by one still more terrible — a voice like a rockslide, crashing down a hill...

Andromache screamed herself awake. "I left them! I left them!" She'd left her neighbors, left them to be crushed between the two groups of raiders!

(*You left them,*) the snide little Voice agreed. (*You left Eriopis and Myrine. They gave you shelter when no one else wanted you, and you left them to be slaughtered.*)

"I left them," Andromache moaned. "I —" But no, that wasn't right. Eriopis and Myrine, the sisters who'd let Andromache and Auntie stay with them, had died years earlier. Raiders hadn't slaughtered them. She hadn't left them behind.

(*Phaenops, then,*) the Voice argued.

Phaenops — old Phaenops! Andromache sucked in her breath. Phaenops had never said three words to her, but he never spoke to anyone, if he could avoid it — and he'd occasionally hauled firewood for her and Auntie.

(*He's probably the one who left food for you after Auntie died,*) the Voice suggested.

Andromache's flush of shame deepened. She didn't want to think about Phaenops! Of all the villagers she might have seen in her nightmare, why had her mind chosen the three kindest ones? The three who hadn't shunned her?

(*Fine way to repay them.*)

As Andromache thought about the ship drifting landward, and the raiders sweeping down from the hills, and the Lyrnassans caught in the middle, her heart began to pound. Her lungs caved in. She needed to think of something calm. *The trees*, she thought. *The platana tree grove*. She tried to picture their leaves, swishing in the wind, and the soft smell of the air beneath them. *That's where I was sitting when the ship came...*

Her heart beat faster. Her room was too small. She needed air. *The courtyard...*

She hurried down the stairs and out to the courtyard. As soon as she breathed in the cool evening air, she felt better. She walked slowly toward one of the raised boxes and peered over the rim. Inside, she saw a feeble row or two of celery, surrounded by weeds. The few remaining celery plants were dried almost to a crisp from the summer sun.

Reflexively, Andromache pulled out one of the weeds, then another and another, relishing the moment of resistance before they slipped out of the earth into the air — *schluuup*! Then, with a satisfying *thwack* they hit the stones at her feet.

She quickly finished weeding the first box and moved on to a second, in which a young medlar shrub was growing. Before she could attend to it, though, she heard the soft scuff of sandals coming toward her. She peeked over her shoulder and saw the priest, Priam. His sudden presence made her nervous. She'd never really talked to him or been alone with him before. Warily, she huddled against the box.

"Gardening, I see," said the priest, his toe nudging one of the weedy corpses.

Was he upset to find her meddling with his plants, the way Hecuba had been angry with her for tidying the kitchen? "I'm — I'm — s-sorry, sir," stammered Andromache. "I should have asked, first, to see if it's all right."

"To garden? Of course it is! And please, little one — call me Priam."

"Priam," she said timidly.

He smiled. "You're our guest. This house, and its gardens, and its kitchen, and its baths are yours. You don't have to ask." Sighing, he sat down, near her but without touching her. "In fact, I should be thanking you. It's a great help to me, my knees being what they are — to say nothing of all the time I must spend at the temple."

Andromache risked a glance to the side. Head bowed, the older man was serenely running his hands along the branches of the medlar shrub. The fading light cast a gentle glow on his face. She imagined him decades younger, kneeling out under the stars, frantic over the fate of his unborn baby. It seemed unfair to her that, after all his suffering, he'd wound up with Paris.

"For the past twenty years or so, I've been a priest down there," said Priam. He bent closer to the shrub, to inspect it. "Here's the sign of my neglect." Frowning, he showed her a host of thick, green caterpillars on the underside of the medlar leaves.

"Oh," said Andromache, eager to be helpful. "I can take care of those." She plucked one off the leaf, intending to smash it, but when she felt the firm heft of its little body, she found she couldn't. She instead set the creature on the end of her sash, on the side farthest from Priam. One by one, she took the other caterpillars, and when she had all of them, she secured her sash with a knot. *Hopefully, he'll just think I'm wiping caterpillar juice off my hands*, she thought, grateful for the fading light. "How — why did you decide to become one?" she asked.

"A caterpillar?"

Her lips curled slightly. "A priest."

Priam told her much the same story his son had, although he didn't use the phrase '*got zapped*,' and he added other tidbits of information. For one, he wasn't just a priest — he was the *high* priest. No wonder he was never home! Andromache had little notion of what priests did, but she supposed that the high one would have his hands full wrangling the low ones, if nothing else.

"And you're on the council, too?" she asked.

Priam nodded. "You can see why I haven't been tending properly to the gardens…but no matter. Soon enough, my daughter will be ready to take over my council seat, and I'll be able to spend more time at home. There are projects I've been meaning to do."

"The bath house cistern is really clever," Andromache said shyly.

Priam looked surprised and touched. "That's kind of you to say."

"What other projects do you want to do?"

"Well, at one point, I had thought about running a system of canals, or troughs, throughout the garden, to make it easier to water everything, but time got away — and I'm afraid the plants have suffered for it."

Andromache looked down. "I had my own vegetable garden in Lyrnassa," she whispered, tears welling in her eyes. "A good one."

Priam touched her hand. "I know ours isn't the same, but please use it, little one. Work in it as much as you like, and let us know if we can help in any way." He shifted on the garden box and cleared his throat. "What else do you enjoy doing, besides gardening?"

"I've read a few texts in the library," she said.

"That's right! My wife mentioned that you can read Truvan. Remarkable. It was your father who taught you, wasn't it?"

"Yes."

"And he was Trojan?"

"He was born here, but once he grew up, he left and never came back. He met my mom," Andromache explained, "and stayed with her in the Lukka lands."

Priam laughed. "Love! That'll do it every time."

"For them, anyway."

"But it's too bad none of his people here are left," the priest said gently. "My wife told me…"

Andromache nodded, allowing Priam, like his wife, to believe that her father's whole family was dead. Who knew? Perhaps they were…

"I wonder if I knew them," said Priam. "What were their names?"

"I don't know," said Andromache. "My dad never told me. It upset him to talk about them."

Priam nodded as though he understood, which he didn't. He couldn't. Had *his* father forced himself on a servant girl and made her pregnant? Taken their son as an apprentice, only to reject him later when a so-called legitimate heir came along? Of course not. But Andromache's grandfather — her dad's father — had done all of those things. He'd aroused feelings of hatred and betrayal that Priam could never understand…

'Someday, you'll want to see him again,' Andromache's mom whispered one night, when everyone was tucked in and supposedly sleeping.

Andromache's ears perked up. She'd learned many interesting things during those hushed, nighttime conversations.

'Never,' her dad hissed fiercely.

'But he's your father…'

'He worked my mother to death. Worked me half to death, too. It's no fun being an apprentice.' His words were bitter. 'I did it, though. Everything he said. And then, after all that, he threw me out! You're calling him my father?'

'But — '

'He never treated me like a son! Look, I don't even know if he's still alive. And if he is, he's dead to me…'

Whenever Auntie had sighed about the genteel Trojans she and Andromache might have met, Andromache had thought of her grandfather and snorted. Trojan gentility, indeed! Auntie must have been thinking about someone else.

Andromache couldn't picture Priam associating with a man like her grandfather, but for the briefest of moments, she wished he did. She wished that hateful old man would come to Priam's house, so she could spit in his face. But then the moment passed.

She probably wouldn't have had the courage, anyway. *Maybe in time*...

Priam looked as though he wanted to press Andromache about her family, but he didn't. "Well, in any case, reading is a wonderful skill to have, especially for those bored by semi-convalescence." He winked at her. "I hope our library will have enough to keep you busy. Some of the texts are a bit dry — inventory lists from my farms, that sort of thing. But Troy is also the home of many fine poets, historians, artists, and observers of the natural world. Explore — enjoy."

"Thank you," said Andromache.

"You may have noticed that we have tablets in the eastern script, as well?" asked Priam.

She gave him a startled look. "I *thought* I saw some that were different!" she said, remembering the script that looked like Truvan but with too many symbols.

The priest nodded. "Different indeed. I'm assuming that you can't read it, then?"

She shook her head.

"Myself, I can read some," said Priam. "But it's a much more complex system of writing than ours. Less practical. The same is true for the script used by the Achaeans, across the sea. I've heard their writing is so complicated that most people can't read it, and from the small bits I've seen, I believe it. Truvan is so much more approachable." Priam smiled and gave a small cough. "Speaking of languages, how is my son doing in his lessons?"

"Fine," said Andromache. "He picks things up quickly."

"He's a bright boy." In a slightly anxious voice, Priam asked, "And he's been coming every day?"

Andromache nodded.

The priest sighed. "I'm glad to hear it. I wasn't sure how he'd make the transition."

Transition? Andromache stiffened. In the context of the Rider, the word had an ominous ring. "Wh-what transition?" she whispered.

Priam plucked a weed from beneath the medlar shrub and began to strip its leaves. "The very fact of taking lessons at all, after so much time off. Beyond that, having to live in the city again. For the past few years, he's spent most of his time riding out in the countryside — sleeping in the fields, more often than not."

Andromache's heart was pounding — she couldn't catch her breath — a stream of sweat was running down her back. The priest was confirming all her worst fears. *The Raider!* she thought. She could see him riding across the countryside, spreading terror. Stabbing — killing — setting fire to houses — draining people of blood. She could see the black hollows staring down at her, fixing on her throat —

"He loved being captain of the patrol," said Priam.

Patrol? The word jarred Andromache out of her gruesome visions. Patrolling was what *victims* did! Her Lukkan neighbors had often gone on patrols, to see if raiders were nearby. The raiders themselves had never patrolled — only attacked — but perhaps Trojan raiders were different. "Patrol?" she asked.

Priam nodded.

"To look for what?"

"For danger, first and foremost," said Priam. "For threats to Troy or our neighbors. But also just to keep an eye on things, to stay aware of everything going on across the protectorate."

Andromache felt more lost than ever. "Protectorate?" she asked. "What does that mean?"

The priest stripped off the weed's final leaf and threw its bare stem to the ground. "Troy isn't an empire and doesn't care to become one. We don't use our army to conquer other lands. However, we do use it to patrol, protect, and defend our own lands."

An army of defenders? Protecting what was theirs? Andromache had never heard of such a thing. Hurapi, her Lukkan village, hadn't had an army of defenders. They'd had to make do with running away during a raid and rebuilding afterward. The only armed men Andromache had ever seen were raiders and pillagers, swarming in to take what *wasn't* theirs.

"By '*ours,*'" Priam went on, "I mean the city of Troy and the croplands that support us. Then there are villages in our vicinity who are allied to us but too small to maintain their own army, or who need extra forces in case of an attack. They are part of our protectorate."

Andromache's throat swelled. "L-Lyrnassa?" she croaked, knowing what the answer would be. As she'd expected, Priam nodded solemnly. "I didn't know," she whispered.

"There's no reason you would, unless you were a Lyrnassan village elder," Priam soothed.

Protectorate. Andromache closed her eyes. The courtyard had begun to swim around her. All the time she'd lived in Lyrnassa, she'd been in the Trojan protectorate? Everyone there knew about Troy, but the powerful city had seemed distant — separate — a world away from sand-whipped little Lyrnassa.

Priam cleared his throat. "Given the short amount of time you've been here, I doubt my son yet has enough proficiency in Lukkan to tell you himself, but he was in charge of patrolling the sector that includes your village. That's why he was there, that day. He saw the smoke in the sky and rode over to investigate."

The Raider — that hollow-eyed, blood-soaked horror from her nightmares — in charge of *protecting* Lyrnassa? Riding out to investigate, rather than to plunder the invading ships? No wonder he'd agreed to help keep a girl from crying herself to oblivion. Helping people was his life's work.

Andromache's head was spinning wildly. The world as she'd known it for the past six weeks was dissolving around her. At the same time, it was finally beginning to make sense. She'd never understood how someone as mild-seeming as her student could ride out to loot, pillage, and burn when he wasn't at lessons. Now, she knew: his whole mission was to stop *other* people from pillaging.

The old priest asked, "And I suppose you remember the rest of the story, from the council meeting the night you arrived in Troy?"

Weakly, Andromache said, "I remember a few things. There was yelling..."

"No shortage of that." Priam sighed. "So many hot tempers in one room! I'm sorry you had to witness that, little one. I blame myself. Penthesilea brought you to our house so that my wife could tend to you. Little did she know, the council was meeting there to spare my knees the agony of walking to the council chamber. I was having a particularly difficult night." His mouth looked sad beneath his greying beard. "Although not, I'm sure, as difficult as yours."

Andromache blinked back a fresh round of tears and looked at her hands. They were streaked with dirt and the green juice of plants. "What's the rest of the story?" she asked in a small voice. "About — about your son, I mean."

"Are you sure you want to hear it tonight?" asked Priam with concern. "You look tired, my dear. Maybe you'd prefer to go upstairs and sleep?"

By now, the sky was fully dark, but Andromache wasn't tired. A feverish energy had taken hold of her, ever since learning why the Rider — why her student — why *Hector* — had come to Lyrnassa. "I want to hear it."

"All right," said Priam. "But stop me whenever you like."

"Your son saw smoke..." she prompted him.

"And took his patrol down to Lyrnassa to engage with the invaders that were burning it. My son and his soldiers managed to take many of them prisoner."

Prisoner! Andromache moaned to herself. She'd heard that word come up in the meeting. If she'd really thought about it, she would have known all along that Hector wasn't a raider — raiders didn't take *men* prisoner! She'd learned that long ago, during her childhood in the Lukka lands. How stupid she'd been not to remember!

"That's why he came back to Troy, to arrange a ship for the prisoners' transport. We bring prisoners back here to ransom them," Priam explained. "Or, if no one is willing to pay the ransom, we find them work somewhere on Trojan territory. It's a good system. We've turned many enemies into useful members of our society." The priest's face turned grim. "But as for Lyrnassa, and the invaders who refused to surrender — well, they won't be troubling any more villages."

Blood-spattered armor — a gore-streaked golden horse. Andromache shuddered.

"I know, little one." Priam gave her hand a squeeze and went on. "I don't like it either, but it's not as though the raiders were invited to pillage our coasts."

Andromache nodded without looking up. She ground a weed beneath her heel.

Priam went on: "No one would have expected one patrol to defeat an entire ship. Hector was supposed to send for reinforcements — the next patrol over — before doing anything else. I don't know why he didn't. I don't know why he charged down there with only five other soldiers behind him! The fact is, though, that they accomplished an astounding feat. Laoganus, my son's commander, even accused him of lying. He insisted that some other group must have come to Hector's aid."

Andromache shook her head. Whatever else was fuzzy about *that day*, she'd been keenly aware of anyone who seemed dangerous. No one else had been there — no one but the ship of invaders and the six riders thundering down the hill. "Only six people came by me. Only one small group."

Priam nodded. "As you said in the meeting. I might add that the council members were grateful for your testimony, as added support, but most of them never thought Hector was lying. I doubt even Laoganus did. For one thing, who would the extra soldiers have been? A battalion of merpeople? Other than the next patrol, no one down there could have come in time. And my son most emphatically did *not* call the next patrol for help.

"That was the real source of trouble in the meeting. Laoganus was outraged that my son had taken his whole patrol down to Lyrnassa rather than sending one person to fetch reinforcements, as he was supposed to do. Laoganus said that Hector had violated the protocol. My son argued that, in his judgment, his group was capable of defeating the invaders, and that to wait for reinforcements would have been to waste time and innocent lives. Laoganus called my son all kinds of names — reckless glory hog being the kindest of them — and he argued that if Hector's patrol had all been killed, Troy might never have known about the invasion. At least, not until it was far too late to do anything. My son shot back that he'd been right, that his plan had worked, and that the invaders hadn't even managed to wound him, let alone kill him.""

The priest paused to clear his throat. Andromache wrapped a weed around her finger, so tightly that the flesh turned white.

"Laoganus told Hector that he would be stripped of his captaincy," Priam went on.

"Oh — no," said Andromache, feeling worse than she had in weeks. The Raider — that frightful, hulking, hideous brute from her nightmares — had not only rushed in to save Lyrnassa from the sea invaders, he'd done so in defiance of his commander. He'd risked his life and ruined his career, and she'd shown her gratitude by reviling him. *I'm a monster*, she told herself. *An eater of tripes*.

She then thought of how clean her student always was. He'd been less fanatical in his scrubbing ever since her comment about his hands, but only by a degree. His skin was immaculate, if no longer raw. She thought of how embarrassed he'd been to have fresh dirt on his clothes. For the first time, she thought about how ugly *that day* must have been for *him* — for her student, plunging into the smoke and spears — for Hector, befouling himself with gore. He might have scrubbed all that night and still not wiped the feel of it from his skin or the smell from his hair. He'd made a thousand sacrifices for villagers he didn't even know — the same ones *she* had deserted, even loathed. But she'd never hated them as much as she now hated herself. She was covered in fungus, in speckles of mold. What she wouldn't give for the past six weeks to be scraped from her, like skin from a radish!

"Oh, my girl!" murmured Priam. "You're crying. Here — take my arm. I'll help you to bed."

But Andromache refused. "I left them!" she shrieked. "I left them!"

"Left who?"

"The villagers!" She couldn't bear to tell Priam all the vile thoughts she'd had about his son, but this, at least, she could let out. "They were — on the — b-beach and I j-just — just left them. I ran! I ran! I ran!" Even knowing what would happen to them, she'd left them — she'd left them at the mercy of the raiders from the sea! She could see their livid white bodies...

Priam wrapped an arm around her heaving shoulders and pulled her close. "There, there. There, there. You did right."

"I didn't even *try*!" she sobbed.

"You were hurt, little one! You were battered and bruised." He rocked her like she was a little girl. "You did the same thing most everyone else in your village did. A few women had been taken prisoner by the invaders — my son freed them as soon as possible, of course. As for the rest of the villagers, some must have run along the beach instead of up into the hills, while others took a different ravine than you did, but in any case, by the time my son and his patrol got down to your village, most of your neighbors had scattered."

Andromache peeked up from Priam's shoulder, a disbelieving look in her eye. "They scattered?"

He nodded. "They're in Thebe, now. They started to arrive there not long after the attack. Gradually, just a few at a time. It took a while for the news to reach us."

"They scattered!" cried Andromache, feeling a strange ache. Was it relief? "So all the villagers are in Thebe, now?"

Again, Priam looked grim. "There are a few — who are not," he said. "And others probably chose to go elsewhere. But from what the survivors have told us, it seems as though most of your village is there, now."

Was Priam saying this to comfort Andromache, to relieve her guilt? Or had other villagers actually escaped? The priest's eyes were clear and guileless. He didn't seem to be lying to her. She had to pull herself together.

"I didn't know," murmured Andromache, sniffling. Slowly, she drew back from Priam's side. "About the villagers, that they — I mean —" She swallowed hard. "Thank you for telling me."

Priam patted her arm. "Of course, little one. I thought you knew, or I would've told you sooner."

So many things she hadn't known! So many...

"I'm sorry about your son," she whispered. "About — about *Hector*. I'm sorry he got punished for what he did."

Strangely, Priam chuckled. The sound had an echo of Hector's black laugh. "*He* might argue that it's a punishment," said the priest, "since he doesn't get nearly as much opportunity to ride across the plains, half-wild, as he used to. But in fact, he was promoted."

"Promoted?"

"One of the council members, Ucalegon, was most impressed with my son. He said that the way Hector had acted — quickly, decisively, forcefully — was what Troy needed in her military leadership. He also argued that for my son's patrol to defeat an entire ship required a very disciplined captain, one able to inspire trust and loyalty from his subordinates. Ucalegon convinced enough council members of this that instead of being punished, my son was made commander of the city's forces."

"Oh!" Andromache exclaimed.

"I should clarify — *half* of the city's forces. He was made responsible for any campaigns outside the city walls. Meanwhile,

Laoganus is to be in charge of defending Troy herself, should she come under attack." Priam laughed. "I'm telling you this so matter-of-factly, but in truth it boggles my mind. My son, commander of half of the city's forces? Managing the stables, hearing reports from the field patrol captains, running combat practice? As though just yesterday he wasn't sitting on my knee…"

Andromache looked over at Priam's knee and tried to imagine Hector sitting there, bouncing and giggling like one of the little boys from Lyrnassa. She couldn't see it.

"But now he's a full-grown man, and I'm an old man," sighed the priest. "An old man who needs his sleep. What about you, little one? Are you coming in?"

"Maybe in a while," she murmured.

Smiling, Priam took a deep breath of herb-scented air and said, "Then I'll leave you to enjoy the lovely night."

෨

THE NIGHT WAS INDEED lovely, but Andromache couldn't enjoy it. After checking on the caterpillars, she went inside and climbed toward her room. All the way up the stairs, she thought about what Priam had told her.

You did right,' his voice echoed in her mind. *'You did right.'* If only that were true! Had Priam been in her place, *that day*, she was sure he would have tried to coax another person or two to safety with him. Probably more than two! In any case, he wouldn't have fled cravenly, like she did. Hecuba, too, would have herded frightened villagers before her. Even Cassandra would have thought to slip an arm around a frightened child! The girl could be silly sometimes, but she had a warm heart.

As for what Cassandra's eldest brother would have done — no, what he *did* do…

Andromache reached her bedroom door. Not yet ready for sleep, she turned around and walked back down the stairs.

She thought of the villagers teeming on Lyrnassa's beach. Which ones had escaped? Which ones hadn't? Of course, there were a number of villagers unable to run — old men and women, young people with injuries. Maybe those were the ones who hadn't made it. Then again, even they might have survived, if they'd had a secret hiding place, like the hillside cave her dad and Auntie had always fled to back in Hurapi...

At the bottom of the stairs, Andromache made an about-face and began to climb once more.

But who knew? Maybe none of the villagers had escaped. None of them! Maybe all of them had been slaughtered by the sea invaders, and Hector had lied to make himself look better in the eyes of the council. Maybe he'd altered the reports from Thebe. Who would know the difference? She doubted that anyone in Troy had a list of all the former Lyrnassans...

That's not fair! Andromache scolded herself, quickening her pace. *He risked everything to defend them, and he wasn't even supposed to*...

She reached the top of the stairs much faster, this time, and when she headed back down, she was practically running.

Fair! When had she ever been fair to him? To Hector? All the nightmares she'd had about him were like rocks hurled in his kind face. She thought of him, looking at her from across the library table, smiling. Laughing. Making jokes. That was who he *really* was! That other thing was just a shell, a costume — and he wore it only to protect the innocent.

For the next several hours, Andromache marched up and down the stairs. When she was too exhausted to think anymore, she climbed to her room, placed her sash gently on the clothing chest, and sank into bed.

Chapter 14

Andromache awoke with a new and urgent problem: what to do about the caterpillars she'd rescued from Priam. Overnight, two of them had died.

Thinking they'd starved, she ran down to the courtyard, grabbed a handful of medlar leaves, and brought them back up to her room. When she untied the sash and spread the leaves out on it, a few of the bolder caterpillars came over to munch, but the others lay curled in a ball, looking peaked.

They need fresh air, she thought sadly. If she took them back to the courtyard, though, the priest would be sure to exterminate them. They would have to go into exile or perish. She knew that the city must have other medlar plants, but to leave the house — to go out among all those people — to feel them milling about her, pushing her, tripping her, crushing her — to pass by dark alleys chocked with dagger-wielding thugs —

Her heart was pounding in terror. She looked down at the insect larvae and began to cry. Even for them, she knew she couldn't leave the house. She was a coward.

What about Cassandra? she thought, rejecting the idea as soon as it came to her. The girl's tenderheartedness might not extend to insects — and what if she squashed them? Their rescue from the priest would be for nothing.

The little creatures' dire situation grew bleaker when Muka put her feet up on the bed and began to snuffle at them. "No, Muka!" Andromache scolded her. But the dog, intent on her prey, quickly snapped one into her mouth.

"No!" Before Muka could eat any more of the caterpillars, Andromache dove for the sash and tied it up again, holding it high above her head. Muka smacked her lips contentedly and curled up on the floor. Meanwhile, Andromache began to weep.

Her tears didn't give out until the sun had reached its zenith. Around the same time, Hecuba's sturdy knock sounded: *thock, thock, thock*. Andromache hastily hid the bag of caterpillars behind a pillow and walked over to the door.

"Hello, Andromache, dear," said Hecuba. Her arms were brimming over with fabric in shades of tan, grey, and white, the same colors she and her daughter wore. "I have good news — your dresses are finally finished."

"Oh, thank you," said Andromache, accepting the clothes. "They're beautiful." They were. Their fabric was light and fine, far lovelier than anything she'd worn since her mother's death. At the moment, though, all she cared about was that she no longer needed her sash to hike up her dress. She could devote it to the caterpillars.

"Besides dresses to wear around the house, there are also a few sleeping gowns and a robe to wear after bathing. Do you think they'll fit?"

Andromache unfolded one of the dresses and held it up to herself.

"Much better," said Hecuba, nodding her approval. "But *you*, on the other hand...you look like you didn't sleep at all. Are you feeling well, dear?"

Andromache was *not* feeling well, but she didn't want to explain the reasons behind her long nighttime march. "I'm fine," she said. "Just a little tired."

"Well, take a nap, then," ordered Hecuba. "You don't want to come down with a fever again, do you?"

"No," murmured Andromache.

"Of course you don't. Have you had anything to eat, yet?"

Andromache shook her head. When she'd fetched the medlar leaves for her caterpillars, she'd forgotten to get breakfast for herself.

"I'll bring you something in a little while," said Hecuba. "For now, get some sleep — oh, and do try on those dresses before too long, dear. If they don't fit, we'll have them altered."

Andromache nodded. As soon as she was alone, she lay down and unknotted her sash to check on the caterpillars. During her brief exchange with Hecuba, two more had died.

଼ଡ଼

TEARSTAINED AND EXHAUSTED, Andromache slipped into one of her new dresses and trudged downstairs to the library, the sachet of doomed insect larvae in her hand. She laid it carefully on the table and sat down to wait for her student.

Just a few moments later, she heard his cheery, "<u>Hay-lo</u>." He strode into the room, swung his cloak off his shoulders, and was about to throw it onto the table when Andromache cried:

"Stop!"

"Oh!" It was too late for him not to release the cloak, but he managed to divert its path toward the floor. "What? Why?"

Panting at the narrow escape, Andromache scooped up the sash and clutched it to her chest.

"<u>Ahndromahk</u>?" he asked.

She took a deep breath but said nothing.

"What is it?"

By this time, she had begun to tremble and her student was staring at her, alarmed. "All right," she whispered. Carefully, so as not to disturb the little creatures, she unknotted the sash and tilted it toward him.

He peered in and, upon seeing the remaining seven caterpillars, stared at them in disbelief. Whatever he'd been expecting, this wasn't it. "<u>Ahndromahk</u>?" he whispered, his voice shaking ever so slightly. "What's going on?"

Why did he sound so strange? Was he angry? Andromache wasn't sure, but the fact that he hadn't immediately squashed the insects gave her courage. "They — they need a medlar plant," she whispered.

Her student bit his lip.

"Please don't tell your father I have them," she begged, her voice growing louder.

"What does Dad have to do with these worms?" he asked.

"Caterpillars," she corrected.

"Caterpillars," he conceded. "Well?"

"They were eating his plants," she explained. "He thinks I — *eliminated* them. If he sees they're still alive, he'll —"

"I see," said her student. For a moment or two, neither of them spoke. "There's a garden by the stables," he finally said. "Do you want me to take them there?"

Andromache clutched the caterpillars protectively as her old fear bubbled up: *He'll kill them — he'll crush them — he'll grind them to a pulp*.

"It wouldn't be any trouble," he added. "I go down there every day, anyway."

When she looked up to see him watching her with dark, gentle eyes, she felt utterly wretched. Oh gods! How could she still be afraid of him, knowing what he'd risked to defend Lyrnassa? She was atrocious — sick — rotten and black inside!

"Ahndromahk?"

Her student's voice held neither hurt nor rebuke. He didn't seem to have noticed her insulting look of fear. Wordlessly, she thrust the open sachet of caterpillars toward him.

He accepted them with a strange expression on his face. Was it derision? Mockery? Andromache didn't think so, although he looked like he was trying very hard not to laugh.

The caterpillars edged their way out of the sachet, crawling around his palm and down his fingers while he watched. "They're cute," he said.

Andromache nodded. "Five are already…gone," she said in a choked voice.

"Oh." Her student frowned. "Do you think I should go now, then?"

Now? He'd rushed down to Lyrnassa to defend villagers he didn't even know, and now he was rushing out to save her caterpillars? Andromache looked up at him with something close to worship. "You'd do that?" she whispered.

His eyes snapped to his hand. Carefully, he tucked the insects back into their carrying case. "Sure. No problem. What kind of plant did you say?"

"Medlar shrub."

"All right. I'll be right back."

"Thank you, Hector," whispered Andromache. It was the first time she'd called him by his name.

He looked up in surprise but said only, "*Pssht!* It's nothing."

156

When he was gone, Andromache laid her forehead on the table. She was so weary that she fell immediately to sleep...

She was walking along the beach at Lyrnassa when she saw a ship, fast approaching. On board, there was a host of hideous wraithlike warriors, spears at their sides. When they were within several boat lengths of Lyrnassa, they took aim.

'Come on!' she called to the villagers. 'Come with me!'

They followed as she led them up the hill to safety, but toward the top, she let them pass her. She would bring up the rear. She was going to protect them. Once the last of the villagers had disappeared over the rise, she followed — only to discover a cloaked figure blocking her path. It was even larger than the ones on the ship. At the parting of its cloak she saw the glint of armor, dulled by smoke and wet with blood.

The phantasm fixed her with its blank-eyed gaze, and she knew that the villagers hadn't made it far — and neither would she...

Andromache awoke drenched in sweat. When she opened her eyes to find herself in the library, alone, she remembered what had happened earlier and began to cry.

Now, at the exact moment when Hector was transporting her caterpillars to safety, she was dreaming him into a monster. *He might have squashed them*, she told herself, to justify her feeling of terror. *He might have killed them. You don't know*. But then she pictured his hands, covered in green larvae, and heard his voice: *'They're cute.'*

What was wrong with her, that she would *still* be having such nightmares? They'd been understandable at first, back when she thought he was a raider. But *now?*

The Voice seemed to shrug. (*Blood is blood, and you saw what you saw*.)

What she saw...

She looked up and saw a brutal monster, covered in gore. Blood ran tracks through soot on its skin and armor. Two black hollows filled the space where there should have been eyes. Its vile stench surrounded her — acrid smoke, sweat, putrescence, the heavy smell of blood. The thing's mouth gaped open, ready to sink its teeth into her — drink her blood — leave her, pale and still, facedown upon the earth...

Andromache had seen the image when she was at her weakest. The Raider had come upon her right after she'd lost her Auntie — been trampled half to death — fled raiders — torn her feet — scorched her skin — vomited — fainted — and hit her head. Fever had seared his every gruesome, gory detail into her mind.

Blood is blood, she agreed, shuddering. *And none of it was his.*

But she'd seen other things since *that day*. A hand patting Muka. Vivid green on brown...

In panic, in confusion, Andromache ran out of the library and up to her room. Hector might be back at any moment, and just then, she couldn't face him.

℘

ONCE THE REST of the family was asleep, Andromache crept out to the back stairwell. All night long, she walked up and down the stairs. Each time her head began drooping toward her chest, she thought of the little sachet in Hector's hand and redoubled her efforts. She stopped just before dawn and huddled, exhausted, in a little alcove off the second floor landing. It was full of dust and spider webs, none of which she cleared away. She lay down among the debris and slept.

Muka found her there, later, and snuffled her awake.

"Hi, girl," whispered Andromache, clutching the dog to her chest. "I know you didn't mean it. You didn't mean to eat the caterpillar."

Muka wagged her tail softly.

"On second thought," sighed Andromache, "you probably *did* mean to eat it...but that's just what dogs do, isn't it. You can't help it."

The plumy tail waved harder until it was thumping against the wall.

"I shouldn't have yelled at you," murmured Andromache. "I was wrong. Do you forgive me?"

Muka gave her arm several long, slow licks.

"I know," said Andromache. "Salty. I need a bath." Not that she, the black-hearted ingrate, deserved to use this family's water or bath oils...even less the new bathing robe that Hecuba had given her.

The dog's tongue grew more insistent.

"All right, you've made your point." Groaning, Andromache rose to her feet and then, with Muka, she limped out to the bath chamber.

∾

THAT AFTERNOON, Andromache sat on the library's porch, her knees tucked to her chest, her eyes fixed on the paving stones below.

Ten...eleven...twelve...

She was exhausted, and counting took all of her energy. She had none left to think about her nightmares, or her student, or how she could manage to be around him without melting into a sludge of guilt and misery.

Twenty-seven...twenty-eight...twenty-nine —

Andromache stopped. Down below, footsteps were falling in time with her numbers. She peeked over the edge of the railing and saw Hector striding across the courtyard. His expression was sober and remote. It was a commander's expression, weighed down by the responsibility of leading half an army — of protecting an entire countryside. His step was firm as he disappeared into the banquet hall.

How could she ever have confused *him* for a hot-blooded raider?

Andromache shot to her feet. She couldn't face *him!* She was too awed by him to face him. If she hurried, she might be able to get out of the library before —

"Hay-lo?"

Too late! she thought, although she whispered only: "Hi." She looked up, noticing how lean and solid his arms were — the right kind of arms for defending hapless villagers, and —

"Thees?" asked Hector, in response to her staring. He held out the text that he'd been carrying.

Too embarrassed to say what she'd really been thinking, Andromache nodded.

"Ah-ee reeting een my betroom. Eet hass mohre *weent*," he said, looking delighted with himself.

Weent'…wind. Andromache's sense of awe vanished. The man before her was just her student, again. "What were you reading out there?" she asked.

His dark cheeks flushing, Hector handed over the text.

"*On the — Breeping? Breading?* No, wait — *Breeding! On the Breeding of —* of — *Champion — Horses,*" she said, slowly reading the title aloud.

Hector brushed a lock of hair out of his eyes and nodded, looking as sheepish as though he'd been caught with drawings of naked women.

Andromache returned the text to him, and he slid it hastily onto the nearest shelf. Once it was out of sight, Andromache cleared her throat and asked, "So, um, how are you?"

"All rahght," said Hector. "Beezy."

"Busy?"

"Yes — uh — beu-zy."

"With what?" asked Andromache, hoping he wouldn't ask her how to say '*horse breeding.*'

"Today, I go plahnts," said Hector. With a triumphant look, he corrected himself: "I go *to* plahnts."

"Plants?" Andromache furrowed her eyebrows. "You mean the garden?"

"Gahten?"

Andromache pointed out the window, toward the courtyard. "Garden — did you go out in the garden?"

Again, Hector shook his head. "*Thees* gahten, no."

"Oh…" She wasn't sure how to prompt him.

"Is — on? — on ze hohrse house."

"By the stable?" she asked.

He nodded.

"You went to the garden by the stable?"

He nodded again. "Zey am — zey *ahre* — all rahght."

They? What does he mean? The vegetables? And then Andromache's sluggish mind finally grasped what he'd been trying to say: "The caterpillars?" she asked breathlessly.

Smiling, he said, "<u>Yes</u>."

After all the nasty thoughts she'd ever had about Hector, he'd checked on her little refugees! It was too much — much too much. Tears in her eyes, Andromache gave him a moony look.

Hector engrossed himself in tracing the edges of the table. "It was no big deal," he mumbled, embarrassed. "I was down there anyway and —"

Andromache shook her head. "It *is* a big deal." The tears were falling in earnest, now, and with them, words began to fly out of her mouth. "And s-so w-was Lyrnassa!"

Hector's face froze.

"I know — I heard — what — what you, and — and —"

"Ssh — stop." Hector's tone was gentle, but he folded his arms stiffly in front of himself and looked out the window.

Now that she'd started, though, Andromache couldn't stop herself. "But I — I — the villagers — and *you* —" She swallowed hard. "Thank you," she said, her voice cracking.

When Hector didn't answer, Andromache realized she'd made him so uncomfortable that he couldn't speak. It was a strange reversal of their usual roles. She wasn't sure why he was upset but didn't want to make things worse, so she decided just to let the matter drop. "<u>Your dad didn't see them, did he</u>?" she murmured, changing the subject.

Still guarded, Hector looked back at her. "<u>Zeym</u>?" he asked.

"The caterpillars," she said.

He laughed. "<u>Dad see zeym, no</u>."

Hector's laughter filled Andromache with the warmth of a youthful conspiracy. She was nine again, with Haliosh, her childhood friend, keeping his parents occupied while he swiped cakes and wine for them to feast on up in the old hollow tree...

For the first time since Auntie's death, Andromache found herself smiling.

Late summer into autumn

Chapter 15

Neither Priam nor Cassandra had overstated the shabbiness of the courtyard garden. Andromache knew that the end of the summer season was an unfair time to judge it — plants all across the countryside were semi-dormant in the heat. Still, her garden in Lyrnassa had never looked so bedraggled, even at the driest time of year.

The first day Andromache went down to survey the garden, she could only walk among the beds, scandalized that the family had shown such disregard for its botanical riches. Limp daisies, nodding down to the earth — browning lily leaves — desiccated rose bushes — whole boxes lost to weeds. The herbs and vegetables were in similar dishevelment; all were leggy and underwatered. No wonder Hecuba had to *buy* the ingredients for her healing mixtures!

Once the initial shock wore off, Andromache got to work.

Despite the woeful state of the garden, she loved spending time out there, taking in the life around her. In the cool of the morning or evening, birds filled the courtyard with their songs. They flitted about, hunting seeds and insects. One had even built a nest in the tallest apple tree earlier that year, before Andromache's arrival in Troy. She hoped it would come back in spring to build a new one, so that she could see the baby birds hatch from their eggs and grow.

The insects, too, enchanted her: bees humming among the white lemon balm flowers, their transparent wings a blur — butterflies, quietly swooping — ants and beetles hurrying along the ground, intent on mysterious tasks. Andromache had missed watching all of those creatures during her self-imposed exile on the third floor.

Insects and birds weren't the only beings she saw more of. Her increasingly frequent trips downstairs also brought her into contact with the family members. With some of them, anyway — Hector never seemed to be home, except during lessons. As for Paris, Cassandra had let slip enough details about his schedule for Andromache to avoid him.

Andromache liked seeing more of Cassandra and her parents, though, and they seemed just as glad to see her. Each had a different way of encouraging her. Priam helped her weed and made florid references to the way dormant life resurges, more beautifully than ever, upon the coming of the rains. Hecuba offered to track down seeds or bulbs that she thought Andromache might like to plant in autumn.

Cassandra went a step beyond either of her parents. One evening, as Andromache was sitting beside Muka, taking a break, the girl dashed out from the kitchen. A radiant look on her face, she cried, "Do you want to come with me?"

"Come where?" asked Andromache. "To the kitchen?"

"Oh, no!" laughed the girl. "To a friend's house."

Andromache recoiled.

Arm bones smashing into her throat — knees bludgeoning her — heels crushing her stomach — sand in her face — in her mouth — in her lungs — choking, fighting for breath —

"So, what do you think?" asked Cassandra.

"I can't," said Andromache, shuddering. Leave the house and its thick walls? Never! She'd finally found a haven from the buffeting forces of the world, and she intended to stay there.

"It's a concert soiree," wheedled Cassandra. "You like music, don't you?"

Andromache *did* like music — in fact, she loved it. When she was a child, in the Lukka lands, her neighbors had come over every evening to drink wine and play music with her dad. Those had been the most wonderful evenings of her life...

Cassandra seized on Andromache's moment of hesitation. "It'll be fun!" she sang. "You'll love my friends — I can't wait for you to meet them."

Friends? In the plural? Andromache shivered. "Oh no, I couldn't —"

"Wait, I haven't told you the best part!" Cassandra dangled her ultimate bait: "Paris might come over later!"

Well, that decided it! Andromache would be staying home for sure. She wasn't about to slog through the crowded streets of Troy, only to spend time with Cassandra's obnoxious middle brother. Horror upon horror upon horror!

"I couldn't tell you where he goes most evenings — and it's probably better not to ask," Cassandra added with a little laugh. "Once in a while he'll come to a play or a concert, though, and he always livens things up."

"I'll bet," Andromache said dryly.

Cassandra laughed again. "Hector used to come, too. Of course, that was back when Mom said I was too young to go. It's so unfair! I mean, Paris went to his first soiree when he was *two years* younger than I was at *my* first." She sighed in frustration. "It would've been nice to go with *both* my brothers, you know? Hector hasn't been to a soiree in ages. Between patrolling and living at Uncle's, he hasn't been able to, and even now that he's back in the city, I guess he just has too much work to do. I'm sure he's off stealing time with his lady, too, whenever he can. If you ask me, they should just get married and done with it — then we could have the fun of a big wedding!"

"Oh," said Andromache, her voice hushed. "Get married?" Hadn't Cassandra only said '*sweethearts*,' before?

"Yes, married!" sang the girl. "And it'll be the most beautiful wedding *ever* — here, in the courtyard, of course, with Dad officiating. For his own son! Can you imagine?" She sighed happily. "Oh, I can't wait!"

I can, thought Andromache. Once Penthesilea moved into the house, Hector would find better uses for his time than daily Lukkan lessons — and then, what would happen to *her*? She liked being able to speak her native tongue; Hecuba had been right about that. She didn't want to lose it, now that it was back in her life. She couldn't simply switch students, either, since Cassandra was supposed to be learning Hittite and Luwian. There was *always* something! Always some new threat! "When are they getting married?" she whispered, her lower lip trembling.

"Who knows?" sighed Cassandra. "It might be a while. Now that she took over his old job as patrol captain, she's not in the city much."

Ah! thought Andromache. When Penthesilea had offered her a place to live, the woman had said she was gone a lot. Now, Andromache knew why — she was out patrolling the hills and plains of the Trojan protectorate. That explained why she and Hector weren't married, yet. Then again, if they'd wanted to, they could easily have gotten married while they were both out on the plains. Perhaps Hector wasn't ready for a wife. Most men waited until they were older. Some, till they were much older…

Andromache shuddered.

Cassandra blithely chattered on: "We've been wondering when they'd get married ever since Uncle sent her here, a year ago. Believe me, if anyone could answer *that* question, Mom would lay a striped egg." First looking around to make sure no one else had come out, Cassandra whispered: "Between us, I'm not sure how much she likes Hector's fiancée, but she trusts my uncle to know what's good for Hector. They're really close. Besides, she's *dying* for one of us to get married."

"Do *you* have a sweetheart?" asked Andromache, reassured that Hector and Penthesilea didn't have any imminent wedding plans, at least.

Cassandra's laughter tinkled through the courtyard. "Let me rephrase that — she's dying for one of the *boys* to get married. As for me, '*You have too much else to think about!*'" She mimicked her mother's severest tone: "'*Relationships, my dear, are a hindrance to ambitious women.*'"

Andromache's lips twitched into a tiny smile. "Well. That doesn't mean you aren't in love with someone," she hinted.

Cassandra smiled back. "Oh, I know. But really — I don't have anyone special." She lowered her voice. "I mean, I've kissed with lots of boys, but who hasn't? What about you? Do you have a sweetheart? Oh!" Frowning, she corrected herself. "I mean, did you, before — oh honey, I'm — I'm so sorry!" She stammered on, growing more dismayed with each word. "I shouldn't —"

"It's all right," Andromache reassured her, and she meant it. She hadn't had a lover in Lyrnassa — hadn't even thought about lovers. As much as possible, she'd tried to avoid men, at least the ones who made ravening eyes at her. She'd avoided them ever since she was thirteen...

Don't think about that*!* she warned herself.

"Oh, honey!" cried Cassandra. "Now I've upset you! You're shivering!"

"It's all right," said Andromache, collecting herself. "Really, it's all right. In Lyrnassa, I lived with my aunt and two old women — sisters — who took us in when we first got there." Andromache didn't add that those two sisters had been the only Lyrnassans to offer shelter to her and Auntie. Either they hadn't believed the rumor that she was cursed, or they'd been too pragmatic to care; they'd had first choice of Auntie's blankets, cloaks, and other woven goods. "Once they died," Andromache went on, "it was just me and my aunt. I didn't have a sweetheart."

Cassandra grasped her hand. "Then you *really* have to come with," she said, bright-eyed and insistent.

"Maybe another time," said Andromache, with what she hoped was enough firmness to deflect the girl's plea.

"All right," said Cassandra, letting her go. As she walked away, though, Andromache thought she heard a faint whisper: "For now..."

Chapter 16

*S**he was at the top of a hill, baking in the sun. All around her, lizards were crawling into their dens, but she couldn't follow them. The last one disappeared, and she was alone. The sun was beating down worse than ever. Her skin was sizzling. But then it went dark — the sun went dark — and that was worse than being scalded because she knew what was blocking it — who was blocking it — whose blood-drenched armor was blocking out the light...*

Andromache screamed. Muka, sleeping next to her, awoke and began licking her cheek. As Andromache's scream faded to a whimper, the dog's plumy tail waved softly. '*See? You're all right,*' she seemed to be saying. '*I'm here, and you're all right.*'

Andromache slid her fingers deep into Muka's thick fur. <u>*You don't know me that well,*</u> she argued sadly to the dog. <u>*I'm not all right.*</u> She was sick. Mean. A shame upon the very air she breathed, to still be having nightmares about the Raider! Once, twice a week — they were an insult to Hector, the hero who had tried to save Lyrnassa. They were an insult to her student, a diligent worker and a likeable person. They were an insult to her hosts, Hecuba and Priam, Hector's parents, who, far beyond simply feeding and clothing her, showered her with every sort of kindness. What more did she need, for the nightmares to stop?

She considered going down to the library but didn't think that reading would help. Written Truvan was coming back to her, and reading didn't take as much energy as it once had. The biography of Sarcho might, but that text brought other problems. Seeing the flawless scrolls would only reaffirm how unworthy she was of this house — of the peace and comfort she'd found there — of Hecuba and Priam's generosity — of Muka's love — of Hector's tolerance. This last most of all, because the Sarcho scrolls reminded her of how she'd cringed against the shelves in fear of Hector, as though he were a monster, aching to slaughter her...

No, the library wouldn't help her. She needed to *run*.

As a child, Andromache had fled raiders so often that running had become her reflex any time she felt scared, upset, or out of control. For a time, at least, the physical pain of running deadened whatever was hurting her emotionally...

She and Auntie were coming back from a nearby town, where they'd been selling cloth and lutes. She was excited to see her parents — she couldn't wait to tell them about everything! But when she got to where the house should have been, all she saw was fallen rock.

'Mom! Dad!' she called. 'Mom! Dad!' She tried to find the cave behind their house, but the entrance was blocked. She picked up rocks one by one and flung them over her shoulder. 'Mom! Dad!'

'Stop, Ahndromahk.' Auntie took her arm.

She tore away from Auntie and went back to throwing rocks. 'Mama!' Thunk, thunk. *'Daddy!'*

'Stop! Stop, child.' Auntie was hugging her. 'It's no use...'

Then Andromache was screaming, shrieking, running off down the rocky shore. Auntie was pounding along behind her, yelling at her to come back, but she didn't stop running. Not until she collapsed from exhaustion.

She awoke in Auntie's arms.

'You silly girl!' chided Auntie, crying and kissing Andromache on the cheeks. 'You're lucky there aren't any raiders about! You're lucky you didn't slip and fall down into a chasm, or I might never have found you — and then what? Oh, my poor, poor, silly girl...'

Andromache's family had lived on the flank of the mountains. They'd built their house right in front of a tiny cave where her dad and Auntie hid during raids. It was a safe little house, tucked in among trees. Raiders seldom went up that far from the shore.

Her friend Haliosh and his family had lived on the other end of Hurapi village, closest to the sea. They'd suffered more during raids, but the rockslide hadn't caught them. Andromache's closest neighbors had been out tending their goats or had heard an odd sound from the mountain and run just in time. Her dad couldn't have run. Years earlier, he'd been injured while helping another family rebuild their house. Even walking was a struggle. He could only do it with someone supporting him...

'I heard your mom ran inside when the mountain started rumbling,' Haliosh told her. 'Your dad was inside, but your mom was out front.'

Had Andromache's mom run into the house to help him? Or had she known it was a lost cause and run inside to die with him? Had she chosen to abandon her child rather than her husband? Had they suffered long, or was it all over in an instant? The weight of these unanswered questions had been too much to bear...

'It's not good for you to stay here,' Auntie decided. 'We'll go to Taruisha. That way, you can get to know your father's culture.'

Andromache didn't care where they went, whether they left or stayed. She didn't care about her father's culture, either. What did it matter? Her parents were dead. The mountain had swallowed them, and she would never see them again.

Neighbors helped them move rocks away from the cave's entrance. Auntie went in to gather what had been stored there — a few lutes, some cloaks, and other woolens. She packed a basket of food for Andromache to carry and told her it was time to go.

As Andromache left Hurapi, she barely noticed Haliosh waving at her. She didn't wave back. She started running, and Auntie had to catch her again...

They'd been forced to end their journey at Lyrnassa, but Andromache had never stopped running. Running had dulled the agony of losing her parents. It had allowed her to escape the Lyrnassans' looks of suspicion — their refusal to get too close to her. Back in Hurapi, everyone had adored her. The neighbors had all sung songs with her, talked to her, hugged her. They'd given her treats — little nut breads they'd baked, or bright feathers they'd found. Nothing had prepared her for the way the Lyrnassans would shun her, from the moment she set foot in the village...

She and Auntie stumbled down the path to Lyrnassa. When they arrived in the village, a crowd of Lyrnassans gathered. No one spoke to them, at first — there were just hushed murmurs of horror.

'What's that on her dress?'

'Blood! It's blood!'

'Oh, by all the gods, no!'

'Get her out of here!'

As the chorus of disapproval grew louder and louder, Andromache and Auntie turned to leave. Before they reached the edge of the village, though, an older woman stopped them. 'Wait!' she murmured. With a look of admiration, she reached out to touch Auntie's cloak. 'Who made this?'

'Sh-she did,' whispered Andromache. 'She's a weaver.'

'Indeed,' said the woman, nodding appreciatively. She turned to another woman beside her, and for a few moments, they murmured back and forth. Finally, the first woman said to Andromache, 'My name is Eriopis, and this is my sister, Myrine. If you like, you can stay with us.'

Life with the two sisters had been quiet; it was even quieter after they died. No one else in the village would speak to Andromache, except briefly, to negotiate for Auntie's fine woolen goods. Blood appalled the Lyrnassans. They saw it as a sign of divine anger, and Andromache was forever cursed in their eyes. But even the most tolerant group would have shunned her for what had happened in that wagon —

"No!" Andromache cried aloud. "No!" Her stomach gave a violent heave. *Don't think about that! Not ever!*

Once again, Muka began licking Andromache's cheek. Insistent but soft, the dog's tongue slid over her skin. That comfort wasn't enough, though — not when Andromache was being hounded by guilt and nightmares and the horrors of her past. She needed to *run*! If she ran, she wouldn't have to think!

Only one place was available to her — the stairwell. *It's nighttime,* she told herself. *No one will see me there.* For what felt like hours, she ran up and down the stairs, until finally she collapsed on her bed and slept a blessedly dreamless sleep.

Chapter 17

*S*he came into the kitchen and saw the table piled high with food. There were breads of all kinds: breads filled with walnuts, breads filled with cheese, breads filled with raisins. There were dried fruit stews and fresh salads. There were thick, savory chick pea soups. There were honey cakes, pistachio-fig rolls, and quince tarts! Quince tarts! Her favorite! She reached for one — she could almost taste it...

As Andromache's eyes fluttered open, she could hear her stomach growling. She'd been running a lot, lately. Whenever she dreamed about Lyrnassa or the Raider, she took to the stairwell, running up and down until she could run no more. The punishing regimen dulled her guilt and pain, but it only sharpened her appetite. She had consciously been eating more, ever since Hecuba had ordered her to, but '*more*' never seemed to be enough.

That morning, she felt ravenous. She could still see all the delicacies from her dream — walnut bread, cheeses, quince tart — and the table downstairs in the kitchen was sure to have some of them. Unfortunately, late morning in the kitchen meant Paris, and she did *not* want to see Paris!

Hoping to find the remains of an earlier meal, Andromache looked around her room. She would have been glad for an old crust of bread or even a desiccated grape — anything! But the one tray she saw was empty. She bit the inside of her cheek, forcing saliva to flow. When that didn't satisfy her hunger pangs, she tried to lie back down and ignore them. That worked for a while, but her stomach finally gave such a loud growl that Muka barked at it. Andromache knew then that she would have to risk a trip to the kitchen.

Furtively, she crept down the back staircase, through the banquet hall, and into the kitchen. She thought at first that she'd gotten lucky — that the room was empty — but then the face she'd dreaded seeing peered out from behind a shelf.

"So, you *are* real!" quipped Paris, without bothering to say hello to her. "And here I thought I'd had too much wine, my first night back, and only imagined meeting you!"

Andromache glared at him and sat down at the table. She devoured a slab of bread and cheese without saying a word.

Unfazed, Paris continued to taunt her: "My brother and sister insisted that they'd had sightings —"

Sightings? Andromache longed to spit in the little jerk's handsome face. He was making her sound like some horrid beast of legend! Pointedly not responding, she stroked Muka's back with her feet and tore off another hunk of bread.

"— but you can't trust either one of them, without proof. My brother likes to joke around, and as for the Songbird —" Paris scoffed. "She sees whatever she wants to see."

"All right!" snapped Andromache, through a mouthful of food. "What's your point?"

Paris smirked. "My point is that you were starting to seem more like a rumor than a reality, Hermie."

Hermie? Didn't he know her name? "Hermie?" she asked.

"As in *hermit.*"

Andromache scowled. "Well, now you know. I'm real."

"I can see that," he said, leering. "You've already eaten half the kitchen."

Andromache dropped the cheese she was holding. "What's it to you?"

"*I'm* the one who has to carry the baskets back from market, Hermie, and you have the makings of a real back-breaker."

"My name's not '*Hermie!*'" she cried.

"And mine's not '*Hand-me-the-chickpeas,*' but if you're going to keep eating like that, the least you can do is help me put this stuff away." Paris pointed to a basket on the table.

Frowning, Andromache peered inside and saw a large jar of beans. "They're already cooked," she said with disgust. "And so are the vegetables."

"Yes, O Wise One!" sneered Paris. "You truly do have the sight! No wonder my parents chose you to tutor my brother!"

Andromache glowered at him. "Cassandra told me that you *cooked!* What *cooking* can you possibly do? It's already done!"

Paris tilted the jar toward her. "Taste the chickpeas now, and then taste them this afternoon, after I've added my secret blend of herbs. You'll see."

"I don't think so," she said with disdain. "You seem like the type who'd slip a sleeping herb into the mix."

He laughed. "All you've done for two months is sleep. Why would I give you sleeping herbs now, when there's finally some potential for you to be interesting?"

"Don't count on it!" she huffed.

He laughed again. "You win, Hermie...you're as thrilling as a thirty-verse song."

"And you're even *more* horrible than your brother said," she muttered.

Paris gave a lazy shrug. "He always underestimates me."

Andromache snorted. In spite of everything, she found herself almost *liking* Paris — she liked, at least, that he didn't tiptoe around her. He hadn't been home, when she first came to the city. He hadn't seen her at her weakest. To him, she was a normal, if slightly reclusive, person.

"Just like I underestimated *you*, Hermie. Next time I'll be sure to get a triple jar of chickpeas." He grinned.

Defiantly, Andromache shoved another hunk of bread into her mouth and stalked back up to her room. She *might* end up liking Paris — as long as she didn't see too much of him.

Early autumn

Chapter 18

wo months, thought Andromache. *I've been in Taruisha for two months.* No time at all, yet in some ways an eternity. The house felt normal, now, with its corridors and stairs, its library, its bath chamber, its great hall, and its kitchen. Andromache had grown so used to walking on rugs, tiles, and polished wood that sand and wild grasses would no doubt feel alien to her feet.

Two months! When she'd come to Troy, summer had been blazing through the countryside. Now, the wind was cool, even during the day, and soon the rains would come. Grapes had been harvested from the surrounding lands. The courtyard trees were heavy with ripe apples.

Meanwhile, Andromache had set about planting seeds, cuttings, and bulbs, so that the plants would have all winter to drink in the rains. She shivered through the work, aghast that she'd ever lived somewhere as harsh as Lyrnassa. Here in Troy, if she took a chill, she could retreat to the comfort of her thick-walled house. She could warm herself beside the hearth or cuddle under a blanket with Muka.

Lately, though, she was feeling less need to cuddle. The energy of good health made her want to run instead. Every day, and not just after nightmares, she ran many flights of stairs. She liked the exercise, and she liked having another element in her daily routine.

When she grew too tired to run any further, she turned to exploration. Little by little, she poked around the parts of the house she wasn't already familiar with — the various nooks of the banquet hall, as well as the third floor rooms.

Until then, she'd been shy about wandering through them, but she didn't see why anyone would mind. Most of the rooms were even smaller than hers. One had nothing inside but a chest full of moth-eaten ancient clothing — robes Cassandra's grandparents had worn, perhaps. A second room held spare jars and, weirdly, a heap of broken sandals. Inside the third, though, there was a loom and a basket of thread.

Andromache skimmed her finger down the frame of the loom, inscribing a line of rich red-brown into decades of accumulated dust. She couldn't help gasping. Even in its grimy, neglected state, the object before her was clearly of the highest quality.

A piece of cloth sat beside the loom. The threads were cut — it was only half-finished, a sweet, soft, pale green cloth with pink flowers woven in. It made Andromache think of fruit trees, blossoming in spring. Perhaps Hecuba had begun it as a blanket for one of her unborn babies, only to abandon it when the baby was lost...

Andromache swallowed hard and turned away from the little green cloth. Idly, she pawed through the basket of thread. Dozens of colors, more than her mom had ever had, were just sitting there. What a waste! Even with poor quality thread in dull colors, her mom and Auntie had been able to weave fine, even beautiful, cloth. Andromache ached to think of what they might have made from the forgotten riches in that basket.

Sighing, she picked up a spool of dark brown thread. She could weave, too, although she wasn't very good at it. She'd never had the patience to learn. A lively, laughing child, she'd always been eager to run around collecting roots or berries for dyes, but working at the loom hadn't suited her...

'*When you're older, I'll teach you,*' her mom had said, indulging Andromache's youthful restlessness. '*For now, Little Cricket, run out and find me some more brown slakeroot...*'

As a weaver, Auntie had been more interested in sturdiness and practicality than aesthetics. Even if she were still here, she couldn't have shown Andromache how to weave ripples, diamonds, or intricate floral patterns. Only Andromache's mom had known those tricks.

Andromache placed the thread back into the basket. She would never learn, now — never know her mom's secrets. With sadness flooding through her, she ran out of the room and all the way down to the kitchen.

Hecuba was in there, warming herself. "Andromache, dear, what on earth are you rushing around for? Are you all right? Goodness — you're crying! Come, come, sit by the fire and tell me what's wrong."

"There's a loom," wailed Andromache. "Upstairs."

"Why, yes — yes, there is," said Hecuba, sounding surprised. "I'd almost forgotten about it. Did you hurt yourself on it, or something?"

Andromache shook her head. "My mom was a weaver. My Auntie, too."

"Oh," Hecuba said gravely. "I see."

Neither woman spoke for a moment. Andromache sat sniffling as tears streamed down her face. Hecuba touched her forehead and cheeks, checking for signs of fever. When she found none, she brushed Andromache's tears away and gently patted her hand.

"If you'd like to use the loom, dear, please help yourself," she finally said. "Cassandra never took to it, and while I used to enjoy weaving, I don't have time for it anymore."

Thinking of the little green cloth, Andromache grew tearful once more. She'd lost her mother; the woman beside her had lost her baby. Several babies, desperately wanted...

"There, there! No need to cry," tutted Hecuba. "Weave as much as you'd like, and let me know if you run out of thread. I can send someone out for more."

"Thank you," whispered Andromache.

"I was about to brew a tisane — rose petals with a drop or two of honey. It's just the thing to warm you on a day like this. Would you like one?"

Andromache nodded and gave Hecuba a watery smile.

AFTER THAT DAY, Andromache devoted her early afternoon hours to weaving. Hecuba's loom was larger and finer than any she'd ever seen, but it worked by the same principles, and she was able to use it. The work frustrated her — no matter how hard she tried, her cloth looked tangled and ragged — but she liked doing it, all the same.

Chapter 19

Every evening, after lessons and a last inspection of the garden boxes, Andromache went into the kitchen to sit by the hearth. Family members came in and out while she was there, and she lingered with them, eating dinner downstairs rather than taking a tray up to her room.

These meals were much quieter than Paris's welcome dinner had been, as the whole group was never there at once. Someone always had a meeting, a patient, a training, an observation of the sky, or some other commitment. Most nights, Andromache dined with Paris and Cassandra. She said little but listened closely while the two traded stories about the goings-on in Troy. Those were the best dinners — the stories were never quite as juicy when a parent happened to be around.

After the meal, Paris would pull out his lute. If his family members were there, he tended to play respectable songs, although he would occasionally slip in a barroom ditty. One night, though, when he and Andromache were alone, he played nothing but bawdy drinking songs. He seemed to take it for granted that she wouldn't mind.

In fact, those were just the sort of tunes her dad had liked best — mischievous, rollicking songs. For a while, Andromache sat with her eyes closed, imagining herself back on the mountain slopes of her Lukkan homeland. She was spinning around in a circle, breathing in the flower-scented air. Dusky pine boughs floated above her, and lively, joyous melodies surrounded her...

Andromache's eyelids fluttered open. The music sounded more like her dad's than any she'd ever heard! She began watching Paris closely, to see what the connection might be. His fingers moved differently than her dad's had always done. They flew about the strings in unusual rhythms and made strange jangling sounds — ornaments, she supposed. The instrument was also tuned to Paris's voice, which was slightly lower than her dad's. Beneath the strangeness, though, Andromache heard a familiar quality — something beyond the Trojan modes that both Paris and her dad had used. Frowning, she studied the lute more closely.

Her confusion turned to shock. The bowl had a distinctive shape to it; the neck, a particular length. How could she *not* have noticed before? Had she somehow forgotten?

"Hermie? Hermie!" called Paris, breaking into her thoughts.

"What?"

"You were staring at my —"

"At your *lute*," she said sharply.

He shrugged.

"It's just — nice."

"'*Nice?*'" Paris scoffed. "It's a lot more than nice! It's the best lute there is! My parents had it specially made for me in my seventeenth summer."

"Could I —"

"What?"

"Could I hold it?" Andromache asked meekly.

"You want to hold my *lute*?" Paris grinned. "I'm not sure we know each other well enough for that, Hermie."

"Never mind!" she snapped. Her cheeks were flaming red.

"I'd let you," he said, his tone serious. "But if you dropped it, I couldn't get another one."

"What do you mean?"

"The guy who made it was a master luthier, the best in Troy. He used to have a shop down in the lower town. He was a nasty old coot, but he knew his craft. Other people have tried to copy his lutes, but —" Paris made a face. "I've played on those, and believe me…they're not the same."

Andromache swallowed hard. "Used to?" she prompted Paris. "Was?"

"Huh?"

"You said he *used to* have a shop and he *was* a nasty old coot. What happened to him?"

"Oh. Food poisoning, a year or two back. He ate some rotten meat and croaked."

Andromache shuddered.

"I know," said Paris. "It sucks, right? He never wrote down his trade secrets or told them to anyone but his worthless son — I say '*worthless*' because the guy couldn't pile two rocks on top of each other, much less make a lute — but the point is, information wasn't the only thing they shared." He paused for dramatic effect. "They also lived in the same house…and ate the same food."

"The son died, too?" whispered Andromache.

Paris nodded. "And the secrets with him. Like I said, the old master never told them to anyone else. His wife died years ago, and they only ever had one kid, the son."

Andromache's vision blurred with tears. Secrets! She had more secrets than Paris would ever believe. For one, she knew that the old master *had* once written down a description of his methods. Everything he knew had been recorded on four leather scrolls. For another, he *had* taught his craft to someone else — his first son, the child he'd had with his servant girl. Andromache had learned many secrets while she and Auntie were living in Lyrnassa…

'*Auntie?*'

'*Yes, pet?*'

'*Why did my dad leave Taruisha?*'

'*You know — he was angry with his father.*'

'*Yes, but why, exactly?*'

'*I shouldn't tell you such things. You're still a child.*'

'*Oh, Auntie! No, I'm not!*'

Auntie sighed. 'I suppose you're not. Now, you have to understand, this is all according to your mom. I can't swear the story is true word for word.'

'*That's all right. Just tell me what she said.*'

'*Very well. You know who your dad's parents were?*'

'*Yes. A luthier and his servant.*'

'*Exactly. Well, by Taruishan standards, your grandparents weren't married — and years later, your grandfather formally married another woman, had a son, and that was it for your dad. Your grandfather wanted nothing more to do with him once he had a 'real' heir. Of all the foolish things I've ever heard!' Auntie shook her head in fury.*

'I can see why he was mad,' Andromache said softly.

'Oh, yes! And then, on top of it, his mother died.'

'The luthier's servant?'

'Mm-hmm. Once she died, there was nothing left for your dad in Taruisha. He decided to leave the city.'

'How old was he?'

'Nearly a man. Not a bad time to make a journey, if you have to make one. Now, your dad had many friends in his Taruishan neighborhood, and among them were some people from Lukká. As he was growing up, they taught him their language and told him about their homeland. It turned out to be a very lucky thing for your dad that he'd made friends with them. Right around the time he was hoping to leave the city, the Lukkana folk made plans to head south, back to Lukká. When your dad heard about that, he asked to go with them. They said yes, of course.'

'Of course!'

'When he left the city, he took a few things with him — things the luthier sorely missed, I imagine. You know what I'm talking about, don't you?'

'The scrolls?'

'That's right. The scrolls. How anyone could make sense of them I'll never understand, but your dad treasured them. They had all the luthier's secrets. Your dad took them, along with a set of lute-making tools, and then he left Taruisha forever...'

Once Andromache's dad had finally reached the Lukka lands, he'd stayed there, making lutes, for the rest of his life. It was a trade he could do even after injuring his legs. His instruments were enormously popular, not only for their high quality but also for their distinctive shape, so different from the native Lukkan lutes...

'We'd be rich if each one didn't take so damn long to make,' he sighed.

'Who cares about riches?' Andromache's mom responded, nodding toward their daughter. 'We have everything we need.'

Andromache considered Paris's lute. She was awed to be in its presence. There were only a few like it in the world, and she'd landed in a house with one of them! Of course, her dad couldn't possibly have made it. By Paris's seventeenth summer, her parents had been dead for years. No, her dad's father — her grandfather, the master luthier — had made it. Lutes like this one had served as a model for her dad, during his apprenticeship.

Her grandfather had made it, and now he would never make another one. Andromache felt a sudden strange sense of loss. A door was closed. It was a door she hadn't wanted, but somehow she regretted it anyway. Her half-lie to Hecuba had been the whole truth after all. Her entire family was dead.

"Aw, Hermie, don't cry," Paris broke in. "If the secret for making these is lost, that just makes mine all the more valuable." He gave the instrument a gentle, proprietorial pat.

Red spots appeared on Andromache's cheeks. "Then maybe you should lock it away in a treasure chest," she hissed, running out of the room.

ANDROMACHE SPENT THAT entire night on the staircase, marching up and down, thinking about the master luthier. She didn't know how to feel about the news of his death. She'd hardly ever thought about him as a person, much less as family. He'd been filthy and lecherous, forcing himself on a servant girl. He'd been cruel, taking his own child's inheritance and future away from him. He'd made the people around him miserable.

More than sorrow, Andromache felt shock over Paris's story. Shock at the unexpected link between his family and hers. Shock at the finality of how it was severed. Shock at the thought that if she and Auntie had made it to Troy in the first place, she might have met her grandfather...

(*So what?*) asked the Voice. (*He didn't want your dad, and he wouldn't have wanted you.*)

The Voice was right again, as always. The master luthier had thrown her dad out into the world — the bastard son, the uninvited guest.

Guest. Andromache repeated the word to herself. She was Hecuba's guest, Priam's guest. They'd treated her better than her own grandfather would have. Despite all of her ingratitudes, her nightmares, her odd ways, they'd shown her every kindness. She was better off with them than she would have been with her grandfather.

(*They're better people than your grandfather was,*) the Voice pointed out.

Andromache couldn't argue.

(*But* you're *just like him.*)

Andromache wilted into the second floor alcove. The Voice was right about that, too. Oh, gods, it was right!

The Voice gave a nasty laugh, and Andromache started to cry. She was a monster, just like her grandfather. She was the kind of person who deserted her neighbors and accused good men of brutality. She didn't deserve to live here — if she deserved to live *at all*. If she stayed here in the alcove, curled up in a ball, maybe the family would forget about her. Maybe she could weep herself into oblivion before they thought to look for her...

Something soft and wet slurped its way across her face. Andromache blinked back her tears to see Muka's cloudy brown eyes staring at her.

"You keep finding me here," she whispered to the dog.

Muka sniffed her nose.

"Why do you want to? Why do you like me? I'm not from good people. Even Paris could see how bad my family was."

The dog once again licked her cheeks.

"I get it," sobbed Andromache, but somewhere deep inside, she was laughing. "I'm a never-ending source of salt."

Muka waved her tail.

"What time is it? Do you want to come upstairs and sleep a little?"

When she stood to climb the last flight of stairs, the dog followed her. Andromache opened the door to her room, crawled into bed, and cuddled under the blanket with Muka. She fell immediately into a deep, peaceful sleep. In her dreams, Cassandra was playing a song with rude lyrics and everyone was laughing — Hecuba, Priam, Paris, Auntie, Andromache's parents, and her childhood friend, Haliosh.

ℰↄ

ANDROMACHE AWOKE stiff and cranky. She'd forgotten to close the curtains, and a cold wind had blown in her window while she slept. Her muscles were aching as she struggled downstairs to the kitchen.

All she wanted was to eat a quick snack and go back to bed, but luck was against her. Paris was sitting there, looking as dour as she felt.

"Hermie," he snarled, ostentatiously massaging his upper arms. "Just the person I wanted to see."

"Why?"

From behind his stool, he pulled out his lute and shoved it roughly toward her. "You can hold it whenever you want," he said darkly. The words sounded practiced — forced, as though they weren't his own.

Andromache was too dumbfounded to react.

"Take the damn thing!" Paris glowered at her through slitted grey eyes.

"All right!" she cried.

As soon as the lute was in her hands, Paris sulked his way out of the kitchen.

Andromache stared at the instrument, raptly tracing the line of the bowl. It was made from a single piece of wood, just like all the lutes she'd held in her hands as a child.

She plucked a pair of strings and they made a familiar, discordant *twang*. *'Careful, Cricket!'* she could hear her dad saying. *'Don't treat the strings like a flower you're trying to pick.'*

Tears dotted the leather face of Paris's lute. *I'm not giving it back,* Andromache thought fiercely. *It's more mine than* Paris's. And that was true. Her grandfather had made it.

Her grandfather. Old coot though he might have been, he'd taught her dad the art of lute-making. And if her dad hadn't been disinherited, he might have married some Trojan woman and had Trojan children. The master luthier had made Andromache's life possible — he'd made *her* possible. He'd made this lute, as well. They were both his creations, in whatever twisted way. She was linked to the instrument.

Paris was not.

It's mine, thought Andromache, clutching the neck of the lute.

(*Oh, really? And what are you going to do with it?*) sneered the nasty Voice in her head.

Love it, she sneered back.

(*That's just what your dad would want — right?*)

Of course it is! He'd want his daughter to have it!

(*Why, so it could sit in a corner?*)

I could learn to play it!

(*You'd never sound like* Paris.)

Although cruel, the Voice was also — as always — right. Andromache could practice every night for a thousand years and never sound anything like Paris. He had a natural spark that she was lacking. *But it's mine*, she whimpered.

(*He told you that you could hold it whenever you want.*) The Voice laughed, knowing what cold comfort it offered.

For hours, Andromache sat in the kitchen, clutching the lute. She tried, from time to time, to pick out a song, but all she could bring forth from the strings were jangles. If her dad had been there, he would have winced — *Here, Cricket, let me show you*. She would have handed over the lute, and he would have delighted her by playing dozens of her favorite songs...

At last, she collapsed against the table in defeat. The only way she would ever hear the lute's music — her family's music — again was by giving it back to Paris.

Then I want to get it over with, she thought bitterly.

Paris, however, never came back to the kitchen. Andromache waited all afternoon for him, but in vain. When it came time for her lesson, she was forced to take the lute upstairs with her. It was far too precious to leave sitting around.

Hector was in the library, waiting for her. Right away, he noticed the instrument. "Yeuh — uh —" He made strumming motions with his fingers.

"Play?" asked Andromache. "No."

"Oh," he said.

"It's Paris's," she explained. "He let me look at it."

"Ah." Hector gave a single, grave nod.

"Now, I'm done. I want to give it back. But I can't find Paris." Andromache frowned. "Do you know where he is?"

Hector, too, frowned. "<u>The betroom? Fohr a sleep?</u>"

He was right: lazy Paris was probably napping in his bedroom. If so, he was beyond her reach. Sighing, she asked Hector, "<u>You're not — I mean — you weren't going to see him later, were you?</u>"

"<u>See</u> Paris?" he asked. "<u>Fohr to — to giff — the —</u>"

"<u>The lute,</u>" said Andromache. "<u>Would you do that?</u>"

Hector nodded. "<u>Yes. Ah can giff the *lute*.</u>"

Andromache handed the instrument to Hector, who took it very gently. He played the first few notes of a song, only to stop and grimace when he heard the music's tinny quality.

"It's all right," Andromache said sadly. "I wasn't the musician in my family, either."

Chapter 20

For several days after the lute incident, Paris kept his distance from Andromache. He limited his market purchases to food that could be eaten the same day and therefore didn't need to be put away. He ate dinner early, while she was still in lessons, and volatilized immediately afterward.

Andromache missed hearing him play, but she wasn't left alone in silence. Cassandra pounced on her to teach her how to play roodles, Troy's most beloved board game.

"It's the best game in the world!" Cassandra trilled. "You *have* to learn it — you're a Trojan, now, and everyone plays it, here. Even old men and women play it — even my *brother* plays it!"

Despite her ancestry and current home, Andromache didn't feel Trojan, but she liked roodles and took to it so quickly that she was soon beating Cassandra.

"You're a natural!" the girl squealed on their third night of tournaments. "I thought winter was going to be *so boring,* now that the soirees have stopped. We always hold them out on Demuchus's courtyard, and with the cold and rain, we can't have them there, right now. His uncle — Demuchus lives with his uncle because his parents aren't around, anymore, and — oh, honey!" Cassandra stopped when she saw tears in Andromache's eyes. "I'm sorry! I wasn't thinking!" She squeezed Andromache's hand.

"It's all right," said Andromache. She forced the tears back, although she still felt sorry for Demuchus, whoever he was. She knew what it was like to be an orphan. "Why — why can't you just meet inside Demuchus's house?"

187

Cassandra cleared her throat. "Well, his uncle doesn't like us meeting there. He says we're too noisy — can you *imagine*? He says we disrupt all the reading he has to do for council business. It's enough to make me crumple to dust on the spot, hearing that he *still* spends all his time reading, old as he is! Not that I don't love reading or learning new things, but honestly — by the time I have as much white hair as Demuchus's uncle, I would have expected to know everything already!"

"I roodle you," murmured Andromache, moving her game piece into position.

"Sprat!" swore Cassandra. "Here I was talking, and all that time you were planning a sneak attack! Maybe *you* should be an army commander, what with your ruses and strategies."

Andromache shuddered involuntarily. Any thought of armor and fighting led inevitably to visions of the monster she'd seen in her nightmares — hulking, blank-eyed, and covered in blood. She'd tried to stop having nightmares. When that failed, she'd reminded herself that Hector was a defender, not a raider. But despite everything, her instinctive fear still lingered, which made her feel guilty. The best way for her to cope was not to think about the army at all.

Cassandra stared at her, and for one horrible moment, Andromache thought the girl had guessed her secret feelings about Hector. But Cassandra said only, "You almost *look* like one, lately. An army commander, I mean."

"What?" Andromache scoffed.

"I don't know — when you came here, I wouldn't have thought that you could lift a bowl of soup over your head — not that that's a good idea for *anybody*! — but now, I'll bet you could lift a whole stack of bowls."

Andromache frowned. She saw no connection between commanders and soup bowls. "What do you mean?" she asked.

"Commanders have to be strong, honey!" Cassandra giggled. "I'd be a bad one, for sure! You can't tell my brother this — he'd flip over onto his head and spin circles, if he knew! — but one time, years ago, I went out to the shed and tried on his chest plate. Oh, gods, honey! Was I ever in a state! I got it on over my head, but I couldn't for the life of me lift it *off*! I thought I'd be stuck out there, trapped like a tortoise on its back, waiting for Hector to find me and yell at me — but just when I thought that, it made me realize, *'If I were on my back, I could slide out the bottom!'* And you know what, honey? It worked! But I'm getting off track, aren't I? What I meant before is, you look so much stronger than when you came here."

Whatever Cassandra's convoluted way of making the point, Andromache knew that the girl was right. Her arms weren't quite as reedy as before. Her stomach was firm, and her legs were strong. She was no Penthesilea and never would be, but now, at least, she wasn't a weakling, either — unlike that poor, younger version of Cassandra.

Andromache didn't like to think about armor, but at least the girl's story had put it in a silly light.

"Honey? What are you smiling about?"

"You really got stuck?" asked Andromache. The image of Cassandra squirming around on the floor was almost making her giggle.

"Yes! It was horrible. Oh, you won't tell my brother, will you?"

"I don't know…it might be funny to see him spin on his head."

"Please!"

"I won't tell," promised Andromache.

"Tell what, Hermie?"

She turned around. Paris was there, and apparently he was speaking to her again. "Tell everyone how badly you lost to me at roodles," she taunted.

Paris narrowed his eyes. "Game on, Hermie."

Chapter 21

The blanket Andromache had been faithfully weaving, a little each day, was looking worse than ever. Scarlet poppies on a field of brown had been a poor choice — every time she looked at the blanket, she thought of diseased skin.

There was, she realized, no point in finishing it. *She* wasn't about to sleep under the thing, and it would be unfair to ask anyone else to do so.

Defeated, she stuffed it deep inside her clothing chest — and, as soon as it was buried, she began to cry. All that beautiful thread, wasted! What would her mom have said about it? *'Oh, Ahndromahk…I'm so disappointed. What a disaster! Why didn't you listen to what I told you?'* Andromache cried at that thought, too.

By the end of the day, though — after lessons and dinner, roodles and music, and a run on the staircase — she reflected once more on her failed blanket and knew that she'd gotten her mom's reaction wrong: *'You need a simpler project, Little Cricket, that's all. You can try flowers again when you've been at it longer.'*

The next afternoon, Andromache began weaving a new cloth, this time in solid dark grey. It grew a little each day, plain but tightly woven and not at all lumpy. She was pleased with it and decided that when it was long enough, she would make it into a cloak. She had a cloak already, a rosy-pink one that Cassandra had grown too tall for, but she wanted something different. She didn't feel pink, at heart. Hecuba would surely have bought her a new one from the dressmaker's shop, but Andromache was determined to finish her own. Then, one day, she could try poppies again. They had been her mom's favorite flowers.

Chapter 22

During her first few months in Troy, Andromache had thought little about the city itself. She hardly felt a connection to the place, even though her dad had been born there.

Inside Hecuba and Priam's house, she had all the basic necessities plus a dog, a garden, a library, people to talk to when she craved company, and space when she didn't. There was even music to listen to and her recent success at weaving to take pride in. She'd had no real reason to think about the rest of Troy.

Lately, though, the house had started seeming too small. She blamed the weather. If gardening were more pleasant, she might not have felt so cramped, but the rain and cold winds often trapped her in the house. She began to wonder about the city around her. Her dad had told her that Troy was large and rich and full of people from different countries, but he'd never given her specifics about the city's size or layout.

Since Andromache wouldn't — *couldn't* — leave the house, she turned to the library for information on Troy. She learned that the city wasn't just large, but enormous — many, many times larger than Lyrnassa or Hurapi. Thousands of people lived in Troy, according to most of the texts, although one insisted on counting only the population of the upper citadel, who numbered at most in the hundreds.

Quickly, Andromache deduced why the text made this distinction: it had been written by an elitist. Within the walls of the upper citadel were Troy's largest houses, some verging on palatial, as well as the council's meeting hall, the main temple, and several gardens. Only the wealthiest families lived there — her hosts obviously among them — and this text seemed to argue that these were literally the only Trojans who counted.

Other texts, though, revealed the lower town sprawling beneath the citadel. This part of the city sounded livelier, with its abundant small dwellings, markets, and shops. She thought of the luthier's shop, which Paris said had been down in the lower town. But where, exactly? None of the texts mentioned a luthier or even a general musicians' quarter. Troy was plainly so immense that the luthier's shop got lost in it.

Andromache chewed her lip in frustration. What about other landmarks? Her dad had mentioned frequenting a tavern on the corner of his street. She scoured the texts for mention of it but found nothing. What she needed was a good map, or maybe different texts.

(*What you need is to go out and look for it*,) the snide little Voice suggested.

Andromache shuddered. She wouldn't — *couldn't!* — do that.

ဆာ

IN BETWEEN TEXTS, Andromache ran the back stairwell. Down, up. Down, up. Flat wooden stair after flat wooden stair. For variety, late one night, she strayed out to make laps around the banquet hall.

"Who's there?" someone demanded.

She nearly fainted.

"Hello?"

Oh! Andromache sighed in relief as she recognized Priam's voice. "It's me," she called back. "Andromache."

Priam, who had been in the kitchen, came out to the banquet hall. His hair was mussed, and he was wearing a long night robe. Andromache tried not to stare.

"I needed a midnight snack," he explained, adding sheepishly, "Please, don't tell my wife on me. She thinks it's bad for the digestion."

Andromache shook her head. "I won't tell."

"Are you here for a bite to eat, too, little one?"

"No, I — I couldn't sleep."

Priam nodded. "I have trouble with that, myself. I have to keep such strange hours, what with studying the stars, that I hardly know when to sleep anymore."

"Oh," said Andromache. She hadn't considered that problem, but it made sense.

"And you, little one — I imagine the winter weather has left you restless."

She nodded. "I wish I could spend more time out in the garden."

"I can understand that," said Priam. "Sometimes it feels like the warmth will never return, and the flowers will never bloom."

"At least the weeds aren't warm, right now, either," sighed Andromache.

Priam laughed. "How true! But that comfort plainly hasn't helped you to sleep. Have you tried reading? Sometimes that works for me."

Nodding once more, she said, "I can't always find the right text, though."

"There *are* a lot to sift through."

"How did you get so many of them?" she asked, thinking of her dad's four meager scrolls, what he'd gone through to get them, and how jealously he'd guarded them.

"Oh, dear," said Priam. "It's a rather long story...and so late. But since neither of us can sleep, I suppose I might as well tell you. Would you like to have something to drink in the kitchen? Wine, perhaps, or an herbal tisane?"

"Tisane, please."

In the kitchen, Priam set a pot of water over the hearth and began his story: "Years and years ago, there was a man from the far south — from the lands of the great cedar forests and the trading cities of Kinahna. Have you heard of them? There's Sydon, Ugarit, Tsyre....no? Well, the names matter little, as I'm not certain which one he called home. Family lore has it that he could speak all the languages of Kinahna. In any case, the man sailed all the way up here with some of his countrymen. It was quite a journey. Whether they were blown in by a storm, or got lost while out exploring, or were running from some sort of danger, I don't know, but the end result was that they stayed here.

"They must have liked the local culture. It *is* appealing, I must say. Did you know that Troy is different from all the surrounding states? We don't have a king. We used to, but the last one died without an heir, and the council took over in the interim, until such a time as a suitable replacement could be found." Priam winked and added, "We're still looking."

Andromache smiled.

"It might be a strange system, but it works for us. We're unique in many ways. Troy, as a trading port, has long been accepting of foreigners. You might not realize it, but Truvan is a mix of languages: Thracian languages from the north, Hittite and its relatives from the east, even some Achaean from across the Western Sea."

The Mudder language, Andromache thought with disdain. She was glad that Lukkan had no Mudder words.

"The name '*Truvan*' comes from an old name for this land, Taru-wa. No one is quite sure which language it comes from — perhaps an ancient form of Hittite. In any case, as I said, this region has always welcomed the contributions of other cultures. My family, in particular, has a history of embracing foreigners." Priam's dark eyes twinkled. "One of my ancestors married the man from Kinahna and brought all the richness of his new ideas into the family. He knew, for instance, about papyrus from the Nile lands. Are you familiar with papyrus, little one?"

Andromache shook her head.

"We have a few papyri in the library — thin material, off-white? Well, you can look for them sometime. As I said, there are only a few. They don't date back to the man from Kinahna, of course. Those would never have lasted this long! Papyri may be fine for the arid Nile lands, but up here, with our rainy season, the mildew eventually destroys them, no matter what I do." Priam shook his head.

"But I digress. I was telling you about my ancestor from Kinahna and the knowledge he brought with him. His country, for instance, had a writing system where each symbol stood for a different sound — '*rrr*' or '*sss*' or '*lll*.'"

"Like written Truvan," Andromache interrupted.

Nodding, Priam said, "Exactly. But much different than the reed-writing from the east, where symbols represented whole syllables, like '*ra*' or '*si*' or '*le*.' Those systems are harder to learn than those of my ancestor from Kinahna because they require a great many more symbols — every language, you see, has far fewer sounds than it does words or syllables. You could make up thousands of words with only a few dozen individual sounds. Does that make sense?"

Andromache nodded.

Priam went on: "Back in those days, there were some in Troy that read Hittite, but very few. My ancestor from Kinahna never made much headway, himself. He did, however, share his knowledge of writing systems from his homeland. He convinced his wife and other influential Trojans that a system with fewer symbols had its advantages. Eventually Hittite was adapted to those purposes — that's why Truvan and the eastern script look similar. Written Truvan uses some of the Hittite symbols, but for representing sounds, not syllables or words.

"Once it was a question of memorizing a few dozen symbols, rather than thousands, learning to read became more attractive. As I said, my family members were among the first to use this new script, and they prospered from it. Their endeavors — farming, shipping, trading — had always been successful, but once they started making detailed ledgers and inventories, their wealth increased many times over. They were able to keep track of everything, and no one was able to cheat them.

"Other families soon noticed and took up writing, too, and these families likewise grew richer. Troy grew richer. Wealth was the main advantage promised by my ancestor from Kinahna, and he'd been right."

Andromache nodded.

"Some of the other advantages of a simple writing system are harder to quantify," Priam went on. "One of my ancestor's younger sons was born with no head for business. He learned how to write Truvan, but instead of keeping ledgers, he jotted down observations of the natural world, stories about ancient heroes, and love poems to his mistresses — and of those, he had many, it seems."

Embarrassed, Andromache looked down.

Priam sighed. "Despite their tasteless origins, though, some of his poems are very beautiful indeed, and his observations astute. He traveled to the Hittite capital, Hattusas, and wrote a description of a Tumanan oyster shell mosaic that was so detailed, craftsmen here could read it, follow the instructions, and duplicate the mosaic to a remarkable degree — several other travelers went to verify. After that, jewelers, surgeons, weapons makers, and others began to write down their methods. They recorded their knowledge so that it would never be lost, even if the master craftsman himself were to die. Of course, writing down trade secrets has its risks, too…"

In saying that, Priam gave Andromache an odd look.

She glanced away. Troy was an enormous city, by her standards, but people there seemed to know each other's business. It was likely that Priam had heard about her altercation with Paris over the lute — and possible that he'd remembered a story from years ago, when an apprentice luthier had stolen his master's tools and scrolls and run away. She didn't want him to ask her about it. No matter how she felt about her dad, Priam might see him only as a thief. '*Thieves…vilest…criminals,*' she remembered from a text she'd once tried to read…

The old priest veered back to their original subject. "You were asking how my family wound up with so many texts in our library. As one of the inventors of written Truvan, my ancestor taught many others to write and, as payment, took a copy of whatever they produced — ledgers, chronicles, tales, poems, or methods of craftsmanship. Everything. That tradition remained in place for many years. Now, of course, most works are given to the council library, but my wife and I continue to purchase nearly every text that comes across our path."

"I didn't know the council had a library," said Andromache.

"Oh, yes!" said Priam. "A most wonderful library. You can't imagine all the ways it's helped us to govern. Long ago, if there was a dispute between two families — about where to pasture their sheep, for instance — whichever family won got to paint the story its own way. They might say, '*Those scoundrels tried to run us off our old family plot, but we repelled them.*' Perhaps the land had never belonged to them, but no one could prove them wrong. The victors could, in effect, rewrite history to suit their own needs.

"But things have changed. The city's libraries hold countless records. If a similar dispute were to take place nowadays, the council would consult descriptions of land-holdings. Perhaps the victor would be in the right; perhaps not. Either way, the council would have a fair and impartial way of deciding which family deserved the pasture land."

Priam gave a single firm nod. "Troy is rich in many respects, but the libraries are our most precious treasures. And such *fragile* treasures! — I worry about them, you know. There have been earthquakes in the city, and of course there's always the danger of a fire." He frowned. "As soon as I have time, I'd like to start making copies of all the texts. Store them somewhere safe."

The mention of fire made Andromache think of Lyrnassa, of the ribbons of smoke in the air above it.

"You're shivering, dear," said Priam. "Why don't you sit closer to the hearth?"

Andromache did as he suggested, but her shaking didn't stop until she thought about the good, strong Trojan walls. Thick, steep walls, rising from the plain. Another ring surrounding the citadel. Yet another protecting the house.

"That's better. And look — our water is ready. I'd forgotten all about it, windbag that I am." Priam smiled and poured a tisane for her.

Andromache smiled shyly in return. "Thank you," she said, accepting the cup. "For the story, too. I liked it."

Late autumn into winter

Chapter 23

"I saw Hippodamia today," Paris murmured slyly, as he and Andromache were unpacking his market baskets.

"So?" Andromache shrugged and tucked the late onions onto their shelf. She'd never met anyone in the city, outside of Paris's family and a few council members. It made no difference to her, whom Paris saw while out haggling for bread.

"I'm just surprised she's willing to show her face, that's all, after she broke that wine jar over the head of her husband's hussy. Oh — sorry," he said, seeing Andromache's shocked face. "Her husband's *paramour*."

"Where was she?" whispered Andromache. "I mean, when she broke the jar over the hussy's head?"

Paris grinned. "Her husband was throwing a lavish end-of-summer party, complete with music and a small troupe of actors. He was trying to establish their reputation as the most sophisticated family in Troy." Smirking, he added, "Hmm…I should ask him how that's going…"

"Well, I don't blame her!" cried Andromache. "She had every right to smash a jar. She should've smashed two — one for each of the cheaters."

"It was a waste, Hermie — a waste of good wine."

"You *would* say that!" Andromache glared at him.

Paris shrugged. They finished unpacking the baskets in silence, and then he sauntered to the doorway. "If anyone needs me, I'll be upstairs," he said, excusing himself.

You would _say that too_, Andromache huffed silently. _Lazy-bones. Napper!_ She imagined some woman smashing a jar over _his_ head and smiled at the satisfying picture. It occurred to her then that the wife in Paris's story must have used a thin-walled jar, because it had broken so easily. Had she grabbed the first thing at hand, or had she deliberately chosen a jar that wouldn't hurt the hussy? And what had happened afterward? Had the husband apologized? Had the wife stormed out in anger? Had the rest of the partygoers pulled out more jars of wine, hoping to forget the whole incident?

Her thoughts were interrupted by a rustle, followed by the sound of two women's voices: someone was with Hecuba in the banquet hall.

The cool weather had been bringing a whirlwind of neighbors, friends, and acquaintances into the warmth of Hecuba and Priam's house. They came at all hours of the day, alone or in pairs, to seek healing or advice or simply to visit.

Andromache had heard all their comings and goings for months, but she'd been too shy to meet anyone. If she happened to be on the first floor when visitors arrived, she would dart, deerlike, to the safety of the back stairs — even if it meant interrupting dinner or a roodles match with Cassandra. The family had long since accepted her reclusiveness.

In truth, however, Andromache was lonely. She'd been in Troy for five months now and had only talked to a handful of people — all from a single house. Before that, she'd spent a decade being shunned, in Lyrnassa. A deep, old part of her missed the hustle and bustle of life in her home village, Hurapi.

When she realized that there was no avoiding Hecuba's latest visitor, then, she wasn't wholly upset.

As the two women entered the kitchen, the guest, heavy and bejeweled, caught sight of Andromache and stared.

Nervously, Andromache whispered, "Can I offer you something to drink?"

The woman smiled. "So, Hecuba! After all your protestations, you've finally gotten yourself a servant. Very sensible. Although, you might want to feed her a little…they work better if they're not starving."

Hecuba silenced the woman with a single, withering look, which she then turned on Andromache.

Andromache shrank. Half expecting a jar to be smashed over her head, she squeezed her eyes shut. She remembered, too late, how Hecuba had yelled at her for brushing crumbs off the table. Apparently, Hecuba had once made a stand against having servants, and ever since, Troy's elite had been waiting for her to break down.

"Andromache eats what she likes," said Hecuba with great dignity. "And she is *not* a servant — she's tutoring my son, Hector, in Lukkan. Now, then." Her expression shifted from frosty to merely businesslike. "Do you want your poultice or not?"

℘

AFTER THAT FIRST, ill-fated interview, word of Hector's Lukkan tutor spread around Troy. Everyone was curious about her. Still, wary of Hecuba, none of the visitors dared admit that they'd come to meet Andromache. They asked instead for an unneeded herbal tonic or permission to consult a text they might just as easily have found in the council library. As long as other family members were around, the visitors smiled politely to Andromache, bade her hello, and welcomed her to Troy. That was it.

If the visitors happened to find Andromache alone at some point during their visit, though, they gave free rein to their curiosity. Most conversations went more or less the same way:

"So, you're tutoring Hector?"

"Yes."

"He's extraordinary," the visitors would say. "Famous all along the coast! They brag about him clear down in Thebe, as though he were theirs. Can't blame them, though. He's the greatest warrior Troy has ever seen — he's invincible in battle." Some visitors even claimed that Hector was *'favored by the gods'* or *'beloved in the light of the stars.'*

Eventually, they would invite Andromache's opinion: "What do *you* think about him?"

At a loss for what to say, Andromache would just nod. It was pointless explaining to these people that she tried *not* to think about her student dressed in armor, fighting.

They told her many stories about Hector's feats: he'd won a footrace by fifty strides, or he'd fended off five other warriors using only his shield, or he'd disarmed the mighty Thestor before the man could even let out his war cry.

"He's ambidextrous, you know," said one. "I didn't believe it until I went to the training field to watch him spar, but then I saw for myself. Have you been down there, yet?"

In fact, most of the visitors asked if she'd been down to the training field; Andromache always tried to suppress a shudder as she shook her head.

Sometimes, the visitors hadn't heard the full story of her whereabouts *that day* in Lyrnassa. They would assume that she'd been down on the beach during Hector's battle with the Mudders. "Oh, of course — how silly of me!" they would say. "You don't need to watch him practice — you've seen him in *action*."

Although that wasn't exactly true, Andromache had all but seen him in action. She'd seen him just after, and the image still haunted her...

A monster was looming over her — a hideous giant with hollow black eyes. Trails of ash blurred his bronze armor, and he was spattered with gore from head to toe. He reeked of smoke — of sweat — of blood —

Not a single drop of *his* blood had been spilled, though; all of it had come from the Mudders. No, Andromache didn't have to watch Hector practicing to know that he was Troy's greatest warrior — she'd seen proof. She *knew!* She just didn't like to think about it.

Her face crumpling, Andromache would then shake her head, leaving it up to the visitor to interpret that as *'No, I don't need to watch him practice'* or *'No, I haven't seen him in action.'* One of those who assumed she'd been on the beach, watching him, muttered, "Lucky!" That time, Andromache had purposefully spilled a full jar of water on herself so that she had an excuse to leave.

In every conversation, talk eventually turned from Hector's supremacy on the battlefield to his weakness in the field of languages. The Trojans knew every detail of his history and delighted in cataloguing the string of his past language tutors, none of whom had lasted more than a few months. According to some guests, Hector just didn't have the brains to learn another language; others warned that he was bright enough but hostile toward other cultures. All agreed that Andromache wouldn't last with him much longer than the other tutors had.

"How long have you been here?" the visitors would ask.

"Five months," she would reply.

"Ah," they would say. "And how are things going?"

"Very well," she would say stiffly, in defense of both herself and her student. It was no lie — Lukkan lessons *were* going well.

Even so, the guests would then give her a look of knowing pity and bid her a pointed farewell.

Andromache wished she had a jar to smash over each of their heads. Five months ago, the last thing she'd wanted was to meet Hector in the library every afternoon. Now, she couldn't imagine life without that part of her day. She liked speaking Lukkan, and she was in a good place with Hector. She was having so few Raider nightmares that she could, for the most part, think of him as a normal person.

In fact, she seldom thought about him at all, unless she was with him or preparing for lessons. He'd become part of the background to her day — an important part, to be sure, but nothing to worry or obsess about. There had been no calamities, no incidents, no further talk of weddings or Penthesilea.

Andromache told herself not to listen to the nosy neighbors. They might be right about Hector's skill as a warrior, but they were wrong about languages, or at least about Lukkan. Hector didn't act like he wanted to stop taking lessons. He'd never been anything but kind, hardworking, and funny. He'd done everything she asked of him and often more. He had his idiosyncrasies, but he'd picked up hundreds of words and understood far more than he could say. Even his accent was improving. He seemed to like Lukkan...

Of course, Andromache knew that he didn't *really* like it — that he was only being polite — that he'd only agreed to the lessons to keep a poor, orphaned girl from crying herself to oblivion. Furthermore, she understood by now that he worked hard at Lukkan because he worked hard at everything. The pots were never brighter than when Hector had scoured them, the Chute never tidier than when he'd been ordered to clean it, but hard work didn't mean that he liked those jobs. Anything that he felt obligated to do, he did well, and he felt obligated to take Lukkan lessons.

(*For now,*) sneered the Voice. (*Those Taruishans know him better than you do. They've known him his whole life. Paris said the same thing they did, and don't you think he knows his own brother? Besides, why would he want to take lessons long-term? It's not like they're useful to him…*)

Andromache began to pick at her cuticles. It was true, she didn't know Hector very well. What if the Voice — and the visitors — were right after all?

Don't listen to any of them! she told herself firmly. The visitors would be easy enough to avoid — she would just have to start running upstairs again whenever guests came to the house. She would have loved to flee the Voice, too, but it was inescapable.

Chapter 24

The courtyard stones were silver in the light of the midnight stars. As Andromache hung her head out the window, a chilly breeze blew down the back of her dress. Shivering, she wrapped her cloak more tightly around herself and tried to forget the latest visitor's pointed, ottery face.

Andromache had been too slow to escape the Otter. With a feeling of dread, she'd begun talking to the woman, expecting the usual line of conversation. The Otter, though, was different. She'd probed and prodded uncomfortably into Andromache's past, but she hadn't mentioned Hector's military prowess. Not once. Andromache was just beginning to relax when the Otter had frowned and said something even worse:

'No offense to you, dearie, but what was Hecuba thinking, adding Lukkan lessons to Hector's regimen? When's the poor boy supposed to sleep?'

The Otter, who plainly cared about Hector, was worried about him wearing himself into the ground: *'When's the poor boy supposed to sleep?'*

<u>*Don't listen to that woman. She's crazy*</u>, Andromache had told herself. But the truth was, she knew nothing of Hector's sleeping patterns. She'd never even imagined him with his eyes closed, much less lying on his back. What if he *wasn't* sleeping enough? What if he *did* wear out?

And, if he did, what would that mean for *her*? If he was running himself into the ground, he would have to drop something, wouldn't he? That *'something'* wasn't likely to be overseeing the stables, or running combat practice, or listening to patrol reports. No, before any of those, Hector would drop Lukkan lessons, and Andromache would be the one to suffer for it. She wouldn't have to fear homelessness — out of compassion, Hecuba and Priam would probably let her stay. Instead, her problem would be boredom. Even *with* lessons, she'd been restless, of late.

That evening, long after the Otter had left, Andromache sat near her bedroom window, looking out. She watched the sky over the sea change from red, to orange, to the deepest of blues. As stars popped out in speckles and clusters, she studied the reflections their light made in the spring's flowing water. She spat down onto the courtyard, wondering if she would be able to see a reflection in that water, too. She couldn't. She shifted from one hip to the other, one elbow to the other.

Night sounds came with the stars. Weird little birds flapped through the air, their movements quick and frantic. The voices of tavern-bound revelers carried up from the lower part of the city, growing louder and louder as midnight approached. Were they fighting or just singing songs?

As she listened more closely to the voices, Andromache almost missed the faint scuff of sandals on the courtyard — almost. Hastily, she looked downward. It was *him*. She recognized Hector's walk, his dark hair, his plain tunic. Unaware that he was being watched, he sat down on the wall of the spring, took a drink, and scrubbed his feet before disappearing into his room across the courtyard.

Andromache stared at the place where he'd just been. The night was half over. When morning came, in a few short hours, he would likely be the first person out of the house. *The Otter was right*, she thought in dismay. *He's hardly sleeping at all!*

How long had this been going on? Since her arrival in Troy? Since he'd been promoted to commander and simultaneously started Lukkan lessons? Had he been limping by on half-rations of sleep for the past five months, or was this some sort of fluke?

Hoping for the latter, Andromache spent the next few evenings spying on Hector. Each night, he came home at midnight or later, stopped at the spring, and then went to his room. Each morning, he was gone long before she went downstairs.

Each afternoon in the library, the shadows under his eyes looked deeper and greyer.

AFTER A WEEK of standing vigil, exhaustion began to show on Andromache's face, too. Concerned, Hecuba came up to see her at bedtime. "Drink this, dear," she said, handing over a cup.

Andromache gulped down the liquid, but immediately, she gagged. "It tastes like Muka's breath!"

"Hector always said '*armpit*,'" Hecuba clucked. "The things you children say, as though I mix these tonics purely to torment you! The fact is, you need it. You haven't looked right, these past few days. Are you ill?"

Andromache shook her head.

"Then what's the matter?"

Normally, Andromache would have hedged, but her defenses were low. All she wanted was to know what was in store for her, and Hecuba might be able to tell her. "It — it's about your son," she murmured.

Hecuba stiffened. "Which one?"

"Hector."

Sighing, the woman asked, "What's he done? Is he giving you grief? Skipping out on lessons?"

"No," Andromache assured her. "He's doing fine. It's just — people have been talking about his work load, and how he must not be sleeping, so I was wondering —"

"Who *is* this '*people*?'" Hecuba asked suspiciously.

"I — I don't know — a neighbor, I guess. I'm sorry. I forget her name." Andromache didn't want to add that the woman had looked like an otter.

"Well! I don't suppose it's *the neighbors'* business whether or not he's sleeping! Hmph! Nosy old she-buzzards, using a guest to meddle in the affairs of *my* family!" Hecuba sniffed. "I can only guess who said *that* — her with her ancient and juvenile fancy for *my* husband, playing at being *my* son's mother!"

Andromache's eyes widened in alarm. "I didn't mean to —"

But the woman stormed on. "Of course you didn't! This has nothing to do with *you!* And if *certain people* continue to harangue you, I'll thank you to tell them that Hector has always been able to sort out his sleeping schedule well enough on his own, without their input."

Mutely, Andromache nodded. She was sorry she'd broached the subject.

Hecuba sighed, looking calmer but grave. "Although, just between you and me, I must admit the situation with Laoganus *is* a trying one for Hector."

"Laoganus?"

"The other commander — formerly my son's superior."

"Oh, that's right." Andromache furrowed her brow. "What situation?"

"I know you were feverish the night you arrived, but surely you heard all the insults my son was bellowing!"

'You ponderous old ass,' thought Andromache, dredging up one of the phrases from that night. *'Are you too old and fat?'* "I remember," she said — although she hadn't realized at the time whom Hector was addressing.

Hecuba primly tightened her lips. "Hector's mouth is foul on a good day, but that night he outdid himself. I suppose he thought there was nothing to lose. Now, of course, it's all come back to hit him on the nose. He's had a lot of hasty diplomacy to perform with his co-commander, I imagine. Perhaps this will teach him to watch his language in the first place," she concluded with grim satisfaction.

Andromache nodded, even though she was skeptical. The words, *'Lahfe ees a bakhoff gotsheet,'* ran through her mind.

"Yes, placating Laoganus has been a challenge for my son." Hecuba sighed again and lowered her voice. "And everyone knows that Troy herself — Laoganus's responsibility — is most unlikely to be attacked. Hector was given the harder assignment, to say nothing of the soldiers he's now in charge of! Every Trojan man has to serve at least a few years in the army, and some women choose to, which means that there are people of every temperament doing jobs of all kinds. When the army was split, the council decided to siphon off all the hot-heads and place them with Hector, on the assumption that he, as the very worst of them, would be the only one able to keep them in check. Not that it's easy, even for him."

Andromache tried to keep her face from falling as Hecuba confirmed the Otter's fears: Hector was exhausting himself, after all, and sooner or later he would drop Lukkan lessons.

Hecuba patted her hand. "Don't look like that, dear. It's sweet of you to worry about him, but things are settling down. Nothing is as hectic as right after that debacle at Lyrnassa, and —" Hecuba broke off abruptly as Andromache's eyes filled with tears. "I'm sorry, dear," she said softly. "I shouldn't have —"

"Why did they come?" asked Andromache.

"My son's patrol? They were —"

"Not them," Andromache interrupted. "The invaders. What did they want?"

Her Lukkan village of Hurapi had been raided many times. Ships had landed on the shore and men had stormed up, taking animals, grain, fine crafts — whatever they could get their hands on. No one had ever raided Lyrnassa, though, not in all the time Andromache had lived there with Auntie. That was the reason she'd never wanted to leave, despite not feeling welcome there. Then, on *that day*, everything had changed…

Hecuba hesitated. "It's up for debate why exactly they chose your village," she said carefully. "For the past several years, now, towns up and down the coast have seen these Mudder sorties."

"So, it *was* Mudders who attacked us!" Andromache exclaimed. What Cassandra had told her was true.

Hecuba's cheeks flamed. "Please, Andromache — I beg you *never* to tell my daughter that I said that word! She'll think I condone such language, and I do *not*. Not even in reference to those people who have willingly become our enemies, rather than remaining our partners in trade."

"I won't tell her," Andromache promised.

"Thank you, dear." Hecuba sighed in relief. "Let me start over. For a while, now, the Achaeans have been coming to the area, making small raids. There doesn't seem to be any greater plan behind the attacks. However, Lyrnassa is the first village within the Trojan protectorate to be raided, so some say the Achaeans were testing how we would respond. Others say the Achaeans had no idea about the relationship."

Andromache thought of Hector, Penthesilea, and the rest of the patrol, galloping down the hill toward Lyrnassa, their armor flashing in the sun. "I guess they found out," she said softly. A tear rolled down each cheek.

"Oh, dear girl," murmured Hecuba, slipping an arm around Andromache. "That your poor village should have suffered! You can't imagine how terrible we all feel — my son, most of all."

"For *what?*" Andromache frowned. Why would Hector feel terrible? Lyrnassa may have suffered — it may have burned — but at least Hector had *tried* to help. He'd run toward the invaders, not away from them like *she* had.

"For not getting there sooner. For not anticipating that Lyrnassa would be a target. He thought that of the towns in his sector, invaders would most likely strike Thebe, what with the ships that stop there to take on fresh water. He blames himself for the destruction of Lyrnassa." Hecuba sighed. "As though anyone can see the future or foretell the wicked plans of men."

"Oh," said Andromache. Her stomach was feeling strangely cold.

Hecuba frowned, first at Andromache, then at the cup she was still holding. "I have to say, dear, the tonic doesn't seem to have done you much good. Perhaps I should bring you something stronger?"

Andromache shook her head. "No — I just need to sleep," she murmured.

"All right." Hecuba worriedly kissed her forehead. "If you change your mind, I'll be in the kitchen for a while."

Even once Andromache was alone, though, she didn't lie down. She continued to sit on the edge of the bed, staring at her hands and mulling over everything that Hecuba had told her. No matter how she twisted the pieces, they only fit together one way.

He blames himself...he blames himself...

Hector had always been kind to her. His patience had been boundless, through all of her fevers, tears, insults, and cringing. He'd worked hard at Lukkan, never questioning her choices but learning whatever she asked him to learn. He'd set aside time each day to sit in the library with her — time he might better have spent fulfilling his new duties, placating his old boss, wrangling his subordinates, or sleeping. He'd even run errands for her, shuttling caterpillars and lutes around the city.

Now, she knew why. Hector was racked by guilt — ravaged by guilt — sodden with guilt — caked in guilt from the soles of his well-scrubbed feet to the top of his head. Even if some of the villagers had escaped, Lyrnassa was gone. Destroyed. The houses were burned, the animals scattered.

No wonder he'd refused her *'Thank you'* for defending the village! He didn't believe he deserved gratitude. He'd come too late to save Lyrnassa, and he couldn't bring it back. The most he could do was salvage one Lyrnassan.

'Give the poor girl something to do, so she doesn't cry herself to oblivion…' The words from the hallway all those months ago came echoing back to Andromache. Hector had indeed been out there with Hecuba — had indeed been convinced to help save poor Andromache —

Oh, she was livid! She'd been able to stomach the thought of him studying Lukkan with her out of pity. Pity at least meant that he looked at her and saw a *person*, one who needed help. Guilt, on the other hand, reduced her to a reflection of his own failure.

As for dropping Lukkan, she could see now that he never would, not even if he hated foreign cultures, as some of the guests had said — not even if he wore himself out to stay with it. Andromache was his cause. If, in the process of rehabilitating her, he made himself miserable, so much the better! Suffering would only help him atone for his failings. She was a sharp-edged pebble he left in his sandal to remind himself of where he'd been.

Tears of anger and humiliation stung her eyes.

Sensing Andromache's desolation, Muka tried to leap up onto the bed beside her. She missed.

"No!" cried Andromache. Her world was falling apart, and now her dog was dying — her *one true friend* was dying!

Muka wagged her tail, looking bemused but unharmed. She pawed at the ground, circled three times, and lay down.

Andromache sank down beside her, weeping with relief. "You're getting too old to jump onto the bed," she scolded. The plumy tail waved just a little. "You'll have to be more careful. I need you, Muka — now, more than ever. I love you, girl…"

Chapter 25

The next morning, Andromache ached all over from having slept on the floor. Her first thought was how soft she'd become, a slave to her cushy bed. How many nights had she slept on the hard earth of Lyrnassa without even noticing it? First she'd lost her tolerance for cold, now for sleeping on hard surfaces. She was becoming citified.

Andromache unwound herself from Muka, helped the dog onto the bed, and climbed in right beside her. There, the soreness drained from her, leaving her to think of other things besides physical discomfort.

Hector. She hated him. Oh, how she *hated* him! She hated him as much as she'd ever feared him — more, even!

Andromache had lost everything, in her short life — her childhood home, her parents, her Auntie, Lyrnassa. She'd been drowning, when she first arrived in Troy. She'd had nothing and been nothing. Just when she thought she was finally breaking the surface, with a safe home, a loving dog, kind hosts, and the self-respect of a worthwhile job, Hector had plunged her back into the depths of nothingness. She was no more than a tool he was using to restore his damaged pride...to free himself from guilt. *Well, screw that — screw him! Screw him!* she thought.

She wouldn't go to lessons, today! Instead, she would lie there in comfort while Hector fidgeted and squirmed, denied the release of penance. The thought made her smile an icy smile — until she imagined what his mother would say in response: *'She what? She refused to give you your lesson? I see. Well, then she can find some other house to haunt, if she's not going to do her job.'*

Andromache quailed, thinking back to the old saying she'd shared with Cassandra — *The future is stable like a rotten roof.* Here, in this house, Lukkan lessons with Hector were her rotten roof. Hecuba and Priam wouldn't evict her if Hector was the one to quit, but *her* quitting might enrage them.

'I'm better, now,' she imagined telling them. *'I won't cry myself to oblivion, I promise. I won't bring you the shame of losing a guest.'*

But she feared that wouldn't be enough for them. Hecuba had been adamant about the lessons. They weren't just about Andromache's well-being, she remembered now, but also about Hector's. Hecuba was tired of the black mark on her son's reputation, tired of the mockery heaped on him for his failure to learn another language. She was tired of feeling humiliated by him and didn't care whether he studied Lukkan out of interest, pity or guilt — only that he was making progress. If Andromache sulked in her room today, her hosts might no longer want her as their guest. They might make her leave forever. And then what?

'You can stay at my place, if you want to,' the warrior woman, Penthesilea, had told her many months ago, but Andromache felt less desire than ever to leave her current house. No — she *wanted* to stay! It was here that she'd dug in the garden — read texts — started weaving again — cuddled Muka — shared clothes with Cassandra — chatted with Priam and Hecuba — bickered with Paris — listened to his lute. Her *family's* lute! She couldn't imagine living anywhere else.

Andromache pressed her face to Muka's fur and wept. How she hated Hector, for ruining everything!

℘

"EET EES COLE," said Hector, shivering as he gestured toward the courtyard.

"Do you mean '*cool*' or '*cold*'?" Andromache enunciated both words carefully. Her tone was neither cool nor cold, but glacial.

Hector frowned, unsure. "Zey ees different?"

"Ugh — I can't understand what you're saying, with that stupid thing in your mouth," snapped Andromache, pointing at his mint sprig. "Either spit it out or swallow it."

"Oh." Hector removed the stem and wound it around his finger. "I said, <u>zey ees different</u>?"

"I guess it wasn't the mint after all," she muttered. "Yes, '<u>*zey ees different*</u>.'"

Andromache had long since gotten used to Hector's accent. She'd never commented on it, let alone mocked it, and she'd always been gentle in her corrections. She knew that, as his teacher, ridiculing him was the meanest, most detestable thing she could do.

She no longer cared. If he was going to make her miserable, then he deserved to be miserable, too.

That day, and the next, and the next, Andromache said whatever nasty comments came to mind. If Hector made a mistake, she bluntly told him so. If he mispronounced a word, she belittled him for it. She spoke far too quickly for him to understand, used words she knew he didn't know, and then berated him when he asked her to clarify.

None of it made her feel any better.

The worst part was that he never got angry. A normal person in his position would have exploded, but Hector never lost patience, never failed to treat her with courtesy, never complained, never skipped a day. Under her cruelty, he remained gallingly serene.

As the week wore on, Andromache grew despondent. If she'd had any doubt that Hector's studies were motivated by guilt, that doubt was now gone. When she'd seemed to be offended by dirt, he'd washed his hands raw to placate her. Now, he was feeding off her abuse as another form of penance — there was no other reason that he would have put up with it.

Her plan to make him suffer was only giving him what he wanted. How she *hated* him!

AFTER SEVERAL NIGHTS in a row of staying up late, hating Hector, Andromache arrived at the library to find it empty. *Ugh!* she thought irritably. *Why does he have to be late? Let's get this stupid lesson over with!*

But Hector didn't come.

Andromache squinted at the door, wondering if she'd finally driven him away by skipping back and forth between present and past time words, the day before. *He didn't know whether he was do-ing or done*, she remembered. *That's what finally broke him.* And since *he* was the no-show, his parents wouldn't evict her. She would be able to stay!

Thinking that she heard a sound at the door, Andromache turned around. There was no one there. *I won! He gave up, and I still get to stay here.* She wanted to feel smug — triumphant — but instead, she felt empty and tired. There was no reason not to rest her head against the table…

She was walking down a dark alley. There was no way out, and it was time to go. She was supposed to meet Auntie, and if she didn't, Auntie would get mad and tear out all her garden plants. She couldn't let that hap-pen! Just then, she saw a wooden stairway. Climb it, she told herself. One step — squish! It wasn't wood, after all — it was thick mud, or gruel. Her leg sank in up to the thigh. Just get up the stairs! Auntie's waiting! Other foot — squish! Now what was she supposed to do with her first foot?

'Leave it,' called a voice. So she went on, leaving her leg behind.

'Hay-lo? Hay-lo?' it called to her, softly at first, then more urgently: 'Ahndromahk? Hay-lo?'

"Ahndromahk?"

"Euh!" She awoke with a start, eyes wild, head snapping up from the library table.

"You sleep?"

"Ye-ye-yes," she stammered, trying to catch her breath.

"You ahre all rahght?"

She nodded.

"You — you see — stahff — in — in the head?" Hector asked carefully.

"Stuff in the head? Oh — dreaming. I guess I was."

"You — treaming — what?"

Andromache's head was still thick with sleep. She forgot all about her anger toward Hector and began describing the dream for him — slowly, so that he could understand. When she got to '*staircase*,' she marched her middle and index fingers at a slant through the air, as though they were climbing steps.

He laughed.

"<u>What</u>?" she asked. "<u>You think my fingers are funny</u>?"

"<u>No. The treamings. They ahre fahnny.</u>" He laughed again. "<u>I walk. I am all rahght</u>..." His own fingers marched through the air with an unmistakable kick to their imaginary heels. "...<u>then, oh, no!</u>" His hand sank downward, fingers thrashing in helpless despair. They landed in a heap on the floor before sailing back to the tabletop in a final grand apotheosis. It all looked ridiculous — as ridiculous as her nightmare now sounded.

Andromache smiled. She couldn't help herself, although she regretted it instantly — she was, as she now remembered, supposed to be hating Hector.

Hector smiled back. He brushed the dust off his hands, then coughed as it flew back in his face. "<u>Dihrts</u>," he said, grimacing. "<u>They haff a bad tasty.</u>" He bent to fumble in his pocket.

Andromache's smile faded. It was so unfair! She didn't *really* hate Hector. In all honesty, she *liked* him. She thought he might have liked her, too, if he wasn't weighed down by guilt — if they just hadn't met *that day*. In another reality, they might have been friends...

"<u>It is all rahght</u>?" he asked, holding a sprig of mint near his lips.

Andromache noticed his more polished accent and winced. What had she *done*, this past week? Maybe he *was* using her, but at least he'd never been cruel. What was more, if not for him, she wouldn't be speaking Lukkan every day — not unless she wanted to leave the house. What did it matter, *why* he was doing it? She would be wiser just to enjoy it for what it was. "<u>Yes</u>, Hector," she murmured. "<u>Have all the mint you want.</u>"

"<u>Meeent</u>," said Hector, in a thick accent. Very thick. Ludicrously thick, it seemed...

When Andromache peered up at him, she saw that his eyes were dancing. "<u>Meeent</u>," she offered timidly.

"<u>Meeeeeeent!</u>" Hector laughed and laughed, and it felt good to hear him laughing again.

Mid-winter into late winter

Chapter 26

"Oh, honey! I just heard the strangest rumor!"

Andromache groaned. "What now?"

"This one makes the others look tame!"

"Tell me! What is it?"

"That you're a sea goddess in human form, testing the Trojans' piety!" Cassandra giggled.

Andromache groaned again. A sea goddess? She'd already been called the daughter of a wealthy pirate, being held for ransom — an orphaned princess from a foreign land, fleeing hordes of dangerous cousins — a prophet — a spy. Now, she was a sea goddess?

Another month had passed since her entry into Trojan society, and the neighbors were at odds to explain why Hector was still taking lessons from her. They'd all heard that she was from a small village near Thebe, and that she spoke Lukkan, but few accepted that as the whole story. There had to be a deeper reason why people like Priam and Hecuba would take in a backwater villager and ask her to tutor their son.

When Cassandra had brought home the first rumor, Andromache had asked her not to deny it. She'd told Cassandra she was curious to see what else they would come up with, which was true. Secretly, she also hoped the rumors would distract people from wondering about her real past. She didn't want to talk with anyone about *that day* in Lyrnassa — nor did she want to be connected to the master luthier. *That* story hadn't surfaced yet, so if Priam had deduced her family history, he hadn't told anyone. The speculations about her had all been absurd.

Cassandra, who loved the fun of the rumors, had cheerfully agreed not to dispute them.

"So, honey — I mean, O Sacred One!" Cassandra giggled. "What do you think about all this? Are you going to whip up a storm to drown us, or do we get a pass?"

"Well, I don't know…maybe you can appease me by dumping a thousand jars of your best wine off the next ship to sail out of Troy."

Cassandra whooped with laughter. "I said a sea goddess, not a wine nymph!"

"Girls!" barked Hecuba. "This is no time for revelry! Have you forgotten about the wedding?"

The two young women sobered.

"No, Mom, of course not," murmured Cassandra.

"Wedding?" asked Andromache, a queasy feeling in her stomach. Had Penthesilea come back to Troy?

Hecuba's eyes bulged. "What else do you think that couple was here for, yesterday — a tour of the gardens?"

"What couple?" asked Andromache.

"She was in lessons, Mom," Cassandra said hastily.

"Oh." Hecuba looked mollified. "Well — then I see why you wouldn't have known. But that reminds me, where on earth have those boys gone? I swear, they were right behind me!" She hustled back out of the kitchen, toward the entry hall.

"Mom freaks out about weddings," whispered Cassandra. "They make her crazy! There's so much to do, to get ready for them."

Andromache nodded. Her stomach stopped churning. Her teaching post was safe, for now. The bridal couple *couldn't* be Penthesilea and Hector — not if Andromache had been in Lukkan lessons when they came. And now that she thought about it, surely Cassandra or Hecuba would have said *something*, if Hector were about to get married! "What *was* the couple doing, here?" she asked Cassandra.

"Practicing," the girl explained. "Dad always has them run through the ceremony once or twice, so none of the rituals catch them off guard. There's nothing worse than a blind-sided bride! Well, I mean, there *are* worse things, of course. Lots of them! We both know that — oh, not that I'm suggesting *you* know in particular, honey, I —" Cassandra's cheeks reddened.

"It's all right," soothed Andromache. "Really — I know what you mean."

"Well, anyway, I think Mom feels a little blind-sided by this wedding — such a warm day, in winter, with the stars in such auspicious alignments! Days like this are rare, honey — you can't expect them, and when they come, you have to pounce on them. Dad says there's no better time for a ceremony."

"Do you know the couple?"

"Oh, yes." Cassandra made a face. "I like the bride, but the groom isn't very nice. At least, he didn't used to be. When I was little, he spit on *my* almond cake! Can you believe it? We were both here, at a wedding, in fact — now, I don't remember whose wedding it was, but I do remember that he spit on *my* cake, thinking it would make me give it to him." Cassandra's expression turned stubborn.

"Cassandra!" cried Andromache. "Tell me you didn't eat it!"

"I wanted to," said the girl. "Just to see the look on his face. But I was too grossed out...so I gave it to Muka, instead."

"Thank goodness!"

"Thank goodness, indeed!" echoed Hecuba, from the kitchen doorway. "The five of us are finally all here — no thanks to *you*," she said sharply to her sons, who were a few steps behind her, one cowed, the other disgruntled. "I thought you'd followed me into the house!"

"I *told* you," said Hector. "I saw someone I needed to talk to — someone from work."

"Your most important *work* today is to support your father!"

"Oh, I forgot...most days I do nothing useful for him or for anyone else in Troy," muttered Hector.

Hecuba pretended not to hear him. "In any case, we'll be losing the light soon enough, so you'd better start by putting out the lamps. Go, all of you! Move, I say!"

In a flurry of activity, strings of garland were hung, lamps were set out, and foods of every kind were piled onto tables in the banquet hall. Hecuba marched around, inspecting, adjusting, and perfecting. Nothing satisfied her.

"Cassandra! Where *have* you gone with the broom? Ants have invaded our courtyard — *ants!*"

"Coming, Mom."

"Hurry! Ants, in winter! Now I've seen it all! And Paris — how is the cup coming along? Simmering stars! What have you been polishing it with, grime? *This* is the cup the couple is supposed to drink from during the ceremony? Is a simple scrap of sanctity too much to ask, these days? Now, here's a clean rag. Start over, and keep going until you can see your reflection in it!"

"As long as I don't have to see my reflection in it during the ceremony," muttered Paris. "I'd rather die than marry that apple-faced bride."

"Don't be so mean!" Cassandra cried out in defense of her friend. "You're just mad because Dad won't let you play the wedding song. It serves you right, after what you did last time!"

"Oh, stuff it, Songbird!"

"Both of you, to your tasks!" ordered Hecuba. "And *you!*" She eyed her eldest son with disfavor. "You're a grub! Just look at your clothes!"

"They're clean," said Hector, shrugging. "I scrubbed them yesterday."

Andromache knew that he was telling the truth. She'd been out on the courtyard the evening before, taking advantage of the warm spell to spend extra time with her plants. Across the way, she'd seen Hector with a wash tub, attacking his dirty clothes as he would his archenemy.

"They're *stained!*" cried his mother.

"*Old* stains," said Hector, as though this news would mollify her.

Andromache understood the distinction he was making. She knew from their earliest meetings that he disliked having fresh dirt on his clothes. Spots that survived the laundering process, however, didn't seem to faze him.

Judging by Hecuba's scowl, the woman loathed stains of any kind. "Well, there's no time to change, now," she seethed. "I need you to set out the wine jars. And you, Andromache, would you please help Cassandra arrange the fruit? She's just not quite — oh no, girls, not like *that!* It needs to be *artful.* Here, try adding some more dried apricots."

"Like that?"

"No! Overlap them a bit. Oh, *honestly,* girls!"

Andromache tried to follow Hecuba's advice, but her tray looked far from artful. In frustration, she gave all her apricots to Cassandra. "You try," she said. "No matter what I do, it still just — *sucks!*"

Everyone fell silent, except for Paris, who made a choking sound.

"What did you say?" gasped Hecuba, looking scandalized.

Andromache's face turned purple.

"Where did you learn that kind of language?" Hecuba demanded. "No, never mind. I have two guesses." She glared at each of her sons in turn.

Paris's mouth was practically turning inside-out in his effort not to laugh. Meanwhile, Hector looked ill.

Andromache turned away from the group. Tears were welling in her eyes. Soon, she would no longer be able to hold them back, and on top of everything else, the family would see her weeping again. It was too much. She fled from the room.

"Oh, for goodness' sake!" sighed Hecuba. "Boys, stay where you are! I think you've done quite enough, and anyway, I still need your help with the wine. We can *chat* while we work. Cassandra, you run upstairs and check on her."

Andromache doubled her pace. She'd run many thousands of flights of stairs by that point, and Cassandra had no hope of catching her. She was safely curled up on her bed before the girl called out to her.

"Honey? Can I come in?"

"I guess," mumbled Andromache.

Cassandra slipped into the room and sat down beside Andromache. "Are you all right?" she asked.

"I'm fine."

"Mom sent me up to check on you..."

Andromache sniffled. "How bad *was* what I said?"

"Not that bad," Cassandra assured her. "Kids say it all the time, around each other. Adults don't like it — I'm not sure why. I guess it's just kind of slangy for a wedding — or a party — or the neighbor's house — or most places where adults go, other than taverns, where you can say pretty much anything you want. Not that I'd know! I'm too young to go to *those*, of course, but I've heard plenty about them from —"

"Can you tell your mom I'm sorry, for me?" Andromache interrupted.

"Oh, no! You have nothing to be sorry for. It wasn't *your* fault! And anyway, you're coming down, aren't you?"

Andromache shook her head. "I'm tired…and my stomach hurts."

"Oh," said Cassandra. "Well, all right then, I'll tell her. But she's not mad at *you*, honey, she's —"

"You should go," Andromache said softly. "The guests are coming soon, aren't they?"

Cassandra gave her a hug. "I hope your stomach feels better," she whispered.

"Thank you."

With a backward glance or two, the girl left.

A short while later, Andromache heard the sound of voices on the courtyard. Two or three, then eight or ten, then a multitude. The guests had arrived. She wondered bitterly if they were enjoying the dried fruit arrangements.

From down on the courtyard, there came the soft strumming of a stringed instrument.

They must be getting started, thought Andromache. In spite of everything, she was curious about the wedding ceremony. She'd never seen one before. Back in the Lukka lands, there were no rituals, no ceremonies, no hunting for auspicious dates. People just decided to be married, and then they were. The families usually had a meal together to celebrate, but that was the extent of things. *I could watch from the library porch. No one would know I'm there.*

By the time Andromache reached the library, the ceremony had already started. The bride and groom were standing together, facing Priam. Both wore robes of blue — the loveliest, warmest, deepest blue Andromache had ever seen. During the ceremony, they chanted, sipped spring water, and crowned each other with circlets made of leaves. Priam gave several long orations. Andromache watched everything with interest, but what charmed her most were the couple's evening-blue robes.

ॐ

WINTER RETURNED THE NEXT DAY, after the brief warm spell, and with it came a dark bank of clouds. Andromache imagined the newlywed couple sighing in relief: their ceremony had been conducted just in time. She didn't think they would have wanted such grey weather for their wedding.

At the same time, she felt grateful that the gloom had returned — it gave her an excuse to spend most of the day upstairs, avoiding Hecuba. She left the safety of her bedroom only in the late afternoon, when it was time for lessons.

Hector was already in the library when she got there. He was sitting very stiffly at the table, drawing lines in the dust with his finger. As soon as he saw her, he stood up and blurted, "I'm sorry! I didn't think to tell you not to say that in front of my parents." He looked chastened.

"It's all right," said Andromache, shrugging as though the incident hadn't bothered her. She didn't want Hector to have anything else to feel guilty about. "Life is a bag of goat shit, right?"

Hector gave a cautious smile.

"Is your mom still mad?" asked Andromache.

He shook his head. "Not at *you*. And the wedding went well, so she won't be mad at anyone, for long."

"I'm glad it went well."

Hector accepted the switch to Lukkan as a peace offering. "Yes," he said, relaxing.

"I was wondering, though…" Andromache let her words trail off.

"Yes?"

"Are all Taruishan weddings that complicated?"

"You see it?" Hector looked surprised.

"Mm-hmm. From here — from the porch, I mean."

He looked out toward the porch, where she was gesturing. "'*Complicate*' mean what?" he asked.

"Complicated? Oh. That means there are lots of parts to it. Singing, and poems, and —"

"And plahnts in the haihr." Hector used both hands to form a circle around the top of his head.

"Crowns," said Andromache, thinking of the leafy head-dresses the couple had worn. "And blue clothes. Why blue?" she asked.

"It is fohr the sea," said Hector. "Fohr the sky." He paused. "Fohr the happy."

"Blue is a symbol for '*happiness*?'"

As Hector nodded, a wistful look flashed across his face.

The intensity of it startled Andromache. She'd assumed that he didn't want to get married, yet, but obviously, that wasn't true. Perhaps the wedding would already have taken place, if not for Hector's lingering guilt — his inability to move on from Lyrnassa, even though he seemed to want to.

Unless...

Unless perhaps *he* wasn't the only reticent one. Penthesilea had said that people from Troy's citadel could be hard on outsiders, and now Andromache knew what she meant. While the neighbors hadn't been openly mean to her, their snide, knowing looks had shredded her self-confidence. Even Hecuba seemed to have suffered at the hands of the wealthy Trojans. It was possible that Penthesilea couldn't reconcile herself to living among them — at least, not yet.

Either way, the whole topic made Andromache feel strange. "Well," she said, clearing her throat. "That's a pretty presumptuous symbol. Marriage isn't always happy."

Hector laughed. "Oh yes — that is true," he said teasingly. "Sometimes it *sucks*."

Blushing, Andromache changed the subject. "What about those plant crowns? What are *they* symbols for?"

Hector rolled his eyes. "Those? Fohr the crazy."

Chapter 27

Andromache looked down contentedly at her clothing chest — the day had come to store Cassandra's old pink cloak inside it. After hours of diligent work at the loom, she'd finally woven enough grey cloth. She'd asked Hecuba to look at it...

'Good workmanship,' the woman said approvingly. 'Your mother and aunt would be proud of you.'

Andromache's eyes grew misty, but she managed a polite, 'Thank you.'

'What are your plans for it?'

'I — I — thought maybe a cloak.'

Hecuba nodded. 'Very sensible. Shall I have Cassandra take it down to the dressmaker, to have it tailored?' She made no mention of Andromache going outside.

'Thank you,' said Andromache.

Just a few days later, the grey cloak was hers. Cassandra had brought it up to her after dinner. *'Oh, honey! It's beautiful!'* the girl had cried, and Andromache couldn't help smiling. The cloak was nowhere near as lovely as those her mom had made, but it was thick and warm. Hecuba was right: her mom and Auntie would have been proud.

Andromache modeled her new cloak for Muka. The dog sniffed appreciatively and waved her plumy tail. She seemed to like the garment, perhaps because its color so nearly matched her fur.

"You like it? You like it, huh, girl?"

Wag, wag, wag.

"It's warm, isn't it? Almost like your fur."

Wag, wag, wag.

"I don't think I'll even need a blanket tonight." Andromache smoothed the cloak over her legs and lay back against her pillows. In no time, she was asleep…

She was on the beach, in Lyrnassa. The sea was black. The sky was black, writhing with white tornadoes. Five of them, twisting all around each other in a cluster that was bearing down on her. All of the other villagers had run away — along the beach, up ravines. No one had thought to take her with. Even if they had, she was rooted to the spot, blocked by —

Andromache shrieked herself awake. Her skin was clammy. Her heart was racing. She leapt out of bed and ran for the stairs. On the way down, though, something felt wrong. Her legs felt heavy — encumbered, almost like in the dream. She stumbled — tripped — landed hard on her bottom —

The cloak! she thought in disgust. Her feet had gotten tangled in the hem. For a moment or two, she sat with her head propped against the wall, willing her heartbeats to slow. They didn't.

I'll go to the library, she decided. Maybe reading would help her calm down.

In the library, on a shelf near the window, she found a text called *On Lorani*. The title intrigued her. *Who's that? Who's Lorani?* As she read, she discovered that Lorani was not the author of the work, or even a person at all. Instead, *On Lorani* was a treatise about certain objects in the night sky. According to the author, these Lorani looked like, '*hazy blotches larger than stars.*'

Hazy blotches? thought Andromache. *I've seen those before!* She hadn't seen them since coming to Troy, though, and wondered if the text would explain why.

> *The Lorani swim in a vait ocean in wach our earth is*
> *bull emote within a bubble of air.*

Swim? So, they were creatures? And the sky was an *ocean?* She'd never thought of the sky that way before, but it made as much sense as anything. Except…if the earth was inside a bubble, what would happen if the bubble popped? Andromache shuddered and read on.

The fact that certain features in this ocean appear and reappear throughout the year seem to indiquet that we are caught in an eddy of fantamastical poporpoises. The celestial ocean reaches far beyond our completion, and most of the Lorani divell a great distance from us. Yet we see them. We see them, and they pull at our imagriation. What are these entreaties, whom the Achaeans call 'galaxias?' (Although it must be said that we poffer the Palaan word 'Lorani,' manning 'cloud creature,' for which ration we have adapted this word ausis into Truvan.) After much study, the collusion has been reached that they are vait fish, or more likely sea jellies, due to their hazy appeasance.

Appeasance? That was a tricky one. Appeasance. Appreasance? — oh, that was it! — ap*pea*rance! Hazy appearance! Andromache nodded her head. *They look like giant, hazy sea jellies.* The blotches she'd seen had indeed looked rather like jellyfish. She'd always thought they were small, but if they lived far away, they might be truly immense, like mountains seen from a distance.

Many people have stood on our earthly seashore at night, in awe of the lurmanous —

Lurmanous? What was *that*?

— creatures drifting on or beneath the waves.

Did *'lurmanous'* mean *'drifting?'* The way earthly jellyfish drift?

Illymander, an observer on the shore of the celestial ocean might watch the great Lorani drift secrinely past each other, lurmanous like certain creatures in our tempestrial seas. Our world wombly invisible, bring comploable, assomend before, to a tin emote within a bubble of air. Forturately for us, it is a transparent bubble, hallowing us to see wonders far beyond our scoop.

For a moment, Andromache set the text down and stared out the window. Floating in a celestial ocean, surrounded by scores of gigantic drifting jellies…what a thought! And was that gigantic ocean, with its gigantic observer, itself only a bubble in a still larger ocean? What sort of creatures might drift through *those* waters? And what sort of observers looked upon them? Andromache expanded the idea until she got to the fifth level of ocean, at which point she got dizzy and had to stop.

> *To view these creatures, the Lorani, one must flecent the darkest plossable cantations. While we tend to consider the Lorani gentle giants, we don't yet know the entorlty of their nature. Lorani have been spotted logged together in what is either a matting riptial or a battle to the death. In this state, they appear to swallow each other, distregging until they become one.*

In her childhood, Andromache had spent a lot of time looking at the sky and knew it well. She'd seen the hazy creatures — the Lorani — many times, but *never* two of them swallowing each other. She wasn't sure that she wanted to — the thought was a little gruesome.

> *It suseritain that any of the Lorani cod swallow the earth, ifkey sochey. In all lariahold wood do so inavertedly, dew —*

Andromache frowned. *When did we start talking about dew?*

> *— to the differences in size. Then again, perhaps this has already happened, and instead of flirting in the celestial ocean, we are flirting in the belly of one of its great beasts, among the other debits…*

"Hi honey!"

Andromache shrieked.

"Are you all right?"

"I just didn't hear you come in."

"Oh, sorry!" said Cassandra. "I get like that when I'm reading, too. What do you have, there?"

Andromache showed her the wooden tablet, which Cassandra didn't recognize.

"Is it any good?" asked the girl.

"Yes. It's — well, it's a little strange, but interesting." Andromache was sure it would have been even more interesting if she'd understood all the words. For a moment, she was tempted to ask Cassandra about them, but then she remembered Cassandra saying, *Do you know there are places where people can't read?'* The girl's horror still rankled, so Andromache held her tongue.

"Of all the times to run across it, when my history tutor is due to arrive!" pouted Cassandra.

"Oh. I should probably leave, then," said Andromache.

Reluctantly, the girl nodded. "Maybe you can show it to me, later?"

"Sure. Have a good lesson."

Cassandra brightened. "Thanks, honey. I will. We're talking about the institution of the first city donkey cart ordinances!"

Andromache smiled to herself. Cassandra never ceased to surprise her. With *On Lorani* in hand, she walked down to the kitchen.

Paris was in there, eating a breakfast of cheese, olives, and bread. "Oh good, Hermie, it's you," he said without other greeting. "This saves me the trouble of trying to find you, at any rate."

"Why do you have to find me?" she asked suspiciously.

"I was just with the taskmaster," he sighed, rubbing his arms and seeking a sympathetic look from her. Instead, he received a blank one. "He instructed me to pray you meet him in the kitchen this afternoon instead of in the library."

"Oh, *that* taskmaster," she said.

"So you agree…"

"With what?"

"That he's a taskmaster."

"No! I — I wouldn't know, it was just what *you* said!" Andromache scowled. "What were you doing with him, anyway?"

Paris mimed shooting an arrow. "Evidently it's some sort of honor that I get to practice with him one-on-one," he snorted. "As if group practice four times a week weren't enough! I'm always down at the archery range when a civilized person should be in bed. The city commanders are conspiring to take away my sleep."

Andromache ignored him and picked up *On Lorani*.

"What's that?" asked Paris, wrinkling his nose.

"Oh, just something I was reading…"

"No kidding."

Andromache scowled again but passed the text over to him.

He examined it briefly, only to pass it back with a look of disdain. "So what's your answer?"

"To what?" she asked him. *To the secrets of the universe? To the nature of the Lorani?*

"Can you meet my brother in the kitchen?"

"Oh. Sure," said Andromache.

Paris sat there, staring at her, making her increasingly uncomfortable until she asked, "Are you going back to him with the message, or what?"

"I suppose I'll have to, though not till I'm sure he's well away from the archery range." Paris paused, adding, "Unless *you* wanted to tell him…"

"No!" cried Andromache.

"That's right, I forgot about your phobia —"

Andromache caught her breath. Did Paris mean her Raider phobia? It hadn't been much of a problem, lately. That night's dream had been a rarity — and she'd woken up before actually seeing the Raider. But, in any case, how could Paris know? She'd never told *anybody*!

"— of leaving the house," finished Paris.

"I don't have a phobia!" snapped Andromache, cross but relieved. "I just —"

Paris held up his hands, cutting her off. "All right, all right, Hermie. I'll leave you to read…whatever that thing is." Grabbing another hunk of bread, he did just that.

For Andromache, though, the magic moment had passed, and she could no longer focus on the text.

Instead, she walked through the garden. It was chilly outside, but not raining. Her new grey cloak kept her warm as she pinched off dead foliage and broken branches. She stayed out till her fingers were red and raw, then returned to the kitchen to warm herself by the hearth. Muka, already stretched out before it, wagged her tail in greeting.

After heating water for a tisane, Andromache picked up the Lorani text. *I'll go over some of those passages again*, she thought. *May-*

be they'll make more sense, this time. The warm kitchen and warm drink made her sleepy, though, and at last, she gave in and laid her head on the table.

🙰

SHE WAS UP ON A HILL of cherry trees, gathering fruit into a basket. Scuff! Scuff! Each and every cherry fell out the bottom. Looking around, she saw that the hillside was paved with flat stones. The cherries were going to be ruined! Stop putting them in there. Put them in the other basket, *she told herself, and sure enough, there was another basket behind her. She began loading fruit into it —* Scuff! Scuff! *— they dropped to the ground as the others had.*

Scuff, scuff!
Andromache shook herself awake.
The sound from her dream continued: *Scuff, scuff.* Not falling fruit, but falling feet.
Oh, great gods! she thought, unpeeling her face from the table. There was a small puddle of drool where her open mouth had been. Hastily, she wiped it with the edge of her cloak.
"I am late," said Hector, crossing from the banquet hall into the kitchen. "Sohrry."
Andromache blinked her eyes, which felt grainy. "That's all right."
Hector smiled at Andromache, then at Muka. "Hey, girl," he called.
Wagging her tail in delight, Muka ran over to him, flung her feet up on his waist — and promptly fell to the floor.
"Muka!" shrieked Andromache.
Hector crouched beside the dog. "You poor old thing!" he murmured. "What were you trying to do, dance with me?"
Muka licked his hands.
"Is she all right?" gasped Andromache.
"She's fine," said Hector. "Just feeling a little silly."
Muka stood up, made a slow pass through the kitchen, and finally settled down beside the far set of shelves.

"She *must* be all right," Andromache murmured in relief. "She's sitting by the food."

Hector smiled. "Her first love — it always has been, ever since she was a puppy." He paused. "Speaking of food, I'm short on time tonight. I have to meet Lee."

"Lee? Who's Lee?"

"She rode with you here, from Lyrnassa."

"Oh!" said Andromache. "You mean Penthesilea."

Hector nodded.

He'd never mentioned his fiancée before now, Andromache realized. She would certainly have remembered the pet name '*Lee*.' It sounded so intimate, compared to '*Penthesilea*' — as though by shortening her name, Hector had cut the two of them off from the rest of the world...

"She has a report for me," he added. "Anyway, I won't have time for a meeting, a lesson, *and* dinner —"

"Oh." Andromache gulped. "So, you need to cancel?" She could see why he would want to. Penthesilea — *Lee* — wasn't in the city much, or so she'd said. Her presence there was a stroke of luck — at least for Hector. Andromache, however, didn't *want* to skip the Lukkan lesson! And what if one day turned into several, the duration of *Lee's* stay in Troy? Andromache thought of Hector's wistful look, when he'd told her the meaning of the blue wedding robes, and her stomach began to churn.

"Not cancel," said Hector. "I just wanted to make sure it was all right if I ate during our lesson."

Relieved, Andromache said, "Sure. Why wouldn't it be?"

Pause. "If you couldn't understand me..."

Andromache thought back to her anger, when she'd first learned about Hector's guilt, and how she'd excoriated him for chewing mint. "I'll understand you," she mumbled, embarrassed.

Hector nodded. He took one plate off the shelf, looked at her, and hesitantly asked, "Uh, you — you eat?"

Why not? She was hungry — she'd hardly eaten all day. "All right," she said, setting *On Lorani* beside her.

Hector handed her a plate before filling his own from the bowls sitting out on the table. He took food from each one without pausing to see what it was. After helping himself to a large chunk of rare, roasted meat, he remembered his manners and passed the serving dish to her: "Here."

Raw meat — ragged meat — torn flesh — glistening red — bloody, ragged shreds of meat —

Reflexively, Andromache gagged, then covered her mouth and shrank back from the plate. So far, she'd managed to avoid such a reaction in front of the family — she hadn't wanted to draw attention to herself — but until now, no one had thrust bloody meat in her face.

Hector was staring at her. Andromache collected herself enough to offer a more polite, "No, thank you. I don't eat that."

"You eat no — um — um —" He frowned in concentration. "Baby sheeps?"

Andromache shook her head. "No lamb. No meat."

"No meat neffer?"

"Never."

"Why?"

He sounded genuinely curious, not mocking, so she told him: "I think about the animals dying."

"Dah-ing?"

"Dying," she repeated, drawing a finger across her throat.

For a long moment he said nothing, as he processed what she'd said and tried to understand the new words. Then, suddenly, he broke the silence: "Befohre, you see the dah-ing." His eyes had the piercing look they got when he was sure of something.

Andromache stiffened. "Yes," she whispered.

She was five or six, walking along the shore with her mom, when they saw a fisherman. They stopped to watch him pull in several large, silvery fish. They were so beautiful, catching the light as they flopped about on the sand! The fisherman was standing over them — Andromache thought it was to admire them — but then, to her horror, he struck each one over the head. They went still.

They're dead!' shrieked Andromache.

Well, yes,' said her mom, confused as to why Andromache was upset.

He killed them!'

Of course he did. He caught them for his family to eat.'

You mean he didn't bring them up to let them play?' Andromache wailed. But they looked so happy, the way they were jumping!'

'Ahndromahk — ' Her mom was giving her an odd look. They were jumping like that because they couldn't breathe. Fish can only breathe underwater, just like we can only breathe on land.'

'I know that!' cried Andromache. 'I just thought they were playing, like we play underwater. Sometimes Haliosh dives down to find rocks or shells for me.'

'Well, he should be careful,' her mom said sternly. 'But that's not the point. Fish don't play, Ahndromahk — at least not on land. Up here, they suffocate. They die very slowly. The fisherman killed those fish so they wouldn't suffer.'

Andromache started to cry. 'Then he never should've brought them up on land! He should've left them in the water!'

'Oh Ahndromahk,' sighed her mom. 'He has to eat, doesn't he?'

'Well, not me! I'm never eating fish again!'

'Poor sensitive little thing,' Andromache heard her dad whispering, later that night. 'I wish she hadn't seen that.'

'I know,' her mom whispered back. 'I don't know what to do with her. What if she really won't eat fish again?'

'Then she'll eat other things,' her dad replied. 'She won't go hungry, between the nut trees, and your sister's vegetable garden, and bread, and the meat and cheese we get from the animals.'

'You're right,' said her mom. 'We'll just let her be.'

Years later, her parents would have yet another round of hushed discussions about her, far more serious ones. It all started when Andromache was twelve or thirteen, walking out in the mountains by herself...

She wasn't supposed to go there alone. She would be in trouble for sure if her parents found out, but what did they know? She wasn't a baby anymore! She would be fine.

And everything was fine, until she heard the screams — piteous, wrenching screams. What's that? she wondered. It sounds like someone's hurt. She ran toward the sound, which got louder and louder until finally, she found the source of it — a baby goat. The little animal was lying on his side, weakly moving his legs. His belly was torn open, the insides spilling out.

'Oh, gods,' moaned Andromache. 'Oh, gods!' The goat screamed again. Andromache tried to imagine her own belly open that way, and her vision fogged with pain. I have to get him home, she thought. But when she

tried to move the goat, even the tiniest bit, the little creature screamed. He was suffering. Deep down, Andromache knew that no one could save him. <u>Mom</u>? *she thought in panic.* <u>Mom, what do I do?</u> *That was it! She needed her mom.*

(<u>Yes, go get your mom,</u>*) said a Voice inside her head. (*<u>She's not as cruel as *you* are. *She* wouldn't run away while a baby animal was dying. *She* wouldn't just let him suffer</u>…*)*

Andromache knew that she'd been silent for a long time. Hector was looking at her, waiting for her to continue.

"<u>I was in the hills, and I found a goat</u>," she said. "<u>A baby goat. I don't know what happened. I don't know why, but his belly was open</u>." She made a slicing motion up her own stomach.

Hector winced.

"<u>He was suffering</u>," Andromache whispered. "<u>He was crying and screaming</u>…" She paused again. "<u>But he couldn't die. He was not able to die.</u>"

"<u>Not able to dah</u>," Hector repeated. Then, the truth dawned on him. "You killed the goat?" His eyes were shocked, his tone appalled.

"I had to!" she cried. "I didn't *want* to, but he was suffering! You think I should've just let him —"

"No, no — sssssssssh, it's all right," Hector soothed. "I only wanted to make sure I understood."

"Oh — I— oh —" stammered Andromache, fighting back tears. "Yes, you — you heard right. I killed him. <u>Killed him</u>," she repeated in Lukkan. "<u>With a rock. I didn't know what else to do.</u>" Looking down at her hands, she told Hector the worst. "<u>I hit him on the head. Then the skin broke. It looked like meat. It looked like shreds of meat. He kept crying. I hit him again. The skull — the head — went *crack*! — and then</u> —" She gulped down a thick lump of horror.

She ran home, blood on her hands, blood on her dress. She didn't stop running until she was inside.

'<u>*Ahndromahk*</u>*!' shrieked her mom, just as her dad yelled,* '<u>*Where have you* been</u>*?'*

'<u>*We've been worried sick!*</u>*'*

'Oh gods! Your dress!'

'<u>*Are you all right?*</u>*'*

234

'All that blood!'

'What the hell happened, Ahndromahk?'

But Andromache could only cry. She threw herself down onto her blankets and lay there, sobbing. When she finally calmed down enough to tell them about the goat, they comforted her. They told her that the animal could never have survived such injuries.

'You did the right thing to end his suffering,' they said. Andromache couldn't believe them, though. Everything had changed…

Hector was staring at her. "It is ahgly," he finally said.

Ugly. That was the word for it. "I feel dirty."

"Oh, Ahndromahk…I know," he said softly.

Andromache felt a chill. Of *course* he knew! She thought about the rot and grime in his black laugh — about the gore and blood on the Raider's armor. He *knew!* But then, hadn't that been why she'd told him in the first place? She didn't want sympathy or absolution, yet it was a relief to tell the story to someone who understood.

"No person — no person is there?" asked Hector. "When you find this goat?"

"Oh, no. I was alone."

"Alone…"

She nodded.

"And young?"

"Maybe thirteen. I was old enough — strong enough — to kill."

"And from this day…" Hector glanced at his plate.

Andromache shook her head firmly. "No meat, not since then. It makes me sick."

For a long time, Hector said nothing — he just sat there, chewing on his thumbnail. When he finally spoke, it was to say, "I see." He then stood, removing not only the serving dish of meat but also his own plate. He placed them in the farthest corner of the room, under a heavy cloth.

"Oh, no!" Andromache protested. "You don't have to —"

He waved away her objection and came back carrying a clean plate. He gestured to one of the bowls on the table. "This one haff all — plahnt — um — plahnt fings."

"Vegetables?" she asked, smiling faintly.

"Vay-ge-tables," Hector repeated. "This one haff — *has* — umm — well, you can see." He pointed to a different bowl, one filled with fruit in honey. After taking a large helping out of each dish, he began to eat.

Andromache's smile died as she watched him. By removing the meat, was he being kind to her? Or had he just found a new way of atoning for *that day*, purposely denying himself something he enjoyed? "Look —"

"Hmm?"

"I don't care if other people eat meat, as long as I don't have to," she said. Her voice had a hint of frost.

Hector shrugged, his expression mild. "And I am happy to eat all vay-ge-tables."

Andromache had to admit that he looked happy enough. He was probably one of those people who didn't care what he was eating, provided there was plenty of it. During his time on that far-flung patrol, he'd no doubt gotten used to eating whatever was available.

"Some people think it's weird," she said, excusing herself. "Not eating meat." As she scooped stew and fruit onto her plate, she told Hector about how her parents had indulged her decision, but only after a series of teary fights. She also told him that Auntie, worried about what the villagers in Lyrnassa would think, had tried repeatedly to slip meat into her food.

"But they found out anyway," she said. "And sure enough, they thought I was crazy." Indeed, they'd looked upon her with even more suspicion than before. "My Auntie made me tell them all that I belonged to a religious group that didn't eat meat." She hadn't dared disobey her Auntie, either: the woman had always refused to speak Truvan herself, but she could understand it well enough to monitor what Andromache was telling the villagers. "They stopped talking about it, after that. People accept anything, no matter how weird it seems, if you call it a religious practice."

"Lahke Dad?" asked Hector, a twinkle in his eye. "Talking to stahrs? Listening to stahrs?"

Andromache covered her mouth with her hands. "Oh, I didn't mean —"

Hector laughed. "*I* meant it! Dad talks to stars, and people call him holy. If a drunk man did it, he'd be crazy." Glancing at the text beside her, Hector amended his words: "Or *hazy*."

Andromache's eyes widened. "You've read it? You've read *On Lorani*?"

Hector nodded.

"But not even Cassandra has read it!"

"It's not on the lists most tutors assign."

Andromache flushed with excitement. Was *On Lorani* a forbidden text? Was that why no one in the house, except Hector, had read it? She lowered her voice and asked, in Lukkan, "Did you like it?"

"No." Hector shook his head. "It is so stringy."

"Excuse me?"

"It's bizarre."

"Oh — do you mean *strange*?"

"So strange," he agreed.

"But interesting," she persisted. "How else can you explain them?"

"Excuse me?"

"The hazy blotches."

"They ahre not stahrs?"

"No!" Andromache said vehemently. "They're bigger and blurrier. I've seen them."

"Hmmm…"

"You've never seen them?" she asked, scandalized.

Hector shook his head.

"Then you have to look for them. You *have* to!" she insisted. "They're beautiful."

"Even if you've seen those things, do you *really* think they're glowing sky jellies?" Hector's skepticism stood out far more in Truvan — which was no doubt why he'd made the switch.

"Well," said Andromache, "there are creatures that glow in *our* seas, and the whole point of the text is that beyond the earth is an ocean —"

"And that we're in an air bubble," finished Hector, making a face. "I don't like that idea."

"Well, I don't *like* the idea that stars are metal," Andromache countered. "But I accept that you — or someone — saw something fall from the sky, that the thing is in your dad's temple, that it's metal, and that you think it might be a star."

Hector gave a sober nod. "It *is*. And metal wouldn't glow like stars do unless it was over a very hot fire...which means that stars can't possibly be underwater."

Andromache thought for a moment. "Maybe the celestial ocean isn't made of water — maybe it's made of strong wine. *That* would burn."

Hector laughed so hard that he dropped the bread he'd been holding. "An ocean of wine! What an idea!"

"Or maybe," Andromache went on, triumphantly, "the metal you saw is just part of the creature — its skeleton — not the part that glows. Maybe stars are creatures, like the Lorani but smaller, and what glows is their flesh. Then it wouldn't matter what the celestial ocean is made of, because the metal wouldn't have to be hot."

Hector nodded again, this time to yield. "Perhaps. There are lots of different reasons something might glow."

Andromache almost choked on a bite of her honeyed fruit. *Glow?* she thought. The word had slipped past her in the heat of the debate, but now she felt its full impact. So many things that had confused her suddenly made sense. "Glowing sky jellies!" she cried.

Startled, Hector looked up from his plate. "Glow — what?" he asked.

Andromache scanned *On Lorani* until she found the passage she wanted:

> *Many people have stood on the seashore at night, in awe of the lurmanous creatures drifting on or beneath the waves.*

"So — is that what that word means?" she asked, pointing. "*'Lurmanous'* means *'glowing*?'"

Hector leaned over to examine the text. "*Luminous*," he corrected. "Yes, it means *'glowing'* — or, um, ah — *'brahght.'*"

He looked delighted at having come up with the word in Lukkan, but, for once, Andromache was more interested in Truvan. One by one, she asked Hector to explain all the words she hadn't understood. Having watched him flail through Lukkan for the past seven months, she was less embarrassed to ask him those questions than she would have been with Cassandra.

Less embarrassed, that is, until they reached the end of the passage.

"And this one?" She pointed to the phrase *'matting riptial.'*

Hector cleared his throat. "*'Mating — ritual.'*"

Cheeks reddening, Andromache peered again at the text and was mortified to discover that he was right.

When she didn't immediately respond, he mumbled, "That means —"

She cut him off. "I know what it means." Her eyes were fixed on her plate. She was trying to think of a way to salvage the conversation when Muka came to her rescue.

Schlarp!

Hector looked toward the far corner of the room, his face wrinkling with disgust. "Stop that," he called.

Schlarp! Schlarp!

"Muka — that's disgusting!"

When Andromache turned around, she saw that Muka had nosed aside the cloth covering the roast lamb and was now gobbling it down.

"Bad dog!" scolded Hector.

Muka unapologetically licked the plate clean.

Good girl! thought Andromache. In more ways than one, the loyal dog had saved her.

೮つ

SOON AFTER, Hector had to leave, and Andromache, too, fled the kitchen. She didn't want to be there when the rest of the family came in to find that their dinner meat had vanished. She went upstairs to her room, where she reread by lamp light the passage that Hector had helped her decipher:

> *The Lorani swim in a vast ocean in which our earth is but a mote within a bubble of air. The fact that certain features in this ocean appear and reappear*

throughout the year seems to indicate that we are caught in an eddy of fantastical proportions. The celestial ocean reaches far beyond our comprehension, and most of the Lorani dwell a great distance from us. Yet we see them. We see them, and they pull at our imagination. What are these entities, whom the Achaeans call 'galaxias?' (Although it must be said that we prefer the Palaan word 'Lorani,' meaning 'cloud creature,' for which reason we have adopted this word as is into Truvan.) After much study, the conclusion has been reached that they are vast fish, or more likely sea jellies, due to their hazy appearance. Many people have stood on our earthly seashore at night, in awe of the luminous creatures drifting on or beneath the waves. In like manner, an observer on the shore of the celestial ocean might watch the great Lorani drift serenely past each other, luminous like certain creatures in our terrestrial seas. Our world would be invisible, being comparable, as mentioned before, to a tiny mote within a bubble of air. Fortunately for us, it is a transparent bubble, allowing us to see wonders far beyond our scope. To view these creatures, the Lorani, one must frequent the darkest possible conditions. While we tend to consider the Lorani gentle giants, we don't yet know the entirety of their nature. Lorani have been spotted locked together in what is either a mating ritual or a battle to the death. In this state, they appear to swallow each other, disintegrating until they become one. It is certain that any of the Lorani could swallow the earth, if they so choose. In all likelihood they would do so inadvertently, due to the differences in size. Then again, perhaps this has already happened, and instead of floating in the celestial ocean, we are floating in the belly of one of its great beasts, among the other debris…

Andromache set the text down. It was the hardest one she'd ever tried to read, and she now understood it better than any other. What if she revisited some of the texts that had previously thwarted her — the one about '*trush*,' for instance? What if she assigned them to Hector, the way all tutors assigned readings? He could help her sort out the difficult words. He was using *her*, after all; she might as well get something from *him*, too.

Besides, it would be good to have new material for lessons. She'd liked talking about the Lorani with Hector. He had interesting ideas, far-fetched though some of them were. As long as the discussions were in Lukkan, from now on, she could justify having them during lesson time. Even if Hector had to resort to Truvan on occasion, to explain something particularly complex, he would probably end up learning a lot of new words.

Andromache looked down at *On Lorani* and was embarrassed to see that she'd left a sticky fingerprint on the text. As she wiped it off with her cloak, she thought of the honeyed fruit and vegetable stew she'd had earlier, with Hector.

No one had ever reacted so compassionately to her vegetarianism, before, not even her parents — and Hector had been kind about the goat, too. His kindness had come out of guilt, of course, but Andromache was grateful all the same. She wished she could show her appreciation without having to say anything. He wasn't an easy person to thank. When she'd tried to thank him for his actions at Lyrnassa, he'd refused to look at her…

He can pick the first text on the reading list, she thought with a sigh. It was a small gesture, but the only one she could come up with. The more she considered the idea, the more she liked it. Hector had read *On Lorani*, after all. He had a wide knowledge of texts, and she was curious to see what he would find for them to read. He might introduce her to a new part of the world, to a new way of thinking, or to creatures and cultures she'd never heard of before.

Part of her wished that he would choose the biography of Sarcho — that most daunting of texts — so she could have his help deciphering it. She knew he wouldn't, though; he clearly hated Sarcho. If she ever wanted to read those scrolls, she would be on her own.

Early spring

Chapter 28

A ndromache awoke with a start, not sure what had disturbed her sleep. Not sun — it was too early; not wind — her curtains were drawn mostly shut. Had it been a nightmare? Feeling troubled, she reached down to pet Muka. The dog didn't stir.

"Muka?" asked Andromache, shaking her gently.

Muka still didn't move.

Andromache leapt to the floor, putting her ear to the dog's muzzle, but she heard and felt no breathing. That was probably what had awoken her — silence. Because Muka usually snored. *Muka usually snored!*

Muka, gentle Muka, the sweet old dog who seldom left her side. Muka, who comforted her. Muka, who found her when she was crumpled in the alcove. Muka, who never judged her. Muka, who loved her — the only one in the world who wasn't just kind to her, but *loved* her.

Andromache was alone. She was all alone — *again!*

She was coming back from the fair with Auntie. She was running toward her home, but something was wrong. The mountain was wrong — it had slumped over. Her house was gone. Her parents were gone. They were lost forever inside of the mountain. 'Ahndromahk, stop! They're gone. There's nothing we can do!' And she was screaming, flying down the shore, all alone...

She was in her old shack in Lyrnassa, lying on the floor beside Auntie. 'Wake up,' she said, tugging on Auntie's arm. 'We need to get going

<u>*before it's too hot.*</u>*' But Auntie never stirred — never groaned herself awake...*

She was doubled over, pulling Auntie's body out of the shack. She was struggling across the shore, toward the water. She was dragging Auntie out into the sea, all alone...

She was leaning over Muka — her sweet, gentle Muka — and Muka's breath was gone...

<u>*No! Not again!*</u> It was a dream! It *had* to be a dream! This couldn't be happening *again*! She couldn't face this, *again*!

Tottering, Andromache drew back from the sad, unmoving mound of fur. She threw on her grey cloak. Downstairs, there would probably be someone to help her. Priam might be there, eating breakfast before his early temple rounds. Or maybe Cassandra would be studying. Even Paris would be a welcome sight — anyone, anyone at all!

The kitchen doorway shone with lamp and hearth light, and from inside came the noises of someone moving around. Relieved, Andromache ran across the banquet hall and into the kitchen, where she saw Hector. He was standing near the table, his back to her.

"Good," he said. "Finally! I thought I was going to have to go upstairs and drag your sorry little a —" He turned around at that moment, blushing faintly when he saw her. "Oh, sorry, <u>Ahndromahk</u>...I thought you were Paris. He's always late for archery practice." Taking a closer look at her, he asked, "What's wrong?"

"Muka," she mumbled. It was all her swollen throat could manage, but he understood.

"Oh, no — I'm so sorry! Here. Here, sit." He motioned toward the table.

Mechanically, she sat.

"Where is she?" asked Hector.

"Upstairs. In my room."

"I'll take care of it," he said, looking around as though he hoped someone else would come. "It'll be all right." His own fingers rigid, he gave her hand a tentative pat.

Andromache didn't respond. The inevitable tears were beginning to roll down her cheeks.

Just then, Paris — the real one — skulked in. "All right, I'm here, so let's — oh, hi, Hermie," he interrupted himself. "What's the matter?"

Hector answered for her. "Muka died."

"Who? Oh, the dog. Poor Hermie." Paris crossed the room to Andromache and slid a surprisingly gentle arm around her, rocking her as she began to cry for real. "What's wrong with you?" he hissed at his brother. "Don't you know how to comfort someone? Maybe I could give you lessons in *that*, today, instead of doing archery."

Paris pulled Andromache's head to his shoulder, but not before she saw a murderous look cross Hector's face.

"*You* — stay here!" he growled, leaving the room.

Andromache pressed closer to Paris, who had begun softly stroking her hair. Why he would have chosen to console her rather than mock her was a mystery, but she was grateful. He was being so nice to her…

Just as that thought crossed her mind, Paris began to talk.

"Poor Hermie. I know you're going to miss that old mutt."

Andromache sniffled.

Paris squeezed her shoulders. "She was a good girl, even to the end. Her last good deed may have been to get me out of archery practice with the task master."

"Oh, shut up, Paris!" snapped Andromache. She wriggled out of his embrace — away from the spicy, overpowering scent of his bath oils — but once free, she thought about what he'd said. "What exactly do you mean?" she asked. "Why won't you be practicing?"

"Well, the corpse can't just stay in your room, can it? Someone — in this case, my brother — has to get it out of here."

Andromache swallowed hard. "Where's he taking her?" she whispered.

"Maybe to a carrion pit, or out in the hills, somewhere —"

"No!" shrieked Andromache, leaping out of her seat and running back through the banquet hall to the bottom of the staircase. When Hector got there, she would be waiting. Hard, cold Hector, who had no feelings, who couldn't even console a crying girl — she wasn't about to let *him* take her dog! She wasn't going to let him leave poor Muka out in the hills, for crows pick at!

The main door slammed.

Andromache cried out in dismay: *he'd taken the other staircase!* He was already outside, on the street! Without another thought, she flew across the room to the entry hall and out the front door, after him.

Weighed down by the large, sorry bundle, Hector had made it no farther than the bottom of the front steps. His shoulder was at just the right height for Andromache to reach out and catch hold of Muka, who was balanced there.

"Hey!" gasped Hector when he felt the dog being yanked away from him. He half spun to face his assailant and wound up losing his grip.

Andromache lunged protectively after Muka. "You can't have her!" she cried, throwing her arms around the dog. "I won't let you! I won't let you leave her out in the hills, for birds to pick at!"

"Ahndromahk — stop!" In spite of her obvious agitation, Hector knelt and tried to retrieve the blanket-wrapped dog.

"Don't *touch* her!" screamed Andromache, clinging to Muka. She would kick Hector, if she had to! She would hurt him! She would —

Ah! Even better!

She wrapped her arms and legs tightly around the dog. "Go ahead and chuck her in some offal pit," she wailed. "But you'll have to throw me with." Let him throw them in together, if he had the strength to lift them both! She didn't care!

"Relax. Relax. Blistering gods, breathe!" ordered Hector, careful now to stay back.

"I *won't* breathe! Go away! Just leave her alone!"

"It's all right — it's all *right*. Ssssh...listen. I wasn't going to chuck her into a pit."

Andromache eyed him suspiciously, not loosening her grip on Muka. "Then where were you taking her?"

"To bury her. I left our spade in the stables."

Andromache didn't move or speak.

"Muka was my buddy," Hector said softly.

At last, Andromache unpeeled herself from the dog. The fight in her was gone; all she felt now was emptiness. "I didn't know," she said dully. "Paris said you were —"

"Paris." Hector's face went flat. "I see." He walked back up to the door. Opening it, he let loose a terrifying roar: "Paris!"

Paris arrived at the summons more quickly than was his wont. Andromache couldn't blame him; she, too, had all but leapt to her feet at the sound of Hector's cry.

"Yes?" said Paris.

"Go down to the range once you're done eating," ordered Hector. "Someone will meet you there."

Paris gave a gloomy nod, and Hector slammed the door. Then, moving slowly, so as not to spook Andromache, he knelt down once more beside her and Muka.

"Can I take her now?" he murmured.

Muka. Andromache's first and best Trojan friend, her comfort during so many long, sleepless nights. Muka, crushed beneath dirt and rocks — obliterated, just like Andromache's parents — swallowed by the earth —

"No," moaned Andromache. "You can't bury her."

"Uh…" Hector frowned. "Then what —"

"The sea."

"The sea?"

"It's the best way." Andromache nodded firmly. "I'm taking her down there."

"That's crazy," Hector protested.

Andromache shrugged.

"Even if you *did* know how to get there, you couldn't carry her that far."

"I'll drag her," she said hollowly, thinking, *I've done it before*.

Hector sighed. "Ahndromahk, let go. I'll do it."

Andromache shook her head. "She's *mine*."

"I told you," he said. "I won't chuck her in a pit. I won't let birds pick at her. I'll take her straight to the sea — you have my word."

She looked at him and saw no mockery in his eyes. Exasperated though he might be, his offer to help was sincere. She laid a hand on the blanket-wrapped body. Muka *was* heavy, and the sea *was* far…and, as Hector had pointed out, she didn't know how to get there…

"All right," she whispered.

"Good."

"But I'm coming with."

"I promise — I *won't* —"

"I need to be with her," she murmured.

Hector sighed again. "Let's go, then." Heaving the bundle back onto his shoulder, he started out from the door.

Andromache tiptoed after him, reeling at the enormity of her decision. *She'd left the house!* She was even going to have to leave the city walls! And she —

Dammit, Ahndromahk — you idiot! Wincing, she looked down at her feet. They were bare. She would have to fetch her sandals. There was no help for it. If she shredded her feet again, Hecuba would never let her hear the end of it. But, if she went back inside the house, would Hector wait? Probably not. She would just have to keep going, then, and hope for the best.

They began to walk.

"I need to make a stop," said Hector.

Andromache nodded, although he couldn't have seen her do so, since she was walking directly behind him. As long as she stayed there, she could focus on his ankles. She didn't have to see the streets yawning around her.

Gods, she was exposed! Early morning darkness was cloaking the city in shadows. Thugs might well be hiding in any of the streetside hollows, waiting to stab her or drag her away. Terrified, she kept her eyes locked on Hector's familiar form.

They walked the streets in silence. Andromache wasn't sure if Muka's weight made talking uncomfortable for Hector, or if he simply had nothing to say. She didn't care either way. Just walking was enough of an effort.

They passed through a gate in the citadel wall and entered the lower town. To her dismay, Hector took them down ever narrower streetlets and lanes — dim, twisting alleys, always downhill. It all looked the same to her — equally frightful — but Hector seemed to know where he was going. At a narrow black door, he stopped, lowered Muka to the ground, and knocked.

A moment later, Penthesilea ducked her head out. Her only sign of surprise was a raised eyebrow in Andromache's direction.

"Sorry it's early," said Hector.

Penthesilea shrugged away the apology. "Come in," she said to both of them.

Andromache demurred. It wasn't just that she wanted to stay with Muka, or that the warrior woman was even taller and more intimidating than she remembered. She also couldn't bear to see the inside of the little house. If she'd accepted Penthesilea's offer to live there, she never would have grown so attached to Muka — she wouldn't be in the position now, as she'd been so many times before, of losing someone she loved.

Hector disappeared through the doorway, and Andromache sat down, burying her face in her arms. Muffled bits of conversation drifted outside:

"...meet...morning?... care of," said Hector.

"...fine," Penthesilea responded.

"...'xtra time..."

"'fcourse."

"And...thing...ooze?"

Rustle, rustle, rustle. "Here."

"Thanks again."

The door closed, and Andromache sat up, hitting her head against a light but solid object. "Oof!" she exclaimed.

"Sorry," said Hector, pulling back the pair of shoes that he'd been dangling. "They're Lee's. Will they fit?"

Andromache mutely accepted the shoes. So, he'd noticed her bare feet. Why hadn't he said something earlier, when they were still by the house — where she could have fetched her own shoes? Why hadn't he sent her home? Deciding it was better not to ask, she slipped her feet into the shoes. They were enormous. "They're fine," she mumbled.

"Good," said Hector, lifting Muka back onto his shoulder. As they walked the remaining distance to the lower city walls, he explained their side errand. "Lee got in from the field late last night. She was hoping to sleep in a little — not meet Paris for morning archery practice." With a grim sort of gusto, Hector added, "He's really going to hate this. If he thinks *I'm* tough on him, well — ouch! Dammit!" He swore as he stubbed his toe on a jagged cobblestone. After that, he again fell silent until they reached the western gate.

"We're going out," he announced to the gatekeepers. Immediately, Andromache, Hector, and Muka were let through, out into the horror beyond the lower wall.

A third layer of city fanned out from the gates, and none of its inhabitants seemed to know that they should still be sleeping. Nearest the walls were merchants, selling and trading their wares, while further out, workers hauled goods to and from ships in the harbor beyond. Everyone was shouting — pushing — swarming.

There was no way to get around this zone, Andromache was aghast to see. It made an enormous semicircle around the gates so that no matter which way they turned, they would have to pass through a section of it.

"The best way," said Hector, "is probably over there." With one hand he steadied Muka, while with the other he pointed toward the most thickly roiling area. "Stay close."

Andromache nodded. She didn't need to be told twice. As long as she stayed in Hector's wake, those people couldn't jostle her — they couldn't hit her — they couldn't knock her to the ground.

Shadowing Hector seemed to be the perfect solution until one of her sandals flopped loose. As she bent down to adjust it, a man stepped between her and Hector, and she stopped short to avoid bumping into him. Once the first man had passed, there was another, and another, and because Andromache was too hesitant to push back at them, the horde soon swallowed her. She fell to the ground, moaning, reliving the horror of the past…

Legs on every side — dozens, hundreds, thousands of legs — everywhere, legs and feet — heels battering her shins, crushing her sides — her face pushed into the ground — no air, only sand —

She was done. Finished. She would be crushed, and her corpse would be left facedown in the outer market —

"Ahndromahk?"

Andromache raised her head to see a hand right there, in front of her — a large, brown hand with short nails.

"Are you all right?"

Hector had come back to find her. She *wasn't* going to die there!

"Are you all right?" repeated Hector. He looked irritated with her — or perhaps his face was knotted with the strain of carrying Muka.

"Fine," mumbled Andromache.

"What happened?"

"I fell." Andromache took the hand he was still extending and scrambled back to her feet.

Once she was upright, Hector tried to retract his hand, but she held fast. *No way* was she going to risk another separation!

He stiffened but didn't pull away. "Do you want to go on?" he asked, a little sheepishly. All around, people were now staring at them.

She nodded, tightening her grip on the dry, callused digits. She and Hector began walking again.

"Not much further," he said after a while, as they passed through the fringes of the outer market. Once they were free of the crowd, she dropped Hector's hand and looked at the harbor before them.

There was a light fog, but several jetties were visible poking out into the water. Hector pointed to the westernmost one and said, "The water's deep at the end of it."

Andromache nodded.

They walked out onto the jetty. Near it, a ship was docked — a hollow ship bobbing on the mist-swathed waves. Andromache shuddered and hugged the far side of the jetty. She hadn't seen a ship since Lyrnassa.

She hadn't seen the sea since then, either. She'd forgotten how hypnotic the waves could be…

"Almost there," said Hector, over his shoulder.

When they reached the end of the jetty, he set Muka on the ground, groaned softly, and stood there, rubbing his shoulder. He was free of his burden — ready to end this silly errand and return to the city. To *Lee*.

Andromache shivered again. "I know you all think I'm crazy," she whispered. "She's just a dog, that's what you're all thinking. Not worth this fuss."

Hector shook his head. "No one thinks that."

"*Everyone* does — especially Paris."

"Paris!" spat Hector, rolling his eyes. "He's just bitter."

The word startled Andromache out of her misery. "Bitter? Why?"

"Because." Hector sat down next to Muka. "He's the one who found her and brought her home, back when Cassandra was just a little girl. My parents let him keep her, but my stupid brother pulled her tail all the time and she ended up hating him. Whenever he came into a room, she left it, or crawled under a table."

"Really?" The picture pleased Andromache enough to make her smile a little. She sat down on the other side of Muka.

"Uh-huh."

"I never noticed that."

"It was more when Muka was younger, but Paris has never forgotten. It drove him crazy that she was more my pet than his. She even slept on my bed, till I finally grew and there wasn't enough room for her, anymore."

Hector went on to tell Andromache about feeding Muka from the dinner table when his parents weren't looking, about walking her all around the city and out into the countryside, about spending less and less time with her as the army began to take up more and more. While Andromache listened, she pulled back a corner of the blanket to pet Muka one last time. The fine sea mist left a veil on the dog's soft fur.

"She loved me," sighed Andromache, when Hector finally fell silent.

He didn't answer.

She gazed out to sea. "The fish are going to pick at her," she said in a thick voice. "Aren't they? Just like the vultures."

If Hector was alarmed at the sudden danger of having to lug Muka all the way back to the city for a different type of burial, he didn't show it. "Ahndromahk, it is all rahght," he said gently. "She cannot feel."

He's right, she thought. Muka was a husk. No matter what happened to her body, she wouldn't feel it. But what about Andromache? How was she going to bear the thought of her friend being chewed to pieces? "She'll be covered?" she croaked. "By the water?"

Hector's face froze.

"I need to know she'll be covered," pleaded Andromache. She needed to be sure that Muka's disintegration would be private. That passers-by wouldn't look upon her corpse with revulsion. That she would be swallowed by the waves.

"Ohff couhrse," Hector assured her.

Andromache nodded. "All right," she whispered.

"I am back, all rahght?" he said, standing once more.

Panicked anew, she asked, "Where are you going?"

"I am back. One moment."

While Andromache stayed with Muka, Hector walked back toward the ship they'd passed. She could see him only dimly in the fog and didn't know what he was doing.

She shivered. It was cold, sitting still. While the days were growing longer — when there was sun to be seen — the spring-time warmth was fickle. The last time she'd buried someone, it had been high summer. She'd dragged Auntie down to the water's edge, to the place where the currents pulled out hard...

"I am back."

Andromache turned around. Hector was there, clutching something to his chest.

"A fishing weight," he explained. "From the ship. For —" He pointed at Muka.

Andromache didn't answer, but she also didn't stop Hector from bending down to tie the weight inside the blanket. "I love you," she murmured, looking at the still, white form: her final farewell to the last being on earth who had loved her.

Hector lowered Muka's body into the waves. Andromache watched as the white blanket sank little by little.

"Let's go back, now," said Hector, after a moment.

Andromache turned away from him. "I almost washed out to sea, once."

"What? When?"

"When I first got to Lyrnassa. I didn't know how strong the waves could be. One of them pulled me off my feet."

The wind rose, drowning out Hector's response. Andromache imagined flying down under the waves, tumbling, weightless as she could never be on land. The water's force would sweep her out among the luminous earthly sea creatures, and, from below, they would look just like stars and Lorani...

"Ahndromahk," hollered Hector. "Come on." It was the same imperious voice he'd used on Paris, but its power was muted by the tumult of wind and surf.

Andromache's eyes were fixed on the blurry patch of white in the sea. Soon, Muka would be torn from her blanket, and then she would fly beneath the waves. She would soar out to meet Auntie, and together they —

Out of nowhere, a forceful clamp seized Andromache's wrist, right at the pulse. It was a strange hold, decided and grim, promising safety without giving warmth. She was hauled back off the jetty, her feet sloshing piteously in Penthesilea's sandals.

Hector didn't release her wrist even when they'd reached land. Instead, he marched along, towing her behind him, never speaking. His legs were long. She had to run to keep up with him.

In the chaos of the outer market, dozens — hundreds — thousands of people slammed into them. They were pushed about by countless hands, arms, elbows, and knees, but Andromache wasn't thrown to the ground, this time. The clamp on her wrist held fast.

She kept her eyes closed as she was pulled along. She didn't open them even when Hector bellowed to the gatekeepers and dragged her back inside the outer walls. She didn't want to see the lower city. Its streets would now be thick with people. Better that she not know how many there were. Better that she imagine herself up in the sky, among the Lorani, watching them float around together. Time would have to slow down — or perhaps speed up — to allow her the privilege of watching the giant creatures dance...

"Here you are."

Andromache looked up. They were back at the house.

"Get some rest. Get warm," said Hector.

His face was tight — furious, she thought. Furious at having been dragged out on that errand, furious at having to drag her back. He opened the door just long enough to push her over the threshold before pulling it shut behind her. With an emphatic *thunk*! he separated himself from her. He was free!

Inside, Andromache fell against the door and slid to the ground. As she sat there, alone again, she began to cry, and then to sob. Anger that had been building all morning — for eight months — for years — poured out in a torrent of sobs.

It's not fair! It's not fair! It's not fair! she thought.

She hated everything — *everybody*! She hated them all! She hated her mom — hated her dad — hated her aunt! It didn't matter if they hadn't had a choice — she hated them for deserting her! She hated them for leaving her to become an exile in a city that didn't want her. She hated Troy! If she hadn't been brought here, she wouldn't be hurting, now — she wouldn't have lost yet another loved one. She wished that she'd never met

Muka. She *hated* Muka, her only real friend, her last comfort, for abandoning her — for leaving her alone and unloved! And more than anyone else right then, she hated Hector. She hated him for dumping her there, in the entry hall! She *hated* him!

Get some rest. Get warm. Get some rest. Get warm.

Warm! What a strange word for *him* to use, cold as he was! He'd helped her bury Muka, but only out of guilt — his plan to salvage a Lyrnassan would fail if Andromache got herself lost or killed in the outer market. But once she was safe, that was his duty done! He hadn't even cared enough to see her to the kitchen. He'd barely been able to stomach patting her hand, and *then* he'd held her wrist as though he was disgusted by it, as though it was diseased! Why couldn't he have just left her by the sea? She didn't want to be here, in a world where no one loved her. Everything would have been so much easier if she'd just —

"Oh, honey, I'm so sorry!" cried Cassandra, interrupting her thoughts. The girl then threw her arms around Andromache and squeezed her, hard.

Andromache collapsed. She cried and cried, blubbering to Cassandra about Muka — about her blanket — about the white-wrapped body sinking downward —

"Oh, you poor thing!" murmured Cassandra. Her eyes, too, looked red. "How long have you been down here?"

"I don't know..."

"Can I get you something? A hot drink, maybe?"

Andromache shook her head and tried to pull herself together. With a shuddering breath, she said, "It's — all right, I — I'm fine."

"You're shivering, honey, and your clothes are damp. You need to change your dress. Come on — I'll walk you upstairs."

Once again, a hand took hold of Andromache, but this time it was a gentle, girlish hand, and the fingers wove comfortingly through hers. Other than the *flap, flap, flap* of Penthesilea's sandals — which Andromache finally kicked off in irritation — the two young women walked in silence all the way up the stairs, to the door of Andromache's room.

There, Cassandra gave her another hug. "I loved her, too," she whispered. "She used to sleep on my bed, sometimes, when I was younger..."

ॐ

SOMETHING WAS FLUTTERING against Andromache's foot when she awoke. At first, she thought it was Muka's tail, and that the whole morning had been a dream. She looked up.

Just the curtains, she thought sadly. As they waved, she alternately saw and didn't see the dark grey sky of a rainy evening. She'd slept most of the day. *No sense getting up now*, she decided, pulling her blanket over her head.

Wait — blanket? Immediately, she resurfaced to eye the coverlet. As she'd suspected, it wasn't *her* blanket. Hers was new, white and scratchy — and it now lay at the bottom of the sea. The striped blanket covering her was old, shabby, and soft to the touch. She'd never seen it before.

Cassandra, she thought. Cassandra must have left it for her — sweet, thoughtful, Cassandra. Andromache had babbled all her woes to the girl, including her lost blanket. Her eyes filled with tears, which she wiped away with the soft striped cloth of the blanket. Someone loved her, after all.

Scritch, scritch, scritch.

Pause.

Scritch, scratch.

Pause. "Andromache? Honey? Are you awake?"

"Y-yes," stammered Andromache, hastily dabbing at a fresh round of tears. "Come in."

The door opened a crack and Cassandra slid through. "How are you feeling?"

Andromache sat up. "All right," she sniffled. "Cassandra?"

"Hmm?"

"Thank you so much for — for —" Andromache couldn't finish the thought. Her throat was constricting, her eyes brimming over again.

Cassandra sat down beside her and kissed her cheek. "Of course, honey." Slipping her hand into Andromache's, she asked, "Say, are you hungry?"

"A little, maybe."

"Good! Mom's made a dinner, for you — for the whole family. She sent me up to fetch you."

Andromache shrank, feeling suddenly cold. A family dinner? The noise, the inevitable squabbling...she couldn't face it. Not today.

"Everyone's down in the kitchen, already," coaxed Cassandra, tugging gently on Andromache's hand — gently, but firmly.

Andromache's eyes fell on the blanket, and she knew that she couldn't refuse.

As she walked down the stairs with Cassandra, she noticed that Penthesilea's shoes were gone. Either someone had returned them to their rightful owner, or they'd been taken to the room of broken sandals, from which they would never emerge.

∾

THE MEAL BEGAN with one of Priam's orations.

"No being on our earth lives in separation from other beings. All share the same air, the same water, the same land. Much as the stars are linked together in a great celestial web, so are we creatures of the earth interconnected. When one life ends, sorrow flows through the other lives touching it. Tonight, we sit in remembrance of one such creature — Muka, beloved friend to this household, and most of all to our Andromache..."

He spoke on at length, and Andromache was moved. Everyone there sat in solemn silence. No one sighed or smirked, not even Paris — although, from the way he was rubbing his arms, Andromache suspected that training with Penthesilea, not grief over Muka, was responsible for his reserve.

Once Priam finished speaking, Hecuba tried in her own way to honor Andromache's loss. "Here, dear," she said, passing a plate of roast lamb. "You should take the first serving."

Andromache stared at the glistening, reddish slab of meat. Why hadn't Hecuba just passed it around, like usual? Now, everyone was staring at her! What was she supposed to do? One thing was certain — there was *no way* she was putting *that* on her plate! Any other day, she might have been able to ignore it, but after the morning she'd had —

256

"Go on." Hecuba smiled, taking Andromache's hesitation for meekness.

Hector broke in: "Mom, for pity's sake — she doesn't eat meat!"

"Oh! Oh my," spluttered his mother. "Why on earth not?"

Andromache stared at her plate, wishing she could pass through it into another realm.

Realizing the position he'd put her in, Hector said hastily, "She said it's a religious practice, I think — but maybe I misunderstood. Her Lukkan is too fast for me, sometimes."

Annoyed at him for blabbing, and still hurt by the way he'd deserted her, Andromache shot him an evil look. His face and hands were red from windburn. He'd probably been out joyriding with Penthesilea — no, with *Lee* — while Andromache lay slumped on his entry hall floor.

"Is that true?" asked Priam. "Did my son hear your words right, little one?"

There was nothing for Andromache to do but nod.

"How interesting!" the priest exclaimed. "It's true that I've heard vegetarianism is the purest way of eating, since it doesn't cause the suffering of fellow creatures. Perhaps I'll have to try it."

"Me too!" chirped Cassandra.

"Andromache, you might have advised us of this," sniffed Hecuba. "We would have been happy to make accommodations for you."

"Oh, I don't need — I didn't want — I mean —" Andromache gulped. "I didn't want to make trouble," she whispered. Once more, her eyes were filling with tears. Why couldn't they have left her upstairs, in peace?

"It wouldn't have been any trouble." Hecuba sniffed again.

"When did your sect begin this practice, my dear?" probed Priam, still fascinated by Andromache's supposed religion. "Are there any other dietary exigencies?"

"Yes, Andromache," Hecuba said acidly. "Are there any other *exigencies* of which you have not yet made us aware?"

"Mom!" protested Cassandra. Under her breath, she hissed an explanation to Andromache: "Sorry, honey! Mom doesn't do well with surprises."

"No," murmured Andromache, in response to Hecuba's question.

"Too bad." Paris smacked his lips on an extravagant mouthful of lamb. "Your exigencies — *smack* — are working out — *smack* — in my favor."

Andromache scowled at him.

"Paris, once and for all!" barked Hecuba. "You needn't inflict that cacophony on us!"

Chastened, Paris closed his mouth and swallowed.

"And *you*!" Hecuba's finger now pointed at her eldest son. "Since you knew so much, why didn't you tell *me*, and save me from looking like a fool?"

"Once again, I wasn't sure if I'd understood," said Hector. "And *I* didn't want to look like a fool by saying the wrong thing. Glaring gods, Mom, I'm not fluent *yet*."

"Even so, you can watch your mouth a little, I think!" his mother snapped. "There's no reason for blasphemy at the dinner table!"

Her fury, however, had abated the instant Hector said '*yet*.' After that, a mollified Hecuba passed plate after plate of bread, dried fruit, honey cakes, and lentil stew to Andromache, who tasted everything — dutifully at first, then with real appetite.

Once night had fallen, Paris pulled out his lute and played a surprisingly tender dirge. Andromache thought of her empty bed upstairs — of the burned shack in Lyrnassa — of the crushed little cottage in Hurapi — and her eyes grew so misty that she had to turn them toward the ground. Before any tears could fall, though, Paris switched to a merrier tune. She was soon tapping her fingers against the table.

Hector, noticing the movement, caught her eye and smiled.

After a moment's hesitation, Andromache smiled back. She couldn't really hold his dinner faux pas against him, once he'd turned it to her advantage. As for leaving her by the door — well, if Paris was right, Hector simply wasn't good at comforting people. He got things done, instead. She had no right to fault him for being who he was, especially not after he'd lugged Muka all the way down to the sea.

"Thank you," she mouthed at him, from across the dinner table.

He blinked in surprise, and then his smile deepened. "<u>Thank you, too</u>," he mouthed back.

Andromache looked away again. *Thank you, too?* What did he have to thank *her* for? Had he always had a secret wish to conduct a sea burial? Or was he glad to have gotten out of archery with Paris? Or was it just the only response he could think of, in Lukkan? She decided not to worry about it. Whatever the reason, he'd finally accepted a *'thank you'* from her.

Chapter 29

All the Trojans Andromache had met liked to call the city '*hilly*' or '*steep.*' She supposed they were right. Troy was built on a hill, or rather a spine of rock thrust up from the plain beneath it, and on top of the rock lay the debris of a thousand years of settlement. To walk from the walled citadel to the sea was indeed a steep journey. Andromache now knew this better than most.

Even so, she found Troy flat. She could see distant mountains, to the south and on the islands just offshore. Those mountains were a tease, though — easily seen but unreachable.

Andromache had grown up in the Lukka lands, on the flanks of a towering mountain range. It was a country of crystal skies and dazzling scree slopes. When alone, she hadn't been allowed to climb too far from her house; her parents had worried about rockslides, about raiders, about her getting lost. Still, she'd gazed ceaselessly up at the mountaintops. She'd imagined walking off of one, into the air, and being carried by the wind to the highest summit, the one so high that trees couldn't grow there.

Lyrnassa had taken some adjusting. There *were* mountains inland from the village, but only cliffs along the coast…

'It's ugly!' she cried to Auntie. 'It's flat!'
'You're used to mountains,' said Auntie. 'And these are hills. Give it time — you'll get used to them, too.'
'Anthills, maybe. I hate it, here.'

In truth, Andromache hadn't so much hated the countryside as her circumstances in coming to it. The longer they'd lived in

Lyrnassa, the more the place had grown on her. She'd climbed into the cliffs, gathering wild oregano to plant in her garden or watching the flight of large, black-and-white striped butterflies. From those heights, she'd discovered the thin band of pale turquoise water hugging the shore and the deep blue farther out. It was beautiful.

Andromache didn't think she could ever see beauty in Troy. While she enjoyed the gardens in her current house and took comfort in the strong walls of the citadel, gardens weren't wildflower fields and walls weren't rock faces. Her life was flattening out. She'd gone from mountains, to cliffs, to a low plateau, and it seemed that she hadn't stopped sinking.

Spring should have been a happy time of year, for her, no matter what the topography. The days were growing warmer. Each morning, new flowers opened in the garden — the courtyard was no longer just brown and green, but also yellow, soft pink, violet, orange, and scarlet. The vegetables, too, were growing furiously. Andromache had been looking forward to this season all winter long, but now she barely noticed its arrival.

Around her, in the shadows of the lengthening day, she saw plumy tails waving a ghostlike *hello*. She moved her foot under the library table, expecting to feel soft fur instead of just the floor. When she climbed the stairs, she sometimes crept into the alcove and sat there, wishing that Muka would find her.

Nighttime was the cruelest part of each day. Andromache had never had a room to herself, before. Someone had always been with her: her parents, her Auntie, Muka. Without the soft sounds of breathing, she had trouble falling asleep. Even if she managed to do so, padded footsteps followed her through her dreams — and when she awoke, sobbing, there was no one there to comfort her.

It was a lonely time. Andromache was no longer the center of anyone's world, as she had been for her parents — for Auntie — for Muka. Their main concerns had been loving her and making her happy. Now, everything had changed. No one cared about her in the same way, not even Cassandra. The girl may have hugged her, and talked with her, and brought her a new blanket, but the truth was, their worlds just barely overlapped. Cassandra had a full life without her.

Even worse than having no one to love her, though, was having no one to *love*. There was no center to *her* world, no one to adore, no one to shower affection upon, no one who needed her. Before Andromache's arrival, poor Muka had been all alone! Even Hector and Cassandra had gradually pushed her aside in favor of other pursuits. Andromache, however, had had all the time in the world to give Muka love and companionship. One housebound, the other old, the two of them had filled the voids in each other's lives.

Now, Andromache was left in a world without a center, where there was no one to call her own.

She tried not to make an issue of her sorrow. She kept to her usual habits of reading, helping in the kitchen, bathing, weaving, teaching Lukkan, gardening, and exercising. She avoided guests but not the family members. Most of the time, she didn't cry in front of anybody.

The family knew the loss she'd suffered, though, and they gave her space for her grief. They left it up to her to heal as she saw fit, on her terms and at her own pace — all except for Paris, who nourished himself, leechlike, on the woes of other people.

"I see you brought the sunshine down with you, Mopey," he jeered one morning, when Andromache came into the kitchen just as the brothers were leaving for archery practice.

She glared at him. Just what she needed, a new nickname! And just like him, to attack her when she was at her lowest! He reminded her of the weeds out in her garden, thriving where gentle plants — tender plants — died.

"You'll be more than mopey if you don't hurry up," Hector warned him.

"All right, all right," said Paris. "I just need to run upstairs to get —"

"To get *what*? What did you forget this time — your left eye?"

"My bow."

"Oh, Paris," Hector said in soft disgust. "Hurry!"

Paris sauntered out of the kitchen and up the stairs.

Hector gave Andromache an apologetic look.

"Is he really worth all the trouble?" she muttered.

"Yes," sighed Hector. "He's good — *really* good — but he won't practice unless he has a —"

"Taskmaster?" she interrupted, using Paris's favorite nickname for his brother.

Hector laughed. "I was going to say, '*nanny.*'"

"Oh."

"Thing is, if I didn't work with Paris, the whole city would think he's worthless. I can't let that happen to my own brother."

Andromache thought of the weeds in her garden and felt guilty. Should she be coddling them, instead of tearing them out? Was she missing out on some secret potential of theirs? Or was Hector wasting his time, cultivating a horrid little plant?

"Besides..." Hector went on in a low, mischievous voice, "The better he is at drills, the more it annoys Laoganus."

"Laoganus?" asked Andromache. "Oh — you mean the Ass General?" Ever since Hecuba had told her whom Hector had once addressed as '*You ponderous old ass!*' she'd thought of Laoganus that way.

Hector fell silent and began to turn purple.

Horrified, Andromache clapped a hand over her mouth. "Oh, gods! I didn't mean —"

Hector cut her off with a burst of laughter. "The Ass General!" he crowed in delight. "Oh, that's perfect! This afternoon, can you teach me to say it in Lukkan?"

Andromache rolled her eyes. "I'm supposed to be teaching you '*phrases of politeness and refinement,*'" she said stiffly.

"<u>Lahke</u> '*<u>goat sheet</u>?*'" he teased.

"Fine!" she said. "<u>Ass</u> — <u>ass, ass, ass</u>!"

As Hector's laughter redoubled, Paris returned from his mission upstairs.

"All right — here I am," he announced from the kitchen doorway. Noticing his brother's state of hilarity, he said, "Hey, thanks, Hermie! He'll go easier on me now that he's in a good mood."

"<u>Ass</u>," Hector shot back. He tried to glower at Paris but couldn't keep a snicker from escaping.

Andromache wanted to stick her tongue out at both of them and was glad when they finally left the kitchen. Paris needn't thank *her* for anything; Hector's merriment had nothing to do with *her*. He'd been that way ever since Muka's burial — laughing for a '*yes*' or for a '*no.*'

That was the day that he'd seen *her* — Penthesilea. *Lee.*

Their meeting had been a pleasure he hadn't been expecting, the joyous result of Paris's nasty sense of humor. Perhaps there had been more to their exchange than Andromache, sitting on the stoop, had been able to hear. Perhaps *Lee* was softening toward life in the citadel — *that* would explain the joy on Hector's face. Perhaps Hector was considering a move to the lower town...

Andromache thought back to *that day*, when Lyrnassa was invaded. More than eight months had passed — enough time, perhaps, for Hector's guilt to have run its course. He might see his project of salvaging a Lyrnassan as near-finished. He might be ready to move on, and meeting with Penthesilea — *Lee* — had been a reminder of all that life held for him. No more guilt, no more wistfulness, just towering mountains and crystal skies.

Mid-spring

Chapter 30

He's late, thought Andromache, tapping her fingers against the table. Late was an understatement. She'd been waiting in the library for over an hour. Hector had never been more than a little late, before — not without sending word.

Maybe he's skipping.

But he'd never skipped a lesson, either — he'd rescheduled them, or moved them, but even then he'd always let her know ahead of time.

Maybe he's sick, she thought, beginning to worry a little.

Sickness, however, seemed no more like him than tardiness, so she decided to keep waiting.

Another half hour slipped by without sign of him. That was when a dread suspicion hit her: *He's quitting.* Just as she'd feared, he was now moving on with his life. And what lay before *her*? Andromache closed her eyes and saw a plain as smooth and level as the surface of a stagnant pond.

(*Crying, again?*) sneered the Voice. (*There was a time when you wanted him to quit.*)

That was true. But she didn't, anymore. '*Lahfe ees a bakhoff got sheet*,' she remembered: her family's ancient refrain, brought back to life by Hector. She hadn't realized how sweet it sounded until now, when she might never hear it again.

(*You have other things to remind you of them*,) said the Voice.

And, as always, it was right. Andromache had found other tokens of her lost family. Weaving brought her close to her mom and Auntie. Written Truvan was a link to those long-ago lessons with her dad. And then there was Paris's lute — actually *made* by her dad's father — whose sound carried her back to her childhood in the Lukka lands.

Before, though, she'd always read *with* her dad, sat *with* her mom and Auntie while they wove, and listened to music *with* her whole family. Now, all of those activities were solitary, even the music. When Paris played the lute for her, he had no idea of its significance.

Only Lukkan allowed her to interact with her past. Share it with someone. Lukkan was the most meaningful link she had to her family — and it could only exist through Hector.

Andromache drew her legs up to her chest and sat there, rocking back and forth, staring out the window.

"Honey?" called a soft voice.

Andromache blinked back unshed tears.

"Mom sent me to find you," said Cassandra, as she entered the room. Her face was pale.

"He's quitting lessons," said Andromache, trying to sound resigned rather than desolate.

"Oh, no, honey," Cassandra shook her head and sat down beside Andromache. "Not quitting — leaving the city. He had to get ready. That's why he's not here."

Andromache frowned. "Where's he going?"

"I don't know. Why would they tell me?" Cassandra tried but failed to force breeziness. "I'm not on the council, yet, so I don't get to hear much about what the army's up to."

"Oh!" said Andromache, feeling stupid. She was aware of Hector's profession — *well* aware! Still, in spite of all she knew, she'd never actually imagined him leaving for a military campaign. To make sure that she hadn't misunderstood, she asked, "You mean, he's going off with the army?"

Without looking up from the table, Cassandra nodded.

"The army..." As Andromache spoke the words, she felt a surge of relief — knee-weakening relief. Lukkan lessons would be interrupted, but only temporarily. Hector wasn't quitting, after all!

"He doesn't have much time, tonight," murmured Cassandra. "We have to go downstairs now, if we want to say —" The girl's voice broke.

Alarmed, Andromache asked, "What's wrong?"

"Oh gods!" wailed Cassandra, bursting into tears. "What if tonight is the last time I ever see him?"

"Cassandra!" Andromache gasped in disbelief. "Why would you say that?"

"Because! What if — and he could be — I mean, all those — if he got hurt, or — oh, honey!" The girl let out a wrenching sob.

Andromache was at a loss to see the cheerful — sometimes *maddeningly* cheerful — Cassandra in such despair. Missing her brother was one thing. Andromache knew how much the siblings cared about each other, and she understood the sorrow of being separated from loved ones. But despair made no sense for a temporary separation!

Who was Hector, after all? The greatest warrior Troy had ever seen! No one could compare to him; he was invincible. All of the visitors had said so, and Andromache had proof that they were right. She didn't put much stock in godly blessings, but she *did* believe what she'd seen with her own eyes: Hector's greatest feat of all. On the day that Lyrnassa was invaded, his lone injury had come from *her* — and that had been a fluke. How many Mudders had there been on that ship? How many attackers had Hector fought off? Enough that his report had been met with skepticism — and yet *not one* of those invading Mudders had touched him!

Judging by Hector's blood-slicked bronze armor, the Mudders hadn't fared so well that day...

Andromache shuddered. The thought still horrified her. But however she felt about that aspect of Hector's life, the facts were indisputable — he'd made it unscathed through the melee at Lyrnassa and obviously knew what he was doing. What was more, the council had such confidence in him that they'd given him command of half the army. Cassandra was tying herself into knots over nothing.

"He'll be fine," said Andromache, putting her arm around Cassandra. "He'll be fine."

The girl shook her head. "You don't know that!"

"Yes, I do!"

Once more, Cassandra shook her head. "Anyway, we have to —" She hiccupped. "He's leaving soon, and —"

"Then let's go."

"Oh — but I can't let Mom see me crying! She'll give me a piece of her mind!"

"No, she won't," said Andromache, although she couldn't help hearing Hecuba's voice in her own mind: *My dear, this isn't doing you any good!'* "But if you're worried about that, just take a deep breath. Maybe two." She inhaled, and Cassandra imitated her.

After a few more breaths, the girl managed to compose herself. "Thank you, honey," she said, giving Andromache a hug. "I'm ready now. Let's go."

$$\wp$$

THE FAMILY WAS GATHERED in the entry hall to see Hector off. He was wearing his new commander's field cloak, looking so proud and official that Andromache wasn't sure it was him until he joked: "What do you think of the vomit orange?" He spread the sides of the cloak, showing off its improbable hue.

"Hector, dear, for pity's sake!" sighed Hecuba. "Can't you just say *crimson?*"

"Not with a straight face, Mom. Just look at this thing!"

Hecuba grimaced at her son but nevertheless hugged him fiercely, cloak and all.

"Careful, Mom," warned Paris. "He doesn't have his armor on, yet."

"Oh, Paris!" hissed Hecuba. "Honestly! Must you?"

"Do you need help with your armor, son?" asked Priam. He was smiling, but in a bittersweet way.

"No thanks, Dad. I'm set."

Priam nodded.

Hector shifted slightly from side to side. He coughed and said, "So…"

Cassandra flew over to him and kissed his cheek. "Love you, brother," she whispered.

"Love you, too." He kissed her cheek in turn. "See you soon."

Hecuba and Priam then approached Hector for their hugs and kisses, and after them, Paris did the same. Andromache was the only one who hadn't. Assuming that she, too, was supposed to participate in the ritual, she took a step toward Hector.

He stood stock still and gave her a little wave.

The message was clear — *she* wasn't family. Andromache recoiled, feeling as gauche as she'd ever felt in her life. She tried to cover her gaffe by muttering that her foot had fallen asleep and even stomped it against the ground several times for good measure.

"See you," said Hector.

In a muffled voice, she gave him the traditional Lukkan farewell: "Stay well and come back quickly."

He nodded once and was gone.

Chapter 31

When Andromache had said '*quickly*,' she'd pictured Hector returning in two or at most three days. After all, the fighting down in Lyrnassa had taken only a few hours. But three days came and went with no sign of Hector. Then five days. A week. Ten days, and still no Hector. At that point, Andromache resigned herself to uncertainty about when he would come home. He couldn't be depended on to send messages, after all. He hadn't even done so the day Lyrnassa was attacked.

Perhaps he was too far away for messages to be practical. Andromache didn't know where he was or which ally he was defending, and although Priam or Hecuba probably could have told her, she didn't truly *want* to know. Knowing where he was would make his actions concrete — and she didn't like to think about what he would be doing...

A smoke-streaked giant — a monster with cavernous eyes — black hollows in a gore-spattered face — blood dripping down bronze armor —

No, she didn't like to think about all that, even now that she knew what Hector was really fighting for — and even if the very horror of those images proved that he would be safe. *He'll be safe*, she told herself repeatedly. That fact was enough; she didn't need to think about the '*why*.' *Hector will be fine*...

His family, on the other hand, had begun to concern her.

Cassandra was walking around with a peaked, woeful look. Foolish though the girl's fear was, Andromache wanted to help her. She suggested roodles matches and tried gossiping about the neighbors, but Cassandra took no interest in either activity.

When Andromache pretended to have heard a new rumor about herself — that she had no physical substance at all but was merely a trick of the moonlight — Cassandra just gave a dull nod and said, "Oh. That's nice."

Most of the time, Cassandra stayed in her room or in the library, away from anyone who might pester her — and ordinarily, Andromache wouldn't have pestered. She understood the need for solitude. The change in Cassandra alarmed her, though. The girl's normally sparkling self had frozen over like a brook in winter. As Andromache observed her, she had a troubling thought: was that what she, Andromache, would have looked like to her parents? If they could see her now, would they recognize the laughing little girl who had danced herself to sleep every night? They'd nicknamed her Little Cricket less because she liked '*The Cricket Song*' than because she sang and chattered all day. The Andromache of Lyrnassa and Troy would have been unrecognizable to them.

That thought bothered Andromache, but she didn't know what to do about it, and she didn't know how to help Cassandra.

No one else was offering to help the girl, either. Her parents were too anxious about Hector to notice anything around them. Priam spent more time than ever at the temple, and Hecuba whisked about, preoccupied and tense as a bow string. Andromache could sympathize with their worry — their son's future rested on this campaign. Priam and Hecuba were more grounded than Cassandra and surely knew that Hector was in no physical danger. They knew about his skills and his feats at Lyrnassa. All the same, he was facing his first real test as commander. If he didn't accomplish the goals set out for him, who knew what might happen? He might be relieved of command for good, this time. Understandably, his parents were consumed by thoughts of him.

Paris alone seemed unworried about Hector, but rather than helping his family, he only added to their problems. Without the structure of morning archery practice, he never bothered to rouse himself till midday — and by the time he slogged to market, nothing good was left. The family's cuisine was slopped together from a few uninspired ingredients, and no one had the wherewithal to scold Paris for it.

The situation first irked Andromache, then spurred her into action. While she could do nothing to ease the fears of Cassandra or her parents, she could at least make sure that they were decently fed. She didn't waste time goading Paris because she knew that he wouldn't listen to her. Instead, she put all her energy into the garden. The plants were now flourishing, thanks to the care she'd given them back in fall. It was the season for tiny, tender vegetables, which the garden gave and gave. The herbs, too, were surging back, as though to repay her for taking notice of them.

Armed with produce, Andromache did her best to improve the family's meals. She crept down to the kitchen every day to slip vegetables and fresh herbs into whatever mediocre stew Paris had made. Her garden had only a limited number of choices, and her culinary skills were pale compared to those of Paris, but at least the family was getting some nourishment. Once, when she spied Hecuba sitting down to eat a fresh green salad — actually *sitting*, not scurrying from place to place — she felt the warm glow of pride. She felt needed again.

It wasn't flashy or exciting — she wasn't hurtling down a cliff on a galloping horse — but in her small, quiet way, Andromache was coming to the family's rescue. It felt good, after all they'd done for her.

She knew, too, that their slump wouldn't last forever. Sooner or later, Hector would come home, unharmed, from wherever he was, just as he had from Lyrnassa. Lessons would start again, and the family would go back to normal. Until then, they would fumble through as best they could — and she would do her part to help them.

Chapter 32

Andromache dipped a crust of stale bread into the stew and tasted it. _More oregano_, she decided, making a face. _I hope that's enough to save it_. She doubted that it would be; she'd never tasted anything as bland as the brackish stew now bubbling over the hearth.

Paris was utterly useless, these days! Andromache thought back to what Hector had told her, not long before he left: *'If I didn't work with Paris, the whole city would think he's worthless. I can't let that happen to my own brother.'*

All that effort, all that time, every day, dragging Paris down to the archery range! Andromache shook her head. If *she* were Paris's elder sibling, she would have let him drift away into idleness long ago and closed her ears to what the city said about him. It hadn't struck her until that moment what a good brother Hector really was.

'You're a good brother,' she imagined saying to him, instead of asking if Paris was worth all the trouble. *'You're a really good brother.'* How would Hector have responded? She imagined him brightening, the way he had when she'd mouthed *'Thank you'* across the dinner table...

'You're a good brother,' she told Hector. 'A really good brother — a lot better than Paris deserves.'

Hector laughed his warm laugh, and his eyes lit up. They were bright and sparkling. His lips curved into a smile...

But imagining the look wasn't enough — Andromache wanted to see it for real. How much longer would it be before he came back? How much longer until she could tell him that he was a good brother — until she could make him smile? *How much longer?* she sighed. *I can't wait anymore!*

Andromache dropped her bread crust into the stew, she was so startled.

She couldn't wait.

She knew that feeling! She remembered it from when she was a little girl, when she'd woken up in the middle of the night...

'Mom...Mom...'
'What is it, Ahndromahk?'
'When's the sun going to come up?'
'Not till morning.'
'I know that! How much longer till morning?'
'A long time. Go back to sleep.'
'But I want to see if the yellow sparrowslip is blooming!'
'You can bet it's not, Little Cricket — it's still dark out.'
'But Dad —'
'Go to sleep, Ahndromahk.'

Andromache remembered sighing — flopping onto her left side, then her right — picturing herself skipping up the mountainside, up to the old hollow tree, where the first yellow sparrowslip of the year always bloomed — seeing the tiny flowers in her mind, almost touching them, almost smelling them — and sighing again because the picture in her mind just wasn't enough.

She couldn't wait!

The feeling was strange and foreign. Andromache had all but forgotten what it was. The last time she'd felt it, she was coming home to Hurapi, bursting to tell her parents about the big city market Auntie had taken her to, imagining the looks on their faces when they heard her news...

And what had come of all her anticipation? It had been crushed. Destroyed. Buried beneath the mountain, with her parents. After that, she'd seen no point in looking forward to anything. The future would only bring more horror. Why think about it at all? It was easier, less painful, just to drift wherever life's currents took her. Not to fight, not to dream. Ever since her parents' death, her feelings toward the path ahead had ranged from indifference to fear. Never once had she longed for the future, only the past.

Just now, though, she'd *seen* the future! She'd *seen* the look on Hector's face and wanted to be in that moment! *'You're a good brother.'* What a strange thing to look forward to!

Because of their Lukkan lessons, she'd spent more time with Hector than with anyone else in the family, but for all that, they weren't close. Hector was kind to her. He felt guilt, pity, and obligation toward her, but none of that meant he *liked* her. And while she admired and even liked him, now, she'd spent weeks in utter terror of him. He'd haunted her nightmares for months.

(*Then why do you want to see him so badly?*) asked the snide little Voice. (*Why do you want to give him a compliment?*)

Because it's true, said Andromache. *Because he deserves it...*

(*And?*) prompted the Voice.

Because he could have been my friend. Andromache had thought this before — that if only she and Hector had met in a different time, a different place, they might have been friends. He might like her, now, instead of just pitying her and feeling guilty for what had happened to her. He was funny, and nice, and he understood things no one else did, like the reason she couldn't stand to eat meat. He knew what she meant by, *'Life is a bag of goat shit.'*

Why did she want to see him so badly?

Andromache added to the answer she'd given the Voice: *Because maybe things will be different when he comes back. Maybe we'll be friends, after all*. The thought wasn't crazy. So much had already changed in such a short time.

Less than a year ago, Andromache had been ruined — exiled — unable to stand on her own. She'd been a mess when she came to Troy. Luckily for her, her host family had taken care of her, kept her safe, and soothed her wounds and fevers. They'd given her space when she needed it, and they'd given her a purpose, too, by suggesting that she teach Lukkan lessons. All the while, Muka's gentle, uncritical, and unfailing love had pulled her back from despair.

Then, all at once, she'd lost everything she'd come to rely on. Muka had died. Hector had left, putting Lukkan lessons on hold. The other family members had more or less disappeared from her life. Was she crying herself to oblivion, though? Was she wasting away? Was she dissolving back into the mess she'd been before? No! She was helping her host family in their hour of need, and she was even feeling glimmers of anticipation. She couldn't wait to see Hector. She wanted to make friends with Hector — Hector, who, less than a year ago, had terrified her.

She was a very different person from the one who'd come to Troy. If Hector hadn't left, she might never have noticed the changes — and he might not have, either. But now, after their time apart from each other, they might be able to move past awkwardness and guilt. They might be able to start over as friends.

(*What about Lukkana lessons?*) asked the snide little Voice. (*If he stops feeling guilty, he won't take them, anymore.*)

Andromache paused. *Maybe he'll start liking them for real, once his guilt fades. Or maybe he'll want to keep taking them out of friendship to me.* Far-fetched though both of those ideas seemed, as Andromache imagined Hector's bright-eyed look in response to *'You're a good brother,'* a tendril of hope wound around her.

In the days that followed, Andromache thought of more and more items to share with Hector when he came back. There was the poem she'd found, transcribed from a well-known song, but not faithfully: the prim transcriptionist had left out a section where the hero drank a lake of wine. Then there was the neighbor who had, in the guise of religious fervor, tried to foist an old robe on Priam. He'd sworn the light of an auspicious sign had fallen upon it. Although Priam had thanked the man, he'd later said slyly to Andromache: *'Too good to be thrown away, too old to be fashionable, is my bet.'*

That story would be sure to make Hector laugh!

There was also a growing list of Truvan words Andromache wanted to ask him about. She was so used to visiting the library in the late afternoon that she continued to go, even though Hector wasn't there to meet with her. She read many texts in those hours. More and more of the words were clear to her, but some still stumped her. She made a pile of texts that she had questions about, to look at with Hector when he came home.

Then, one day, she was aghast to see that the texts she'd set aside were gone. *No, not gone,* she sighed in relief, after inspecting the table more closely. *Just buried.* Someone had heaped a mound of other scrolls and tablets on top of them. The library was in shambles! Afraid that her little pile might be lost for good, Andromache spent hours wandering up and down in front of the shelves, trying to put the other texts back in their proper places. Should *On the Extraction of Arrows From Fleshy Parts of the Body* be put with texts on weaponry or with those on the healing arts? Should *Ersha Kills the Giant* be shelved among hero tales or among stories from foreign lands? In such cases, Andromache took her best guess and checked the next day to see if her placements had been corrected. They never were, but perhaps no one had gone looking for the texts, yet.

Hector would be able to tell her if she'd been right…

Either way, she was glad to have cleared off the table. Beneath the mess, she'd rediscovered not only her pile of texts, but also something far more personal: the drawings she and Hector had made during their Lukkan lessons. There, on broken bits of pottery, were the bowl of fruit; the frightened horseman; the river Scamander; the garbage heap Hector had laughingly tried to draw, the day she'd asked him to explain the word '*trush*'; and the Three-Legged Dolphin, his favorite constellation. She remembered them all.

The drawings were unnecessary, now. Hector knew all of those words without having to look at pictures for cues. Hecuba had said to get rid of the potsherds when they were no longer needed — '*No sense leaving things around to gather dust.*' But as Andromache glanced down at the drawings, her eye fell on the horseman with his round mouth and squiggly hair.

What if he comes back and doesn't remember anything? He might need the pictures, after all, she told herself. *It would be silly — a waste — to have to do them over. I'd better save them.*

Gently, she collected the used potsherds and took them up to her room. There, she tucked them into her clothing chest, all the way at the bottom, where they would be safe — just in case.

Chapter 33

"I'm so glad we found you *in*, Hecuba — you're never home these days!" cooed a woman's voice from the banquet hall.

Andromache, who was tidying the kitchen, froze. Visitors! Visitors were there, and she had no way of escaping them. She was trapped.

"It's your lucky day, then," said Hecuba, smiling, as she led her guests — two eleant, long-robed Trojan ladies — into the kitchen. "Oh, hello, Andromache, dear. Have you met Theano and Periboea?"

Andromache made an odd little bow. "Can I get you something to drink?" she asked the women, whose names she'd already forgotten.

Hecuba flashed a look halfway between a glare and a manic smile. "Only if you're free to join us, dear. We're going to sit out on the courtyard."

As she trailed the others outside, Andromache cursed herself. *Can I get you something to drink? Can I get you something to drink? Idiot!* If she'd just said '*Hello*' to the women, she might have been free to leave. Instead, she'd played into their suspicions that she was really Hecuba's servant — and now, she was stuck going with them, proving herself their equal!

Andromache sat where Hecuba indicated but tuned out the ladies' conversation, preferring to watch as a troupe of caterpillars munched their way through Priam's beloved medlar shrub. They were the first brood of the year.

Better stay out of sight, she warned them silently. *No one's here to save you, this time.*

Her attention remained fixed on the insect larvae until the phrase, "…such a noble figure," made her look up.

Hecuba stiffened almost imperceptibly, then said, "Thank you," in her loftiest, most gracious tone.

"You must be proud," the guest added.

"Yes, certainly," said Hecuba.

"And at *his* age!" the second woman breathed.

Her companion nodded in agreement. "What an honor!"

"Assuredly." Hecuba's agreement sounded pinched.

"I'm certain he'll succeed in his mission," the first woman proclaimed.

"And he'll return covered in glory!" the second concluded.

"If the stars will it," amended Hecuba, regally bowing her head.

"If the stars will it," echoed the other two.

'Covered in glory?' Andromache pictured Hector with lengths of garland streaming off of him and had to cough to hide her smile. When Hector got back, she would tell him that line, too — *'covered in glory.'*

The first woman went on in graver tones. "You know, Hecuba, we were thinking…"

"Oh?" asked Hecuba, a hint of sarcasm in her voice.

"His return would be the perfect opportunity for him to formalize his — ahem! — *irregular* relationship with that warrior girl —"

"Penlesteria," interrupted the second woman.

"Do you mean Penthesilea?" Hecuba was gritting her teeth.

"With Penthelestria, then, or Pantherstellia, or Pans-on-the-ceiling." The second woman waved away the matter of names. "The point is, it's not proper to have our commander —" She lowered her voice to a hoarse whisper. "— *living in disorder.*"

The first woman coughed delicately. "That is to say, conducting an illicit liaison."

"I know the meaning of the phrase!" snapped Hecuba. Her ears and cheeks were pink.

Andromache almost jumped in, then. She almost told the women about Hector's wistful look when he'd said *Blue is fohr the happy*; she almost told them how complicated his situation really was. Then, just as the words were about to spill out, she stopped them.

She didn't like how nosy these guests were. What business was it of theirs, what Hector did in his free time — with or without Penthesilea? And even if they'd had a right to know, Hector's wistfulness wasn't *her* secret to reveal. He'd once promised not to tell Priam about the caterpillars, and, as far as Andromache knew, he'd kept his word. She would guard his secret, now.

In any case, his mother was ready to defend him. "There's no disorder under *my* roof!" Hecuba said icily. "And my son will marry *Penthesilea* when he sees fit."

The women gaped, spluttered, and finally regained their aplomb.

"Well!" said the first. "If it's when they get back, there'll be a celebration like the city's never seen, between the wedding and the victory."

"If the stars will it!" insisted Hecuba.

"If the stars will it," chorused the women.

The first one added, "And you'll be glad once and for all that he was chosen for this path."

"I thank you for your kind thoughts," said Hecuba. The words sounded like a hex.

"And prayers, Hecuba," assured the second woman.

"Indeed," said the first. "The stars will see to it that everything is as it's meant to be."

Noticing a twitch at the corner of Hecuba's eye, Andromache intervened. "Can I get you more water?"

"Thank you, my dear," said Hecuba, and this time her gratitude was sincere.

After all the cups were refilled, talk turned back to trifles, and Andromache went back to watching the caterpillars.

Hecuba's polished dignity cracked only after her guests had left.

"It was very kind of them to visit," she said, as she and Andromache were cleaning up.

Presuming that she was meant to nod in agreement, Andromache did so.

"Yes, very kind indeed," Hecuba went on, "although I hope we shan't live to regret the time it took away from their *prayers.*" She practically spat the last word.

Andromache stared at her.

Hecuba took no notice of the staring but rolled her shoulders once or twice as if to calm herself. "Now, Andromache dear, let me serve *you* a little something." She replaced the water jar, took a small flask from the top shelf, and poured a cup of liquid for each of them. "Gulp it down, my girl."

Andromache gulped, then began to gag.

"Trust me," said Hecuba. "It's just the thing to wash the old biddies away."

Still gagging, Andromache added another item to her list of things to tell Hector: he'd been right about his mother's healing tonic tasting like armpit.

Chapter 34

Andromache contemplated the library with a deep sense of
satisfaction. The room looked tidy. Cared-for. Not a single spider web was sullying the corners; apart from her
small stack, not a single scroll or tablet was lying on the table.
Even if the texts weren't all in their proper places, they were at
least sitting neatly on the shelves.

The afternoon shadows were growing long. *Almost time for
dinner,* she thought. *I'd better hurry.* Earlier that day, she'd seen
Paris mixing a wan spray of herbs into a soggy, uninviting pot of
lentils. There was probably nothing she could do to save the
meal, but she owed it to her hosts to try. If *she* didn't, no one
would.

As Andromache opened the library door, she gave the room
one last peek. *Looks good,* she thought, but before she could step
out into the hallway, several scrolls near the table caught her eye.
They weren't sitting crookedly — indeed, they had an almost insistent straightness, a refusal of disorder. They were texts that
had seldom been taken from the shelf.

Without even having to go near the scrolls, Andromache
recognized them: the three-part biography of Sarcho. This text
was the first one she'd ever touched — the first one she'd ever
tried to read — on the first day she'd ever set foot in Priam's library. Stirred by a flood of memories, she forgot about the dinner lentils and walked back toward the table.

She looked up at the biography of Sarcho.

(*You wouldn't dare!*) sneered the Voice.

Andromache wanted to retort, but the truth was that she
hadn't dared. The scrolls had always reminded her of the way

she'd felt during her first days in Troy. Ignorant — worthless — a failure who couldn't read. Someone so low that a raider despised her. Someone who didn't belong in Priam's library or anywhere else in Troy. The uninvited guest, tolerated out of pity. The intruder.

Her future in Troy didn't rest on these Sarcho scrolls, of course. She'd made other connections and laid down other roots. All the same, she also knew the importance of one's first steps in a new place...

She was stumbling down the path into Lyrnassa — *Auntie was dragging her by the arm, urging her on* — *'You heard what he said. There's a village down here, Ahndromahk. We can find food. Shelter. Come, my girl!'* — *but Andromache was weak* — *covered in blood* —

(*They never forgave you for that,*) the Voice reminded her.

As always, it was right. From the moment Andromache had set foot in Lyrnassa, the villagers had seen her as cursed.

(*And just think about how much worse it would have been if they'd known about the wagoner* —)

SHUT UP! She wasn't going to let the Voice make her think about *that!* There was no point, least of all now, when she wanted to move forward! That whole hideous episode only mattered for the lesson to be taken from it: entrances were crucial. Unless Andromache could somehow retake her first steps in the library, part of her would always feel like an intruder. Part of her would remain the exile she'd been when she came to Troy.

Fortunately for her, no one in Troy knew about her failure to read the biography of Sarcho. Rumors and gossip had blocked her from having a second chance in Lyrnassa; this time, she would only have to battle her own mind.

Only her mind! Andromache sighed. In her mind, the Sarcho scroll loomed above her like the tallest mountain of her homeland, the one whose snow never melted. What if she tried reading it, only to fail again? What if the words were still scrambled? How many chances would she have before her exile became permanent?

Just do it, she told herself. *Look at everything else you've done since you came here.* She'd tutored Hector, the Raider of her nightmares. She'd walked out into the streets of Troy, at the risk of being trampled. She'd faced those fears. What was one little text, compared to all that?

Now was the perfect time to read the biography of Sarcho, with Hector away. He'd called the text '*painful*.' He'd drawn himself fleeing it! If he found out that she was reading it, he would mock her for sure. She no longer thought of him as an ignorant raider — far from it! — but she wanted to be able to answer his mockery with substance. He had strong opinions and could ask piercing questions. If she was going to discuss Sarcho with him, she had to be prepared.

Trembling, she took one of the Sarcho scrolls and sat down with it at the table. Slowly, gently, she unrolled the fine linen. Despite the numerous other texts she'd read since coming to Troy, she half expected Sarcho's biography still to be a mess of squiggles. Instead, she saw words — words that she could understand, words that had meaning. Many of them were difficult, but she'd run across harder ones in other texts.

You can do this, Andromache told herself. *You can do this*.

She began to read in earnest. The material included many of Sarcho's own words, introduced by his unknown biographer:

> *And yea, Father Sarcho guides us to our breathless*
> *oneness: 'with firlamingts —*

Andromache frowned. *Wait* — *firmaments? No* — *filaments!*

> *— filaments of learning to link yore and rarest*
> *might-have-been, our plunderous —*

No, wait — *ponderous*. Andromache smiled. *Maybe that's what made* Hector *think up* '*ponderous old ass.*'

> *— our ponderous selves do climb ever upward on the*
> *god-spangled tree of infinity.'*

Ponderous...thought Andromache. *Oh, I can think of a few other things I'd call* '*ponderous!*' Reading Sarcho's biography sapped her energy. Her head began to droop toward the table. *A little more*, she told herself. *Just a bit more. Maybe it gets better*. On the next line, the biographer interceded once again:

That inert —

<u>*No, Ahndromahk,*</u> she corrected herself. *Inner.*

> *That inner chime of which so many do despair ever to
> catch its ring shall onward 'wing the smacktrolds
> rithor — '*

<u>*What?*</u> Andromache's head snapped up. She shook it to clear
her mind and then read back through the passage:

> *And yea, Father Sarcho guides us to our breathless
> oneness: 'with filaments of learning to link yore and
> rarest might-have-been, our ponderous selves do climb
> ever upward on the god-spangled tree of infinity.' That
> inner chime of which so many do despair ever to catch
> its ring shall onward 'wind the slack-rolled river.'*

In disgust, Andromache stopped reading. '*Wind the slack-
rolled river?*' Was that really any better than, '*Wing the smacktrolds
rithor,*' as she'd first understood the words to say? She didn't
think so. In fact, she was sure that if her dad were there, he
would throw Sarcho's biography into the sea — or onto a garbage heap with all the other '*trush.*' He would be heartsick that
precious resources had been wasted on it!

Hector had been right all along about the biography of Sarcho. If anything, he'd understated just how painful the text really
was! Andromache had been wrong to discount his opinion —
but then, she'd been wrong about many things…

A light breeze ruffled her hair. When she turned toward the
window, she saw leaves of every shade of green — gem green,
ice green, night green — waving patterns on the silvery courtyard walls. Beyond, the roofs of the nearby houses were just visible, silhouetted in the rich light of late afternoon. The city was
aglow.

Andromache had seen the same tableau every day for almost a year, but now it moved her as it never had before. She
felt sorry for the harsh judgment she'd made after Muka's death.
Even without mountains, even without cliffs, Troy no longer

looked flat to her. It was a lovely, peaceful city, where strangers were cared for; where girls could hope to join the city's ruling council; where art and music and writing were cherished; and where the army was used only to defend. Troy wasn't perfect — the story of her own dad and grandfather proved that — but it was a remarkable place, a city worth belonging to.

Out in the hallway, someone heaved an extravagant sigh. Paris. Andromache knew that she was needed in the kitchen.

Gently, she re-rolled and re-shelved the Sarcho scroll. *When Hector gets back, I'll tell him all about Sarcho*, she thought. *About that, and everything else.* In her mind, she saw a brief image — not of cavernous eyes, or soot, or blood — but of caterpillars crawling across a large, brown hand. Perhaps he would have things to tell her, too. Perhaps he would see her differently, too.

PART TWO:

Beyond the Walls

Late spring into summer

Chapter 35

Troy had come into that loveliest of all seasons, the height of spring. The earth, recharged, now, by the winter rains, had swathed itself in greenery. Warm winds were blowing the scent of flowers to every corner of the city.

The days were long, now, too. Extremely long. In fact, for the past month, they'd been longer than any days Andromache could remember or imagine. Each day felt like a week, each week like a month or more. Half a year seemed to have passed since she'd last spoken Lukkan. Since she'd last seen —

Hicca hift!

Andromache's thoughts were interrupted by a soft sound. *How many does that make?* she wondered. *Five? Six?*

That afternoon, a particularly tedious one, she and Cassandra were sitting downstairs in the kitchen. Cassandra was reviewing one of her lessons, and Andromache was tallying how many times the girl coughed or cleared her throat.

I think it's six. No, wait — was that a cough or a sneeze? She has a really weird sneeze! I never noticed that, before...

Andromache had *nothing* to do. That morning's lush growth of weeds now lay in heaps on the courtyard tiles. Until Paris got back from market — he'd gone out later than *ever*, and he was taking his sweet time! — there was no point in starting dinner. The library had *nothing* in it for her to read, and it was far too hot to run stairs, even if she'd wanted the exercise.

Just as Andromache was letting out a sigh of utter boredom, Priam came rushing into the kitchen.

"They're coming!" he cried, so sharply that Andromache was afraid he meant raiders. Her face drained of color and she grasped the table for support. A wave of terrifying memories crashed over her...

A ship full of raiders was bearing down on Lyrnassa — she was flee-ing up the hillside — her feet were torn and bleeding — she could hear the sounds of screaming from below — they were coming for her — gore-spattered raiders with hollow eyes — they would find her — they would leave her corpse face-down upon the earth —

<u>*No*</u>*!* thought Andromache, while fear seethed in her belly. Her whole field of vision was turning red. <u>*Not here, too! Please, no!*</u>

Priam, noticing Andromache's look of panic, asked, "What's wrong, little one?"

"Who's coming?" croaked Andromache. "Mudders?" Mud-ders, those raiders from across the Western Sea! Mudders, those brutes who had invaded Lyrnassa and —

"Oh, honey!" Cassandra protested. "I told you, that's a bad word! You have to call them '*Achaeans*.'"

"Either way," Priam said soothingly, "that's not who I meant. The Trojan army is coming, girls. They'll be back in un-der an hour."

Andromache relaxed against the table. Meanwhile, Cassan-dra dropped the text she'd been studying, ran to her father, and threw her arms around him. Priam's message was happy news: the return of the Trojan army meant that Hector was coming home at last! Yet both Priam and Cassandra seemed subdued.

Priam, she supposed, was worrying over how well his son had fulfilled the mission. If Hector came back in disgrace, having failed his first test as commander, he would be done. Laoganus, the other commander, would regain control over the whole ar-my. He would send Hector to the far ends of the earth, or per-haps have him shackled to the oars of a slave ship, as he'd once threatened to do. He would take joy in it, too! He'd probably been yearning for vengeance ever since Hector had called him an ass in front of the whole city council. Hector's future was tied to the outcome of the mission, and his parents didn't want to bring bad luck to him by celebrating too soon. *'If the stars will it,'* Hecuba had insisted, each time her friends had spoken of Hector's imminent victory. And as for Cassandra —

"Where *is* everyone?" asked Priam.

"Mom's next door," said Cassandra. "And Paris said he was going to market. Oh, Dad — do you know if —"

"No, my girl," said Priam, shaking his head gravely. "We'll have to see. Why don't you go down with Andromache, and I'll find the others. We'll meet you as soon as we can."

As Priam rushed off, Andromache asked, "Go down *where?*"

"There's a place," explained Cassandra, "on the walls, where you can look down at the gates and watch the soldiers coming in." Her voice dropped to a whisper. "The ones who — who make it back, I mean." Choking back a sob, she added, "We'll be looking for — for *vomit orange.*"

Andromache shook her head. Cassandra was *still* worried that Hector wouldn't be coming home, that his orange commander's cloak wouldn't be there at the gate with all the others! Andromache opened her mouth to chide the girl for her fears — to remind her just who her brother was! — but Cassandra broke in first:

"So," she murmured. "Let's go."

Go...Andromache's eyes widened. *Go*...Her mouth went dry. *Go*...

"I know, honey." Cassandra's tone grew more prodding and she took Andromache's hand. "I'm nervous, too, but we *have* to check."

Andromache's terror, however, had nothing to do with Hector. She wasn't at all scared for *him!* He was the talk of the entire region — the pride of towns that couldn't even claim him — the greatest warrior Troy had ever seen. He was invincible! What harm could possibly have come to *him?*

As for what harm could come to *her*, if she left the safety of the house...

Heels battering her shins — arms blocking her escape — feet crushing her stomach — sand in her mouth —

Andromache shook off Cassandra's hand.

"Come *on*, honey!" cried Cassandra, vexed. "If we don't hurry, we won't be able to see through the crowd!"

Crowd. Andromache was trembling. *Crowd…*

The Lyrnassans were surging around her without seeing her — they were crashing into her — heels were battering her shins, arms were blocking her escape — she stumbled and was lost in a sea of legs — feet were crushing her stomach — grinding sand into her skin and face — she was suffocating on sand — struggling, fighting for breath — choking on the earth —

In a Trojan crowd, though, there would be even more people. Thousands upon thousands of feet — elbows — knees. Andromache would be crushed before anyone even noticed!

"We *have* to get to the walls!" Cassandra went on. "If we can't find a place, we'll be stuck going to the gate instead, and it's a real whirlwind down there! Believe me, we're better off on the walls — you can see a lot more. Besides, even if we go down by the gate, we won't be able to talk to Hector. He'll be too busy. We can chat with him later, w-when he comes back up to the house, for the party." The girl choked superstitiously on the word *when.* "Anyway, honey, we have to run!"

Andromache shook her head.

Cassandra frowned. "Don't you want to look for Hector?"

Much as Andromache might have missed Lukkan lessons with Hector, she wasn't about to risk being trampled just to catch sight of his cloak. "I'll see him later," she said.

Cassandra gasped. "It's not — oh, honey, tell me it *isn't!* Tell me it's not because you're afraid to leave the house!"

Of course Andromache was afraid to leave the house! She'd decided long ago never to leave it, as Cassandra and her family well knew. Even on a normal day, she wouldn't have wanted to go out, but now, after her sense of fear had been sharpened by memories of raiders, of being crushed half to death —

Andromache shuddered. *Not a chance!* she thought.

"But you did it for Muka." Cassandra's tone was rebuking.

Andromache's cheeks reddened. *That* wasn't at all the same situation! *That* had been a last goodbye for a cherished, loving friend; *this* would be a hot, crowded, needless search for someone who wouldn't even know she was there. *This* wasn't worth being trampled for! Besides, that other time, she'd been with someone who could protect her from the mob. Who was supposed to protect her now — *Cassandra?!*

When Cassandra didn't get a response, she said indignantly, "Don't you care *at all* that they're back?"

Care? Of course Andromache cared — she'd been looking forward to this moment for weeks! But even if she weren't afraid of being trampled, she wouldn't now be following Cassandra down to the walls. She didn't want to see Hector in his armor, the way he'd looked at Lyrnassa. She didn't want to risk awakening her old Raider fears...

A gore-spattered monster was leaning over her. It reeked of smoke and blood. Its eyes were two cavernous hollows, and its teeth were gleaming fangs. They were bared, yearning to tear out her throat — to drain the blood from her body —

Again, Andromache shuddered. She wanted a new start with Hector, not a return to the old ways! No more fear, no more guilt. She wanted to share all the stories she'd been saving — to watch his face light up when she told him that he was a good brother. She wanted to be friends with him, too. Anything had seemed possible in recent weeks, and she didn't want to spoil that feeling by —

"Andromache!" Cassandra cried in outrage. "I said, don't you care that they army is coming home?"

"Yes!" Andromache exclaimed. "Yes, of course, but —" However much she cared, she didn't see what difference it would make if she went down to the walls. "Isn't there something I can do *here*, to help out?"

"There's the party tonight, as long as..." Cassandra didn't finish her sentence, but Andromache knew what she meant: there would be a party as long as Hector numbered among the returning soldiers.

Which he will be, Andromache told herself firmly. To Cassandra, she said, "I'll clean — set out lanterns — get things ready."

"Fine," Cassandra said coldly. "I'm leaving, now — *Hermie*." With one last reproachful look, she stalked out the door.

Hermie? If the girl hadn't already left, Andromache might have slapped her. Cassandra had *never* called her Hermie — '*as in hermit!*' Only Paris did that! *How dare you judge me!* Andromache thought at Cassandra. *You have no idea! Cassandra was judging *her*, Andromache? Cassandra, who had never stepped outside of her nice, pink, little world? What a laugh! The girl had experienced so little trauma that she had to invent things. To her, life was an endless string of beauties, like pearls wound around her neck.

And even if something had happened to Hector — which it *hadn't* — but even if it did, Cassandra had an entire family to comfort her. People would stand in line to take her in their arms and let her cry; she was almost sickeningly beloved. She certainly didn't need Andromache to join her entourage!

Andromache set about furiously cleaning the kitchen. She whisked back and forth between the table and the shelves, her arms heavy laden with dishware, her mind hurling insults at Cassandra. It was the shattering sound of a fallen jar that snapped her back to reality. She froze, savoring a moment of satisfaction at the wreckage she'd caused, before sweeping up the pieces.

For another two hours she marched around, cleaning this or setting that out, doing what she imagined had to be done to make the house ready for a party. She even scrubbed the rim of the Chute, the moldering pit where chamber pots were emptied. There was no one to ask what other tasks needed to be done. Everyone else was down at the walls, awaiting news of Hector.

They'll be back when they're back, Andromache told herself, but still she jumped at every sound.

When at last she heard the unmistakable tinkle of Cassandra's laughter, she dashed through the banquet hall to meet her.

"Oh, honey!" Cassandra threw her arms around Andromache's waist and spun her in a circle. It was as if their earlier scene in the kitchen had never happened.

Andromache knew then that the orange cloak must have been spotted. *I told you so*, she wanted to gloat, but rather than saying anything, she hugged Cassandra back.

More footsteps sounded at the door. A moment later, Cassandra's parents had joined them in the banquet hall.

"*There* you are, dear," said Hecuba to Andromache. "What in the name of the heights have you been doing, here?"

"Oh, uh — cleaning — decorating — getting things ready for — for — the party."

Hecuba pursed her lips. "It looks lovely, dear. But you really didn't have to. You should have come with." She sighed. "We'll take it from here. Why don't you go wash up? Cassandra, help her heat some water, will you?"

Andromache peered over Hecuba's shoulder, but no one else was there.

"He'll be home in a few hours," Priam explained with a smile. "There's always a lot to take care of — people to herd, horses to stable, chariots to stow. You can imagine the chaos."

"Oh, I wasn't —" Andromache began, but she didn't know how to finish the sentence. She wasn't *what?* Luckily, Priam had already turned to his wife, and the two were discussing details for the party.

Cassandra took Andromache's arm and led her away.

"How do your parents manage to throw it together on such short notice?" Andromache asked as they walked across the courtyard to the bath chamber. Although she hadn't been idle while the family was away, the place seemed far from ready. There wouldn't even be much food for the guests to eat until Paris came home from the market. *And who knows if he'll bring back anything at all?* thought Andromache. *He's gotten so lazy, without* Hector *here to prod him.*

Cassandra laughed. "Oh, Mom and Dad have their ways! Parties are their specialty. Step one is to pull lots of wine off the shelves. Any party is a success if there's enough wine, you know! Step two is to ask their friends to bring things over — food, musical instruments, more wine." Cassandra's eyes were twinkling. She had transformed back into her merry self. "But the best part is the dancing!" While helping Andromache to prepare a bath, Cassandra chattered on happily about all the dances she'd ever learned and all the boys she'd ever danced with. "Promise me you'll dance tonight!" she cried when the bath was ready.

"Oh, I don't know," said Andromache, shrinking. It wasn't that she disliked dancing. As a child, back in the Lukka lands, she'd danced almost every night. That had been a long time ago, though, and in a rather small group of people — her parents, a few neighbors. Nothing like the mob that was sure to be there at the house, welcoming Hector back! Andromache was going to have a hard enough time just *breathing* among all those people, let alone dancing. She might have thought up an excuse to skip the party altogether, if she wasn't so stung that Cassandra had called her '*Hermie.*'

"Someday, then!" Cassandra smiled knowingly. "All right, I'll leave you to your bath. I have to go help Mom."

Once Cassandra had left the room, Andromache locked the door firmly behind her. When Hector came home after his other tasks were done, he would no doubt want to clean up — and if he were to interrupt her bath, all hope for a new start with him would vanish because they would both die of embarrassment.

Chapter 36

Early afternoon had turned into early evening. Andromache was alone in the entry hall, sweeping the floor, when she heard the soft *creeeak!* of the door opening. She looked up to see Hector, his hair damp — he must have stopped to wash at the public baths — and a normal grey cloak around his shoulders.

He shut the door and smiled at her. It was a sweet smile, almost swallowed by an unfamiliar beard.

Andromache didn't smile back. However much she'd been looking forward to Hector's return, she was unprepared to meet him so suddenly. On top of that, a scent was distracting her — something green and fresh that the open door had let in from outside. She knew the scent from childhood but from somewhere else, too. *Where? How?* She couldn't quite grasp it —

"Did I hear the door, Andromache?" called a voice from the next room.

Hector's smile evaporated but was quickly replaced by another one. "Hi, Dad," he called back.

Priam appeared in the entry hall. In no time, the tiny space was flooded with the other family members. Cassandra ran to her brother, kissed his cheek, and hugged him, while Hecuba gleefully embraced both of them at once.

"Where's Paris?" she huffed, searching for her other son. "Where has that boy gone, tonight of all nights? Oh, when I get my hands on him, I'll —"

"It's fine, Mom. Don't worry about it," said Hector. "I'm sure he'll show up once the wine starts flowing."

Priam laughed. "Then let's beat him to it. We should have a cup to celebrate. You, too, little one." He beckoned to Andromache, the intruder, who had flattened herself against the wall so as not to interrupt the family reunion. "The guests are only going to drag in more dirt, anyway."

Andromache let the others go first so that she could linger a moment in the entry hall. She opened the door — just a crack — in order to catch the scent the wind had brought in moments earlier.

Thyme? she thought, wrinkling her brow. *Apples? No, that's not right. And now it's fading...*

She sniffed harder. Too late. The wind had shifted, and the scent was gone.

℘

WAVE AFTER WAVE of guests swept into the house. As they were filling the banquet hall, Andromache ducked into one of the room's many alcoves. There, she sought protection from the maelstrom.

Meanwhile, Priam steered Hector and his captains to the front staircase, where they could be seen by all, and toasted them with a lengthy oration.

"My friends. My neighbors. Tonight, it brings me deepest joy to celebrate with you the return of the army, in particular my son —" Priam beamed at Hector. "— and his captains. Palmys. Dolops. Orthaeus. Medon. Penthesilea." He nodded to each of them in turn.

Penthesilea...*Lee*. Hector's fiancée and comrade-in-arms. Andromache had never really seen them standing together. She'd been too sick and scared to observe them when they'd found her on the cliffs above Lyrnassa, and on the day of Muka's death, Hector had entered Penthesilea's house alone. Now, finally, Andromache saw how *right* they looked together. Tall, strong, and confident, they made an elegant couple. A regal couple. Perfect, except —

They're not touching at all!

Hector was standing as aloof from Penthesilea as from his male captains. Not that an oration was the proper time for full-on groping, but the two of them never so much as brushed arms. Andromache would have expected Hector to do at least that much, as wistful as he'd been about Trojan wedding symbolism.

He wants *to brush arms with her*, Andromache told herself, with another glance at the stunning woman beside Hector. *And a lot more than that. Remember what Hecuba's friends said?*

'It's not proper to have our commander living in disorder.'
'That is to say, conducting an illicit liaison.'

If the women were to be believed, Hector and Penthesilea were, if anything, *too* affectionate. *He doesn't touch her in public*, Andromache reasoned, *but when they're alone* —

At that precise moment, Penthesilea caught her eye. Andromache felt her cheeks flush under the piercing gaze. *None of your business, Ahndromahk!* she thought, hoping the warrior woman hadn't read her mind.

"...an announcement," Priam was saying.

Oh, gods! Andromache's stomach began to churn. Was this it? The announcement of their marriage, as Hecuba's friends had hoped? If so, what would that mean for Andromache?

As best she could guess — no one had ever confirmed her theories, but they made sense — Hector and Penthesilea had different reasons for delaying their marriage. Penthesilea — *Lee* — was reluctant to live up in the citadel, among the Trojan elite. Meanwhile, Hector still felt lingering guilt over the destruction of Lyrnassa, and studying Lukkan with Andromache was his way of atoning. His way of punishing himself, his way of helping one survivor of the Lyrnassan raid rebuild her life. He couldn't move on with his own life, with *Lee*, until his guilt faded.

Had that day finally come? Had he decided once and for all to let go of his guilt and marry *Lee*? Perhaps move down to the lower town with her? Andromache had been hoping that Hector's return would bring a different kind of change. She'd been hoping that Hector might grow to like Lukkan lessons, so that even as his guilt faded, he would still have a reason to take them. She'd been hoping that they might become friends...

Andromache's stomach roiled once more. A sudden marriage would dash all of her hopes.

"…pleases me greatly," said Priam.

Andromache held her breath.

"Following the success of their most recent mission, Penthesilea will be promoted to a new post created especially for her, as the direct subordinate of my son, here in Troy."

So, there was to be no marriage, yet! Sighing with relief, Andromache looked over at the two warriors to see Penthesilea exchanging a most professional nod with Hector. No simmering passion, no delight — and still no touching.

They're good, thought Andromache. *They're hiding it well*. Or maybe they just weren't affectionate people. She remembered the trouble Hector had had patting *her* hand, the day that Muka died…

Penthesilea once again looked over at Andromache. Her gaze was neither friendly nor hostile, just persistent. Andromache couldn't think of any reason the woman would take such an interest in her. Unless —

Oh, gods! Andromache swallowed hard. Of course — Penthesilea resented her! It was one thing for Hector and Penthesilea to delay their own marriage, quite another for a third party to thwart it. *Well, she doesn't have to stare at me like that*, thought Andromache. *It's not my choice, how Hector deals with his guilt!*

"— I'll just end with a few last words, the most important of all," Priam was saying. He gave his son a tender look. "That we're all ever grateful for the benevolence of the stars."

With that signal, Paris — who had finally shown up — began an interlude of soft lute music. It made Andromache think of home, of the far-off Lukka lands, of the songs her dad had once played. She was a little girl again, lying on a blanket her mom had woven. She was breathing in the fragrant breezes that blew through the pine-covered mountains…

Paris switched to a livelier tune and the room began to move. Guests milled freely, filling plates with food and cups with garnet wine. They hollered and guffawed, but the chaos didn't bother Andromache as much as she'd expected. So long as she clung to the walls, out of the main fray, no one pushed or shoved her. No one even noticed her. They were all there to see and talk to Hector.

He'd come down from the stairs and was now standing in the middle of the room, seemingly untroubled by the jostling horde around him. He gave a kindly smile to everyone, kissed cheeks with many, and exchanged a variety of other greetings.

Middle-aged men slapped him on the back — and, at least twice, caused him to spill his wine. Meanwhile, the women of that generation cupped Hector's chin when they spoke to him, waggling it back and forth in their hands as though in disbelief of his beard. Adolescent boys were ushered over to him by their parents, but they looked awkward and shy about being near him and quickly slunk away. Girls and young women, however, approached Hector with ease. Not only did they kiss his cheeks, they even held hands with him while they talked.

They were relentless, those young Trojan women with their fluttering hands and robes in butterfly colors!

Andromache looked around for Penthesilea but couldn't find her. Perhaps she'd left for the night, too irritated by the whirlpool of wings around her fiancé to stay. The cheek-kissing was so pervasive that it had to be a local custom, empty of romantic meaning. Still, Penthesilea was foreign, wasn't she? According to Cassandra, she came from Santiya, a land to the east. She was unused to Trojan ways, and the kisses might bother *her*. She might resent the fact that Hector was stiff with *her*, yet affectionate toward the fawning, clutching Trojan girls…

The crowd finally swallowed Hector. As he was cut off from view, Andromache shuddered, taking comfort in the fact that no one had come to see *her* — that *she* wasn't the one being engulfed. She would never have been able to endure what the guests were doing to Hector. At the periphery, though, she felt almost serene. She was a jellyfish, moving along with the currents, aloof from the shining silver shoals of fish below.

৪৩

SEVERAL HOURS AND several cups of wine later, Andromache was perched on the staircase that led up to her room. She felt odd. It was the wine, or perhaps the overstimulation. She'd grown used to her host family's boisterous conversations, but *this!* — gods, the party magnified their squawking by a thousand! To make matters worse, the dancing had begun. Dizzied by the rush of people, Andromache pressed her head to the cool wall and closed her eyes.

She was falling asleep in that position when fabric brushed against her left arm.

"Yeuh — ahre — all rahght?" asked a familiar voice, deep and husky.

Andromache opened her eyes and turned to look at Hector, who was sitting beside her. "I — I'm fine," she said. "And you?"

He smiled. "Yes, all rahght."

She looked back at him without smiling.

He touched his beard self-consciously and asked her, "Yeuh fink what?"

"I don't know," she said. She was just drunk enough to stare openly. "It's different."

"Betteh?" he asked gravely, "ohr wohse?"

She thought about it for a moment. "I don't know," she said again. "Just different."

"Oh," he said, looking uncomfortable.

Andromache tried to think of a way to change the subject. She had a month's worth of things to tell him, but none of them were coming to her. "Where's Penthesilea?" she finally asked, kicking herself even as the words left her mouth. After the stare Penthesilea had given her, and the likely reason for it, she didn't want *that* topic to come up!

Hector looked surprised but said only, "Gone. Home."

"Is she mad?" whispered Andromache.

"Mad?" Hector now looked perplexed. "Why?"

Andromache thought of all the butterfly girls grasping his hands, but that was none of her business. She didn't want to be like Hecuba's friends, those old biddies who'd accused Hector of '*living in disorder.*' "I don't know," she murmured.

"Oh," said Hector, still sounding confused.

A group of dancers swirled briefly in front of the stairway.

"Crazy parties," muttered Hector.

"You don't like them?" asked Andromache. She was surprised. He'd seemed happy enough, earlier.

He shrugged. "They're all right. Just a lot of people you'd never want to talk to."

Andromache looked out at the guests, and so did Hector.

"Yeuh see those one?" He gestured to a pair of gaunt, reptilian men who could only have been twins.

Andromache didn't correct his phrase: the two were indeed one, an ancient bicephalic turtle. She nodded.

"They hate *heem*." Hector pointed this time at a red-faced little man. "Becahse they haff grahntfathehs."

Andromache looked at Hector in confusion. Two — or, in this case, two-and-a-half — people didn't hate each other simply because each had a grandfather, did they? She was used to connecting a certain number of dots when Hector spoke Lukkan, but this time he'd given her too little to work with.

"There was an old wool rivalry between the grandfathers," he clarified, seeing her confusion.

"Over whose wool was best?" asked Andromache.

"Not quite," said Hector. "They were always feuding about whose cloth should be used to make the temple priests' winter night shirts."

"What?" she cried. "You're not serious!"

"Unfortunately, I am." He smirked. "Each man accused the other of high blasphemy."

Andromache giggled somewhere deep in her chest, although the sound was lost well before it reached the surface. "And the grandsons still hate each other?"

"Like blood hates the air," Hector said cheerfully.

"How do you know them all?" Andromache gestured at the partygoers.

"They all know my pahrents. Efferyone know theym." He heaved a sigh. "Now ah haff to go back out thehre…" His words trailed off as though he had more to say.

"But?" Andromache prompted.

"Baht I want sleeping." He looked at her, his eyes bright but ringed in shadows.

Andromache didn't blame him. She would want to sleep, too, after returning from — from — from wherever he'd been. "Can't you sneak off to your room?" she whispered.

Hector rolled his eyes meaningfully toward the courtyard, where people were jubilating. If he tried to pass through them to go to his bedroom, he would be trapped for sure.

"Oh," said Andromache.

"It is all rahght. Ah am — am — used to this."

"Oh."

"Anyway, I wanted to say hay-lo."

"Welcome back." Looking up at him, Andromache finally offered him a smile. "See you tomorrow?"

Hector smiled back. "Tomorrow," he agreed. "Oh…and you might want to stay away from Paris tonight."

Andromache hadn't planned to seek Paris out, in any case, but Hector's odd emphasis on '*tonight*' caught her ear. "Why?"

"When he gets really drunk, he dances on the tables — and sometimes he pulls people up with him."

Grimacing, Andromache said, "Thanks for the warning."

Hector gave a nod before diving back into the melee on the banquet hall floor.

Alone once more, Andromache rested her head against the wall. The whirling of the dancers had coaxed a breeze in from the gardens, a breeze that carried a hint of the same green scent she'd smelled earlier, by the main door. *Laurel?* she wondered, with increasing irritation. *Oregano? No and no. Lemon balm? Hmm — maybe a little, but there's something else…*

It was time for bed, she decided. There was no one else she cared to talk to, she didn't want to dance on a table, and she'd clearly had too much wine to drink. Teetering, she took the staircase up, away from the party.

In the small alcove where the second flight of stairs met the third, a dark-haired man was standing with his back to her. *Paris,* thought Andromache, feeling alarmed. She had to get past him before he saw her! He would no doubt find it hilarious to make '*Hermie*' dance on a table! In taking a second wary glance, though, she realized that Paris wasn't alone: there was a woman's hand buried in his hair and another clutching at his back. The two lovers were kissing with a writhesome frenzy that reminded Andromache of eels.

Hardly daring to breathe, she crept past them and on up the stairs. She'd barely gone halfway, though, when she stopped and whipped around.

So smug in their stupid little world! She ripped off one of her shoes and hurled it at the lovers. It missed them but struck the wall and landed with a loud *plop!* That sound was followed by the clatter of Paris and his girlfriend scurrying out of the alcove and back down to the party.

Her heart much lighter, Andromache retrieved the shoe and climbed up to her room. *They'll think twice, next time they run off to grope each other!* she thought, letting out a cackle and flopping onto her bed. She lay there, reveling in the glow of victory, but eventually a question began to gnaw at her: *Why?* Why had their kissing bothered her so much? Why had she ruined their tryst? Why hadn't she simply let them be?

(*You're jealous, you idiot,*) spoke up a familiar, sneering little Voice.

Andromache sat up and frowned into the night. Jealous? Well, it *had* looked like a nice kiss. A *very* nice kiss. When she thought back to what she'd seen, her pulse began to thud as though she were running flights and flights of stairs. No, she wouldn't mind having a kiss like that...

(*From* Paris?) taunted the Voice.

No way!

But, frowning harder, Andromache considered the idea. There was no denying how handsome Paris was, with his grey eyes and striking dark face. She supposed he could even be charming, in his slinky way. Then again, when Muka died, he'd wrapped his arm around her, and she'd felt nothing. Shouldn't she at *least* have wanted to kiss him, if not to thrash around, massaging his scalp?

(*Not necessarily,*) the Voice opined. (*You didn't know about that kind of kiss, then. Now that you do —*)

Andromache pictured kissing Paris the way the stairway girl had — one hand in his dark hair, the other on his back — and felt a tingle of excitement.

(*Jealous,*) repeated the Voice, savoring her unrest.

No! Not Paris — not lazy, malicious Paris — not Paris, who called her Hermie! Andromache couldn't possibly want *him* to kiss her!

(*Why else would you be so bothered?*) nagged the Voice.

Why, indeed? Andromache had no good answer. The Voice must be right. She must, after all, be attracted to Paris. *Oh, gods!*

she moaned to herself. *He can't find out!* But he was bound to, eventually. She knew from all the gossip he'd shared with her that romantic intrigues were his favorite. He relished ferreting them out, especially when they involved him. Once he discovered *her* secret, he would mock her, or try to seduce her, or crow the humiliating truth to his family. Possibly all three.

In drunken despondency, Andromache began to cry. If anyone found out, she would be expelled from the house! She knew how Hecuba felt about '*disorder*' under her roof. Andromache might soon lose her home — her friend, Cassandra — her Lukkan post — and all because of some stupid, mediocre lust!

She cried and cried, miserably clutching her striped blanket to her chest as though it would be the first thing prised from her hands when she was thrown out in disgrace.

Chapter 37

A fter a night of fretful sleep, Andromache went down to the kitchen. She hoped it would be empty. Now that she was aware of her shameful lust for Paris, the last thing she wanted was to face his family. Surely they would all sleep late, the morning after such a party! She could gobble down her breakfast and leave again before the others even awoke.

To her dismay, though, the kitchen was full. Cassandra was at the table with Priam, engaged in an animated conversation about her new astronomy tutor. Hecuba was standing near the shelves, pulling at Hector's cloak and murmuring something to him. Her voice sounded serious, although Hector — beardless once more — was smiling at her.

Maybe the cloak needs a repair, thought Andromache, before realizing that a certain family member was absent. She'd lucked out after all!

One by one, the others greeted her:

"Good morning, dear."

"Hello."

"Hi, honey!"

"Good morning, little one."

"Good morning," she replied to everyone at once. The others then went back to their conversations, and Andromache sat down to nibble quietly on her breakfast. Every so often, she froze, thinking that she heard sandals scuffing down the staircase, but Paris never appeared.

At least I'm lusting after the laziest person in the house, she thought wryly, to comfort herself.

A sudden silence made her look up. Had Paris joined them after all? No, everyone was staring at *her*.

"See yeuh layteh," said Hector — loudly, as though he'd already said it once.

Andromache flushed. "See you later," she mumbled.

Hecuba was beaming. "Well, Hector dear, you seem to have remembered your Lukkan! You'll be in fine shape for your lesson today. Oh, and afterwards, I want both of you to come to dinner."

"All right, Mom."

A short while after Hector had left, Priam drifted off to the temple, and Cassandra headed up to the library, leaving Hecuba alone with Andromache.

"Andromache, dear?" said Hecuba, as she too rose from the table.

"Yes?"

"Would you mind tending to the garden this morning?"

"Of course not." Indeed, Andromache welcomed the chore. It meant that she was needed in the house — and therefore less likely to be banished, even if someone caught wind of her attraction to Paris.

"Thank you. There's so much work that needs to be done — replanting, I mean. I don't know if you've seen the wreckage. You'd think our herbs had insulted one of the guests, the way they're strewn about! Can you imagine?"

Andromache shook her head.

"Of course you can't!" cried Hecuba. "You'd be the very last person in this city to lay waste to a garden, what with all the time you spend taking care of those poor plants. You have quite a knack, dear — as fine a touch as any I've seen."

"Thank you," Andromache said shyly. "But it's your spring water that makes the difference."

"The plants would never benefit from it without your dedication," Hecuba replied. "And they're not the only ones who should thank you! You've transformed my healing practice—I rarely have to run out for herbs, anymore. Almost everything I need is here — winkswort, lemon balm, snow root. Although, I *will* say it's a shame we have no owlsburr. I could use a good, steady supply of that! Down at the herb market, I usually can't find more than a dry sprig or two, and it costs a fortune." She clucked with disapproval. "And you can bet I'll be needing more soon, if we get the usual outbreak of summer rashes."

"I could try to grow it," offered Andromache.

"Would you really do that, dear?" asked Hecuba. "Everyone says it's a perfect headache to cultivate. Most vendors gather it in the wild, and they bring precious little to market, the rascals!"

"I'll try," Andromache repeated.

"Well, now! That would be something." Hecuba nodded stoutly. "I'll see what I can do about getting seedlings for you."

"And I'll go out to check on the other plants," said Andromache. "I'm done eating, anyway."

"That's for the best, dear," said Hecuba. "Otherwise, the poor things will wither down to nothing. I'm afraid we're going to be scalded, today. Honestly, the heat comes earlier every year! I suppose I should rustle my younger son out of bed. Have you noticed, dear — has he been sleeping in a lot, these past few weeks?"

Andromache's cheeks turned pink. She didn't trust herself to say anything about Paris. "I — I don't know," she murmured. "I should see to the garden…"

"Of course, dear," said Hecuba. "And thank you."

Once safely outside, Andromache tried to catch the green scent that had eluded her the night before, but the air was still and the fragrance nowhere to be found.

A night-blooming flower? she wondered. *I'll have to come out later, to check.*

ℰↃ

AFTER REPLANTING THE HERBS, Andromache spent most of the day behind a myrtle shrub. Hecuba had, if anything, underestimated how hot the day was going to be, and the shrub offered shade as well as a hiding place. Andromache knew she would have been cooler within the house's thick walls, but outside there was less risk of running into Paris. He seldom ventured onto the courtyard except at night.

Tucked away in her little haven, Andromache planned for that afternoon's lesson. *Maybe I can catch* Hector *up on news about his family*, she thought, *unless he's forgotten too many words, and we just have to spend the time reviewing*. He'd been away for a full month and had spoken no Lukkan during that time; he probably didn't remember as much as Hecuba thought he did.

Then again, the night before, he'd held up his side of their conversation in the stairwell. He'd understood her words of Lukkan, even when he'd answered in Truvan.

Andromache smiled into the greenery of the shrub before her. Oh, it had been nice to speak Lukkan again! With all her turmoil over Paris, she hadn't had a chance to appreciate just *how* nice. She was glad — very glad! — that no mention had been made of Hector marrying Penthesilea. Lukkan lessons were in no imminent danger of ending for *that* reason.

They were, however, still very much at risk: from inside the house, Andromache heard a voice that sounded like Paris. She gasped and huddled closer to the myrtle shrub.

ಠಂ

WHEN THE SUN was slanting at just the right angle, Andromache made for the back staircase. She refused to look at the second floor's shadowy alcove but instead hurried down the hall to the library.

Hector was already there. He was looking out the window, his back to her, his arms wrapped around himself so that one hand grasped the opposite shoulder and the other, his waist. The peculiar embrace reminded Andromache of what she'd seen in the stairway alcove, how —

At that moment, Hector turned around and smiled.

An embarrassed warmth welled through Andromache, from her stomach up to her cheeks. She would *have* to stop thinking about that kiss, before the family noticed her strange behavior!

"I'm late," she mumbled, fanning herself. It was even hotter in the library than it had been outside. Here, there was no wind at all. "I'm sorry."

"Yeuh ahre not late," said Hector, sitting down. Although beads of sweat were glistening on his forehead, he didn't remove his cloak.

Andromache joined him at the table. "Aren't you hot?" she asked, eyeing the wool garment around his shoulders.

Hector brushed a lock of hair out of his eyes. "Well — yes," he admitted.

"Then why are you wearing that thing?"

He looked down at the cloak in surprise, as though he'd forgotten he had it on. "Fohr thees," he said, first shrugging out of his cloak and then extending his right arm.

A jagged line of stitches ran from near his shoulder all the way to the elbow. The flesh was swollen, bruised, and covered in grey ointment, which gleamed sickeningly on Hector's otherwise brown skin.

"Oh!" gasped Andromache, her troubles with Paris forgotten. *Name of all the gods!*

"Ah am lah-cky," Hector observed.

Lucky! she thought. Lucky that the arm hadn't been broken, or hacked off entirely? Lucky it hadn't rotted away? Lucky his artery hadn't been severed? She supposed he had a point, if a grim one. "I guess it could've been worse," she murmured. "And it looks clean…"

"No dihrts," he agreed. "Baht Ah want to say, Ah use bohff ahrms the same. Remember?"

Andromache thought of the sketch that Hector had made in a long ago lesson: grapes and figs, drawn ambidextrously. She nodded.

"If one arm gets clobbered, I've got a spare. That's why I'm lucky," he explained. His tone was light.

Andromache looked away from him, and especially from his arm. How *stupid* she'd been! Despite Cassandra's dire croakings, she'd never believed that Hector might be wounded. It wasn't possible! Not a single Mudder had hurt him, the day of Lyrnassa's invasion. He was invincible — invulnerable — perhaps even charmed…

Oh, gods! Andromache moaned to herself. *How could I have been so stupid?* She took a peek at the awful wound. *Oh, gods!* Had he lost a lot of blood? How long — how excruciating — had the stitching process been? Andromache had been stitched once, after cutting her leg open on a rock. She'd passed out cold from the pain, and *that* cut had been a lot smaller. Had Hector passed out? Had he screamed? Had someone had to hold him down? Oh no! Had Penthesilea been there to see it all? Poor Penthesilea, watching her lover endure *that* — although, tough as the warrior woman was, she'd probably been the one to restrain him.

And now, Hector was sitting there, making jokes about it! Smiling! Did he expect Andromache to find his wounds funny? How sick did he think she was? How sick was *he*?

As though he knew what she was thinking, Hector looked down at the table and gave a soft sigh.

It was the loneliest sound Andromache had ever heard. She wished that she could tie her own eyebrows into a knot; it would serve her right! Who was she to judge him, for the way he dealt with his wounds? If he wanted to make jokes, he had every right! Hadn't she once admired his black laugh, the way he could shrug off painful things? She should help him, not condemn him!

She tried to think of a joke to tell him, to make him feel less uncomfortable, but she couldn't think of any. Polite interest was the most she could muster. "Don't you have armor?" she asked.

He looked up. "Of course — but I'm not a beetle, covered in plates from head to toe, Ahndromahk." He was teasing her, smiling once more.

She felt her cheeks turn red. "I know *that*, it's just —"

"Just what?"

Maybe you should *be a beetle!* she thought at him. What she said was: "So, the cloak is supposed to hide — uh, *that* — from your mom? So she doesn't worry?"

"Oh, no, not Mom. Ah show eet to her," said Hector, adding, "She knows how to keep wounds from putrefying. That's what the grey salve is for."

Putrefying! Andromache shuddered at his matter-of-fact tone.

Hector, who was picking at a loose thread, didn't seem to notice her trembling.

Andromache gulped. It her turn, now. "Your mom — uh, knows a lot about healing," she said.

Hector stopped fiddling with the thread. "Yes — *healing*," he repeated in a grave, scholarly voice.

"Healing." Andromache fanned herself once more. "So, if you weren't hiding your arm from your mom, why *did* you wear your cloak?"

"Fohr ahther — ah, peoples, ah, ohff Troy."

"Oh…"

Understanding that she wanted more of an explanation, he gave her one. "Peoples — they lahke — um, victory?"

"Victory," she said.

"Victohry," he repeated. "Baht they do not lahke see — uh — *to* see — wands? No — that means something else, doesn't it?"

"Wounds," she said. "That's the word you meant."

"Yes, that. *Woooooounds.* Peoples do not lahke wounds. Peoples lahke us — clean — and — and — um — entahre?" Hector frowned.

"Whole?" Andromache suggested.

"Yes — yes. Whole. It is mohre easy fohr them." Rolling his eyes as if at a child's lame joke, he added, "Then they can pretend we were just away on a pleasant trip to the sea."

"Oh," said Andromache.

"They want only the pretty. The clean. They see thees —" He pointed to the gash on his arm. "— and they look so fast away! They fink, '*Eet ees so aaaaaahgly.*'"

Andromache reproached herself for having been one of the ones who looked away. Well, she wouldn't do that again. She didn't want to be someone Hector had to wear his cloak around. "They'd rather not know," she summarized for him. "They don't want to see ugly things."

He nodded.

"And you wear the cloak so no one sees the wound — and so *you* don't have to see their stupid looks."

"Yes," said Hector. "Baht sometimes Ah fohrget the cloak. A person sees me. He fink, '*Eeet eees so aaaaahgly.*' And Ah *want* to say thees —" He made a rude hand gesture.

Andromache almost laughed. "And you *could* say it under the cloak, so —"

"So, next time Ah am mohre careful. Next time Ah wear the cloak. Maybe Ah see that one person again —"

"And then you can say what you really wanted to say the first time," said Andromache, repeating the gesture Hector had made but less vigorously, as though her hands were covered by a cloak.

"Exactingly," said Hector. His eyes were sparkling.

They went on to discuss everything that had been going on at home, the main news item being Cassandra's new astronomy tutor.

"Why new?" asked Hector.

"The old one had a fight with your dad."

Hector froze. "I don't understand."

Andromache started to repeat her words, more slowly, but he interrupted her.

"No — I understand what you said, just not — I mean, *no one* fights with Dad!"

"Oh, I see. He's just been —" Andromache paused. "A little tense."

"But —"

"And the fight was about the *stars*," she added, as though that explained matters.

Hector shook his head. "Still, it *really* takes a lot to rile him. I've only seen it once…when someone was attacking one of his kids."

Andromache made a connection — that unknown, terrible voice in the meeting her first night in Troy: *'You're speaking out of turn!'* "You!" she said sharply to Hector.

"No," he said. His eyes were dancing again. "I only attack Paris and Cassandra when they deserve it, and Dad backs me up."

But Andromache refused to joke with him. "No," she said, shaking her head. "*You* were the one being attacked! By the Ass General — I mean, Laoganus." She blushed; Hector snorted in amusement. "Laoganus was attacking you," she repeated.

Hector studied his hands, turning them over and over as if to make sure that they were intact. "And when Ah am gone, Paris makes trahble?" he asked, changing the subject. He clearly expected an answer of 'Yes.'

"Not as much as he's made since you got back," Andromache muttered without thinking.

"What?" Hector looked startled, then stern. "What trahble does he make now?"

Andromache cursed herself. Why hadn't she just kept her stupid mouth shut? Hector was canny — shrewd — all too likely to figure out that she was lusting after his brother! Knowing that she couldn't brush him off entirely without arousing his suspicions, she gave him a cautious, abbreviated version of what had happened the night before.

At the end of her story, Hector laughed. "Paris wouldn't be the first to get caught there, although he's probably spent more time on the Make-Out stairs than most."

"Make-Out?" asked Andromache, frowning.

"Oh, sorry," said Hector. "That's Truvan slang." He cleared his throat. "For — uh, kissing. I mean, young Trojans are always going up there to —" His cheeks flushed.

So did Andromache's — the Make-Out stairs, indeed! A sly comment Cassandra had once made came back to her — something about not using *those* stairs for climbing. Why couldn't the girl have warned her that young couples went there to kiss? Andromache would have been spared a whole slew of embarrassments — like finding out the stairs' true purpose from Hector — and seeing Paris in the midst of a stairway kiss — and discovering her own indecent lust for him!

"So yeuh — yeuh frow shoes?" asked Hector, sounding sheepish.

Andromache nodded. "They hit the wall near Paris."

"Yeuh ahre too nice. Ah fink Ah frow them by his head."

"I was *aiming* for his head," she admitted.

"It is hahrd to see in that stairs," he said. "So dahrk." Then, to Andromache's relief, the subject of Paris was dropped. "What on yeuh?" asked Hector. "What yeuh do, these weeks?"

"A lot of reading," said Andromache. "I found some texts we can use during lessons."

"Good," said Hector. "Ah am happy to read."

"There's one about a sea — the Muranda Sea?"

"The Munnanda Sea," he corrected. "It's through the straits, up to the northeast."

Andromache nodded. "That's the one! I couldn't figure out much else about it, though — there were lots of words I didn't know…"

"Ah can help," said Hector, smiling.

Andromache smiled back. "And then maybe you can tell me where to shelve the text, when we're done? I found it sitting out on the table with a bunch of other ones, and I'm not sure where everything belongs."

"Yes, Ah can look."

"Oh!" cried Andromache "And I wanted to tell you — I *did* finally read '*The Biography of Sarcho*.'"

Hector looked confused. "Finally? Fohr a long time, yeuh want to read this?"

She nodded.

"Why yeuh want to read it?" he asked skeptically.

"To see if it was really as awful as you said."

Smiling once more, he prompted, "And?"

"'*Our ponderous selves do climb ever upward on the god-spangled tree of infinity*,'" quoted Andromache.

Hector shook with laughter. "I warned you!" he said.

"You were right!" It felt good to be able to tell Hector some of what she'd stored up during his absence — especially since the compliment she'd most longed to give him, that he was a good brother, would have to wait. Now was not the time to turn his thoughts back to Paris! "You were definitely right about Sarcho."

"Baht *yeuh* ahre rahght to make sure."

Andromache smiled. "You've remembered so much Lukkana!" she said approvingly. His accent wasn't as crisp as before, but he'd retained a lot of words.

"Ah haff some practice," he said.

"Practice? How?"

"Wiff myself," he explained, adding, "Inside the head."

"You thought out conversations to yourself?" she translated. "You didn't say them aloud?"

With a wry smile, Hector said in Truvan, "It's not good for a commander to look crazy, talking to himself."

Andromache nodded. "I suppose not…" Silence returned. The air was hot and still, so thick it was almost unbreathable.

Hector idly ran his fingers through the tabletop dust. A line appeared, then a curlicue. When he noticed Andromache watching him, he cleared his throat. "Yeuh, ah, yeuh go to eat, now?"

She nodded, remembering that his mother had asked them both to be at dinner.

Hector retrieved his cloak and headed for the door. There, he paused to let Andromache go first, explaining, "<u>Yeuh can get mohre vay-getables</u>."

Vay-getables, she thought, as they walked downstairs. *Vay-getables — lahff — lahke — exactingly —* how she'd missed it! And not just Lukkan in general, but Hector's peculiar version of it. He'd remembered far more than she ever could have hoped. Review? No, he wasn't going to need a review. In fact, she would have to think of something new, or he might get bored. He was doing as well as if he'd never left.

In fact, it already felt like he'd never been away. He was just as easy to be with as before, although he almost seemed friendlier. *Friendlier!* Had she been right, after all, to hope for a new start with him? Had enough time passed since *that day* in Lyrnassa? Was his guilt finally fading? Was he going to start being friends with her, instead of just seeing her as a cause? She'd often thought he could have liked her, if not for their past — and if that no longer mattered...

And what about Lukkan? she wondered. Did he like it, now? He'd been practicing it in his head, after all. Would he want to keep taking lessons, even once his guilt was gone? Andromache hardly dared think these thoughts, but something seemed different, and maybe —

"Hey there, Hermie."

Andromache gasped and stopped short, stubbing a toe. She cursed herself for not anticipating this meeting. Of *course* Paris had been invited to the family dinner! How could she have forgotten that she would have to see him?

"Oh, and look who else is here — my brother, the quilt." Paris nodded at Hector's wounded arm.

"It still works better than yours," snapped Hector, elbowing his brother. Paris returned the shove.

"Paris!" squawked Hecuba. "The things you say!"

"Me, Mom? Didn't you see him shove me?"

"If she didn't, I can do it again," offered Hector.

"Oh, honestly!" griped their mother. "You boys have all the manners of two feral pigs!"

No one noticed the way Andromache was staring at Paris.

She was in shock. After all the torment and tension of the past day, the strangest thing happened when she looked at Paris

— *nothing*! His face wasn't ringed by a rosy aureole! The sound of his voice didn't stir her into even the most minor of ecstasies! And *Hermie*? *Hermie*! A giggle bubbled forth from deep inside her.

"What's up, Hermie?" asked Paris, surprised. He smoothed his hair with a self-conscious gesture and turned to the others. "Did you know Hermie could do that? Make that sound?"

The hair! A hand in the hair! Andromache giggled again, harder, looking right at him.

"What's wrong with her?" A now-irritated Paris directed the question at his brother, this time. "Is this *your* doing?"

"I'd say she's laughing at *you*, you puckering gnat!" Hector retorted.

Puckering gnat! Puckering gnat! Oh, that was it exactly — an obnoxious little creature ever miring itself in one's eyes! Andromache snickered. It must have been the wine that had brought on her surge of lust, the night before! She was no more attracted to Paris than to her dinner plate. Attracted to Paris? He was a baby — a silly, puckering gnat baby! Another stream of giggles rippled out.

"Seriously, Hermie, what's your deal?" Paris hissed darkly.

"Do — do you think she needs a tonic?" whispered Hecuba, sounding concerned.

For the very first time since coming to Troy, Andromache laughed. She laughed wildly, exuberantly, until she was bent over double. Oh, gods, it felt good! Still laughing, she staggered over to Paris, hugged him, and kissed him on the cheek just as Cassandra often did. By now, everyone was gaping at her. *They must think I've lost it!* thought Andromache, laughing even harder. Paris shrugged out of her embrace, and she stumbled over to an empty seat by Cassandra, who had started giggling along with her.

Paris threw an olive at each of them. Although Andromache's struck true, the one he'd lobbed at Cassandra ricocheted off her, hitting Priam in the eye.

"Oh, for the sake of the roiling seas, Paris!" chided Hecuba. "Why must you blind your father at every opportunity?"

"Tomorrow we'll work on your aim, little brother," Hector teased good-naturedly.

Priam gave an oration, and the family began to eat. It was the best meal any of them had had in a month, now that Paris was back to his old cooking routines, but Andromache hardly tasted it. Every time she thought her giggles were finally spent, she would catch a glimpse of Paris and think, *Puckering gnat.* Then she would start laughing again. So would Cassandra, and Hector, and even their parents, although Paris maintained the emphatic silence of the wronged. At the end of the evening, however, he surprised Andromache by returning her hug and kiss. While the embrace gave her no rush of lust, it did give her new respect for Paris: she never would have dreamed that he could be so gracious after suffering hours of mockery.

Andromache walked upstairs feeling lighter of heart than she had in a long time. Hector was back and seemed ready for Lukkan lessons. She wasn't attracted to Paris. There was nothing to worry about, no reason not to get a good night's sleep. She lay down on the bed and covered herself with her blanket. She uncovered herself. She turned onto her right side, then her left, and then tried curling into a ball. Nothing worked. Sleep would not come.

All she could think about was the kiss she'd so vindictively interrupted.

Cut it out! she told herself. *Stop obsessing! Just go to sleep and forget about the damn kiss.*

The more she tried to bury the thought, though, the more insistently it came forth — and with it, the same shudder of excitement she'd felt before. Plainly, her lust was no mere trick of the wine. It was real enough, even if it had more to do with the type of kissing than with the man she'd seen doing it: *One hand buried deep in the man's dark hair, the other on his back, pulling him close...but where were* his *hands? In the woman's hair? On her back?*

Andromache felt a pang of jealousy even more vicious than the first. She would gladly have given a week's — no, a month's! — worth of sleep for another chance to throw her shoes at the lovers. It wasn't fair! What had that girl done to deserve such a spine-tingling kiss? What had she done to deserve the excitement of slithering against a boy for a few moments without worrying that he might hurt her? Nothing, that's what, aside from being born in Troy! Apparently, *all* young Trojans kissed that way.

Well, Andromache was half Trojan, too! Her dad had been born in the city, and she lived there now. She had just as much right as anyone else to dabble in stairway romances!

Unless…was she too old? *Was* she? She sighed. Probably. However young she looked, she was older than Cassandra — older than Paris. In all likelihood, Trojan women her age didn't go around kissing boys indiscriminately, the way Cassandra did. Trojan women her age got married.

Well, if that was the case, she would just have to do without boys. She would live out her days gardening, reading, and teaching Lukkan. She would be like Auntie, living to quiet old age. Andromache could see the allure of going somewhere safe, like Priam's stairwell, to kiss a good-looking boy, but marriage was another story. Marriage, and everything it entailed, were most emphatically *not* for her!

Andromache thrashed back onto her left side and looked out the window.

A breeze was blowing through the treetops. As the branches moved about, they seemed almost to touch the stars. She stared at the optical illusion, wishing she could climb up the trees and out into the sky. How many steps would it take to reach the celestial ocean? And how far out could she swim? *Nowhere near the Lorani,* she thought.

Lorani — they were like the glowing sea jellies in the earth's own seas, but much, much larger. They were so large and far away that they didn't even know the earth was there…

Chapter 38

Andromache rose very early to tend her garden while the day was still cool. Hecuba was already in the kitchen, and Hector arrived a moment or two later. At first, Andromache was glad to see him. Their lesson had been fun, the day before, and so had dinner. As he was sitting down, though, she noticed that his face had a surly, ominous look. Fun was forgotten; she didn't even dare greet him.

Hecuba frowned almost imperceptibly. "Good morning, Hector, dear," she said.

He gave a curt nod.

"How are you this morning?"

"Fine."

"Is your arm healing well?"

"Yep."

"Do you have a lot to do today?"

"Yep."

Hecuba forced a smile. "Oh, I forgot to tell you, dear — Socus and Hypsipyle will be getting married later this summer, or perhaps in autumn, depending on what your father sees in the sky."

"Great."

"The wedding will be here, of course."

"Mmm."

"It'll be lovely, I'm sure. You know how excited the city gets about big weddings!"

Hector made no response but instead began tearing his bread into chunks.

"I wish you wouldn't pick apart your food like that," said Hecuba in irritation.

Andromache wished that she was invisible, or at least that she'd waited another hour before coming down to breakfast.

Hector threw the remaining bread onto his plate and left without a word to either woman. As soon as he was gone, his mother, too, tossed her food aside and muttered something that sounded like '*uncle.*'

Hector's mood was fouler than any Andromache had seen, but she assured herself that it wouldn't last. *He didn't sleep well,* she told herself. *Or maybe he was mad because* Paris *skipped archery practice. And I'll bet his poor arm hurts. It's probably stiffest in the morning. He'll feel better by the time I see him for lessons.*

When Hector entered the library that afternoon, though, Andromache saw instantly that his humor had, if anything, deteriorated. To her tentative, "Hi, how are you?" he responded only with a raise of the eyebrows.

All of her plans for the lesson — mostly regarding stories she'd forgotten to tell him the day before — flew out the window. For too long, she could do nothing but silently watch him examining the backs of his hands.

"How — how are your guys readjusting?" she finally managed to whisper.

Hector looked at her but said nothing.

She tried again: "Are they happy to be back in Taruisha — in Troy?"

"Oh," he said. "Eet ees deefferent."

Well, at least he'd answered. "Different, how?" she asked.

He stared at her as though she were stupid.

Andromache flushed. Her question hadn't been *that* absurd, and she was sure he'd understood it. Still, she offered a few suggestions: "Sleeping at home? No more riding?"

Hector shrugged. A lock of hair flopped over his eye, but he didn't move it.

"Seeing family and friends?"

He shrugged again and went back to examining his hands. Andromache gripped the table until her fingers went white. How naïve she'd been, the day before, to think that things might have changed — that she and Hector might finally become friends!

(*But something has changed,*) murmured the snide little Voice, and, as always, it was right.

Something had changed. Hector squabbled with his family at times, but he'd always been courteous to her. He'd shown boundless patience for her nervous ways and had even endured her insults and abuse without complaint. He'd transported live caterpillars and dead dogs at her behest, accepting it all as punishment for what had happened in Lyrnassa. Now, he was punishing *her*. Abusing *her*.

Well, forget that*!* huffed Andromache. If Hector was done flogging himself, and if he still didn't want to be friends with her, so be it, but she wasn't going to let him start flogging *her!* He might have gotten away with it when she first came to Troy, but she was a different person, now.

In that moment, Andromache came to a very rash decision. "I know you must have a lot to do," she said. "And I don't want to take up your time with a bunch of silly questions."

Without giving Hector the chance to stop her — not that he would have! — she ran from the library and down the hall. Cutting the lesson short gave her a sense of freedom — of triumph. She never would have had the guts to do it before that day! On impulse, she stopped before coming to the staircase. *Might as well go all the way*, she thought, knocking on Cassandra's door. "Cassandra!" she called.

"Honey?" asked the girl, as she opened the door. "What are you doing here?"

Andromache froze. Her sense of daring was beginning to fade, leaving her terrified by what she was about to say. "I was just — um, wondering —" She couldn't quite choke the words out. *This is a bad idea*, she told herself. *Go straight back to the library, and —*

The library — Hector's arrogant look —

"I was wondering if you were going out tonight," she blurted. She knew that on warm evenings, Cassandra met up with her friends to discuss whatever they were studying with their tutors. Many times, the girl had asked her along, as a guest. She'd always made excuses...

"Well, yes," Cassandra was saying. "I'm going to a concert."

Music. You love music, Andromache reminded herself. Music was at the root of her oldest, sweetest memories.

"Why are you asking, honey?" Cassandra furrowed her eyebrows. "You don't — you don't want to come, do you?"

"Yes," said Andromache, more definitely than she felt. Going to Cassandra's soiree was a stupid idea! Months ago, Cassandra had told her which subjects the city council hopefuls had to study: history, poetry, astronomy, music, foreign languages, plants and animals, numbers, painting, and so much more. *To be on the city council, you have to know everything!* Cassandra had said. Andromache knew only the barest fraction of *'everything.'* She was nothing but a silly village girl! Everyone would know that she didn't belong there. They would all laugh at her, and —

"Oh, honey, I can't believe it!" Cassandra's face shone with joy. "We're going to have so much fun!"

Fun? Andromache doubted it, but now she was stuck. "Are a lot of other people coming?" she asked timidly.

"No," said Cassandra. "Just a few of my friends."

A few friends, Andromache repeated to herself. That didn't sound *too* bad...

"Oh, let's make a plan for when to meet up! I'd love to just go downstairs and relax until it's time to leave, but I have *so* much reading to finish first." Cassandra sighed. "I'll probably have to skip dinner. Hmm, how about this — I'll come find you in the kitchen right around sunset. I can grab something quick to eat, and then we'll go!"

"Good," whispered Andromache. Now that a plan was set, her triumph had all turned to terror.

"Oh, honey!" squealed Cassandra. "I can't wait! I can't wait! I can't *wait*!"

&)

THE EVENING BREEZE was warm and sweet with the perfume of apple blossoms, but Andromache barely noticed. She was too busy trying not to throw up.

I'm leaving the house! Not spur-of-the-moment, as she had for Muka's burial, but in a deliberate, pre-meditated act. And for what, a stupid tiff with Hector? One by one, she pulled weeds from the garden boxes, strewing their bedraggled remains beside her — *schluuup! Schluuuuup!*

As she finished weeding the first box, she heard the soft *scuff!* of sandals crossing the courtyard. *Oh, Priam must be home*, she thought. Good! Talking to him might take her mind off the horror of what she was about to do. When she looked over, though, instead of the priest, she saw his eldest son. Hector caught her eye and gave her a tentative wave.

In anger, Andromache dug her fingernails deep into the wood of the garden box. That stupid wave! It reminded her of how gauche she'd felt the night he left with the army, when he'd hugged everyone else while giving her a horrid little wave. She'd never hated a gesture more!

Hector waved again, more vigorously this time.

Andromache refused to acknowledge him. Not only was he *waving* at her, it was his fault that she was exposing herself to the danger and ridicule of a night out — *his fault!* If he'd just been civil to her during their lesson, she *never* would have asked to go with Cassandra to her soiree. Hector definitely did *not* deserve a greeting!

He began moving toward her.

Oho, feeling lost without your daily dose of penance, I see! Andromache thought spitefully. *Well, leave me out of it! Go wallow on your own side of the courtyard.*

"Hay-lo," he said, sitting down beside her.

Andromache raised her eyebrows the way he'd raised his own at her, earlier. "Off to bed?" she asked pointedly, hoping he would take the hint to go sooner rather than later.

"Yes, finally." His voice was grey and repentant.

Andromache turned toward him, noticing dark smudges under his eyes. She began to feel guilty for her curtness — and a little worried, too. She'd known Hector for the better part of a year and had never seen him upset, except at the council meeting the night she came to Troy. His black mood was something new, and he seemed to have little control over it.

His arm is hurting, she chided herself, *and he probably had a lot of work to do, today. Maybe he didn't get to see much of Penthesilea, even though she's living in Taruisha, now. Or maybe the two of them had a fight. Or maybe he's just exhausted, after being away so long, trying to defend another village like Lyrnash...*

Whatever the reason, Hector was obviously suffering, and he deserved a little slack from her. "Good night, then," she said, in a softer voice.

He nodded but made no move to leave. "The lesson ees so shohrt today," he said apologetically.

Andromache didn't respond. She could pardon his earlier rudeness, but only so far. She was still going to be in hell for the rest of the evening because of *him*.

Poking at the weeds with his toe, he spoke again: "The night ees pretty."

Andromache took a deep, involuntary breath of the evening air. Beneath the scent of apple blossoms, she caught a different, tangier, smell — the elusive green one. This time, it lingered long enough for her to seize it.

Cedar! she thought. *The next house over must have a cedar tree in their courtyard.* No wonder she'd been reminded of her childhood, high in the pine-covered mountains of the Lukka lands. Cedars had grown there, too. She exhaled slowly, holding the fragrance in her lungs as long as possible. The sky had turned deep blue, the last shade before black, and silvery stars were strewn across it. *'The night is pretty . . .'*

"Pretty," she whispered. "Like home."

"Yeuh want to say Lyrnassa?" asked Hector.

Andromache shook her head. "No, I meant before Lyrnash. With my mom and dad and Auntie." She felt very close to them, just then.

Hector paused, the look on his face balancing between interest and caution. He knew that the subject of her family was an extremely sensitive one. "So, when yeuh liff een — *in* the lahnds ohff Lukka?"

"Lukká," she agreed, giving the country's name its native pronunciation.

"Eet — *it* is lahke what?" he asked.

"Beautiful," she murmured. "We lived on a mountainside, and every night I used to lay out in front of our house and look up at the stars. There were pine trees all around, and flowers, so the air always smelled sweet. It was even more beautiful than here."

Hector didn't challenge her. He asked only, "Pine?"

"Pine," she translated. "There were so many pine trees in Lukká..."

Pause. "Yeuh leaff why?"

Andromache gulped. "Because my parents died."

Pause. "How — uh, how ahre —"

"How did they die? A rockslide."

"Rockslahde..."

"You understand?"

"I fink so."

"Part of the mountain collapsed and buried our house."

Pause. "Yeuh — *you* ahre not — in — in —"

"Inside? No. Auntie and I were at a market in another town. Mom and Dad were home."

Long pause. "I see."

"The rocks fell on top of them." Andromache swallowed hard. "That's why I wanted to take Muka to the sea. Remember? I couldn't stand to bury her in the ground, under all that dirt."

"Ahndromahk —" Hector's voice was inexpressibly gentle. "I am so sohrry."

Andromache blinked rapidly several times. She didn't want to cry, least of all in front of Hector, who didn't know how to comfort people. She thought again of the stiff way he'd patted her hand, the day that Muka died. "When we found the house," she said hurriedly, "or what was left of it, Auntie decided to leave Lukká, to live in my dad's country." She cleared her throat. "He was from here. From Taruisha."

"He is Trojan..."

Andromache nodded. In a soft voice she went on, telling Hector more than she'd ever told anyone. "He was apprentice to a luthier — luthier. That's what my dad did — he made lutes. Lutes."

Hector's look sharpened; she'd plainly just confirmed a suspicion of his. "The lute ohff Paris?" he asked.

She shook her head. "The master luthier made that one. My dad left Taruisha when he was about as old as Paris."

"He leaff why?"

"His own mom died, for one thing."

Pause. "And his dad?"

"My dad really didn't like his father, the luthier," Andromache whispered. "That man wasn't nice to him at all. His father and mother weren't married, and when his father married some-one else and had another son, he didn't treat my dad like a son, anymore."

Hector nodded in understanding.

"My dad took his father's lute-making texts — he took a lute, those texts, and some tools, and he ran away." Andromache said this defiantly. She knew about the deep contempt that Tro-jans had for thieves. '*Thieves…vilest…criminals,*' she remembered having seen in a text, once.

Hector's face was grave but not disapproving. "You know," he said quietly. "He is died…"

"Who? My dad?"

Hector shook his head. "No. Your grahntfatheh."

"I know," said Andromache. "I heard."

Pause. "From Paris?"

She nodded. "Yes. He told me."

Pause. "The lute shop — it is down by Lee. By her street. You can see it…"

Andromache took a sharp, painful breath. By *Lee*? By Pen-thesilea? *Andromache had been to that house!* So, that meant she'd been near her grandfather's old shop — where her dad had grown up — where he'd been rejected and disinherited — where his mother, the luthier's servant girl, had died! At times, Andro-mache viewed her grandfather with a philosophical eye. His cru-elty had pushed her dad away from Troy, toward her mom. But tonight, after telling Hector about the rockslide, she felt only rage. Her dad might be alive today, making lutes down in the lower town, if his own father hadn't betrayed him. *Both* her par-ents might be alive, far from each other but happy, on some al-ternate life's path.

"I don't *want* to see that shop!" Andromache snapped. "My grandfather was an asshole!" She could feel the prickling of tears. "I don't want to see his shop, and I don't want to talk about him anymore!"

"All rahght, Ahndromahk," Hector soothed. "All rahght. No mohre."

Andromache took several deep breaths; Hector sat beside her in silence. She wondered if he was going to ask her a differ-ent question, or if by '*no mohre*' he meant that the conversation was over. She didn't want it to be over. She certainly didn't want it to end on heated words about her grandfather. "I think —" She cleared her throat. "I think I was telling you about my aunt — Auntie."

He nodded. "She brings you to Troy?"

"Toward Troy — Taruisha," said Andromache, using both the Truvan and Lukkan words for her father's city. "She picked it because Dad came from here. But also, Auntie was a weaver, like Mom, and Dad always said that lots of wool thread and cloth are made in Taruisha. She thought we could support ourselves, here."

"Baht here is too fahr?" asked Hector. "And so you stay in Lyrnassa?"

"Taruisha is a long way from Lukká," Andromache agreed. "I guess we got tired of traveling. I was young — thirteen or so — and Auntie was pretty old. It was hard, especially early on, because we had to carry a lot of stuff with us. Blankets," she explained. "And cloaks, and scarves."

"To be wahrm," said Hector.

Andromache shook her head. "No, no — to trade for food. They were all things Auntie and my mom had made back in our village, Hurapi."

"And lutes?" asked Hector. "You carry lutes?"

"Those — those were the first things we traded," Andromache said softly. "For boat passage up the coast." She had a memory, the image of a man walking away, a lute slung carelessly over his shoulder. The last lute her dad had ever made...

"So you take boats, wiff Auntie?" Hector prompted.

"Partway. Sometimes we had to walk." Andromache gulped. "Or go by wagon..."

It was dark now. Hector didn't seem to have noticed her shudder of revulsion. "Your Auntie, she lahke Lyrnassa? You lahke it?"

"Lyrnassa — Lyrnash — was nice," said Andromache, deciding on the spot not to tell Hector that the Lyrnassans had always shunned her. That they'd seen her as cursed...

She was stumbling down the path. 'Come, Ahndromahk!' How much further? 'Keep going, my girl.' She wasn't going to make it! 'Just a little more.' A little more. A few more steps. Then, the villagers saw her. 'Oh, gods!' they cried. 'She's covered in blood...'

Don't think about that! Andromache warned herself. Insistently, she went on with the answer to Hector's question: "It was nice. There were sheep, and goats, and gardens. There were things for us to do. Auntie's health wasn't good, though. She died about a week before — before —"

"Andromache? Honey? Where are you?" called a voice from the kitchen.

Both Andromache and Hector jumped.

"Cassandra?" asked Hector.

"Oh, hi, big brother!" sang the girl, dancing over to them. "And there you are, honey! What are you guys up to?"

"We had to reschedule a lesson," said Hector.

"Oh." Cassandra tried to hide her disappointment. "But Andromache and I were supposed to go out, together."

"*Out?*" Hector asked in disbelief.

"I should stay," Andromache said hastily. She was delighted to have an excuse that Cassandra couldn't fight. In this house, she was first and foremost Hector's tutor. "We have to finish the lesson."

"No, you should go," Hector insisted.

Andromache forgot any warmth she'd been feeling toward him. It was *his* fault she'd made these reckless evening plans, and now that he had a chance to save her, the traitor was refusing!

"Have fun," he added.

Andromache chewed her bottom lip until she tasted blood. Fun? Fun! He was mocking her, too. All that was left was for him to wave at her! She turned away from him before he had the chance.

"You should come, too!" trilled Cassandra, her face glowing in the moonlight.

"Not tonight. I'm too tired," said Hector. "Maybe another time."

"I'm going to hold you to that," warned Cassandra.

"All right," said Hector. "Now go. You don't want to be late."

ℰℭ

THE CONCERT was to be at the house of a certain Demuchus, who lived — or so it seemed to Andromache — an interminable distance away. The only other time she'd been outside of the house, she'd stayed fixedly behind Hector so as not to see the frightful city around her. Cassandra, however, made a point of walking side-by-side. Andromache had nothing to look at but Troy itself, now cloaked in layers of frightful evening shadowry. She shivered. All the pockets and alleyways she remembered from her earlier trip were more ominous than ever...

Cassandra, noticing the shudder, took Andromache's hand. Either gestures of comfort came more naturally to her than to Hector, or she was preventing Andromache from turning back toward home. If it was the latter, she needn't have worried: they hadn't even left the citadel, but Andromache was hopelessly lost.

"Demuchus's house is gorgeous," gushed Cassandra. "You won't believe it! His uncle's on the council, and they're *obscenely* rich!"

Andromache pursed her lips. What incredible wealth must Demuchus have, to impress someone of Cassandra's status?

"Demuchus is going to be on the council, someday, too. Just like me. He's much further along in his studies, though. I mean, he's older than *Hector!*"

The emphasis Cassandra put on her brother's name suggested that Hector was himself just shy of being as old as the earth or the sea.

"Ancient," mumbled Andromache.

Cassandra giggled. "I only meant *learned.* That's why Demuchus gets to host these soirees. He knows so much more than the rest of us."

Andromache raised an eyebrow. "And he has a gorgeous house," she said.

"That doesn't hurt," Cassandra admitted. "But we don't get to see much of it, because his uncle —"

"Thinks soirees are too noisy," said Andromache. "You told me that, once."

"Well, it doesn't matter, anyway — his courtyard is just *gorgeous!*" sang Cassandra.

When they arrived, a man opened the door for them and showed them inside. There, a dozen or so young people clamored to greet Cassandra with the usual round of cheek kisses.

Andromache hung back. *A few?* she thought in horror. To her, a few meant three, maybe four.

"Everyone? This is Andromache." Cassandra dragged her forward. "She's staying with us!" To Andromache, she introduced all her friends.

The only name Andromache caught was that of their host, Demuchus. He was shaped like a fennel seed — tall and thin with a slight bulge in the middle. He didn't look like someone who would know more than Cassandra.

His house, however, lived up to its reputation of gorgeousness. It was even larger than Cassandra's home and positively choked in finery. Delicate fabrics were draped over elegantly carved tables; dozens of painted vases sat on jewel-encrusted pediments. While the others chatted, Andromache gawked at the riches around her.

"Let's go to the courtyard, shall we?" proposed Demuchus, with a nervous look toward the stairs.

Andromache presumed that he was worried about upsetting his uncle, the one who didn't like noise. She felt sympathy for the old man and wished that she could sit with him and read, instead of attending the concert. The young people moved outside, though, and Andromache was pulled along with them. On the courtyard, she had her second disappointment of the evening: there were no garden boxes out there, just a few potted plants and three trees. Three spindly, little trees.

That's not their fault, Andromache rebuked herself. *They're doing the best they can.* They couldn't help it that their courtyard had no spring! There was no sense in covering the place with garden boxes, either, when they would have been almost impossible to care for. Andromache looked at the barrenness around her and felt grateful she lived where she did, in a house lush with vegetation and bathed in the sweet scents of apple blossoms, roses, cedar, and herbs.

The group of friends, Andromache in tow, made their way to four long benches arranged in a square. Cassandra and most of the others sat down on three sides of the square, leaving the fourth side open for the performers.

"Are you a musician, too, Andromache?" asked one of the young women, extending a lute as if in offering.

Andromache stared at the lute. It wasn't like the ones her dad and his father had made; it was too new and had the wrong shape. Her eyes tingled with imminent tears. *No!* she told herself. *Don't cry in front of these people! Just answer the question.* "No — I — I — no — my — but —" she stammered. To herself, she added a sarcastic, *Well done, Ahndromahk!*

"That's all right," said the woman with the lute. "It's not for everyone." She sat down on the far bench with two other musicians, who had likewise picked up their instruments — a drum and a reed flute.

Andromache suspected that she'd failed some kind of test, but she didn't have much time to fret about it. A hush fell over the group, and everyone sat still as the first song lilted through the courtyard.

They sat still.

Perfectly still.

Perfectly and utterly still.

Perfectly and utterly still through song after intricate song.

Andromache fixed her bottom to the bench and tried to keep her breathing to a minimum. While the music was lovely, she didn't know what to make of the silence beneath it. Back home, when her dad was playing his lute, all her neighbors had whooped and cheered. They'd twirled Andromache in circles until she collapsed to the ground, watching the sky's misty streaks turn back into precise and brilliant stars.

Cassandra's family never danced to Paris's music except at parties, but when they listened to him play, their quiet was comfortable. They at least permitted themselves to fidget once in a while.

Here, all was still.

Deep in the back of her throat, Andromache felt the twinge of a cough. *Oh, no!* she moaned to herself. No one else had even scuffed their sandals against the ground, and yet here she was, about to cough? She *couldn't* bring that shame on herself! She pretended that her lips were sewn together so tightly that no air could escape — she pictured a wide stream of water pouring down her throat to squelch the cough — she imagined that she was in a cave with thick walls, where she could cough herself inside out and no one would ever know.

The last song faded to nothingness.

"What did you think of the music, Andromache?" Cassandra asked her.

"Pret — ty," gagged Andromache, struggling to hold back the worst of her hacking. Why, oh why, had Cassandra chosen to address her, just then? Now *everyone* was looking at her!

"Pretty!" interjected a man in robes of a toxic green color. "That's a *pretty* tepid description of it." He paused to let the others admire his word play.

Andromache frowned, then coughed. She wasn't sure how to feel about the man in toxic green. She disliked him on sight, yet he'd at least done her the favor of taking the group's attention away from her.

"And what *was* the inspiration for those songs?" he went on. "Did I detect a southern influence?"

"Indeed," approved Demuchus. "Although the southern elements are far more nuanced than in some pieces…"

He launched into a scholarly discourse on music theory that Andromache couldn't begin to follow. She felt lost. On the other hand, the many interruptions, clarifications, and questions made more than enough noise to drown out her coughing.

From music, the discussion branched out to other topics — history, law, and literary works the young people were reading with their tutors. Andromache sat back and listened, both fascinated by the group's learnedness and relieved that no one asked her opinion on anything. Cassandra's friends made her feel stupid. They didn't read for pleasure, like she did, but with purpose — they were trying very hard to know everything. Each of them had a close relative on the council, and they all intended one day to take that relative's place. Studying was, if not life or death, at least the means to their future.

Andromache drifted in and out of the conversation, not fully listening until Demuchus made a different sort of comment:

"The council was pleased with — *ahem* — your brother's report this evening," he said to Cassandra.

Hector had spoken to the council? It must have been just after the failed Lukkan lesson, and just before Andromache saw him on the courtyard. Well, no wonder he'd been so ill-tempered all day — worrying about the meeting would do that to anyone! But if Demuchus was to be believed, everything had gone well for Hector — which perhaps explained his gentler mood when she saw him out on the courtyard.

"Did *you* go to the meeting?" asked the man in toxic green. He seemed awestruck.

"No," Demuchus said with gravity. "Now is not the time to interrupt my studies. Uncle told me all about it, afterward."

Andromache stifled an ironic laugh. Was she the only person there who'd been to a council meeting? Spoken at one? That seemed to be true, yet she was the last person here who would want to. *What a world*, she thought, knowing that even the man in toxic green couldn't have disagreed with her.

"He also said that as soon as I begin my final writings, I'll be asked to serve as attendant," added Demuchus.

The others nodded solemnly.

Andromache remembered that all would-be council members first had to spend a period of time serving the council — by fetching texts, doing research, and other such tasks. They also had to write a long essay about something of interest and importance to the city. That was no doubt what Demuchus meant by *'final writings.'*

"What are you writing about?" asked one of the guests.

Demuchus's already-pinched nose narrowed further with distaste. "Uncle thinks that I should write about — *ahem* — the Achaeans. He's convinced our future is tied up with theirs."

A chorus of mumblings rose up among the guests, but Demuchus shushed them with a raised hand. "And he may be right, no matter what some of us think. But, regardless, I feel drawn to a more universal topic — the injuriousness of kingship to civilized societies. In countries all around us, our brethren suffer under the yoke of monarchs both feckless and cruel, while here, in Troy, we enjoy…"

Andromache stopped listening again. Wind was gusting through the courtyard trees, making their branches whip and thrash. From one of them, a leaf escaped — it was a fig leaf, large, shaped rather like a hand. It leapt into the river of wind and swept past the house, then back around to the square of four benches, where it skimmed over Demuchus's hair.

"What was that?" he said sharply.

"What was what?"

"I felt something — on my head."

Andromache watched as the leaf, unseen by the others, flew over the courtyard wall.

"A ghost crown!" said someone, giggling.

"Crowns and sovereigns are *not* to be joked about," Demuchus said sternly. "Not even those of the spectral variety."

"It was just the wind," someone else chided.

"It *is* getting windy…"

"I know. I'm cold."

"Me, too."

The young woman with the lute yawned. "And tired."

"Shall we adjourn for the evening?" proposed Demuchus.

To Andromache's relief, everyone agreed. After a prolonged round of cheek-kissing and farewells, she was allowed to stroll back home with Cassandra. The whole way, the girl chirped excitedly, highlighting this point or that idea from the debate. Andromache nodded along without really listening. While the soiree hadn't been the disaster she'd feared, she was exhausted.

When they got back to the house, all was dark and quiet. Andromache excused herself from Cassandra, saying that she had to check on a night blooming flower. In truth, she just wanted to breathe in the air from her own garden — she didn't want to fall asleep with the dust of Demuchus's courtyard in her nose.

She inhaled. *Apple blossom…oregano…lily.* No cedar, though, which was strange. The wind was blowing harder, but it hadn't changed direction. Nothing was different except —

And then, Andromache understood. It all made sense, why she'd smelled cedar earlier but didn't now — and why the scent had two resonances for her, one from her childhood and one from Troy. She remembered one of her first meetings with Hector, when his hair had been damp and his hands scrubbed raw, and he'd brought a green scent with him into the library…

Andromache's cheeks grew hot. All that time, wondering what the fragrance was and where it came from! Well, at least now, she knew — and she would never have to think about it again.

Chapter 39

"Andromache!" sang a bright voice. "I have wonderful news!"

Andromache blinked. Wrinkled her brow. Stared at the door. Was it talking to her? *This must be a dream.*

"Andromache! Honey, open up!"

Not a dream...Cassandra. Andromache yawned.

"Honey? Are you all right?" The lilting voice took on a hint of worry.

"Just hang on," muttered Andromache. "I'll be right there." Her striped blanket had wound itself in knots around her legs. She took so long untangling it that Cassandra called out to her again:

"Hurry!"

"All right!" Andromache opened the door. "So," she asked, a little peevishly. "What's your great news?"

"My tutors aren't coming today!" Cassandra clapped her hands with joy. "Isn't that wonderful?"

Andromache rubbed her eyes. "But I thought you liked lessons," she said.

"I *love* them!" chirped Cassandra. "But Dad gave my tutors a holiday so I could show you around the city. It means we can go for a walk! Oh, I just love walking around Troy in the morning! You've never seen anything so beautiful. I don't get to do it very much these days, what with all my studying, but Dad says I work so hard, all the time, that it's really not a bad thing to take a break for *one day*. He says studying from texts is a complement to being out in the world, but one can't replace the other, and I've been too heavy on the text end, lately. Besides, he and Mom thought you might want to know your way around the city, now that you've started going outside of the house, so it all works out *perfectly!* You'll come, won't you?" Cassandra's eyes were shining.

Andromache was worn out from her late night, but she couldn't refuse — especially not when Cassandra hugged her and started dancing them both in circles. "All right," she agreed. "As long as we're back in time for my Lukkan lesson."

"Goodness, listen to you!" Cassandra giggled. "I'm not suggesting an all-day trek around the city walls, or anything. Just a stroll through some of the parks, maybe a garden or two. We'll just brush your hair a little — there! — and braid it — hang on, hang on — don't wriggle — just a little more — that's it! Now, I'll wait outside the door while you put on some clean clothes, and then we'll be off!"

Andromache picked out the first clean dress she found in her clothing chest but took her time putting it on. The combination of Cassandra's chatter and being spun in circles had left her dazed.

"You look ravishing!" gushed Cassandra when Andromache finally reopened the door. "You'll be surrounded by clouds of admirers!"

Alarmed, Andromache took a step back into her room. A stairway kiss would have been one thing, but *clouds of admirers?* "Cassandra — I'm not sure I feel so —"

"Come on, now!" A deceptively strong hand locked around Andromache's wrist. "Before it gets too hot."

∞

ON THE WAY down the stairs, Andromache steeled herself to face the sinister alcoves and alleyways found along every Trojan street. She gritted her teeth when Cassandra sang, "Here we go!" and swung her out the door. She raised her elbows, preparing to fend off villains. And as she looked out between the protective bars of her forearms, she saw —

Nothing. Oh, there were alcoves — and alleyways — and people, some of them questionable — but no immediate danger. She could feel her fears crumbling, falling away.

"Over here," said Cassandra, pointing to the north. "There's something I've been dying to show you."

Walking hand-in-hand with Cassandra, Andromache gave the city a wary once-over. Tall houses rising on either side of theirs. Vine-covered walls surrounding courtyards; trees poking up over the top. Large streets studded with stones and narrow ones made of packed earth. Donkeys pulling carts. Elegant little girls, like Cassandra in miniature. Men and women, laden with baskets. More buildings. Angry voices soaring out the windows.

Andromache scooted closer to Cassandra.

"Almost there," whispered the girl. "You're doing fine!"

Ashamed, Andromache took a step — a small one — away from her friend.

"Let's turn in here," said Cassandra, indicating a doorway.

When Andromache stepped through it into a garden of frozen people, half-emerging from stone blocks, she turned around at once and tried to leave.

"Come on," coaxed Cassandra.

"What *is* this place?" whispered Andromache. She'd heard stories about monsters who turned people to stone with a glance, but she'd never believed them. Now, though —

"It's just the sculpture garden."

Sculptures! Andromache felt impossibly stupid. *Sculptures!* But then, she'd never seen sculptures this large before, or this lifelike. Even if the figures were just partially raised, rather than fully three dimensional, they made the rough-carved wooden animals of her childhood look like clods of earth.

"Don't you want to look at them?" asked Cassandra.

Hesitantly, Andromache nodded and re-entered the garden.

As they approached the first sculpted block, Andromache felt more and more foolish for her fear. Up close, the sculpture wasn't at all like a person frozen in stone; it was far too smooth, too serene, too beautiful. Flawless.

"This is Councilman Pisander," said Cassandra, as though introducing him to Andromache at a party.

"You mean — it's — a real person?" Andromache asked skeptically.

"Well, yes. I mean, he's not actually encased in stone —"

"I know that!" snapped Andromache, reddening. "I meant that this is supposed to *represent* a real person?"

Cassandra nodded.

"Does Councilman Pisander really look like this?" Andromache thought of the pot bellies she'd seen on the Trojans who came to their house. She thought of their liver spots — their pouchy eyes — their mismatched ears.

"I don't know." Cassandra shrugged. "I never met him — he died years and years ago."

Andromache frowned, and they walked down the garden path to the next sculpture.

"The great commander Atymnius," said Cassandra.

Except for their poses, Atymnius looked identical to Councilman Pisander. Andromache stepped close enough to palpate the commander's implausibly smooth skin.

"Andromache!" Cassandra cried in shock. She turned her head quickly from side to side, making sure that no one had seen the transgression.

"What?" cried Andromache, blushing once more. "Don't people ever touch them?"

"I'm not sure," Cassandra said primly. "I've never seen it done."

"I'm sorry! I won't do it again. I was just seeing if he had any scars."

"Of course not!"

"Why not?"

"Because the sculptures are supposed to show ideal beauty."

'*Eet ees so aaaahgly,*' Hector had said about his wound. Andromache thought of him, sweating under his cloak, making rude gestures with his hands. "But people have them, sometimes," she argued. "Scars, I mean."

A look of pain crossed Cassandra's face. "I know it!" she snapped, raising her chin. "But maybe that's not how *people* want to be seen. If you'd been born with two noses, would you want to be sculpted that way, for children to gawk at centuries from now?"

The honest answer was '*no*' — she most certainly would *not!* — but Andromache didn't want to back down. "Sure, I would, if that's how I looked," she said, her own chin in the air.

Cassandra pursed her lips. "Well, I suppose things must be different, back where you're from. Come on! There are lots more sculptures to see!"

Andromache let herself be dragged.

The man swelling outward from the next block stood on a chariot drawn by two horses. He was indistinguishable from the other men, with the same broad shoulders, thickly-muscled legs, and straight, perfect nose. Andromache didn't bother to study him but instead looked at the horses.

They were a magnificent team — surely the demigod behind them wouldn't have settled for anything less — but also interesting. The artist hadn't sculpted two identical beasts. One was slightly taller at the shoulder, the other slightly wider around the middle. Their feet kicked up asynchronically, and some of the hooves were chipped. Careful not to touch the sculpture, Andromache bent down to inspect the chips. They seemed to be intentional rather than the result of weathering. One of the horses even had sweat on its neck, while the other's eyes were rolling in terror. The animals were fascinating. Andromache could tell that the sculptor felt something for horses that he — or she — didn't feel for people. *I can sympathize with that!* she thought.

Cassandra caught her smiling. "You like this one?"

"Yes," said Andromache. "It's my favorite."

The girl gave her an excited squeeze. "So far! Let's go see the others."

After their tour of the sculpture garden, Cassandra took Andromache through two smaller parks and past the colonnaded council hall. On the way home, she pointed out the houses of her closest friends. They then spent the rest of the morning playing roodles out on the courtyard and chatting about upcoming soirees.

Andromache was surprised to find herself looking forward to them.

"HI, AHNDROMAHK," said Hector, late that afternoon.

Nervously, Andromache looked up from the text she'd been reading. She wondered which Hector had come — the black-tempered one from yesterday's lesson, or the kind one from their talk out on the courtyard. "Hi. How are you?"

"Good," he said. His face had a bright but fragile look, like someone whose fever had just broken.

"How's your arm?" Andromache asked timidly. "Does it hurt?"

Pause. "You effer haff these?" He indicated his stitches.

She nodded. "I had stitches in my leg, once."

"Then you know," he said, smiling wryly. "Sometimes, it is all rahght. Sometimes…"

Andromache didn't smile back. "I'm sorry," she said.

He shrugged. "And you?" he asked. "You ahre all rahght, today?"

After the morning she'd had outside the house, Andromache felt radiant — victorious — but she was reluctant to say so with Hector in pain, sitting right across the table from her. "Fine. Maybe a little tired."

"You hate — the eefening?" he asked, sounding strangely apologetic.

She frowned. "No — uh, I like it. I don't like the afternoon, when it's hot out, but the evening is nice. So is the morning —"

Hector was shaking his head. "Wiff my sister, yesterday. You hate the eefening?"

Ah! So that was it! He felt guilty for not having saved her from the previous night's soiree. Andromache had almost forgotten. She certainly wasn't mad at him, anymore — in fact, she was grateful. If not for his perfidy, she would still be doing nothing but skulking around the house. "Oh, no," she said to Hector. "I didn't hate it at all. It was fun. Cassandra's friends were very nice."

"They ahre who?"

"I don't remember their names," she admitted. "Except Demuchus. We were at his house."

"Demuchus?" asked Hector, clearing his throat.

"I think that's right. You know him?"

"Ohff couhrse."

"I suppose you know everyone. It's probably a requirement, for your family," she teased.

He nodded. "<u>When we ahre babies, Mom giff tests</u>."

Andromache frowned again. Had Hecuba *really* given them tests? Hector's tone had been so serious, and yet —

He smiled to show her that he'd been teasing, too.

"<u>Well, I wouldn't put it past her</u>," mumbled Andromache.

"<u>No</u>," Hector agreed. "<u>So, you see some nice peoples, at the house ohff</u> Demuchus?"

"<u>Yes, very nice</u>," said Andromache. "<u>And they're smart, too — they know *so* much!</u>"

"<u>Oh? On what?</u>"

"<u>Everything! Music, and history, and politics</u>."

"<u>You lahke these fings?</u>"

"<u>Yes, but — but — well, I just felt so *foolish* next to them, and —</u>"

"<u>Foalish?</u>" Hector frowned. "<u>Lahke a baby hohrse?</u>"

Andromache gave a rusty giggle. Laughing still felt strange, even awkward.

"<u>What?</u>" asked Hector.

"<u>Not *'foalish'* — foolish. I felt ridiculous. Silly. Stupid</u>."

"<u>O-o-o-oh!</u>" Hector laughed. He, too, sounded a little rusty. "<u>Why *'stupid?'*</u>"

"<u>Where to start?</u>" asked Andromache. "<u>I haven't read half of what they've read. It's been ages since I've studied anything, and when I did — well, it was different, with Dad. I guess we weren't as serious. He taught me to write with a stick on a dirt floor. He only had four texts, and —</u>"

Hector broke in. "<u>You cannot feel foalish. You ahre mahch smahrter. You fink new ideas. Those peoples, they only say again...say again —</u>"

"<u>Repeat?</u>" guessed Andromache.

"<u>Yes.</u>"

"<u>Repeat.</u>"

"<u>They *repeat* old ideas. They say not *new* ideas</u>."

"<u>What do you mean?</u>"

"<u>They jahst repeat stahff from texts. From older peoples. To sound mohre smahrt</u>." Hector smiled. "<u>Lahke me, when I speak Lukkana</u>."

Andromache shook her head and snorted. Hector's Lukkan was nothing if not original; *'foalish'* was proof of that.

"What, '*no*?'" asked Hector, wondering why she'd shaken her head. "You fink they repeat not?"

"I don't know," she said. "I haven't read enough to catch them at it."

"Me, I know that they do it," he assured her. "Ago — befohre — it is not lahke this. When Dad is young. When I am young. People then fink new ideas. Say new ideas. Now, it is bohring."

"Is that why you stopped going?" asked Andromache, remembering that, according to Cassandra, both Hector and Paris used to attend the soirees.

"This…and ahther reasons." After a small pause, Hector asked, "You talk, the entahre ohff the eefening?"

"No, not the whole time. We listened to music, too."

"You lahke the music?"

"Mm-hmm…"

"Baht?" Hector prompted.

"But it was so — so quiet. It just wasn't what I'm used to, when music's being played. Nobody laughed or danced. I mean, it went on for hours and no one moved at all. Not a bit!" Andromache squirmed in memory of her discomfort, the evening before.

"They haff asses ohff stone!" Hector laughed again, more normally this time.

Andromache let out another rusty giggle. "They're too polite for asses," she said. "For them, you should say, '*tush*.'"

"Tush," repeated Hector, with relish. "So, you sit…"

"Yes, and the whole time, I had to cough," said Andromache. "You know how it is, how you have to cough more if you know you're not supposed to? Anyway, I made it through the songs, but once they started talking, I coughed — and coughed — and coughed."

Hector looked perplexed, making Andromache wonder if she'd said too much at once. She was about to ask what he'd missed when he posed a question of his own: "First you say '*cough*.' Then, '*coughED*.' Why? These ahre different?"

"Oh," said Andromache. "Yes, they are." She was a little surprised, in retrospect, that the question hadn't come up sooner, but she supposed that Hector had been absorbing too much else to notice the slight difference in pronunciation between '*cough*' and '*coughed*.' He'd relied on expressions like '*yesterday*' and '*now*' to separate the past from the present.

"They ahre different how?" he asked.

Worried that she would confuse him further by explaining in Lukkan, Andromache switched to Truvan: "The two are talking about different times. '*Cough*' happens in the present. If you say '*coughED*,' that means it happened before."

"In the past," said Hector.

"Mm-hmm. Hey…" The turn in conversation had given Andromache an idea. This was just what she'd wanted, a new Lukkan challenge for Hector, to keep him from getting bored.

"Hey, what?" he asked.

"You should start using the different times," she said. "All you really have to do is add that extra sound — '*cough, coughED*.'"

"All right."

"Maybe you can tell me about your morning. For example, here's mine: I walkED with your sister. She showED me some city parks." Andromache made sure to emphasize her past time words.

Hector gaped. "You *what?*"

"You didn't understand?"

"It is not that," he said, shaking his head. "I ahnderstand. Baht — baht — you ahre *serious?*"

"I'm serious!" Andromache couldn't help but sound pleased with herself.

Hector, too, looked proud. "You can say to Paris, '*No more Hermie!*'

"No more Hermie." She smiled. "So, anyway, now it's your turn."

"All rahght. This mohrning, I feed, uh, feedED my hohrse." Hector's face grew serious as he concentrated, until finally he was frowning. "That doesn't sound right."

"You're right." Andromache nodded. "That one's different. You say 'I FED my horse.'"

"All right. I FED my hohrse, and I eatED." He looked up for confirmation, but she shook her head.

"Ate," she said.

He frowned again. "You said that usually —"

"I know." She bit her thumbnail. "You've just been unlucky."

"No kidding," he muttered.

"What else did you do?"

"I — FED — my hohrse. I — ATE — breakfast. I seeED my dad." He looked up at her expectantly, but again she shook her head.

"Saw. You say, '*I saw my dad*.'"

Wrong for the third time in a row, Hector was seeping exasperation. "Does your rule work for *anything*?"

"Sure," said Andromache. "Talk, talkED; march, marchED; dance, dancED; like, likED; touch, touchED."

"Come? Go? Take? Haff?"

"Came. Went. Took. Had."

"So it doesn't work for anything very useful."

"Listen, listenED," suggested Andromache, now sorry that she'd proposed this topic. For the first time, she saw signs of what the city had always gossiped about — Hector balking at his language studies. His eyes were clouding over. He looked a breath away from going dark, as he had the day before. She bowed her head, examining the grain of the table, afraid of what she might see if she looked up.

"Today I fed my hohrse," Hector said softly. "I ate breakfast. I saw my dad. I learnED many foalish, reediculous words."

Beaming, Andromache turned her face back to his. "Exactly!" she cried. "You *learned* them! I *told* you — I *told* you it was a good rule!"

"Told?" Hector protested. "Not *tellED*?!"

Andromache swallowed hard before whispering the fatal word: "Told."

Hector narrowed his eyes; Andromache widened hers. They stared at each other for a moment. A tentative laugh escaped — Andromache wasn't sure whose — and then more laughter.

"All rahght," ceded Hector. "You *told* me."

ℰↃ

ANDROMACHE SIGHED as she walked down the hall. She didn't understand this new Hector — not at all!

(*You wanted things to be different when he came back,*) the snide lit-tle Voice reminded her. (*You got what you wished for.*)

That's not what I meant! she shot back. She'd hoped Hector would want to be friends with her — not that he would turn dark and tense! *And unpredictable,* she added to herself.

There were times now when she felt as close to Hector as she'd ever felt to anyone. She'd shared some of her most painful memories with him, even how her parents had died — she'd never told *anyone* about that! He was so easy to talk to, though. He understood so much without her even having to say it! He was easy to talk to — easy to smile with — easy to like —

But then, other times, he might as well have been a stranger — a remote, silent stranger with a shadow-darkened face.

He's probably acting this way because of his arm, Andromache told herself, although without much conviction. *Moody when it hurts, nice when it doesn't. He'll be his old self once it's all better.*

(*Unless that's not the reason he's so moody.*)

Andromache's stomach knotted up. *What else is there?* But she knew…

(*Penthesilea,*) said the Voice. (*Who knows what she's been saying to him? How she's been badgering him? She might not be too happy with him, still wallowing in guilt after all this time.*)

For guilt it was. Only guilt could have kept Hector in the li-brary, that day, enduring their catastrophe of a lesson. Lukkan was still just a form of penance to him. *That* hadn't changed!

(*No, but his guilt will fade eventually,*) said the Voice.

Andromache sighed. She knew that the Voice was right — and now that *Lee* was living in Troy, Hector had more incentive than ever to let go of his guilt and move on with his life.

(*He'll do it even faster if you don't stop squabbling with him during your lessons.*)

We didn't squabble! Andromache protested. *Not really.*

(*Almost,*) the Voice insisted. (*And that's close enough. His pen-ance is to learn Lukkana, not to fight with you.*)

The Voice was right again. Fighting was a waste of time for Hector — and if lessons weren't giving him what he needed, he might quit, even if his guilt hadn't faded away yet. The past few fights and near-fights had been easily resolved, but that might not always be the case.

I'll just have to keep lessons calm, Andromache decided. *As long as I do that, everything will be like it used to be.*

(*And you were so happy with that?*) jeered the Voice.

In hindsight, Andromache thought she was. At least back in the early days of their lessons, she always knew that someone gentle and patient would be meeting her in the library. She now saw the folly of wishing for their relationship to change. The dream of making Hector smile by telling him '*You're a good brother*' seemed silly and childish, and Andromache was glad she'd never said the words to him. While he was away, she'd let herself get sentimental — she'd let herself forget what really bound them together. But their old, strange symbiosis wasn't all bad. She certainly preferred it to fighting.

In the meantime, some things *had* changed for the better since Hector's return. Andromache was leaving the house, now! She was socializing — going to soirees! That would have been unimaginable, just a week earlier. And several times, now, Hecuba had come to her with new herb requests. She was needed. She had a good life in Troy, with or without Hector's friendship.

I'll keep peace with him, Andromache told herself. *Other than that, I'll just forget he's even there.*

Chapter 40

No one tapped on Andromache's door the next morning, or cajoled her into going for a walk. She awoke to the fluttery sounds of birds chasing each other across her window sill and walked downstairs in a somber, lonely mood. She wished Cassandra's tutors had been given a two-day break.

Dutifully, she plucked her way through the garden boxes that needed weeding and sloshed water over those that were too dry. Once the gardening was done, she went on a search for novelty among the courtyard's trees and shrubberies.

Nothing.

Her plants were sweet, and lovely, and growing, but no matter how many circuits she made among them, she couldn't find anything new. The space inside the high courtyard walls was too small — inadequate, like the sachet where she'd once kept her troupe of caterpillars. She thought of how the little creatures had languished, with only a few dry leaves to munch on.

Her dreary thoughts were interrupted by a sudden cry: "Hey, Hermie!"

Andromache stopped short. Her path had taken her back around to the kitchen. "Hi, Paris," she said.

"Are you dizzy, yet?"

"What?"

"That's your fourth circle around the courtyard."

It was her tenth.

"If you're bored, you can come to the market with me."

"I'm not bored!"

Paris raised an eyebrow. "Reeeeally," he said sarcastically, stretching out the word.

"Really!"

"Well, you can come anyway. Then I won't have to carry as much."

"No, thanks." Andromache shivered at the images brought to mind by the word '*market*.' A seething crowd of shoppers, bumping into her — two vendors going in opposite directions, crushing her between their bulging stomachs — her reedy little body, slipping — falling — lost in a rush of feet. The markets were located in the lower town, which was home to far more people than the citadel…

"Look, Hermie," said Paris. "The jig is up. I know you've been going outside. Everyone knows. The whole city knows."

Great! Her trip around town had been yesterday's hot item. Over cups of tisane, all throughout Troy, gossips had gabbled about that poor little ex-recluse living in the high priest's house!

"What do you say, Hermie?"

Andromache sighed. "What if we went to the sculpture garden, instead?" she suggested. The sculpture garden was safer. It was inside the citadel.

"Why would I want to hang around a bunch of stone women?" Paris asked with disdain.

"I thought most of them were men."

"Even worse," he said, grimacing.

"I think I'll stay here," Andromache decided.

"What are you so afraid of — the meat tent?" Paris looked disgusted. "I won't make you go in. You can wait for me outside."

"No!" she shrieked. "I don't want to be left, there!"

"All right," said Paris. "Then you can come with. I'll make sure you don't get lost, Hermie."

Andromache considered the idea. The day of Muka's burial, Hector had kept her safe while they were down in the lower town. Paris was no Hector, but he looked reasonably sturdy. "You will?" she asked cautiously.

"Of course. My parents would kill me if I lost a guest." Paris offered her his arm. It had a certain heft, thanks to the morning archery sessions. "Come on — just for a little while."

Again, Andromache looked around the now-tiny courtyard. "All right," she murmured. "A little while."

∽∂

'A LITTLE WHILE!' <u>*That's the last time I take him at his word*</u>, Andromache thought irritably.

Paris had decided that, instead of going straight to the market, he would give her a tour of the lower town. Along with a few of his favorite taverns, he'd pointed out the stables, the city gates, and finally the arena, which looked like a giant, curving staircase...

'What's it for?' she asked.

'For exercise, during the day,' said Paris. 'People run around the bottom or up and down the stands. Let me specify, Hermie — crazy *people use it for that. You might like it.'*

Andromache scowled. 'And what do sane people use it for?'

'At night, people come here to see plays or concerts,' said Paris, grinning. 'But I can't say they're sane, either. Sane people stay away.'

Then, once they'd entered the market, Paris had begun towing her along on a tortuous path through row after row of stalls. Hours later, they were still at it.

"What do we need *here?*" hissed Andromache, when Paris steered them toward a booth full of flaccid celery and spotted greens. "Everything here is disgusting."

"Not so!" Paris nodded at the young woman peddling the vile produce. "*She's* not disgusting."

"Oh, Paris," groaned Andromache. "Leave the poor thing alone! She's got enough trouble already, sitting with her slimy vegetables."

The vendor, however, seemed delighted by Paris's attentions. She gave him an alluring smile — which changed to a pout when she noticed Andromache, clinging to his arm.

<u>*You can have him!*</u> thought Andromache. <u>*Once I'm back in the house in one piece, that is*</u>. It was comical to think that, so recently, her wine-soaked brain had dreamed up an attraction to Paris! She'd just spent hours glued to his side without feeling the slightest hint of lust. He was her anchor in the flow of the market crowd, no more.

Andromache turned her attention back to Paris, who was kissing the hand of the vendor. The latter snatched her hand away, but not in anger. Instead, she reached beneath a pile of unsightly vegetables, pulled out an exquisite head of crisp, green lettuce, and handed it to Paris. He kissed her other hand, paid, and left.

"Sorry I ruined your fun," Andromache said drily.

"Ruined?"

"The salad queen didn't look happy to see me with you."

Paris laughed. "She *wasn't*. It was fantastic."

"What do you mean?"

"'*The horse of the greatest worth is always the one in another man's stable*,'" quoted Paris. "Or, in this case, another *woman's*." He gave Andromache a sly, sidelong look. "Seeing me with another girl made her realize *my* worth. I should thank you, Hermie. In fact, we *all* should — these are the best vegetables she's ever given me."

"You don't deserve a stable," muttered Andromache. She didn't scold him further, though. They *had* gotten beautiful produce, and the vendor had received a fair price. Paris was probably right to do things his way. Alone, Andromache would have brought home nothing but a pile of limp, mold-ravaged greens.

Paris flirted his way to a large sack of almonds, several jars of honey, a hunk of roasted meat — which he was chivalrous enough to carry, rather than shoving it into Andromache's basket — and two round loaves of bread. While he teased the vendors, Andromache concentrated on staying close to him, and on holding her breath.

The day that Muka died, Andromache had been too upset to notice the foul flood of city stenches, or perhaps the cool spring weather had stifled them. Now, though, she had to fight the urge to gag. She'd been sheltered in her house. Cassandra, Paris, and the others bathed often, and afterward they smelled of plants — of flowers — of spices. There were other scents she associated with the house, ranging from neutral to pleasant: healing unguents, library dust, stable smells, incense, garden loam, mint, and the occasional honest, hard-earned sweat.

There was nothing honest about the marketplace odors. Ancient garlic stewing deep within the mouths that heckled her — curdled sweat, thick-caked in the armpits at her nose level —

forgotten bits of fish fermenting under booths — rotten cheese ground to jelly in the cracks of the pavement stones. Every time Andromache turned a corner, she was enveloped in some new, more hideous aroma.

"So, what did you think?" asked Paris when they'd returned to the house, their baskets too heavy to lug any further. "Are you going back with me, tomorrow?"

Andromache took a deep breath of the kitchen's air. *Thyme and rose petals*. Hecuba must have just been there, making a tisane.

"Well?" prodded Paris.

The market *had* been interesting, with its breads, cheeses, and produce — varieties of fruits and vegetables not growing in her own garden. Andromache wouldn't have minded seeing more of what the vendors had to offer. But oh, the smells! What if she somehow spoiled Paris's flirtations, rather than helping? He might get back at her by abandoning her in a cul-de-sac of evil smells.

"I don't think so," she said. If she stayed home, she could have a tisane. She could inhale rose petal steam instead of rotten fish.

Paris shrugged. "Suit yourself, Hermie. Scour a ring around the courtyard, if that's what makes you happy."

Andromache scowled at him and fled to the bath chamber, where she opened each bottle of scented oil and breathed in deeply. Little by little, the market faded — first the armpit, then the sour breath and the fetid air of the meat tent — till the only aroma in her nose was the soft, breezy perfume of her favorite bath oil.

She filled the tub with water and scrubbed and scrubbed. When her skin was red, she lay back, resting. She let the morning soak away and thought about what might lie ahead of her, that evening. Another soiree, she hoped. It had been nice to get out for a while, and whatever else might be said about Demuchus's house, it didn't stink. If there was another concert, she would pay better attention to the notes and lines of melody. She would be ready with comments. This time, she wouldn't sound — what was the word? — *foolish*.

Andromache took a little extra care rubbing in the scented oil. She wished she'd paid more attention to how Paris and his lady friends flirted, so she could be ready for that, too. At the last soiree, she thought a few of the men had been eyeing her. Maybe someone would flirt with her, tonight — maybe he would even try to coax her into a stairway for a dark, sly moment or two. She imagined the kiss in the alcove and felt a tingle of excitement.

To hell with it! she thought. She wanted a kiss like that, even if it meant going back to the market with Paris, to learn how flirting worked. Surely a stairway kiss would be worth a few nasty smells.

Chapter 41

"Phew!" said Cassandra, making her move on the roodles board. "It's scorching, today!"

Andromache nodded. They were sitting in the shade of the fig tree, the only one large enough to hide them from the mid-afternoon sun.

"I love this weather," whispered Cassandra.

Andromache hated it — she hated the headaches, the lethargy, the sweat running down the inside of her clothes. She hated it all! Spring had been short, that year, and summer had come early. She saw no reason to cheer about *that*. If she wasn't careful, the wild owlsburr plants that Hecuba had brought her would wither before they had a chance to take root in her garden. What could Cassandra possibly like about the weather? And, for that matter, why had she been whispering?

"What's so great about it?" Andromache asked suspiciously.

First looking around to make sure that they were alone on the courtyard, Cassandra murmured, "Well, sometimes when it's hot like this, combat trainings get scheduled for the morning or the evening, when the breeze is cooler."

"Oh," said Andromache, and then, "So?"

"So, we — my friends, I mean — go to the evening ones. To watch, not to train. Can you imagine *me* with a spear?" Giggling, Cassandra thrust her arm skyward.

Andromache shivered. She could understand why Cassandra and the others might watch the occasional training. Future council members had a duty to understand combat, since they would one day have to make decisions about the army. But to *enjoy* the sight of people fighting — pretending to hack each other to death? She shuddered again, harder this time.

"What's wrong?" asked Cassandra. "You can't possibly be cold, unless — oh, no, honey! You didn't go and take another fever, did you? Oh! There's a training tonight, and I was hoping you'd go with us!"

"I don't have a fever!" Andromache snapped. "It's just — why do you like watching people fight each other?"

"Oh, no one gets hurt, honey! They're just practicing — you know, having fun. It's like running a foot race or having a stone-throwing contest. And besides —" Cassandra's eyes began to sparkle and her voice dropped back to a whisper. "I don't go to watch the *fighting.*" She giggled.

When Andromache didn't immediately giggle back, Cassandra added: "Some of the guys are *really* sexy!"

Paris in the market, Cassandra at the training field…did this family do nothing but flirt? Something in the air here turned everyone's thoughts to romance. *Including mine,* Andromache admitted, remembering her secret hunger for a stairway kiss. She'd gone to two more soirees but was no closer to a kiss than she'd ever been. After several mornings spent at the market, studying Paris and the vendors, she now knew the signs of flirting — the tilting of the head, the fluttering of the eyelids, the body's languid look — but she felt too shy to use them. What if she flirted the wrong way and everyone laughed at her? What if she flirted the right way, but the kiss didn't turn out to be harmless? What if the man hurt her? She was just scared enough not to try.

"How can you even tell they're sexy, under all that armor?" she asked Cassandra.

"Who says they wear it all?" the girl murmured slyly.

Andromache blushed and cried out, "Oh!"

"They don't take off the bottoms, of course," Cassandra whispered. "I imagine any soldier with *that* exposed would be too worried about protecting it to fight properly. Although —" The girl furrowed her eyebrows. "I've read that some cultures fight without *any* clothes or armor on at all! I wonder if it's true. I suppose Hector knows, but it's not something I want to ask my *brother* about." She made a face of disgust.

"No." Andromache shook her head vehemently.

"You're coming with, right, honey?" asked Cassandra.

Andromache shook her head again.

"Please?" Cassandra wheedled. "If you don't want to look at the boys, you can always just cheer for Hector."

Spears. Swords. Blood. A helmeted face. Empty, cavernous eyes. Andromache caught her breath as the dormant image of the Raider flashed through her mind. She never wanted to see Hector like that again! She didn't want to relive those nightmares! *Wax-white corpses, drained of blood. Blood-spattered armor. Torn flesh. Raw meat —*

No, Ahndromahk! she hissed at herself. *Don't think about that — especially now.* Before, the Raider of her nightmares had been covered in someone else's blood. He'd been cutting and stabbing other people. Now, the blood and torn flesh were Hector's. She thought of the gash on his arm. Of his skin splitting open. Of his pain. Of —

"What do you say?" Cassandra prodded. "Won't you at least come to cheer for my brother?"

"Isn't — won't he —" Andromache took a deep breath. "Won't he be sitting out, anyway? Because of his arm?"

Cassandra sobered instantly. "You're right. He *should* sit out, not that that means he *will*. But either way, you ought to come."

"Maybe some other time," Andromache deflected. "I'm already exhausted, today, and I haven't even had lessons yet."

"All right," said Cassandra, winking. Her devious look had returned. "Some other time…"

ॐ

THAT DAY'S LUKKAN LESSON was unremarkable. Calm. Hector's face looked pinched and his manner was subdued, but he talked without having to be prodded. When Andromache commented on the strong wind from the northeast, he painstakingly explained that this wind kept ships in Troy's harbor for weeks at a time. If they wanted to head further east, they had to wait for the winds to shift. He then added that Troy had grown rich from the business of these trading vessels. Andromache told him that she'd read a text proclaiming horses as another source of Troy's wealth. He nodded, modestly describing the Trojan horse herds as *'pretty good.'*

That's how lessons ought to be! thought Andromache.

Afterward, Hector bolted out of the library and down the stairs. Andromache followed him, much more slowly, and ran into Hecuba, Cassandra, and Paris in the kitchen.

"Where on earth is *he* rushing off to?" asked Hecuba, gesturing toward the blur that had been her eldest son.

"He's got training down on the field," answered Paris.

"Again?" Hecuba asked sourly. "They had one this morning, too, I heard! He won't be satisfied until he's driven himself and his army into the ground."

Paris laughed. "Drive has nothing to do with it. They're showing off for the girls."

Cutting. Slicing. Bruising. Hacking, thought Andromache. She shuddered. What kind of girls would get a thrill from *that*?

Hecuba's lips tightened into a line. "Not that *he* shouldn't think about something besides work, for a change," she muttered, "but I wouldn't think — *certain women* — would be much impressed by that."

Penthesilea, thought Andromache. Hecuba had a point. Penthesilea was unlikely to be wowed by the sight of men in armor.

Paris shrugged. "*Certain women* probably aren't, even when the men aren't wearing chest plates. But as for the Trojan girls who go there —"

"To *ogle*?" squawked Hecuba. "Where's their dignity? I certainly hope *you* don't go down there to watch your brother's subordinates flail about, half-dressed!" Her finger pointed accusingly at Cassandra.

The young girl blushed. "Everyone goes!" she squeaked. "Andromache's going!"

"No, I'm not!"

"Honey, please! You *have* to!"

"No, she does *not*," decreed Hecuba. "And *you're* not going either — not unless Paris goes with you."

Cassandra turned the pleading look on her brother.

He shrugged. "Fine by me, Songbird." Under his breath, he added, "Maybe *certain women* won't wear their chest plates tonight, either."

Fortunately for him, Hecuba didn't hear the last part of what he said. "Go, then, if you must!" was all she snapped.

Paris and Cassandra scurried out before their mother could change her mind.

"What are you up to tonight, dear, since you have the sense not to join my two absurd younger children?" Hecuba still looked peeved.

"Probably some gardening," Andromache said softly. "The beds need water again."

"Indeed." The woman nodded. "With this heat —"

"Oh, I know. It's terrible."

There was a pause.

"How are you doing, otherwise?" asked Hecuba. "Have lessons been going well? I was a little concerned that after my son's — *hiatus* — he might have trouble falling back into the routine."

Andromache thought of the lesson she'd run out of, because of Hector's sullenness, and the other where he'd almost lost his temper. "They're going fine," she said. It wasn't quite a lie. She knew how to make the lessons run smoothly, from now on.

"Good. I'm glad to hear it. What are you covering, these days?"

"The past time — talking in the past. And we read texts and discuss them in Lukkan."

"Very impressive," Hecuba said approvingly. "Let me know if there's anything you need."

Andromache nodded.

"Well, I must run down the street. One of the neighbor's daughters is due any day now, and I wanted to check on her condition. It's her first baby, and the poor thing is frightened to death, but if you ask me, it's just as well to have the baby out before high summer. There's nothing worse than going through the hottest months all swollen about the middle. I should know." She groaned at the memory. "Paris was a late summer baby."

Hecuba left on her healer's errand, and Andromache went outside. She hauled water around to the garden boxes, pulled a few weeds, and finally lay down on a bench, looking up at the sky. It was still blue, with deep orange at the horizon. The first few stars were showing. Soon, with the dark of night, the rest would appear, and the sky would be covered with stars. With the Lorani.

She thought of Muka — of Auntie — drifting out among the earth's own luminous sea creatures. She thought of her parents, inside the mountain that had once been their home. She thought of the house, empty behind her. She thought of Cassandra, Paris, and Hector, down on the practice field with the rest of the city's youth. She thought of Hecuba, holding a squalling newborn in her arms, and of Priam, conducting rituals down at the temple.

Andromache closed her eyes. The earth was immense, the sky, unfathomable — and she wasn't a part of any of it.

Chapter 42

Andromache shifted on the hard stone bench and sighed. She was disgusted with herself. *Sails, Ahndromahk? Now, where did you get the idea that they'd be talking about* sails?

Hoping to impress the soiree group members, she'd slogged through a particularly dry text about sail-making — that evening's assigned reading, or so she'd thought. She was determined to make comments, this time, or at least nod along intelligently rather than drifting off.

As soon as the young people had gathered on Demuchus's courtyard, though, they began a heated discussion on Troy's relationship to other nearby states. Andromache was interested but so lost among the unfamiliar names that she couldn't hope to follow the group's comments. Once more, she sat in cowed silence on the bench.

"Troy ought no longer allow herself to be treated as the Hittites' vassal," said the man in toxic green.

"We aren't a vassal," Cassandra objected.

"The treaty of Alaca would suggest otherwise."

"That doesn't make us their vassal. It just keeps them out of our business."

"It's *tribute!*"

"I think of it as a tax."

"I agree with Cassandra," a young woman said pensively. "What we send to Hattusas is so little that Troy never feels it."

Because Troy is rich, thought Andromache, feeling a little less dimwitted. *Because of the wind and the horses.*

"And what will stop the Hittites from demanding more, in the next treaty?" challenged the man in toxic green.

"If they ask too much, we'll simply refuse," said Demuchus.

"But then they'll attack us," argued Cassandra. She sounded almost shrill.

Andromache felt sorry for her. She could understand why Cassandra, even more than the others, would want to prevent an invasion. While the Ass General — Laoganus — was technically in charge of defending Troy, Hector was sure to be drawn into the fight. In her mind, she saw his arm, covered in bruises and a long red gash — the skin torn open — the blood pouring out —

"The Hittites won't attack us," Demuchus assured Cassandra. "They have other problems on their other borders."

Cassandra's ally shook her head. "We couldn't risk it. Especially now, when *we* have other problems on *our* other borders."

"You mean the Mudders?" asked a boy even younger than Cassandra.

"Don't call them that!" hissed Demuchus. "For goodness' sake, say '*Achaeans*!' And yes — of *course* that's who she means."

"They're just making little raids," scoffed the man in toxic green. "They're no real threat to *us*."

Andromache didn't know about Hittites or tributes, but she certainly knew about Mudder raids. On that point, she was an expert. "They were a threat to *me*," she interjected. "When they attacked Lyrnassa."

The young people fell silent. They looked right at her, then awkwardly away, as though she were foaming at the mouth and they didn't want to draw attention to her. She learned in that moment that uncomfortable truths were social ruin.

The group splintered. Several people clustered around Cassandra, while others drifted off in twos and threes. Andromache found herself alone, sitting under a spindly olive tree, flattening the wrinkles in her dress and picking at her cuticles.

"May I join you?"

She looked up to see Demuchus smiling down at her. She nodded.

"You're Andromache? Is that right?" he asked, once he'd settled himself beside her.

"Yes." Andromache folded her hands together so that she wouldn't pick at them. "And you're Demuchus."

He nodded.

"You have a gorgeous house," she said. The words came out too quickly.

He smiled. "Thank you. You're very kind to say so."

Andromache gave a tentative nod and glanced down at her hands. The thumbs looked raw. Furtively, she tucked them up against her palms.

Demuchus cleared his throat. "So, Cassandra tells me that you're staying with her, now, tutoring her brother?"

"Mm-hmm."

"What excellent news! I never thought that Paris would return to his studies, but this is just the thing to straighten him out."

If Hecuba or Priam had said this, Andromache would have agreed wholeheartedly, but Demuchus's pompous tone irritated her. She felt a wave of protectiveness toward Paris. What did Demuchus know, anyway? What gave *him* the right to make such proclamations?

Before she could reply, though, Demuchus went on: "What subject do you teach him?"

"Lukkan," said Andromache. "But not to Paris — I'm Hector's tutor."

"Oh!" exclaimed Demuchus, his eyes goggling. "You'll have to forgive me. I'd heard that — ahem — *he* — had a Lukkan tutor, but naturally I thought it was one of those ridiculous rumors that sometimes make the rounds of the city." He smiled as though expecting her to understand his confusion.

Andromache frowned back. Demuchus had a point about rumors, as she well knew. Trojan gossips had once speculated that she was actually a pirate princess or even a goddess in human form. But surely the idea of Hector taking Lukkan lessons wasn't as outlandish as all *that!*

"Since, against all odds, the rumor appears to be true," said Demuchus, "— perhaps you can resolve a question it brings to mind: how did a woman from Lyrnassa come to speak Lukkan?"

Andromache relaxed. This question, at least, was legitimate. "I used to live to the southeast, in the Lukka lands."

"Ah!" said Demuchus. "That makes sense. What made you settle in Lyrnassa, then?"

"It's — a long story," she murmured, hoping he wouldn't ask her to tell it.

Demuchus affixed a look of concern. "Your journey was most difficult, I'm sure. What means of travel —"

He was interrupted by Cassandra darting suddenly over to them.

"Honey?" said the girl. "It's time for us to go." In Andromache's ear, she whispered, "Mom said no later than midnight or I've got Chute duty for a month."

Demuchus stood and bowed to them. "It's been a pleasure to make your acquaintance, Andromache — you who are a lady well-traveled and a tutor, wise far beyond the scope of us mere students. I trust that we shall meet again."

Andromache was too flustered by his embroidered way of speaking to answer.

"You can trust," sang Cassandra, clutching Andromache's hand in hers. "She'll be back."

Chapter 43

Back she was indeed, more often than not. Andromache refused to join Cassandra and her friends when they went down to watch combat training, but she never missed a gathering at Demuchus's house.

At that point in the evening when the large group dissolved into smaller ones, Demuchus always sat with Andromache and asked her questions about Lyrnassa or the Lukka lands. He was the only one at the soirees to take an interest in her past.

Some of his questions flummoxed her: *'What do you think about life under a council, rather than a monarchy? There is a Lukkan monarch, is there not?'*

Was there a Lukkan monarch? If so, Andromache had never seen or felt the sovereign's authority. The Lukka lands were a wild, mountain country, regulated locally if at all, and prone to disruption by raiders. However, she couldn't say that Demuchus was wrong. There might well have been a Lukkan king or queen.

At first, Andromache wasn't sure what to do in cases like that, when she wanted neither to lie, and risk getting caught , nor to look stupid by admitting her ignorance. She soon learned that deflections were best. Her reply, *'There's really no comparing the two,'* had won a nod of approval from Demuchus.

Once Andromache had mastered that trick, she enjoyed visiting with Demuchus. He'd read hundreds of texts and had traveled widely. It was true, he had strong opinions and a tendency to pontificate, but he also inquired about her thoughts and didn't discount them. He asked questions about Lukkan traditions, culture, philosophy, music, and art as though the answers mattered to him.

Andromache had never had a conversation partner like Demuchus. Back in her Lukkan homeland, she'd been too young to have intellectual talks with her parents; Auntie had been too tired to have them with her during their years in Lyrnassa.

Now, to be sure, she discussed a wide range of topics with Hector, but the real point of *those* conversations was to strengthen his grasp on Lukkan. His thoughts about texts, other lands, and the natural world came out haltingly, as he hunted through his mind for the right Lukkan word or fought to understand what Andromache had said. He bumbled. He erred. Their lessons were often a stew of Lukkan and Truvan mixed willy-nilly together.

With Demuchus, everything was different. He and Andromache chatted easily in Truvan and only because they wanted to. No one had ordered Demuchus to talk to her. He wasn't doing so out of guilt. He simply enjoyed spending time with her.

ℰℭ

"WE'D BEEN AT SEA for four days, tossed mercilessly about by the waves," Demuchus said one evening, as he was telling Andromache about his voyage to the island of Lesbos.

Andromache knew Lesbos. It was visible from Lyrnassa, not far from shore. She couldn't imagine a voyage there taking four days — more like four hours! — but she supposed the timing would be different from Troy, so she let Demuchus go on.

"Our vessel threatened to capsize at any moment and deliver us to the dreadful maws of the creatures lurking in the depths. You can't imagine the fear gripping our hearts."

And then, as though to illustrate the grip of fear, Demuchus grabbed her arm.

Andromache gasped and wrenched away. Brief though it was, his touch had been unmistakably clammy. She could have overlooked a rough hand, or even a cold one, but clamminess made her think of worms — of innards.

Demuchus looked hurt by her violent reaction.

"I'm sorry," she said, blushing. "I wasn't — you just — you surprised me." And he had. He'd never touched her, before.

Demuchus made no response but instead went on with his story. "The wind calmed enough for us to make landfall, but that hardly left us any better off. The king of that country is no friend to Trojans, mind you. He greeted us with appropriate pomp but we all knew he was just waiting for our backs to turn, that he might thrust a dagger into them. I didn't sleep the whole week we were there. The danger was beyond anything I've experienced before or since."

Demuchus touched her arm again; once more, Andromache flinched. This time, she didn't excuse herself and Demuchus, looking disappointed but resolute, went on to describe the interior of the great palace of Lesbos.

Andromache paid little heed to his story. *He's going to do it again*, she told herself, both fascinated and dismayed by his persistence. *He's going to do it again — I* know *it*.

"That said, the stone carvings in the palace garden *are* magnificent," Demuchus was saying. "I understand you've taken an interest in that art form. You might like to visit there, one day — in the company of someone who could protect you from the dangers of the journey, of course."

Demuchus laid his hand on her arm once again. This time, Andromache was ready and forced herself not to recoil. He rewarded her with a kind, if oddly paternal, smile and recounted the tale of his voyage back to Troy.

Andromache pretended to listen, but really, she was studying Demuchus. Other than the too-slim nose and pouchy lips, he was decent-looking. True, she felt no tingles of excitement when she thought about kissing him, and she couldn't imagine herself pawing wildly at his hair, but maybe she would want to once they were in an alcove with their arms locked around each other. His third touch hadn't seemed as clammy as the first two. Most importantly, he was harmless, incapable of hurting her.

Andromache smiled to herself. Demuchus's story was a bit overblown, perhaps, but she liked its unexpected twist: finally, here was her first real prospect for a Trojan stairway romance.

Chapter 44

After the arm-touching episode, Andromache started making an effort to beautify herself before the soirees. She brushed the tangles from her hair and braided it carefully. She wore her most flattering dresses and wished for the first time that she had something prettier. Wistfully, she thought of the butterfly girls who had swooped around Hector at the party, but she was leery of asking Hecuba for a dress like theirs. The woman was too likely to ask why she wanted one.

'But, my dear, you've always preferred simple dresses,' Hecuba might say. *'Just like my daughter and I do. Why the sudden need to bedeck yourself like a flowering almond tree?'* It was a conversation Andromache did *not* want to have! Instead, she wore her plain dresses to the soirees and hoped for the best.

Late every evening, when the large group had broken off into twos and threes, Andromache lingered with Demuchus. She sat as close to him as she dared and suffered the moistness of his palm, hoping that he would finally lead her away to an alcove and kiss her. Each night, he stayed attentively beside her, talked to her, and touched her arm. He never kissed her, though, or tried to kiss her, or even hinted that he might want to.

Hector had said that all young Trojans kissed, and Cassandra had implied that they did so constantly. At soirees, Andromache had seen for herself that couples often withdrew to dark corners. Why, then, was Demuchus refusing to kiss her? Why didn't she, Andromache, merit a kiss? Was she *that* unappealing? Was she too little? Too plain? Too dull? What was wrong with her? Or was something wrong with *him?*

Whatever the problem, it was aggravated by the fact that Demuchus had become her *only* hope for a kiss. He'd effectively sequestered her. All of the other boys were ignoring her now that their leader was talking to her and touching her arm every night.

At a loss for what to do, Andromache finally crept down to Cassandra's room for advice. "Cassandra?" she hissed through the door.

"Andromache?"

"Yes. Can I talk to you for a moment?"

"Sure! I was just getting ready for bed, but come on in."

Andromache opened the door and slunk over the threshold.

"Are you all right?" asked Cassandra.

Andromache shrugged. "I don't know."

"Come — sit down," said Cassandra, patting the bed. "Tell me what's wrong."

"Nothing's wrong. There's just — uh, I was just wondering something."

"Oh. What's that?"

"It's silly, really. I just —"

"Honey, what's the matter?"

"Well, it's — how do you know if a Trojan boy wants to kiss you?"

Cassandra frowned. "First of all, '*kiss*' is very generic. What kind of kiss do you mean?"

"There are kinds?"

"Well, of course! Do you mean a little kiss to say hello — or *more?*"

Andromache blushed. "More, I guess."

Cassandra giggled. "I figured. You say '*Kiss with*,' then. Or you can say '*make out*,' as long as there aren't any grown-ups around. Mom hates the phrase. She says it's crude."

The Make-Out stairs, thought Andromache, remembering Hector's words. "All right. How do you know when a Trojan boy wants to — to *make out* with you, then?"

"They're like any other boys, honey."

Andromache looked down at her lap, ashamed.

"Are you telling me you've never had that kind of kiss?" asked Cassandra in a hushed, shocked tone.

"It's not like here, where I used to live," snapped Andromache. "People don't just — *make out* — all the time."

"But why not?" asked Cassandra, scandalized. "It's nice! It's fun!"

Andromache sighed. "I just want to know how you *know*."

"Well, usually they'll tell you," said Cassandra. "Either that, or pull you away by the hand." She giggled. "You know — to somewhere *private*. That's the easiest way."

"Of course it is," muttered Andromache. Just her luck, to be stuck with the one Trojan boy who didn't do things the easy way! "What if they don't tell you, or drag you away? What if they're shy, or something?"

"Trojan boys aren't very shy."

"*Some* must be!"

"Well…" Cassandra pondered. "They might send someone to ask in their place."

"And if not?"

The girl frowned. "I don't know — maybe we could find something about that in the library."

Andromache let out a sigh of disgust. Instead of a romance, she'd wound up with a research topic.

"You know, honey, if there's someone you want to kiss with, just tell him! Or drag *him* to a dark corner. You don't have to wait for him to do it. In fact, sometimes it's better not to. Boys are so thick, they don't always know you want to make out with them. Although," Cassandra pouted, "in my case, there are other problems, too." She sighed heavily but didn't elaborate.

Andromache fought back the urge to roll her eyes. She didn't have time for Cassandra's problems, just then, especially not imaginary ones. Cassandra was lovely and flirtatious. There was no good reason a boy wouldn't want to kiss with *her*.

The more Andromache thought about it, she didn't have time for Cassandra's advice, either. Tell Demuchus? Interrupt their next conversation about Trojan history or Lukkan agriculture with a request to make out? Take his clammy hand in hers and pull him off to a stairwell? What a ludicrous idea! Besides, he might not want to kiss, and she couldn't think of anything more humiliating than throwing herself at a man who didn't want her.

"There's no one I want to kiss with," Andromache said stiffly. "I'm just interested in Trojan customs, that's all."

"Remember what my dad says!" Cassandra gave her a sly little smile. "You need life experience to go along with study. You can't learn everything just by asking me questions."

"Oh, you told me what I needed to know. Thanks. Sorry to keep you up."

"Any time, honey. Sleep tight!"

"You, too."

Andromache, however, didn't go to sleep. She crept down the hall to the library, intending to do as Cassandra had suggested — to look through a few texts for information on boys who didn't kiss. She made a brief search of the shelves but soon gave up in favor of sitting on the balcony.

Black leaves blotted out much of the sky above her, but here and there, a fleck of silver starlight shone through. She inhaled deeply. *Flowers. Herbs. Fresh-turned earth.* The mornings she'd spent weeding, the evenings she'd lugged water across the courtyard — all of it was paying off. Her garden was thriving. The irony of it was that she, the gardener, didn't belong there. She was the winter-shriveled berry, the twig that never greened. She'd made the garden into a place fit for people whose lives were in bloom, people like Cassandra.

Oh, well, sighed Andromache. It was a disappointment, but not a tragedy. She'd lived through enough tragedies to know what didn't count. She would just have to enjoy Demuchus's company for what it was and forget about her silly obsession with kisses.

ॐ

AFTER HER LATE night, Andromache was so tired that she fell asleep at the breakfast table. She was in the midst of a dream about plucking dry leaves when someone prodded her awake.

"Hermie — oh, Hermie!" sang Paris. "It's marketing time!"

"Go away," mumbled Andromache. If she was never going to get to use the Make-Out stairs, the last thing she wanted to do was watch people flirting.

Paris's face loomed before hers. "You look terrible," he sneered.

Andromache closed her eyes to block out the sight of him.

Tauntingly, Paris said, "I think I know why…my sister told me all about your problem."

"What?" cried Andromache, her head flying up off the table. "What problem?" What had that wretched Cassandra told him?

"That you have loner lips!" Paris made several wet, repellent kissing sounds.

Andromache turned purple with humiliation and rage. "Go away!" she snapped, shoving at Paris's shoulder. "I don't need *you* to fix them."

He tweaked her nose. "Good. I wasn't offering. You're cute, Hermie — but not *that* cute."

"Thanks." She flopped back down against the table.

"Are you marketing or not?"

"Not."

"But I hear there's a sexy new onion merchant…"

"Then whoever wants onion breath can have him."

Paris laughed and slung a basket over his shoulder. "Later," he said, heading for the door.

Andromache scowled. Three things were certain: first, that if she *had* to have a nickname, she much preferred '*Hermie*' to '*Loner Lips.*' She hoped the latter wouldn't stick.

Second, she would *not* be in the kitchen when Paris came back! She would rather do *anything* than see him again. *I'll go running*, she decided. That way, she could burn off some of her anger. *Maybe I'll try out the arena.* She'd been curious about the place, and today seemed like a good day to head down there — today, when the house was full of gossips!

The third and last of Andromache's certainties was that she wouldn't be speaking to Cassandra for a *very* long time.

Chapter 45

Andromache stared at the poem in her hand. The script was exquisite, the words, unusual. They sounded pretty when she read them aloud, but she didn't understand much of what they said, either individually or strung together in verses:

> *Flaring damsel slight of timbre*
> *Singing woodsilk scant of tile*
> *Isle of while of guile of beauty*
> *Moot sweet trial of clinging night...*

The poem went on in like manner for another forty-four lines. Demuchus had given it to her that evening at the soiree. When he'd beckoned her to the courtyard doorway with a furtive wave of his hand, she'd thought he finally wanted to kiss with her. Mildly nervous and very curious, she'd followed him. Instead of kissing her, though, he'd reached into a box...

> *'Here,' he said, producing a fine linen scroll. 'For your reading pleasure. I might advise you that the opening lines are suggestive of —— '*
> *Before he could finish his thought, though, Cassandra darted over to them.*
> *'Andromache!' she hissed. 'We really have to go!'*

Andromache wished now that she'd stayed, even at the risk of angering Hecuba, to hear Demuchus's take on the poem. On her own, she couldn't make sense of it. *'Singing woodsilk scant of tile?'* <u>*Is that a code? Do I even have the words right? Maybe I should just*</u> <u>*wait and read it in the daylight. The lamp's burning low, anyway*</u>...

Sighing, she tucked the poem carefully into her cloak and went to bed.

ဆဂ

THE NEXT MORNING, after several hours of gardening and exercising, Andromache settled down once more with the poem and tried to decipher it. She read it — re-read it — sounded out the words — even muttered whole passages aloud. By the end, she was sure she understood each word, yet together, they still meant nothing.

"What do you think of the poem?" asked Demuchus, later that evening.

Andromache tried to deflect him. "It's extraordinary," she said.

"Which images do you find particularly intriguing?"

Unable to answer, she looked down at her hands.

"You didn't read it?" He sounded hurt.

"No — no, I read it, it's just — I —" She took a deep breath. "I had a hard time understanding it."

"Perhaps you should have read it more carefully," he said, a hint of frost in his voice.

Andromache shrank. "I'm sorry," she murmured. "I'll try again."

Demuchus nodded stiffly and left to join another conversation. For the first time since he'd started talking to her, she spent the evening alone. She wished he would come over to grab her arm, so things could go back to normal. She wished he'd never given her the poem. How sad it would be to lose a friend over something so small!

ဆဂ

THE WHOLE NEXT MORNING and much of the afternoon, Andromache did nothing but wrestle with the poem. The more she read it, though, the less sense it made. The words were like wild berry jam, oozing all over the scroll — she simply couldn't get a firm grasp on them.

When Hector came to the library, later, he found her sweating and close to tears. "What's that?" he asked, peering over her shoulder.

Andromache turned to face him. "Just some poem," she muttered.

He frowned. "It isn't from *our* library."

"How would you know?" she snapped, her exasperation with Demuchus's verse shifting over to Hector. Too late, she remembered that she was trying to avoid having conflicts with him.

Hector, however, didn't bristle at her tone. His eyes looked less shadowed than they had in weeks. He gestured to the library shelves with his right arm, moving it as though it had never been injured. Indeed, where the stitches had once been, there was now a line of shiny pink scar tissue. "I know because I've read everything here," he said.

"Everything?" she asked skeptically.

"Everything," he confirmed.

"Even the poetry?"

He nodded.

Andromache cocked her head. "Do you understand it?" she asked.

"Some of it...most of it."

"Do you understand *this* one?" Painful though it was to have to ask, after all the hours she'd spent on the poem, dumbly facing Demuchus a second time would be worse.

Hector took the scroll from her and scanned it.

"Well?" she whispered. "What does it say?"

"Not much," replied Hector. "Dad collects some pretty crazy things, but even so, this would never make the cut." He gave the poem a sniff of disdain. "This is *trush*."

'*Trush*' — her misreading of the Truvan word '*trash*' was an old joke between Hector and her. Just then, however, Andromache didn't find it funny. Her face turned red. Her eyes prickled with tears. Of *course* Hector was right! Of *course* the stupid thing was trush! What *else* could she inspire but poetry worthy of the garbage bin?

Hector shifted uncomfortably. "Maybe I lookED too fast," he offered.

Andromache peered up at him. "*Looked*," she murmured. "*Looked!* You spoke in the past! You did it!"

"I doed it?" Hector teased. Behind a stray lock of hair, his eyes were dancing.

Andromache gave him a watery smile. Then, forlornly, she asked, "Do you really think this poem is trush?"

He hedged. "This — this poem — it is precious to you?"

"I don't know," she said.

"Oh…"

"Please — your honest opinion."

"Honest?" Hector coughed. "I haff readED better."

"Oh," said Andromache. She wasn't surprised. "Like what?"

Hector stood and walked over to a shelf, reached out, paused, and then went on to a different shelf. He selected a wooden tablet and brought it to her.

Andromache read it through once, then again. The third time, she murmured the words aloud:

> *Time to take the horse to the old tin alley,*
> *Time to walk the foxes past the old tin door.*
> *Hey! With the pretty goat, hand it up slowly!*
> *Hey! With the hen and the cockerels four.*

"So?" said Hector. "You fink what?"

Andromache frowned. "It doesn't mean anything. No more than *my* poem does…"

"No," he agreed. "Baht?"

"But," she said slowly. "There's something about it — I don't know what, exactly."

"It is *fahn*," he said. "A good poem has fahn. Or feelings. Or boff. Not pretty words only."

"Fun." Andromache nodded. Hector was right: these verses, unlike Demuchus's, were *fun*. She could imagine her dad, or even Paris, plucking out a jaunty tune to go with them. "Did you write this?" she asked.

Hector laughed. "No, no, no. It is a old Táruvan poem. A song fohr little boys, little girls. Mom singED it, when I am little." In Truvan, he added, "No one knows where it came from. Dad wrote down a whole bunch of these old songs, so they won't be forgotten if people stop singing them."

"This is Priam's writing?" asked Andromache, touching the elegant script.

Hector nodded.

"And your mom sang it to you?"

"'*Sang*,'" he repeated, making a face. "She *sang* it to me." He laughed again. "And wiff the last words, she does this wiff her hand —" He wiggled first his thumb, then his four fingers, chanting, "*Hey! With the hen and the cockerels four.*"

"Oh!" exclaimed Andromache. "So it *does* mean something. The hen and cockerels are a hand!"

"In Mom's version, anyway."

"That's cute."

Hector smiled. "You haff poems lahke this, in Lukká?"

Andromache thought back to the songs she'd sung with her family. "Yes," she said. "We do —

> *Sunny, sunny, sunny meadow,*
> *Grasses tall, grasses high,*
> *All around the sunny meadow,*
> *Crickets jumping by and by.*"

She choked on the last line, on the word '*crickets*.' Little Cricket had been her family's pet name for her...

"*That*," Hector said gently, "is a good poem."

Andromache sniffled and gave a little nod.

ॐ

AS ANDROMACHE WALKED down the hall after the lesson, she paused at Cassandra's door. Things between them had been tense ever since the girl had told Paris about Andromache's '*loner lips*.' They'd walked to and from soirees together and had seen each other around the house, but Andromache had spoken only the bare minimum of words, and she'd snubbed Cassandra's repeated attempts to make amends. Now, she decided, it was time to move on.

"Cassandra," she called.

Cassandra arrived at the door, her cheeks pink and her eyes remorseful. "Andromache! Do you want to come in?"

Andromache nodded. "Can I?"

"Of course!" Cassandra grabbed her hand and pulled her over to the bed, where they could sit beside each other. "I'm so glad you're here! You have every right to be mad at me, but I just hate fights. We're not in a fight anymore, are we? Oh, honey, I'm so sorry! I wasn't thinking, when I said — when I said *that* to Paris. It just came out."

Andromache squeezed Cassandra's hand. "It's all right — really. Don't worry about it."

"Has he been horrible to you?"

"No," said Andromache. "He hasn't said much." In fact, after the first day, he hadn't said *anything*. It was unlike Paris not to mock her, but after wondering briefly why he wasn't, she'd decided just to be grateful for his silence.

Cassandra breathed a sigh of relief. "Oh, good! I told him to leave you alone, but he doesn't always listen to me." She rested her head on Andromache's shoulder and so noticed the text Andromache was holding. "What's that?"

"Oh — a poem," said Andromache. "Demuchus gave it to me. I —" She gulped. "I'm having trouble understanding it." The Lukkan lesson had lifted her spirits, but it hadn't given her any further insight into the poem. She couldn't very well tell Demuchus that his work was '*trush.*' "He was really disappointed, last night, so I told him I'd try reading it again, but honestly —"

"Let me see." Cassandra held out her hand.

Andromache passed the text over to her. For several agonizing moments, the girl read through it.

"What do you think?" Andromache finally asked.

"It's —" Cassandra frowned.

Trush, thought Andromache, with a private sigh.

"— hermetic."

"Hermetic?" Andromache frowned in turn. "Is that your idea of a '*Hermie*' joke?" she asked, feeling hurt.

"Oh, no!" Cassandra laughed. "It just means that the poem is so elevated that it's closed to common understanding."

"Hermetic," mused Andromache. Demuchus might well accept that word in lieu of comprehension. "Thanks, Cassandra."

ℰↃ

IN THE END, '*hermetic*' so pleased Demuchus that he wrote Andromache another dozen poems. She wrapped them in one of Cassandra's old dresses and tucked them carefully into her clothing chest. There they stayed, unread but safe, as a warm spring turned into an even warmer summer and Andromache and Demuchus resumed their companionable old ways.

Early summer

Chapter 46

ap, rap. There was a soft knocking at Andromache's door. She ignored it.

Rap, rap. "<u>Ahndromahk? You ahre there?</u>"

Go away, she thought. *Go away, Hector!* He would just have to do without a lesson, today!

He knocked again, louder. "<u>You ahre sick, Ahndromahk?</u>"

Go away — just go away!

"Listen, my sister saw you come in all doubled over."

Damn that spying, babbling Cassandra! Damn her once and for all!

"She sent me up to check on you. Puke freaks her out."

"I'm fine," Andromache finally croaked. "I'm not puking."

Pause. "You don't sound good." Hector's concern was transmitted clearly through the door. "I'll go find Mom. Will you be all right till I get back with her?"

No! Andromache began to panic. She was trapped! The last thing she wanted was for Hecuba to come to her room — far better to take a risk on Hector. "Wait!" she cried, throwing the door open wide.

When Hector saw her, he exclaimed, "What the hell!"

Andromache clutched the little, white, spotted puppy to her chest. "They were *hurting* her!" she shrieked.

"Who was?"

"The boys! They were holding her up in the air by her back leg! She was squealing — and I — I — they were *hurting* her!" Inadvertently, Andromache gave the puppy such a hard squeeze that she grunted. "I had to stop them! I had to *stop* them!"

"Sssh," soothed Hector. "Sssh. It's all right."

Trembling, Andromache sat down on the floor of the hall-way. Hector sat beside her.

"What happened?" he asked.

"I took her from them."

"I kind of guessed that. I meant your eye."

Oh — that. "They didn't just give her up," Andromache said cautiously. "We struggled, and I fell against the wall." There was no way she was going to tell Hector the truth — that one of the little shits had hit her on purpose, blackening her eye, and that she'd hit him back. She was too embarrassed to admit that she'd been brawling with adolescents.

"I see," Hector said quietly. "So there were two boys? Three boys?"

"Two."

"How old?"

"I don't know. Maybe thirteen, fourteen."

"What did they look like?"

"Like each other."

"What?"

"I think they were twins."

"Oh. Did you recognize them?"

"No!" cried Andromache. "And even if I did, I'm *not* taking her back to them!"

"Ssssh —"

"Shush me all you want — *I'm not taking her back!*"

"I never said you should," soothed Hector. "I was asking because something has to be done about those boys." His face hardened, and menace seeped into his voice. "Consequences."

Andromache blanched. *Black hollows where there should have been eyes — gore-streaked bronze armor — the reek of blood and smoke.* The images were still there, lurking in her mind. "They were just a couple of stupid kids," she muttered, leaning as far away from Hector as she could in the narrow hallway.

"That doesn't make it all right."

Andromache kissed the puppy's ears, which were the exact reddish brown of fallen pine needles. "She's safe, now. That's what matters. I don't care about the boys."

Hector didn't respond.

Assuming that he'd let the matter drop, Andromache went on: "The real problem is, I don't know what to do with *her.*" She giggled as the puppy chewed on her finger.

"Keep her?" suggested Hector. His voice had returned to normal.

"Your parents would never let me."

"They let Paris keep Muka."

"He's their *son*! I'm just —"

"I can talk to them, if you want — put in a good word for her."

Andromache eyed Hector warily, but he didn't seem to be mocking her. "All right," she said, wincing as her bruised eye crinkled.

Hector frowned. "Still hurts?"

Andromache nodded.

"Then I think we should skip our Lukkan lesson today. Instead, I'll track down my mom so she can take a look."

At that suggestion, Andromache groaned. Hecuba would have more than a few choice words for *her*!

"She'll see it anyway," argued Hector.

"Not if I stay up here."

He shook his head. "A door won't stop her. You might as well show it to her so she can give you something to make it feel better."

"She'll be so annoyed with me, she'll say '*no*' to the puppy!"

"No, she won't."

"How do you know?"

"After all the times I've annoyed her, believe me — I *know.*"

"But then, your dad —"

"— will praise the stars for guiding you to the puppy in time to rescue her."

Andromache sighed.

"You need to see my mom, <u>Ahndromahk</u>."

Reluctantly, she nodded.

Hector watched her stroking the puppy's ears. "Can I hold her?" he asked.

Andromache turned to look at him. His earlier aura of menace had faded, but the fact that it had been there at all made her nervous. She shook her head and murmured, "I'm the only one she trusts."

"Oh," he said, nodding. "That's understandable. Well, I'm off to find Mom, then."

"Listen — Hector?"

"Hmm?"

"Please — don't ask her to come up here. I'll come down, when — when I'm —"

"When you're ready." He nodded again. "Of course."

"Thank you," said Andromache. "<u>Um…I guess I'll see you later.</u>"

"<u>See you.</u>"

ဢ

ANDROMACHE DIDN'T GO downstairs until late that evening. She would have put it off longer, if the puppy hadn't needed food and a visit to one of the courtyard's private corners.

Once the puppy had relieved herself, Andromache carried her back to the kitchen. She was hungry and knew that the puppy must be, too. At the threshold, though, she stopped short: Priam and Hecuba were inside.

Dammit! Andromache had hoped to find the place empty. Instead, she would have to face both of the parents at once! On the bright side, Cassandra, Paris, and Hector had already left on their nightly outings. If Hector was wrong about his parents' reactions, Andromache would at least be able to suffer their wrath in private.

Holding her breath, she stepped into the kitchen.

Priam was the first to notice her. "Hello, little one," he said. "Oh! And who's that, with you?" He nodded toward the puppy in her arms.

Andromache launched into her story. "I found her on the streets — some boys were — they were hurting her, and I was hoping I could — she's a really good puppy! — she doesn't make messes, I swear, and if she does, I'll —"

"Of course, you can keep her!" Priam beamed at her. "We needed a dog. I didn't realize until now just how much I've been missing poor Muka."

Andromache smiled shyly.

"And the one you've found is a funny little thing, isn't she? All covered in spots!" Priam laughed. "What are you going to call her?"

"I don't know, yet."

"You'll think of something," said Hecuba. "Bring her over here so we can pet her."

Andromache felt guilty doing so, since she hadn't let Hector pet the puppy, but she could see no graceful way of refusing. Besides, Hector would never know.

Hecuba held her arms out to take the puppy. "Little monster!" She laughed as the creature nibbled her chin. "We'll have a dinner tomorrow night, in honor of her arrival." She looked as pleased to have found an excuse for a family gathering as she was by the puppy herself. "Now, Andromache, dear — let's talk about that eye..."

Chapter 47

"Ahndromahk?" called Hector. He was breathing heavily, as though he'd run all the way there. "Sohrry so late…"

"Oh. It's fine," said Andromache, forcing a light tone. She'd been pacing for the past half hour, waiting for Hector to arrive. He was *never* late! Why today, then, when she least wanted to linger in the library? Her puppy was downstairs with Cassandra — Cassandra, who was well-meaning, to be sure, but untried as a babysitter. What if the puppy had an accident because she wasn't let outside in time? What if Cassandra let her eat a bee?

"The baby dog is where?" asked Hector.

"With Cassandra." Andromache tried not to let her misgivings show.

Hector nodded.

"Your family seems to like her," Andromache said softly. "You were right. And I think she's going to like it, here, a whole lot better than —" She winced, thinking of what the puppy had been through the day before.

"Sssh, it is all rahght, now," murmured Hector. "They cannot hurt her —"

Andromache nodded.

"Ohr any ahther baby dogs."

Andromache gaped. *They cannot hurt her — or any other baby dogs.* Priam had once used similar words to describe the Mudders at Lyrnassa, the ones who hadn't surrendered: *They won't be troubling any more villages.'* Theirs was the blood, red and slick, on Hector's armor…

Andromache began to tremble; her vision clouded over. She was a little girl again, running up the mountainside, fleeing raiders who had come to plunder her home in the Lukka lands. She was on the beach in Lyrnassa, watching a Mudder ship come closer and closer to the village. She was up on the cliffs above Lyrnassa, and a monster was leaning over her — the monster her parents had always warned her about...

His eyes were two black hollows, fixed on her throat. He reeked of gore — of smoke. His bronze armor was wet with blood, but still, he yearned for more. His teeth were bared. He was going to tear her throat — drain her blood — leave her stiff body facedown upon the earth —

Panic boiled through Andromache, making her forget everything she'd learned about Hector over the past year. He was no longer the kind, gentle man from the library. He was no longer part of an army of defenders. Now, he was nothing but a brutal, gore-spattered monster, seeping menace and thirsting for blood. He was the Raider.

They cannot hurt her — or any other baby dogs. Andromache's stomach filled with cold slime as she pictured the boys, lying in some dusty Trojan street. They'd been stabbed a thousand times. Their blood had poured out, leaving their bodies waxy-pale — just like the corpse she'd seen long ago, in her Lukkan village of Hurapi —

"I told you to leave them alone," she croaked.

Hector's jaw was set. "This is *my* city. I'm not going to stand by and let that kind of thing happen, here."

"I told you to leave them alone!" she cried. Her hands were shaking. Clammy. The words seemed to be coming from somewhere else. "I told you to leave them alone, not —" She paused, searching for just the right word. "Not *gut* them!"

"Whoa — *what*? What did you say?" Hector stared at her in disbelief. "Is *that* what you think of me? That I go around, gutting *kids*?"

Andromache didn't answer — her lips were trembling far too wildly for her to speak. Now that Hector had said the words aloud, they sounded crazy. And yet, there was the aura of menace she'd felt from him when he'd said that the boys needed '*con-*

sequences.' *They won't be troubling any more villages. They cannot hurt her — or any other baby dogs—*

"I see," spat Hector, his baleful eye glaring into her black one. "Then I'd better go." With that, he left the library, sucking all the air out with him.

Andromache couldn't run after him — couldn't move — couldn't breathe. All her life, family and friends had been leaving her: first her grandparents, then her parents, her Auntie, and, most recently, Muka. They were dead — gone forever — and yet she could still feel a hint of their presence.

Not so, with Hector. He was just gone.

No one had ever withdrawn from her so completely — so violently. He'd slashed through her insides. The cold slime was now oozing out, and hornets were pouring in to fill the cavity.

What had she *done?*

(*You made him hate you,*) said the snide little Voice.

Andromache couldn't respond. She was still in shock.

(*But why should that matter? Why would you want to spend time with someone who goes around, gutting kids?*)

The more times those words were uttered, the more outrageous they sounded. Andromache couldn't imagine the Hector she knew doing anything like that. Fear had made her say it — the old, thick fear that came on strong and was impossible to reason with. Fear had made her say it, and now Hector hated her.

(*He never really liked you, anyway,*) said the Voice. (*This whole time, he's just been using you — learning Lukkana to punish himself.*)

I know, murmured Andromache.

(*And his guilt is fading…*)

I know! And she'd just given him reason to leave it behind for good. To leave Lukkan lessons behind for good. To leave *her* behind for good.

(*Oh, well. What can you do?*) the Voice replied, shrugging. (*Life is a bag of goat shit.*)

Andromache blinked back tears. The Voice had struck a cruel blow with '*life is a bag of goat shit*' — the first words of Lukkan she'd ever shared with Hector. She could still hear the black sound of his laughter as she explained the phrase to him: *Bad things happen. What can you do? Life is a bag of goat shit. He knows,* she'd thought, even then. *He understands dark things.* Because of that laugh, she'd been able to tell him about Auntie, and her parents' death, and the goat she'd had to kill. She'd known that he would understand in a way most others never could. And now, Hector was gone.

Andromache felt a hornet sting the inside of her belly.

(*Gone,*) the Voice agreed.

There were several more stings. Tears rolled down Andromache's cheeks — first as a trickle, then a flood. Unaware of the passage of time, she covered her face and cried and cried while the hornets boiled on inside her. She didn't stop crying until loud voices from below, on the courtyard, broke through the sound of her sobbing.

"Paris, dear, where on earth is everybody? Are Hector and Andromache still in their lesson?"

"I don't know, but here comes Dad."

"Priam! Well, thank goodness — that's *something*, anyway. Now, Paris —"

"Yes, Mom?"

"I need you to run to the kitchen. There's one more platter of fruit to fetch."

"All right."

"And if you see your sister or Andromache — whoever's looking after the puppy right now — tell them I've saved a few tidbits for her."

"Right — I'll tell them you saved a few tidbits for Hermie."

"Paris! You give them the *proper* message, or I swear to you, I'll —"

"All right, Mom! All right."

Andromache wiped her nose and straightened her dress. She'd forgotten about the family dinner. Worse, she'd forgotten about the puppy! As if making Hector hate her wasn't enough, she was now a rotten mama to the puppy, too! There just didn't seem to be a bottom for her to hit.

388

AS ALWAYS, Priam opened the dinner with a beautiful oration, this one about the joy of welcoming new members of the family. When the puppy began to punctuate his words with little yips, he laughed and cut short his speech. Food was passed around.

For the others, it was a normal family dinner, full of chatter, laughter, and eating, but Andromache didn't join in any of it. All of her energy went to wishing that Hector's stony countenance wasn't at the table with them. He neither talked to anybody nor ate anything. He had mustered far too much dignity to eat, and his sole purpose in being there, as far as she could tell, was to make her feel wretched.

At first, he succeeded. The hornets stung her insides to a misery of welts and sores. She loathed herself in every possible way and wished that Hector and Penthesilea had passed by her on their way out of Lyrnassa, leaving her to perish on the cliff. At some point, though, as she sat hunched over the table, dragging her bread crust through the stew she couldn't choke down, she began to feel angry.

What right did Hector have to get mad at *her?* He hadn't seen himself *that day* above Lyrnassa, when he'd been looming over her, covered in gore! Mudder gore — *They won't be troubling any more villages,* she thought, shivering. Given Hector's fearsome alter ego, the burden was *his* to explain what '*consequences*' he'd inflicted upon the boys! Yes, that was it! If he'd done nothing horrible to them, then he should have explained himself, rather than evaporating like some bilious fog!

Andromache looked up. Hector was disdainfully refusing the platter of fruit that had been passed to him. Suddenly, she longed for nothing more than to launch a cupful of stew at his face and watch the rivulets slop down the hollows in his cheeks. If he never spoke to her again — even if that meant the end of Lukkan lessons — it would be no great loss!

No great loss, she repeated to herself, trying to ignore the hornets still buzzing inside her.

AS ANDROMACHE lay tossing on top of her blanket that hot, airless night, she heard a knock.

Hector! she thought, wrenching herself upright. He'd come to straighten things out — to tell her what had really happened. Her heart raced. She brushed several strands of hair off her cheek.

"Honey?" said a girlish voice, uncharacteristically sober.

"I'm here, Cassandra," said Andromache. Disappointed but not really surprised, she lay back down and curled around the sleeping puppy. "Come in."

Cassandra slipped in, sat on Andromache's bed, and sighed.

"What's wrong?" asked Andromache.

Cassandra turned pleading eyes on her. "Don't be mad at my brother."

"What?"

"I could tell you were mad at him, at dinner."

"Oh, I'm not mad at anyone. I was just tired, that's all."

"I heard you in the library," whispered Cassandra.

Andromache gaped at her. "What?"

"I was bringing the puppy up to my room to take a nap with her, and I heard yelling, so I stopped." Cassandra gave Andromache a reproachful look. "I heard what you said. Hector isn't like that."

"Oh, I'm sure!" snapped Andromache, who was in no mood to hear a catalogue of Hector's virtues — especially not from a *spy*! "He's as gentle as a baby rabbit, with all his swords and spears!"

Cassandra recoiled as though she'd been slapped. "He *needs* those, when people are trying to — to *hurt* him."

Andromache's cheeks flamed. "We're not talking about an army of Mudders, Cassandra. It was two teenage boys!"

"I told you — don't say that word!" gasped Cassandra, covering her mouth in horror.

"Mudders!" cried Andromache. "Mudders, Mudders, Mudders!" With each repetition of '*Mudders*,' she raised her voice further until finally she was shouting.

The puppy awoke and anxiously licked Andromache's chin.

"Ssssh," soothed Andromache, feeling guilty. "It's all right. Go back to sleep."

"My brother feels like you do," murmured Cassandra, once the little dog had curled up again. "He just wants the puppy to be safe."

"Well, she doesn't *want* him for a nursemaid," Andromache hissed.

"You think *I* do?" Cassandra hissed back. "You think it's easy for me to meet up with boys, with *him* around, scaring them half to death, shooting looks at the ones that come over to me? You think they're all eager to kiss with *his* little sister, after seeing him down on the training field?"

Andromache blinked. She hadn't expected *that* retort, although it explained why Cassandra, lovely as she was, sometimes had trouble finding boys to kiss with.

"It was better a year or two ago, before he realized I was old enough for all that. But *these* days —" Cassandra sighed. "Hector might be annoying, sometimes — believe me, I'd know! — but that's just how he is. He can't help being protective. One night, Mom was out on the courtyard when she saw him sleepwalking. She told him to go back to bed, and he knocked her to the ground! He was dreaming that an axe was flying at her head. Lucky for her, she landed in a bed of herbs."

Andromache chewed a raw patch into her lip. She'd never thought about Hector having nightmares, and she didn't want to. Feeling sorry for him just made the frenzy of the hornets worse. "He did *something* to those boys," she reminded Cassandra. "He told me himself that they wouldn't be bothering any more dogs. Do *you* know what happened?"

"No," admitted Cassandra. "But I know what *didn't* happen — and so do *you*."

Andromache felt more despicable than ever. "I'm tired," she said, looking away from Cassandra.

"Oh," said the girl. "I should leave, then. Good night, honey." She stroked the puppy. "And good night, sweet little baby." Cassandra got up walked toward the door.

'*I know what didn't happen — and so do you,*' Andromache mouthed at the girl's self-righteous back. Who did Cassandra think she was, saying a thing like that? She only knew the kindly older brother or, at most, the Hector from the training field. Andromache alone knew the *other* Hector — the battlefield Hector

— the living nightmare, hollow-eyed, caked in gore and blood, and reeking of smoke!

Her mind refused to produce the image of the Raider. Instead, she saw Hector carrying Muka on his shoulder.

Caked in gore and blood and reeking of smoke! she insisted.

Hector, pushing his mom to the ground to rescue her from a flying axe. Hector, saying *'It is ugly'* when Andromache told him about the goat she'd killed. And meaning it.

Caked in gore! Hollow-eyed!

Hector's hands, covered with crawling caterpillars. His dark eyes, bright when he smiled — soft when he glimpsed the puppy — hurt and angry when he was accused of gutting the puppy's tormentors.

If only he would tell me what really happened! sighed Andromache.

(*He probably thought he didn't have to,*) said the Voice, snide as ever. (*He probably thought you trusted him.*)

And why *wouldn't* he think that? What reason had he ever given her not to trust him?

The hornets redoubled their stinging, turning her whole stomach into a carpet of angry welts.

***

LICK. LICK. SCHLUUURP.

Andromache groaned. The puppy was slobbering all over her face.

Lick. Nibble, nibble.

"You have to go outside, don't you."

The puppy panted gleefully. So far, she hadn't made any mistakes in the house — she seemed to dislike soiling her living space — but there were limits to how long she would be able to endure.

Andromache peeked out the window. The courtyard was empty, but soon Hector would be meeting Paris for archery practice. "I'd sooner clean up a thousand of your messes than face *him*!" Andromache said to the puppy.

The little creature moaned.

"Please, baby! Just a little longer. Here, let's find something to chew on." Andromache dug through her clothing chest until she found the monstrous spotted cloth that had been her first weaving project.

The puppy seized the cloth and yanked on it much more forcefully than Andromache had expected. Andromache pulled back. The puppy growled in delight and moved up her grip until she was biting Andromache's fingers.

"Ouch!" cried Andromache, letting go. "Stop! You play too rough."

The puppy moaned again and shook the cloth furiously.

"Just a little longer," Andromache pleaded. She looked once more down onto the courtyard and this time saw someone. A man, straight-backed and tall.

Hector.

He looks scary, she told herself. *Even without the smoke and blood and armor. He looks like he could gut someone without breaking stride.*

On his way over to the kitchen, he stopped by the spring. He drank a cup of water, stretched his arms overhead, yawned, and brushed a lock of hair out of his face. He couldn't have looked more benign.

The hornets awoke and started buzzing around.

Andromache tried desperately to conjure the image of the Raider...

He was on the cliffs above Lyrnassa, riding a golden horse, barreling down toward the village, risking his career and his life for people he'd never met —

In frustration, Andromache slapped her hand against her forehead. The puppy licked her face once, then again. And again.

"Sssssssh...stop," said Andromache, taking the little animal in her arms. "We'll go down as soon as he's gone."

৪০

ON THE PRETEXT of her black eye, Andromache begged out of marketing with Paris and instead sat outside on the courtyard. She'd imagined a peaceful morning of cuddling with her puppy, but the little creature had no interest in sitting still. Instead, she romped around the gardens, batting at ants and butterflies with her paws and shoving her snout into plant after plant — most of which made her sneeze. Eventually, she collapsed on the ground with her legs in the air.

"Nap time," said a gentle voice.

Andromache turned to see Priam, home at an unusual hour.

Noting her surprise, the priest explained: "One of my associates has a daughter with heat rash, and Hecuba asked me to fetch her some of your owlsburr. I must say, little one — she's enormously impressed that you've been able to grow it here."

"Oh," Andromache said softly, embarrassed by the compliment. "Thank you."

Priam sat beside her and asked, "So, what are you up to?"

"Just watching the puppy. She was running around, chasing bugs, and then all of a sudden —"

Priam interrupted with a loud snore, then laughed. "That's babies, for you."

The puppy moaned. Her feet began to churn.

"Oh, no!" cried Andromache. "Something's wrong! She's sick, or —"

"She's just having a dream," Priam assured her.

"Probably a nightmare," Andromache said dolefully.

Priam gave the puppy a somber look. "The very idea that someone could hurt a defenseless little creature…" He was too sickened to finish his thought.

Andromache nodded, feeling like a hypocrite. Just the day before, she'd accused Priam's son of a similar crime. The priest would probably yell at her, if he ever found out. That was the only time he'd ever yelled, wasn't it? To stop the Ass General from attacking Hector, her first night in Troy? Or maybe Priam wouldn't yell, in her case, but just look at her, his dark eyes sad and wounded. She didn't know which would be worse.

A volley of hornets bombarded her insides.

"Well, I'm sure you'll fill her life with good dreams, from now on," said Priam, patting her hand.

Involuntarily, Andromache shrank from him. She didn't deserve to be patted and comforted — especially not by Hector's father.

"Little one, what's wrong?" he asked gently. "Did you hurt your hand, yesterday, too?"

She shook her head, unable to speak. Any moment, tears would start flowing.

"You're still worried about the puppy?" he asked.

"What if it's too late?" She sniffled. "What if she's afraid forever, even though she's safe, now?"

Priam put his arm around her shoulders. "You saved her life. Apart from death, anything is fixable. Give her time."

෫෮

LATE IN THE afternoon, when the day's heat had reached its peak and the breeze off the sea had stopped blowing, Andromache went to the library. She sat down with the puppy on her lap, fully expecting to spend the afternoon alone with her pet — *And that's fine by me!* she told herself repeatedly.

To her surprise, though, Hector arrived a short while later and sat stiffly on his usual stool. He looked as welcoming as a prickle plant, but he'd come.

At a loss for words, Andromache just sat there, staring at the table in front of her. Hector, too, was staring, but at his hands. Andromache sighed. In response, Hector peered out the window.

"Hector…" she finally murmured.

He turned back toward her.

"I —" There, she got stuck. What exactly did she want to say to him? *I'm sorry* — really *sorry* — *I know you wouldn't gut anyone?* The words sounded insane. *Dammit!* she moaned to herself. She wasn't good at expressing her feelings! She'd never even managed to tell Hector what a good brother he was, the compliment she'd once so longed to give him. *Dammit!* He was eyeing her, waiting for her to speak, but she couldn't. Nothing sounded right. *Dammit, dammit, dammit!*

Reflexively, she did the one thing that came to mind — she walked around the table and placed the puppy in his arms. Delighted, the little creature slathered kisses all over his neck and chin.

The effect on Hector was immediate, much like a gust of wind stirring a barley field into motion. "Silly!" He laughed at the puppy. "Cut that out!" To Andromache, he added, "I tell — *told* — you, my parents say you can haff her."

His friendly tone flushed the hornets from Andromache's stomach and excised the past day from their lives. Her apology was accepted. Weak with relief, she said, "Yes, they liked her."

Laughing again as the puppy sank needle-like teeth into his finger, Hector asked, "You haff a name fohr her?"

"No," said Andromache. As a further gesture of reconciliation, she asked, "What do you think it should be?"

Hector's face flooded with surprise and flattery. "Cutie."

Andromache laughed. She'd been expecting something a little grander — the family's first dog had been called Mukadiah. "Cutie?" she asked.

"It is good, no?"

"Yes. It's perfect for her..."

"Baht?"

"But what if Paris makes fun of her for it?"

Taking her objection seriously, Hector said, "You can call her '*Cutie*,' but in Lukkana. You can say it mean '*brave wolf*' ohr somefing."

"Cutie," mused Andromache. "I like it."

"I lahke *her*," said Hector. He laughed again as the puppy licked him squarely on the lips.

Andromache's smile turned wistful. What she'd told herself at dinner, about not caring whether Lukkan lessons ended, had been an out-and-out lie. She was relieved — so relieved! — to see Hector across the table from her.

Watching Cutie wriggle about on Hector's lap, Andromache had to blink back tears. How could she have said what she'd said to him? How *could* she? Would Lyrnassa always be a stain on her life? If only she'd never seen him dressed in armor! If only they hadn't met *that day*, they might have been friends, unshadowed by guilt and fear...

(*But you* did *meet in Lyrnassa,*) the Voice gloated. (*And you can't change that.*)

No, Andromache couldn't change where, and under what circumstances, she'd met Hector. It was useless imagining a life that might have been. Instead, she needed to refocus her energy on keeping peace with him. Things between them had been calm for so long that Andromache had let herself slip. *No more!* she told herself. From now on, she would remember what his limits were and avoid topics likely to trigger a fight. They might never be friends, the way she would have liked, but at least she could avoid becoming his enemy.

Chapter 48

While her black eye was healing, Andromache spent most of her time with Cutie. The little dog shadowed her even more closely than Muka had, and with a lot more energy. When Andromache gardened, Cutie chased grasshoppers through the courtyard. When Andromache swept the floor, the little dog yowled in protest and snapped at her bitter enemy, the broom. She hated the broom — yet she never left Andromache's side to escape it.

Andromache was equally devoted to Cutie. Sometimes, she found herself locking eyes with the little dog, gazing at her until Cutie's tail began to wag. At bedtime, she curled up around the puppy, stroking her fur, while Cutie lay on her back with her legs in the air. Those moments gave Andromache a bubbling of joy like none she'd ever known, not even with Muka. No one had ever been hers like Cutie was.

Although they didn't take it to Andromache's extremes, the rest of the family members also adored Cutie. No one — not even Paris — could look at the dog's pointed ears or the smudge of black on her lips without smiling. No one could watch her wriggling on her back without cooing. Everyone laughed at Cutie's stiff-legged trot, at the way her back legs made circles rather than moving back and forth. Everywhere Cutie went, she was surrounded by smiles, giggles, hugs, and squeals of delight.

Hector was especially fond of her. Andromache had worried, at first, that he might resent Cutie — that he would see her only as the cause of a terrible fight. Far from it, though, Hector doted on the little dog. He held her on his lap for as long as she would let him and brought lengths of old rope for her to chew when she got restless. He steered Lukkan conversations toward the subject of dogs — what Muka had been like as a puppy, or the best way to housetrain a pet. He even made jokes about Cutie squatting over the Chute.

In all, Andromache was housebound for almost two weeks. No one made her stay home, but she was too embarrassed to leave. Once the color of her eye returned to normal, she went back to marketing with Paris. She tried bringing Cutie along and discovered that the three of them were an even more effective team than she and Paris alone. Meat merchants and bakers, charmed by Cutie's white, spotted fur and perky ears, gave tidbits to the little dog and slipped extras into Paris's baskets. After that, no marketing trip was complete without Cutie.

Whenever Andromache *did* leave Cutie home — like when she went down to the exercise arena — the dog greeted her afterward with sharp, angry-sounding little barks: *'Where were you? What took you so long? You left me here! I'm mad, I'm mad, I'm mad!'* She writhed around Andromache's feet, licking her frantically.

Besides the exercise arena, the only other place Andromache didn't take Cutie was to Demuchus's house. His uncle, who was immune to cuteness, didn't allow animals within his walls. Andromache resented the rule so much that she might not have gone back to the soirees at all, except they tended to start after Cutie had bedded down for the night, anyway.

At the gatherings, Demuchus resumed his place by Andromache's side. He never mentioned her injury, although she knew he'd heard about it from the fleeting way he glanced at her eye. He also touched her arm more lightly than before, as though she were a vase in danger of shattering. He occasionally muttered about *'unsafe situations'* but changed the subject when she asked what he meant.

Andromache liked being back at the soirees, back among the young people discussing texts and politics. She liked spending time with Demuchus and knowing that he, too, enjoyed it. She liked returning to Cutie, afterward, and snuggling down into bed with the warm, wriggling little creature beside her. Her life in Troy was rich and full. She was as happy as she'd been in a long, long time.

High summer

Chapter 49

Andromache grimaced at the text she was reading — an historical treatise on the great earthquakes. It was interesting, but not easy. She'd arrived early at the library to review a little before Hector arrived for his lesson.

> *...yet on the forty-third day after the origiant upheamable, another tremor of the earth took place, one large enough (or so claim the sourshas) to move a cow notoriously up and down. Others claim the animal in question to be a goat or small deer — petite comparted to a cow, but neverthorlens of snignifiant size...*

Cutie, hot and restless, was patrolling around the library.
"Sit, Cutie. Sit. Come over here," ordered Andromache.
Cutie ignored her.
"Hector will be here any moment, now, and I don't need you running around. I can't spend the whole lesson yelling at you to sit. Come here, Cutie. Cutie — I mean it!"
The little white dog galloped past, tripping over her long legs and falling face-first beside Andromache.
"Oh, no! Are you all right?"
Cutie looked up at her, panting and wagging her tail. The tongue dangling from her snout looked to be half as long as her body.
"How on earth do you fit all that in your mouth?"

The dog's ears perked. She leapt up, throwing her front feet onto Andromache's lap, and Andromache couldn't resist giving her a hug.

"<u>All right — all right, sweetie. But you have to go down, now. And I need to read.</u>"

Cutie slid to the floor, where she began nibbling on the hem of Andromache's dress.

Andromache sighed but didn't protest. At least the dog was finally sitting still.

> *...but nevertheless of significant size. Several hundred of these tremblings were noted, although not all coniformed and of those not many great enough to shake a cow. Next on the falsimer —*

Falsimer? thought Andromache. She frowned and glanced back through the reading, but the context didn't help her. She would have to wait for Hector, for that one.

She frowned again, more deeply. Where *was* he? He was almost an hour late. He should have sent a message — that would have been the decent thing to do! She certainly wouldn't have sweltered up here in the library, if she'd known he was going to be late. She would have waited on the courtyard, or maybe in the kitchen. Even now, she might be sipping cool water infused with herbs rather than sweating half to death!

> *— flowsing aggan, trimmeled zenistically —*

<u>*An hour?*</u> Andromache's stomach lurched. The last time he'd been this late to a lesson, he'd been about to leave Troy — with the *army*. Did he have to leave again? Would he be going that night? Was he already gone?

Suddenly, vividly, Andromache saw him. He was lying on the ground — his arm sliced open — the skin torn back — all the inner parts red, raw, and exposed. She covered her mouth and ran for the door, half tripping over Cutie on the way. The dog leaped up to join her, and the two of them careened down the hall to the back staircase.

Andromache didn't know where she was going. To the courtyard, to rip out weeds, or perhaps to the exercise arena —

yes, there! She would run up and down the stands as she'd once run the stairs in the house, lifting her knees higher and higher with each step. She would run until her legs were screaming, until she had blisters all over her feet. Anything, anything to erase that picture from her mind! The picture of —

"Andromache?" Hecuba called out to her from the kitchen.

Andromache stopped short. Was *he* in there? Was the whole family in there, having a hasty farewell meal to which she hadn't been invited?

"Where are you off to in such a hurry?" asked Hecuba, coming into the banquet hall from the kitchen. She looked calm, tranquil — not at all how she'd looked the last time Hector was about to leave for a military campaign.

Confused, Andromache stammered, "I was going to — I mean, I was waiting — reading, to prepare — maybe I — maybe I missed a message, or something." She took a deep breath. "It's just, he's never late, except — so I thought —"

"Late? Who's late? You mean Hector?"

Andromache nodded.

"Oh, when I get my hands on that wretched boy!" muttered Hecuba. "Here, dear — sit." She gestured to a bench. "Sit!"

Andromache sat.

"So, I'm assuming he didn't think to tell you he'd be leaving for a few days on a patrol inspection."

Patrol inspection? The spinning inside Andromache's head began to slow.

"Dear?" prompted Hecuba.

Andromache shook her head.

"Typical," Hecuba spat in disgust. "Not even the common courtesy to alert people to his comings and goings! You may find this hard to believe, Andromache, but I did *not* set out to raise a pack of wild boars."

"It's all right," said Andromache, too relieved to care about manners. "He just forgot."

"'*All right?*'" Hecuba sniffed. "I think not! Not telling one's teachers when one must miss several days' lessons is the height of impropriety. Well! He'll be gone for a few days, and when he returns, believe you me —" Her eyes narrowed dangerously. "My son and I will be having a little *chat*."

Chapter 50

That evening, at the soiree, Andromache met Demuchus's comments with less than usual enthusiasm.

"What's wrong?" he asked, touching her arm.

She flinched. "Nothing."

"It can't be *nothing*." Demuchus smiled beneficently. "If *nothing* were upsetting you, you would have given my thoughts on standardizing axel length a heartier nod."

Andromache sighed. "I'm sorry. It's just —"

"What?"

"I know the next few days are going to be boring."

Demuchus looked miffed. "Oh. Well, I apologize that the scheduled topics aren't of interest to you."

"Not *here*," Andromache said quickly. "It's not *here* that things will be boring. I meant at home. Hector is away, so I won't be having Lukkan lessons. That leaves a big block of empty time in the afternoon, when it's too hot to exercise, too late to market, and too early for soirees." She sighed again.

"Oh!" Demuchus's inflection had changed entirely. He squared his shoulders and said, "*That's* not a problem. My lessons end well earlier, and I'd be happy to keep you company."

"Oh — oh —" Andromache stammered. "I — oh — I —"

"Shall I come over in the late afternoon, then?"

Andromache considered the idea. Although meeting with Demuchus couldn't take the place of Lukkan lessons, it would be nice to visit with a friend. "All right," she agreed. She hoped her nod was hearty enough to suit him.

෨

THE NEXT DAY WAS BRUTALLY HOT. Andromache invited Demuchus to sit out on the courtyard, in the shade of the fig tree. Cutie went with them. She made a single, timid approach to Demuchus, who rebuffed her. After that, she lay panting at Andromache's feet.

Demuchus cleared his throat several times. "It has come to my attention," he finally said, "that you appreciate the art of music, particularly lute music."

Andromache braced herself to hear Demuchus recounting the story of how her lecherous old grandfather had forced himself on a servant, fathered a child — Andromache's dad — and taught him the art of making lutes, only to reject him when a legitimate heir came along.

But Demuchus never mentioned her unseemly origins. Instead, he gave a dissertation on musical lore. He seemed interested only in showing off his knowledge.

Cassandra must have told him I like listening to Paris *play, that's all*, Andromache thought with relief.

"...Of course, I only know half of this because my father was a great historian on the subject," Demuchus admitted humbly in one of his few pauses for breath. "Possibly the greatest ever to live. His writings describe the subtle differences between eastern and western music in exquisite detail. If you're interested in reading his text, the library here probably has a copy. They have a *fair* selection." His tone implied a much greater abundance of reading material at his own house.

"It sounds interesting," Andromache agreed. "Maybe I'll look for it, later."

"We could look now..."

"I'm too tired to go upstairs, right now," she said, although she wasn't tired. She just wanted to avoid visiting the library with Demuchus. *He'll complain about how small it is*, she told herself. *And I never got around to straightening up the table*. She thought of his long, thin fingers seizing her reed pen and potsherds — of his long, thin nose wrinkling over the text on earthquakes. She didn't feel like explaining her teaching methods to him.

Looking concerned, Demuchus touched her arm. "Can I bring you anything? Some water, perhaps?"

Andromache reached down to pat Cutie, incidentally breaking contact with Demuchus's hand. "No, thanks," she said. "I'm fine."

₨

THAT NIGHT, Andromache dreamed that she'd been buried up to her throat in garden loam, and that Demuchus had summarily plucked her out and tossed her behind him, with the rest of the weeds. She awoke feeling depressed and threw an arm around Cutie for comfort.

₨

DEMUCHUS LAUNCHED the next afternoon's conversation by asking if Andromache had found his father's text.

"Not yet," she said, stroking Cutie with her bare feet. "But I haven't been able to search all the shelves."

Andromache held her breath, hoping Demuchus would believe her. The truth was that early that morning, she'd searched until she found his father's history of music. She'd read it — or tried, anyway. It was just as hermetic as Demuchus's *'flaring damsel'* poem and just as stodgy as the biography of Sarcho. *I can't talk about this with Demuchus!* she'd thought, setting the history of music aside. *It would hurt his feelings if he knew I didn't like it.* The text no doubt stirred the same emotions in Demuchus that joyous lute music did in her.

"Keep looking," Demuchus encouraged her. "Perhaps you'll find it tomorrow."

"I hope so," she said.

Demuchus cleared his throat. "For today, I was thinking…"

"Yes?"

405

"You've missed speaking Lukkan, these past few days, isn't that right?"

For no good reason, Andromache flushed. "Oh, I guess so, but it's not a big deal."

"You don't have to miss it at all, you know." In response to her blank look, Demuchus said, "You could teach *me*. And I could, of course, meet with you earlier in the day, once your — *student* — returns."

Andromache fell speechless. Teach Lukkan to Demuchus? Was he joking? She could hear him now: *Why did you say at and not to?*' he would ask, demanding that she explain every nuance of the language. When she had no better answer than *Because it's like that,*' he would frown in disappointment and refuse to drop the matter. Hector's way of learning — to sacrifice absolute accuracy for speed — allowed her to have fairly normal conversations with him. Demuchus, on the other hand, would want to stop every few words to ask for a precision. Their chat would slow to a crawl. And what if he wanted to compose poems in Lukkan? The very thought gave Andromache a headache. The place Demuchus held in her life had nothing to do with speaking Lukkan. He talked to her at soirees; sometimes, he touched her arm. Their relationship had long since solidified, and Andromache was content with it as it was.

"I feel ready to take on the challenge of learning Lukkan," said Demuchus. "And besides —" He fixed her with a molten look. "It would give me a chance to get to know you better."

Suddenly uncomfortable, Andromache turned away. She'd told him all about Lukkan culture. What else did he want to know? "I — I'm really not that interesting," she murmured.

"You fascinate me," he said. "It would give me great pleasure to study you empirically."

With those words, Andromache saw herself huddled in a corner while Demuchus stared at her and made notes. Was *that* what he meant by getting to know her better? Before, she'd been flattered by his interest in the Lukka lands, but his '*study*' comment put everything in a sinister new light.

"What do you say?" he asked, oblivious to her discomfort.

She shook her head. "I — I —" She stammered, trying to think of an excuse he would accept. "I can't take on another student. Lessons are tiring."

"Ah," said Demuchus. "I can imagine."

There was something about his '*Ah*' — a knowing tone, a snideness — that Andromache didn't like. Someone was being insulted, and she wasn't sure whom. With her big toe, she poked the largest spot on Cutie's back. The dog rolled over, kicking her feet in the air.

Demuchus frowned.

"What's wrong?" asked Andromache.

"That — the dog." Demuchus gave a stiff nod toward Cutie, sprawled at their feet. "Does it do anything but lie there?"

"*She* is *hot*," Andromache said tightly. "What else would *she* do?"

"Do? I know little about the mindless pursuits of beasts, but I'd expect her at least to stand guard. Dogs are for protection, no?" Demuchus wrinkled his nose. "That one doesn't seem very — *useful*."

"She's a baby!" rebuked Andromache, crouching down beside Cutie and taking the little dog in her arms. Cutie squirmed but didn't pull away as Andromache cuddled her.

After a moment, Demuchus sighed. "I apologize," he said. "It was rude of me not to make allowances for her age."

Andromache gave him a cold nod. His apology didn't sound entirely sincere.

"Well. I must prepare for the soiree, now," he said. "Shall I see you later, then?"

"I don't think so," she replied. "The heat's affecting *me*, too."

Demuchus closed his eyes. "Of course," he said solemnly. "Till tomorrow, then."

ᔐᔑ

AT DUSK, when it was cooler, Andromache went back out to the courtyard with Cutie. They played tug-of-war with an old rope — at least until Cutie bit Andromache's hand instead of the toy. After that, Andromache watched the little dog chase insects and snuffle plants. When Cutie tired of making her rounds and collapsed on the ground to sleep, Andromache lay down beside her.

She looked up at the sky. The moon was nearly full — no chance of seeing the hazy Lorani. Even in the mountains of the Lukka lands, or on the cliffs above Lyrnassa, the floating giants would be invisible, swallowed by the bright light of the moon.

℘

THE NEXT AFTERNOON, Demuchus looked chastened. Even before speaking to Andromache, he patted Cutie on the head and threw a stick for her to chase. Because of his tentative hold on it, the stick landed only a few arm's lengths away, but Cutie didn't care. She dove for it, brought it back to him, and danced around in front of him, daring him to take it. Demuchus made a half-hearted grab for the stick. Cutie whisked it away in triumph and sank down onto the ground to chew it.

Looking just as victorious as the dog, Demuchus turned to Andromache. "So," he began. "Were you able to find my father's text?"

Andromache thought fast. She didn't want to be mean. He'd at least tried, with Cutie. "I — I — well, they don't keep it in the library," she said.

"They don't?" Demuchus frowned.

Andromache shook her head. "It's *far* too precious. Priam keeps it locked in a chest in his bedroom." She was delighted by her off-the-cuff lie: even Demuchus couldn't expect her to go snooping around in Priam's bedroom.

"Too precious," he murmured, looking tenderly at her.

She coughed and turned away.

"In that case, we'll have to renounce reading it for today."

Trying to look regretful, Andromache nodded.

"No matter," said Demuchus. "There's another question I wished to address. Is there any chance you might have reconsidered giving Lukkan lessons to me?"

Andromache's stomach twisted. She didn't answer.

"I've mastered Thracian, Achaean, and even Ugaritic," he said with bored pride. "North, west and south. That leaves a single chink in my armor — the east."

Andromache raised an eyebrow at his pompous tone.

"I know what you're thinking," he said. "That with the increase of Achaean attacks in recent times, it's unnecessary for me to master any language other than theirs. But what of allies, I ask you? It's all very well to cultivate them to the north and south, but we'd be fools to ignore the east and southeast. Particularly the latter," he said, nodding to her. "It would be wise to strengthen our relations with the Lukka lands, before they are invaded by or make an alliance with the Achaeans."

The thought of the Lukka lands being invaded by Mudders gave Andromache a shiver of horror. Far better for her home country to ally itself to Troy!

"What do you think?" asked Demuchus.

"Learning Lukkan sounds like a good idea," she said. "I know that at one time, there were some Lukkan people living here, down in the lower town. You should see if any of them are still there." Her dad's friends had long since moved back to the Lukka lands, but others might have come in the meantime.

Demuchus looked her squarely in the eyes. "I would prefer to study with someone whose record is proven."

As he spoke, a single long whisker waggled on the end of his chin. Andromache couldn't help but stare at it.

"Andromache?" he prodded.

"Oh!" she gasped, blushing. "I'm sorry, but I really — it's just — well, I can't."

"So you won't reconsider?"

She shook her head. "I only have time for one student."

Demuchus gave a gracious nod. "Very well."

IT WAS SO HOT in her room, that night, that Andromache had trouble falling asleep. She crept down to the courtyard and lay on a bench, staring up at the moon. When she finally drifted off to sleep, she dreamed that dozens of people were yelling at her in Thracian — which she didn't understand at all, and which, in her dream, sounded like a drunk person speaking Truvan backwards.

ℰℐ

THE FOLLOWING DAY, the inevitable happened: Demuchus brought his own copy of his father's text.

"These lines are written in his hand," he said. "Have you ever seen such a fine script?"

"It's beautiful," Andromache said sincerely. Beneath Demuchus's boastful tone, she could hear real affection and longing for his father, whom he'd lost as a boy. Andromache thought of the time she'd held Paris's lute and felt sympathy for Demuchus — so much so that when he touched her arm, she smiled at him.

"Shall I read to you?" he asked.

She nodded.

He read for the better part of an hour, stopping here and there to explain his favorite passages. Andromache didn't understand the text any better than she had on her own, but she nodded at the appropriate times and Demuchus looked content.

When he'd finished reading, Andromache murmured, "That's very beautiful."

"Thank you," said Demuchus.

"Your father was your uncle's brother, wasn't he?"

"That's right."

"And did your uncle write about music, too?"

Demuchus furrowed his brow. "For his final project, at the end of his studies, you mean?"

Andromache nodded.

"My uncle Ucalegon wrote about the Achaeans," said Demuchus. "In particular, their pottery. Trade with them was really starting to grow in his father's — my grandfather's — time."

"All those vases in your house are *Achaean*?" Andromache asked in shock. Demuchus had never said a kind word about the

Achaeans. She wouldn't have expected him to have a house full of Mudder pottery!

"They are objects of *research!*" he cried, his cheeks coloring.

Andromache held up her hands. "I didn't mean anything! I — um, I just didn't realize I'd actually *seen* Achaean pottery. It makes sense," she said quickly. "The vases in your house are — are — gorgeous, and I'd heard Achaean work was — of *excellent* quality."

"Indeed," said Demuchus, mollified. "Perhaps we can take a closer look at them tonight."

"All right," Andromache agreed.

෭

ANDROMACHE AND CASSANDRA arrived at Demuchus's house before the other group members and were given a private tour of Ucalegon's treasured vases. There were some painted with people or animals, while others had geometric patterns.

The longer Andromache studied the vases, the more troubled she felt. They were lovely. Exquisite. She didn't understand how the same people who'd produced them could also have destroyed Lyrnassa. The thought made her sick. She wanted to go home, where the only pottery was simple, grey clayware native to the region near Troy. She'd never properly appreciated it, before.

As the tour ended, Andromache told the others that she needed to lie down. "The full moon is giving me a headache," she said, moaning outlandishly. Neither Demuchus nor Cassandra suspected her deceit. Indeed, they were all sympathy as they told her to go home and get some rest.

411

Chapter 51

In the early hours of the morning, before the sun had even peeked over the city walls, Andromache awoke to a terrible clamor.

Cutie was attacking her dresses — her shoes — the hem of her striped blanket — anything within reach. In between sallies, the little dog tore mindlessly around the room.

"All right," mumbled Andromache. "I get it. You need to pee." She would have to start leaving her door cracked at night, so Cutie could go downstairs and take care of that business on her own.

Cutie gave a sharp bark.

"All *right*!" Andromache exchanged her sleeping dress for one she wore around the house and hurriedly tucked her hair behind her ears. When she opened the door, Cutie dashed down the stairs and was outside relieving herself before Andromache had made it to the banquet hall.

"Cutie?" she whispered, finally stepping out onto the court-yard. No one else seemed to be up, yet. "Cutie?"

"Yip! Yip! Shrieeeeeeek! Yip! Yoooooooowll!" wailed the dog from the other side of the garden. She was barking in the petulant way she did after she'd been left at home by herself.

"I'm right here, stupid dog," muttered Andromache. "Why don't you just come over here instead of waking up the whole house?"

"Aaaaahoo! Mmaaaaooowl! Yip! Yip!"

"All right! Then I guess I'll have to find *you*, so you stop yelling at me."

But as Andromache drew closer to Cutie, she realized that the dog had been yelling at someone else. The other voice was low and soft and had been drowned out until then by the ruckus: "Hey, girl. Hey, baby. I know. I missed you, too."

Andromache rounded one last corner to see Hector, his arms overflowing with the wriggling little animal. "Ssssssh," he murmured. "Stop — stop!"

Cutie was busily biting and licking his chin. When she saw Andromache, she gave another sharp bark and her tail, pinned by Hector's forearm, did its best to wag.

Hector turned toward Andromache. His hair and clothes were disheveled, as though he, too, had just woken up.

"You're back," Andromache said stiffly.

Hector nodded. "Last night. You were asleep." Under five days' growth of stubble, a hint of red was visible as he said, "I'm sorry, Ahndromahk."

"Oh." She gave an icy shrug.

"I should've told you I was leaving," he added, setting Cutie on the ground. Immediately, the dog leapt after a bird, leaving the two humans to their discomfort. "Mom said that you were worried..."

"No!" Andromache shook her head vehemently. The last thing she wanted was for Hector to think she thought about him! He thought so little of *her*, he'd left without saying goodbye. He hadn't even given her one of his horrid little waves, this time! "I wasn't *worried.*"

"Oh," said Hector.

His '*oh*' was as frosty as hers had been, and now Andromache was the one who felt compelled to continue: "I mean, I'm sure you can take care of yourself." She tried not to look at the long scar on his arm. "It's just that I put in all that time preparing for our lesson, and waiting in the library, and then you never came."

"I'm sorry," Hector said again.

After a long stretch of silence, Andromache asked, "So — where did you go, anyway?"

"Out into the countryside. I was inspecting patrols..." He wouldn't make eye contact with her.

"Your old one?" she asked, with a flash of intuition. "The one near Lyrnassa?"

Looking sorrowful, Hector nodded. "That's kind of why I didn't tell you I was leaving. I didn't want to bring it up."

"Oh." Andromache sat down hard on a bench. To her surprise, the mention of Lyrnassa had caused a surge of homesickness. Homesickness, of all things! Her last few days there had been nightmarish: burying Auntie, fleeing raiders, suffocating, shredding her feet. But even before Auntie's death, life in Lyrnassa hadn't been easy. All but a few of the villagers had shunned her, and she'd ached constantly for her parents and her home in the far-off Lukka lands. How could she possibly feel homesick for that place?

She was sitting beside Auntie on a hot day. Their feet were in the creek. Butterflies were fluttering all around, their black and white stripes reflecting on the water...

It was winter, and Auntie was tucking a newly woven blanket around her...

She was running wild through the hills, collecting herbs. She was telling Auntie about everything she'd seen from up high, and Auntie was smiling at her. Auntie was hugging her...

Andromache blinked back tears. "Did you see any butterflies?" she whispered.

Hector looked puzzled.

"When I lived there, I saw lots of these big, white butterflies with black stripes," she explained. "They could fly so fast!"

Hector thought for a moment. "Yes — I'm pretty sure I saw some."

"What about lizards? On sunny days, big lizards — as long as your lower leg, if you include the tail — always came out to lie on the rocks."

Hector sat down beside her. "I wish we'd seen those, but we were making too much noise," he said regretfully. "We probably scared them off."

"Oh," said Andromache. "Well, did you look down at the sea? From what I remember, it was mostly dark blue, but if you went up into the cliffs and looked down, you could see a band of turquoise right by the shore."

"Yes," said Hector, nodding. "I definitely saw that."

Cutie finished her rounds and came over to them. Absent-mindedly scratching the dog's ears, then her belly, Hector murmured, "<u>Ahndromahk</u>…"

"Hmm?"

"You sound like you miss it."

Andromache sucked in her breath. "I do. At least in some ways."

"Would you ever want to —"

"No!" she snapped. Just because she missed some things about Lyrnassa didn't mean she *ever* wanted to go back there! If any Lyrnassans had resettled the village, they would remember her. They would gape at her with horror, just as they had when she first arrived there…

They were blanching at the sight of her blood-soaked dress. They were holding up their hands to ward her off. They thought she was cursed…

They'd never stopped looking at her that way, not in all the years she lived there, and she didn't want to return to that old life. Not even to visit! She didn't want to ruin the few pleasant memories she had.

Hector went back to rubbing Cutie's belly. The little dog kicked her legs in glee.

"What about the village?" Andromache whispered. "Is — has — have any people —"

"Have any people moved back there?" Hector finished her thought. "Some. Not like — like — *before*. There aren't as many houses." Making an effort to look brighter, he added, "But they have more animals, now. Lots of goats and sheep. And they built a bridge over the creek, too. That made getting around a little drier."

Drier. The way he said it left no doubt in Andromache's mind. A survivor might have told Hector about the houses and animals, but he'd obviously had personal experience with the creek. "You were there," she croaked, her face going white. "You were there *before*."

"Once," said Hector. "About three years ago. When I was first named patrol captain, I wanted to visit all the towns and villages in our sector. But I didn't go back, not until —" He gulped. "Lyrnassa's elders have never wanted Trojan patrols to spend much time there. They wanted to keep the village quiet. Private. I respected that." He gulped again, harder. "At least, until —"

"You never told me," Andromache accused.

"I know," said Hector. "But whenever Lyrnassa came up, you —" This time, he coughed. "There wasn't any *need* to tell you, so I didn't."

Andromache looked down. "I could've handled it."

"I'm sorry."

"I remember the Trojans coming," she murmured, peering up at him again. "Everyone was talking about it. Lyrnassa didn't get many visitors."

Hector nodded.

"I wasn't there, that day," she said. "I was out digging wild herbs for my garden." Her voice sounded strange and airy. "If I'd been there..."

"I know," he said. "It's weird to think about."

She nodded.

"I'm not sorry you weren't there." Hector's look was wry. "It wasn't my finest hour."

"Why? What happened?"

"Let me start by saying I got the nickname '*Dancer*' out of it."

"'*Dancer?*'"

"Mm-hmm."

"How?"

"Well," said Hector, "I was walking around, just to get a feel for the place, and I ran into this tiny old woman carrying water from the creek. Her baskets probably weighed eight times what she did, so I asked if she wanted help."

Andromache caught her breath...

Little village ladies, carrying water — trips back and forth to the creek — villagers passing with their heavy baskets — water for drinking, for washing, for gardening —

How long had it been since those things had come this close to her? "And did she?" she whispered. "Want help, I mean?"

Hector shrugged. "Honestly, I don't know. She didn't say anything."

Andromache turned sharply toward him. "Nothing?"

"Nothing," he said. "I didn't know what else to do, so I just took her baskets and carried them for her."

Andromache's breathing grew ragged. "That — that's *sweet*," she whispered. "Not embarrassing."

"Just wait," Hector said drily. "We started walking back to her little house, and that's when I tripped and fell — *crash!*" He threw his arms out wide. "All the water spilled, and I split my shin open on a rock. It was a mess — blood and creek water everywhere. You can still see the scar." He stretched out his leg and pointed to a thin line of pink tissue.

Andromache made herself look.

"That's where '*Dancer*' came from — because I was just *so* graceful!" Hector gave another wry smile. "I think the lady felt sorry for me. Or embarrassed. Anyway, she took me the rest of the way to her little house and wrapped up my leg."

Wrapped his leg…Andromache was reeling. As she well knew, Lyrnassans shrank from touching a stranger's blood. Blood, they thought, was a sign of the gods' anger. The belief had come as a shock to her. Back in her country, people saw no hidden meaning to blood. It was nothing but a sign of injury, of a wounded person needing care…

Hector went on with his story: "It was a good bandage — tight." He smiled again, adding, "I guess she was used to wrapping things. She had a scarf wound around her head."

Andromache didn't smile back.

"After she fixed me up, I went and fetched her more water. When I got back, she tousled my hair and patted my cheek like I was a cute but stupid three-year-old."

Even now, a lock of Hector's hair was falling over one eye. Had it always done that? Andromache couldn't remember. She couldn't ask him, either. Her tongue was dry; her throat felt sticky and full, as though she'd been swallowing spider webs.

"I liked her," Hector said quietly. "I wonder about her. She wasn't with the captives that the raiders tried to take. I wonder what happ — <u>Ahndromahk?</u>"He interrupted himself, finally noticing her stricken face.

Andromache shook her head and stood up, turning away from him.

"Wait," called Hector. "Wait!"

But Andromache didn't wait. She ran, and ran, and ran, all the way down to the exercise arena, where she kept running until she was exhausted. She sat panting in the shade for a while, and after that she got up to run some more.

༄

THE AFTERNOON SUN was beating down on Andromache as she made her rounds of the garden boxes. The spring flowers had long since faded, and the garden was going dormant for the summer. The place looked almost as desolate as Demuchus's courtyard.

Cutie had fled the heat and was now inside, lying under the kitchen table. Andromache, however, was too agitated to sit still. She poked feverishly at each of the boxes without much regard for what she was doing.

Schluuup! Out came a weed, its roots ceding after a moment of suction. Andromache flung it to the ground.

Soon, it would be time for Hector's Lukkan lesson — the first one in five days, and she'd ruined it before it ever started. After the way she'd run from him, that morning, the afternoon was sure to be awkward. Hector was sure to be annoyed with her.

Schlup! Schluup! Schluuuuup! Out came a few more weeds — or perhaps they'd been herbs. Andromache didn't care.

She couldn't blame Hector for being annoyed. All he'd done was tell her a story — a *sweet* story — about helping someone fetch water, and she'd run away as though he'd confessed to drowning the villager instead. Annoyed? No, he would be angry! He would be offended, just like when she'd accused him of gutting Cutie's attackers.

Schlup! She ought to explain, or at least apologize. She didn't want things to be tense between them. Now, less than ever!

Hands, old and cracked, ruffling a boy's hair, winding a bandage around his leg. Hands, firm but gentle. She could feel them in her own hair, smoothing it back from her forehead…

Schlup! Schluuuuup! She *had* to explain! What Hector had told her changed everything! There was a real connection between them, something neither of them had realized before. He was, tangentially, a part of the life she'd shared with her Auntie…

A little shack. Her blanket in one corner, Auntie's across the way. Baskets of water. Baskets of thread. A small, rickety loom…

Hector seemed to care about the old woman. He still thought about her. If he learned who she was, and why she didn't speak to him, he might feel differently about Lukkan. He might start seeing the language as more than something to punish himself with. It was Andromache's best hope yet for a new, better relationship with Hector — especially now that Lyrnassa was being rebuilt, and he had less reason to feel guilty. All she had to do was explain.

Schlup! Schlup! But what if she explained, and he *didn't* care? What if their connection *didn't* matter to him? How could she face him, then, when it meant so much to her?

Schluuuuup! Andromache tossed a weed viciously to the ground. Hector was right. Telling her about Lyrnassa had been a mistake! Everything was more complicated now, and she couldn't handle it!

Schlup! Schluuuuuup!

"Ouch!" cried Andromache, popping a bloodied finger into her mouth.

Behind her, someone coughed delicately.

Andromache whipped her head around. "Oh — hello, Demuchus." Her heart was pounding. She hadn't heard anyone come out. "H-how are you?"

Demuchus frowned at her finger. "Quite well, thank you," he answered, with a gracious little bow. "And yourself?"

Andromache thrust her hands behind her back. "Oh, fine. A little tired."

"The work you're doing is too much for you."

Too much for you. Too much for you. What *wasn't* too much for her? She yanked at a few more weeds.

Demuchus watched her, his disapproval deepening. "I was wondering," he began after an uncomfortable moment, "if you would care to spend our afternoon talking about the roots of Lukkan music."

Andromache sighed. *Anything* sounded better right now than apologizing to Hector — explaining to Hector — but she was stuck. "I'm waiting for lessons."

"Oh, I see," said Demuchus. "So — *Hector* — has returned safely from his — *excursion* — then?"

Not wanting to invite further talk about the — *excursion* — Andromache gave only the briefest of nods.

"Five days away…hmmm. But then, I'm sure he'll return to lessons in excellent form." Demuchus's tone had all the sincerity of someone complimenting a tawdry gown.

Right then, Andromache wasn't sure whether she could face Hector — talk to him — have a normal lesson with him — but she was certainly in no mood to hear him belittled. While things might have been simpler if she'd never learned about Hector's meeting with her Auntie, now that she knew, she couldn't just forget about it. "Of *course* he will," she answered coldly.

Demuchus missed the warning, or ignored it. "Good, good. I'm glad he's not being — *difficult* — for you."

Andromache scuffed her toe against the stones. *Scuff. Scuffa, scuff. Scuff, scuff, SCUFF!*

Demuchus fixed his eye on her foot. His shoulders tensed. He opened his mouth, no doubt to ask her to stop, but said nothing.

Scuffa scuff! "So, you wanted to talk about *music?*" Andromache punctuated the last word with a final, pointed *scuff.*

"May I wait with you, then?" he asked.

Andromache nodded and folded her hands in her lap. She'd lost interest in gardening.

Demuchus sat down. There was a faint whiff of sulphur about him, like the crumbly heart of a boiled egg. Despite having suggested a conversation, he seemed to have nothing to say. They sat in perfect stillness. Nothing stirred on the courtyard — neither the birds, nor the insects, nor even the wind.

At last, Andromache heard the sound of footsteps ringing out from the banquet hall. She looked up, thinking that Hector had arrived at last, but instead, she saw only Paris.

(*Maybe* he's *not coming,*) sneered the Voice. (*Maybe after what happened this morning, he's too furious even to look at you.*)

"Hello, Hermie. Hello — um —" Paris paused eloquently.

"Demuchus," said Andromache.

"Ah. Yes. Well, hello, then — Demuncus." After nodding to Demuchus, Paris kissed Andromache's cheek with unusual gusto.

"Paris." Demuchus nodded back. Turning to Andromache, he said, "'*Hermie*?' Is that short for something?"

"Hermie's short, all right!" Paris interjected.

Andromache glowered at him; he laughed impishly at her. Poor Demuchus just looked lost.

"I have something for you," Paris announced.

"What?" she asked.

"A message, from my brother—he has to stay late in the main stables and won't be able to make it back here before his meeting tonight."

Looking pleased, Demuchus sat up straighter.

"So, he wants to know if you'd be willing to have your lesson at the stables, instead of here."

"He does?" gasped Andromache.

"Yes. To be sure, he begs your pardon for the unusual nature of the request —"

"I'll go right over." She shot to her feet. However angry Hector might be, he wasn't refusing to see her. At very least, she could apologize to him for running away.

"Very well, then," said Paris. "And Hermie?"

"Yes?"

"Would you be so kind as to give *him* a message from *me*?"

"What's that?"

"That I am far too busy to be his errand boy." Paris turned and sauntered back indoors.

Andromache, too, took several steps toward the banquet hall.

"You don't have to go," said Demuchus, rather severely.

Andromache stopped. "Of course I do," she said. "I'm his *tutor*. It's my job to give lessons."

"In the stables?" Demuchus scoffed. "You shouldn't have to lower yourself like that."

"'*Lower* myself'?" she asked.

"Tutoring amidst all that filth and dirt." Demuchus gave a disdainful shudder. "It's troubling enough for one of our city's commanders to be mucking out stables or whatever he's up to, when he could easily have someone else do it —"

'*Troubling*,' that Hector should spend time in the stables? Even Andromache, as far removed as she was from military matters, could see why a leader would want to keep an eye on the operation he was running. Perhaps what was *troubling* was that a future councilman could *not!*

"— but to involve *you* in this madness!" Demuchus shook his head. "And when there's a perfectly adequate library at his disposal!"

"I don't mind," said Andromache. Actually, she liked the idea of seeing the stables — and the *horses!*

Demuchus's face looked grave. "I suppose I *could* walk you down there..." he said, as though pondering a request she'd made. "It would give us a chance to talk about music, after all."

"All right," agreed Andromache. She was far too anxious about what she was going to say to Hector — and what he might say to *her!* — to chat normally with Demuchus, but she didn't remember quite where the stables were and so was glad to have a guide.

Demuchus seemed unfazed by her silence. For the whole of their long, hot promenade, he gave a discourse on southern music and the way it had influenced Lukkan songwriting. He was completely immersed in the subject; not once did he comment on Andromache's failure to nod.

"...some of the more intricate melodic chains," he was saying. "They reflect the values of the mountain culture and its — oh!" He interrupted himself. "Well, then — this is the door to the stables."

"Thank you for bringing me," said Andromache.

"You'll be all right?"

"Of course."

Demuchus's eye twitched, but when he spoke, all he said was, "Will I see you tonight for the play? It's in the arena."

"Oh — oh, that's right," said Andromache, dimly remembering that Cassandra had mentioned a play. "And a discussion afterward, at your house?"

"Exactly. Shall I come around later, to escort you and the lovely Cassandra?"

Andromache hesitated. If things went badly with Hector, she might not feel like going out that night. Still, it would be easier to send an excuse later than to refuse Demuchus now. "That sounds fine," she said, nodding. "See you then."

Demuchus bowed his head in farewell.

After bobbing her own head, Andromache entered the stable. The building's dim, cool environment was a welcome change from the scorching city streets. The air inside smelled of well-kept horses. From all around, she could hear the sounds of them snorting, stomping, and munching on grain.

Which way? she wondered. Paris hadn't said where to go. There were three aisles in front of her, and no sign of Hector.

As she hesitated, a guard accosted her. He was an old lobster of a man, arisen from the sea at roughly the same time as the hills — and apparently, he'd been watching over the stables ever since. "What do *you* want?" he demanded.

Flustered, Andromache found herself stammering: "I — I'm here to — to see — Hector."

"Eh? Hector? You can go gawk at him on the practice field like everyone else."

Gawk at him? Andromache blushed in mortification. She wanted to turn tail and flee to the house, but the fact that she'd already run away from Hector once that day stopped her. "He sent me a message to meet him here."

The old man scowled. "Oh he did, did he? Poppycock!"

"But his brother told me to —"

"His brother, eh? That one's playing tricks on you, Missy! Now run along."

"No, you don't understand. I have to —"

"You have to leave. We're too busy for this kind of nonsense." With that, the guard attempted to shuttle Andromache back through the stable door.

"Stop!" she shrieked, switching to Lukkan out of distress. "Stop that! Leave me alone!"

There was a faint rustling from the middle aisle, and then, "Ahndromahk?"

She froze.

The guard frowned but stopped trying to expel her.

The rustling grew louder — closer — and finally, Hector emerged. "Ahndromahk!" he cried. "What are you *doing* here?"

The guard made as if to start shoving her again, but Hector stopped him: "A cup of water! *Now!*" he ordered.

Surprised, the old man left on his mission.

"And *you*, <u>Ahndromahk</u>!" barked Hector. "Sit down!"

Andromache sat. She looked at the floor, her cheeks flushed in shame. The guard had obviously been right about Paris playing a trick on her. His message had been a fraud. Hector didn't want her there, hadn't asked for her to come — and from the way he was yelling, the incident that morning had left him even angrier than she'd thought.

"What are you *doing* here?" he demanded again. Without waiting for an answer, he began to lecture her: "Someone who's been as heat-sick as you were, the day you came to Troy, has no business going out in weather like this. You'll always be vulnerable to it. You could have fainted, or worse! You're showing signs already! Your face is all red."

Andromache gaped at him. Heat-sick? Hector wasn't mad at her for coming here — he was *worried!* And if he was worried that she might get hurt, or sick, then he couldn't be too upset about that morning, could he? No, worry meant that he *cared* about her! The anxiety she'd been feeling all day melted into relief, then hope. She'd been right! Even after everything that had happened, there was still a chance for them to become friends. "I'm sorry," she said, trying indeed to sound sorry rather than delighted. "I didn't know how heat-sickness worked."

"Someone should have told you." Hector's voice had softened. "We didn't think to, I guess. For so long, it seemed like you were never going to leave the house. *I'm* the one who's sorry, <u>Ahndromahk</u>."

"It's all right," she said, and it *was* all right. More than all right! The meeting she'd so dreaded was going miraculously well.

"No, it's not. You have no idea what my parents would say if they knew you'd gone out in this heat."

Andromache's stomach turned cold. His parents? Was *that* all Hector's worry boiled down to — fear of what his *parents* would say? Fear of bringing shame upon them by letting their guest cook herself to death?

(*See?*) said the Voice. (<u>*Nothing's changed. To him, you mean nothing but guilt...obligation...*</u>)

SHUT UP! snapped Andromache. Aloud, she said crossly, "Then maybe *your parents* should have explained my illness to Paris."

"Paris?" asked Hector, narrowing his eyes.

"He told me that you told him to ask me to come here *now* because it was the only time and place you could fit in a lesson."

"Oh," said Hector, his eyes now aglitter. "Well, that's interesting! Because when I ran into him, earlier, what I asked him to tell you was that I'd be stuck here all afternoon finishing things up and that, if it was all right, I'd meet with you in the evening." Hector's tone was ominous. "Paris and his stupid pranks! This time, he's gone too far. Did he at *least* walk you down here?"

Andromache shook her head. "But Demuchus did."

Hector gave a tepid nod as if to say that that was — slightly — better than nothing.

The mention of Demuchus reminded Andromache of her plans. Apologetically, she said, "I can't meet you for a lesson tonight, anyway. There's a soiree."

"Oh," said Hector.

"I guess I should go, then...sorry for bothering you." Andromache turned back toward the door, her spirits plummeting after their all-too-brief lift. Not only did that morning's incident remain unresolved, she would also probably faint or die on the way home. Assuming that she could even find her way back there...

"Wait," said Hector. Perhaps he, too, had an image of her melting into a puddle — and of how his parents would respond to the liquefaction of their guest. "Stay. You can teach me the words for all of this stuff." He nodded toward the equipment on nearby shelves. "And you can meet Buzzy."

Andromache looked tentatively at the guard, who had just returned. "Buzzy?" she asked.

He shot her a dark look and handed her a cup of water.

Hector laughed. "No — that's Xanthus, the stable master. Xanthus, this is Andromache, my teacher."

"Your teacher, eh?" asked Xanthus. "So what are you teaching him, Missy? Riding, I hope."

"Lukkan," she murmured. "The language."

"Too bad," cackled the stable master. "His riding has really gone to hell. So, what's a Loo-kan teacher doing down here, in the stables?"

"That's my brother's doing," muttered Hector.

Xanthus grimaced. "Just as I suspected! Is your water cool enough, Missy?"

"Yes, sir. Thank you," Andromache said shyly, taking a sip of the water.

The old crustacean nodded once before scuttling back to his post at the door.

"Well, I'm working on some things over there," said Hector, indicating the middle aisle. "Would it bother you if I finish up while we —"

"No," said Andromache, feeling a new surge of lightness. Bother her, to go among the horses?

Hector nodded and motioned for her to follow. "That's Thunderbolt," he said, pointing to a reddish horse on their right. "And here's Hellsteeth." Hellsteeth had a beautiful black coat and small ears. "And Gold Fury. Hey there, buddy." The horse — who was brown, not gold — blinked at Hector and gave his shoulder a playful nip. "Hi, Warbright. Hi, Jagged Ray. Hello, Arm of Bronze."

Andromache longed to pet them, but Hector never stopped long enough to let her. He seemed anxious to reach the back of the stables. As they continued, a horse on their left began to stamp her feet and whinny nervously. Hector swore under his breath.

"What's wrong?" asked Andromache.

"Just go," Hector said brusquely. "Hurry! All the way to the end!"

Confused, Andromache rushed on to the end of the aisle. None of the other horses bucked or stamped as she passed. What was wrong with the one? Looking back, she could see Hector trying to calm the creature down.

"What happened?" she whispered, when he'd finally rejoined her.

Hector bit his lip to stifle a laugh. "That's Lee's horse, Battleblaze," he explained. "I think she remembers you."

Lee's horse — the very horse Andromache had ridden from Lyrnassa to Troy! In her struggle to stay astride, she'd pulled out many handfuls of the poor beast's hair. She couldn't blame Battleblaze for hating her.

Hector started walking again and didn't stop until they'd reached a large stall in the left-hand corner of the building. Within it, Andromache saw a tall, vaguely familiar, pale gold horse.

"Hi, Buzzy," said Hector, stroking the horse's neck. The look in his eye far surpassed pride — Hector was plainly in love with his horse.

"Oh," said Andromache. "So *this* is Buzzy."

Hector nodded.

"Buzzy…" Thinking of the names of the horses they'd passed, she asked wryly, "Why not Deathneck Thunderdome?"

"That name was taken," said Hector, smiling.

Andromache smiled back. "Is it all right if I pet him?"

"Ohff couhrse."

As she buried her hands in Buzzy's mane, he butted his nose against her and nuzzled her with his velvet lips. "What's he doing?" she asked, giggling.

"Looking fohr to eat. Always, he looks fohr to eat. Celeries, apples — anyfing! Maybe a better name is 'Greedy.' You see, he has mahch to eat already." Hector gestured indignantly at the horse's full trough.

Buzzy snorted, making Andromache giggle again.

"You lahke him?" asked Hector.

"He's beautiful!"

"You lahke Grandma Thisbe, also?"

"Grandma Thisbe?"

Hector gestured to the next stall, from which a grizzled pony was whickering for his attention. "A frahnt ohff Buzzy," he explained.

Andromache stroked the pony for a long moment before Hector's words registered. "*Frahnt?*" she asked. "What do you mean?"

"You know — um, Buzzy lahke Thisbe so mahch. They haff the fahn together…"

"They have fun together? Oh, you mean *friend*!" Andromache laughed. "Not fern leaf."

"What?"

"I thought you said *frond*, which is a kind of leaf."

"<u>Oh</u>." Hector gave a self-deprecating smile that morphed slowly into smugness. "<u>Baht yes</u>, Thisbe *is* <u>lahke a plant</u>."

Andromache raised an eyebrow. "<u>How</u>?" she asked.

"<u>Becahse, she is</u> — um, <u>not nerffous</u>?"

"<u>She's calm</u>?"

"<u>Calm, yes, lahke a plant</u>."

Andromache snorted, but Hector went on as assuredly as though she hadn't. "Buzzy <u>has need fohr calm</u>."

"<u>He's jittery — excitable — spirited</u>?"

"<u>Speerited</u>." Hector considered the word. "No — *crazy*."

"<u>Crazy</u>."

"<u>Crazy</u>."

By that time, Buzzy had begun to eat his dinner. Andromache caught an odd smell coming from the trough. "<u>What exactly is he eating</u>?"

"<u>Grains</u>," Hector answered slyly. "<u>Special grains</u>."

Andromache finally placed the smell. "<u>Wine</u>!" she accused.

"<u>A little only</u>," Hector assured her. "<u>One time the week</u>."

She narrowed her eyes.

"<u>It is effer this way, in</u> Troy," he said. "<u>They lahke it. You lahke it</u>, Buzzy, <u>rahght</u>?"

The horse's face was buried in his food.

"<u>You see</u>?" said Hector.

Silently, Andromache watched Buzzy and Thisbe gobble their wine-soaked grain.

Hector cleared his throat. "<u>Ahndromahk</u>?"

"Hmm?"

"<u>You ahre all rahght</u>?"

"Hmm? Oh — of course. <u>I'm sure you know what's best for them</u>." Gently, she patted Buzzy's shoulder.

"<u>No</u>," said Hector. "<u>I want to say, you ahre all rahght from this mohrning</u>?"

Andromache froze. The pleasure of visiting with the horses had made her forget all about that morning, but now, her stomach started churning again. "<u>I'm fine</u>."

"<u>You ahre</u> — *were* — <u>you were so *trah*bled</u>," prodded Hector, looking concerned.

"<u>My onions</u>," Andromache said stiffly. She wasn't going to open old wounds for someone who didn't care about her. If he hadn't mentioned his parents, before — if *he* had been the one to feel worried about her — she might have been able to give him a full explanation. She might have been able to tell him why his story had upset her. But since she couldn't be certain he would really care…

"<u>Your *onions*?</u>" Hector asked in confusion. "<u>You want to cook somefing? Ohr — ohr it is onions that make you to cry?</u>"

Andromache suddenly bit her lip.

"<u>What?</u>" asked Hector.

She started to laugh.

"<u>I say somefing crazy?</u>"

"<u>No!</u>" Andromache laughed even harder. "<u>No, it's just that if you say, '*My onions*,' it means you don't want to talk about it. I mean, I could say, '*Hector, what are you up to after our lesson today?*' and you could say, '*My onions, Ahndromahk*.'</u>"

"Butt out," he mused.

"<u>Exactly.</u>"

"<u>All rahght</u>," he said, sounding a little stiff, now, himself. "<u>Your onions.</u>"

Hector's hair looked as unkempt as it had that morning. The stray lock was still flopping over his eye — and Andromache had a sudden, wild urge to smooth it back. She felt sorry for freezing him out and wished that she could take back her '*onions*.'

(*So, what is it?*) jeered the Voice. (*Are you mad at him or do you want to pet him?*)

Neither! Andromache blushed hotly. What a stupid thing to say! *It's just weird to know that he knew my Auntie.* He'd known her Auntie — *liked* her Auntie! He'd helped Auntie, purely out of kindness. He'd rushed down to Lyrnassa to save her from the Mudder raiders, never knowing that she was already dead.

(*He liked your Auntie more than he likes you,*) taunted the Voice. (*He didn't see her as a cause — a responsibility — a burden —*)

Andromache tried to ignore the pain the Voice was causing her. Now wasn't the time to let it draw her into an argument. She had to smooth things over with Hector. Whatever his faults, and however he felt or didn't feel about her, the fact that he'd been good to her Auntie meant something. And Auntie had liked him, too. *Sweet boy with hair in his face*…

"Hector?" she whispered.

"Hmm?"

"It's hard for me to think about Lyrnassa. That's why I was so upset this morning."

Hector thawed visibly. "I'm sorry, Ahndromahk," he said. "I shouldn't have —"

"I'm glad you did," she interrupted. "And I'm glad —" She swallowed. "I'm glad you helped that old woman."

"Oh," he said, blinking. "I was happy to."

Andromache thought about what he'd said earlier: *'I liked her. I wonder about her. She wasn't with the captives.'* He cared about the old woman…and so he deserved to know at least part of the truth. "I remember her," she said. "The woman you described — the one with the scarf on her head. And there's something you should know about her."

"What's that?"

"She — she died before the invasion."

"She did?" Hector's voice was quiet. Stunned.

Andromache nodded. "It was peaceful — very peaceful. She died in her sleep."

Hector's features relaxed as a longtime worry was removed from him. His eyes shone with gratitude. "Thank you," he said. "Thank you for telling me that!"

The look far surpassed what Andromache had once hoped for by telling him, *'You're a good brother.'* Suddenly, she wanted to tell him the rest — who the old lady was — what she'd really thought of him —

But then, before she could say another word, Hector started laughing. "Oh, Ahndromahk!"

"What is it?"

"I was just thinking about what happened, the day I met her. It's a lot funnier to me, now."

Andromache thought of his stumble, of the water spilling everywhere. "So…do people still call you *'Dancer?'*" she asked, smiling.

"Well," he said, "these days, they drop the *'Dan-'*"

Maybe I'll tell him the whole story another time, she decided. *Things are calm, now — better to leave them that way.* Aloud, she asked Hector, "What are you working on?"

"I mahst look at this," he said, gesturing to a stack of boxes sitting on the floor near Buzzy's stall.

"What are you looking for?"

"I mahst see if it is all rahght. No wounds — er —" Hector laughed and corrected his error. "No *dahmage*."

"Oh, you're inspecting it."

"Yes, *insecting*," he agreed, taking a box from the stack. He bent to set it down, then opened it.

Andromache peered inside and saw a labyrinth of tangled ropes. "Is that normal?" she asked hesitantly.

"Nohrmal?" Hector gave a snort of disgust. "I fink not!"

"Oh…"

"No one can put stahff away rahght," he grumbled. "Why not?"

"I don't know," murmured Andromache.

Hector seized a length of rope and savagely began yanking at the knots.

Andromache could only stare in dismay. She'd grown up around sheep, wool, and thread. What was more, she'd grown up poor. She knew everything there was to know about untangling thread, about salvaging every last bit. Hector's methods were maddeningly sloppy. "Can I help?" she asked. Pleaded.

"It is not necessary," said Hector.

"But you're doing it wrong."

"I am?"

"You have no knot strategy."

"Stre-te-gy?" He frowned.

"Strategy — um, it's an overall plan, or idea, for how to do something complicated. Something with a lot of steps." Seeing how lost he was, Andromache gave up and said, "Strategy."

Hector laughed. "Oh, that's one I should know! Stretegy!" He tossed the rope from one hand to the other. As he did, Andromache saw the scar tissue on his right arm catch the light. She thought of her vision from the other day, of Hector's arm laid open, and shuddered.

"When I worked with my mom," she said, to hide the queasiness bubbling inside her, "there were times I had to untangle a whole flock's worth of thread." Seeing Hector's quizzical look, she clarified. "A *lot* of thread. If I didn't want to spend all day doing it, I needed a strategy."

"Oh," he said. "You can show to me?"

Andromache took a snarled piece of rope and turned it over several times, considering it from all angles before attempting to unknot it. Once she began, though, she worked quickly, untangling it with only a few deft motions. She then coiled the rope neatly and presented it to Hector.

He nodded in solemn approval and said, "That is pleasant."

"Thanks," she replied, trying not to giggle. *Pleasant?* "What are they for?"

"Hmm?"

"These ropes. What are they for?"

"Oh, one can use them to — uh — to make together — uh — groups ohff these." Hector gestured to an array of blankets, daggers, and wineskins.

"Bundles," said Andromache.

"What?"

"When all of those things are together, it makes a bundle."

"Oh!" Hector laughed. "It sounded like a swear word. Like, '*Paris borrowed my best cloak and vomited wine all over it. Oh, bahndles!*'"

Andromache laughed with him. "Maybe it *should* be a swear word," she said.

"Maybe," said Hector. "All rahght. Then I can try now your stretegy." He bent his head over his work.

Andromache had to stifle another urge to brush the lock of hair out of his eyes — and an even more inappropriate one to lay her hand on his leg, on the place where he'd cut himself while in Lyrnassa. She imagined other hands on his shin — old hands, roughened and cool. She imagined them bandaging Hector's leg. First up, then around, tucked in just so at the top. A very particular way of tucking —

The knots, Ahndromahk! she warned herself, taking another rope. Before she could start untangling it, though, it was pulled from her hands. She shrieked.

"Buzzy!" scolded Hector. "Knock it off!"

The golden giant continued munching placidly on his prize. Hector tried several times to tug the rope away from him but finally threw up his hands in defeat. "Well, there you are," he said. "These ropes are obviously doomed."

"Oh, bundles!" swore Andromache, giggling.

"Oh, Buzzy," Hector amended. He took another tangle of rope out of the box, gave it a thoughtful look, and then tossed it back.

"Giving up?" teased Andromache.

"You have plans tonight, right?" asked Hector. "A soiree, or something?"

Unsure why he was asking the question — and so suddenly, and in Truvan — Andromache hesitated. "Yes," she said quietly. "With Cassandra and Demuchus."

Hector nodded. "It's getting late. I can finish the rest at home." He tucked the box under his arm, stood, and waited, his eyes fixed on the floor.

"Oh," said Andromache. She understood. It was still hot outside, and he wanted to see that she made it back from the stables without fainting, melting, or worse. "All right." Privately, she added, *We wouldn't want your parents to worry*...

℘

THE WALK HOME was quieter than the walk out. Unlike Demuchus, Hector had nothing pressing to lecture her about; the only sounds he made were occasional '*aachs*' and '*oofs*' as the box he was carrying poked him in the side.

Andromache said nothing at all. Even with a few awkward moments — and even though nothing had truly changed between her and Hector — that afternoon had been more fun than any she could remember. She would gladly have gone on talking about Buzzy, knots, and bundles all evening. After the abrupt way Hector had cut off their conversation, though, she couldn't think of anything to say to him.

When they reached the house, Andromache made for the stairs, while Hector waved and headed toward the kitchen. The whole way up the staircase, Andromache seethed. That wave, again! Why did he have to keep *waving* at her? What was *wrong* with him?

Her hurt and irritation built until she reached the bedroom door. There, Cutie greeted her by leaping up on her, writhing against her, and yipping every bit as angrily as she had that morning for Hector. Andromache couldn't help but laugh at the little dog's antics.

"What are you so mad about?" she teased, gratified. "I was only gone for the afternoon, not five days."

Cutie alternately licked Andromache's face and nibbled her chin.

Andromache sighed. It was so easy, with animals — so plain when they liked you. Horses nuzzled, dogs licked. There were no subtleties, no mysteries, and the only hidden agenda was food.

"I won't worry about it," she told Cutie, who gave her face another *schluurp*. "It doesn't matter what *one person* thinks, anyway. It doesn't matter if *one person* spends time with me because he feels he has to. I have other friends, now. It's not like when I first got here. I've got Cassandra, and sometimes even Paris. I've got you, of course." She sighed. "I've got Demuchus…"

Demuchus. He would soon be arriving at the house.

"I'd better change clothes, then," Andromache said to Cutie. "The way you've been sniffing my dress, it must smell like horses." And she didn't like to think of all the comments Demuchus would make: *'What's the new — aroma — you're wearing? It's quite — earthy.'*

It's not — worth it, thought Andromache, slipping a new dress over her head. When she threw the old one to the ground, Cutie snuffled eagerly at it. "Cut it out!" said Andromache, more sharply than she'd intended.

Cutie put her ears back and raised her nose to the ceiling.

Andromache had seen a shark once, long ago, at a market, and Cutie's down-turned mouth looked just like that of the great fish. "I'm sorry, Cutie," she murmured.

The dog gave a timid, slow wag of her tail.

"Let's go downstairs."

გე

DEMUCHUS HADN'T ARRIVED, YET, but much of the family was gathered in the kitchen — everyone but Hecuba and Cassandra.

"Good evening, little one," said Priam when he saw Andromache. "To you and to Cootie."

"Thank you," she said, without correcting his pronunciation. She knew by his earnest, dark eyes that he wasn't making fun. Cutie wagged her tail.

"Hey, Hermie." Paris grinned at her.

Paris! Lying little brat that he was, he received a scowl. Hector, who hadn't said anything, got an ironic wave. He waved back unironically. As he shifted on his stool, Andromache noticed the box of tangled ropes sitting at his feet.

"Do you have time to join us for a bit?" asked Priam.

Andromache nodded and chose a seat beside the priest.

"Good," he said. "It's nice to see you, even if just for a moment or two. This seems like a busy night for everyone. Hecuba is off assisting another birth, and goodness knows where my daughter is."

"Primping," suggested Paris.

"You'd know about *that*," said Hector.

"It wouldn't kill *you* to learn a thing or two about it."

Hector glowered through the hair flopping over his eye. In spite of everything, Andromache still felt the urge to brush it back.

"What are *you* up to tonight, Dad?" asked Hector.

"The summer initiation ritual."

Hector gave a whistle. "Already?"

"I know. Time is flying by, as always. Which reminds me...I must be on my way." Priam rose to leave. Groaning, he said, "If only *I* could fly back here after the ceremony, late as it'll be, by then."

"If I'm still out, maybe I'll run into you, Dad. We could stop by a tavern."

"Oh, Paris!" Priam chuckled. "I should be so lucky! Have a pleasant evening, all of you."

"Thank you," murmured Andromache.

"Good luck, Dad."

"Yeah, Dad, good luck — but don't forget the tavern."

"All right, Paris." Priam laughed again.

They heard the soft *tip tap tip* of Priam's feet and then the *squeeeak!* of the main door. After that came the unexpected, clipped rapping of different feet: *clock, clock, clock.*

Andromache knew that sound. She'd been hearing it all week, in the late afternoon, out on the courtyard.

"Good evening," said Demuchus. From the kitchen door-way, he gave a formal bow. "Your honored father let me in."

Paris frowned. "We don't have one of those."

"Shut up, Paris," said Hector. He leaned down to take a length of rope, then sat up and began to untangle it.

To her chagrin, Andromache noticed that he was once again tugging at the knots without first examining how all the loops fit together.

"Or, if you have to talk," Hector went on, "try just saying '*hello.*'"

"Hello." Paris returned Demuchus's bow, adding a flourish or two.

Demuchus frowned first at Paris, then at Hector. "Didn't I hear that you have a meeting tonight?" he asked the latter.

"Cassandra must be almost ready," Paris interrupted, before talk could turn to his prank.

"That's right." The rope thumped dully to the table, and Hector fixed his eyes on Demuchus. "Didn't *I* hear that *you're* go-ing somewhere with my sister?" His voice was soft. Menacing.

"No — no," Demuchus hastened to say. "With Androma-che." He touched her arm.

Unblinking, Hector pressed: "*And* Cassandra."

Hesitantly, Demuchus nodded.

Hector busied himself once more with the rope.

Demuchus turned pale, as though he was imagining the ob-ject wound around his neck.

Meanwhile, Andromache sat in humiliated silence. However protective Hector might be of Cassandra, he couldn't spare a single stern look for *her* sake! As long as she wasn't offending his parents' hospitality by getting heat-sick, he didn't seem to care *what* happened to her — boys could paw at her all night, and he wouldn't care!

Another set of footsteps sounded in the banquet hall. "Honey? Where are you?" cried Cassandra. Before Andromache could answer, the girl had dashed into the kitchen. "There you are!" she sang. "Oh, my stars — *everyone's* here! Are you coming with us, Paris?"

Paris shrugged. "We'll see. I may have other plans, tonight. You should ask Hector."

At the suggestion, Demuchus blanched and looked like he wanted to protest, but Cassandra didn't notice. She kissed her eldest brother on the cheek and chirped, "Good idea! Come with us!"

Hector gave the knotted rope another yank or two.

Turn it over, Andromache thought in frustration. *Fire in the sky! At least* look *at it.*

Giving up on the knot, Hector turned to Cassandra. "Sorry, little sister, but I can't, tonight. There are some things I have to do."

Paris raised an eyebrow. "If that rope is all that's keeping you here, just give it to Hermie. She's foaming at the mouth to take it from you."

"Paris!" shrieked Andromache. *Foaming at the mouth?*

Hector set the rope back on the table and looked over at Andromache. "<u>Sohrry</u>!" he apologized. "<u>I fohrget to stre-tegy</u>."

Furiously red, Andromache looked at the floor.

"Oh, Paris — honestly!" chided Cassandra. "I'm sure he doesn't mean that stupid rope, anyway."

Hector stood up. "Cassandra's right. I've been away for a while and I really need to —"

"Ah!" interrupted Paris, a knowing leer on his face.

Ah, thought Andromache, *he's off to see* Penthesilea. *I mean,* Lee.

"Have fun, all of you," said Hector. He paused to smile at his brother. "Oh, but Paris? Not too much fun — you and I have practice, tomorrow morning."

"I don't like that smile," Paris muttered to himself.

Cassandra made one last attempt to wheedle her eldest brother. "You could meet up with us later..."

"Maybe another time," said Hector. He then put the lid back on the box of ropes and left.

Andromache wasn't all that surprised. She couldn't picture *Lee* mingling with Demuchus and his crowd at one of their soirees; *Lee* didn't even like the people of the citadel. But although not surprised, Andromache was sorry. The evening would have been different — interesting — with Hector and Penthesilea there. *Too bad we aren't going somewhere they'd want to meet us,* she thought. Then, with a twinge of embarrassment, she reflected that *not* meeting up with the likes of Cassandra, Demuchus, and herself was precisely the point. As Cassandra had mentioned, *Lee* never even came to the house — and why would she? Far better to meet Hector down at her place, in the house with the narrow black door, far from Hecuba's eagle eye...

Demuchus cleared his throat. "Well. Now that *that's* settled, we really must be going, those of us who will be attending the play. The opening scene is crucial."

Andromache's gaze drifted toward the one rope left on the table. When she looked up again, Paris was eyeing her. "Take it!" he whispered.

Pointedly ignoring him, she stood and followed the others to the door.

୫୦

IT WAS MIDNIGHT before the young women returned home, and long past that hour when they finally fell asleep. Cassandra, who had been studying a treatise on theater, had left the play brimming with commentaries. The problem was, so had everyone else in her group. Cassandra had been forced to let most of her thoughts simmer until she was alone with Andromache.

Curled up on her bed, wrapped in her blanket, Andromache listened willingly. She was learning much more about the play from Cassandra than she had at the soiree, where arguments were hard to follow and silly questions were not appreciated.

"...and the use of symbolism was brilliant," Cassandra was saying.

"Symbolism?" asked Andromache.

"Well, for instance, when the characters mentioned the sea, they weren't *really* talking about the sea — they were using it as a symbol for old men."

"Oh." Andromache frowned. "So then, what were young men?"

"Rivers," Cassandra explained patiently.

"Oh," said Andromache, perplexed. The symbolism seemed backwards, to her. If anyone should be the sea, it was *young* men — vibrant, energetic, and strong.

"And boys are streams," added Cassandra. "All men are water, just different kinds."

"What about women?" asked Andromache.

"They're the earth."

"Different kinds of earth?"

Cassandra nodded. "Exactly, honey!"

Pleased with herself, Andromache tried to imagine which kinds of earth would symbolize which women. She found it hard to characterize whole groups, though, and focused instead on individuals. Cassandra struck her as a range of gently rolling hills. She herself would be an unimpressive flatland like the one beyond the city walls, whereas Hecuba would have to be something formidable, like a cliff, or even a mountain. The same went for Penthesilea.

Lee, on the other hand — *Lee* sounded like a meadow, soft ground for a man to lie upon...

"For instance, old women are fields grazed over by sheep," said Cassandra.

Blushing, Andromache stammered, "What? Sheep? Who are the sheep? Men? No — wait, I forgot — they're water, right?"

"Mm-hmm. The sheep are babies and young children."

"But what if the old woman never had any children?"

"Well, then maybe she's been grazed over by *other* people's children."

Andromache nodded. That, at least, made sense. Auntie had looked a little grazed-over on occasion. *Auntie*... Gulping, she whispered, "And young women?"

Cassandra giggled. "River banks, of course!"

River banks! Andromache blushed even harder than before.

"Well, you asked, honey! You *asked!*"

Chapter 52

Exhausted from her late night with Cassandra, Andromache awoke just long enough the next morning to push Cutie out the door. She then stumbled back to bed and slept for several more hours.

The sun was high before she showed her face in the kitchen. *Paris <u>must already have gone to market</u>*, she thought, looking expectantly at the table. On it, however, she saw only a sad loaf or two of bread and a miserly heap of fruit. Paris was sitting at the table, glowering and rubbing his arms. He gave a curt nod to Andromache as she sat down.

"What else did you get?" she asked him, eyeing the meager spread. "Is this all?"

"'*Is this all?*'" he mimicked. "Is this all, Paris, you donkey — you camel?"

Andromache drew back, surprised at his ill humor.

"What else shall I haul for you, my lady?"

"I'm sorry — I — I —"

"You — you — slept late!" he accused. "If you wanted a feast, you should have helped carry it."

"I'm sorry!" she cried earnestly. "I'm so sorry, Paris. Are — are your arms going to be all right?"

Paris, who hadn't stopped rubbing them, gave her a venomous look and stalked upstairs to his room.

လ

AT FIRST, Andromache didn't take her altercation with Paris too seriously. The most pampered, indulged family member, he was also the most easily offended. His fits of pique seldom lasted long, though. Andromache went about her afternoon as usual: bathing, reading, and meeting Hector in the library.

Nervous about what his mood would be like after all the strange episodes the day before, she tried hard to keep the lesson calm. She avoided all mention of Lyrnassa, old ladies, Penthesilea, Demuchus, ropes, and plays. Hector was similarly cautious. Their lesson was cordial, almost dull. She asked Hector what he'd had for breakfast; he asked how the garden was doing. She asked him which text he wanted to read next; he asked her if she liked reading travel narratives.

The only moment of levity came when Hector asked if the market had been busy.

"I didn't go. Cassandra and I were up late last night, talking." Andromache sighed.

Hector frowned. "There is trahble?" he asked, his voice soft and dark. "You talk trahble?"

"Oh, no — she was just explaining the play," Andromache said hurriedly, not wanting Hector to think that there had been '*trahble*' between Cassandra and Demuchus or any of the other boys. "But we were up late, and I overslept, so I missed out on marketing." Again, she sighed.

"And so, you ahre sad?"

"No, it's just that Paris got mad at me because I wasn't there to help him."

Hector laughed. "Paris is mad fohr this? He is mad becahse you sleep?"

Andromache nodded.

Hector laughed even harder. "Oh, this is fahnny!"

Andromache, too, began to laugh. It *was* funny, the very idea that Paris — the family sluggard — might condemn someone else for sleeping late! Not to mention the fact that he'd pulled a nasty trick on her, the day before! His footing on the moral high ground was precarious at best. "Still," she said. "I feel bad about it."

"Do not," advised Hector. "He cannot be mad fohr long."

ℰℭ

BUT FOR ONCE, Hector was wrong: Paris held his grudge long into the evening. He rebuffed Andromache's offer to help him clean the cooking pots and ignored her queries about his plans for the evening. The only question that got any response from him was when she asked, in a plaintive voice, "Are we going marketing tomorrow?"

"That," Paris said disdainfully, "is as her ladyship wills it." He made a deep bow to her and backed out of the room, his fingertips scraping the floor.

Andromache sighed. The acting troupe was still in town, and that night they were putting on a different play. Now that she knew to expect symbols, she was sure to understand this one better. She'd been looking forward to it all day. On the other hand, the longer Paris dragged out *his* theatrics, the more unpleasant her life would be. She didn't want him to be mad at her. So he called her Hermie! So he gave her false messages! Mischief and mockery were his ways of showing affection. She could skip *one* soiree, just to make sure she didn't sleep late and —

Andromache shrieked. Someone was grabbing her arm! Cutie, who had been asleep, started barking at her cry.

"I'm sorry for startling you," said Demuchus.

"It's all right." Andromache tried to collect herself. Meanwhile, Cutie sniffed Demuchus, her tail circling dubiously, the hair on her back standing up. "I didn't hear you come in."

"Cassandra opened the door for me." He had a strange look on his face, a mix of solemnity and glee. "She told me the most unfortunate news."

"She did?" asked Andromache, alarmed. "What's wrong?"

"The poor girl was in a tearful state." Demuchus clicked his tongue. "It appears that she fell asleep during morning lessons and won't be allowed out, this evening."

"Oh," said Andromache. "I can't go, either, tonight. I — I have a headache." *And his name is Paris,* she sighed to herself.

Demuchus nodded. "I suppose the play last night *was* a lot to take in, especially if you're not — *used* to them."

442

"That's not why!" Andromache shot back, aggrieved. "It wasn't too much for me! I understood it just fine — young men are rivers!"

Demuchus smiled in a condescending way.

"*Aren't* they?" she asked, reddening.

"Of course," he said. "That's the characterization made by the work, in any case. I just happen to disagree with it."

"Oh." Andromache brightened. "Me, too."

Demuchus went on. "It's too base, not aspirational enough. Plays should present us with ideal versions of ourselves — people as they *ought to be*, not as they *are*. Why watch them, if not for edification?"

"For fun?" suggested Andromache, immediately sorry that she'd spoken. Demuchus, she could now see, hadn't been asking her opinion but was pausing solely for rhetorical effect.

"*Fun.*" He gave her a look of pity. "Mere fun, with all the ills there are in the world? With men's degradation? No! In plays, and other arts, we seek our own betterment."

Andromache couldn't argue that the world had ills, or that most people were in need of betterment. Even so, she didn't like the way Demuchus had said '*fun*,' as though he were spitting out a slug. Demuchus, if anyone, could use a little fun! Peevishly, she asked, "Well, what *should* have been the symbol for young men, then?"

"The wellspring," said Demuchus, with somber tranquility. "The source — ever-pure and unfailingly noble."

"Oh," said Andromache, thinking, *Wellspring? Who says 'wellspring?' Why can't he just say 'spring' like everyone else?*

"At least," he added humbly, "that's *my* opinion. But you, too, disagreed with the river symbolism. What did *you* think it ought to have been?"

"I-I forget," she murmured.

"Oh. I see. Well, if you remember…"

She nodded.

"I'm very sorry to hear about your headache." Demuchus touched her arm. "Try drinking some water with rose petals and honey — *if* there's honey to be found, here," he added, frowning at the kitchen shelves as though they offered nothing but dust.

"There's honey," Andromache assured him.

"Excellent." He stood. "I must be off to the play, then."

Andromache opened her mouth to say, '*Have fun,*' caught herself in time, and instead thanked him for coming to fetch her. When he was gone, she went up to bed and fell asleep thinking about wellsprings, rivers, and the sea.

Chapter 53

"Well, hello, Andromache, dear," said Hecuba, when Andromache came down to the kitchen for breakfast the next morning. "Come in, come in — we were just talking about you."

Andromache froze in the doorway, looking nervously from Hecuba, to Priam, to Hector. Was this about her quarrel with Paris, or had she done something *else*? "You — you were?"

Hecuba nodded and patted the seat to her left. "Come. Sit."

Andromache sat down where she was told. Once she was settled, Priam passed her a tray of walnut cakes and Hector flashed her a sunny smile. He seemed to be in a particularly good mood; he, unlike herself and Cassandra, must have gone out the night before...

"Here's the problem, dear," Hecuba began. "I'm in need of windbane, today. When I went out to check our patch in the courtyard, however, I noticed that it's ailing."

"Oh!" cried Andromache, blood rushing to her cheeks. "I'm so sorry!" Ailing? Dying was more like it. She hadn't been paying proper attention to the garden, lately. Her mind had been wandering to too many strange places.

"Goodness! I wasn't criticizing!" Hecuba clucked. "You've done wonders with the winkswort patch, and everyone's still in shock that your owlsburr is growing here. I've never had such a fine array of healing herbs on hand! No, don't feel a bit bad, dear. Sometimes one or another plant sickens, and it can't be helped. There are other ways to get windbane."

To Andromache, the words sounded ominous. What was Hecuba suggesting? That she steal windbane from a neighbor?

"I'll translate for you," said Hector, noticing her look of confusion. "Mom wants you to go to the herb market, today."

"I was getting there!" Hecuba hissed.

"But by the time you did, Mom, all the booths would have closed."

Hecuba rolled her eyes. "Oh, for goodness' sake!"

"Wh-what about the herb market?" asked Andromache.

"I need that windbane, and Paris can't be trusted. *He'd* bring back an oak gall as though it were gullweed and expect to be thanked for the trouble he'd caused!" Hecuba sniffed. "If a plant can't be eaten, he's useless at finding it."

"Normally, I'd go," Priam explained to Andromache, "but today, my plate is full. It turns out that several priests inducted last year were extorting gifts from *this* year's initiates."

Priam's exasperated face looked just like Hector's, the moment he'd opened the box of knotted ropes. Andromache glanced from one man to the other in surprise. Except for the eyes, she'd always thought Hector looked more like his mother than his father. Family resemblances were fickle, though. When she was a little girl, she'd been told many times that she was the image of her mom and mom's sisters. But as she grew older, her dad's features — except for his height — had asserted themselves, to the point that she had to be standing beside a member of her mom's family for anyone to see the resemblance...

"You're right to be startled, Andromache," Hecuba was saying. "Extorting gifts! I was scandalized, myself, when I heard. And to think, that you'll have to waste *your* time sorting out this mess, Priam!"

"Believe me, it's not my first choice," the priest said darkly.

Hecuba flashed him a sympathetic look before directing a question at Andromache: "Since my husband will be off steering his villainous underlings straight, perhaps *you* could pick up the windbane, then?"

"Oh — oh, sure. Yes."

"Thank you, dear."

"Since that's settled, I'd better go see to the underlings," said Priam, rising from his seat.

"Come home early for a cup of honeywine, dear," said Hecuba. "I'd hate to see them ruin your whole day."

"In any case, my day won't be *nearly* as bad as theirs," Priam assured her.

Hector laughed. His father winked at him before leaving.

"The poor man." Hecuba shook her head. "Thank you for running that errand for me, Andromache. I'd go myself, if I didn't have so much else to do, today. Medesicaste will no doubt keep me occupied all morning, but if you could have the wind-bane back here before noon, dear, I'd be most grateful."

"Of course!" said Andromache. She still felt guilty over having let Hecuba's own windbane ail in the first place. "I could even bring it to you, at — um — your friend's place."

"Well…" Hecuba hesitated. "It *would* save me a trip. Do you know which house is hers?"

Andromache shook her head.

"It's the large one, whitish-yellow plaster, near the council hall."

Andromache knew of at least five or six houses matching that description.

Once more, Hector clarified the matter for her: "It's the one with the pair of seven-headed vultures by the door."

Shuddering, Andromache said, "Oh! I know *that* place."

"A charming invitation to guests, I'm sure." Hecuba sniffed indignantly. "But what about the herb market? Do you know how to get there?"

Again, Andromache shook her head.

"Never mind, I won't try to explain. Paris can take you." Hecuba frowned. "And speaking of him, where on earth *is* he?"

"Probably still asleep," said Hector. He gave Andromache a knowing look.

"Isn't he supposed to be meeting you?" asked Hecuba.

"Not today," said Hector. "I've got a double training session, this morning."

Hecuba sighed. "I suppose I'll never get those plants, if I don't go shake him loose, myself, then — and now is *not* the time to be short on windbane, what with all the pustule flare-ups I've been seeing!"

"Pustules?" Hector looked peaked. "Mom, please — I'm eating!"

"Well, it's not as though you're eating yogurt, in which case I'd see your point."

Hector's jaw stopped moving. He seemed unsure whether to swallow or spit out the mouthful he'd been chewing.

"Besides," Hecuba said sternly. "There are afflictions far fouler than pustules."

"It's not the affliction," said Hector. "It's the *name*. Listen: pustule. Puustule. Puuuus-tule."

Andromache stifled a giggle.

"Since when have *names* bothered you?" Hecuba demanded.

"I don't know, Mom. They bother me now."

"Would you prefer that I say boil? Abscess? Or furuncle?"

Hector snorted, then bit his lower lip. When he lifted his cup of water to take a drink, his hand was trembling.

Andromache tried not to look at him.

"Pimple? Eruption?" goaded Hecuba.

The water Hector had just drunk flooded from his nose at the same time as Andromache lost control of her giggles.

"Oh, honestly!" snapped Hecuba. "Both of you!"

"Sorry, Hecuba," murmured Andromache.

Hector mopped his face. "Mom?"

"Yes?"

"Please pass the yogurt?"

Despite Andromache's best efforts, another giggle escaped.

"Shouldn't you be on your way, by now?" Hecuba scowled at her son.

"You're right," said Hector, giving his face a final, graceful dab. "Xanthus will pop a pustule if I'm late."

"Well, we wouldn't want *that!*" huffed his mother. "Just in case, I'd better go wake your brother so he can help Andromache find my plants — provided she can stop whinnying long enough to do so." With a last, icy glare, Hecuba swept from the room.

Andromache sobered up. She would have stayed sober, too, if Hector hadn't whispered, in leaving, "I hope you know a pustule plant from gullweed, Ahndromahk — for both our sakes."

ဢ

ONCE ALONE, Andromache fed Cutie and tidied up the kitchen. She hoped Paris wouldn't be too much longer in coming downstairs. Not only did she want to make up with him, she was also anxious to fetch Hecuba's windbane. The whole pustule episode had been funny at the time, but now she was at odds with *two* family members.

What was taking him so long, anyway? Surely Hecuba had roused him, already. Had he gone back to sleep? Had he gone down the main staircase and out the door, bypassing the kitchen — and her — entirely? That was it! He knew what would happen if she didn't produce the windbane, and he was making her pay! The brat — the jerk — the —

"Hey, Hermie."

Andromache whipped around. "Finally!"

"You missed me?" asked Paris, leering. "That's sweet."

She forced herself not to scowl. "I missed marketing with you, yesterday."

"And now you need me to take you to the herb market, so you're making nice?"

"I wanted to go marketing with you anyway!" she said defensively. "*That's* why I was up. It's not my fault your mom asked me to fetch windbane for her."

"Hey, relax!" said Paris. "You think I don't how these errands can crop up? Believe me, I understand. In fact, today, I myself have been enjoined to take a lunch down to the taskmaster. Mom's worried that he forgot to pack one in all of this morning's hullabaloo."

"Oh," said Andromache. "Then you'll take me to the herb market?"

"Sure, Hermie. Are you ready to go?"

"Mm-hmm. You?"

"Do I look ready?" Paris smiled. His curls were gleaming and neatly coiffed; he was wearing his best tunic and smelled richly of spices.

Andromache rolled her eyes. Now, at least, she knew what had taken him so long — he hadn't been plotting against her, just primping for the girls in the market. "Let's go," she said. "Come on, Cutie!"

The dog followed joyously after them.

"All right, Hermie," said Paris, when they were out on the street. "Let's get your errand over with."

He led the way down to the herb market, which was tucked away in an odd corner of the lower town. Once Andromache had found the freshest-looking windbane from among the many stalls, Paris helped her haggle down the price, and they left with a basket full of the healing herb.

Andromache wished that she could have had more time to peek at the plants in the market, but she was so glad Paris was speaking to her again that she didn't dare ask him to slow down.

No further mention was made of their squabble the day before. All was forgiven and forgotten — or so it seemed until they arrived at the main market. There, Paris saw to it that Andromache was loaded down with enough food to cover that day as well as the day before. Her basket was so full, in the end, that she could hardly carry it.

"We'll need these," said Paris, tossing a bulging packet of figs her way. "And you still eat almonds these days, don't you, Hermie? Good. A measure — no, make that two measures of almonds. And a dozen or so pomegranates, for my brother."

"He doesn't —"

"There! You don't mind carrying *that*, do you, Hermie?" Paris interrupted.

That proved to be a monstrous sack of apricots, which landed with a *plop*! on top of the almonds. Andromache stumbled but managed to bear the weight. "No," she muttered. "I don't mind at all."

"Excellent! That leaves *me* free to carry the oysters."

Andromache was about to ask what he wanted with oysters, since no one in the house liked them, when two young women lanced a jealous look her way and a covetous one toward Paris. The latter pretended not to notice, but his maneuvering of the heavy basket had the same self-conscious gravity as a lion-slayer shouldering his prey.

Andromache choked and spluttered, but she couldn't quite keep the giggles in.

"What now, Hermie?" Paris asked suspiciously.

Not wanting to renew their quarrel by bruising his ego, Andromache said the first thing that came to mind: "I was just thinking of something funny from a soiree the other night."

"What's so funny about *those?*" asked Paris, turning toward home.

"A question," she said. "If you were a body of water, what kind would you be?"

"You're nuts, Hermie!" He scoffed. "As nuts as the nuts in your basket."

"I know it's silly! That's why I was laughing, remember?" Andromache giggled again, for good measure. "Well? Answer it."

"Why?" Paris looked more suspicious than ever.

"For fun." Now that she'd asked, though, she was genuinely curious. What if Paris answered, '*the sea*,' siding with her against both Demuchus and the playwright?

"Then I'd be saliva in the mouth of a beautiful woman."

"Oh, Paris!" she cried in disgust, as much at herself as at him. She should have known better than to ask.

"Well, you *said* fun…"

"Never mind." Andromache closed her mouth and resumed the walk in silence. *Saliva…* The word made her shiver, this time neither with revulsion nor with cold. Paris's crude comment was affecting her more than she liked to admit. Her old desire for a stairway kiss resurged suddenly. She let her mind drift to a dark alcove, where she was with a man — and *not* one whose pallid yearning dribbled forth like a wellspring. No. He was someone vibrant and strong, who seized her and held her tight against him while they kissed, who —

"Whoa, Hermie!" called Paris. "Are you moving out?"

"What?"

"You walked past the house."

"Oh!" Andromache walked back to where Paris was holding the door for her.

"Do I even want to know?" he sighed, as she passed into the house.

She blushed.

"Never mind."

They went to the kitchen. Paris began to put the food away, leaving a substantial pile in front of himself. "For the task master," he explained. "Who's no doubt lounging on a silken couch while I toil about like some toady, readying his lunch."

"Oh," said Andromache. "That's right."

"It's *not* right," Paris groused. "It's not right at all!"

An idea glimmered in Andromache's mind. "I could take it down to the stables for you, after I deliver the windbane," she suggested. "To make up for yesterday."

"Why, Hermie! Is this a peace offering?"

Andromache nodded, not quite meeting Paris's eye. While true, that was only part of the reason she'd offered to go. Above all, she wanted an excuse to see the horses again, to pet Buzzy and Thisbe and give them celery to munch. Then, too, there was Hector. She wouldn't mind running into *him*, either! He'd been so much fun, that morning, joking about vultures and pustule plants. Maybe she could make him laugh again by telling him how Paris had behaved in the market.

"I don't know…" Paris hedged. "It's my understanding that you're not supposed to go out in the heat." Unconsciously, he rubbed his arms.

"It won't be *that* hot till later," Andromache coaxed. "And, like I said, I promised to get the windbane to your mom, anyway. There's no sense in *both* of us going out on errands."

"True," said Paris. "Very true. All right, Hermie, here's the lunch." He handed her a basket full of the items he'd set aside. "If my brother's not in, just drop it off by his horse, Bertie."

Andromache didn't bother to correct the horse's name, as Paris was already headed back upstairs. She did, however, remove the pomegranate that Paris had slipped into Hector's lunch. Pomegranates were the one fruit that Hector hated. *'Eet taste not,'* he'd once complained to her. *'Eet hass no tasty.'*

Andromache smiled. *Eet hass no tasty*…

⁊

"HELLO?" ANDROMACHE SAID TENTATIVELY, poking her head through the stable door. She gripped the lunch basket, ready to flash it in the stable master's face if he tried to expel her.

"Uh — hello," said an unfamiliar, gangly young guard.

"Oh. Uh — uh —" Andromache struggled to remember the old man's name, but couldn't. "The — the stable master isn't here?"

The boy shook his head. "Training field," he mumbled.

"Oh." More confidently, now, Andromache held up her basket and said, "I need to leave this for — for someone."

"Oh — uh — do you know where to —"

"Yes," said Andromache, taking pity on the young guard. He was even more awkward than *she* was!

"All right." He nodded.

"Thanks, uh —"

"Thoas," he said softly.

"Thoas." Andromache turned down the leftmost aisle.

Without Hector there to whisk her past them, Andromache was free to pet other horses on the way to Buzzy's stall. Reddish ones, black ones, spotted ones — she passed through a wonderland of soft manes and velvet lips. It was bliss. She didn't linger too long near any of them, though, but saved most of her caresses for the two horses she'd already met.

As soon as she rounded the corner, the pale gold horse and the small grey pony began to whicker. Their long necks stretched out toward her.

"<u>Hi</u>, Buzzy," she said softly. "<u>Hi</u>, Thisbe. <u>How are you guys?</u>"

Andromache set the basket on the floor and hurried over to them. As soon as she was in range, Buzzy nuzzled her side with his head.

Giggling, she asked, "<u>You want a piece of celery? Here you go.</u>"

With a great crunch, Buzzy bit off half the celery. Green juice dribbled out from the corner of his mouth. As he chewed, Andromache stroked his face. Having barely finished the first bite, Buzzy nibbled her hand in search of the next. She gave him the other half-celery, holding it firmly against his mouth so that he didn't drop it.

Thisbe began to sniff the air, quietly waiting for her treat.

"<u>I'm sorry, sweetie! I didn't mean to ignore you.</u>" The pony ate more delicately than her friend — *Frahnt*, thought Andromache. Deliriously happy, she stood between the two horses, stroking the grey hide and the gold.

Meanwhile, feet wandered, sped, or marched up and down the aisles. Amongst the footsteps, muffled bits of conversation filtered through:

"…riding today?"

"Maybe…'fternoon…"

"If…wife…you. Heh, heh."

"Go soak your…!"

"…filthy hay, will you!"

"All right!"

The banter went on and on in a similar fashion. Andromache didn't pay it much heed until a ripple ran through it, changing it suddenly to a chorus of vocal salutes. Then, she froze, listening carefully. What was happening?

Buzzy whickered. Andromache shushed him. After the ripple faded, new voices started up:

"…*too* bad…"

"Not too bad? You're…"

"…about it."

"…really?…hell, if…me…"

Then, Andromache heard it — Hector's laugh. She wiped the celery juice and horse spit off her hands and straightened her dress.

"…expect, in…goddamn heat?"

Goddamn heat…

Andromache had a twinge of misgiving. Maybe Paris was right. Maybe it *was* already too hot for her to be out, at least without provoking Hector. He'd been upset, the other day, and this time he might be furious. She could hear him now:

What are you doing out in this goddamn heat? What did I tell you? It wasn't a joke. Are you trying to kill yourself? Don't you care about my parents, after everything they've done for you? How would it look if their guest cooked herself alive?

If she and Hector were to quarrel now, all the friendliness from breakfast that morning would disappear. Depending on how bad the fight was, the hornets might even come back to nest in her belly.

Andromache looked at the basket she'd brought. Leave it, or give it to him in person? Sneak out before Hector got there, or wait for him? Stay at peace with him, or risk war? Either way, she had to decide. His voice was coming closer.

"…tomorrow. I demand a rematch!"

Again, the laugh. "I'm all yours, Buttercup." Hector's voice had a cockiness to it, an audible swagger, a certain exhilaration that Andromache had never heard before. He sounded playful, although in a very different way than he had been at breakfast.

Rematch? she wondered, and then it hit her: *Oh, gods!*

Hector had been training. He'd mentioned that, of course, but she'd forgotten all about it. She hadn't really considered what it would mean to see him at the stables, that morning.

He might be bruised, even bloody — certainly sweaty — after spending the past few hours on the training field, pretending to fight his comrades to the death. He would be filthy, appalling to look at — and after she'd struggled so long and hard to forget the gore-spattered Raider!

I'm all yours, Buttercup. He'd enjoyed himself, too! He'd gotten a thrill from whatever they'd been up to on the training field…

That did it! Andromache ran off, stumbling over the lunch basket in her haste to escape. Apricots, bread, and figs rolled out onto the ground, tantalizingly close to Buzzy's nose. Andromache rounded the corner of the far aisle and fled down it as quietly as she could. She'd made it halfway to the door when she heard a muffled:

"What the —" followed by a bellowed:

"*Thoooo-as*! Come over here *now*!"

She kept running. So, Hector had found the strewn lunch and called the guard back to interrogate him. So much the better for *her*! No one would be at the door to see her leaving. Thoas didn't know her and she couldn't remember telling him her name, or whom she was visiting. He would have nothing to report to Hector except that a girl had come in with a basket. So the basket was near Buzzy! She could have dropped it on the way to or from any other stall — nothing on it said it was for Hector! He and Thoas might spend some time searching for the mysterious girl, but then the incident would be shrugged off.

(*Unless Hecuba asks him how he enjoyed his lunch*,) said the snide Voice.

I'll figure out how to deal with that later, thought Andromache, running out of the stables and onto the street. *If I have to*. For now, though, she was safe.

࿇

CUTIE'S EARS perked up. She stood, and her rear end began to wiggle.

Restlessly, Andromache drummed her fingers against the table. Hector was coming, and she didn't know what to expect from him. Would he be funny, as he'd been at breakfast? Troubled by the mysterious goings-on in the stable? Irritable from having missed lunch? Angry, if he'd learned about her errands out in the heat?

"Hay-lo?"

Andromache's cheeks colored. It was worse than she'd imagined! His voice still had a hint of that cockiness from earlier: *'I'm all yours, Buttercup…'*

"Ahndromahk?"

"He — hello," she stammered. He looked clean, now — no sign that he'd been sparring. No grime, no sweat, no blood…yet Andromache could have sworn there was something different in his face. And the way he was *talking* —

You're imagining things, she told herself.

(*But why* that?) demanded the snide Voice.

Why, indeed? And why exactly was Hector's voice making her nervous? Was nervous even the right word? She didn't feel scared, although her pulse *was* flying the way it sometimes did after nightmares —

"Ahndromahk? You ahre all rahght?" Hector brushed back the lock of hair that had once again flopped in his eyes.

Aware that she'd been staring, Andromache murmured a quick, "Yes," and looked elsewhere.

A fly was buzzing at the window. Cutie snapped at it, missing the insect by a snout's length. Vexed, she pounced after it several more times and left a trail of tongue prints around the library. Andromache wondered what would happen if the fly landed on the biography of Sarcho — if Cutie would manage to take out both pests in a single lunge. A chorus of loud smacking sounds from the far corner of the room, however, announced that Cutie had given up on the fly and begun to groom herself.

The dog's unspeakable noises released Andromache from her daze. "How are you?" she asked Hector.

"Good," he said, sitting down.

"What did you do today?"

"Oh, trainings. Rahtings. Many fings."

"You went riding?"

"Yes." Hector cleared his throat. "Buzzy, he say '*hi*.'"

Andromache froze. Was it a trap? Did he know that she'd already seen Buzzy, that day? Cautiously, she answered, "Well, tell him '*hi*' back."

"In Lukkana?" Hector was smirking now, looking a little too much like Paris. "Or in *hohrse*?"

Ah! That explained the smirk, at least. It had nothing to do with the lunch basket. Hector just wanted to tease her for her long ago '*neigh*!' He'd probably been awaiting the opportunity ever since her first visit to the stables. Andromache laughed in relief. "Your choice," she said.

"And the plahnts fohr Mom?" asked Hector. "You find — *finded* —"

"Found."

Hector made a face. "You *found* the rahght plahnts?"

"I did. She was very happy."

"No mohre — how can you say, '*pustules*'?"

"I don't know." Andromache laughed again. "We don't talk about them, in Lukká."

"So smahrt," approved Hector. "And Paris? He is — he *was* helpful?"

"Paris was Paris," sighed Andromache. "One moment, he was helpful. The next, he was saying that he wants to be saliva in the mouth of a beautiful woman."

Hector blinked. Inured though he might have been to his brother's ways, the statement seemed to shock him. "Sa-*lah*-va?" he asked. "You want to say *spit*?"

Andromache nodded.

"I am scary to ask, baht he say this, why?"

"It was my fault. I asked him what kind of body of water he would be. The question came up after we all saw that play, the other night."

"Body ohff water?" Hector wrinkled his brow. "I do not ahnderstand."

"It just means a *form* of water," said Andromache. "Like a lake, a river, a spring, a pond, the ocean —"

"I see." Without debating the validity of her question, Hector declared: "Paris is sa-*lah*-va? Me, I am a fall ohff water."

"Waterfall," Andromache corrected automatically.

"Waterfall," Hector repeated.

Waterfall. The word took Andromache back to the mountains of her youth, to the Lukka lands, where she'd seen many waterfalls. Some coursing, ribbon-smooth, over rounded rocks. Others crashing to the bottom of a cliff, making a cloud of mist that billowed back upward. Dazzling waterfalls, joyous and alive.

Without warning, her mood turned sour. "There aren't any waterfalls around *here*," she muttered. "Only wellsprings."

Taken aback, Hector tried to placate her. "All rahght, all rahght. I am then a — a *wellspring*."

"It doesn't work that way!" she snapped. "You can't just change your answer!"

Hector frowned. "Calm down," he said. "It's just a stupid question, for fun — right?"

"*Fun!*" spat Andromache, choking on the word as though it were a slug. "Plays aren't for *fun*." Haughtily, she added, "They're for *edification*."

"I see." Hector borrowed her tone. "Well, then — thank you for *edifying* me."

Wordlessly, they studied each other, and then Hector stood to leave.

Andromache didn't stop him. She didn't know what to say, and this time she couldn't make things right by handing him a puppy. She felt like crying; she felt ashamed. Once again, she'd forgotten to keep things calm! All by herself, without the help of Paris's mischief or the heat, she'd snuffed out any good feelings Hector might have had for her.

Cutie reappeared. Her ears were standing tall and her eyes were fixed on the door.

"Go on," Andromache said bitterly. "Go ahead and follow him."

The dog's ears shriveled. Her eyes turned bleak. Her right front paw rose up from the floor.

"I'm sorry," murmured Andromache, melting. "I'm so sorry. Come here. Come here."

Delighted, Cutie galloped over to Andromache and licked her hands in forgiveness.

Things were definitely easier with animals.

Chapter 54

Two days later, Andromache was sitting out on the library's balcony, watching soft light shimmer through the apple leaves. Cutie lay beside her. Every so often, the little dog sighed in contentment — all was right with *her* world.

Andromache's world, on the other hand, felt shrunken. Withered. The worst hadn't happened, at least not yet: Hector was still coming to lessons every day and working diligently. He showed no signs of rancor toward her. But who knew how much longer it would all last? In any case, the warmth she'd recently been noticing between them was gone. She'd squandered it all in a flash of hostility that she didn't even understand.

(*You didn't squander it,*) said the Voice. (*It was never there.*)

Sometimes it felt like we were closer, Andromache argued. *Like that afternoon in the stables, and that one morning at breakfast.*

(*You weren't any closer. That was all in your head.*)

The Voice was probably right. Andromache had seen what she'd wanted to see, knowing what she now knew about Hector.

(*You mean, about* 'the boy with hair in his face,') jeered the Voice.

Abruptly, Andromache stood up. No sense thinking about *that.* "Come on, Cutie. Want to go for a walk?"

The little dog flew to her feet.

"Where should we go?" Andromache had an hour or so before she was supposed to meet Cassandra and Demuchus for the soiree. She didn't feel like going to the sculpture garden or the exercise arena, and the stables were out of the question. What did that leave?

Cutie wagged her tail.

"I know!" cried Andromache. "The herb market!" Without Paris to rush her through, she could explore the different stalls of plants, seeds, and flowers at her leisure.

She and Cutie retraced the path that Paris had shown her, through the southern gates of the upper citadel, down narrow streets bearing west. She felt pleased with herself for remembering the route. When they reached the herb market, though, she was disappointed to see that all was quiet. The vendors had already gone home.

"Tomorrow, we'll come here earlier in the day," she said to Cutie. "But that doesn't help us much for tonight, does it? I don't know, girl. I don't really want to go home, yet. I suppose we could walk around here for a while. Want to do that?"

Cutie wagged her tail in response. Her jaws were slightly parted in a dog smile.

"All right, then," said Andromache.

Slowly, she led Cutie through the streets beyond the herb market, paying little heed to where they were going, deciding on a whim which way to turn at each intersection. She stayed mainly on large streets until an especially tiny alley caught her eye. She turned down it, looking at the houses with interest. *Reddish roof...brown curtains...narrow, black door...*

Narrow black door? Her heart began to pound. *This is Penthesilea's house!* She recognized it from the day she and Hector had buried her first dog, Muka, in the sea. *Penthesilea's house!* Her breath caught in her throat. Hector had told her that Penthesilea — *Lee* — lived near the old luthier's shop. Her grandfather's shop. The place where her dad had grown up...

Hector hadn't given her any specifics — neither a landmark nor a direction with respect to Penthesilea's house — and small wonder! *'I don't want to see that shop!'* Andromache had cried. *'My grandfather was an asshole! I don't want to see his shop and I don't want to talk about him anymore!'* Hector had taken her at her word. Since that night, he'd never again brought up the luthier's shop.

Andromache was sorry, now, that she'd cut him off. She had a sudden urge to see the place. From the moment of her birth, she'd known her mom's childhood home. If only she could find the luthier's shop, she would have a chance to know her dad's, too.

She peered up and down the alley, not sure what she was looking for. An old, weathered sign over a door? Lute pegs littering the ground? Or something less concrete — a feeling, perhaps, a pull to a particular building? She began to walk, but none of the structures called out to her. In one, she saw a tavern, which made her catch her breath — her dad had mentioned going to a nearby tavern! — until she saw several more down adjacent streets. Most of the houses, other than Penthesilea's, were bigger than she'd imagined. She'd always pictured her dad living in a one-room hut, like her own homes in Hurapi and Lyrnassa.

A bigger place makes sense, though, she thought. *The luthier must have been rich, or at least well-off, if he had all those texts*. Grimly, she added, *Not to mention a servant girl*.

As Andromache walked along, she dodged children herding flocks of ducks and chickens. She tried not to get in the way of neighbors chatting from opposite sides of the alley. All of them, she couldn't help noticing, spoke Truvan — apparently, no more Lukkan immigrants had come to replace the ones who had left with her dad. Yet somehow the scene reminded her of her first home, the Lukkan village of Hurapi. It was the ease these people had with each other, the familiarity, as though they were all family. The adults teased each other while fussing over and gently chiding the children. It seemed like a nice place to grow up…

He was four years old, maybe five, running through the streets on his chubby little legs. He was chasing a bronze-colored hen, trying to touch her gleaming feathers. Women were passing him treats — warm bread, figs, walnuts. They were smiling as he played hide-and-seek with the other neighborhood children…

The clarity of the vision left Andromache breathless. Slowly, she looked around at the people on the street. Some of them — the older ones, at least — might actually have known her dad! They might have seen him darting around, playing chase with all his little friends! Did anyone down here remember him? Did *she* look familiar to them? Was that why they were staring at her?

(*They're staring at you because you're staring at* them,) said the snide Voice. (*You're making them nervous*.)

Hurriedly, Andromache turned down a side street. *The shop might not be on the same alley as* Penthesilea's *house anyway*, she told herself. With Cutie beside her, she turned down one street, then another. They meandered through much of the quarter but never came across a building marked as the luthier's shop.

The sign must be gone, she sighed to herself.

Some of the passers-by must have known the location of the old shop, but Andromache couldn't summon the courage to ask them. She couldn't ask Hector, either. Even if they *had* been on friendly terms, she'd made too much of a fuss, before, about never wanting to see the place. And while Paris could surely tell her the location of the luthier's shop, he would be suspicious about why she cared. She didn't want to explain herself to him.

In the end, Andromache decided that it might be better not to know, anyway. What if the shop was rotten and falling apart? What if the next door neighbors were horrid? What if no one remembered her dad? What if they *did* remember him — as the unwanted bastard of an unlikeable man? What if they'd thrown pebbles at him? As long as Andromache didn't know the truth, she was free to imagine her dad as a little boy, chasing chickens…as a teenager, calling out to his friends across the alleyway. She was free to imagine the neighbors making him their pet, just as she'd been the pet of everyone in Hurapi.

She could almost see him there, beside her! It made her feel happy — less alone — more Trojan — to walk the same streets her dad had once walked, to see people he'd once known. She was glad she'd never met the master luthier, even if he was her blood. She'd never heard a good word said about him. But oh, to be surrounded by her dad's old neighbors! It felt almost like having a family again.

Andromache stopped and looked up. The blue of the sky had deepened. Soon, it would be time for the soiree. She would have no trouble finding her way home, though — she'd come full circle and was back on Penthesilea's street.

Penthesilea's street? Andromache gasped. She was on Penthesilea's street — *Lee's* street — in the evening. The *evening*! The hour when young people went out. The hour when lovers met…

"Come on, Cutie!" she cried. They ran all the way back to the citadel.

Chapter 55

"Have you ever considered living somewhere else?"
Demuchus asked Andromache one evening, while
they were out for a walk together before the soiree
gathering.

"I used to live in Lyrnassa," she reminded him.

"No, I mean somewhere else within the city walls."

Andromache thought of Penthesilea's little house. She could
have lived there, if she'd accepted Penthesilea's offer of lodging,
back when she first came to Troy. At the time, she hadn't seen
any reason to do so, but that was before she knew her dad had
grown up in that neighborhood. "No," she said to Demuchus.
"It wouldn't make sense, at this point."

"Oh, no?" he asked.

"Since I have Lukkan lessons, I mean." Not that those had
been particularly pleasant, of late. Andromache often found herself wishing for the lesson to end, so she could poke around
down in the luthier's quarter. Maybe, after all, she would have
been better off living with Penthesilea…

"Ah," said Demuchus. "Lukkan lessons."

Andromache looked down. They'd turned onto a street with
large, smooth stones for pavement — a major thoroughfare.
"Where are we going?" she asked.

"To the sculpture garden."

"But that's —"

"By a roundabout way."

"Oh." Andromache welcomed the extra exercise. The past
few days, it had been too hot for her to do much. Even the na-

tive Trojans were complaining, now — those same Trojans who wrapped themselves in warm cloaks at the first sign of a mist.

Everyone's habits had changed. Animals panted piteously in the shade, refusing to work or play. Cutie had almost stopped eating, although she sucked down many bowls of water each day. Paris and Andromache had taken to marketing right at sunrise, or even before.

While at the market, Andromache had noticed a change in costume, too: all the men were walking around bare-chested. How she envied them! No matter how handsome or unsightly their bodies, all were at liberty to shed half their clothes.

'It's not fair,' she'd complained that morning to Paris…

'You men only have to wear half the clothes we do. I wish I could walk around in nothing but a skirt!'

Paris snickered. 'No one would complain if you did. All the same, Hermie, I doubt anyone would be that excited, either.'

Andromache struck out with her elbow, jostling Paris's basket but missing his body. Which was, she noticed, as she gave it a sidelong look, rather unimpressive. There was a fuzziness to it, a lack of definition. 'You look like you could use a few extra archery sessions yourself.'

Paris refused to speak to her the rest of the morning, but Andromache didn't realize how deeply she'd wounded him until dinnertime. Then, out of nowhere, he threw a cup of water at his brother's face.

Droplets ran down Hector's nose and darkened the front of his tunic. 'What was that for?' he asked quietly.

'Something stinks in here,' said Paris. 'I'm just assuming that you forgot to bathe — '

From her place beside Paris, Andromache had a perfect view of Hector's dark eyes narrowing.

'— so I wanted to help you out. You know, for the sake of the ladies.'

'And what makes you think the problem isn't you?'

'Logic. I wasn't the one out there on the training field, sweating a river under nine layers of rotten leather armor.'

'Oh, we can fix that,' muttered Hector. 'Tomorrow morning, little brother — you and me. We'll see who stinks.' He then stalked off — or so Paris's comment about ladies led Andromache to assume — in search of Penthesilea. Lee.

Meanwhile, Paris looked delighted with himself. He flashed Andromache a triumphant smile and flexed his arm…

Demuchus cleared his throat. Andromache turned slightly to consider him. Demuchus, unlike most of the city's men, was fully dressed. She wondered why. What shame could *he* be hiding, when other men walked around with slicks of pimple ichor on their chests? Did his belly button have a crust? Was his chest hair strewn about in unsightly patches? Did he have a —

Again, phlegm rattled in Demuchus's throat. "I ask about housing because —"

"Housing?" Andromache frowned.

"If you'd ever thought about living somewhere else in the city," he reminded her.

"Oh, that's right. Why do you ask?"

"Because," he said gravely. "Where you are, it's not — *ahem* — the healthiest environment."

"What could be healthier than living with a healer?" said Andromache, in an effort to lighten the mood. She mistrusted where the conversation was going.

Demuchus refused to acknowledge her joke. "That dreadful woman!" he spat.

"What?" His vehemence caught Andromache off guard. "What are you talking about? Hecuba has done nothing but take care of me."

Demuchus stopped to face her, seizing her arms with unusual vigor. "That family is trying to consolidate power, Andromache, don't you see? Controlling the priesthood — the military! A councilman married to an ambassador, spawning commanders of the army! That's not how Troy is supposed to work! We're not supposed to be ruled by one family! They're well on their way to a coup, and *you* don't want to be swept up in that!"

Small flecks of white foam dotted Demuchus's lower lip, as though he'd just drunk milk straight from a sheep's udder. Andromache shrank from him. "Let me go!"

He dropped her arms and licked his lips. "I apologize," he said stiffly. "I am deeply concerned about the future of Troy."

Andromache said nothing. She could still feel the rabid pressure of his fingers. Demuchus had finally shown real passion, and the effect was horrifying.

"I'm sorry, Andromache."

He looked miserable indeed, and the tingle where he'd grabbed her was fading. Still, she wasn't going to absolve him quite that easily. "How much farther to the sculpture garden?" she demanded.

"Just one more street."

To her relief, he didn't broach the subject of her living quarters again, and he kept his hands in the small of his back. The stance made his chest puff out a little.

"Here we are," said Demuchus, once they'd reached the sculpture garden. "Shall we start left, or right?"

"Left," said Andromache, knowing full well that he favored the other direction.

"Left it is."

As they walked among the blocks, Andromache's already-foul mood worsened. The carvings irritated her. Bloated mounds of muscle coated the arms and chests. Swollen legs, as thick as middle-aged trees, hulked down from the fluttering stone tunics. Should those sculpture people ever come to life, they would collapse under their own weight. They didn't look a thing — not a thing! — like *real* athletes. *Real* athletes' arms were taut, not engorged. Their legs were lithe and lean. Andromache wasn't certain about the chests, she but knew — just *knew!* — that they wouldn't bulge like the cancerous knots on trees.

"What's wrong?" asked Demuchus when she snorted. "Are you too warm? We could rest a moment, or go back for water. A delicate maiden such as yourself —"

"I'm fine," Andromache interrupted.

"Then what's wrong?"

"*He* is." Andromache gestured to the sculpture before her, a simpering oaf with his sword raised to the sun.

"What's wrong with him?"

"He looks like he's been inflated."

"Inflated?"

"Yes! Like when someone blows air into a sheep's bladder."

Demuchus frowned. "You're referring to his muscles?"

"Is *that* what they're supposed to be?"

"Those are the *ideal* of human musculature," he informed her.

She snorted again. "They look ridiculous."

"You only think that because perfection is seen so rarely," he argued. "The fact that few, if any, humans can achieve it is what makes these sculptures an *ideal* — that is to say, something of the mind, pertaining to the spiritual rather than the physical realm."

"Then they're a *stupid* idea," she spat.

"Andromache," murmured Demuchus, touching one finger to her cheek.

She stiffened.

He gazed patiently at her, as though she were a child in a tantrum. "Don't be stret-e-gy."

Andromache drew back, eyes blazing. He'd stolen the word! He'd *stolen* a Lukkan word, and he hadn't even used it right! Worst of all, his voice had sounded like worms! She felt sick — violated.

"Andromache?"

"I'm sick," she moaned. "Heat-sick. I have to lie down — I have to get *home*." She purposely stressed the last word.

Without argument, and without even mentioning the soiree she was going to miss, Demuchus escorted her back. She insisted on being left at the door, and when it was closed, she went straight out to the courtyard.

Cutie, who was taking a drink from her water bowl, wagged her tail slowly and came over.

"Hi, there, baby," said Andromache. She flopped down beside Cutie and hugged the little animal. Then, without knowing why, she began to cry. She felt empty. She was a sheep's bladder with the air squeezed out. She was shriveled. Void.

As the tears rolled down her cheeks, Cutie earnestly licked them away. It started as a comforting gesture, meant to soothe Andromache. Then the dog grew more persistent. She sat up, then stood, then finally put her paws on Andromache's shoulders in order to lap up as much of the salt as possible.

"All right, all right." Andromache laughed wearily. "I'll stop if you will."

For hours, she lay on the cool paving stones, beside Cutie. They watched bats swooping overhead, while down near ground level, moths were visiting the night-blooming flowers. Andromache breathed in the garden's perfumes and tried to forget about her walk with Demuchus.

Little by little, she calmed. She was falling asleep when a soft sound startled her: Hector, walking out to his bedroom. His step sounded calm, not huffy as it had when he'd left the house, earlier, after the scene with Paris. He was walking so quietly that Cutie hadn't stirred. Had an evening with Penthesilea — with *Lee* — cooled his wrath?

Andromache peered through a nearby shrub. Hector's hair looked no more or less tousled than usual; it was impossible to tell whether *Lee's* hands had been buried in it. His tunic was rumpled, but that, too, was typical — his clothes always looked bedraggled. *'You're a grub!'* Hecuba had once chided him, and she wasn't wrong. It just —

Wait — tunic? That can't be right. Andromache interrupted her thoughts to squint at Hector, who was indeed wearing a full tunic. For the past few days, she'd seen no one else but Demuchus dressed that way.

Where Demuchus's choice of clothing unsettled her, Hector's depressed her. She knew exactly what *he* must be hiding: old scars, new bruises, scrapes. Everything the Trojan elders considered too ugly to include on their monstrous sculptures. *At least his fiancée wouldn't care about that kind of thing*, thought Andromache.

She watched as Hector sat down on the spring's wall and scrubbed his feet. When he was done, he stood. His body tensed as though he was about to start walking again, but before he did, he peeked over his shoulder at the sky.

The gesture nearly prompted Andromache to run over to him. If she had, she felt sure that he would have pardoned her remark about edification and her snappishness about wellsprings. They might even have had a laugh or two about the sculptures…

She hesitated, though, and Hector turned back toward his room.

Just as well, she thought. It was just as well he'd left before she could make a fool of herself with someone who didn't *really* want to talk to her…

She gave a loud sigh. At the sound, Cutie awoke and began wagging her tail.

"Come on, baby," murmured Andromache. "Let's go up to bed."

Chapter 56

*J*ust focus on the music, Andromache told herself. *You should be flattered.* For weeks, Demuchus had been planning a special concert in her honor. He'd tirelessly researched music from the Lukka lands, as well as its roots and influences — talking about music with her had been his way of solidifying the concepts in his mind. Once ready, he'd arranged for some of the songs to be sung at a soiree. A surprise soiree ! Until Andromache arrived at his house that evening, she'd been led to believe that the night's discussion would center on an obscure collection of poems.

He put a lot of effort into this. Stop thinking about the argument. But no matter what Andromache told herself, her mind kept spinning back to earlier events, when she and Cassandra had crossed paths with Hector out on the courtyard…

'*Hector!*' *sang Cassandra, running over to him.* '*Andromache and I were just about to leave for a soiree at Demuchus's house. Come with us!*'
'*Maybe another time.*'
'*Please?*'
'*I can't. I'm too tired.*'
'*You* always *say that.*'
'*I'm always tired. I'm old, remember?*'
'*Ha, ha. Demuchus is even older than you, and* he's *not too tired!*'
'*Of course he's not. He does nothing all day.*'
'*Oh. Is that what you think of* me, *too? That I do nothing all day?*'
'*No — no, of course not! Not you, Cassandra. You're different.*'
'*What's so different about me? I don't do anything different.*'
'*It's just —* '

Just what? You might as well say it — you think I'm a walking joke!'

'Oh, Cassandra, come on! Shhh. Stop it.'

Hector hugged his sister to him, but too late to stop her weeping. Over the top of her head, he looked at Andromache, who was picking her cuticles.

'Go on ahead,' he muttered. 'She'll catch up.'

Half an hour later, Andromache was on Demuchus's court-yard, still picking her cuticles, worrying about Cassandra and Hector, yet thinking a most ignoble thought: _At least_ I'm _not the one fighting with him, this time_. Despite all her worries, they'd been on civil, if stiff, terms ever since the waterfall flare-up...

"The music is about to start," murmured Demuchus, look-ing with disapproval at her hands.

She laid them flat in her lap.

The words to the first song were identifiably Lukkan, but peculiar, as though they were being sung into a bronze kettle. It took Andromache one full verse to recognize them as belonging to her favorite childhood lullaby. The singer plainly didn't under-stand the words — she sang them as though cheering on an ar-my rather than lulling a child to sleep.

Andromache wasn't sorry to hear the song end, but when Demuchus looked over at her, she smiled like she'd enjoyed it.

From the back of the courtyard, there came a soft commo-tion. Andromache turned around to see Cassandra walking in, tear-stained but triumphant, Hector in tow. Rather than settling down at the far end, the natural choice for latecomers, Cassandra headed straight for the middle bench. Hector sat beside her, rigid and aloof.

Everyone began to murmur. From the little Andromache was able to catch, she could tell that the young people were argu-ing over how long it had been since Hector's last soiree.

Demuchus sniffed.

"What's wrong?" asked Andromache.

"It was good of them to come..."

"But?"

"But did he have to wear *that*? His tunic is old!" hissed De-muchus. "Shabby. Stained. This is supposed to be a nice event!"

"Oh." Andromache sank further into her seat, hoping De-muchus wouldn't notice the plant juice on the back of *her* dress.

Cassandra hadn't had a chance to clean it off with spring water, as she'd been about to do before the fight with Hector.

"And his hair! Why can't he cut it, or comb it, or *something*?"

The boy with hair in his face...

"Farmer prince," grumbled Demuchus.

Before Andromache could ask him what he meant, another song began.

It took her even longer to place this one, between the garbled words and the dragging tempo — but once she did, she had to stifle a giggle. Demuchus had unwittingly chosen an old Lukkan drinking song.

"When ahlt he glahcked his driiiiiiiiiiiiiink, to ze grount dit he siiiink, ahndt his maw dribbelt styew on ze flooh."

Across the way, Hector stiffened. Had he noticed? Did he understand? It was impossible to tell from the blank expression he was wearing.

"Den he crowled lahke a stowt, dit zat wheeeeskery gowt," crooned the vocalist's earnest, melodious voice — oh, gods, she might have been singing about silver raindrops on the petals of a rose, rather than some filthy old drunk! At home, when Andromache's dad and neighbors had sung this song, they'd always used a lot of extra spittle, and between that and their laughing, they'd rarely made it through all the verses.

"Ahnt sodden begahn he to snoooh."

The young Trojans listened with rapt attention; they sat perfectly erect with their hands in their laps.

Meanwhile, Andromache coughed to hide another giggle. Whatever she did, she couldn't look at Hector. If he caught her eye, she would lose it! She would dissolve into laughter, hurt Demuchus's feelings, and humiliate herself in front of everyone.

"Wiff neery a drope een hees leeathery crope —" Oh, the caterwauling of the singer! "— he fah-eented fahst deeat bah-ee ze dooooh."

Andromache couldn't stand it anymore! She *had* to share the joke with someone! Peering at Hector, she thought, *Look over here!* But his glittering eyes never wavered from the singer's forehead. Why wouldn't he look at her? Was he, too, trying not to laugh? She coughed again, this time purposely, to get Hector's attention. Instead, it was Demuchus who turned toward her — Demuchus, the picture of solemn contentment as he imagined trickling streams, moonbeams, rosy maiden cheeks, or whatever else this song conjured up for him.

Andromache glanced hurriedly away. *No more!* she warned herself. *You can't look at either one of them!*

"And theeehre ent hees days, wiff hees legs twenty ways, ahnt his heeeead in ze lahp ohff a whoooooooooh!"

Andromache coughed to hide the laughter that she could no longer hold in.

"Are you all right?" whispered Demuchus, touching her arm. His hand was exceptionally moist, that night.

Andromache nodded. "Inside — a moment —" she spluttered, excusing herself. By the time she'd made it to an alcove in the banquet hall, her giggles had mercifully dissipated. She nevertheless stayed there through the next song, just in case, before returning to the courtyard.

The final two songs were harmless and short. After finishing them, the vocalist sat down among the other members of the group. "I just couldn't memorize any more of *that* language!" she explained, sighing in exhaustion.

"*That* language," said Demuchus, "is Lukkan, spoken southeast of here in the mountainous Lukka lands. You may ask why we —"

"Aren't *you* studying Lukkan, Hector?" interrupted one of the guests.

Hector looked startled at having been addressed but managed a nod.

The voices began to buzz:

"Is that why you came, tonight, Hector?"

"How would he have known? The topic was a secret, remember?"

"Well, yes — but Demuchus might have told *him*, to get him to come —"

"I told no one!" snapped Demuchus. Haughtily, he added, "And this has *nothing* to do with *him*!"

"Could you understand the songs?" someone asked Hector.

"What were they about?"

"Exile, perhaps?"

"Or lost lovers?"

"Or the mountain thorn?"

"What?"

"I was just joking!"

"Well, don't! He's about to tell us what the songs said."

"I don't know," said Hector. "You should ask the expert." He gestured politely to Andromache.

The group gave her a cursory glance before turning back to Hector.

"Forget about those songs. Welcome back, Hector! We've missed you."

"That's kind of you to say." Hector gave another nod, with more grace this time. "I've missed your company, as well."

"Are you going to start coming to soirees, again?"

"Yes, when will you be back?"

Cassandra brightened, and Andromache gasped. Hector, rejoin the soirees? He certainly *could* do that, if he wanted to. He was just as bright and well-read as the others, and among them, he somehow seemed regal — disheveled hair, shabby clothes, and all.

Demuchus, meanwhile, looked pained, as though troubled by a faint but offensive smell.

"With the constraints of my schedule," said Hector, "I'm afraid I'll have to ask you to accept my regrets."

Andromache grimaced. He sounded unnatural, like he was quoting Sarcho. The others didn't seem to mind his stilted tone, though — they were all nodding.

"Of course we will."

"We understand."

"You don't have to explain to *us*!"

"We know about all the responsibilities you have, now."

Cassandra, formerly radiant, began to wilt: she was sensing the short duration of her victory over her brother.

Hector nodded gravely. "Indeed. Even tonight, I'm afraid there's a matter of great importance…"

As he stood to leave, the guests pooled around him, exchanging farewells and kisses on the cheek. Unwilling to give him the thrill of waving at her in front of everyone, Andromache stayed in her seat.

Demuchus, who had felt obliged to see Hector to the door, returned to Andromache's side as quickly as he could. "I apologize for that," he sniffed.

"For what?"

"For the way *he* leapt in and dominated everything. This was all supposed to be for *you*. I never meant for your music to be upstaged by that scruffy, tattered has-been."

Andromache opened her mouth to joke that shabby clothes fit well with the drinking song Demuchus had chosen, but just in time, she stopped herself. Demuchus wouldn't see any humor in the song's real words — far from it, he would be humiliated. Why provoke him? He'd made a monumental effort for her; he'd set up a whole night around her. No one had ever done that for her, before.

"Never mind all that," she said. "The concert was perfect."

ℰℭ

TOUCHED THOUGH SHE WAS by the musical soiree, Andromache couldn't help but laugh inwardly at the true meaning of the songs, and afterward she walked home bursting with the need to share.

"Do you want to sit up and chat awhile?" she asked Cassandra when they arrived at the house. "It's such a nice night. We could go out on the courtyard."

"No, thank you," the girl said dully. She'd been quiet most of the evening. "I'm tired. Maybe another time."

Andromache stared at her, uncertain whether Cassandra saw the irony of her words, the very same ones that had sparked the fight with her brother. "You could come up to my room, then, or we could go to yours," she cajoled.

Sad-eyed and pale, Cassandra shook her head. "It's been a long night. I just need to sleep." Her shadowy form floated up the stairs into darkness, leaving Andromache with a frustrated desire to socialize.

She went to the kitchen where, to her surprise, she saw Hector sitting at the table. His '*matter of great importance*' seemed to be a large bowl of stew. Cutie lay beside him, so focused on the bone she was gnawing that she barely wagged her tail to welcome Andromache.

Hector's greeting was even sparser: he just glowered at her, daring her to comment.

Andromache would have preferred Paris, right then, but even a surly companion was better than none. "Can I sit?"

"Mmph," Hector grunted.

She sat down at the table. Cutie, after a moment's hesitation, came over beside her. As she stroked the dog's ears, Andromache reminded herself that this time, she wasn't the target of Hector's ill humor. "Did you like the music?" she asked.

He nodded noncommittally.

Cutie smacked her lips on the bone.

"My favorite was the second one. Didn't you think it was funny?"

"Maybe."

Aha! thought Andromache. *He's talking — a little, anyway.* "Could you understand the words?"

Hector shrugged.

"It was about a guy who gets drunk."

"Hmm."

"And hangs around with a woman who —" Andromache coughed as color rose in her cheeks. "Who was also drunk," she finished, wondering if Hector would notice her editing.

He just nodded and dipped a piece of bread into his stew.

"At the end, he falls asleep," Andromache added.

"Great," said Hector.

Maybe the song wasn't as funny as I thought, Andromache decided. "It was nice that you came," she said, changing the subject. "It meant a lot to Cassandra."

"Oh, I'm glad of that," Hector said sarcastically.

Cutie whined.

Andromache acknowledged neither the sarcasm nor the whining. "She was sad to see you leave, though. Why didn't you stay?"

Hector's face was tight. "*My gahrlics, Ahndromahk,*" he growled.

The laughter that had been building all night in Andromache's belly finally escaped.

"What?" Hector demanded hotly.

Giggling, Andromache explained, "*You say 'my onions,' not 'my garlics.'*"

Hector froze, blinked once or twice, then finally began to laugh with her. "<u>My gahrlics</u>!" he said over and over, between bouts of laughter.

Perturbed by what she took for another fight, Cutie scurried over to Hector and licked his toes.

"Stop that!" he yelped, howling with laughter.

As Cutie slunk away, her tragic expression made Andromache, too, laugh harder.

"Honey?" asked a soft voice from the kitchen doorway.

Andromache turned around and saw Cassandra. The girl's eyes were red and swollen.

"I came down to find you. What's so funny?"

"Hector's garlics!" cried Andromache.

Hector, who had just taken a breath, released it through his nose.

"Oh," Cassandra said earnestly. "Do you think you might start gardening, too?"

Hector looked at his sister, then at Andromache, before dissolving once more into laughter.

Cassandra didn't seem to know whether to laugh with him or cry.

Noticing her expression, Hector sobered. "Little sister," he said gently, "Andromache was just telling me what those songs were really about. Do you want to sit?"

Cassandra brightened. At the next soiree, she would have the scoop. "Oh, yes! Was it sunsets? Boat trips? A love story?"

"A love story?" Andromache coughed. "Not exactly…"

Chapter 57

The plain beneath Troy was gold and dry. It was the end of summer. During the day, the air was still hot, but evening was falling sooner, and with it came cool air.

Out in the garden, Andromache had begun preparations for the rainy season. Her second rainy season in Troy! Was it possible? The memories of her first few tentative steps into the garden, the first few weeds she'd plucked, were still vivid — and yet, the person who had done those things seemed separate from her. Had she ever *really* been afraid to leave the house? Had she ever *really* had nightmares about Hector?

Hector. Their relationship had fallen back into old patterns, after the Lukkan soiree; the mood between them was no longer stiff or civil, but calm. Andromache directed their conversations toward safe topics and made sure not to sound haughty. Hector, in turn, was kind — funny — very much his old self. After a close call or two, balance had been restored.

Andromache was glad to be leaving summer, the season of hot tempers, behind.

Autumn would bring many joys to her. On days with fine weather, she would go down to the herb market to explore its botanical riches and find new plants for her garden — and afterward, she would head over to Penthesilea's neighborhood to hunt for the old luthier's shop. She still wasn't entirely sure she wanted to find the place, but she hoped to see more visions of her dad as a little boy, running through the streets.

On rainy days, when it was best to stay inside, she would work on her new weaving project, a cloth with green and white stripes. She hadn't touched the loom all summer, and she was out of practice. Three times she'd had to start over — digging down farther into her memory each time, to recall the tricks her mom and Auntie had used — before the cloth satisfied her. Now, though, she was ready.

The cool months of the year were almost there. It would be a time of quiet contemplation. For the last few nights of summer, the soiree group would gather to discuss chronicles, treatises, and travel narratives. Soon, though, the group would stop meeting. Andromache wondered what the end of soiree season would mean for her and Demuchus. He often dropped by to escort her and Cassandra back to his house, but he never came over just to see her, the way he had during that string of afternoons in high summer. What if he went the whole winter without visiting? She wasn't sure how she would feel — perhaps disappointed, perhaps a little relieved. Even at the best of times, he had a way of getting under her skin.

Andromache nodded to herself. Plants needed winter, the time of rains and slow growth that allowed them to burst forth in spring. It made sense to her that people would have similar needs. A few months of quiet evenings, playing roodles with Cassandra and listening to Paris strum his lute — her family's lute — would restore her. In the springtime, when she met up once more with Demuchus, she would be well-rested and ready.

Early autumn

Chapter 58

"A little more," said Cassandra.
"Here?" asked Andromache.
"No — over there."
"I can't reach that."

"We'll have to wait for Hector, then. He's usually the one to string the garland, anyway."

"Because he's the tallest?"

"There's that," said Cassandra. "But the fact is, he's just got a knack for it."

The two young women were decorating the courtyard for a wedding. It was to take place later that evening, a warm fall night with just the right sliver of moon.

"Where is he?"

"Scrubbing the Chute."

"Oh. Could Paris do it?"

"The Chute, or the garland?"

"Either."

"I don't think so." Cassandra frowned. "He's busy polishing the marriage cup."

"Not again! Remember what happened last time?"

"I know, but there's not much he *can* be trusted with. At least no one really sees the cup, because the couple's hands hide it."

"I guess," said Andromache. "Anyway, here he comes. Here they all come."

As Hecuba marched over, flanked by her sons, Andromache gave the woman a wary look. She'd learned the hard way just how tense Hecuba could be before weddings; anything, even the accidental blurting of an obscenity, could send her into a rage. For the moment, however, Hecuba looked calm.

"Refreshments!" she announced. "Have a cup of cool grape juice, girls."

"Thanks, Mom!"

"Thanks."

"You're welcome, little finches. It's lovely so far." Hecuba gave an approving nod to the garland. "Though we'll need a few more touches." She looked meaningfully at Hector.

"All right, Mom."

"It's going to be quite the event, tonight," gloated Hecuba.

"Who all is coming?" asked Paris.

His mother rattled off a list of dozens of friends, then added, "plus, whoever is coming from your young set."

Cassandra rattled off a similar list of friends, ending with, "and Demuchus of course." Her eyes twinkled at Andromache.

Andromache blushed and looked away.

"Which one is Demingus, again?" asked Paris, in his lazy drawl.

"Oh, Paris!" said Cassandra, exasperated. "You know *Demuchus*! You've talked to him — in our *kitchen*!"

"I've talked to a lot of people there, Songbird."

"Demuchus is the one whose face is always dripping off his neck like beeswax," interjected Hector, his features taking on a lurid melting look.

"Oh, that's uncanny!" Paris laughed. "I know exactly who you mean, now!"

Cassandra ignored her middle brother, the better to frown at her eldest one. "There's no need to be nasty," she scolded.

Hector shrugged. "It's not nasty if it's true."

"It's *not* true!" Cassandra said reproachfully. "And even if it was, it wouldn't hurt you to be nice. He'll be a council member, someday. You'll have to work together."

"Your sister's right," Hecuba approved.

"Oh, relax, both of you," said Hector. "On my honor, I swear that I hold him in the highest possible esteem."

"Oho!" said Paris. "Then why not marry him, brother."

Hector snorted. "Maybe I will."

Andromache pictured Demuchus and Hector in matching floral crowns, chanting lovingly to each other. She let out a loud snicker.

"Boys!" barked Hecuba. "Honestly! Paris!"

"Why *me*? Why not Hector?"

"*You*, I said! And don't egg them on with your giggles, Andromache — they mustn't be allowed to think they're funny!" Hecuba's eye swept over them, finding fault on whomsoever it fell.

"Hector isn't coming to the wedding," said Paris, to deflect his mother's ire away from himself.

"What!" she squawked.

"There's training for new patrol members, Mom," explained Hector.

"That *you* planned, I don't doubt! Why on earth would you schedule it for tonight?"

"It was an auspicious night for training."

Hecuba gave her eldest son a thunderous look.

"I can't reschedule it now," he said, a little sheepishly.

Andromache wondered if he'd planned the training that way on purpose, so he wouldn't have to go to the wedding — and face reminders of his thwarted wish for marriage to Penthesilea. To *Lee*.

"You, of *all* people not to be here!" cried Hecuba, shaking her head.

"Why *me*, of all people? Why not Paris?"

Hecuba turned purple. "Because he's not the one *living — in — disorder!*" she hissed through gritted teeth.

Andromache gasped. Time seemed to stop. It was the first time the relationship between Hector and Penthesilea had ever been mentioned in front of him. What would he do now? Capitulate, admit that he was languishing for *Lee*? Storm out?

"Paris? Not living in disorder?" Hector laughed. "You must not have looked in his room, lately — not that I see what that has to do with weddings." There was no sign whatsoever that he'd understood his mother's euphemism.

Hecuba glared at him.

"Oh, Mom," he sighed. "What's the big deal? I don't even know the happy couple."

"Of course you do! Why, the bride is our neighbor's niece. Your sister practically grew up with her! As for the groom, I can't say I'm as fond of him," Hecuba admitted with a sigh. "He's the one I caught feeding mud to your brother, all those years ago."

"Mom!" howled Paris.

Hector guffawed. "Maybe I *should* reschedule — that guy sounds all right!"

Paris dug his elbow hard into Hector's side.

"Boys! Once and for all!"

"Sorry, Mom."

"Sorry."

"So, you won't be here, then?" asked Hecuba.

Hector shook his head. "Not physically. But I assure you, Mom, my heart will be here."

Outraged, Hecuba lobbed a strand of garland at her son. It landed pertly on his head and wound around one shoulder.

Cassandra giggled and tossed another strand, which came to rest in the crook of Hector's elbow. Paris, too, joined in on the game, and soon Hector was barely visible under the strings of flowers.

"Now you *have* to come to the wedding!" Cassandra trilled. "Without you, we'll have no decorations."

Hector laughed and stretched out his arms, letting the garland stream to the ground.

"Look!" cried Andromache, shaking with laughter. "Hector is *'covered in glory*!'" The scene before her was just what she'd pictured months earlier, back when she'd first heard the phrase.

Hector threw a strand of garland at her. It landed on her head. They all started laughing, then, even Hecuba.

Andromache wished there didn't have to be a wedding. She didn't want the guests to come or Hector to leave. What she wanted was for the fun of the garland-throwing to last a little longer.

THE WEDDING had been perfect, as were all Priam's ceremonies, and the hour had come for guests to mingle in the banquet hall. Andromache stood with Cassandra and her friends, half listening to their chitchat about different traditions of marriage.

"I read that in some countries, they throw the groom into a lake."

"What! Why?"

"Is it some kind of ritual bath?"

"The writer wasn't sure."

"Was it just one groom or all grooms?"

"Does it matter?"

"Of course! If it was just one, the writer can't claim that it's a cultural tradition."

"That's a good point."

"Is such a marriage even valid?"

"Why wouldn't it be?"

"What if the lake washed off the — the *marriedness?*"

"So are you saying that if we threw *this* groom into the river, or the sea, he wouldn't be married to the bride, anymore?"

Rivers…the sea…Andromache did *not* want to start thinking about bodies of water! She did *not* want to unleash those strange feelings, the ones that made her start fights about wellsprings and waterfalls! It was a dangerous subject that had to be avoided. She concentrated instead on the wine cup in her hand, feeling tiny bumps and declivities on what appeared to be a perfectly smooth surface.

"Andromache," said a voice.

She looked up to see Demuchus and smiled in relief. Cassandra's babbling friends would have to break up the conversation to greet him, and by the time all the kisses were exchanged, the group would have found a new topic.

Rather than joining the others, though, Demuchus pulled Andromache aside. "There's something I wanted to talk to you about," he said.

"Oh, sure." She turned away from Cassandra's friends to face him.

He looked around hesitantly. "Not here. It's too noisy. Let's go outside."

"Oh." Andromache frowned. The evening air had grown chilly. "Let me get my cloak."

"Please," Demuchus said firmly. "This will only take a moment or two."

"All right," Andromache agreed. "Just a moment."

She took a deep breath of sweet-smelling air as Demuchus led her out to the courtyard. Her gardens were reviving, now that the shock of summer heat had passed. No guests were out there to appreciate the plant life, though. Everyone had flocked to the warmth of the banquet hall as soon as the ceremony was over.

Demuchus paused beside a bench.

"Andromache," he said, his tone even more serious than usual. "I've been wanting to talk to you about this for a while."

"About what?"

He furrowed his brow. "About your servitude."

"My *what?*" she squawked.

"Your servitude," he repeated, with more force. "Always having to go places at other people's bidding — having to march all over the city, in order to secure a place to live." He shook his head disapprovingly.

Servitude? thought Andromache. *That's ridiculous!* There was only one time per day that she was required to be in a certain place: for Lukkan lessons, which she enjoyed, especially now that she and Hector weren't fighting. She would have gone to them even if she didn't have to. "I'm *not* in servitude."

"Cleaning, pulling weeds, shopping for food —"

"Everyone in the house helps out," said Andromache, with exasperation. "They don't have servants."

"Not officially, perhaps."

"Not at all! Everyone pitches in."

"Even the young princes?" Demuchus sneered.

Andromache was startled by his harsh tone. "I'm *not* a servant," she said defensively. "I'm a guest. And a teacher."

"It amounts to the same thing."

"How? I *like* teaching."

He gave her a hard look. "You still are not free to choose your day's activities. All that could change," he said, taking her hand.

While Andromache had grown used to the clammy touch of Demuchus's hand on her arm, she was shocked by this latest caress — by the way his fingers slunk through hers, at once overly bold and apologetic.

He touched her cheek with his other hand and said, "You could marry me."

Marry him? Andromache raised her eyes to find a liquid expression on his face. *What*? she thought frantically. *What? What*?

Demuchus mistook her silence for assent. He swept her into his arms and kissed her, drowning her in the scent of the lamb he'd eaten for dinner. It was *not* the kiss she'd so longed for! He plainly wasn't comfortable in his own skin, let alone pressed against hers, and he had an inexplicable sweatiness that she found unnerving. Worst, though, was his tongue — that slinky muscle poking hesitantly around her mouth!

Andromache twisted away, but Demuchus only looked at her more meltingly than before. *Oh, gods! He* can't *think I want him to kiss me again!* Unbidden, the phrase *'the one whose face drips off his neck like beeswax'* popped into her head, and she began to laugh.

Drawing back from her, Demuchus asked, "Andromache, what's wrong?"

She wanted to stop laughing. Oh, gods, she wanted to stop laughing! But it was too late — each peal of laughter triggered the next. She laughed until her sides throbbed, until she felt like she was going to throw up.

In one motion, Demuchus stood, swirled his cloak around his shoulders, shot her a look of betrayal, and swept back into the house. Still, she couldn't stop laughing. She hated herself for it, but it was beyond her control.

Cassandra, who had seen Demuchus storming in from the courtyard, rushed out to find Andromache with tears streaming down her cheeks.

"Honey! What's the matter? Why are you crying? Did Demuchus upset you?"

Andromache shook her head, unable to respond.

Cassandra touched her shoulder in concern. "You're scaring me!"

"I'm sorry!" Andromache finally managed to gasp. "So sorry!" Half choking, she told Cassandra the gist of what had happened, finishing lamely with, "He caught me by surprise."

"Oh, dear," sighed Cassandra. "That *was* silly of him. But everything will be all right. He'll forget all about this once you're married." She gave a devious smile.

Instantly sober, Andromache recoiled. "Married? What? You're crazy!"

"What do you mean?"

"What do you think I mean?"

"Don't you like him? Why were you asking me all about kissing? I thought you wanted him to —"

"I didn't! I don't! I mean, maybe I did, before I really knew him, but just a kiss — not *this*!"

"You don't want to marry him?"

"No! Gods, no! And I don't know why he'd think I do!"

"Maybe because that's what I told him," said Cassandra, in a small voice.

Andromache stared at her. "Why would you do *that*?"

"When you brought up kissing, I figured you meant *him*, so I asked him when he was going to get around to kissing with you."

"You *asked* him?" Andromache shrieked in mortification.

"Yes, honey —I did! *Someone* had to! *You* weren't. He said he couldn't kiss with you — yet — because he had more serious intentions. He said it was important to wait for the right moment — which answers your question about why a Trojan boy might not give you a kiss! I didn't want to tell you, though. I wanted you to find that out for yourself. Anyway, it seemed so perfect, the two of you getting married! That's why I encouraged him."

"Wait — no kissing means it's *more* serious?" asked Andromache. What bitter irony!

"Yes! Isn't that something?" Cassandra's voice held the thrill of discovery, as though she were a shell-collector stumbling upon a new type of snail. "I've never been to that stage, so I didn't know!"

"How exciting for you, to find out about it!" Andromache hissed.

Cassandra looked chastened. "Demuchus likes you," she whispered. "And I thought you liked him. And then you didn't have a sweetheart, so — well, it seemed like you were lonely! I thought it would be good for you. He's well-off, too, so you'd never have to worry about that. And..."

There was more? "And *what*?"

Cassandra squared her shoulders and said with great dignity: "And I thought it would be advantageous to have a link between his family and ours."

"'*Advantageous?*'"

"You may not have noticed, but he and my brother don't seem too fond of each other."

Andromache *had* noticed their mutual dislike, between Demuchus's cracks about shabby clothes and Hector's deadly beeswax remark. She'd noticed, but she hadn't thought much about it until tonight.

"It's always been that way," Cassandra went on. "Not that I know *why* — it's not as though anyone tells me *anything*! — but Hector stopped going to soirees when Demuchus started hosting them. Whatever their problem is, though, their — *animosity* — could be dangerous for the city. I mean, if the council and the army can't get along, who knows what might happen, down the road! I thought your marrying Demuchus would heal their rift, since you're a part of our family now."

"A pity marriage!" snapped Andromache. "*And* a political alliance!" She didn't know which was worse.

"He adores you," whimpered Cassandra.

"Well, I can't stand him!" Andromache shot back.

"But why not? He's so cute."

"He's a rotten kisser!"

"Oh!" Cassandra clutched her chest and fell back several paces. "How bad?"

"*Really* bad."

"Maybe he could learn…"

"I doubt it."

With that, Cassandra gave up trying to foist Demuchus on Andromache. "What's everyone going to think?" she moaned.

Andromache shrugged. It wasn't as though she had much popularity to lose, in Trojan circles.

"And Demuchus! He won't believe a word I say, after this! Forget about Hector — my whole life, *I'll* have to work with Demuchus, and he's going to think I'm a liar, a giver of false promises!" Cassandra's eyes looked swollen, as though she were about to cry. "I really thought you liked him, honey, or I swear I never would have said — oh!" She gasped as tears started rolling down her cheeks.

"Don't cry," Andromache heard herself saying. Exasperated though she was, she felt sorry for Cassandra. The girl had meant well. She wanted Andromache to be happy. She thought of her as *family*. "Don't cry, Cassandra. It'll be all right."

ℰ◯

ANDROMACHE CLIMBED the stairs to her room and curled up on the bed with Cutie. *Smart dog!* she thought, wishing that she, too, had stayed upstairs instead of attending the wedding and party. She rubbed the little dog's belly, all the while fretting over what had happened that evening.

It wasn't that she regretted turning down Demuchus's offer. The most she'd ever wanted from him was a good stairway kiss — then, barring that, a good soiree companion. She had no interest in marriage, period, and even less in marrying *him*. Marriage to Demuchus would mean listening to his overmannered speech — his talk of '*honored fathers*' and '*delicate maidens*' — all day, every day. His airs wore thin after an evening; she couldn't imagine what a lifetime would do to her.

(*Maybe he wouldn't be like that, once you're married,*) the Voice chimed in. (*He might yell at you or ignore you, instead.*)

Thanks for that, Andromache thought sourly, but she knew the Voice was right. Demuchus might put on one face until the marriage was sealed, then change his ways. She had no idea what he was like in private.

(*You do! You know a* little *of what he's like in private!*) the Voice said salaciously.

Andromache shuddered. Oh, that indecent flailing of Demuchus's tongue! What a sad end to all the fantasies she'd cherished about Trojan kisses! She'd never really thought much about tongues before that evening and was sorry that Demuchus had given her reason to.

(*And then, husbands do more than kiss…*)

That time, Andromache didn't just shudder — her stomach heaved. "No!" she cried aloud, before her mind could turn any further in that direction. Cutie looked up in alarm and licked

Andromache's chin. "It's all right," soothed Andromache. "It's all right."

But nothing would be all right if she married Demuchus. Even if he promised never, *ever*, to touch her, she wouldn't want to live in his house. What would she do, there? Sit around and stew? He'd made it clear how he felt about gardening, marketing, wandering down to the stables, and everything else she enjoyed. He would, no doubt, do his utmost to discourage those activities. Not that she would have a choice, where gardening was concerned: his courtyard was so barren that she would have little to tend. *Three spindly trees and a few sad little potted herbs*, she remembered. The work of a single morning. She would have to leave behind all the vegetables — the flowers — the mint — to instead be surrounded by vases and fineries.

"Vases and fineries," she said aloud.

In response, Cutie grunted, rolled onto her stomach, and stretched her back legs straight out behind her. Her red-brown ears stood erect, slightly to the sides of her head.

Smiling, Andromache stroked first one ear, then the other. Cutie didn't belong in a house with vases and fineries, and no animals were allowed there, anyway. If Andromache married Demuchus, she would be dogless once more. No padded feet would follow her down the stairs; no little muzzle would prod her awake in the morning. She would be alone. Cutie, meanwhile, would remain here, where she would transfer her love to the others and forget all about Andromache.

In fact, the whole family would forget about Andromache! Cassandra and her parents might visit, once in a while, but would Paris? Andromache doubted it, and the truth was, she would miss the little brat. She would miss his stupid pranks, and she would even miss being called '*Hermie*.' But more than anything else, she would miss the sound of Paris's lute — her *family's* lute. Never again would she hear the music that took her back to the Lukka lands — to the pines — to the sweet breezes. She would lose that connection to her long-dead family.

As for Hector, who tied her even more tightly to her family, she might never see him again. Visiting Demuchus's house had been excruciating for him, a sacrifice he'd made once for his beloved little sister but would never repeat. Not that Demuchus would want him to: *What's that scruffy lout doing in my house? This is a nice place. We don't need him dragging his stable filth in here.'* And for all the run-ins Andromache had had with Hector, lately, there was no doubt that she would miss him.

She couldn't return to *his* house for Lukkan lessons, either. If Demuchus didn't try to forbid the practice outright, he would make it so unpleasant for her that she would quit of her own volition. *'Let me know if he gives you any — difficulties.'* Every day Demuchus would say this, making his unctuous little pause, until she could bear it no longer.

A hornet stirred inside her.

She would never speak Lukkan again. That part of her life would be over. It would shrivel up and die. *'Teach me,'* Demuchus would offer as an alternative, thinking he was doing her a kindness, and she would have no reason not to accept. Demuchus was intelligent, a devoted student. He could probably learn to speak Lukkan better than she did — certainly better than Hector. Demuchus would never say silly things like '*horse house*' and '*foalish*.' Demuchus wouldn't pronounce *life*, *laugh*, and *love* identically, as *lahff*. He would say every word correctly, and they would still sound wrong. He had no place in her Lukkan world.

Andromache clenched her stomach against the barrage of stings. Looking out the window, she saw the tops of the courtyard trees and, far beyond them, the light of the moon glinting off the sea. From there, her mind wandered south, along the shore, then over plains and rolling hills to a cliff rising over a valley. Down on the valley floor, a small, clear stream ran through a grove of platana trees. A boy — a sweet boy with hair in his face — had once — no, twice — carried water from that stream to a little old woman's shack...

'What is it?' asked Andromache, when Auntie gave a deep sigh. It was nighttime, and they were lying on their sleeping rugs.
'Some Taruishans came today.'
'I heard.'
'They were nice.'
'That's good.'
'One boy cut his leg. He was bleeding pretty bad.'
'Oh, no! What happened?'
'He tripped when he was helping me get water.'
'What did you do?'

'What do you mean, what did I do? I bandaged him, of course! Do you think I'd just leave him there to bleed?'

'No, of course not.'

'He was a nice boy — a sweet boy, with hair in his face. Maybe that was why he tripped, because he couldn't see. But he carried my water, and I didn't even have to ask him to.'

'That was nice of him.'

'He had good manners. He smiled and said "thank you" when I bandaged him. He even asked if there was anything else I needed.'

'You answered him, I hope.'

'Of course not! He was speaking Táruvan.'

'Oh, Auntie! It wouldn't kill you to try a word or two!'

'I've been speaking Lukkana my whole life. Why should I change now?'

'You could've at least said, 'No, thank you." That boy probably thought you were a rude old cow…'

As a light breeze ruffled her hair, Andromache shivered. Back then, she'd never dreamed that she would hear the other side of this story. The shock, when Hector had told it to her, was so terrible that she'd run away.

For Auntie's '*sweet boy*,' Andromache had always pictured a gawky adolescent — not someone like Hector, who had been, even three years ago, a man. A young man, perhaps, but fully grown. Auntie had been using the word '*boy*' affectionately; she'd *liked* the Trojan soldier. She'd tousled his hair and bound his leg. He, in turn, had liked the old woman. He still remembered her and thought about her. He'd risked his life to save her.

Hector was a living connection to Auntie — to Andromache's dead family. How could she relinquish *that*? Even if she wanted to marry Demuchus — which she didn't — cutting herself off from Hector this way was unthinkable.

(*Laughable, even.*)

Laughable…Andromache cuddled closer to Cutie. She felt colder than the wind should have made her feel. *Laughable…oh, gods!*

What had she done, by laughing? She hadn't meant to. Between the comment about wax and her own surprise and nervousness, it had just happened. Now, though, she was beginning to worry about the consequences.

Because of her, Cassandra was going to have a miserable future career on the council, working with someone who hated her. For that matter, because of her, Priam's *current* career was in jeopardy — oh, how could she have forgotten that Demuchus's uncle, Ucalegon, was Priam's colleague?

However Ucalegon found out about Andromache's laughter — whether from Demuchus himself or from the chatter of Trojan gossips — he would surely fly into a rage over it. She was a nobody from Lyrnassa who had no business rejecting someone like Demuchus, much less laughing at him. Ucalegon might have her jailed or banished. He might force Priam and Hecuba to kick her out of the house, as retribution.

They might kick her out voluntarily, after the disgrace she'd brought on them.

No! thought Andromache, digging her nails into her palms. *I like it here! I want to stay.* But refusing Demuchus now seemed just as likely to spoil her life there as marrying him would have done. As soon as Ucalegon found out, she was finished.

Then he can't find out! she swore. She would go to Demuchus first thing in the morning and beg his mercy — mercy for the sake of Cassandra and her parents, if he wouldn't have mercy on *her.*

Once again, Andromache looked out her window at the silver speckling of stars. She imagined the slow dance of the Lorani, who could swallow the earth without even noticing it. Her plight would be nothing to them.

Chapter 59

"Andromache," someone hissed, as Andromache was creeping through the banquet hall toward the main door. "Where are you going?"

"To see Demuchus," she hissed back, relieved that it was only Cassandra.

"You changed your mind?" asked the girl, her face rosy and bright with hope. "You'll make such a beautiful coup —"

"No!" cried Andromache, more loudly than she'd intended. In a whisper, she added, "I just want to apologize for making a scene."

"Oh," said Cassandra, looking disappointed. "Well, I don't think he'll be up yet. Have something to eat with me, before you go."

Andromache shook her head. The last thing she wanted before the Demuchus question was settled was to see the other family members. "I'll just wait till he's up, then, and eat when I get back."

Before Cassandra could say anything else, Andromache hurried out the door and over to Demuchus's house. She was glad to have made so many nighttime trips there; otherwise, she might have lost her way in the dim morning light. Cassandra had been right about how early it was — far too early to pay a visit.

Determined not to leave before talking to Demuchus, but without anything better to do, Andromache paced up and down the street, memorizing the arrangement of the cobblestones. *Kidney shape, grey. Greenish-black circle. Next comes the white wing. No, wait — the tan mountain.*

When at last the sun was high enough, Andromache approached Demuchus's house. At her knock, the door groaned open, revealing a man she didn't recognize. She looked hastily down the street, horrified that she'd gone to the wrong house. *No, this is it*, she told herself. *This guy must be a friend. Or maybe a new servant. Yes! That's why* Demuchus *knows so much about servitude!*

The man sighed. "Can I help you?"

"Please — uh, Demuchus —"

"Yes? What about him?"

"I need — I need to speak with him."

"He's unavailable at the moment."

Dammit! Andromache swore. It just figured! He was probably in some lesson, and wouldn't — but no, she wasn't going to give up that easily. "Please tell him that Andromache wants to speak with him. *Please*," she added when the man gave her a dubious look. "It's important."

With a shrug, the man left to deliver her message. Andromache paced back and forth at the door the whole time he was away. It felt like an hour — two hours — ten. When he finally returned, he was alone.

"Master Demuchus can meet with you this afternoon," said the man.

Andromache sagged. "But now —"

"Is out of the question," he said firmly.

So that was Demuchus's game, to punish her by making her wait? So be it — *she* wasn't going to play! "Now," she said, her tone anything but meek. "It has to be *now*."

The man sighed.

"I have to see Demuchus," she cried. "I *have* to see him!"

"You *can* — later." The man made a brushing motion with his fingertips. "But for now, off you go, little miss. Shoo!"

Andromache's cheeks flamed. She *wouldn't* be shooed! She sat down right in the path of the door so that the man couldn't close it.

"Away with you!" he hissed.

"No!"

"Now, listen! You can't just —"

"What is the *meaning* of this ruckus?" interrupted a dignified voice.

"Demuchus!" Andromache cried with relief.

"Andromache! You *are* here," he said.

"Yes."

Demuchus turned away from her. "Go see if my uncle needs you," he said, dismissing his servant with the same finger-tip brushing the man had used on Andromache.

The servant left.

"Come in," Demuchus said solicitously to Andromache.

She hesitated. "Demuchus, I — I came —"

"I see that," he interrupted, looking mawkish. "It means a lot to me." His cheeks took on an unbecoming flush.

"You didn't let me finish," she murmured, wary of his look. "I came to apologize for —" She paused. "For my outburst. I don't know what came over me."

"There, there," said Demuchus. "You needn't apologize. I shouldn't have rushed things. It was too much of a shock on your delicate nature." He paused to touch her arm and bestow a tender look.

Andromache swallowed her growing annoyance. She had to deliver her message—and if she couldn't do so without snapping at him, all would be lost! "Demuchus," she said. "I *do* have to apologize. I shouldn't have reacted like that. I don't want there to be bad feelings between you and Cassandra, or her parents."

Demuchus blinked. "Of course there won't be. We'll be like family, Cassandra, and her parents, and I."

Andromache's stomach turned over. *Oh gods, he thinks I came here to marry him after all!*

Demuchus squeezed her arm. "We'll *all* be family."

"No!" said Andromache, recoiling.

"What do you mean, '*no*?'"

"I'm sorry, but what Cassandra told you — it was a misunderstanding. Don't blame her, it's not her fault, but —"

"But you don't want to marry me."

Andromache hesitated, hoping to find a kinder way of saying it. Since there wasn't one, she simply shook her head.

Demuchus squared his shoulders, attempting to recapture his poise. "All that time you spent with me, at the soirees…were you just playing a little game, seeing if you could hook me?"

Andromache bristled. A number of sharp retorts came to mind — that *he* had sought *her* out, more than the reverse — that even if she'd had the bad luck of '*hooking*' him, she'd at least had the good sense to throw him back — and that if she'd known what he was really cooking up, she would have done so a lot sooner. She bit them all back, though. Her goal was to smooth things over, not to further upset Demuchus. "I just thought it would be nice to be friends with you," she said quietly. *Friends*. The friendship *had* been nice, for a time, before ending up spoiled and warped, like everything else in her life.

"Friends?" Demuchus narrowed his eyes. "Very well. What greater act can one *friend* do than to rescue another *friend*? To save her from a life of toil?"

Andromache stumbled backward from the door. Greater act? So *that* was it? He hadn't he even *liked* her! She'd been a project to him, too! He hadn't cared about *her*, only the grand gesture he could make by rescuing her. *Rescuing* her! Saving her through marriage!

Saving her through marriage…

Andromache was overcome by an unpleasantness far deeper than the present one. In her mind's eye, she saw a wagon. Her real vision blurred. She began to hyperventilate. Forgetting all about her oath to make things right for Cassandra, she turned away from Demuchus's house and fled down the cobblestone street.

"I know what you're up to!" Demuchus wailed after her. "And it's never going to happen!"

She didn't stop to ask him what he meant; she didn't care. She just wanted to get away from him. She wanted to run.

છ

ANDROMACHE RAN FOR the rest of the morning and into the afternoon. She ran until she felt lightheaded, and then she kept going at a walk. She didn't leave the arena until she could see by the angle of the sun that it was time for lessons.

The instant she stepped into the entry hall, she ran into Paris. He turned toward her with a snide grin.

"What?" she snapped.

"You seem upset."

"Well, I'm not!"

"Your boyfriend sure was, last night..."

"Oh, what do you know?"

"I know you went to see him this morning, and by the look on your face, it didn't go so well. *Tut, tut!* And here I thought *laughter* —" He stressed the word. "— was the best medicine."

Andromache's face turned purple. Oh, how she hated Demuchus for that kiss! And Cassandra, for blathering about her errand to Paris! And Paris, for being himself!

Before he could find something even worse to say, she fled up the stairs, to the library. She couldn't get there fast enough! Something would have to be done about the Demuchus situation — she would probably have to see him yet again — but for now, she needed to escape it. She needed a distraction, a sanctuary, and her Lukkan lesson would be both. Hector hadn't been at the wedding, or even in the city, the night before. He was as far removed from the kissing incident as anybody could be.

Once Andromache had closed the library door behind her, she felt better — and better still when Cutie ran over. Andromache rubbed the dog's ears and murmured, "<u>Hey, girl</u>."

Hector, who'd been sitting at the table, poring over a text, looked up. "Andromache?" he said, with theatrical surprise.

She frowned. Why did he sound so strange? And why was he calling her '*Andromache*?' He almost always used her Lukkan name, even when they weren't in lessons. "<u>Hi, there</u>," she said cautiously.

"I'm surprised to see you. I thought you might be —" Hector coughed delicately. "*Busy.*"

Andromache bristled. Had she heard him right? "Ahem — *busy?*" she asked, mimicking his words.

"Yes — busy." Hector's mouth curved into a cruel smile. "Making tongue soup with your *swain.*"

Andromache's knees buckled; her heart skipped a beat. *Hector knew about the tongue!* It was intolerable, the crown of all ignominies! And '*swain?*' Even if he hadn't mentioned tongues, she never could have forgiven him for '*swain!*'

What *was* this? *Who* was this? She might have expected jabs like '*swain*' and '*tongue soup*' from Paris, but not Hector! The Hector she knew had teased her and gotten angry with her, but he'd *never* been mean to her. He'd never looked at her with that cruel glint in his eye, as though he was seeking out her jugular. She had sudden sympathy for how his enemies must feel, as he homed in on their vulnerabilities and struck without pity.

Was it because Demuchus was involved? Did that explain Hector's sudden nastiness — his deep-rooted loathing for Demuchus? *Then I hope whoever blabbed the story to him gets sucked up into the celestial ocean!* Andromache thought bitterly. She looked over at Hector and saw that he was sneering at her. Her cheeks flamed in fury. Was *this* the person she'd been so unwilling to cut herself off from? Auntie would forgive her for having doubts! Very well. She would answer him, then, but she couldn't — *wouldn't* — acknowledge '*tongue soup.*'

"He is *not* my '*swain*,'" Andromache snarled.

"Did I misspeak?" asked Hector. "Is he already your husband? Oh, I don't blame you one bit! In your place, I couldn't have waited, either."

"In *your* place I'd go take a nap!" Andromache hissed back. She longed to shriek at him but kept her voice low for fear of spies in the hall or courtyard. "Or soak my head in the spring!"

Cutie slunk away to a dark corner of the library.

Hector gave a nasty laugh. "If only I'd been soaking it last night! Then I wouldn't have missed seeing your tender, private moment." Idly, he fiddled with the text he'd been reading.

Andromache blanched. *Private moment?* This was *not* to be endured! "I did *not* have a '*private moment!*'"

"Oh?" Hector grinned. "So was it your twin out there, tangling tongues with His Honor, the future councilman?"

"You and your brother are so clever to make fun of me for that!" cried Andromache, outraged to the brink of tears. "Are you always this funny when a woman gets slobbered on against her will?"

The text smacked against the table. Hector changed directly from ice to steam, skipping the liquid state. "*Against your will?*" he fumed.

"Well — I — I mean —" Andromache was too stunned by his sudden metamorphosis to do anything but stammer.

"Against your will!" Hector muttered ominously. "Against your — Paris never mentioned that *that little* — oh, if he were here right now, I'd —" He broke off without saying what he would do, or to whom, Paris or Demuchus. Judging by the igneous look on his face, it wouldn't have been pleasant.

However, the fact that he'd finally mustered a bit of protectiveness toward *his parents' guest* didn't soothe Andromache in the least. What good was this little show now, as horrible as he'd just been to her? "You'd *what?*" she asked crossly. "Whatever it is, don't bother." She was pleased to see his self-righteous look evaporate.

Hector closed his eyes, breathed deeply, then opened them again. Looking calmer, he asked in a penitent voice, "You're all right?"

"Fine," she snapped.

"He didn't hurt you?"

"No."

"Hit you?"

"No."

"Kick you?"

"No! No! No, I said!"

Undeterred by her wrath, Hector continued to question her: "So, what happened? What did you do when he —"

Andromache glowered. "I laughed at him."

"Laughed?" Hector blinked in surprise.

"You mean your brother didn't tell you about *that*, either? I'm shocked! It seems like something the two of you would love to mock me for!"

Hector ignored the jab. "He kissed you — and you laughed?"

"Yes."

"You laughed!"

"Yes, already!"

"Laughed!"

"Yes, a thousand times, yes! Are you happy?"

Hector didn't reply, but plainly his answer was also *'yes.'* Tears were running down his cheeks. His sides were tensing spasmodically, yet his laughter was silent, apart from a few small squeaks.

Andromache had never seen him, or anyone else, in such a state of hilarity. As she watched him choke and splutter, she realized what she must have looked like to Demuchus. It was not a pretty picture.

After several moments more of convulsions, Hector tried to speak. "And th-there he w-was," he stammered, "thinking he'd given you s-some great honor!"

"Oh, and he *did*," Andromache said sarcastically, before she could think. "All smelling of sweat and half-digested lamb!"

Hector's laughter resurged. "Sweat and lamb!" he gasped. He looked close to vomiting. "Sweat and lamb!"

Andromache snorted, then laughed. She despised herself for laughing with Hector — he didn't deserve it, after the way he'd treated her! — but she was as powerless to stop herself as she'd been the night before.

"Sweat and lamb...oh, <u>Ahndromahk</u>, that's funny."

"Demuchus didn't think so," she said, sighing. "And neither did Cassandra."

"My sister? What's it to her?"

"Oh, she's worried about working with him on the council later in life, and him thinking she's a liar, or —"

"A liar?"

"I guess she encouraged him to —" Andromache sighed again. "To ask me to marry him. She told him I wanted to."

Pause. "*Do* you?" asked Hector, now sounding tentative.

"No."

Pause. "You're sure?"

"Yes."

Pause. "*Really* sure?"

"Yes, <u>dammit</u>!" cried Andromache. "I don't need another husband saving me from my life!" She didn't realize what she'd said until Hector's eyes widened in shock.

Oh, gods, she thought. *I didn't!*

But clearly, she *had* — Hector was staring at her, waiting for her to say more.

"I don't need a husband saving me from my life!" she said fiercely, as though repeating herself verbatim. Her cheeks blazed. She sat perfectly still, pretending to study the loops and whorls on her fingertips, hoping Hector would have the good sense and tact to move on without further probing.

After an uncomfortable moment or two, he did. "Did Cassandra even ask *you* first?"

"No, she didn't."

"What a family of busybodies!" Hector complained, shaking his head. The stray lock of hair flopped in his face.

"She meant well," said Andromache.

Hector rolled his eyes. "I'm sure."

"Really, it's no big deal. Everything's fine, now — or it will be. I went up to apologize —"

"To Cassandra?"

"No — to Demuchus."

"To *Demuchus*?" Hector looked disgusted. "For *what*?"

"Well —" Andromache hesitated. "For making a scene."

"That was his own fault."

"Well, I don't know. Maybe. But I wanted to apologize anyway, in case — in case — I mean, I don't want something to happen to your family because I — because I — *laughed*, and — I mean, his uncle's on the council and all, and I figured he might be — I don't know, upset — and then get mad at your parents and —"

"Wait." At long last, Hector interrupted her babble. His brow furrowed in bewilderment as it did when she spoke Lukkan too quickly. "Upset about *what*?"

Andromache sighed. "About some — some little Lyrnassan hick — laughing at his nephew."

"Hick?" Hector laughed.

"It's not funny! I'm serious."

Sobering, Hector said firmly, "Demuchus won't tell his uncle about any of it."

Andromache frowned. "How do you *know*? This morning, I meant to make him promise not to take it out on anyone in your family, but I left before I could." She had to blink back sudden tears.

"Don't worry," Hector reassured her. "Believe me, a future councilman is *not* going to run around bragging that he's been dumped by a Lyrnassan hick."

"But —"

"Trust me."

"What if it's too late? People saw him rush out!"

"Don't worry. He'll think of *some* cover story. He probably already has."

Hector looked so certain that Andromache felt a little better. "I hope you're right," she said.

"I am — you'll see. Right, <u>Cutie</u>?" He offered a conciliatory hand to the dog, who crept out from her hiding place and thoroughly licked each of his fingers. "<u>Oh, Cutie, I haff already a baff today</u>," he joked.

Andromache smiled. The normality of the scene before her had a soothing effect. "<u>So, how was patrolling, last night?</u>" she asked, changing the subject away from Demuchus.

"<u>Pet-rolling?</u>"

"<u>Oh, um</u> — riding Buzzy <u>in the night, watching the countryside, teaching younger people what to look for</u>…"

Comprehension lit in Hector's eyes. "<u>Oh, yes, it go — it</u> WENT <u>— well</u>," he said, adding with a sigh, "<u>More and less.</u>"

Without correcting the expression, Andromache nodded for him to go on.

"<u>One young</u> — uh — *so smahrt* <u>person</u> —" Hector's tone dripped with sarcasm. "— <u>connect-ED</u> — uh — <u>ti-ED himself to his hohrse. Fohr an accident</u>," he assured her, but he still looked disgusted.

"<u>Tied himself to a horse?</u>" asked Andromache. "<u>Poor bastard.</u>" A giggle escaped and was soon followed by another.

"<u>Pooh bahstahd?</u>"

Once she'd explained the words, Hector laughed with her. "Yeah, he really *sucks.*"

'*Sucks*'…the vulgarity that had so infuriated Hecuba the previous year. It seemed that Andromache couldn't make it through a single Trojan wedding without disgracing herself! Yet how insignificant her '*sucks*' faux pas now seemed, compared to the Demuchus debacle! Sighing softly, she asked, "<u>Where were you patrolling?</u>"

"<u>In the hills upon the</u> —" Hector paused to correct himself. "Um, *around* <u>the city.</u>"

Andromache pictured him galloping up and down the silent, moonlit hills and felt a sudden surge of envy. "<u>It must have been very beautiful</u>," she said wistfully.

Hector looked surprised. "<u>Yes</u>," he agreed.

"<u>I bet you'd have a great view of the</u> Lorani <u>from there</u>…"

"Lorani <u>is not real</u>," he said teasingly.

"<u>Yes, they are! Just because *you've* never seen one doesn't mean they're not there.</u>"

He made a face. "That's too many '*nots*' and '*nevers*' for me to understand."

"Lorani — are — real!" she cried.

Shrugging, he said, "Maybe. It is true, I am — I *was* — not looking. There ahre too many ahther fings I was obligate to do." He yawned.

So did Andromache.

"You ahre tahred," Hector observed. With an audacious little smirk, he added, "In your place, I'd go take a nap."

∞

AFTER THE lesson, Cassandra was waiting at Andromache's door.

"Hi," Andromache said cautiously.

"Oh, honey! I'm so sorry!" moaned Cassandra, throwing her arms around Andromache. "About what I said to Demuchus. I don't know what came over me!"

"It's all right," said Andromache, hugging Cassandra back.

The girl sighed deeply. "Mom really let me have it! Oh, dear, if someone had told me I'd be arranging marriages, at my age…"

Andromache managed a small laugh. "You were just trying to be nice."

"Well, remind me to be horrible, next time!"

"Oh, Cassandra!" cried Andromache. "Please don't say '*next time*!'"

The girl smiled. "So, you're not mad?"

Andromache shook her head. "No, but I *am* really tired."

"I'll let you sleep, then, honey," said Cassandra. As she tiptoed down the stairs, she whispered, "Sweet dreams!"

Andromache opened the door to her room, trudged in, and collapsed onto the bed with Cutie. Galling as it had been to have her words thrown back at her, Hector was right about her needing sleep. She felt dried out, like a too-daring worm that had missed its chance to burrow back underground after a rain.

Tap, tap, tap.

Andromache sat up sharply and smoothed her hair.

"Andromache?" murmured a woman's voice. Hecuba.

Andromache groaned. She wished that she'd already fallen asleep. The last thing she wanted right now was a scolding!

"You're not ill, are you, dear?"

If Andromache didn't answer, the questions would keep coming — that is, if Hecuba didn't simply break down the door. "No. I was just resting."

"May I come in for a moment, then?"

"Sure," said Andromache.

"I have a tray of food for you, if you wouldn't mind opening the door."

"Oh! Sorry." Food sounded good. Andromache hadn't eaten all day. "Here. Look out, I'm opening it."

"Thank you, dear," said Hecuba. She presented the tray to Andromache, who took it and set it on a clothing chest.

"Thank *you*," she said to Hecuba. "For the food, I mean."

"You're welcome." Hecuba was chewing almost perceptibly on her thoughts. She clearly had a mission beyond delivering supper.

Andromache waited.

"We were worried sick about you, gone all day without so much as sending word that you were all right," Hecuba finally accused.

"I'm sorry," said Andromache.

"My daughter eventually coughed it up where you were, and my son filled in the '*why*.'"

Well, of course he did! Andromache scowled to herself. *Why wouldn't Paris run to his mother with that juicy tidbit!*

"And I have to ask you, dear — what were you doing over *there*? At *his* house?"

"To apologize," whispered Andromache.

"Apologize!" squawked Hecuba. "What on earth for? Why would you care if that cad is upset with you or not? As though he were entitled to be! In fact, I don't care to have him coming around here anymore. I've never heard of something so ill-mannered, attacking a guest of this house in our very courtyard, where she ought to feel in perfect security!"

"He didn't *attack* me," Andromache said in alarm. Words like '*attack*' might lead to anger between the families, when all she really wanted was for the episode to be forgotten. At the same time, she was pleased to have Hecuba on her side. Whether or not Demuchus invented a cover story, Hecuba didn't seem inclined to throw her out.

"Oh, *don't* defend him! While I can't say that your reaction was — conventional — as far as I'm concerned, you were perfectly within your rights." Hecuba paused to take a closer look at Andromache. "You haven't had enough rest, dear. You should sleep in, tomorrow." She bent down to pat Cutie on the head. "Take care of your mama, you silly little white monster!"

Cutie yowled joyously.

Hecuba gave the dog's ears one last rub before moving to the door. Just outside, she paused to say, "I mean it, dear. Get some rest."

As the door was closing, Andromache flashed Hecuba a look of gratitude. Everyone was exhausting her — Paris, Demuchus, Cassandra, the whole lot of them! Today, though, Hector had taken the bouquet. He seemed wholly separate from the even-tempered person she'd known during her first months in Troy. Anything could turn into a fight, now: Cutie, heat-sickness, waterfalls, Demuchus. This last time was the worst of all. Their other fights had arisen when Hector was grouchy, or else justifiably angry with her. This time, he'd been mean. He'd deliberately tried to hurt her. He'd taunted her about something that wasn't her fault, just to make her suffer. No amount of kindness afterward could change that.

Andromache curled around Cutie and glumly stroked the little dog's flank. No, Hector's kindness meant nothing, now that she'd seen the cruelty beneath it. She thought of what her grandfather had done to her dad, treating him for years as a valued apprentice, then coldly showing him the door when he was no longer needed — when a legitimate heir came along.

Hector and she had a similar relationship, based on need rather than caring. But how long would it be until he no longer needed her? Or until he was overwhelmed by resentment for her, the person he didn't *want* to need? Such questions had been nagging Andromache for months, sometimes at the forefront of her mind, sometimes on a deep, hidden level. Now, she realized just how little control she had over the answer. No matter how hard she tried to keep their lessons calm, Hector himself might light the fatal blaze.

And then what? Andromache wondered. She thought of her dad, sailing down to the warm blue waters and pine-covered hills of the Lukka lands...

℘

LATE THE NEXT MORNING, Cassandra brought up a tray of food. "I'm sorry, honey," she said, gesturing to the mealy apples, stale bread, and bowl of murky stew. "There wasn't much food to pick from. Paris refused to go to market, today."

Andromache yawned. "Why?"

"Oh, who knows? He said his arms weren't working, but he'd say almost anything to get in an extra nap."

Napping versus flirting: Paris's daily conundrum.

"Anyway, we just had a few leftovers."

"That's all right. I'm not hungry, anyway." The tray Hecuba had brought up the night before was so large, Andromache still hadn't finished it.

Cassandra cleared her throat. "I also wanted to tell you that Demuchus has been talking to everyone about — about — well, *you know.*"

Andromache knew, all right. Here it was — the moment of her salvation, or of her disgrace. "So..." She gulped. "What's he saying?"

"That you two had an argument."

"About what?"

"About councils and monarchs, and which one is better for the common folk. He said that he could *never* reconcile himself to your monarchist views."

In disbelief, Andromache asked, "And — and people are buying that?"

"They seem to be. That's a sensitive topic, around here."

"Well, good, I guess."

"It is. The only downside is, with everyone thinking you're a monarchist, you might want to avoid that group of friends for a while."

507

Andromache hadn't been planning to see them, anyway. Soiree season was over, and there was no one from the group whose house she wanted to visit. "I'll do that," she said. "But did — I mean — so, did anyone see —"

"The kiss? No," said Cassandra. "I mean, no one except Paris. You're lucky it was so cold, and no one else was out there. It would've been the talk of the city by now, otherwise. Everyone's been wondering who Demuchus would pair off with."

Andromache let out a long sigh. She didn't ask why Paris himself hadn't spread gossip about the kiss. She didn't care. All that mattered was that Hector had been right about Demuchus inventing a cover story. Now, at least, she could stop worrying and put the whole affair — beginning with her very first soiree — behind her.

Mid-autumn

Chapter 60

Andromache sighed.

"<u>What is abohff?</u>" asked Hector, meaning, *<u>What's up?</u>*

"<u>Nothing.</u>"

"<u>Then why the sigh?</u>"

What could she say? She'd been sighing a lot, recently — and just when all the world was happy! The gold of autumn had shone with particular brilliance, that year. Troy was rich in grain and flowing with wine. In Priam's courtyard, the apple trees had given basket after basket of fruit, which meant an abundance of delicious foods — dried apples, apple breads, apple tarts, apple stews. It was a time of plenty.

But to Andromache, the bounty of the land only served to mock her withered life. The summer, begun in excitement, had ended in disappointment. Nothing had gone as she'd hoped. There was Demuchus, of course, with his slinking tongue. Not only had he crushed her dreams of what a Trojan kiss would be like, he'd also confirmed her fears — she was of marrying age, not kissing age. She was too old to play around on the Make-Out stairs. Worse than anything else, though, was the fact that Demuchus had apparently been trying to rescue her.

A project, she thought wearily. *All anyone sees in me is a project!*

A project — Demuchus's project — Hector's project. In retrospect, she wasn't all that surprised about Demuchus. They'd had so little in common, after all. Why else would he have spent time with her? But Hector was another story. She was sure they would have been friends, if not for how they'd met. Even despite their history, again and again, she'd let herself believe that he might grow to like her — become friends with her — stop using her to punish himself. Again and again, though, her hopes had been dashed. His kindness was a duty, a façade, and now she'd finally seen what lay beneath it.

But why should that surprise her, either? Her whole life was built on fantasies and daydreams — everything she treasured, anyway. Daydreams of friendship — of family — of home.

As often as she could, she went down to the neighborhood where the old luthier's shop had once been, but still, she always looked for it without really trying to find it. She couldn't bear to risk losing the precious visions of her dad...

Now, he was an adolescent, learning the trade from his father, the master luthier.

'Scrape more there, boy. More. A little more. It has to be thin enough to vibrate.'

He was a good student, a quick learner.

'This is where the strings attach. Then you pull them tight by turning the pegs.' The master luthier was pleased with him in spite of himself. 'When everything is just right, she'll sing for you, boy.'

Andromache's dad understood. Somehow, he'd come into the world already sensitive to music, to lutes. He didn't so much need instruction as refinement of the gifts that were already there.

'A little narrower here, on the neck. Lots of places need smoothing. But not bad, boy. Not bad.'

The master luthier was pleased, even if he wasn't affectionate. But then something went wrong — the birth of a legitimate son and heir. 'Go on, then, boy! I'll work no more with you. Your mother was nothing but a servant — and you're nothing at all to me.'

Andromache's dad stormed out of the luthier's shop, furious about his father's rejection and grief-stricken over his mother, who had recently died. He stormed all the way down to the Lukka lands...

He'd always seemed at home in the Lukka lands, but in truth he'd been a transplant there, just as Andromache was in Troy. The neighborhood surrounding the luthier's shop had been his first home. How different his life would have been, if only the master luthier had died sooner! He could have taken over the shop and made lutes for all the finest players in Troy.

Her mom — why not? — might have come up with a group of Lukkan immigrants. Once there, she would have charmed all of Troy with the beauty of her weaving. Andromache could have sat in the corner, watching her parents work their arts to perfection. When she grew tired of sitting, she could have gone out onto the street to chase chickens with the other little boys and girls. The neighborhood would now be hers by birthright. She would fit in there. The people would want her. It would be more than just a shelter she'd been given out of pity…

Why the sigh? Andromache felt like a reflection of the autumn world. If someone were to write a play using weather as symbols for people, she would be a cold, constant drizzle.

During her long silence, Hector nibbled uncomfortably on his thumbnail. "Xanthus <u>asks on you</u>," he said at last.

"Xanthus?"

"<u>In the hohrse house</u>."

"<u>Oh, the stable master. What's he asking</u>?"

"<u>He lahkes you. He asks, maybe you can play</u> roodles <u>wiff him</u>?"

"He *likes* me?" asked Andromache, shocked out of her melancholy. "<u>You mean the guy who yelled at me and tried to throw me out of the stable</u>?"

"<u>He is lahke that wiff all peoples</u>," said Hector, shrugging.

"Roodles…" The stable master had brought her water, too, she remembered. He'd been nice enough once he stopped trying to shuttle her out the door. "<u>All right. I'll play</u> roodles <u>with him, sometime</u>."

If nothing else, she would get to see the horses again.

ℰↄ

THE NEXT DAY, AFTER marketing was done, Andromache plodded down to the stables.

"Well, well," grumbled Xanthus, when he saw her. "Your friend said you might drag your little bones down here, one of these days."

"He's not my friend, he's my *student*!" snapped Andromache, not caring if her tone offended Xanthus. Let him throw her out, if he didn't like it — that walking carapace had asked for *her*, not the other way around!

"Eh? And I should care, so long as he's not a liar?" the stable master retorted. Without wanting to appear too eager, he began setting up the roodles board. "Know how to play?"

Andromache nodded.

"We'll see. You need patience to play well, not to mention brains, which explains why most young grubs can't play worth a damn. Too much fluff crammed into their skulls, these days." Xanthus shook his head and muttered, "Everything's going to hell. Did you hear about that Phegeus whelp?"

"No," said Andromache, making her first move.

Xanthus countered. "He tried to balance a duck on his nose because he'd read a treatise saying that it could be done."

Andromache couldn't help giggling.

"Right in the middle of the market, he did this, for all to see. And what happened? Well, what do you think a duck does when he's getting balanced on a nose, eh? Yep! Splat! He let go all over that fool's face. And everyone around tried to blame the duck — chased it right out of the marketplace, a whole horde of people did, as though it was *his* fault for acting like a duck. The city's short on brains these days, Missy. Back in my day, if a fool balanced a duck on his nose, he'd get what he'd get, and no one would blame anyone but him."

"I roodle you," murmured Andromache.

The stable master gaped. "A trickster, eh?" he crowed. "Of all the sneaky things to do! But no one can say your head is full of fluff, Missy. Half-full at worst, I'd wager."

Xanthus reset the board, and then they played several more matches. All the while, the stable master griped about everything that was wrong with the city: lack of brains, lack of sense, lack of hard work, lack of planning.

Andromache loved it. As with the duck story, most of Xanthus's rants had a humorous side. Even when they didn't, he gave voice to all the irritation she was feeling but couldn't express. Playing roodles with him was cathartic.

After their last match, Xanthus sighed: "Well, Missy, you're no grand champion, but I've seen worse."

Andromache snorted. She'd beaten him three times out of five.

"I guess we could play again sometime," he said reluctantly, as though giving in to her pleading. "Tell you what, Missy. Come a little earlier, tomorrow, and I can show you the late season foals."

That did it. For a moment, Andromache forgot her troubles and fell in love with the cranky old stable master.

Late autumn into winter

Chapter 61

As often as she could, Andromache went down to the stables to play roodles with Xanthus. He never failed to entertain her with his croakings about the dire state of the city.

On the first few trips, she'd been worried about running into Hector, muddied and bruised from the training field — perhaps even wearing his armor. She wanted at all costs to avoid such a meeting. Their relationship was strained enough already, without her having Raider nightmares on top of it. Soon, though, she realized that Xanthus always went to the field during trainings. He never invited her down for roodles at those times, so she was never in danger of seeing an armored Hector.

In fact, she rarely saw him at all. He had other duties besides tending to the stables, and even when he was there, he was too busy to do much more than wave as he headed through the main door.

On one such occasion, Xanthus shook his head. "Everything's going to hell," he grumbled.

Andromache wholeheartedly agreed. She was tired of Hector's stupid waves.

"Especially the council," Xanthus went on, sounding more serious than usual. "Splitting the army! Why not just split the walls right open? Of all the rot-brained things to do! And of all the times to do it, considering what the Mud —" He looked up at Andromache, whose eyes had grown very wide, and coughed.

"Never mind specifics. The army is split, and one of its commanders has all the sense of a tent worm!"

Andromache set her game piece down with unnecessary force. "That's not fair," she muttered.

"You're right." Xanthus nodded in hawk-eyed approval. "Not fair to the tent worm."

Andromache gave him a reproachful glare.

"You needn't look at me that way, Missy. I've known him since he was spitting up on his mama's shoulder, and he's never had much going on inside his skull, if you know what I mean. No, don't interrupt me, Missy! Take those twin nitwits, a couple months back."

Andromache's ears pricked up. Twin nitwits? How many of those could there be, even in a city as large as Troy? Once she and Hector had made peace, she'd never again mentioned Cutie's tormentors, but she'd always wondered about them. Now, it seemed that she was going to learn their fate. "What nitwits?" she asked innocently.

"Young fools! Twin teenage nitwits."

"What about them?"

"Now, don't ask *me* what they did!" Xanthus snapped. "But it must have been bad. They were here all day—scrubbing floors, hauling feed, and shoveling horse crap as though their lives depended on it — and Hector glowering behind them the whole time, missing a full day's work to make sure they did *theirs*. The great buffoon —" Xanthus coughed and shook his head.

Andromache opened her mouth to retort, but the stable master interrupted her.

"Excuse me, Missy. The great buffoon never would've done that. Probably would've given them a public whipping, for all the good that does."

Breathlessly, Andromache digested Xanthus's words: *The great buffoon would've...*' Would have. That had to mean —

"So, Hector's not *'the great buffoon*?'" she asked.

Xanthus cackled. "Some days, Missy, I have to wonder!"

Her cheeks flushed. "I — I didn't mean —"

"Eh? What's that?"

"Nothing."

Xanthus went on: "The *'great buffoon*,'" in this case, is Laoganus. Have you met him?"

Remembering the Ass General's blustery voice, she nodded. "Then you know what I mean."

She nodded again. She thought of the blustery voice threatening to whip Hector or chain him to a slave ship. She then pictured the nitwits working, cleaning, and shoveling, all the while shadowed by a furious, spear-wielding warrior. They'd had a rough day — a frightening day, even — but they'd been safe. They hadn't suffered any harm, certainly nothing like what she'd accused Hector of.

She picked at her cuticles until they bled. Why hadn't he just told her?

(*Maybe he would have, if you hadn't attacked him first thing,*) the Voice said snidely. (*And like I said before, he probably didn't think he had to tell you. He thought you trusted him.*)

Xanthus went on. "Yep! Laoganus would've whipped them for sure, if he'd been as mad as Hector. I've never seen *him* quite that mad. One of the nitwits asked him what they'd done, and he said — I'll never forget it —" The stable master cleared his throat and did a rattly imitation of Hector's voice: "*You know what you did. Shut up and keep shoveling, or I'll rip off your diapers, tattoo 'coward' on both your asses, and chase you through the city.*" Xanthus cackled. "And he'd've done it, too, or so the nitwits wagered. They didn't make a peep the rest of the time."

"I'll bet," murmured Andromache. She'd seen Hector angry, and in the nitwits' place, she wouldn't have peeped, either.

"Scared the bile right out of them, that's for sure. But you know what, Missy? I have a heck of a time keeping them out of here. Two, three times a week I have to chase their sorry little asses away, just like *he* threatened to do. They're always up here, begging to be let into the army, begging to serve with him, as though he'd given them some sort of privilege by making them shovel horse crap. *He* can't stand to look at them — wants nothing to do with them — and so of course it falls on *me* to clear them out." Xanthus scowled. "That said, no one's ever begged to be in Laoganus's army."

Andromache could barely breathe. After everything she'd thought about Hector — everything she'd accused him of — Cutie's tormentors had wound up respecting him. Adoring him, even! She was dirt. She was mold. How she *despised* herself!

"So — you think — the council should put him — Hector — in charge of the whole army?" she stammered.

"Eh? Of course," squawked Xanthus, scandalized that she'd asked. "Don't you?"

"I-I don't know," murmured Andromache. "I don't know much about armies or councils."

"And you're the better for it, Missy." Xanthus gave a nod, accentuated by a tap of his gnarled finger. "Believe you *me.*"

Chapter 62

L ate that night, Andromache hung her head out the bedroom window. How she missed the wind! Everyone in the
city would have called her crazy for saying so. Troy was a
windy place — wind swept down its broad avenues and roared
around its towers. That wasn't the kind of wind she missed,
though, funneled and channeled down a few set paths.

She missed the broad, wild wind.

Long ago, as a child in the mountains of the Lukka lands,
she'd spent much of the day outside, tending sheep and goats,
gathering dye plants, walking with her mom, or running through
the grass. She would come home at night covered in dirt and bug
bites. Sleepy from the open air, she would lie out under the pine
trees, watching their boughs toss and shake above her.

In Lyrnassa, when she went running up in the hills, plants
whipped against her legs until her skin turned red. Along the
shore, she was stung by salt spray and sand. The wind came in
hard in the evening; she would sit beneath the platana trees, her
feet in the stream that cut the valley floor, her hair whipping
around her shoulders.

She could almost see them from her window, the currents
of air weaving patterns into the grass and foaming the tips of the
waves.

Andromache leaned even farther out the window, hoping to
catch a stronger breeze. Instead, all that happened was that more
blood ran to her head — and with it came the dregs of her conversation with Xanthus.

Hector had never hurt the nitwit twins. He'd never touched
them — no, he'd so impressed them that they made nuisances of

themselves trying to be near him. Meanwhile, *she* had accused him of murder.

Tears sprang to her eyes. She felt sick at herself — and angry. The story of the nitwit twins was just one more reminder that things should have turned out differently between her and Hector. He was a good person — someone she liked — someone she *should* have been friends with. And why wasn't she? Because of one simple fact: she'd met the wrong Hector first.

It was so unfair! Why had she gone to the hills that day, three years ago? Why had she been away from Lyrnassa the first time Hector had come? If only she'd stayed, *she* would have been the one fetching water from the creek! He would have liked *her*, just as he liked Auntie! He never would have seen her as a project, a penance, or a responsibility. He would feel no resentment toward her, and there would be no cruelty lurking under his façade of kindness. His kindness wouldn't *be* a façade! And she would have met him as *'the sweet boy with hair in his face,'* not the gore-spattered Raider! She never would have feared him — had nightmares about him! If only she'd met Hector the first time he came to Lyrnassa, there would be no terror, pain, or guilt coming between them.

If only! she thought, with a pang. *If only…*

The way she felt when they laughed together — when they talked about her family, his horses, or Cutie — all of it would be real. The closeness she felt to him, the sense of understanding —

(*But it's not real,*) the Voice jeered. (*You know he's just using you to punish himself.*)

It's not fair! cried Andromache. *None of this is fair, and I can't take it anymore!*

(*Then what are you going to do?*)

What *could* she do? She was stuck!

(*You could quit being his teacher.*)

She didn't *want* to quit! She didn't *want* to break the tie!

(*Then keep having your little lessons,*) said the Voice. (*Keep acting like his true feelings toward you don't matter.*)

Andromache blinked back tears. Of course his feelings mattered — but still, she didn't want to quit. So what *could* she do?

At other points in her life, when she'd had a problem she couldn't solve, she'd gone running. The more upset she was, the longer distance she'd run. In Lyrnassa, she'd been able to run all day without passing the same place twice, and the rushing wind had cleared her mind. Here, she had only the exercise arena. The stairs.

A light mist began to fall.

If she went outside the walls to run, following the path she and Hector had taken toward the sea, she would have to pass through the outer market. Alone, she would have to navigate the jostling chaos of merchants, deckhands, and riffraff. She would be shoved — prodded — perhaps even knocked to the ground — and no one would be there to help her to her feet.

She shuddered. Perhaps there was another way out of the lower town, a gate that avoided the outer market. She'd never come across one, but she hadn't looked, either.

Andromache drew her head back in through the window and smoothed the mist from her hair. Beside her, Cutie stirred. "Want to go running outside, little girl?"

The tip of Cutie's tail wagged. She then rolled onto her back and moaned contentedly.

Scratching Cutie's belly, Andromache said, "Don't worry. I don't mean tonight. I know you're comfy, right now." She lay down with her arm around the little dog. "I should probably try to sleep, too."

Cutie sighed as if in agreement, and Andromache closed her eyes. In her mind, she saw waving grasses — sparkling sand — streams flowing clear and bright beneath the silver stars...

Chapter 63

"It's a beautiful day," Andromache said to Cassandra the next afternoon, when Cassandra had finished her lessons and Andromache wasn't yet due at hers. It was a sunny day, warm for the winter season, and they were sitting out on the courtyard.

"Oh, honey, isn't it? It burned me up to have to stay inside all morning, but there you go. At least the warm weather means we can have a soiree, tonight — oh!" Red-faced, Cassandra covered her mouth.

"It's all right," said Andromache. She hadn't been to a soiree since Demuchus's failed proposal.

"I'm sure you can come back, one of these days. Just give it a little more time to blow over."

"Far from the eyes, far from the heart," murmured Andromache, remembering a phrase Hector had once used.

"Exactly!" Cassandra frowned pensively. "But I *do* hate to think of you being here, by yourself. Maybe I should stay home — we could go for a walk, or something."

Andromache sat up straighter. A walk wasn't the same as a run, for burning off bad feelings, but just being out in the open air of the countryside would do her good. And if she had company — even Cassandra — the outer market might be less daunting. "Where would we walk?" she asked.

"Oh, somewhere pretty. Maybe in one of the gardens."

"What about the countryside?"

Cassandra gave her a blank look. "What countryside?"

"Oh, up on the plateau outside the city, I guess, or maybe down by the sea."

"Why would we want to go *there*?"

"To walk — to look at the view — I don't know."

"I don't know, either." Cassandra sniffed. "If you want a view, the city has perfectly good gardens for that."

Andromache sagged down against her bench. "You know, I'm tired anyway. I think I'll just stay here, tonight. You go ahead to the soiree, though."

"Really, honey? Because I could —"

"Go. I mean it. I'll probably go to bed early, anyway."

"All right," said Cassandra, looking doubtful.

Andromache broke a small branch off the nearest shrub and poked it into the ground. If Cassandra wouldn't walk out to the countryside with her, there was little chance Paris would, either. He was an urban creature, at heart. If only she had another way out, one that didn't involve the outer market, she would just go by herself. Neither Paris nor Cassandra seemed likely to know of one, though. The only person who might was —

No — not him. Andromache's head began to spin.

(*Then you're not serious about wanting to spend time out there,*) the Voice opined. (*If there's another way outside the walls, he's the one who would know it.*)

What if he asks why I want to go? Hector might accept that running out in the countryside would help her release tension, but she didn't want to have to explain why she was so upset.

(*Then I guess you're stuck…*)

৪০

HER RESOLVE CRACKED several days later, when Hector came into the library smelling of horses and looking windblown and happy from a ride through the open air.

Envy surged through Andromache. Almost reflexively, she whispered, "I need your help."

Hector frowned. "What is wrong, Ahndromahk?"

"Oh, nothing," she said. "Nothing's wrong, exactly. It's just that —" She sighed. "I need to get out of the city."

Hector's face froze. "You want to leaff?"

She shook her head. "Just for an hour — two hours."

"You haff the intention to do what?" he asked, frowning more deeply.

"Walk along the sea, or —"

"The *sea*?" he interrupted.

Too late, Andromache remembered how strange Hector had been about the sea, the day of Muka's burial. Too late, she remembered how he'd dragged her back to Troy.

"— or go running out on the plateau," she said hastily, as though he'd never spoken. "Back in Lyrnash, I used to spend a lot of time in the open country. I miss it."

Hector abandoned all efforts to continue in Lukkan. "How do you plan to get out there?" he asked sternly.

Cutie stiffened.

"Well —" said Andromache, "from the main gates, I guess — unless —"

"The main gates," said Hector, cutting her off again. "And from there, through the outer market? Good idea. Your first time there went so well." His tone was now sarcastic. He was plainly remembering her panic, the pathetic way she'd dissolved in the middle of the crowded outer market.

"It wouldn't be like that," she argued.

"No, it would probably be worse," he shot back. "Before, you were with me. No one was going to bother you."

"You certainly think a lot of yourself," she snapped.

Cutie slunk away to a corner.

Hector's look sharpened. "There've been murders down there," he said severely. "I can't do my job if I know you might be running around down there."

"Oh, for pity's sake, Hector! I'm an adult."

"I *know* that." He scowled at her. "But that doesn't mean I'm not responsible for your well-being. You're my teacher — you're our *guest*."

*Responsible…guest…*the words made Andromache sick. "Yes, I'm your *guest*," she said scathingly. "Not another sister for you to nanny!"

"Not my sister? No kidding!" A storm was roiling across his face.

Andromache pulled back. She hadn't wanted to start a quarrel. "You get out of Troy all the time," she murmured, trying to appeal to his sense of sympathy. "I love the wild lands as much as you do, remember? How would you feel if *you* couldn't go?"

"Ahndromahk," sighed Hector. "That's different."

"How?"

He looked at her as though she'd lost her mind.

"Hector…" she pleaded.

Evenly, he said, "I can't order you not to go through the outer market."

"No," she agreed, newly hopeful. Was he going to tell her about an alternate route, then?

"But I *can* order the gatekeepers not to let someone out."

Andromache hissed in outrage and disbelief. A fight was one thing, but she'd *never* expected him to lock her away! And for what? So his parents wouldn't lose face if she ran into one of the outer market murderers? Tears welled in her eyes and she didn't try to hide them; maybe they would soften Hector where arguments had failed.

But when he stared back, his face implacable, Andromache knew she'd lost. Not only wasn't he going to help her, he was actively going to thwart her. So be it — she was done trying to mollify him, to tiptoe around him! She was done trying to deflect their inevitable fight!

Lacing her fingers together until the knuckles turned white, she said, "Yes, *my captain*. We'd better get back to the lesson, then, *my captain*."

That afternoon, she did everything in her power to make life miserable for Hector. She treated him a thousand times more nastily than she had when she'd first learned of his guilt:

"It's *ve*-getables, not *vay*-getables. Aren't you ever going to learn how to say it right? There's no excuse, anymore. And for the thousandth time, you say, '*I ate vegetables*,' not '*I eated vegetables*' — unless you want to sound like a moronic child, that is."

It felt good, giving vent to her bile! Her insults flew out so swiftly that even Auntie would have had trouble following them. Hector had no chance. All the same, he couldn't have missed her tone — her cruelty. She expected him to fight back. She *wanted* him to! A simple '*What the hell is wrong with you?*' from him, and she could have explained. Their farce of a relationship would finally be over.

Just when she was aching for him to fight, though, Hector bowed out. His face was serene; he never complained. Somehow, his calm riled her more than anything else. How galling, that he should goad her and goad her, then meekly refuse to fight!

She supposed that he was content as long as his *parents' guest* was safe.

As the days passed, Andromache's bitterness grew. Why wouldn't he yell? Why wouldn't he quit? She *wanted* him to quit! She wanted to be out from under his suffocating aegis! She didn't want him to have any '*responsibility*' toward her, anymore! She no longer even cared about the so-called link to her family — they were all gone, and there was nothing Hector could do to bring them back, no matter how much Lukkan he spoke, and no matter whose hand had tousled his hair!

For the next week, Andromache continued to assault him, making each lesson more painful than the last. Every sentence ended with a sneering '*My captain*.' Even outside of lessons, she sought to annoy him. She made exaggerated efforts not to notice him when he walked by. She lolled about near windows, staring at the world outside the house but pointedly refusing to leave. She didn't walk with Cassandra, or shop in the market, or go out for any other reason. When the family members asked her what was wrong, she claimed illness or fatigue — unless Hector was in earshot. If he was, she sighed and said it wasn't safe outside the walls of the house.

Hector never complained, nor did he show signs of boredom, anger, or frustration. If anything, he grew ever nobler and more gracious, using all the phrases of politeness and refinement his mother had so desperately wanted him to learn. He thanked Andromache for her patience. He appealed to her indulgence.

The more courteous he was, the more she wanted to explode; the worse her abuse, the more calmly he took it. At the end of their seventh such lesson, when she compared his accent to that of a frog swallowing a withered grape, he nodded gravely and promised to work on it.

"On that note," he added, "I have late afternoon training and an evening patrol scheduled for tomorrow. I fear that we won't have enough time for lessons if we don't meet earlier than usual. Would that be acceptable to you?"

Fed up with his air of gentility, Andromache gave an obnoxious little bow. "Yes, *my captain*. Of course, *my captain*. Demuchus rightly observed that I'm a servant of the house, of the family, of *you*. I have no liberty of my own and must always go where I'm told."

When she looked up, Hector's eyes were snapping.

For the first time in a week, she felt a trickle of warmth. He was mad! She'd finally done it! Something was finally happening! She tried not to look triumphant in the face of his wrath. "I'll meet you whenever you tell me to, *my captain* — my *farmer prince*."

A thousand emotions rolled over Hector's face before glacial haughtiness won. "Fine. Then meet me tomorrow, in the entry hall, before sunrise." Refusing to look at her, he stalked out of the room.

It was then that Andromache felt the first sting inside her belly.

ॐ

HECTOR WASN'T at dinner that evening. For that matter, neither were Hecuba and Priam, which was all perfectly normal. Dinner had always been an informal gathering of whoever happened to be home, except when Hecuba planned a special family banquet. Just then, however, Hector's absence weighed on Andromache. Was he punishing her? Or would he have missed dinner anyway, as he often did?

More hornets joined the first, stinging her one by one. Briefly, she considered *not* meeting Hector the next day, but at that thought the swarm stirred into a frenzy, rising up toward her throat. Their message was clear: under no circumstances could she miss the rendezvous.

Under *no* circumstances!

Andromache frowned. How was she supposed to wake up on time? If he'd wanted to meet just a little later, she could have counted on Cutie's personal needs to rouse her, but he'd said '*before sunrise.*'

She chewed on her lip, wondering what the chances were that Hector would come upstairs to find her if she wasn't waiting by the door. *Not very good,* she decided.

No, not good at all. And she could think of only one way he would be sure to find her in the entry hall...

Chapter 64

"Aaaaah!" Andromache cried in panic. Someone was crouching very near to her, whispering her name. "Sssh, it's just me," murmured Hector.

"Oh…"

"So, how long have you been waiting here?" He was close enough that Andromache could smell the mint on his breath. His features looked gentler than they had the previous day, or maybe it was just the darkness of the hall that softened them.

"I don't know," Andromache mumbled through a curtain of hair. She was ashamed to admit that she'd been there all night, that she'd slept by the door for fear of missing him, and that even Cutie had known it was a silly thing to do and had gone upstairs. "Not that long."

"Oh."

Feeling uncomfortable, she muttered, "Anyway, I'm here, where and when you asked me to be — *Master.*"

Hector's face embrittled. "Well. Let's go."

Andromache was ashamed of herself. She didn't know why she'd ruined the moment — why she'd chosen rancor over peace with Hector. A hornet took flight. "Where are we going?" she asked, pushing her hair out of her face.

Hector didn't answer. "Bring your cloak," he said.

Hurriedly she tugged on the cloak, which she'd been using as a pillow, and struggled to stand. Hector was halfway out the door by then. Still clumsy from sleep, Andromache tripped twice on the hem of her dress in her haste to catch him.

Cool air hit her face as they stepped out onto the street. No one else was there. The only sounds she heard were her own footsteps and the breeze.

She followed Hector out of their immediate neighborhood, across the citadel, and down to the lower town. A few people were walking around down there, but in the taciturn way of early morning travelers, they passed by without saying a word.

As Hector led them onward, Andromache realized that she'd never been to this part of Troy. She could see a grove of fruit trees just ahead, and, beside it, a small building that looked like a stable. Hector headed straight for the building, not so much as pausing until they'd reached the door. Andromache opened her mouth to ask him what the place was, but he didn't give her the chance to speak.

"When it's light out, the swallows that nest here will dive at you," he said at the doorway. "Be careful on the way back."

Before Andromache could ask what he planned to do inside the stable until daybreak, Hector had hurried through the door, past a row of empty stalls, toward the rear of the building. Reluctantly, she followed.

When he finally stopped beside a trio of flickering oil lamps, she gasped to see what their light revealed. *Guards!* she thought. *There are* guards *back here!* Whatever else she might have expected to find, it certainly wasn't guards!

"We're passing through," said Hector after exchanging formal greetings with the guards.

Wary of Hector's obsidian face, the guards merely nodded. One of them handed him a lamp.

Through? Through what?

The answer made Andromache's jaw drop: a square panel was lifted from the floor, revealing a stairway.

Hector indicated the stairway with his chin. Andromache stepped down onto it, and Hector joined her. "Shut the door behind us," he said to the guards.

"Yes, sir."

Andromache waited until the flooring had been replaced before whispering to Hector: "Where are we going?"

He didn't answer but instead set off down the staircase, into a tunnel. There, he kept walking — and walking — and walking. Their silent march through the tunnel went on for what felt like an eternity, until at last they ascended another, much taller, staircase. At the end, there was a panel of wood. Hector rapped on it — *craaaaack, crick crick, craaaaack, crick, craaaaack!*— and it was lifted aside. He then led Andromache out into another building where, like the outpost stable, there were several guards standing watch. Hector nodded to them and handed over his lamp before moving toward the building's door.

Andromache followed him outside. In the predawn light, she could just make out a flat stretch of land. The wind caught her hair, pulling it loose from its braid. She'd never before felt such a strong wind inside the city!

Wait....

Andromache squinted back in the direction they'd come, and there she saw the towering grey walls of Troy. Everything — the stairs, the tunnel, the guards — made sense! They'd crossed under the walls and were now on the plateau outside the citadel. The guard station was one of several small shepherd's cottages scattered around there. Hector had brought her to the countryside after all!

Before Andromache could open her mouth to thank him, he started walking briskly away from the building.

"Wait!" she cried, hurrying after him. His legs were so much longer that she had to run. At a copse of scrubby trees far beyond the guards' gateway cottage, she finally caught up with him.

"Well — here you are." Hector gestured to the open landscape while his voice seeped out, quiet and cold. "Come here whenever you want." The air around him fairly bristled with lightning, but it, too, was cold. Everything about him was cold.

Andromache caught her breath. Inside her, the hornets were ready to surge.

"Bring Demuchus, if you really want to enjoy yourself."

The hornets burst forth. Her guts were a torment of buzzing — of stinging. Hector's guilt was gone. He no longer needed to punish himself. He'd probably brought her here hoping that she would walk off into the fields and never return to Troy.

But Hector wasn't quite done with her, yet. "A servant," he hissed before bellowing, "A *servant!* That's all you have to say about my family? How dare you? How *dare* you! My family loves you — they *adore* you! You have no idea the sacrifices they would make for you!" He kicked at a loose stone, sending it scudding over the ground.

Loves me? Adores me? The instant he said those words, Andromache began to seethe. How dare *she*? How dare *he*! How *dare* he take that self-righteous tone with her, after the way he'd used her! How *dare* he say that anyone in his house loved her! She knew what love was. When people you loved left forever, they tore a hole in you that never healed. Hector's family didn't feel that way about *her*! They liked her, they took care of her, but if she disappeared one day, never to return, would she leave an empty place in their hearts? She doubted it very much. How *dare* Hector throw his family in her face! How she *hated* him! In all her life, no one had ever made her feel worse, and *that* was saying a lot! He was through with her? Good! She was done, too. Done! All that remained was for someone to speak the fatal words.

"I'm done," she said.

"Done?" he fired back. "What do you mean, done?"

"I quit!" cried Andromache. "I'm done with our stupid lessons!" There — she'd made the last gesture she could make to spare her dignity! She'd quit before he could have the pleasure of dismissing her. "I'm done with your family! I'm done with Troy! I'm done with *you*!"

Without another word, she turned and bolted toward a distant copse of trees.

"Ahndromahk?"

Hector! Was he trying to call her back, so he didn't have to explain her disappearance to his family? Oh, well! She didn't care what happened to him and wasn't waiting around to find out! She was going to run as far and as fast as she could, to get away from him!

Escape wasn't easy. Her lungs were burning. The wind tore at her hair and threatened to knock her off her feet. Still, her legs were strong, her need was desperate, and it didn't take her long to reach the trees.

"Ahndro — wait!"

Hector's voice sounded far away, but not far enough! Andromache saw a rocky outcropping further down the ridge and set out for it. Around a tree — down into a trough — then up, up, up again, ever toward the rock! As the gradient grew steeper, she leaned into it, pushing her muscles to the limit.

531

"Wait! Stop!"

Andromache had just reached her goal when the landscape started to shimmer. She stumbled — teetered — and then her toe caught the hem of her dress, and she crashed down onto the rock.

"<u>Ahndromahk</u>!"

She could hear Hector chasing after her and tried to rise, to flee him, but she fell back. The air was too thick. She couldn't breathe.

"<u>Ahndromahk</u>! What happened? What are you doing?" cried Hector, upon reaching her rock.

She was surprised to hear more fear than anger in his voice, but what did that matter? *He just doesn't want to have to tell his parents why I croaked out here*. Once again she tried to get up, but the hill was still spinning.

Hector was leaning over her — his hand was on her back — she could feel it through her cloak, through her dress — it was warm — her skin was softening under it — the warmth was spreading down, to her belly —

(*I thought you hated him.*)

I do!

She wrenched away from his hand.

"<u>Ahndromahk</u>, don't. Ssssh…calm down."

"Go away!" shrieked Andromache. "I said, I'm done."

"Don't quit. Just —"

"I'm quitting!" She sat up. The rock was cold under her bottom. "I *am*! I'm sick to death of being used!"

Hector squinted at her. "What are you talking about?"

"I'm a just penance, to you! I'm your project!"

"Project?"

"Yes! You didn't get down to Lyrnassa fast enough to save everyone, and you've always felt guilty about it. So to make up for it, you took in a Lyrnassan and gave her a job, to keep her occupied…" Tears, instead of dizziness, were now blurring her vision. "To keep her from wasting away to oblivion."

"Oh, <u>Ahndromahk</u>," Hector said softly, sitting down beside her. "I never knew you thought that."

"Of course I do! It's the truth!"

"No, it's not." He shook his head. "No, it's not! Why didn't you say something to me? I could've explained. I could've told you how crazy you were to think all that!"

"I'm not crazy! Your mom said those exact words to you, right after I got here!"

"No, she didn't."

"Yes she *did!* She said I needed something to do to keep me from wasting away to oblivion! I heard her! She was in the hallway, outside my room — I'm *not crazy!*"

"Sssssh...I didn't mean she never said that, but if she did, it wasn't to me." Hector's face was somber but truthful.

In confusion, Andromache blinked back tears. "*Someone* was out there, with her. I wasn't dreaming it. I —"

"It wasn't me. Maybe it was my dad, or Cassandra, but it wasn't me. I swear to you, I'm not taking Lukkan lessons to keep you from wasting away to oblivion. You're not a project, Ahn-dromahk — and you're certainly not a penance."

"I *am!*" Fresh tears rolled down her cheeks. "You look at me and see all the villagers you couldn't save." Pain crossed Hector's face, but Andromache didn't stop. "You feel guilty about what happened in Lyrnassa, and suffering through lessons with *me* is your way of punishing yourself."

"Of course I feel guilty," he said softly. "You have no idea."

She let out a sob.

"But that has nothing to do with Lukkan lessons! I'm not suffering through them — I *like* learning Lukkan."

"No, you don't! You *hate* it!"

Hector looked confused and hurt. "What have I done to make you think that? I've worked my ass off!"

"Exactly," said Andromache. "To suffer as much as possible! You hate learning languages — you always have. Languages are the one thing that's too hard for you. Everyone in the city has told me that, even your parents!"

With his toes, Hector grasped a plant growing at the base of the rock. "I like learning things. I like getting new skills. Yes, languages are hard for me, but I've never hated them. I like hard things *best,*" he said with just a touch of haughtiness. "At least as long as they're worthwhile."

"You *hate* them!" shrieked Andromache. "I heard all about how you —"

"I hated my *teachers*," Hector interrupted. "They were all the same, giving me stupid, useless phrases to repeat, correcting every mistake I made, nitpicking about all kinds of dumb little rules, never just letting me try it." The plant slipped away from him and he frowned. "They gave me headaches, so I gave *them* headaches. I guess people noticed that…although I don't know why they cared."

Andromache swallowed several times. Her throat was too dry for her to speak, and she was feeling dizzy again.

Hector went on. "If my parents had found me teachers who did things like you, right from the start, I wouldn't have given them any trouble."

Andromache frowned, not sure whether to believe him.

When he saw her look of doubt, he added, "Lukkan's not my first foreign language."

"What?" she gasped.

"I can speak a little Luwian."

"Your mom's language?"

He nodded. "I learned it during my remedial military officer training with Uncle. The Santiyan court speaks Truvan, but the commoners only speak Luwian. To get by with the soldiers, I had to learn it." He smiled wryly. "Except, soldiers being soldiers, I didn't learn many words I could share with my mom, so I never told her."

"Oh," whispered Andromache, too surprised to say more.

Hector smiled again. "You teach the same way they did — by just talking to me. You're a lot better, though, and you talk about different things. I never know *what* you're going to say! You make me laugh. You've *always* made me laugh — ever since 'Lahff is a bag ohff goat shit.'"

His words made her feel a strange combination of pleasure and embarrassment. "You really speak Luwian?" she asked, to hide her confusion.

"Mm-hmm." Hector's toes reached out once more for the plant.

"Ayam soo glatt yooer heer," she murmured. It was the only phrase of Luwian she knew, the only one Cassandra had ever shared with her: *I am so glad you are here.*

Hector looked up in surprise, the plant forgotten. "Yooer glatt?"

It was Andromache's turn to blink. She'd uttered the phrase without meaning it to be part of the conversation, but Hector had taken it literally, and now she had to answer. "~~Ayam glatt~~," she repeated.

He gave her the same sweet smile he'd given her in the entry hall, the day he came back with the army. This time, though, she didn't stand there dumbly.

"Hector?" she whispered.

"Hmm?"

"Do you like me? Are we friends?"

"Yes, Ahndromahk!" he said adamantly, so that she couldn't mistake his answer. "Always, *always* we ahre friends."

As her last whispers of doubt faded away, Andromache nearly burst with happiness. *Friends.* She and Hector were *friends* — and always had been! Everything she'd told herself was fake was actually real. He'd *always* liked her! The way they'd met had never mattered, not to him. His kindness to her came from friendship, not guilt or responsibility — and whenever he'd been awkward around her, it was in reaction to *her* awkwardness. She could hardly blame him for *that!* Even their recent quarrels no longer had an ominous meaning. Friends fought, sometimes! She'd had fights with both Paris and Cassandra. If Hector had refused to fight with her, at first, it was because he'd seen her at her most fragile. Once he knew she was strong again, he'd started treating her like any normal friend.

(*And then there's the way you've been treating* him...)

Andromache fought back yet another round of tears. The Voice was right! All those horrible things she'd said to Hector, over the past week! The way she'd mocked and antagonized him — oh, gods! There was so much she had to make right — so much she wanted to say —

"Hector," she murmured. She had to start somewhere! "Hector, I'm so sorry."

"Sohrry?" He frowned. He'd been making another grab for the plant. Once more, it slipped out from between his first and second toes. "Sohrry, why?"

She looked at him, her eyes bright with unshed tears. "For the things I said."

"Lahke what?"

"Like being a servant."

"Oh."

"I didn't mean it! I don't think that about your family…or you."

"Ssssh, I know this," he said gently. "You ahre mad, when you say this. I ahnderstand. I am mad, too, yesterday and today. And I am also sohrry."

"It's all right!" she hastened to say. "I don't blame you for getting mad — I was *trying* to make you mad." Thinking of the phrase that had proved so incendiary, she asked, "What does *'farmer prince'* mean, anyway? Why did Demuchus call you that?"

Hector laughed boyishly. "Really, you want to know?"

"Yes. What is it?"

"Oh, Ahndromahk, it is goat shit!" He laughed even harder. " '*Lahfe is a bag ohff goat shit,*' lahke you say. A big, big, big bag ohff goat shit."

"Goat shit?" she asked.

"Maybe cow. I remember no mohre."

"Hector —"

"I am a little boy, you see? Maybe eight. I go to the land — the lands — ohff Dad."

"The lands?"

"You know, where the *vay*-getables ahre growed. And the bahrleys." Hector grinned. "And my gahrlics."

"Oh, to the farm lands," said Andromache, understanding. "You used to go to the farm."

He nodded. "I work there, and I stay. And then I come to the city again, and he call me *'farmer prince* — '"

"Demuchus called you that?"

"Yes, and — *thwock!* — he frow me in the goat shit." With his hands, Hector indicated the shape of a large mound. "A big poil — pail —"

"Pile," Andromache said softly.

He nodded again. "A big, big pile."

She gulped, feeling sick. She could see now why Hector hated Demuchus — why he reacted so badly to any mention of Demuchus! She could see now why he'd been so cruel!

"He is maybe firty —"

"Thirteen?"

"Yes, and bigger, so he can frow me in. He fink it is so fahnny! After, he calls me *'farmer prince'* again and he say *'You stink!'* <u>and he hold himself on the nose.</u>" Hector mimed pinching a nose much smaller and more delicate than his own. "<u>All the</u> <u>time, when we ahre boys, he calls me this. But he catched me on-</u> <u>ly one time.</u>"

Andromache forced herself not to scrape her fingernails against her lips — her arms — everywhere that Demuchus had touched her. How she wished she'd bitten him instead of just laughing! The bully! The horrid, rotten bully, throwing little boys into manure! "<u>Did — did he get in trouble?</u>"

"<u>No — I never telled —</u> *told* —" Hector proudly corrected himself and went on. "<u>Anyone.</u>"

"<u>Not even your mom?</u>"

"Mom?" He scoffed his way back into Truvan. "Are you kidding? It was between us boys."

Andromache felt oddly pleased. She liked that Hector had confided in her. She liked being the only one who knew. "Well, I hope you at least punched him, once you were bigger," she said. "I would've punched him."

Hector smiled at her, thinking perhaps of the fat lip she'd once given him. "I bet you would."

"Well? Did *you?*"

He shook his head. "By the time I could have, it was too late."

"You weren't mad anymore?"

"Oh, no. I was plenty mad — you don't just get over being thrown into shit, <u>Ahndromahk</u>. But by then I'd been spending more time in Santiya, with Uncle, than on the farm, and I just..." Hector made another grab for the plant, missed it, and shrugged. "It didn't seem right."

Santiya, where Hector had gone for '*remedial military officer training.*' He'd trained hard and come back much stronger than his old nemesis. Punching Demuchus would have been as easy — and as fair — as punching a baby.

"I understand," said Andromache. "But still — I think you should've punched him."

"Maybe!" Hector laughed. "Maybe we'd be friends, now."

"Friends? Really?"

"Sure. Why not?"

"Oh, I can think of a few reasons..." Andromache made no attempt to veil the disgust in her voice. "Why didn't you tell me all this before I went to those soirees at his house? Why haven't you told your sister?"

"Because," Hector said gently. "Demuchus is all right, now. Harmless. A lot of people do shitty things when they're kids, but they grow out of it."

That was true, Andromache knew. Oh, she knew! At least Demuchus hadn't killed anyone! When she was that age, she'd beaten a baby goat to death with a rock — and while she'd been acting out of compassion, to end the creature's suffering, her deed was a lot more violent than Demuchus's. And then, that wasn't *all* she'd done at age thirteen...

She was lying in the back of the wagon — blood was soaking through her dress —

<u>*Don't think about* that</u>! she warned herself. <u>*Forget about it!*</u>
(<u>*So, you don't like reliving your old shame*</u>?) taunted the Voice. (<u>*Think about how*</u> Hector <u>*must feel, after the way you dragged him back through*</u> his<u>*! Calling him*</u> 'farmer prince' <u>*the way you did!*</u>)

Her cheeks flushed red; the Voice was right. "Hector?" she murmured.

"Hmm?"

"I never would've called you — *that* — if I'd known..."

"I know," he said gently. "I know that, <u>Ahndromahk</u>."

She gave him a watery smile.

"Farmer prince!" he said, laughing. "It sounds so silly, now — doesn't it?"

She nodded. "Yes, it does. Especially the '*prince*' part. What was *that* about — just Demuchus's way of being cute?"

"Well, maybe," said Hector. "But it's also a jab at my mom."

"Your mom? What about her?"

"She used to be a princess, before she married Dad."

Andromache gaped. "So you really *are* a —"

"No!" He shook his head vehemently. "There's no royalty in Troy. Mom gave it up to be here, and nothing about her family bleeds down to me or my brother or sister. Even if it did, I'd find a way out. Being a prince is my idea of hell."

"Why?"

"Are you kidding?" Hector's eyes widened. "Uncle — my mom's brother, Asius — has to be a general — *and* an administrator — *and* high priest, although for him it's just a ceremonial role — *and* trick everyone in the kingdom into loving him. It's nonstop."

"It doesn't sound like much fun," Andromache admitted.

"It's *hell*," Hector corrected. "Anyway, some Trojans were — and are — suspicious of Mom. They think she must be plotting some kind of takeover since she comes from foreign royalty. Mom fights back, though. She goes out of her way not to look or act royal, so the gossips won't have anything to accuse her of. She goes farther than most Trojans do. I mean, most of *them* have servants. I'm not saying Mom does everything for herself — she doesn't wash her own clothes, or mill her own grain, or fetch her own firewood — but the people who do those things for her aren't attached to the house. They live independently, and Mom and Dad pay them or trade services for what they need." Hector cleared his throat. "You know — you haul firewood for me, I'll give you a salve to treat your pustules."

Andromache smiled at the joke, even as her understanding of Hector's family deepened. So many things made sense now, from Demuchus's insults to the sharp way Hecuba had once reprimanded *her* for cleaning.

"What's funny about people like Demuchus," Hector added, "is that they hate royalty but still wish they were connected to it."

Andromache didn't answer.

"You think I sound arrogant," Hector said apologetically. "That's why I never talk about this stuff."

"No — you don't," said Andromache, and it was true. He sounded matter-of-fact. "I was just wondering..."

"What?"

"Do you think that's why Demuchus wanted to marry *me*? Because he believed all those stupid rumors that I was a princess? Or maybe you didn't hear them."

"I heard them," said Hector. "And that's *not* why he asked."

"You don't think so?" Andromache hoped not. That possibility irked her as much as the thought of Demuchus trying to rescue her.

Hector shook his head. "He knew you weren't. You'd never pass."

"Why not?" she asked indignantly.

"You're too funny to be a princess."

She raised an eyebrow. "Your mom's funny," she argued.

"Not very," said Hector. "And if she is, it's only because she stopped being a princess. You should meet all my cousins — there's a small army of them, each one as funny as a rotten log. I've tried and tried to make them laugh, but it's no use."

"Maybe *you're* the one who's not funny," said Andromache.

Hector stared at her until she felt uncomfortable. Then, unexpectedly, he crossed his eyes. She laughed; he raised his chin in triumph.

"All right," she said. "You're funny."

He smiled. "<u>Ahndromahk</u>?" he asked, a moment later.

"Hmm?"

"Is that what '<u>*my cahptain*</u>' means? '*My farmer prince*?'"

"No," she said. "Just '*my captain.*'"

"You demoted me!" he accused her.

Andromache shrugged and looked around the hillside. Behind her, the pastel light of morning was spreading across the sky. "It's nice up here," she said softly. "And it was nice not to go through the outer market."

She hadn't meant her comment as a reproach, but Hector nonetheless looked sheepish. "You can go there if you want," he murmured. "I never said anything to the gatekeepers."

"What?" Andromache stared at him. So, her week of sulking and punishing him had been for nothing? Why hadn't he said so before?

"You were right," he went on. "I have no business keeping you from going out there."

"Oh," she said, strangely dissatisfied. "No…but it doesn't matter. I like this place better."

Hector nodded. "I'll show you the knocks and introduce you to the guards. Then you can come here whenever you want."

"Are you sure?" she asked. "We came here so early, I just assumed you didn't want anyone to see."

"We came early because that's when I have time, today."

"The tunnel's not a secret?"

"Well, kind of. Most people in Troy don't use it — just the army."

"But I'm not —"

"I know. But it's all right if you come here. Just be careful." Frowning, Hector looked downward.

As Andromache followed his gaze, she noticed blood soaking through her dress, at the knee, where she'd fallen earlier. "It's nothing," she protested, flushing a little. "I just got dizzy."

"I suppose you never had anything to eat, this morning…"

She shook her head. "I didn't know we'd be taking such a long walk."

"I wanted to surprise you," said Hector, chastened. "Here — take this." He offered her an apple from his pocket, keeping a second one for himself.

"Those are from the courtyard tree!" she said, recognizing the fruit, even in their slightly shriveled state.

He nodded. "I store them as long as I can in a cellar under the floor. Buzzy and Thisbe love them, so I always carry a few with me."

Andromache seized the apple and chomped furiously into it. "Thanks," she said.

"You feel better?"

She nodded. "I was stupid to run on an empty stomach."

Hector gave her a thoughtful look.

"What?" she asked.

"You rahn lahke a hohrse."

She stopped chewing long enough to glare at him. "If you say, 'on all fours,' I swear to you, I'll —"

"No!" He laughed. "I mean, hohrses rahn becahse they lahff to rahn. You ahre lahke that."

"Oh," said Andromache. The compliment both surprised her and made her sad. She *did* love running, in a way, but it had always been first and foremost a way to flee whatever was bothering her: raiders, nightmares, sorrows, anxieties. Hector's admiration was so sweet, though — so innocent, so touching. She didn't want to spoil it. "Thank you," she said. "You too. You're really good."

He shook his head. "Not lahke you. I, ah, ohrder myself to do it —"

"You *force* yourself to do it?"

"Yes." He nodded. "Fohr me to rahn a lot, it is impohrtant. Becahase then I do not get tired as fast as ahther peoples."

"What other people?" she asked.

541

"Ahther soldiers," he said lightly. "Ahther *captains*."

Andromache fought down a wave of nausea. By '*other peoples*,' then, Hector must mean enemy soldiers — those who were trying to hack him to death, the ones he had to outlast. She pictured his arm, torn open — red and raw — leaking blood —

Don't think about that! Andromache warned herself. "I-I must be out of shape," she said aloud, changing the subject. "That stupid little run was too much for me — not that *this* thing helped." She pulled at the dragging hemline of her dress.

"No, this uniform is not optimal fohr the rahnning," Hector agreed.

Andromache gave a startled laugh. "Optimal? Where did you come up with *that* word?" *And*, she thought to herself, *what's with* 'uniform*?*'

"I-I don't know." Hector looked perplexed. "It just came out."

"You must've heard me say it some other time."

"I suppose," he said, seeming troubled that something had slipped so furtively into his mind.

Andromache smiled. Then, holding up the core of her apple, she asked, "Do you have any more of these?"

Hector shook his head and said, "You're as bad as Buzzy!"

Andromache had a sudden image of herself, nuzzling Hector's side like Buzzy on an apple hunt, and turned away to hide the embarrassment she was feeling. She slipped her right arm out of her cloak, threw the apple core, and watched it arc through the air. It didn't go far before hitting a tree and falling down into the brush.

"Nice throw," teased Hector.

"Well, *you* try, then!" she challenged, flushing.

Smugly, Hector brandished his apple core. As he drew back in preparation to release it, though, his arm bumped into hers. His aim went wild, and the core landed mere footsteps away.

"Nice throw," Andromache gloated.

Hector laughed, but his dark cheeks had a haze of red. "I guess I should've used my other arm," he said.

"Or even your *feet*!"

In response, Hector's toes made another grab for the plant growing at the base of the rock. Andromache looked down and saw several more like it nearby. She frowned. Even after all the plants she'd seen in the Lukka lands, Lyrnassa, and Troy's herb market, the ones around the rock were unfamiliar. She wondered if they would be worth transplanting into her garden. "What are these?" she asked, poking at the plants with her own toe.

"Leaffs," said Hector.

She grimaced and kicked a stem at him. "Seriously!"

"I am effer serious."

"What *kind* of leaves?" Andromache tried again.

Hector bent down to inspect the plant, caught his breath, and then recoiled.

"What's wrong?" she asked. Alarmed, she, too, shrank from the leaves. "Is the plant poisonous?"

"Poisonous?" He frowned. "Of course not."

"What do you mean, '*of course not?*' You jumped back like it burned you, or gave you a toe rash or something!"

"A toe rash?" Hector laughed. "A toe rash! You see, Ahn-dromahk? You say the funniest things."

"Well, what *are* the plants, then?"

Hector's laughter faded. "They haff purple flowers," he said, looking out toward the sea, a faint, mysterious smile on his lips.

Andromache could only guess that he was pleased at knowing something she didn't, all the more because she'd mocked him for his throw. *Fair enough*. She didn't press him for a name. "Oh, really? Purple flowers? I bet my mom would've liked them. We could never find a good purple for dyes."

Hector turned back toward her. "Wiff you, she seeked many flowers?" he asked softly.

"Whenever she could. She had a lot of other work to do, though."

"Wiff — what's the word? Weaving?"

"Weaving," said Andromache. "And she was amazing! She could make the most beautiful cloth. I helped her, too, but mostly by taking care of the sheep and goats or untangling thread."

"Wiff knot stre-tegies," said Hector.

Andromache smiled. "With knot strategies. Mom and Auntie did the actual weaving. And then one of them had to go to market to sell everything, since Dad couldn't go."

"Why?"

"There was an accident." Andromache swallowed hard and went on in a whisper. "When he was helping our neighbors rebuild their house. I was little — I don't remember much — just that my dad got hurt. Badly. He couldn't walk much after that, so he never went far from the house." Not even when raiders came to their village, Andromache remembered. In the hillside just behind their home, there had been a little cave. Her dad and Auntie had hidden there while she and her mom fled up into the mountains. He'd said that everyone would be safe, that the mountains would protect them all...

She wiped her eyes with a fold of her cloak. Ultimately, the mountain hadn't protected her dad — it had swallowed him, along with his wife.

"I didn't have any brothers or sisters, either," she went on, sniffling. "Mom told me that she lost another baby right after me —" Andromache gulped. "But then, they couldn't have any more. I think it was because of the accident." She didn't add that she'd been adored, even spoiled, as a little girl, in part because she was her parents' only child.

"Oh, Ahndromahk," murmured Hector, when her words trailed off. "I am sohrry."

"It was horrible for him," she whispered. "The accident, I mean. But Dad had a full life, even after. He had lots of friends in our village — everyone liked him! And he made lutes and helped Mom with the weaving, although he was about as good at it as I was. He loved reading, too. He only had a few texts, but he read them to me and taught me how to read. I used to spend hours listening to him."

Hector nodded. "So, your dad readed — *read* — to you. And your mom?"

"No. She couldn't read."

"Oh..."

"She couldn't speak much Táruvan, either," added Andromache. "Only a little. We spoke Lukkana at home, except when Dad was giving me lessons. He *was* Taruishan."

"I remember," said Hector. "You tell me that night when we ahre out on the courtyahrd. You ahre going out fohr the first time. You tell me about your parents..." He hesitated on the word, and Andromache knew why: he didn't want to upset her by mentioning the rockslide. She nodded to show him that she knew what he meant. "You tell me about your dad," he went on.

"That he is Taruishan. You tell me about his — his *lutes*." Hector strummed an imaginary instrument.

"You remembered *everything*!" whispered Andromache. But then, of course he had! Hector had *always* remembered what she told him, even words of a language that he couldn't understand: *'Lahff eess a bakhov got sheet.'* Her words mattered to him. Her thoughts mattered to him. He'd always listened, even back when she was terrified of him — even when they were fighting. He listened to her as no one ever had. He'd always liked her, too, even when she was at her most difficult — her most unlikeable. She'd had friends before, but never one like *him*...

"What is it?" he asked, and Andromache realized that she'd been staring.

She should tell him. She'd never found the right time to tell him that he was a good brother, or that the old woman in Lyrnassa was her Auntie, but selfishly, she found *this* more important anyway. What would he say? It might seem like a small thing, to him. He might not realize how much it meant to her. "It's just —"

"Just what?"

"Just that — Hector —" She switched to Truvan, to his language: "You're the best friend I've ever had."

The bright-eyed look he gave her in response wasn't quite a smile. Andromache wasn't sure *what* it was, but she liked it. It made her feel like she was being carried off by a flock of birds.

At the same time, both of them spoke:

"Ahndromahk, I —"

"It's cold up here. We should — ."

They both paused. "All rahght," Hector finally said. "We can go back." His face had returned to normal.

They arose from the rock and started walking back toward the building. "So, you have a busy day, today," said Andromache.

"Training this afternoon and petrolling tonight," he agreed.

"Won't you be tired, after getting up so early?"

He shrugged. "Many days ahre lahke this. Tomorrow I can sleep, ohr the next tomorrow."

Andromache's brow furrowed in thought. "I was wondering something..."

"What?"

"How *do* you wake up so early?"

"I say to myself, '*You need to wake up at dawn*' — or before dawn, or whenever."

"That's all? And it works?"

"Mm-hmm." Hector turned toward her, smirking. "And it is mohre comfohrtable than to sleep in the entry hall."

Andromache looked away before he could see her blushing. "I suppose it would be," she said, with as much dignity as she could muster.

He laughed.

"Here we are," he said, a few moments later, when they'd reached the shepherd's cottage with its underground gateway to Troy. "Are you ready for another trip under the walls?"

Under the walls, thought Andromache, imagining the tunnel that would lead her home, to Troy.

Troy. Not two years earlier, she'd arrived in the city half-dead, draped over the back of a horse. All she'd wanted then was a quiet place to languish, but Troy had given her so much more.

Troy! It was a magical world, a city of transformations. The streets that once had scared her were now hers to explore. The walls, so recently her prison, were now the home she couldn't wait to return to. The man walking beside her had changed from the monster of her nightmares, to a student, to her best friend. Of course, nothing about *him* had really changed. He'd always been her friend — '*always, always*,' he'd told her. His transformation existed only in her mind. Still, it felt real enough to her, and she knew that Troy would look different to her from now on.

Back to Troy, the city of new beginnings and new realities. After losing her parents, Andromache had stopped believing in the future. She'd thought her happiest days were behind her. Well, no more! Good things had come to her in Troy, and more would follow.

To Troy, then! That journey, first made in fear and misery, had somehow brought her to a moment of astounding joy. She'd come there with nothing; now, she had the world.

"Ready," said Andromache. "Let's go."

Geography of *The Trojan Peace*

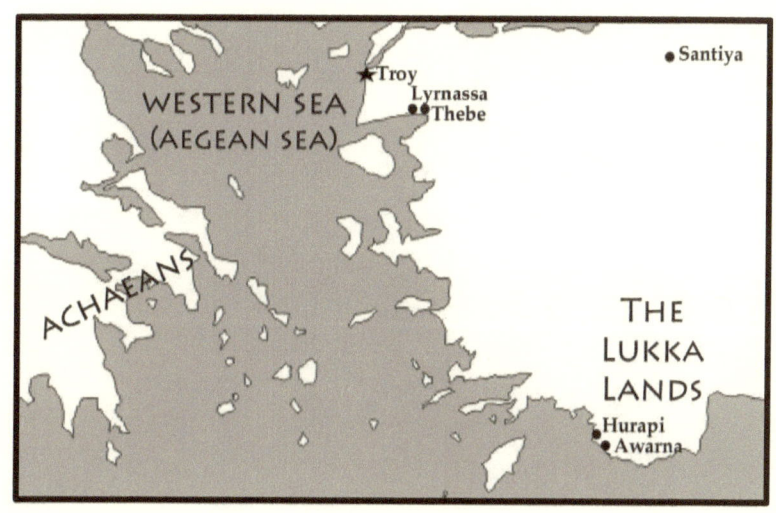

Author's Note

The Trojan Peace began as a single work but grew so long that I eventually divided it into two volumes —*The Trojan Peace: First Light* and *The Trojan Peace: Half-Light*. The original working title of the whole work was *Battle of a Man*, a translation of the name Andromache.

Troy and legend

Andromache is a character rooted in legend. She appears in Homer's *Iliad* and in texts derived from it. Some even bear her name, such as the *Andromache* of Euripides and *Andromaque* of Jean Racine. Countless authors have used her in their works — but is she always the *same* Andromache?

Legendary characters inhabit a strange realm. Readers know them and have certain expectations about their life histories and personalities. At the same time, Andromache, Hector, Hecuba and the others aren't documented historical people. We can't say for certain that they even existed, let alone what they were like. We have no diary or other written record to offer proof of their innermost thoughts. Each author who engages with such characters therefore has freedom in developing them.

The fabric of the Trojan War legend is universal: love, war, grief, rage, rivalry, and family. However, each author — each society — each era — has unique concerns and perspectives, and so the legend is modified. Characters are brought forward or are made to recede into the background. Some are added, others deleted. The storyline is changed to a greater or lesser degree. Where the legend has holes, they are filled in. Ambiguities are resolved — or perhaps deepened.

In the *Iliad*, Homer himself was writing about an era long past. While the *Iliad* is thought to have been written in the eighth century BCE, an historical Trojan War — if there was one — would have taken place some five centuries earlier, in the Late Bronze Age. Does the *Iliad* reflect a Bronze Age society, or is the world of Hector, Andromache, Ajax, and Achilles reminiscent of Homer's own time? Scholars have done extensive research into this question and have found a little of both. An excellent resource on this matter is Bernard Knox's introduction to the Robert Fagles translation of the *Iliad*.

I first encountered Andromache not in the *Iliad*, but in the French tragedy *Andromaque*, written in 1667 by Jean Racine. In his editor's note on *Andromaque*, Bernard Lalande says that "the protagonists of the tragedy are simply men and women of the seventeenth century French [nobility]" (13; my translation). In other words, Racine created characters with values reflecting his own time and place more so than Bronze Age Anatolia.

After *Andromaque*, I read many other works inspired by the legend of Troy, among which the fifth century BCE *Andromache* by Euripides and the twelfth-century *Roman de Troie* by Benoît de Sainte-Maure. In all of them, the legend's storyline, or the natures of the characters — or both — showed variation. What the legend offered was a starting point for exploration of the themes contained in the Trojan War story.

In my own writing, I often had to invent details rather than simply changing them, as *The Trojan Peace* begins long before the events recounted in the *Iliad*. That said, some of the changes I *did* make are large ones.

Most notably, the Olympian gods are absent, and none of the Trojan characters are royal. In the legend, Priam and Hecuba are king and queen of Troy, while Hector and Paris are princes, and Cassandra is a princess. Andromache, too, is a princess. She comes not from the Lukka lands but from the nearby town of Thebe, where her father and seven brothers were killed by Achilles. However, Andromache came into my mind not as a princess, but as a battered, wounded refugee. The others began as Trojan royalty but didn't feel natural that way; early on, they evolved into their current forms. They became, despite the setting, people from my own world — people I could relate to.

Troy and history

The Trojan Peace is not a work of strict historical fiction. It wasn't my goal to paint the most plausible possible picture of Late Bronze Age life or the values and customs of the people who lived it. That said, I didn't altogether ignore the realities of history.

"My" Troy is based loosely on an archaeological site called Hisarlik hill, in Turkey. Ever since Heinrich Schliemann excavated Hisarlik in the nineteenth century, many have accepted it as the location of ancient Troy, the Troy of Homer's *Iliad*. Regardless of its exact connection to legendary Troy, Hisarlik is a fascinating place. The site has nine main layers of settlement, ranging from 3000 BCE through 400 CE or so, in the Roman and Christian era. The commonly accepted date range for Homer's Troy, a Late Bronze Age city, is mid-thirteenth century to early twelfth century BCE, which corresponds to the Troy VI layer (1700-1250 BCE) or the Troy VIIa/VIi layer (1250-1180 BCE).

I used a city plan that roughly follows that of the Troy VI layer at Hisarlik, with a relatively small citadel and much larger lower town. The general orientation and location of the gates reflect the Troy VI layer. As for the buildings, Hector's house is not based on a particular dwelling of Troy VI, but there are a number of large houses on this level, some of which are pillared. To my knowledge, there is no tunnel at Hisarlik quite like the one Hector uses to take Andromache out into the countryside. However, beneath the site there *are* tunnels or shafts that were once used to access a water supply.

I also integrated elements of the landscape around Hisarlik, including the rise of bedrock on which the citadel is built and the harbor outside the city walls. Back in the Bronze Age, the sea was closer to the citadel than it is now; the bay has since silted in. But the winds still blow as they did back then, and I imagine that some of the same local wildlife would have been there: lizards, swallowtail butterflies, squirrels, birds, and tortoises.

I have tried to avoid historical or geographical impossibilities, such as technology that wouldn't have been available in the Late Bronze Age. Historical unlikelihoods are another matter. Rule by council and phonetic writing might seem unlikely elements for a Bronze Age society, but they weren't impossible. Other details that might seem anachronistic — like hallways and proto-toothbrushes — would have been physically possible to make in some form, however simple. If social norms had demanded them, they could have been made.

My Troy is undoubtedly utopic. The arts are flourishing. Learning is valued — even if, by our twenty-first century standards, some of the conclusions are faulty. Women are respected and hold positions of power. Even prisoners are well-treated. *Utopia.* The word means "*no place*," somewhere that doesn't exist — and where, therefore, one can explore what is possible, rather than what *is*. In some ways, *utopia* is the very essence of Troy.

The modern search for an historical Troy is a fascinating subject, and I encourage readers to make their own investigations. Still, those who focus solely on the historical settlement are missing out. Troy is a city on horseback, with one leg dangling into history and the other into legend. It belongs to the imagination as much as to reality.

Names

All of the major character names — such as Andromache, Hector, Hecuba, and Cassandra — are used in their Latinized form. These spellings are reasonably familiar to the English-speaking world, which is why I chose them. There is enough linguistic strangeness in the story already, what with Hector's Lukkan lessons, that I didn't want to add to it by spelling the names "*Andromakhe*," "*Hektor*," "*Hékabê*," and "*Kassandra*." Even so, I used "*Achaeans*" rather than "*Greeks*" to name the Trojans' seafaring enemy. While less familiar to modern readers, "*Achaeans*" is more era-appropriate.

Lukkan

On the Mediterranean coast of modern-day Turkey, roughly between the cities of Fethiye and Antalya, there is a peninsula of land known as Lycia. This area was once its own country, with its own language and great cities such as Patara, Tlos, Pinara, Xanthos, Olympos, and Myra. Lycia even had a reputation: the ancient world knew Lycians to be a fiercely independent people. The citizens of one city, Xanthos, twice committed mass suicide rather than submitting to foreign rule. In Homer's *Iliad*, the Lycian heroes Sarpedon and Glaucus come to the aid of Troy but bristle at Trojan authority.

Even earlier, though, back in the Bronze Age (before about 1200 BCE), this region had another name. It is thought that the Hittites, whose empire stretched across central Anatolia, called it

"*Lukka*" or "*the Lukka lands*" (Cimok 29). I chose to use this older name.

There is, as far as I know, no real language called "*Lukkan.*" Lycian, on the other hand, *is* a real Anatolian language, along with its close relatives, Hittite and Luwian. While the latter are known from cuneiform and hieroglyphic scripts, though, Lycian script is closer to alphabetic Greek or Phoenician. Written Lycian thus comes from an era later than the Bronze Age; I envision Lukkan as its spoken ancestor.

Lukkan speech and thought are underlined throughout both volumes of *The Trojan Peace*: "I like horses." The Lukkan speech patterns have nothing to do with the structures of the real Lycian language. Instead, the more natural these words sound in English, the more comfortable that speaker is with Lukkan.

Naturally, Hector is less comfortable than Andromache. I would caution the reader not to look too deeply into his accent, but just to accept that he has one. There may be some discrepancies in how he pronounces certain sounds, but language learners are not perfectly consistent. Moreover, if Hector's accent were perfectly consistent, it would be unreadable. I tried to strike a balance, giving him a definite and reasonably consistent yet still decipherable accent.

Another word on consistency...Hector's mistakes are sometimes erratic. This is often true for language learners. When they are struggling to master a new word or structure, they might let older material slip. Language learners are always juggling accuracy and fluency, and Hector defaults to fluency. He prefers to keep the conversation going regardless of grammatical errors.

Truvan

Truvan, like Lukkan, is an invented language. Assuming that there were in fact people called Trojans, no one can say for sure which language they spoke, although educated guesses (such as Luwian) have been made. I chose instead to imagine that the region surrounding Troy — called the Troad in the *Iliad* — spoke a language all its own, a blend of nearby languages. Linguistic mixing, especially at a coastal trading port, is a real phenomenon. Unfortunately, a language can also be lost when those who speak it are killed, dispersed, or assimilated by other cultures — which is what happened to the Trojans of legend.

Why not call the language Trojan, then? I wanted there to be a divide between something regional (Truvan) and something or someone pertaining only to the city of Troy (Trojan). A form of *"Taruisa,"* a Hittite name often associated with Troy (Woods 138), would have been an option, but I decided to use a variant of that for the city's name in Lukkan: <u>Taruisha</u>. In Lukkan, Truvan is <u>Táruvan</u> while Trojan is <u>Taruishan</u>.

It follows that written Truvan, is also an invention. To my knowledge, no writing at all has been found at Hisarlik, except for a seal inscribed with Luwian hieroglyphs (Korfmann 39). However, even assuming that Hisarlik is Troy, this seal does not prove that Trojans spoke Luwian or wrote with Luwian script. The seal could have been brought in by an ambassador, a trader, or another visitor. The lack of written documents doesn't prove that the Trojans *didn't* write, though. Later settlements destroyed much of the city center area in the Late Bronze Age layers at Hisarlik. It's impossible to say what might have been there.

While there is no such thing as written Truvan, it's not unreasonable to portray Trojans as adapting Hittite or Luwian symbols to write their own language. The symbols of one language have often been adapted to others. For instance, English, French, Spanish, and many other languages all use the letters of the Roman alphabet.

Truvan, if it existed, could even have been a phonetic script. The written alphabetic forms of ancient languages like Greek and Hebrew — as well as modern ones like English — have roots in the Phoenician script (Robinson 98). This writing system came to prominence in the first millennium BCE, after the Late Bronze Age city of Troy would have fallen, which means that Phonecian itself could not have been used as a model by the Trojans.

There were, however, earlier alphabetic scripts, such as Ugaritic cuneiform from the fourteenth or fifteenth century BCE (Robinson 96). Even earlier writings, such as the Proto-Sinaitic inscriptions found in Sinai and Proto-Canaanite inscriptions found in Lebanon and Israel, as well as a particular set of inscriptions from Egypt, may also have been alphabetic (Robinson 93-96).

The corpus of these writings is small and much about them remains mysterious, but in any case, it would not have been impossible for someone like Priam's ancestor from Kinahna to know about an alphabetic script, whatever its origins, and apply its concepts elsewhere. Incidentally, the word *kinahna* is an Akkadian version of the name Canaan. The name appears in a collection of writings known as the Amarna Letters, diplomatic correspondence between Egypt and other lands (Smith). *Kinahna* is one of several transliterations that I've run across.

Between languages

When Andromache encounters an object for which there is no Lukkan word, like "library," she simply borrows the Truvan word and gives it a Lukkan pronunciation. This practice happens all the time among languages. She treats proper names differently, though. Some names have forms in both Lukkan and Truvan: Ahndromahk/Andromache, Lyrnash/Lyrnassa, Taruisha/Troy, and a few others. Most, however, have no Lukkan equivalent. When Hector and Andromache are speaking Lukkan, but mention Cassandra, Paris, or any other Trojan, they simply refer to these people with their Truvan pronunciations: "I saw Cassandra yesterday." Additionally, the Lukkan forms of names are only used in dialogue or interior monologue, not in narration— that includes Auntie (Auntie in narration), Cutie (Cutie in narration) and of course Ahndromahk (Andromache in narration).

In the course of writing *The Trojan Peace*, I came to view it as one long translation. The characters — especially the younger ones — began to speak in a more and more modern way, even using modern English slang and vulgarities. I imagined them saying something in their ancient language — Truvan or Lukkan — that resonated with them in the same way the modern slang resonated with me. I imagined myself translating or interpreting their words into English rather than recording them verbatim.

Inventions and realities

Languages. Lukkan, Truvan, and the language called Palaan are invented (I wanted a fictional language from which to derive the word "*Lorani*," supposedly meaning "cloud creature," and referring to galaxies, or any object that might, to the naked eye, look similar to galaxies). All other languages mentioned are real.

Place names. Andromache comes from two fictional villages: Hurapi in Lukka and Lyrnassa from the region near Troy. Other place names are real, such as Thebe and Awarna (see map, Cimok 29). Still others fall somewhere in between real and invented. Santiya, the native country of Hecuba and her brother, is adapted from the place name *"Marasantiya,"* from a map of the Hittite empire (Cimok 29). In the *Iliad*, Hecuba's brother, Asius, comes from the Sangarius River region. The map included in the Fagles translation of the *Iliad* shows this river to the East of Troy and south of the Black Sea (73). If the two maps were superimposed, Marasantiya would lie slightly to the east of the Sangarius River. As for the Black Sea itself, I've chosen to call it by a different name: the Munnanda Sea. According to one online dictionary, *"Munnanda"* comes from the Hittite language and is translated as *"hidden"* (Puhvel 153-55).

Plant names. Common names for plants are used throughout *The Trojan Peace*, and while many are obviously real (celery, apple, apricot), others are not. Gullweed, windbane, and winkswort, for instance, are invented common names referring to undetermined plants growing near Troy. If whimsical, these names sound no more ridiculous than many real common names: starry stonecrop, mallow-leaved stork's-bill, shrubby hare's-ear, hogweed, and violet honeywort. Finally, the platana tree falls somewhere in between: its name is an adaptation of the plane tree, a relative of North American sycamores.

Texts. All of the texts that Andromache reads (as well as the songs that she hears) — the biography of Sarcho, *On Lorani*, the Trojan law codes, Demuchus's poem, 'Old Tin Alley,' 'The Cricket Song,' and the Lukkan folksongs — are invented. They do not refer in any way to real texts of the ancient world.

Mudders. The use of *"Mudders"* as a pejorative toward the Achaeans is an invention. However, its origin (as described by Cassandra) has some basis in reality. Mycenaean Greek pottery of the Late Bronze Age *was* beautifully made and highly prized. Pieces of this pottery have been found at Hisarlik, which may well indicate a trading relationship between the two cultures. Just in case it needs to be said, the use of *any* pejorative toward the Achaeans reflects the views of the Trojan characters, not my own personal views of Greek people, past or present. For better or worse, groups of people in conflict tend to give each other pejorative names. It's human nature. If I'd been writing from the Achaean perspective, they undoubtedly would have had a pejorative name for the Trojans.

Elements of Trojan society and culture. Most specific elements of Trojan society and culture are my inventions. These include board games, constellations, religious beliefs and practices, ritual elements, and the organization of the Trojan army. None of these are based on an historical source, nor are they intended to reflect any of the well-described cultures of that era (Greek, Egyptian, Hittite, etc.). Where details are hazy, the reader is free to imagine them.

Sources

Askin, Mustafa. Troy: With Legends, Facts and New Developments. Rev. ed. Antalya (Turkey): Keskin Color Kartpostalcilik, 2010.

Benoît de Sainte-Maure. Le Roman de Troie. Ed. and Tr. Emmanuèle Baumgartner and Françoise Vielliard. Paris: Livre de Poche, 1998.

Blamey, Marjorie and Christopher Grey-Wilson. Wild Flowers of the Mediterranean. 2nd ed. London: A & C Black, 2008.

Blondel, Jacques, James Aronson, Jean-Yves Bodiou and Gilles Boeuf. The Mediterranean Region: Biological Diversity in Space and Time. 2nd ed. Oxford: Oxford UP, 2010.

Cimok, Fatih. Les Hittites. Tr. Marion Feildel. Istanbul: A Turizm Yayinlari, 2010.

Cunliffe, Barry. Europe Between the Oceans. New Haven: Yale UP, 2008.

Fields, Nic. Troy c. 1700-1250 BC. 2008 ed. Oxford: Osprey Publishing, 2008.

Homer. The Iliad. Tr. Robert Fagles. New York: Penguin Classics, 1990.

Homer. The Iliad. Tr. Robert Fitzgerald. 2004 ed. New York: Farrar, Straus and Giroux, 2004.

Homer. The Odyssey. Tr. Robert Fagles. 2006 ed. New York: Penguin Books, 2006.

Korfmann, Manfred O. Troia/Wilusa: Guidebook. Trans. Jean D. Carpenter Efe. 2005 ed. Çannakale (Turkey): Çannakale-Tübingen Troia Vakfi, 2005.

Melchert, H. Craig. "Lycian." In The Ancient Languages of Asia Minor. Ed. Roger D. Woodard. Cambridge (UK): Cambridge UP, 2008.

Lalande, Bernard. "Notice." In Andromaque. Jean Racine. Paris: Librairie Larousse, 1959.

Map of the Eastern Mediterranean. Original at http://www.d-maps.com/carte.php?num_car=3160&lang=en

Puhvel, Jaan. Hittite Etymological Dictionary: Vol. 3 Words beginning with H. In Trends in Linguistics Documentation 5. Berlin: Mouton de Gruyter, 1991. Accessed online 8-31-2014. http://books.google.com/books?id=kghtOX_crPMC&pg=P

A155&lpg=PA155&dq=munnanda+hittite+words&source=
bl&ots=Qs2ICti_xj&sig=W5UPZH93O9X1QSRYERtht2n
hi5k&hl=en&sa=X&ei=CUN_UI-iC-
Tq0gHrtoC4DQ&sqi=2&ved=0CB0Q6AEwAA#v=onepag
e&q=munnanda%20hittite%20words&f=false

Racine, Jean. Andromaque. Paris: Librairie Larousse, 1959.

Smith, Duane. "The Canaanites Were in Canaan." Abnormal Interests: A few thoughts on things that interest me (blog). Posted 9-10-2006. Accessed 8-31-2014. http://www.telecomtally.com/blog/2006/09/the_canaanites.html

Sterry, Paul. Collins Complete Guide to Mediterranean Wildlife. London: Harper Collins, 2000.

Virgil. The Aeneid. Tr. Robert Fagles. 2008 ed. New York: Penguin Books, 2008.

Wood, Michael. In Search of the Trojan War. 1998 ed. Berkeley: University of California Press, 1998.

Woodard, Roger D., ed. The Ancient Languages of Asia Minor. Cambridge (UK): Cambridge UP, 2008.

Acknowledgments

The Trojan Peace has been a labor of love for the past eight years. I have many people to thank for helping me throughout this process.

First and foremost, I must thank Marc Nelson. You're my husband — my love — my best friend in the world — my fellow dreamer — my fellow traveler — my favorite conversation partner — my everything. Thank you for giving me space in the early stages of this project, when I refused to tell you what I was working on. Thank you for reading early drafts of *The Trojan Peace* and giving me feedback. Thank you for always believing in my characters, even when I was frustrated with them. Talking about them with you has helped bring them to life — you have supported me in ways that only a fellow artist would be able to do. There is a lot of you in *The Trojan Peace*, more than you — or perhaps even I — know. Thank you for your laughter, your passion, your willingness to listen, and of course, your love of animals. Thank you for wrangling my computer when I was ready to smash it against the wall. Thank you for gazing at the stars with me. Last but certainly not least, thank you for your beautiful paintings. Ever since I started writing *The Trojan Peace*, I dreamed of having your artwork on the cover. Thank you for making that dream a reality.

Thank you to my parents, Bob and Karen Bartelt, for always encouraging me to appreciate and explore the wonders of the world. Some of my earliest memories involve hiking through the mountains of southwestern Montana and marveling at the geysers in Yellowstone National Park. You took our family to many fascinating places when I was a child; later, you supported my wish to study abroad in France and East Asia. These adventures –all of them — have had a lasting impact on my curiosity, creativity, and willingness to try new things. I also want to thank you for teaching me tenacity, without which writing a book would be impossible. Thank you for your patience, your keen intelligence, and your love. I would need many more pages to list all that I admire about you.

Thank you to my brother, Erik Bartelt, for inspiring me to visit Turkey. Before you went there in 2011, I'd never thought of Troy as a modern-day travel destination! I'd also never dreamed that Turkey would become one of my favorite places in the world. I started writing *The Trojan Peace* long before either you or I visited Turkey, but going there — seeing those legendary landscapes first-hand — has definitely informed my writing. Thank you for opening that door for me, and thank you for everything else that makes you the best brother I could ever imagine.

Thank you to Tom Mayer for encouraging me to write. I think your exact words were, "What? You want to go to grad school for *French*?! Are you crazy? Why don't you write fiction?" Nevertheless, you gave me the letter of recommendation that I'd asked for. I learned so much and had so many wonderful experiences during grad school, yet in the end, I realized that you were right — academia was not for me. I'll never know what you would have thought of *The Trojan Peace*, but I can't thank you enough for that first little push. Thank you also for everything you taught me about close readings of texts and careful structuring of arguments. I may never again encounter another mind as fine as yours.

Thank you to Josh Shepherd and Nikki Dyke for reading early versions of *The Trojan Peace* and sharing their thoughts with me. A fresh eye is invaluable for finding mistakes and pointing out strengths and weaknesses. I'm truly grateful for the time you spent reading my work and helping me improve it.

Thank you to Adrienne Bashista for preparing my CIP data block for me.

Thank you to all the teachers and professors who contributed to my education. I never took a class that wasn't somehow interesting and valuable. It can be difficult for someone who loves science, math, music, literature, languages, history, and everything else to find a path in life; it can be difficult to focus. However, these diverse areas of interest have also been an asset — I've drawn from all of them while writing *The Trojan Peace*.

I'd like to thank a few professors in particular: Professor Hope, for sensitizing me to the rhythms and sonorities of poetry; Professor Laronde, for exposing me to the theories and practices of translation; Professor Heilenman, for sharing her knowledge of language acquisition; Professor Racevskis, for his detailed and thoughtful critiques; Professor Guentner, for giving me a background in aesthetics; Professor Curtius, for her instruction regarding *la créolisation*; Professor Ungar, for his line-by-line analysis of *Le Cimetière Marin*; and Professor Thomas, for securing me a teaching position in France.

Thank you to my Lyle family. You've truly been a bedrock of support for me throughout the past eight years — often in ways you never realized. Your kindness, patience, caring, and compassion show every day in all you do. Thank you for the hugs, for the laughter, and for keeping me grounded.

Lastly, I must say thank you to Luke, my little cattle dog, my very own Cutie. You're a constant source of joy, sweetness, and love. You've snuggled in my lap while I'm writing; you've licked away my tears of frustration; you've taken walks with me whenever I needed a break. You make the world a better place. Thank you for being so innocently, purely, and perfectly yourself.

Also by Jill Bartelt

The Trojan Peace: First Light
The Trojan Peace: Half-Light

Available in print and digital formats

Connect with Jill Bartelt via her author page
on www.calymenepress.com

Connect with Marc Nelson

www.marcnelsonart.com

On Twitter: @Marcnelsonart

www.ingramcontent.com/pod-product-compliance
Lightning Source LLC
Chambersburg PA
CBHW030537020726
47494CB00005B/1400